MURIEL JENSEN

*Mommy
and
Me*

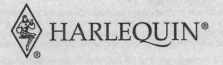

HARLEQUIN®

TORONTO • NEW YORK • LONDON
AMSTERDAM • PARIS • SYDNEY • HAMBURG
STOCKHOLM • ATHENS • TOKYO • MILAN • MADRID
PRAGUE • WARSAW • BUDAPEST • AUCKLAND

If you purchased this book without a cover you should be aware
that this book is stolen property. It was reported as "unsold and
destroyed" to the publisher, and neither the author nor the
publisher has received any payment for this "stripped book."

HARLEQUIN BOOKS

by Request—MOMMY AND ME

Copyright © 2001 by Harlequin Books S.A.

ISBN 0-373-20193-1

The publisher acknowledges the copyright holder
of the individual works as follows:
KIDS & CO.
Copyright © 1997 by Muriel Jensen
MAKE WAY FOR MOMMY
Copyright © 1995 by Muriel Jensen
MERRY CHRISTMAS, MOMMY
Copyright © 1995 by Muriel Jensen

This edition published by arrangement with Harlequin Books S.A.

All rights reserved. Except for use in any review, the reproduction or
utilization of this work in whole or in part in any form by any electronic,
mechanical or other means, now known or hereafter invented, including
xerography, photocopying and recording, or in any information storage
or retrieval system, is forbidden without the written permission of the
publisher, Harlequin Enterprises Limited, 225 Duncan Mill Road,
Don Mills, Ontario, Canada M3B 3K9.

All characters in this book have no existence outside the imagination of
the author and have no relation whatsoever to anyone bearing the same
name or names. They are not even distantly inspired by any individual
known or unknown to the author, and all incidents are pure invention.

® and TM are trademarks of the publisher. Trademarks indicated with
® are registered in the United States Patent and Trademark Office, the
Canadian Trade Marks Office and in other countries.

Visit us at www.eHarlequin.com

Printed in U.S.A.

CONTENTS

KIDS & CO.   9

MAKE WAY FOR MOMMY   255

MERRY CHRISTMAS, MOMMY   509

KIDS & CO.

Chapter One

MALIA: Well, here we are—doing time again. I told you flushing Chelsea's blankie wasn't a good idea. Now she's stroking out and we're in the slammer till our moms get here. Good going, Foster.

GARRETT: Relax. Amy will call a plumber, Chelsea'll get her blankie back, and we'll get to go outside 'cause Amy'll think we need to work off steam.

MALIA: You're such a bozo. It's raining. We never go outside when it's raining.

GARRETT: Well, I'd had about all I could take of that animal-sounds book. I thought a little action would perk up the afternoon till the big kids get here. I like that Truman dude. He can spit Cheerios all the way to the fireplace!

MALIA: I know. That's cool, but he's always getting time-outs in the big chair. Here comes Kate with Chelsea. Tell her you're sorry. Give her your bear.

GARRETT: No way.

MALIA: Okay, but she's gonna scream till it's bye-bye.

GARRETT: Geez. Women! It was just a dweebie blanket, Chelsea. You got to get rid of the thing before you go to school, anyway. Here, you want my bear? Kate? Kate! Take me out, ple-e-e-ease! I don't care if it's raining, I want to go out on the slide. How about the sandbox? I won't put sand in the air conditioner this time, I promise. Kate? Chelsea, what are you doing with my bear? Ow!

CHELSEA: Take that, you macho piglet! That was my blanket. My mom says I can carry it around until I'm forty if I want to and this is what I think of your bear!

MALIA: Not on his head, Chels. It's his weak spot. Come on, you two. Amy's trying to run a respectable day care here. How will it look if some mom comes by to look it over and you're duking it out in the playpen? Hey, look. The bus is here! It's the big kids!

"AMY! THE BUS IS HERE," Kate Murray called out. "But don't worry. I'll get them their snacks, and I'll put on *Babe* for the babies!"

Amy Brown, armed with a plunger and a wire coat hanger she'd pulled apart to serve as a probing tool, sat on her knees in front of the toilet. She was surrounded by wet towels she'd put down to sop up the water. She groaned at her assistant's announcement.

Great. Now Truman, the crime boss, Darcy, the investments queen, and Rodney, who owed the cuss box $112.75, had arrived to round out the lineup of felons at Kids & Co.

"Thank you!" Amy shouted back, not because she

was grateful for the news, but because setting an example with the "magic" words had become a habit for her after six months as a family day-care provider.

She forced the extended coat hanger down the toilet, hoping against hope that the blanket hadn't gone very far, that she wouldn't have to hire a backhoe and dig up the yard to find it—as she had to do three weeks ago when Garrett flushed a twelve-inch stuffed Keiko the Whale to freedom.

The coat hanger refused to go any farther and she drew it back, praying there would be a ten-inch square rag of blanket attached. There wasn't.

From the living room she could hear Chelsea Jeffries screaming over her loss.

"No, no, Chelsea!" Kate was saying to the accompaniment of the sound of something that squeaked hitting something that screamed. "Beating Garrett with his bear, while very satisfying personally, will not bring your blanket back. Here. Give me the bear. Ouch! Chelsea!"

Above that was the sound of two eight-year-olds and a nine-year-old running to the kitchen. She could hear the sounds of the refrigerator door being opened and closed and cupboard doors slamming while Kate was probably preoccupied with the screaming toddlers.

Amy closed the lid on the john, propped her elbows on it and dropped her head in her hands. She didn't know whether to laugh at Kate's textbook-psychology-catchphrase approach to child care, or cry over the chaos that she knew reigned in her living room.

It was a good thing the parents of the toddlers were all friends of hers from her days as promotion and public relations director at Riverview Hospital. Otherwise any stranger walking into this facility this afternoon would probably have her license pulled.

The older children hadn't fit in elsewhere, so she was in no serious danger of losing them, but that was not necessarily a comfort at the moment.

She had two other children enrolled who were blessedly normal—Pete and Eddy Nicholas, nine and twelve, Malia Nicholas's brothers, but they came only two afternoons a week when there was no football practice after school.

But she was getting inquiries all the time, and she needed more space if she was to provide the kind of day care she really wanted to offer. Remodeling the barn behind the house had seemed like the ideal solution.

The building had been wired and plumbed by the previous owner, but it needed many inside amenities before it could be inhabited by children. And she had visions of cupboard and closet space, a second kitchen, a roomy bathroom.

The playground equipment between the house and the barn was perfectly placed for the summer, but in Heron Point, Oregon, it began raining in late September and didn't stop until May. She imagined converting one half of the barn into a kind of indoor playground.

But that would only happen if she could find a builder she could afford. So far the bids were outrageous, and if she had to keep hiring backhoes and plumbers because of The Mad Flusher, her dreams of expansion would be pushed farther and farther out of reach.

Her family might help her if she asked, but she'd come to Heron Point and taken the job her uncle had found for her at the hospital to escape the look of disappointment in her parents' faces.

Her father had inherited a textile factory from his father, and though, as far as Amy recollected, he'd never contributed much to running or improving it, he'd had a competent staff, and so the company had been a success and their family comfortable.

Her mother, a society maven and a beautiful woman, had groomed her three daughters to marry up, as though their home on Long Island was some country place in Regency England.

Jane, Amy's older sister, was beautiful, petite and brilliant, and had claimed the attention of the scion of a wealthy Boston family in her second year at Yale.

Peggy, Amy's younger sister, was beautiful and very tall, and had caught the eye of a photographer at a Junior League charity function. Before she knew it, she was working as a professional model.

The last Amy heard in a birthday card from her mother in April, Peggy was working in Paris through the summer.

Amy had been her mother's only failure. She had no interest in her looks, in social contacts, or in the young men who ignored her for those very reasons. She was happy enough with her degree in education and a position in a school library, but her mother kept shaking her head over her and murmuring ''poor Amy.''

So she'd come to Heron Point to take control of her life. But the illusion of starting over had lasted only long enough for her to launch the Model Mommy campaign for the hospital's birthing rooms opening, fall in love, then have love walk out on her as though she'd been just any old affaire.

So she'd decided to do something for herself—not to meet the family's expectations of her, and not to comply with some societal rule that expected her to find a man whose idea of a wife was a tall, slightly gawky blonde who really wanted to belong but couldn't quite make it happen.

She'd left the hospital and with a small inheritance from her uncle put a down payment on this big old house at the edge of Ethan's Woods. She had to make this work. She would not fail.

She didn't want to hear another "poor Amy."

She groaned and lifted the lid on the john, feeding the hanger slowly down, knowing the future wasn't going to brighten for her until she had the present in order.

"Right," she thought as the sound of dishware crashing to the floor came from the kitchen. "Like that's going to happen."

TOM NICHOLAS HEARD the persistent doorbell and tried to make his way toward it. But with a blinding headache and the remnants of sleep clouding his brain, he wasn't doing very well. He bounced off of the back of a chair, crashed into the coffee table and limped toward the annoyingly cheerful sound while his shin throbbed painfully.

Before he could reach the door, he heard a key turn in the lock and the door flew open, launching two figures into the room. He squinted against the glare to identify them. Oh, God. Just what he didn't need. His brother and his best friend.

He put one hand over his eyes and held the other hand out, hoping to stop them from moving farther into the room. "I know, I know. I should have told you I was back. But I got in late last night and..."

"Oh, shut up." Jave, his brother, walked right past Tom's halting hand and into the kitchen. "I wasn't expecting to hear from you," he called over his shoulder.

"You've been wandering the countryside for almost two years with nothing but a card or a call every couple of months to let us know you're alive, and Mom and Nancy and the kids worried about you. Why would I expect to be informed that you've moved back into town? I'm the one remaining person in your circle of family and friends who's still talking to you, but, hey... Haven't you even made coffee yet? It's almost three o'clock."

Nate Foster, Tom's friend, looked him up and down and fell into the chair that faced the television. "A word of advice," he said. "If you're going to try to sneak into town, you should park your truck in the garage instead of the driveway. Nice one, incidentally. You must have made big bucks with Healey Construction."

Tom sank into a corner of the sofa, resigned to accepting Jave and Nate's loving but brutal concern. But he was not in an accepting mood. He'd been awakened this morning shortly before eight by the sounds of the sanitation truck, and he'd gone to the window and looked out on residential Heron Point and wondered what in the hell he was doing here.

He'd just finished working on a hotel in Tucson four days ago when he'd looked around at the hot, dry landscape and had the very same thought. *What in the hell am I doing here?* With sweat pouring down him and nothing but mesquite and tumbleweed for miles, he'd longed for the four-mile-wide river, for the evergreens, the coastal breeze, the moist and fragrant air that made even the deepest summer day feel like he was rafting on a lake. For Heron Point.

He'd been so homesick for Oregon that he'd quit Healey on the spot, turned down a considerable raise and a plea to stay with the crew as it moved south to Tempe, packed his truck and headed north.

It had been long enough, he told himself. He'd put the specters of his past behind him before he'd even left Heron Point, but he'd still had to get away to learn to live without them. Guilt had governed him for so long, it had pushed him from the fire-fighting career he'd loved, driven him into an aimless isolation that had kept his entire loving family frantic with worry. Just before he left, Nate, who had been treating a homeless woman, proved to him that he hadn't been hearing things the night he and Davey stormed into the burning hotel, that a woman *had* been screaming, even though he hadn't been able to find her. At the time, he'd felt as if he'd sacrificed Davey for a woman who didn't exist. Davey had died while waiting for him.

No one had understood his need to get away. They'd insisted the issue was resolved. He wasn't to blame for anything. Why did he have to go away now?

It had been hard to explain that guilt had become his identity, and that without it, he had to rediscover himself. His mother had told him he'd always overanalyzed everything. Nate told him he was nuts. Jave told him he was running away.

Amy had closed her door in his face. So much for the love and devotion she'd pledged just two nights earlier.

Angry and confused, he'd left town and kept just a minimum of contact, knowing if he was ever going to find himself again, he had to do it without the family and friends who were always so quick to support and defend him.

He'd had to learn to depend upon himself again, to

learn that he was worthy of his own trust, that he was whole once more.

He'd thought he had, until he'd looked out the window that morning and felt the impact of all that was familiar in his hometown It was one thing to feel heroic in foreign surroundings, but quite another to come back and face the demons that had wrestled you down.

"You look like you ought to start a grunge band," Jave said, two steaming mugs hooked in the fingers of one hand, one in the other. He was wearing a suit. He and Nate, Tom guessed, must have just left the hospital.

"How'd you do that so fast?" Tom asked, sniffing suspiciously at the light brew in the cup.

"It's a powdered instant Jo ordered for Mom," Jave replied, sitting on the other end of the sofa. "I made it in the microwave."

Jo Jeffries owned Coffee Country downtown, a coffee bar patronized by everyone in Heron Point.

Tom took a careful sip and found that it was sweet and tasted of almond. He held back a grimace. Construction site coffee often doubled as mortar, but he'd grown used to it.

This stuff tasted like melted candy, but at least it was hot.

"You heard from Mom?" he asked, trying to sustain the mood of civility as long as possible. "She wrote me that you and Nancy and the kids gave her a trip to Europe for her birthday."

Jave leaned an elbow on the back of the sofa and turned sideways to look at him. "Yeah. She's with a tour in Scotland. She's having a great time. She's not due home until Thanksgiving." He looked around at the bag Tom had propped against the coffee table, the tool boxes he'd brought in to clean up, the jacket over the back of a dining room chair, the sandwich plate and empty potato chip bag from the meal he'd made himself when he'd arrived last night. "That'll give us time to bulldoze this place and start over."

Tom drank more coffee, tuning out the sweetness and concentrating on the heat and the caffeine. "Don't nag, all right? I just got here. I'll get organized."

Jave ignored his reassurances. "How are you?" he asked, and waited for an answer with that analytical, older-brother concentration that had always annoyed Tom yet somehow sustained him.

"I'm fine," he said, almost surprised that in some deep-down, elemental way he really was. All he had to do was figure out what to do about his life now that he was.

"You look like the last stages of swamp fever," Nate observed.

Tom ran his hand over several days' growth of beard on his chin and through hair that hadn't been cut in seven weeks, and laughed. "Yeah, well, I'm not a doctor, so I don't have to look like a George Clooney wanna-be like you guys."

"You don't even look as good as the Unabomber."

Tom laughed again. "I know. But the last few days on the job were a real squeeze, then it was a three-day drive home, so don't hassle me. I'll clean up, then you'll be sorry because Karma will be wondering why she married you instead of me."

Nate shook his head slowly. "You *are* in the last stages of swamp fever."

"So, you want to come over for dinner," Jave asked, "and join Nate and Ryan and me for handball tonight?"

That sounded like a lot of effort at the moment, but he was looking forward to seeing Nancy and the kids.

And a homecooked meal—even Nancy's cooking—would be a nice change from the last three days of fast food on the road.

"Yeah. Thanks." He pointed to the suitcase propped against the coffee table. "Somewhere in there I've got some things for the kids."

Nate frowned. "Nothing for us?"

"I've brought you my sublime skill," Tom said grandly. "I'm sure you must have some project on the old A-frame that needs remodeling or repair. How's the deck holding up?"

"Great," Nate replied. "We spent a lot of time out there. You know..." He dug into the pocket of his jacket with a casualness that was almost theatrical.

·Tom knew immediately that something was up. Jave took a magazine from the coffee table and perused it, as though detaching himself from what was about to unfold.

They'd used this trick on him before. They plotted something together, purportedly for his own good, then one or the other of them presented it in a way that would not suggest collusion. It was a device they'd employed many times when he'd been trying to put his life back together after the fire.

He waited while Nate made a production of exploring his pockets. Jave appeared to be completely absorbed in *Needlework Quarterly*.

"Ah, here it is!" Nate handed him a newspaper clipping. "If you're back in business in Heron Point, you'll need work. I just happened to notice this when I was having lunch."

"I thought you just noticed my car on your way home?"

"No. Karma noticed your truck when she drove past

to go to the Scupper. She called the hospital to ask me if I knew you were back.''

Tom blinked. ''Karma...was going to the Scupper Tavern?''

Nate rolled his eyes. ''She does their books, amoeba brain. Read the ad.''

It was a small ad from the classifieds. Accepting Bids On Barn Remodel. Call Kids & Co. Day Care.

Tom looked up. The ad seemed simply to be a good lead on a job. He'd made and saved a lot of money during his two years in Arizona, but he'd stashed it in savings to build his own place one day, and he was eager to get back to the variety of work offered in general carpentry.

And work done at a day care would mean a lot of parents would see it, and that could mean more work.

Had he misjudged his brother and his friend?

He doubted it. Nate was drinking his coffee with studied calm, and Jave appeared to be memorizing a knitting pattern.

''I suppose the day-care provider is a gorgeous single woman,'' Tom guessed, pocketing the ad.

Nate and Jave exchanged a look. ''As it happens, she is,'' Nate replied. ''This could get your business and your social life off to a good start.''

''You two are so transparent. Just because you were involved in a wedding frenzy and a baby boom two years ago, don't think you're getting me involved.''

Nate gave him an affronted look. ''Did anybody say anything about weddings and babies?''

''Not me,'' Jave replied from behind the magazine.

Tom snatched it from him and slapped it on the table. Then he caught Jave's arm and pulled him to his feet.

With his other hand, he caught Nate and dragged him along as he headed for the door.

He backed them up to it and caught each collar in a fist.

"Now, you two listen to me," he said with quiet sincerity. "I'm back in town less than twenty-four hours and you're already working my life like a piece in a chess game. I do not belong to you!" His voice rose despite his efforts to remain calm. He swallowed and began again. "I am no longer your burned-out little brother—" he focused on Jave, then turned to Nate "—or your needy friend. I've got it together, and I'm back. I want to be a part of your lives, but don't try to find me women or create work for me or otherwise manage my life, or you'll need an orthopedist! Do I make myself clear?"

"Very."

"Sure."

"Good." Tom pulled them away from the door, pushed them aside, then opened it. He smiled amiably at his brother. "Then I'll see you at dinner, and you—" he slapped Nate's shoulder "—at the gym."

"So you don't want help of any kind," Jave said, stopping at the porch stairs, "but you don't mind being fed."

"Food is always above the rules. Pleasure to see you both."

Tom closed the door, then peered through the small square of window in the top to make sure they left.

They walked side by side down the steps, two men in dapper suits who looked like an ad for Armani. When they reached the bottom of the steps they turned to each other, exchanged a high five, then laughed as they walked to Nate's car.

Tom didn't like the looks of that at all.

Just to prove to himself that he was impervious to their machinations, he called the number in the ad.

A young woman's voice answered. Children's raucous voices and crying babies were audible in the background.

"This is Tom Nicholas Carpentry and Construction," he said. "I'd like to make an appointment to see the barn you'd like remodeled and offer a bid."

"Oh. Hold on, please."

He waited. She was back in a moment. "Come by anytime," she said. "The barn is in the back. You have the address?"

"Yes, thank you. I'll be there in half an hour."

Tom showered and shaved and wished fervently that he'd done laundry. He went to the closet in his room and found a pair of casual beige slacks he hadn't bothered to pack when he'd left two years ago. He pulled them on and found them snug. He'd acquired glutes in the intervening time.

In the bottom drawer of his dresser was a long-sleeved green knit sweater he'd never liked because it made him look like a dandy. He pulled it on, thinking that if he was going to wander around a day-care facility, he'd better look as little like a reprobate as possible.

Tom rapped on the front door of a big, turn-of-the-century farmhouse about a quarter of a mile from Nate's place at the edge of Ethan's Woods, and introduced himself to an attractive but very serious-looking young woman. He told her he was going back to the barn.

Behind her he could see an empty playpen, a little girl sitting in a big chair watching television, and two boys on the carpet, playing with cars and trucks.

"That's fine," she said with a stiff smile.

Jave and Nate had really lost it, he thought as he made his way across a neatly trimmed back lawn to a red barn the same vintage as the house. The young woman was practically a child herself, and looked as though she wouldn't know how to laugh if she were given directions.

He pulled the barn's big double doors open and turned his attention to the project. He turned on a light switch on the wall, and could see the plumbing and wiring had been brought in, and that there was a deep laundry tub on the far side.

Cheap paneling had warped on the walls, and the floor squeaked. The windows were rotten, and a flimsy partition apparently intended to separate the large space into two rooms was falling down.

The structure, however, looked sound. He climbed up into the loft to check the beams and found them dry and free of rot. The floor of the loft was sound and would allow that space to be made into an interesting room or office, depending on what the owner wanted to do with it.

He climbed down again, pulled a small piece of paneling away and found that the walls, too, were dry. The leaking window frames had probably been responsible for the condition of the paneling.

He sat on a rough wooden bench and made a few calculations. He put together a bid in three parts. The first, a deluxe remodel, included a dropped ceiling, a stairway to the loft on a second floor, a new floor downstairs, new windows and a wall dividing the space into two rooms.

A moderate job included all the features of the deluxe job, except for the dropped ceiling.

If the client was operating on a really small budget,

he could do just windows and floor and whatever cosmetic work was preferred.

He copied the figures legibly onto a piece of letterhead on his clipboard and headed back to the house.

He was intercepted halfway across the lawn by one of the boys he'd seen in the house. He was towheaded, freckled and scrawny in the way of little boys whose metabolism outdistanced even their great consumption of food.

And this one seemed to be made of sheer energy. He sprang along beside him as though his shocks were bad.

"Hi! Are you gonna fix the barn?"

"Maybe," Tom replied. "I'm going to bid on the job."

"We're gonna play in there in the winter. You're the fourth bidder. The other three were too high."

That was good. He'd put together a conservative bid, hoping it would help reestablish him in Heron Point. After that, the quality of his work would build his reputation. When he'd left the fire department and gone into business for himself four years ago, he'd had more work than he could handle within three months.

"I'm Truman," the boy said, still hopping along beside him.

Tom detoured to go around to the front of the house. "Weren't you president once?" he teased.

The boy punched him in the arm. "Everybody tries that joke. That was Harry Truman. I'm Truman Fuller."

Tom stopped at the bottom of the porch steps to offer his hand. "Hi, Truman. I'm Tom Nicholas."

The boy had a good grip—dirty, but good. "I've got friends named Nicholas. Pete and Eddy. And Malia. She's a girl, though, and a baby."

"I'm their uncle." Tom walked up the steps and Truman followed.

"Cool! The hero from the fire?"

Tom felt the beginnings of the old familiar wrenching in his gut. But he could stop it now. He bore no guilt for it. That was over. Resolved. This was now.

"Not a hero," he corrected the boy gently, rapping on the door. "I went to try to save somebody, but she was already gone."

"But if she'd been there youda saved her!"

The boy's eagerness to invest him with heroic qualities touched him.

The door was opened by the grave young woman. She invited him into a large living room. There were toys everywhere, an empty playpen, and rocking horses on springs, rockers and wheels. The girl still occupied the chair, but the other boy was now stretched on his stomach on the sofa, engrossed in the television.

Something apparently happened in the action that the boy didn't like and he said emphatically, "S---!"

"Rodney!" the young woman said. "You owe the cuss box another quarter. And I'll have to tell your father you're slipping again."

"Well the Gargoyles just got attacked!"

"'Darn it' would have been just as effective a response. I understand your need to express distress, but you're in the presence of a lady."

Rodney frowned. "Where?"

The girl, clutching a fairly large box that seemed to be wrapped in plastic, replied, "Me, stupid," without even looking away from the television.

The woman put a hand to her forehead and closed her eyes.

"I can just leave this with you," Tom said quickly,

afraid the woman was about to have a breakdown. "If you're interested, we can talk about it when it's convenient for you."

"Oh." She shook her head. "I'm not the director. She does want to talk to you. She's in the bathroom. We're having a plumbing crisis."

"Garrett Foster flushed Chelsea Jeffries's blankie down the john!" Truman seemed to find it exciting.

Tom grinned. "No kidding." When he'd left Heron Point, his niece, Malia, and Garrett and Chelsea had been a little over three months old. Now they were two years old.

It had been a curious twist of fate that the babies had all been born at Riverview Hospital on the same day, and that their parents had become the best of friends thanks in part to Amy Brown.

First he'd felt lucky to be part of their warm and riotous group. Then, after the holidays, when they'd all settled into their contented routines, he'd been unable to find his own contentment. So he'd left.

But he was back. And getting work was going to be an important part of his readjustment process. So he put the past out of his mind and followed the young woman across the living room and down a corridor that deposited them in the partially open doorway of a bathroom, with Truman still at his heels.

The woman knocked twice on the door, announced, "He's here!" then turned Truman bodily around and led him away with her.

"Hello?" Tom pushed the door open the rest of the way.

The sight that greeted him drew a quick smile and a gusty sigh of masculine appreciation from him.

A woman was bent over the john with a plunger, her shapely derriere in jeans swaying with her efforts.

"Just a...minute," she said, yanking hard with the plunger. She planted both feet more firmly, affording him an even more delectable view.

Then the little rug under her left foot slipped, the plunger went flying, and she fell backward with a little scream of alarm and a wild flailing of arms.

Tom caught her without even having to move. He extended both arms and she fell into them, hers clutching at his as her head and shoulders crashed into his chest, slapping silky silver blond hair against his mouth and chin.

With his arms full of her, he was overpowered suddenly by several alarming familiarities. The shapely tush, the scent of jasmine, the soft breast around which his right hand was shaped—and the fact that he was here at Nate's and Jave's suggestion.

He put the woman on her feet none too gently, spun her around—and found himself looking into Amy Brown's startled gray eyes.

Chapter Two

Amy stared with shock into Tom Nicholas's dark glare and thought that if any one thing could have made this day worse than it already was it was this. Him.

But for an instant she saw the anger shift in his eyes, letting something else take its place. Something gentle and quiet that allowed her to let all the hurt and anger go and remember what it had been like to love him for two months.

Actually, he hadn't loved her all that time; theirs had been a very volatile relationship. She'd come to Heron Point trying to find self-confidence, self-esteem. And then she met Tom, who was at a point in his recovery from the fire when he blamed himself for his friend's death and tried to refuse himself all happiness.

But she'd pushed, and he'd weakened, and for a few blissful weeks she'd been happier than she'd ever been in her life. Then they'd made love for the first time, she'd touched his burned leg when he'd asked her not to, and the encounter had ended in disaster.

Shortly after, Nate had discovered that there had been a woman in the old hotel the night of the fire; that Tom hadn't heard phantom screams. They'd been real—very real.

And just when Amy had expected that Tom, free of the self-inflicted guilt, might turn to her again, he'd come to her apartment to tell her he had to leave—and he didn't know for how long.

She didn't think she'd ever forget the pain of that moment, how it had felt to see him standing there, thinking he'd come to tell her he loved her, only to discover he was leaving.

She'd screamed at him that she was tired of waiting for him to stop running away from happiness and that it was over. Then she closed the door—on him and on all she'd hoped to have with him.

And here he was, one glimpse of his dark brown eyes decimating the control she'd finally acquired over the loneliness, destroying the confidence she'd built in herself one careful step at a time. It had been such a long way back. And that was reason enough to let her anger reignite.

She yanked out of his grip and took a step away, the narrow confines of the room relegating her to the corner between the john and the tub.

Had one of her glamorous sisters met an old lover, she thought wryly, it would have been in a moonlit garden or by the glow of a dying fire. But she had to be caught in the corner of a soggy bathroom.

Still, she was committed to being a new and better Amy. She folded her arms and drew a breath for calm.

"Hello, Tom," she said coolly, lifting her hand to sweep the hair out of her eyes. "What are you doing here?"

In her mind she heard him reply, "I've come for you, Amy. I'm sorry I left. I've been in agony every day since. I've thought about you, longed for you, desired

you, missed you with absolute desperation. Say you forgive me. Please.''

In reality, he said, ''I'm here about your ad.'' He
reached to the floor for a clipboard he'd apparently
dropped when he'd caught her. He turned it over to
reveal a sodden newspaper clipping. The sheet of paper
under it, however, was covered with figures and considerably dryer. ''I've given you three options. If any
of them appeals to you, call me.''

He removed the sheet of paper with the figures,
handed it to her and turned to leave.

She should have just let him go, but this was the new
Amy—no longer afraid to speak her mind. ''I can't believe you had the nerve to come here,'' she said, balling
the sheet of paper in her hands. ''And *three* options?''
She widened her eyes in theatrical surprise. ''I thought
you were a take-it-or-leave-it kind of guy.''

He turned in the doorway, his formidable chest rising
and falling as he drew a breath—for patience, she
guessed. She was pleased that she'd annoyed him. She
remembered that he'd hated having to talk about what
he felt.

''I came here,'' he said with exaggerated calmness,
''because I didn't know Kids & Co. was *your* place.
Otherwise I'd have known there was nothing for me
here. And if we're questioning motives, why did you
let me come? I called for an appointment first.''

''The message I got was that Somebody or other Carpentry and Construction was coming by to bid on the
barn,'' she said, her hand tightening around the ball of
paper in it. ''It never occurred to me it could be you.
And you're right. There is nothing for you here. You
killed it.''

He leaned a shoulder in the doorway with an arrogance she hadn't seen in him two years ago. "*I* killed it?" he asked. "Who slammed the door in whose face?"

"Who ran away?" she snapped back.

"I...left," he said quietly, "to try to figure out who I was, with the thought that that would be better for you as well as for me. But you're the one who closed the door in my face when I tried to explain that. So, metaphorically, I'd say you're the one who ran."

She made a scornful sound and tossed the paper wad in the air. "Yeah, well, you've always had a myopic view of the world. Thank you for coming. Don't call us, we'll call you. We've had several other bids. Would you let me pass, please?"

She tossed the paper wad again and he caught it as it came down. He remained where he was, filling the doorway. "Three bids, I understand," he said. "And all of them too high."

She looked a little disturbed that he knew that. He enjoyed it. "Well. I'd have done a good job for you, but never mind. We'll just consider the bid withdrawn."

She was quiet for a moment, and he thought he saw an instant's flash of regret in her eyes. Then she met his with a haughty glare. "I think that would be best. Goodbye, Tom."

He backed out of her way into the hall and let her pass before him, leaving the bid in his haste, feeling a desperate need to get out of this house and into his truck. She always had the ability to take a simple situation and confuse him about which way it should go. He hated that.

She was the one who hadn't understood. *She* was the one who'd closed the door on him after he'd shared his deepest concerns. Why should *he* feel guilty because for an instant her gray eyes looked hurt and anguished?

She marched past him into the living room.

"Did he get the job?" Truman bounced around her the way he'd bounced around Tom. "I vote for him. He's Pete and Eddy's uncle!"

Amy put an arm around Truman's shoulders, encouraging him to be still. "I know who he is, Truman. But he's not really...what we need."

She went to open the door for Tom, the last three words spoken with subtle significance.

Tom started through the door, headed for his truck and his new life in Heron Point without the irritations this woman had applied to his old one.

Then he stopped. It occurred to him that the door closed in his face had burned in his gut for two long years. During that time he'd accepted that it had been his fault that that had been the final word. He should have banged on the door until she opened it again and told her what he thought of her capacity for understanding. But he'd had his pride.

Well, he still had it, but she wasn't going to close the door on him again.

"You're wrong there, Amaryllis Brown," he said, leaning aggressively over her. "I think I have precisely what you need. Truman!"

"Yeah?" The boy came to him eagerly.

"Will you hold the door open for me, please? I'll be right back."

"Sure!"

Heart thumping with leftover surprise, anger and a trace of excitement she thought of as battle fever, Amy stood in the doorway impatiently as Tom went to his truck. His words echoed in her ears—"precisely what you need,'' "precisely what you need," and the, er, battle fever rose a little higher.

He opened the back of the truck and removed a wide loop of metal that he slung over his shoulder. A plumber's snake.

He ran lightly up the porch steps, marched past her, then went into the bathroom, with Truman in pursuit. The two children who had been watching television crowded into the small space with Amy.

Tom fed the snake into the toilet, assigning Truman to hold the remaining loop of cable while he worked.

He met an obstruction almost immediately and carefully withdrew the snake as though reeling in a trout. The end of the cable appeared, a wad of baby blanket attached to the end of it.

"Chelsea's blanket!" Darcy exclaimed, her cellophane-wrapped box clutched in her arms. She looked up at Amy in wide-eyed disbelief. "He found it!"

Amy gently disentangled the dripping patch of blanket from the end of the snake and lobbed it into the sink. A little soap and disinfectant, and Chelsea could have it back.

"Thank you," she said stiffly, relieved that she didn't have to call a plumber and that Chelsea would be happy once again. But she hated that it was Tom Nicholas who'd accomplished that. And before he could think she considered the gesture anything but business, she asked briskly, "What do I owe you?"

His eyes went from the snake he was recoiling to her, their darkness filled with rebuke. "Perhaps that's a question you should ask yourself?" he suggested.

Then he turned and left the room, the snake dangling from his hand like a lariat. The children ran after him.

"Mr. Nicholas!" she shouted authoritatively, stopping him at the outside door. The children ran ahead of him to his truck.

"Yes, Miss Brown?" he asked politely, the formality between them edged with sarcasm.

She squared her shoulders and closed the distance between them. "I appreciate your help," she said, "but I will not let that be a favor. I want to pay you for your time."

"I'll bill you," he said, turning away.

"Tom!" she said sharply, grabbing his arm and turning him back. "I insist!"

She knew she was in trouble the instant his eyes met hers, dark and turbulent with anger. She braced herself, not sure what form it would take.

Tom looked into her stubborn frown and wanted more than anything to shake the square-shouldered resolution in her, to rattle all that unyielding determination that made her so sure of what she wanted—and made her know it wasn't him.

The children nowhere in sight, he caught the back of her neck, pulled her to him and opened his mouth over hers. In the kiss was anger for two years of loneliness, disappointment that she hadn't fallen on him with apologetic tears as he'd have liked in some old-world corner of his mind, and personal pain that she could look so good when he'd been so miserable.

Then the softness of her, the familiar scent of her that brought back other times, other kisses, the delicious, moist taste of her after two long years of eating sand gentled his anger and made him forget he was taking his payment in punishment.

He felt her lean into him and kissed her deeply, thoroughly. Then she gave him a sudden, vicious shove and he let her go.

"You egocentric Neanderthal!" she shouted at him.

"You parsimonious old maid!" he returned. "It *was* a favor. Live with it." He turned, heady with anger, and suddenly, painfully, discovered what had happened to the children.

They were bunched behind him on their hands and knees, watching something in the floorboards of the porch. He fell over Truman and saw Rodney and Darcy scatter as he began to go down.

He heard shouts, screams, then the staccato thump of his body against the steps as he hit each one on his way down. With a curious clarity in the heart of danger, he saw the terra-cotta pot on the stone walk and knew he was headed for it—quite literally.

Then he was one with a pretty bunch of purple pansies, pain exploded in his head, and the world went black.

Tom FELT AS THOUGH he were being used for croquet practice, as though someone had a foot on his face and was hitting him in the head with a mallet.

He decided against opening his eyes, knowing it would hurt.

"You're *sure* he's all right?" That was Amy's voice, high and concerned.

His heart palpitated in response to her worried tone. Or was it thumping because of his injury?

"Amy, I'm sure." Nate's voice was patient but had an air of finality about it, as though he'd answered the question before. "He's coming around. I know someone losing consciousness is scary, but it isn't as dangerous as it seems. And this guy's got a head like granite."

Tom opened his eyes at that and found that he'd been right. It *did* hurt. He was apparently on the sofa, and the lamp on the end table behind his head shone right in his eyes.

When he winced against it, a hand moved it away.

Three faces leaned over him—Nate's, Amy's and Truman's.

"Granite?" he asked Nate as he put a hand to his throbbing head. "Are you supposed…to talk about patients like that when…they're out?"

Nate pushed Tom's eyelid up and flashed a light into it. "What's wrong with granite? It makes great monuments and lasts forever. What's your name?"

"Elvis. I'm back."

"I could find a reason to inject you with a really big, dull needle. Your name?"

"Tom Nicholas, six foot two, 193 pounds, born August 25, 1963. One brother, James Victor Nicholas, who tends to enter into collusion with one Nathan Borman Foster for the purposes of playing with my life. What else do you want to know?"

Nate held three fingers up in front of Tom's face. "How many fingers?"

"Three. If there were not a woman and a child present, I would break them for you."

"Hostility is not good for your condition."

"You mean because it could affect your condition—negatively."

"Look." Nate leaned over him, his gaze level and purposeful. It was his emergency room face. Tom had seen it several times before. "You've had a nasty blow to the head. You seem all right, but you never know about these things. You need to be watched."

"I'm fine." Tom tried to sit up.

Nate helped him, then steadied him as the room spun. Tom quickly closed his eyes and tried to right the world again. He opened his eyes cautiously. The ceiling was back where it belonged.

"You need to be watched tonight," Nate said, "and your mother's away. I'm going to call Jave."

"No!" Tom said too emphatically. The sound hurt his head and set the room spinning again. He closed his eyes. "No," he repeated more quietly. "You know how he is. He'll sit over me and have his whole house in an uproar. Besides. You guys were going to the gym tonight."

"I think we can forgo that for one night."

"No. I won't go to Jave's. I'll be fine at home. Mom's got a cordless phone. If I feel ill, I'll call you."

"No way." Nate stood. Tom opened his eyes to keep track of him. "If you won't go to Jave's, I'm taking you home with me."

"No. You're as bad as he is."

"Tom. This is not a choice. If you don't cooperate, I'll call 911, have you brought in and admitted."

Tom glared at him. "You do that and I'll rivet you to your front door."

Darcy's face appeared over the back of the sofa. "When you fall on somebody's 'propity,'" she said tutorially, "you can take them to court and get lots of money. My mom works in a lawyer's office."

"Bonehead!" Rodney said. "He fell over *us*. It's our fault."

"So. It's Amy's propity. She's supposed to keep it safe. He can get lots of money."

Amy accepted this last indignity in a day that had been filled with them. "Thank you, Darcy," she said dryly, then turned to Nate with a fatalistic sigh. "Why doesn't he just stay here? I'm not going anywhere and I won't hover. I've got several extra rooms upstairs, I'll see that he has some dinner, and if he has a problem during the night, I'll be nearby.''

Nate's expression didn't change, but she thought she saw a little flare of victory behind his professional firmness. She questioned it with a raised eyebrow, but he turned to Tom, who did not look pleased with the suggestion.

''I'm going home,'' Tom insisted.

''You're staying here,'' Nate corrected him, ''or you're going to the hospital. It's as simple as that.''

Rodney sat companionably beside Tom. ''Hell of a mess, huh?''

''Rodney, the word *hell* isn't allowed,'' Amy said. ''You know that. Please don't say it.''

''My dad says it all the time. And lots worse.''

''I know, but that's the problem we're trying to solve, remember? You're both trying to learn to use real words rather than swear words. And so far, he's doing a lot better than you are.'' Amy smiled at Nate. ''You'd better get home to Karma. Thanks for coming. I should have called 911, I guess, but I thought if you were home, you knew his case history and everything....''

''I'm glad you called me.'' Nate gave her a quick hug. ''If there's a problem, call me no matter what time. Take it slow, Tom. It'd probably be a good idea to stay down until dinner. I'll be back in the morning before I go to the hospital.''

Tom ran a hand over his face, perfectly willing, suddenly, to follow the suggestion. He felt very tired, and since everyone seemed to be squarely set to prevent him from doing what he wanted to do, retreating into sleep seemed like a good idea.

''Sure,'' he said, then with a grudging glance up at his friend, added, ''Thanks.''

"You're welcome. See you in the morning."

When Nate opened the door to leave, a burly man in grubby jeans, boots and a work shirt came into the room. Rodney left Tom's side, calling, "Hey, Dad!" He pulled the man to the sofa. "This is Tom and he just fell over me and Truman and Darcy and the doctor came and he might have a concussion!" That was all reported excitedly like a child might have announced the birth of puppies or the arrival of the ice cream truck. "He has to spend the night 'cause his mom's gone and somebody's gotta watch him!"

The man leaned over Tom and asked tentatively, "Tom Nicholas?" Then, as though a closer look had assured him that he was, he beamed a smile, extended his hand and said in a big voice, "Boomer Sorenson. You built the poolroom at the Scupper. Me and Paulie Petersen held the Sheetrock on the ceiling while you put it up."

Tom remembered the burly giants who'd offered to help when his T-brace collapsed. He tried to surface from his weirdly disconnected state and offered his hand. "Hi, Boomer. You saved my skin. How's it going?"

"Great!" He patted Rodney's shoulder proudly. "My boy, Rodney."

"Yeah. We've met."

"You going to be okay?"

"Sure. Just need to rest."

Boomer turned to Amy. "How was Roddy's language today?"

Tom watched Amy open her mouth to reply, then reconsider and smile. "He's trying hard, Mr. Sorenson, but I hope you'll keep reminding him."

Boomer nodded, looking a little sheepish. "I'll just

have to plainly do better myself. Well, let's go, son. Your mother's picking up a pizza on her way home from work. Good to see you, Nicholas. Thanks, Amy.''

While Amy saw Rodney and his father to the door, Darcy returned with a pillow and a blanket. The cellophane-wrapped box still clutched in her arm, she plumped the pillow for him and urged him down to it with nurselike care. Then she covered him with the blanket.

"You want your shoes off?" Truman asked.

Before Tom could decline the offer, Truman was unlacing his steel-toed Wolverines and pulling them off—or trying to.

"Don't you guys ever go home?" Tom asked.

Darcy knelt on the floor beside the sofa as though ready to be of service. "My mom doesn't come till six. And Truman's dad is always late. Sometimes he gets to eat here. Amy makes good stuff."

Yes. He remembered that.

He tapped a finger against the box in Darcy's arm. "What's in there?" he asked.

Darcy held it toward him so that he could see it. "It's a Beautiful Bride Brenda, 1995." In its original wrapper, the box revealed, besides the smiling doll in all her wedding finery, a bridal bouquet, a garter, a suitcase—presumably for the honeymoon trip—and a casual outfit complete with brimmed hat and tennis shoes.

"Wouldn't you be able to play with it better," Tom asked, "if it was out of the box?"

She shook her head, wide green eyes solemn. "It's not to play with. Brenda is a collectible. It's an investment."

"An investment."

"From Grandma Browning. If I don't play with it,

Mom can sell it in a couple of years and make some money. My dad never paid stuff, so we have lots of dots.''

''Debts,'' Truman corrected her, still yanking unsuccessfully on Tom's shoe.

''Debts,'' she repeated. ''You want a glass of water?''

''I think the best thing we can do,'' Amy said, returning now that the Sorensons had gone, ''is let Tom get some rest. Let me help you with that, Truman.''

Tom, lying on his side, watched her support his leg in her arm as she slipped the other hand inside the heel of his shoe and directed Truman to pull on it. The shoe came off.

Tom had never thought of his ankle and heel as erogenous zones, but as she grasped the other ankle under him, tugged it gently sideways to get a grip on it, then slipped her fingertips inside the heel of his shoe, he felt a jolt of electricity that might have accompanied a far more intimate touch.

His breath caught somewhere in his throat. Fortunately, he wasn't called upon to say anything. She readjusted the blanket over him, told him briskly to rest, then led the children off with her.

When Tom awoke, the room was dark and the tantalizing aroma of dinner wafted toward him. He hadn't eaten anything since the very early hours of that morning, and he reacted like Pavlov's dog.

He sniffed, trying to analyze what it was. Something traditional. Something his mother fixed. Something he hadn't had in two years.

''Pot roast and vegetables!'' Truman announced.

The light behind Tom's head went on with blinding suddenness and Truman's head appeared over the back of the sofa. "I'm supposed to see if you feel like eating, or if you'd rather sleep. Amy says she can fix a plate for you that you can microwave later if you want."

She'd like that, he thought with sudden, inexplicable rancor. Well, if she could invite him to spend the night as though there'd never been anything between them, as though they'd never begun a beautiful night together that she'd ultimately ruined—then he could play the same game.

She no longer meant anything to him except a reminder that women could be good company, but a man shouldn't get serious about one.

He could be as unaffected by seeing her again as she was by seeing him.

Tom made his way to the table, Truman supporting him solicitously if unnecessarily with an arm around his waist. He and the boy sat across from each other at the table in a pretty green-and-beige dining room with an old-fashioned hutch filled with teapots.

He focused on them, spotting a small one sprigged with rosebuds that he remembered Jave and Nancy buying for her the Christmas before he left. When she'd lived in the small apartment, he'd teased her about the collection because there hadn't been enough space for her to display them together, and she'd distributed them around the house.

They'd been on the counter in the kitchen, on the coffee table in the living room, on the dresser in her bedroom.

Somehow their reunion in the antique hutch seemed to express that she'd accomplished something, that she finally had what she wanted, and he couldn't help a certain twinge at the knowledge that she'd done it without him.

Of course, he reminded himself, if a woman was willing to head off on her own without a second thought to
the man in her life, then it would be easy for her to
make strides.

It was the caring that held one back, the attention
given to someone else's needs that took focus and energy away from one's own goals.

Well. He wasn't going to make that mistake twice.

Tom glanced at the clock. It was six-forty-five. Darcy
had apparently been picked up, but Truman still waited.
He wondered what kind of life the poor kid had with
parents who didn't bother to come for him until it was
time to put him to bed.

Amy appeared suddenly with a polite smile and a
platter of succulent-looking beef and aromatic vegetables. She disappeared again and returned with a basket
of rolls and butter.

"Coffee?" she asked Tom.

He smiled with the same removed courtesy. "Please.
No cream, no sugar."

"Straight," she said. "Yes, I know." She gave him
a quick, judicious glance and she was gone again.

He fought annoyance and concentrated on the wonderful food. In deference to her hospitality, though Nate
had forced her to offer it, he was determined to spend
the night in her home without a confrontation. Even
though every glance she sent in his direction seemed to
berate or condemn him. Responding would only mean
it mattered to him, and it didn't.

Over dinner, she asked politely about his two years
in Arizona, and he explained about the chain of hotels
he'd helped put up in five different cities.

"Did you get to Tombstone?" Truman asked.

Tom shook his head. "No. We were in the northern half of the state. Phoenix, Flagstaff, Kingman."

"Did you see any cowboys?"

"Yeah, a few. They use helicopters now, you know."

Truman frowned. "I wish I could time-travel, you know? Like in *Bill and Ted's Excellent Adventure.* Then I'd meet famous marshals and great Indian chiefs."

Tom was a little surprised by his interest in the past. "What about astronauts and basketballs stars? They're right here, today."

"But history's alive with great people."

That seemed like an unlikely observation for a fidgety, physical child, and Tom teased him with a grin. "Really. Where'd you hear that?"

"My mom," Truman replied. "She taught American history. She liked the frontier part best 'cause her great-grandma left Missouri on a wagon train and ended up in Tombstone. Her husband was a marshal for a while."

"No kidding?" Tom regretted his disbelief and turned the grin to a smile of interest. "What happened?"

"She died."

"Your mom's great-grandma."

"Yeah. And my mom. She had cancer."

Tom guessed by the look in the boy's eyes that it hadn't been that long ago. It wasn't extreme pain as much as the simple disbelief that someone he'd apparently considered indestructible could have died.

"Me and Dad moved here from Portland to kinda start over."

"Yeah," Tom said, relating to the need to start fresh, though it didn't seem fair that a little boy should have to. He should be able to remain connected to what was familiar. "Well, this is a good place to do it. Heron Point's a great place to live."

Truman gave a noncommittal shrug. "I like Amy, but school's not so hot. They yell at you for *every*thing."

"Truman's dad is the new principal at the high school," Amy said, reaching for the boy's empty milk glass and pushing away from the table. "He has a lot of beginning-of-the-year work to do, and he's putting in some extra time learning about the school. So Truman's spending a lot of time with me."

Truman smiled at Amy with unabashed heroine-worship. "I like that part."

Tom bit back a smile and turned to Amy with mild reproof in his eyes. "Another conquest," he observed as Truman helped himself to more beef.

"One of my wiser ones," she said sweetly, managing to convey the message that Tom was in another category altogether.

Chapter Three

Tom didn't like Steve Fuller's looks. Oh, he was pleasant enough, shook his hand when they were introduced, behaved in a concerned and apologetic manner when Truman explained excitedly about the fall, even offered to pay for the medical expenses incurred.

But it was all a play for Amy, Tom knew.

She seemed to be gushing. She explained about calling Nate, that he was Tom's friend, and that there probably wouldn't be any expenses. Then she thanked him softly for asking.

Her voice always softened when she was attracted. He remembered. It had happened with him.

And now this tall guy in a suit with a body that said he thought for a living instead of wielding a hammer was bringing her voice down to a throaty murmur.

She helped Truman into a light fleece jacket, then walked him and his father to the door.

Tom pretended to be interested in the paper. Amy and Fuller were lost in their own quiet laughter as they discussed something he couldn't hear, and they didn't notice him watching them over the top of it.

Then Amy leaned down to hug Truman, Fuller put his hand on Amy's upper arm in a gesture that wasn't precisely a rub but was obviously intended to express affection, and Amy walked them out onto the porch.

Tom leaned sideways to try to see what happened next, but they were out of sight.

Then Amy was back and Tom straightened, frowning in concentration over what he pretended to read.

"Got a girlfriend?" Amy asked as she gathered up a cup and plate off the end table. "Or do you just like to look at the pictures?"

Tom lowered the paper in confusion. "What?"

She pointed the cup at the section of newspaper he held. "You've been studying that Magic Moon Lingerie insert for ten minutes." Then she went to the dining room, took a simple green teapot from the hutch and disappeared into the kitchen.

He slapped the paper down and got up and followed, pausing after three quick steps to regain his equilibrium. Rapid movement made his head thump.

Steady once again, he went through the dining room and into the kitchen. It was like walking into a bower—a bower where midgets lived.

The room was green and white, the walls covered with ivy-patterned wallpaper. A large table was tucked into a nook, and a dozen mismatched chairs painted green surrounded it.

"I was trying to remain available," he said with strained dignity, "on the chance that you needed help. I've seen suits operate before."

She put the teapot on the counter and the cup and plate in the sink. Then she filled a teakettle with water. "Suits," she repeated, going to the stove. "You think men in suits operate any differently than men in tool belts?"

He leaned against the counter as she reached into an overhead cupboard for two cups and a flowered tin.

"No," he replied, "but a woman sees a guy in a tool belt, she knows she's dealing with trouble. A guy in a suit creates the impression of being harmlessly cerebral, then you drop your guard and he's got you right where you might not want to be."

She smiled at him over her shoulder as she opened a drawer and retrieved a tea strainer. "What makes you think I might not want to be there?"

"Past experience," he replied. "You're afraid of a relationship, remember?"

He thought he saw the jab register in her eyes, but she turned them to the task of spooning tea from the tin into the strainer, so he couldn't be sure.

"I think the blow to your head," she said as she placed the strainer in the open top of the teapot, "has affected your memory. I've been right here for two years. You're the one who ran away."

"I *went* away," he corrected her quietly. He really wanted to shout it, but he was trying to maintain her level of neutrality. "There's a difference."

"Really." She reached into another cupboard and brought down a package of napkins. "It didn't feel like it to me."

He was suddenly tired of neutrality. "Does that mean you missed me?" he asked.

She took two napkins out of the pack, placed them near the mugs, then tossed the package back up into the cupboard. "I thought I would die," she said with a detachment that belied the words. "Then, after a couple of months, I got word through Nancy via Jave that your hotel job was finished, but you weren't coming home, you were moving on to yet another one, and whatever I felt for you died right there. I knew you were...gone.''

He felt a curious pain from the base of his throat to the pit of his stomach, almost as though he'd swallowed something lethal. It occurred to him grimly that the truth could be hard to swallow.

But it hadn't been his fault. It had been hers. And he wanted to be sure she accepted that.

''I suppose that's a good thing,'' he said, ''because what I felt for you died when you slammed the door on me.''

She turned to look at him then, gray eyes calm. But when she met his gaze, he saw something frantic in hers, something he remembered from the disastrous night when they'd started to make love.

The teakettle whistled, filling the room abruptly with its shrill noise. She looked away, turned the knob off above the burner, then picked up the kettle and poured steaming water over the tea in the strainer.

''Well aren't we lucky, then?'' she asked, her eyes on her task as water filtered slowly through the aromatic leaves. ''This is a good place for us to be. Sexual tension out of the way. Nothing to interfere with the efficient administration of business.''

He struggled to retain his handle on the situation. ''Business?''

''Yes.'' She removed the strainer and put the lid on the teapot. With a hand cupped under the strainer, she carried it to the sink and placed it on the cup. She dried her hand on a towel and gave him that smile again, only this time it was a little warmer, almost friendly. And curiously, that hurt even worse.

''While you slept,'' she said, putting the pot and mugs on a tray, ''I looked over your proposals for the barn. I think I'd be a fool to reject the quality I know you would put into the work for an old grievance over something that's now deader than a doornail. That is, if you think you can work for me?''

''The way it works,'' he said amiably, ''is that we decide together what you want, then I work for me.''

''I see.'' She added the napkins to the tray. ''Well, if I wasn't familiar with your work, I might consider your attitude uppity. But, all right. Can you work for yourself on *my* barn?''

He knew it would be safer to cut and run, but he'd never done that in his life, despite what she thought. So he nodded. ''Sure I can,'' he said.

''Good.'' She picked up the tray and headed for the door. ''Come with me,'' she said. ''I'll show you where you'll sleep tonight.''

He followed her up a narrow back stairway that led from the kitchen into an upstairs corridor. A pretty pot of eucalyptus stood on a little table against one wall.

He took a rough count of six rooms that opened off the hallway. Most of them held cribs, bunk beds and a plethora of toys.

''Your mom told me this was a boarding house in the heydays of the canneries.'' She led the way into a room that had a simple double bed, a dresser and a small round table next to which was placed a rocking chair. She put the tray down on the table. ''It's perfect for my purposes. I often have kids overnight on week-ends, too, so I really appreciate the space.'' She pointed to a box on the wall over the bed. ''There's an intercom. If you don't feel well during the night, buzz me and I'll call Nate. Meanwhile...'' She poured tea into one of the mugs and handed it to him. ''This is chamomile. It'll help you sleep. If you feel up to it, we can talk business in the morning."

She poured tea into the second mug, took one of the napkins and headed for the door with it.

"I'm at the far end of the hall," she said with that pleasant smile, "and the bathroom's across the hall, second door down. There's a Bugs Bunny night-light in it. Can't miss it. Need anything else?"

Tom struggled for equilibrium—and it wasn't physical this time. In the space of five minutes she'd admitted she'd missed him while he was away, told him it was unequivocally over between them, offered him work and now stood in a shadowy room with him, a double bed between them.

Could his life get more complex? he wondered. Then he noticed the neat pile of clothes and shaving bag on the rocking chair. They were his.

"Jave stopped by while you were asleep," Amy explained, "but he didn't want to wake you. Nate called him. He wanted to see for himself that you were okay, and he thought you might appreciate a change of clothes in the morning. He said to tell you you can have a rain check on the dinner invitation."

That was Jave, Tom thought. As much as his hovering irritated the hell out of him, it also often produced just what he needed at just the right moment.

"Well..." Amy went to the door, her mug of tea in hand. "Sleep well. And if you have a problem, call me. See you in the morning."

"Right," he said. Then he added grudgingly but sincerely, "Thank you."

"Sure," she replied lightly, and left the room, closing the door behind her.

He wanted to put a fist through it, but he didn't. His

emotions were turbulent enough to launch the action, but his physical strength at the moment was too uncertain to assure that he could follow through.

How dare she be so coolly removed from the roar of anger and the memory of two lonely years that rode on his shoulders. How dare she be kind and considerate when she'd claimed just a few minutes earlier that his absence had made her want to die. How dare she suggest that they were now in this comfortable place.

He didn't feel comfortable at all. At the moment he felt as though he were half testosterone-fueled fourteen-year-old boy and half deranged psychotic. And he'd finally come home because he thought that after two years of living on his own and learning to be free of the past, he had it together. Ha. Amy had managed to destroy that in him in a matter of minutes.

Tom moved the clothes to the foot of the bed, went to the table, picked up the tea, then sat in the rocker by the window and made himself relax.

He could do this. He could work on her barn because he needed work if he was to get his business going again, and she would be too busy with the children to spend much time getting in his way. And if she could be so relaxed and forget that they'd ever meant anything to each other, then so could he.

He took a sip of tea and gagged the moment the pale brew hit his taste buds. He'd never tasted anything so vile in his life. It reminded him of castor oil with grass in it. It could put you to sleep all right—permanently. He put the mug down on the farthest side of the table, as though its mere presence close by could still gag him.

He leaned his head against the high back of the chair and looked out the window. Somewhere beyond the ev-

ergreens that curved in a semicircle behind Amy's barn
was Nate and Karma's place.

While he felt grateful that Nate had rushed over in
response to Amy's call, he also remembered that it was
Nate and Jave's doing that he'd come here in the first
place.

While he'd been in Arizona, his mother had written
him that Amy had quit the hospital, but that was all
she'd said. He hadn't known when he'd read the clipping that Kids & Co. was Amy's place. But Jave and
Nate had known. And he was going to see that they
paid for the deliberate deception.

AMY AWOKE WITH A START to the sound of a crash. It
vibrated in the darkness even as she sat up, and she
clutched the blanket to her, her first thought that she
had an intruder.

Then her brain awakened sufficiently to remind her
that Tom, somewhat of an invalid, was at the other end
of the hall.

The certainty that something was wrong sent her flying into the hallway without bothering with a robe.

"Tom?" she called anxiously, running toward his
room. "Are you all...?"

"Stop!" he ordered sharply.

She did instinctively, but not before landing in mid-
stride on something that ripped into the pad of her bare
foot. She cried out in pain and stumbled against the
wall.

Tom was there in a minute, his arm going around her
to support her. "You stepped on it?" he asked.

She hopped to redistribute her weight, having no
choice but to put her arm around the arm that supported
her. "What is *it?*"

"Your pot of eucalyptus," he said in a tone of self-condemnation. "I'm sorry. I was headed for the bathroom, forgot about the little table and crashed into it. Before I could grope for the pot, it fell over."

She felt relief despite the pain in her foot. "Thank goodness. I thought something was wrong with you, that you'd...collapsed or something. Ouch."

He had leaned down to examine her foot and made contact with the injury.

"I'm fine," he said, swinging her up into his arms with a suddenness that startled a little scream out of her. "But I think you're the patient this time. It's a good thing we have a lot of doctor friends."

She laughed nervously. "They probably don't think so. I'm not sure you should be carrying me after what you've just been..."

There was no point in continuing. They'd reached the bathroom.

"Can you get the light?" he asked.

She reached out to the right and flipped the switch.

The pink-and-white room came alive in all its minuscule proportions.

He placed her on her good foot, reached to the towel rack for a bath towel, placed it on the counter, then lifted her onto it.

He bent her leg over her other knee and leaned over her to inspect the sole of her foot.

All the air in her lungs left her in a rush. His large, muscular shoulder covered in a cotton T-shirt was a hairbreadth from her breast, his bare arm rested on her thigh, and her foot was caught in the gentle but sturdy grip of his hand. He wore a natty pair of dark blue, waffle-weave Joe Boxer shorts, and the warm fabric rubbed against the inside of her leg, which dangled over the edge of the counter.

His burned leg was clearly visible with its vivid, puckered scars from thigh to ankle, but remembering his extreme sensitivity to attention on it, Amy tried to concentrate on his hands.

But she found she couldn't focus on anything.

Every place in which her body was in contact with his seemed to develop its own erratic pulse. The very small room closed in even more tightly until it felt as though they'd been placed in a box together and someone was closing the lid.

Amy tried to lean back, but there was nowhere to go. She tipped sideways as one hand ended up in the sink.

"Whoa!" He reached up to steady her, his hand connecting with her bare upper arm. "What are you doing?"

"Sorry," she said, her voice little more than a gasp but sounding very loud in the small space. "I...was trying to move out of your light. But there's no place to go."

"I can see," he said, leaning over her again, apparently suffering none of her claustrophobic anxieties. "This isn't deep, but you've got a little piece of pottery stuck in the ball of your foot. Do you have tweezers?"

She pointed to a basket on the counter across from the sink. It held a brush, comb and makeup odds and ends. "In that plastic makeup bag in the basket."

He leaned over her dangling leg to reach for it, unconsciously steadying himself with a hand on her bent knee. Sensation ran along her thigh and into the heart of her like a small bolt of lightning.

He ran the end of the tweezers under the hot water,

then leaned over her again and in one easy pull that pinched removed the splinter of pottery.

He ran a thumb over the spot. "I think that's it. Can you feel anything?"

Oh, yes. She felt a lot, she thought, about to strangle with tension. But she wasn't going to tell him that. "No," she replied. "Feels fine."

"Good. Antiseptic in here?"

He leaned her sideways into his arm as he opened the mirrored door of the medicine cabinet behind her. Her hand closed around the rippled muscle of his shoulder in an instinctive grasp for balance, and she had a sudden, vivid recollection of what it was like to hold him, to be held by him.

Then in an instant he had the tube of cream and the tin of Band-Aids. He closed the cabinet and pushed her upright again with clinical detachment. He handed her the tin. "Want to get one out for me?"

She complied, horrified to find her fingers unsteady. She removed a Band-Aid from the tin and watched it flutter past him to the floor as she lost control of it.

He didn't seem to notice. He removed the top from the tube of antiseptic cream and squeezed out a cold line of white stuff against the ball of her foot.

"That ought to do it." He held his hand up for a Band-Aid.

She ripped the end off one and handed it to him. Then she fumbled the box she held and forty-some Band-Aids fell to the floor.

He teased her with a glance before leaning over her to cover the antiseptic cream with the Band-Aid. "I hope you're more coordinated than this when one of your little kids has an injury. There. Feel better?"

He accompanied the question by grasping her waist

through the cotton nightshirt she wore and lifting her off the counter and onto her feet.

Trapped with him between the half-open door and the counter in the already narrow space between tub and sink, she was an inch from him and completely flustered by his sexily rumpled appearance in shorts and T-shirt, and his competent ministrations.

She looked up into his eyes and saw the dark flare there as he caught the awareness from her as though it were a germ. But it didn't seem to upset him. It seemed to steady him even further. His eyes held hers without reflecting any of the fluster that was rendering her completely useless.

"I'm fine," she said, and turned, anxious to escape.

"Watch it!" Tom warned, but not before she'd collided with the half-open door.

"Damn it," she muttered as she rubbed her forehead. She'd done the same thing in Jave's office the first time she'd met Tom, only with considerably more dire results. They'd had to put her in a wheelchair and take her to Emergency, where ten stitches had been sewn in her scalp.

She remembered how she'd felt when she'd first looked into his eyes—as though she'd come home after a long and trying day. Only her home had never held that degree of comfort for her. She'd never really felt the sense of belonging she'd experienced when Tom looked back at her and smiled.

Then Tom had offered her a spur-of-the-moment invitation to his birthday party and their rocky relationship had begun.

For a moment, the anger she always felt over the waste of what had seemed so promising dissolved in the memory of how wonderful it had sometimes been.

Tom took her face in his hands and tipped it up to the light, combing her hair aside with his fingers to inspect her forehead. He shook his head over her. "You're going to have a lump there. Come on. I'll get you some ice."

"No." She pushed out of his arms. "I don't want ice. I'll be fine." She slapped the door aside and would have stepped out into the hallway if Tom hadn't caught the back of her nightshirt in his fist and prevented her.

"What?" she demanded testily.

"The hallway is full of broken pottery," he reminded her patiently, "and your feet are still bare." In the narrow space, he cinched an arm around her waist, held her to him and lifted her off her feet. He walked gingerly with her over the rubble and into her room.

Expecting to be set down, she was surprised when he swung her up into his arms as he crossed to her bed and deposited her in the middle of it.

"Thank you," she said stiffly, trying to tug down on the nightshirt that had risen uncomfortably high in the process.

"You're welcome," he said. He placed one hand on the mattress on the other side of her, trapping her under the barrier of his braced arm. "Small payment for the dinner and the accommodations, not to mention your call to Nate."

She tried to back farther into her pillows. He'd had a curious alteration of mood, and she was in no emotional condition at the moment to handle it.

"Anyone would have done the same thing," she said breathlessly.

He leaned a little closer. "But *you* did it. After telling me you no longer care."

"I don't."

"Really?"

"Really."

"Then how come you can't breathe?"

"Because you're leaning on me."

"No. I'm not touching you."

Wasn't he? She took a moment to conduct a sensory examination of her body and it was true; he wasn't touching her. It just felt like he was. Or she could imagine he was. Or maybe…wished that he was.

"Is there something else you want?" she asked, using the defensive tone of her voice to counteract the softening inside her.

"I was going to ask you that," he replied softly.

She didn't know as much about herself as she'd thought, she realized, when two years of rebuilding a life could be undermined and nearly negated by a simple question from the man who'd caused her destruction in the first place.

She could put her arms around him now, she knew, and get back everything that she'd had before he left Heron Point. Then it occurred to her that she hadn't had as much as she'd thought if he'd been able to walk away—and stay away for two years.

"I'd like to go to sleep," she said.

Silence rang between them for a long moment, then he leaned over her and she felt her heart slam against her ribs, thinking he was going to kiss her—ecstatic that he was going to kiss her.

But he simply kissed her forehead and pushed himself off the bed. "Good night, Amy," he said, and left the room.

Through her closed door and above the thumping of her pulse, she heard him go downstairs, rummage around, then return, apparently with a broom.

There was a quiet stirring in the hallway while he swept up, then the closing of a door.

The closing of a door. That felt alarmingly significant as she lay alone in the darkness.

She glanced at the clock on her bedside table. It was 2:32 a.m. Her life had been turned upside down in less than twelve hours.

Everything she'd thought resolved within herself had been dug up and turned over like space for a garden. The question was, would it safely remain fallow, or would something grow?

She turned over and pulled the blanket up under her chin. That was just a fancy metaphor for unearthing a relationship that had brought her nothing but trouble.

No. She wasn't going to do it. She'd fallen under the spell of troubled brown eyes and a sweet and funny manner before, and where had it gotten her? Alone, that's where.

Well, she was smarter this time. This time she owned a house and a business, and had many little lives dependent upon her remaining sane and self-confident.

So Tom Nicholas could just get the hell out of her life.

Except that she'd hired him to renovate her barn. Well, that was all right. He would do fine work and for a better price than anyone else she'd consulted.

It would be a business relationship. They'd agreed upon that earlier. And she'd hold him to it.

Down the hall, Tom climbed back into bed with an unsettling sensation stirring in the pit of his gut—and in his groin. He still had strong feelings for Amy Brown, and she'd just closed another door in his face— at least, metaphorically speaking.

Well. He'd be damned if he'd walk away a second time.

Chapter Four

Tom groaned when he awoke to find Jave leaning over him, taking his pulse.

"Will you give me a *break?*" Tom demanded, trying to yank his wrist away, but Jave shushed him and held fast, his eyes on his watch.

Jave finally dropped Tom's wrist and frowned down at him. "Headache?"

Tom sat up and felt a subtle little throb behind his eyes. "No," he lied. If he'd said yes, he was sure he'd have found himself in intensive care.

"Nausea?"

"No."

"Clear vision?"

"No," Tom answered testily, throwing the blankets back. "You're in sight."

Jave grinned dryly. "Hmm. Irritability. But with you that's a character trait and not a symptom."

Tom stood and squared off with his brother. "I thought we had a talk yesterday about you and Nate staying the hell out of my life?"

"Yeah?"

"Yeah. So Nate gave me this clipping while you pretended to mind your business—which, incidentally, I didn't believe for a minute—and I answered the ad to find myself at Amy's house!''

"We thought you needed work." Jave frowned, as though surprised by his indignation. "And Amy tells me you've struck a deal over the barn. So what's the problem?"

"So the problem is that you knew how things were between me and Amy when I left here."

"Did you?"

Tom stared at him blankly for a minute. "Are we having the same conversation here? Did I know what?"

"How things were between you and Amy," Jave replied calmly. That was one of his favorite tricks. He drove Tom to the edge of apoplexy, but remained calm himself. Someday Tom was going to turn the tables on him and remain calm himself.

Someday. But not today.

"Would you get out so I can get dressed?" Tom asked, taking Jave's arm and leading him to the door. "Thank you for bringing my stuff last night, but don't think for a minute that that gets you off the hook about the clipping. I'll get even."

Jave made a scornful sound. "You've been threatening that for thirty-four years, and by my calculations, you could live to be ninety-two and I'll still be way ahead."

"Goodbye."

Jave handed him a ring with one key on it. He recognized it instantly. It started the *Mud Hen*, the late-twenties cabin cruiser he and Jave had bought together two summers ago. It had been an old bucket at the time, but he'd refinished it inside and Jave and Nancy had honeymooned on it. He'd given Jave his key for safekeeping before he'd left for Arizona.

"In case you want to check it out. There're Cokes in the fridge. We'll expect you for dinner tonight. You can bring the wine."

Jave started for the stairs.

Tom stopped him in the hallway with a shout. "Hey!" He leaned a shoulder in the doorway. "Did I tell you it was good to see you?"

Jave looked back at him with an irrepressible grin. Behind it, Tom saw welcome and the stalwart affection that had seen him through most of his life. "No, but it was pretty obvious when you told me to get out. Incidentally, I just dropped your niece off. You might give her a little attention when you get downstairs. See you tonight."

AMY WAS IN THE KITCHEN on a cordless phone when Tom got downstairs, showered, dressed and feeling like himself again. The shower had done a lot to clear his head.

Bright sunlight poured in through long windows in the living room and onto the three occupants of a nylon mesh playpen in the middle of the room. One of them played with a plastic ball, another swung a string of four large plastic beads against the side of the playpen, and the third watched the television where a tall man in a propeller beanie talked about the alphabet.

The toddlers were all dressed in long-sleeved T-shirts and rompers, and Tom found it difficult to determine gender. As he recalled, one of the three babies born on that same day in September had been a boy.

Amy put her hand over the telephone's mouthpiece. "I'll get your breakfast in a minute. Darcy's mother just put me on hold."

He shook his head. "Thanks, but you don't..."

"I want to talk about the barn," she insisted, holding a finger up as a sign to him that she was about to resume her phone conversation. She held one hand to her ear and walked back into the kitchen.

Prepared to wait, he went to the playpen and knelt down beside it to study the children. They all came to the side, like little colts at the sight of hay.

Which one, he wondered, was Malia?

"Malia?" he asked.

All three looked at him with wide eyes, but he noticed no significant response to the name. He looked for family identification. Malia wasn't Jave's flesh and blood, but she was Nancy's. He looked for brown eyes and brown hair.

Two of the babies had brown hair and one was bald. Three pairs of brown eyes looked back at him.

He put his finger to the cheek of the little baldy.

"Hi," he said. "Are you Malia?"

No, I'm Chelsea. Who are you? You look familiar.

"If you are Malia, I'm your Uncle Tom. And no jokes about Uncle Tom's Cabin, okay? Pete and Eddy have already worn that one out."

Say, what? You had a bad fall yesterday, didn't you? I heard about it. Maybe you should lie down. Want to hold this for a minute? I understand you saved it for me. Thanks!

Tom found a little square of threadbare blanket pushed into his face. He recognized the blanket he'd rescued and so identified its owner. "Ah. You're Chelsea."

Told ya!

"Thank you. What about you?" He turned his attention to the baby with the beads. "Are you Malia?"

Look, dude, the name's Garrett. Do I look like a girl?

I know the clothes aren't exactly from the Gap, but hey, I don't have a lot to say about my wardrobe yet, you know what I mean?

Tom pinched a pointy little chin. "You're a pretty little thing."

Oh, yeah? Well, let's put a dimple in yours!

Tom leaned back just in time to avoid the sudden fling of the plastic beads in his face. He went to the third baby, who was trying to climb out of the pen.

Hey, unc! It's me! I'm Malia. Over here.

"Okay, it's got to be you." Tom unhooked the little leg now stuck on the edge of the pen and lifted the toddler into his arms. "Malia?"

She laughed and patted his shoulder. "Lia!" she said.

Feeling as though he'd accomplished something truly brilliant, Tom grinned at her. "Well, how are you? You were just a fingerling when I left here. Bet your brothers have been spoiling you."

She watched him with a broad grin, apparently as fascinated with him as he was with her. She launched into a barrage of sounds.

Yeah, they're cool! How are you? Everybody was worried about you. I don't know why. You look fine to me. Want to watch this with me? It's all about letters. You know, A, B, C...that stuff. I have to know that, 'cause my mom's a writer, and when we work at the computer, she always makes a file for me. She says someday I'll put a story there. Look. A is for alligator. B is for...

Malia, suddenly bored with him, turned her attention to the television. He put her back in the playpen, and she hung her arms over the side closest to the TV and watched.

"Isn't she precious?" Amy asked from the edge of

the fireplace. "We're all convinced Heron Point was blessed the day these three were born. Jave's boys have really become a pair of ladies' men. They're going to be even more handsome than the two of you."

He raised an eyebrow at the compliment. Her cheeks pinked as though that admission embarrassed her. "Well, let's face it," she said finally, as though trying to slough off her discomfort with candor. "We both know that good looks were never your problem."

He shrugged, wondering how to explain without sounding falsely modest that it was something he never gave much thought to. But he did like the notion that *she* thought about his looks—and liked them.

She studied him, her eyes…wistful?

"I know. And your ignorance of it was always part of your mystique. Come on. I've got your breakfast."

"I have a mystique?" he asked in amusement, following her into the kitchen.

"Everyone has a mystique," she replied, pointing him to a place at the table where she'd already placed a glass of juice and a cup of coffee. She took a plate out of the oven and placed it in front of him. Then she pulled a little folding gate closed that separated the kitchen from the living room. She was on one side, he on the other.

She pointed to the coffeemaker on the counter. "Help yourself to more. Kate should be here in fifteen minutes. When you're finished we can talk about the barn."

Then she disappeared around the fireplace, and he heard the immediate scamper of little feet in all directions as she apparently released the trio from their nylon prison.

While Tom ate, two more little children were delivered to Kids & Co. by mothers in a hurry. Tom watched the doorway into the living room with mild trepidation. One child pedaled by on a little plastic trike, another went by pulling a toy, one was waving wildly with a plastic wand that produced bubbles, and Malia, a stuffed dog hanging from her hand by its tail, peered in over the gate and grinned.

"Hi, Malia," he called, waving his fork at her.

She waved back, then ran away with a shriek of laughter.

Kate arrived on time and launched into immediate action as the toddler on the trike tried to extend his tour of the living room to include the great outdoors.

Amy appeared on the other side of the gate and looked at his empty plate. "More toast?" she asked.

He shook his head, thinking she looked like something a man could nibble on this morning in slim black pants and a red, white and black plaid shirt. Her hair was tied back with a narrow length of red ribbon. "Thanks, that was plenty," he said, carrying his plate to the sink. "I've done nothing for the past four days to burn up energy."

"You ready to look at the barn?" She waved the sheet of paper with his proposals. "I have your suggestions, but I also have a few questions."

"Can you get away with all that activity going on out there?"

She laughed. "This is a good time—while Kate's still fresh, and before we serve snacks."

The baby on the trike went pedaling by the doorway at Olympic-competition speed. Tom shook his head as Amy stepped over the gate. "I guess I thought it would be more organized. You know—games, lessons, group things."

She went to the back door and opened it. Birdsong

and sunshine flowed over her. "We try to do that with
the bigger kids who come after school, but these guys
are still too small for that. The best we can do for them
is make them feel happy and at home and let them do
their own thing and make their own discoveries."

He followed her out the door. "But they're all going
in different directions. How do you keep up?"

"You just don't do anything else. You watch them
every minute, keep their tummies fed and their toys
running and they're happy."

The morning was glorious, the field green and fragrant after yesterday's rain, the Douglas firs a jagged
backdrop to the bright blue sky filled with tufty white
clouds. In another few weeks those clouds would bring
incessant rain, but this morning they were simply a
beautiful accent in a picture-postcard landscape.

Nestled in the crescent-shaped line of trees, the ram-
shackle barn stood in faded splendor, a remnant of another time.

"I think I would have liked to be here when the barn
was operational," she said as they strode toward it, side
by side. She seemed perfectly relaxed this morning, as
though she didn't remember their middle-of-the-night
encounter.

He did. He hadn't gotten to sleep for hours. He hadn't
been sure if it was sexual frustration or extreme irritation. He still didn't know. But on a day like this, it was
hard to feel negatively about anything, so he made himself put it aside.

He helped Amy push through the big double doors
and into the musty space poorly lit by one overhead
light on the far side.

"I think the previous tenant used this half of the barn
for storage," Amy said, "so they weren't concerned

with how well lit it was. You can do electrical work, can't you?''

"Yes."

"Good. I'd like to use this side for an indoor playground. Swings, slides, all the stuff that's outside, but I'll put mats all around it. The kids really miss the swing set when it's raining.''

She walked into the lit half of the room. "This I'd like to set up just like a living room with another TV, sofas and chairs, and maybe even a little library in a corner. I have one little girl who comes on Mondays and Fridays and she actually tries to do her homework with the music blaring and the babies crawling over her.''

"Sectioning off a space would be no problem.''

"Good.'' She stepped back to point up at the loft. "I really liked your idea about making an office out of the loft. I was up there once the day I bought the place, but I hadn't even thought about actually using it. Right now I do all my paperwork at the kitchen table or sitting on my bed. But…is the ceiling really high enough? I seem to remember I was ducking the whole time I was up there.''

Tom headed for the ladder. "Come on," he said. "I'll show you." He turned before he began to climb to see that she still stood in the middle of the room, looking a little sheepish. "What?" he asked.

She went toward him with obvious reluctance. "I remember that I didn't like that ladder. It's so… perpendicular.''

He nodded. "It's a ladder. They tend to be that way.''

She scolded him with a look. "I know that. I'm just accustomed to going upstairs on nice solid steps, not little flimsy sticks.''

"Well, you can trust me that it's high enough, but if you come up with me I can show you exactly what I had in mind." He beckoned her. "I'll be just a rung below you. It'll be physically impossible for you to fall."

Amy suspected it was a bad idea, but something perverse inside her wouldn't let her say no. The night before had proved that their attraction for each other was still incendiary, but the new and improved Amy had chosen to put her fears aside. She wasn't going to deprive herself of taking part in the planning of her office just because she used to have a thing for this man.

She pocketed the sheet of paper that held his proposal and went to the ladder. She held the sides and stepped up a rung.

He came up right behind her, his body paralleling hers exactly. The extra inches he had on her were just about the distance from rung to rung. His mouth was right at her ear.

"Just go slowly," he said. "It's only about a dozen rungs."

She counted them, feeling him right behind her, a wall of security and yet a six-foot-plus memory she was determined not to relive.

But when he was being solicitous like this, when he was being tolerant of her shortcomings and quirks and not making her feel inadequate as her family tended to, she felt drawn to him, could almost feel the inclination of her body into his arms even against her will.

She was imagining things, she told herself, because he was so close behind her. Their bodies bumped lightly, her arm against his hand, her head against his shoulder, her hip against his belt buckle. Suspended on the rickety ladder near the shadowed loft still redolent of hay after all these years, Amy felt as though the innocent little touches took on a drama that she fought against with all the forward-driving impetus of her new resolve.

She didn't realize she had stopped until Tom asked, his breath warm against her cheek, "You okay? One more step and you'll be able to see into the loft."

That did it for her. If he was unaware of the tension, it must be an atmosphere she was creating herself out of old dreams and a misbegotten fling. She climbed the rest of the way up, scrambled onto her knees at the top and waited, arms folded over her chest, for him to join her.

Aware that she was breathing rapidly, she strode away from him as he cleared the top of the ladder and stepped off. It was simple exertion, but she didn't want him thinking it was something else.

She went to the open hay doors. Her breathing slowed, and she sat on the wide sill of the opening and looked out, thinking it would be wonderful to be able to work up here and look out at the children at play on the swing set or, when they'd all gone home, to work on the book she had in mind and be able to look out at the moon and the stars and the river visible over the treetops of residential Heron Point.

Tom sat facing her, his legs stretched out over hers, which were folded daintily to her side.

"Wonderful view," he said, letting his eyes scan the panorama. "You can see what's playing at the Liberty from here."

She turned her head to look. "You cannot," she denied in a tone that berated him for exaggerating.

"Well, if I had an office up here," he said, ignoring

the reproof, ''I'd keep the binoculars handy. You'd be able to keep an eye on Rodney's dad at the port.''

''I let his wife do that.''

He ignored her and went on. ''You can watch Nate and Karma coming and going, you can watch the kids walking over here after school. Hmm. If we had that mountain ash cut down, you could probably even see the high school.''

''Why would I want to see the high school? Those kids are watching *each other* after school.''

''Well. You might want to see if Principal Fuller employs the same technique on single lady teachers that he uses on you.''

She rolled her eyes. ''What technique?''

''The heroic single father technique. The 'I don't know what I'd do without you' technique. And that's usually accompanied by an adoring look into your eyes, and the close scrutiny of your backside when you turn away.''

She gasped, half indignant, half amused. The notion was so preposterous. ''He doesn't do that!''

''How do you know? Do you have eyes in the back of your head?''

''As a matter of fact, I do. Anyone who cares for children does. Steve Fuller isn't interested in my backside.''

''I saw him look.''

''You'd had a blow to the head. And so what if he did look? I've noticed that he fills out a pair of Dockers very nicely.''

Tom knew that his stunned expression had to look comical. How Amy had changed. The shy little klutz he'd fallen in love with was becoming a woman of the world—well, of as much of the world as was visible in Heron Point.

"Amaryllis Brown!" he said, unable to hold back the grin. "You hussy."

She hadn't become sophisticated enough to hold back a blush, however. She held her head high, unwilling to appear repentant for her admission, but her cheeks were pink.

"Grow up, Nicholas. The new millennium is coming. We're taking men on dates now."

"And how many men have you squired around town?" he teased.

She lifted a haughty shoulder. "Dozens."

"It doesn't count if they're under eight."

"We're not here to talk about my conquests," she said, "we're here to plan an office." She looked out at the view and sighed, a little smile curving her lips. "I'd like to put my desk right here. Can we glass this in?"

He congratulated himself on having just the right answer for her. "Not only can we glass it in," he said, "but it just so happens that in my warehouse of scrounged materials, I have a window that I think would fit here. It's framed in leaded stained glass squares with clear glass in the center, so you can have beauty but keep your view."

"It sounds perfect." She stood suddenly and wandered across the loft. "I suppose an old-fashioned railing with turned balusters would be a fortune."

"Yeah, it would," he admitted, following her. "If I could scrounge some, it would be less, but I'd need the time to look."

"Of course." She was becoming businesslike again. He wanted to call back those few minutes at the window that reminded him of the slightly combative companionship they'd once shared, but it couldn't be forced, and she was apparently on another track.

He shouldn't be surprised. Even in the good times two years ago she'd been high-strung and changeable.

"What kind of a mood do you want up here?" he asked. "Rustic, nautical, feminine?"

She looked around, her eyes losing focus as she thought about finally having her own work space. "I wish there was such a thing as feminine nautical," she said. "You know. Sort of…ship's-plank walls, but decorated with flowers and stuff instead of brassy ship's wheels and barometers." Then she focused on him. "You know what I mean?"

He was grinning. "Not a clue," he admitted frankly. "But you tell me what you want for walls, I'll put it up, and the 'flowers and stuff' is your responsibility."

"Right." She looked at all the open beams above her head. "It's all in good shape, right? No rot or bugs or anything?"

"No signs that I can see. You do have some rotten windows downstairs, though, that should be replaced."

She tapped a foot on the floor. "And this is good and solid?"

"Very."

"Good." She made a shoulders-up gesture of pleasure that brought the best times of the past back like the stroke of silk across his mind. It felt wonderful for a moment, then it was gone, leaving him with a sense of loss.

"There's good energy up here," she said, looking around again with that pleased expression. "Like happy ghosts still live here or something."

He tried to relate to her fanciful shift in mood. "Well, that's not surprising," he said. "This was probably a rendezvous spot in the old days for the farmer's daughter and some poor hand on a fishing boat who wasn't considered good enough for her.''

She appeared to like the notion. She walked to the wall of the barn and back as though expecting to find them in a mad embrace in the corner.

Then she looked at him with a surprised smile. ''And what kind of binoculars did you have for that particular vision?''

''I'm basically full of bull,'' he replied. ''Always have been.''

''Not bull,'' she corrected him, coming back toward him. ''Imagination. I used to like that about you. You were always more...connected to your environment than men usually are. If they like the outdoors, it's because they like to hunt and fish in it, take something from it. You just liked it—'' she hesitated, then finished the sentence in a quick, quiet rush, as though regretting that she'd begun the explanation ''—because it was there.''

She stopped a foot away from him, folded her arms, then unfolded them in a fluster.

He didn't dare smile. But he tucked away for future consideration the memory of the flush in her cheeks and the watchful little glow in her eyes. He suspected she wasn't as comfortable with their situation as she claimed to be. Considering he was in a total flap, he appreciated that glimpse of truth.

''See?'' he said.

Amy, lost in her loose-lipped admission that she'd liked certain things about him, tried to get herself together and restore a certain employer-employee relationship to this discussion.

''See what?'' she asked flatly, thinking he meant,

"See? Your behavior proves you still have feelings for me" or "See? All I have to do is get close to you and you begin to dither."

When he said neither of those things, but simply pointed overhead, she felt disoriented, confused.

"Lots of headroom," he clarified for her. "You were worried about it, remember?" He ran a hand between his head and the four or five inches that remained between it and the roof's slope. "Fuller would fit up here easily."

She pursed her lips at him. "Suggesting that he's somehow deficient because he's not as tall as you are?"

He widened his eyes innocently. She knew it was an act. "Not at all. Although I'm not sure he's tall enough to hold you to the ladder to get you up here."

"Well, if you're putting in stairs, that won't be a problem, will it? And even though this is absolutely none of your business, I'll tell you one more time that he does not have designs on me."

"Okay, I'll tell you what," he said. "We'll make a small wager. If he doesn't make a move on you in the next couple of weeks, I'll let you have that leaded-glass window as a gift."

She liked the sound of that. And she knew Steve Fuller. He had loved his wife and he still wasn't over her death. She smiled and held out her hand. "Deal."

But when he reached out to take it, she drew it back, aware suddenly of an unfinished detail. "And I'll owe you for it if I lose—which isn't going to happen, but for the sake of argument we should have all details clear."

He nodded. "Absolutely. Fine with me."

"All right." She extended her hand, somehow feeling as though this was more significant than it seemed, as though thunder should roll, or the wind suddenly howl.

He took it and gave it a firm shake. "Do you have time to go over the downstairs with me?"

She glanced at her watch. "Can we do it in fifteen minutes?"

"I think so. Unless you have questions."

Getting on the ladder from above was much more difficult than getting off of it had been. She couldn't see behind her and had the most unsettling sensation of stepping out into space.

But Tom took a firm hold of her ankle and placed her foot on a rung. "Okay," he directed, "just slip your other leg down between me and the ladder and we've got it made."

She made herself comply, though she didn't want to at all. The combination of his closeness and her dislike of the ladder had her nervous and unsure. And the new and improved Amy didn't like that at all.

The moment her feet reached the rung above his, he leaned in, his solidity against her managing to be comforting as well as unsettling. "Okay?" he asked.

"Yeah," she lied breathlessly.

"Good. Here we go."

Because they were going down, his progress placed him two rungs lower, and now she could feel his chin bump against her back, her hips strike his shoulder. At one point she felt her balance shift, kicked out anxiously and got him in the stomach.

She heard his "Ooof!" of surprise, and embarrassed, she groaned an apology.

He laughed. "It's okay. Just keep coming."

She followed his instructions, then suddenly hands

nipped her waist and she was swung to the concrete floor.

She let herself sag against him in relief. Then, realizing what she'd done, she straightened and pulled at the hem of her shirt.

"Thank you," she said, pulling the shreds of her dignity together. "Maybe you could put the stairs in first thing. Show me the bad windows."

Tom followed her across the room, a hand rubbing at his chest, against which her round bottom had bumped several times, and thought he'd leave construction of the stairs till the last possible moment.

Chapter Five

Tom stepped aboard the *Mud Hen* for the first time in two years and went to the afterdeck to simply stand there and absorb the sense of rightness he always felt on the river.

Years ago—another lifetime ago—when he and Jave had bought their first boat, a fifty-foot Fiberglas vessel called the *River Lady,* together, he had just been made battalion chief, and Jave was the new head of Radiology at Riverview. They'd both been cocky, had felt like they were living the American dream and that they deserved it because they'd worked hard and followed all the rules.

Then Jave's first wife had left him and the boys, Tom and his men had responded to the fire in the hotel, Davey had died, and Tom had spent three months in the hospital recovering from a broken leg and third-degree burns from hip to foot.

He and Jave had both needed money, so they'd sold the *River Lady.*

It had taken almost two years, but they'd both gotten on their feet again and they'd responded to an ad in the classifieds that had brought them to the *Mud Hen.* It had been in terrible shape, but had an energy Tom had felt even then.

He remembered touching the lapstrake hull and being aware of how different he was from the younger man who'd bought a share in the *River Lady.* Then, untried and flush with a little success, he'd looked for cosmetic beauty and speed.

When he'd first seen the *Mud Hen,* he'd related instantly to its worn and wounded appearance. He'd felt just like that for so long.

Jave had kicked in his share just to humor him, he was sure. The old sea dog who'd sold it to them had been repairing a hole in the deck and was having her painted when they bought it. But Tom had spent every spare moment he had on the inside, and now the *Mud Hen* was a cleaner, more finished boat that had been through a lot and endured and prevailed, and was now ready to hit the open sea again.

Like him.

He went down into the galley, found the Cokes Jave had told him would be there and wandered into the blue-and-gray stateroom.

He sat on a corner of the bed, downed a long swig of cola and felt old needs begin to prowl through his body.

He ran a hand through his hair and groaned, knowing there was nothing he could do about it. Over the past two years he'd had sex carefully but casually and endured various reactions to his scarred and puckered leg.

He didn't know why he'd been able to deal with the touch of virtual strangers when he'd made such a scene when Amy had placed a hand on it. He'd guessed it had been because Arizona wasn't home to him—it was a sort of limbo where he held his real life at bay while he tried to deal with who he was and what he was going to do.

It had been a little like being touched in a dream.

But the dream was over. He was home, and this was where he intended to stay.

And he didn't want to have sex with just any woman. His body craved Amy.

He wasn't sure why. He was still angry over her re-action when he'd told her he had to leave, though he saw interest in her eyes now when she looked at him. But they'd both been there before.

They seemed to be able to identify qualities in each other they needed, without seeming to be able to reach them. She'd come to Heron Point to escape her family and a part of herself she'd said she'd been unhappy with. And his life had been so confused the past few years that he hardly knew up from down.

But he was home to fix that. And she was on a new track. Was this a second chance? It was hard to tell. She seemed drawn to him one minute and then ran away from him the next.

And he still wasn't sure how he felt, except to know for certain that he wasn't indifferent. He felt the same sexual attraction he'd experienced two years ago, but emotionally there was a lot of old stuff between them still unresolved.

He hated that.

He placed the pop can on the small strip of deck between the berth and the bulkhead, then lay back and closed his eyes.

Maybe he'd been a pirate in another life. That might explain his love of boats and the deep-down wish that a winsome woman could be kidnapped into a man's life and held there by sexual prowess and pretty baubles traded from the Orient.

As far as he was concerned, he thought sleepily, it beat the current system hands down for finding a woman.

"AMY! TRUMAN'S PICKING ON me again!"

Darcy's shrieking voice brought Amy from the kitchen where she was unloading the dishwasher. Because all the babies had been retrieved earlier in the afternoon, Amy had let Kate go home early. Rodney's father had just picked him up, so she was alone with the two warring factions.

"Well, it's stupid," Truman said in his own defense, "for her to play with a doll she never takes out of the box. Now she's got clothes for it that aren't going to come out of the package, either? Give me a break!"

Darcy held her precious packages to her, her eyes wide with hurt and brimming with tears. "I *want* to take them out of the box, but then they won't be worth anything."

"Truman, we've been over this," Amy said, putting an arm around each of them. "The doll is hers. That means she can do what she wants to with it."

"But, it's dumb to…" Truman began.

"To Darcy," Amy interrupted, "it makes sense. And since it's hers, that's all that matters. So butt out, okay?"

"You break everything," Darcy accused Truman. "You can't keep anything nice."

"Well, I wouldn't keep it in a box, that's for sure. What's the good of having something you can't play with?"

''You can't play with it if you break it, either!'' she shot back.

A knock on the front door saved Amy from having to find some wise advice with which to end the confrontation. And she was grateful for that because she couldn't think of a thing.

Darcy and Truman were as opposite as two children could be, and not simply because of their gender. He was rowdy and explosive but deep-down sweet. She was introspective and moody and seemed afraid to have fun.

Truman did break almost everything he touched, but Amy guessed it was a simple problem common to many boys his age—strength outdistancing finesse. But his might have been compounded by anger over his mother's death that exaggerated his naturally impulsive personality.

Darcy, on the other hand, spent weekends with her grandmother while her mother worked a second job, and seemed obsessed with her mother's financial difficulties.

The doll and then the clothes that she'd arrived with that morning had been gifts from her father. Amy didn't know if the notion of ''saving'' the doll until it appreciated had been passed on by Darcy's mother or grandmother, or if Darcy had simply overheard something and imposed this decision on herself.

Either way, the other children had given her a lot of grief over it. And the way she carried it around rather than leaving it on a shelf was proof that she loved it, and that was what disturbed Amy. The child had to be hating the thought that she had to part with it one day.

Amy opened the door to Ginger Billings, Darcy's mother. She was small and harried-looking, and always seemed preoccupied.

But when Darcy ran tearfully into her arms, Amy saw all the mother-instincts come to the fore. She wrapped the child in her embrace and held her close, asking for an explanation. When Darcy wept instead of providing it, Truman admitted grudgingly that he'd teased her about the doll. Then he braced himself, as though expecting her wrath.

Instead, she gave him a sad look that made him shift uncomfortably.

"Her father sent it for her birthday," she explained, rocking Darcy gently back and forth. "And my mom doesn't like him because he never sends money to help me, so she told Darcy if she loved me she wouldn't play with it, she'd save it and sell it when it became valuable." She hugged Darcy more tightly and kissed the top of her head. "So that's what she's doing. I've told her it would make me happier if she took it out of the box and played with it, but she's trying to help with the money."

Her eyes were now filled with tears. She reached a hand out to Truman and cupped his chin. "Please don't tease her about it."

Truman looked at Amy, his eyes wide and horrified. "I'm sorry," he said. "I won't anymore."

Ginger turned to leave, Darcy still holding on to her, and almost collided with Steve Fuller, who stood just inside the door and had probably heard the discussion.

They studied each other uncertainly, then Ginger pulled the door closed behind her.

"Did I hear that you were picking on that little girl?" Steve asked Truman, his expression displeased.

"I don't think he was picking on her," Amy interceded, "as much as having trouble understanding her behavior." She ruffled Truman's hair, knowing he hadn't been malicious. "He's a very practical boy. He didn't understand why she wouldn't unwrap her toy and play with it."

Steve nodded, still frowning at Truman. "Well, now that you do, you'll leave her alone about it, right?"

"Yeah. But isn't it weird to tell a kid not to play with it?"

Steve nodded. "I think so. But it's something her mom has to deal with, Truman, not you."

"Yeah." Truman heaved a sigh and went to the coat closet for his jacket. "I thought she was gonna yell at me," he said as they walked to the door. "But she was really nice. How come you're here so early, Dad?"

"Computer's down. I thought we'd take advantage of it and go to dinner and to the movies." Steve smiled at Amy. "I don't suppose you're free to come with us."

Oh, God. There went her leaded-glass window. Or did an invitation to go out actually constitute "a move"? She wasn't sure. Men had such strange euphemisms for the steps in a relationship.

She looked into Steve's expectant gaze and could find nothing sexual in it. It appeared to be a simple friend-to-friend invitation. And certainly if an invitation did constitute "a move," the definition would change if a child was included.

"Thanks," she said, "but I have a million things to do tonight. Unfortunately, my duties don't end when the last child goes home."

"Sure." He did seem disappointed, but that might just be good manners. "See you tomorrow night."

"And don't forget she has that book-party thing to-morrow," Truman reminded. "Mrs. Nicholas talked about it when she picked up Malia."

"That's right." Steve opened the door, and they all

stepped out onto the porch. "I'm invited also. Fortunately, Truman has a Cub Scout meeting."

Amy walked them down the steps. "I didn't know you knew Jave and Nancy."

"I met Nancy when she came to school to help with Career Day. Like most former English teachers, I have a novel in the bottom drawer of my desk, too. We got to talking and became friends."

"Anyway..." Steve turned to Amy, who'd stopped on the bottom step. "Want me to pick you up?"

Uh-oh. Another invitation. Though this one didn't include a child, it did involve a host of other people. So that couldn't constitute "a move," either.

But maybe *two* such invitations did?

"Ah...thanks, but Diantha Pennyman and I are going together." She smiled too broadly. It was hard to turn a man down twice in the same evening—move or not. "I'll see you there."

"All right. Good night."

Amy tidied the kitchen, did laundry, straightened and vacuumed, then organized food for the following day's meals.

Then she wandered out to the barn with a cup of tea and stood in the middle of the big shadowy room and looked up. She'd have loved to climb the ladder, but she wasn't sure she'd make it, and caring for little children involved too much running to risk having to do it with a broken leg.

So she simply pushed her visions of an office to the back of her mind and walked around on the lower level and imagined it finished with wallboard and paint, pictured new windows that didn't leak and actually *opened,* envisioned new flooring covered in high-traffic carpeting.

She'd asked Sam at the Secondhand Barn to watch for sturdy furniture in good condition, and she pictured it placed around the room. She saw a little library in the corner.

She sat cross-legged in the middle of the room as darkness began to fall and thought about how far she'd come in two years. Her family had thought she was crazy when she'd left the hospital job her uncle had arranged for her.

She'd only taken it in the first place because it had gotten her out of New York and away from her parents' concern and the glow of her sisters' successes. But the job *had* resulted in her friendships with the parents of the September 23 babies, and she considered them gifts from the hand of providence.

She was grateful that she hadn't fallen on her face in this new endeavor. The children seemed to enjoy coming to her home, and their parents seemed to appreciate her approach to child care. If the addition of the barn did what she thought it would do for her in the winter months, she might consider expanding to Seaside.

She could, if she wanted to dream big, have a chain of child-care facilities.

But that was putting the cart way ahead of the rocking horse. She had to make the barn work first.

She raised her knees and wrapped her arms around them, thinking that the only phase of her life that did not seem to be moving forward was her attraction to Tom. She wanted to be over it.

She admitted to herself with a sigh that she was already anticipating tomorrow, when he would arrive in his truck and go to work. She would be too busy with the children to spend any time with him, but she felt a little glow in the pit of her stomach at the knowledge that he would be here.

That was crazy. She accepted that. But it didn't change the way she felt.

Her mother would probably think that typical of her. "Poor Amy" was the only one of the girls who couldn't focus, Amy had once overheard her telling a friend. "She doesn't have the same drive as the other girls. She tries all kinds of things but she fails at most of them. I don't know what will become of her. And, of course, she's too tall and not very pretty."

"This is it, Mom," she heard herself say aloud, her voice hollow in the cavernous room. "Child-care maven and ill-starred lover. Didn't know I had it in me, did you?"

TOM, JAVE AND NANCY sat in a swing in the backyard of Jave and Nancy's home on the hill overlooking Heron Point. Jave had barbecued salmon for dinner, and they were all replete, the boys playing halfhearted one-on-one basketball with Mo, a large brown-and-black dog of doubtful heritage. The adults had alternated pushing Malia on the swing. She was now in Tom's arms, yawning and rubbing her eyes.

"No, I am not coming to your autograph party tomorrow," Tom said to Nancy, who sat between him and Jave, "because you allowed your husband to set me up to run blindly into Amy."

Nancy leaned into Jave's arm, which rested on the back of the upholstered swing, and raised an eyebrow at Tom. "Allowed? You think he consults me before he takes action on anything?"

"He must," Tom replied, bracing Malia's little body as she fought sleep and stood up on his thighs. "Otherwise I'm sure he'd have made a lot more mistakes than he has.''

"Actually," Nancy said, patting his knee, "he didn't ask my permission, but he did tell me that Nate had the clipping and I must confess that I applauded the plan.''

Tom gave her a grimly disapproving look. "I'm appalled.''

"Why?" She smiled, apparently unimpressed with his expression. "You'd have been too stubborn to look her up, and she'd have been too proud to come to you and tell you that she's done nothing for two years but think about you.''

Tom studied Nancy's face, certain she was lying. But she looked clear-eyed and her gaze didn't waver. "She's worked like a fiend to put Kids & Co. together, but she refuses to date, and all she does when she and Jo and Karma and I go anywhere together is watch the faces of people passing by. It was our theory that she was watching for you to come home.''

Malia jumped on his lap. He bracketed her little body with his hands. "Well, I think your theory went down in flames when she took one look at me and told me to leave.''

"Pardon me," she said quietly, "but did you miss the part where she hired you to do the barn?''

"She hired me because I'm the best carpenter for a hundred miles.''

"Then it's up to you to take the opportunity afforded you to prove to her that you're the best husband material for a hundred miles also.''

Tom turned his attention to Malia. "I'm beginning to think your mom is as much of a buttinsky as your dad.''

"Mommy!" Malia said, pointing at Nancy.

"Right," Tom praised her. "Buttinsky. Mommy is a buttinsky. Can you say that?"

Yeah, but I think I'd get in trouble. What's your problem with Amy, anyway? I saw you watching her this morning when she was playing with us. Daddy watches Mom like that. I think it makes babies. I heard Truman and Rodney talking about it. So, watch out. That playpen Amy puts us in when she's busy is pretty crowded already.

Malia pointed to Jave. "Daddy!" she said.

"Yeah, I know." Tom bumped noses with her. "But why are you so happy about it?"

'Cause he can throw me in the air and he never drops me. He rescues me when the boys play too rough, he knows a lot of cool songs and he loves me a lot. He tells me all the time.

"Who's going to watch the kids while we're all at this party?" Tom asked.

"Beachie," Nancy replied. "We made a deal. She'll miss the party to watch the kids for three autographed books."

Nurse Beacham had been at Riverview as long as Tom could remember. She had a reputation for being the classic no-nonsense autocrat, but underneath was a heart of gold. And there wasn't anything she wouldn't do for Jave—and now Nancy.

"Then I guess I'll come. Who else is going to be there?"

"Most of our friends."

"Amy?"

"She's coming with Diantha. Remember Diantha?"

"Of course. She's pretty unforgettable." Diantha Pennyman ran the health food store next door to Jo Jeffries's Coffee Country. She was also an astrologer, and Tom remembered that she'd worked up a forecast for Jo and Ryan's baby at the time of its birth, and Jo had shared it with Nancy and with Nate's wife, Karma.

"Did her predictions about the Libra babies come to pass?" he asked Nancy.

Yeah! She said I'd have a keen intellect, but it's hard to convince anybody that that's true, because I've only got about fifty words in my vocabulary.

"I'll say," Nancy replied. Malia was now leaning out of Tom's arms toward her, and Nancy took her from him and cradled her in her arms. "She predicted she'd be a finicky eater, and that's right on. She also said she'd be hospitable and compassionate and philanthropic. She isn't really into sharing yet, but I swear she's just like Eddy in that she doesn't know a stranger."

Nancy stopped, then she laughed a little self-consciously and smiled across the yard at the boys, now digging the basketball out of a rhododendron bush. "Not that I should expect her to be anything like either boy. I just forget sometimes that they're not related by blood."

Jave bent the arm he held on the back of the swing, gently caught her neck in the crook of it and looked down at her with an expression so intimate, so grave that Tom felt like an intruder. "They're related by love," Jave said softly. "When we got married, you gave her to me and I gave you the boys. The heart pumps the blood, the blood doesn't pump the heart."

She gave him a smile that said things that made Tom blush.

"All right, I'm out of here." He stood. "Every time I'm around you two, I expect birds carrying silk banners to come by and the mice to start singing. If there's a pumpkin parked behind my truck, I'm reporting you to the DMV.''

"It's licensed," Jave said with a grin, standing and taking Malia from Nancy so that she could rise. The boys came running over with Mo bounding behind them.

"How come you're going?" Eddy asked. He was twelve, and Tom swore he'd grown a good six inches since he'd seen him two years ago.

"I can only take so much of your dad," he said, putting an arm around each boy as everyone walked him down the driveway to his truck.

Eddy laughed and grinned at Jave. "I know. Us, too."

Jave swatted at his head and Eddy laughed.

Pete, at nine, was quieter and more serious, though Tom thought he seemed less so since Nancy had come into the boys' lives. "Me and Eddy are gonna bring our basketball to Amy's, and if you take a coffee break in the afternoon when we get there, we can play. She has a hoop in back of the house."

"That might work," Tom said with a wink at Jave. "But we're going to put a library in the barn so you'll have a quiet place to do your homework. Wouldn't you rather do that?"

Both boys frowned up at him. "Maybe," Pete said brightly, "you could talk Amy into changing the plan from a library to a video arcade."

Tom drove home with the sound of family laughter ringing in his ears. Coming home, this part of it, anyway, had been a good idea.

Chapter Six

Amy was out of bed at 5:00 a.m., and showered and dressed and sipping coffee by five-thirty. Children would be arriving by six-thirty, and she treasured the time alone to prepare herself for the day.

When she opened the door to greet her first arrival, Tom's truck was pulling into the driveway.

With a quiet tap of the horn in greeting, he pulled around the back of the house and drove across the field to the barn. The back of the truck was loaded with lumber and tools, and Amy responded with a wave, a sense of excitement stirring in her chest. Kids & Co.'s expansion was officially underway.

She peered out the kitchen window in the middle of the morning while she prepared snacks and felt mild concern when she saw that the truck was gone. Then she heard it turn into the driveway, and as she watched it went bumping across the field, full of more lumber, more tools.

Bless Ryan Jeffries. Chelsea's father was the manager of the bank with some district pull, and he'd gone to bat for her and gotten her the loan that was paying for this.

At lunchtime, she saw Tom sitting outside in the sun,

propped up against the wall, eating a sandwich, a tall thermos beside him.

By afternoon snack break, he was power-washing the barn. All the children who came after school were watching from the backyard, fascinated. They included Pete and Eddy, who didn't give a second thought to running across the field to greet their uncle.

Truman, Rodney and Darcy ran after them, and Kate followed while Amy stayed with the toddlers. She would have liked to go, too, but if Tom was to spend two months at work out there, she had to establish a professional distance from him and maintain it for the sake of her work and his.

By the time he left at five, it looked as though the entire barn had been power-washed.

"My goodness," Amy said, looking out the back door, flanked by his nephews. "He'll be ready to paint tomorrow."

"He has to scrape first," Eddy said.

"I thought the power-washer did that."

"Mostly, but he has to get the stuff it didn't get." He spoke very matter-of-factly. "'Cause he's the best, you know. Nothing gets by him."

She was sure that was true.

"GOOD GRIEF!" DIANTHA exclaimed as the crowd assembled at Booked Solid pressed in around the table where Amy poured champagne and Diantha kept the hors d'oeuvres trays filled. "Murder must be better business than health food."

"Or accounting." Karma Foster, Nate's wife and Garrett's mother, swapped a tray filled with decorated cookies for an empty one. She was dark-haired and pretty, and Amy had always envied her calm control.

"How are the cookies holding up?" Jo Jeffries, who'd taken on the job of catering the affair, held two hot pots of coffee in her arms. She was tall and blond, and always seemed to Amy as though she'd just walked out of a pre-Raphaelite painting. Her hair was wild, her face angelic. She'd been a surrogate mother for Ryan's and her sister Cassie's baby, then married Ryan after her sister was killed.

She seemed to have acquired a serenity with her new life that made her that much more dramatic.

"There's one more tray," Karma replied. "Is that it?"

Jo handed Karma a hot pot, took the empty tray from her, then handed her the other pot. "I've got more in the back room. Do we need more champagne?"

Amy looked under the white table skirt and saw a single bottle of champagne in a tub of ice. "Yes," she replied.

"There's a small fridge in the basement. I stashed a couple of bottles in there. I'll send Ryan down for it if I can find him." She looked around at the sea of bodies.

Amy poured champagne for another taker. "I'll go for it as soon as I can get away. Is Nancy selling lots of books?"

Jo smiled widely. "Last I heard, she was over one hundred. And it doesn't hit the stands till tomorrow." She pointed to the very happy shop owner hovering at Nancy's shoulder and chatting with a buyer while Nancy signed her book.

Nancy looked stunning in a red silk jacket over a black shirt and pants. Her dark hair was caught back in an elegant knot.

"All right." Karma set the pots down at the end of

the table and handed Jo an empty one. "Maybe Heron Point will put her on the bestseller list all by itself."

Jo nodded. "Well, she better remember her friends when she buys a vacation home in Cozumel. I'll get more cookies and be right back."

"I wish we had thought to bring ourselves a tip jar," Karma said with a grin as everyone refilled on goodies and champagne. "We could be making a bundle."

Amy laughed and continued to fill glasses, very much aware of how little of the bubbly was left in the basin filled with ice.

She looked up during a lull to see Jave, Nate, Ryan and Tom collected in a group at Nancy's table. All elegantly groomed and wearing suits, they snagged her attention and held it. Even *GQ* magazine, she thought, would have been hard put to find a more handsome collection of men.

Jave and Nate seemed to have shed the nervous energy their work as doctors required, and appeared relaxed and lighthearted. Nate had apparently teased Nancy with some remark that made Jave give him a punitive but friendly shove.

Ryan had none of the dignified banker about him tonight, but seemed to be in a party mood. When Jo sidled by him, empty tray in hand, he caught her wrist and kissed her lightly. He asked her something to which she responded with a shake of her head and another kiss. Then she headed for the back room.

But Tom was something else. She found it astonishing that a man whom she'd always thought had the slim-hipped, thick-shouldered body made for the jeans and flannel shirts he always wore could look so heart-stoppingly handsome in the more constricting shirt and tie and pin-striped suit. He had a hand in one pants pocket, and a brightly wrapped gift in the other.

Amy watched him give it to Nancy. Jave sat on the edge of the table as she unwrapped it, and Nate, Ryan and Pam, the shop owner, closed in to see what it was.

Nancy held up a pen whose beautifully faceted silver barrel glittered in the overhead light. She stood and came around the desk to hug Tom.

Jave, Amy thought, looked pleased. She knew how much he loved his family, and she could only guess how satisfying it was to find that the woman he loved, loved his family as well.

Amy was momentarily lost in fantasies of what it would be like to feel that kind of bond within one's family. She loved hers and she knew they cared about her, but she was just too different from her parents and her sisters to be able to relate to them—or them to her. While love was a comfort, it didn't completely replace the unity created by people who simply understood one another.

Amy turned at the request of a party-goer for more champagne, then looked up to see Steve Fuller talking to Diantha and trying to sidle away from her toward the refreshment table.

Amy decided it was a good time to retrieve the champagne in the basement. She warned Karma that she would be gone for a few minutes, then pulled off the tea towel that covered her vanilla silk shirt and beige skirt. She wound her way through the guests gathered in little knots of conversation, books tucked under their arms, and opened the basement door.

She flipped on the light over the stairs and made her way down carefully, aware of a sense of awkwardness in her seldom-worn black leather pumps. But once she reached the bottom, she couldn't find another light switch. The light over the stairs lit the forward half of the room, but since she saw no refrigerator there, she presumed it was located somewhere in the dark half under the stairs.

Ignoring all the old childhood stories of creatures that lived in dark and musty basements, she went carefully into the shadows.

She touched spinner racks of books, tripped over old displays, kicked aside a cardboard dump that had fallen over. She paused to peer into the dark but found nothing. Then she turned to her right, aware suddenly of a spine-chilling sense of being watched, and saw a pair of blue eyes under the stairs catch the light from above.

Her heart rocketed against her side and she screamed. Limbs light with the sudden rush of adrenaline, she spun around to run and found a pair of dark eyes looking down on her.

She screamed again and swung out, terror now a galvanizing force within her.

"Whoa, whoa!" a familiar voice said as a pair of hands, also familiar, caught her wrists. "It's me. What are you doing?"

"Tom!" Amy caught his arm and pointed to the stairs. "There! Someone's there!"

She felt the tension in him, but he remained still for a moment, then when there was not a sound or a movement, he reached to the back of a support beam under the stairs and the dark half of the basement was filled with light.

Amy peered around Tom's shoulder and saw the blue eyes. Then realized with a groan of self-deprecation that they were glass eyes—in a molded plastic face that belonged to the animated Santa that graced the shop's window at Christmastime.

She saw Tom struggle to withhold a laugh. "If I kill him for you," he said in a voice strained with suppressed amusement, "it could endanger your Christmas wish list."

She punched his shoulder and went to the refrigerator now clearly visible in the far corner. "Very funny. How come *you* know where the light switch is?"

"Easy," he replied, coming to stand behind the open refrigerator door. "I installed it when I built some shelves for Pam."

"Well, you couldn't have hidden it better if you'd tried."

"Pam knows where it is, and she's usually the only one who comes down here."

Amy removed two bottles of champagne from the rack on the bottom and held them out to Tom. "Would you take these upstairs for me, please?"

"Sure." He took them from her by the necks and rested them on the top of the door.

"You don't have to wait for me," she said, wishing he would go. She bent to reach two more bottles, feeling as though the musty basement had sapped all her energy and her air. It was difficult to breathe, to think. "Go on. Karma's waiting for those."

"I'll wait for you," he insisted with a grin. "Just in case Santa comes to life and decides you belong on the naughty list."

She rose with the bottles and closed the refrigerator door with her hip. She made a scornful sound. "Ha. As though you'd come to my defense."

She tried to walk around him, but he stepped into her

path. His eyes were clearly puzzled. "You think I wouldn't?"

He would come to her defense in any physical danger; she was sure of that. But when she'd needed him emotionally, he ran. And she hated that she still reacted to him this way, pulse racing, breathing shallow, heart yearning.

"I think you wouldn't," she replied, and tried again to move past him.

Again, he sidestepped. "Why?"

"Because," she said quietly, looking him straight in the eye, "you're afraid of me."

She got as far as the stairs before Tom caught her and turned her around. He had put the champagne bottles somewhere between the refrigerator and the stairs, and his hands were closed around her upper arms like manacles.

Tom didn't know a man in town who would react with any patience to the suggestion that he was afraid of a woman—nineties' political correctness notwithstanding. But more than that, he knew what this particular woman meant by it, and he was getting tired of the issue.

"*Afraid* of you?" he asked flatly.

"Why else would you have run off just when we were becoming intimate?" she retorted, her stubborn jaw set, her hands white-knuckled as she continued to hold the bottles of champagne trapped against his chest. She was tired of the issue, too. "When you finally *knew* you could absolve yourself of even a suggestion of blame in Davey's death? Why?"

He tightened his grip on her and gave her a shake. "If you'd listened to me instead of slamming the door on me when I came over to explain it to you," he said, his temper just under control, "you'd have the answer to that, wouldn't you?"

"Oh, I have it," she said with that frosty tilt of her chin that always made him long for a tub of icy water to dump her into. "You're afraid of me. You think if I become important to you, you might be happy. And if you're happy, you'll have to get on with your life, and you're afraid that you can't. You're no longer the story-book hero in the fireman's hat running to the rescue of a screaming woman. You're just a guy with a scarred leg that still causes him a lot of pain, with memories that still give him nightmares, and with a heart that's just a little empty without sirens and firetrucks, and the call of the flames. And deep down, you think it's over. And maybe you want it to be."

He had to punish her for that. She couldn't fill his brain and his dreams, then stake him out over the coals of his past and poke him with a stick.

He took the bottles from her, set them on the stairs, then yanked her back when she tried to escape him. "*You're* the one who's scared," he said. "You're the one who can't love and trust without knowing every thought in my head, without understanding every little corner of my soul. You can't just want me, you have to *own* me. Well, that isn't love, that's slavery."

Her face paled with anger. "Then consider yourself emancipated," she said, and tried to pull away again.

He held firm. "You can't free me," he said angrily, "because you never did own me. That's what you're afraid of. That you never will."

"I do *not*," she shouted at him, "want to own you. I just wanted to be allowed close enough to try to figure out what the hell was going on with you."

"All right," he said, drawing a breath to calm himself, "you want to read me? You want to prove you're not afraid? You want proof that I'm not?"

He dropped his hands from her, and she knew what he intended instantly. She was free to go, but she would prove her claim—she would understand his—only if she stayed.

He rested his hands on his hips and challenged her with a look, his anger slipping into something even more elemental, more dangerous—masculine arrogance.

"Make me believe you could care about me," he dared her, "without having me under lock and key."

Amy looked into his unrelenting stare with the thought that hurrying back upstairs would be the wiser course of action. But she'd taken up child care as a profession; obviously she hadn't a clue about wisdom.

And this was something she was not going to be able to go around in her life. It was going to keep getting in her way. She had to deal with Tom Nicholas. She had to show him.

Unsure if she was being brave or reckless, she slipped her arms inside his open coat and around him and put her hands to his back, just above his belt. She tried to use them to pull him toward her, but he remained firmly planted. Part of his independence manifesto, she guessed. She had to go to him.

So she did. She came right up against him, breast to chest, thigh to thigh, and everything in between in direct contact, except for the cotton-and-wool blend of her skirt and his slacks.

She saw the flare of reaction in his eyes, felt the guarded alertness in him as he maintained his hands-on-hips position.

"The question," she asked very quietly, "is does a woman want to put all this effort into a man who will not only keep his heart locked away from her, but his body, too? Even a very determined woman works best with a little response.''

''A man responds best,'' he said, still not moving, ''to a woman who isn't trying to change him.''

Amy remembered their days together so clearly, and the abject misery she felt when he held her in his arms and still managed to exclude her from what he thought and felt.

''I never wanted to change you,'' she said with all the sincerity with which she had once loved him. ''I just wanted to *know* you.''

His eyes darkened, and he dropped his hands, distracted, it seemed, by something he saw in her face.

She took advantage of his vulnerability, and with the added height her heels afforded her, she stretched up just a little and claimed his mouth.

He did not resist. In fact, she congratulated herself on her consummate skill, as he seemed to become pliable in her arms. He leaned down to accommodate her, his arms came lightly around her, and he responded to her searching kiss with surprising cooperation.

He parted his lips when her tongue probed for access, then he parried with it as she explored. He held her kiss as her hands wandered into his hair, teased his ear, then went back inside his jacket to rove his back.

She finally drew away, nipping his chin for good measure. His expression was unreadable but his body wasn't. He'd liked that. She'd been close enough to know. She thought she deserved to gloat a little.

''So,'' she said breathlessly, with a superior glance at him, ''I guess we've proved that I'm not afraid.''

He seemed to take exception to the look in her eye; his own expression darkened further.

Now, she thought, was a good time to leave. She turned to pick up the bottles, but he caught her arm and pulled her back to him, his eyes filled with purpose.

"Now," he said, "it's my turn to prove a thing or two."

Oh, no. They'd already pushed the limits of conduct at a business party. She looked at him warily and he raised a questioning eyebrow. "Or is the issue of your courage in question again?"

Before she could answer, he combed the fingers of one hand into her hair, used them to tip her mouth up to him, and claimed it with all the proprietary conviction of a lover.

All the gentleness with which he'd responded to her kiss was gone, and in its place was a ruthless command of everything his lips and hands touched—and both seemed to be everywhere.

His lips roved her face—her eyes, her earlobes, her mouth, her throat—as his hands swept all the way from her shoulder blades to her hips and remained there to hold her to him as he kissed her so deeply she felt her heart leap up in response, as though trying to reach him.

It felt as though fire roared through her, flushing her cheeks, stinging her eyes, heating every part of her in contact with any part of him.

He raised his head, and she felt as though she were made of rags, as though she might flop to the floor if he let her go.

The door at the top of the stairs opened, and Jo's voice shouted, "Amy? Are you down there?"

She had to draw a breath to find her voice. "Yes," she replied, hidden from view by a turn in the stairs. "It took me a few minutes to find the fridge. I'll be right up."

"Okay. Steve Fuller's looking for you."

Amy caught Tom's eye and saw amusement there. "Tell him I'll be right up," she said, pulling out of Tom's arms.

The door closed. Amy picked up the bottles off the stairs as Tom went to retrieve his.

"So, neither of us is afraid," she said, her emotions in turmoil, her heart beating too rapidly for her to think clearly. "You're emancipated, and I'm a business-woman now with new priorities. We should be able to function like two reasonable people."

She started up the steps, but he stopped her again, the two bottles caught in his left hand. She looked down into his even stare. He came up two steps until they occupied the same one. "If we're to 'function like two reasonable people,'" he said quietly, giving added emphasis to her words, "you have to get straight on the notion that you've freed me."

She nodded quickly, wanting nothing more at the moment than to get out of this damned basement. "Poor choice of words. I apologize. You're not emancipated because I never owned you. I forgot. I just meant you were..." Now she'd talked herself into a corner and didn't know where to go with her explanation. Mostly, because she didn't understand their status herself. "You know...that I have no hold on you."

He stunned her when he shifted his weight and admitted gravely, "Actually, you do. What I meant was that *you* can't free me from what I feel for you. I feel it just because I do, because I want to."

While Amy stared at him open-mouthed, trying to decide how to react to that admission, he loped up the stairs and disappeared into the buzzing crowd.

Amy managed to avoid Steve Fuller until the party

wound down and nearly everyone had left except Jave, Nancy and Tom. Nate and Karma helped Jo and Ryan clear away and clean up while Amy turned the serving table over to fold the legs. She became suddenly aware of Diantha's absence.

"Where's Diantha?" she asked the group. But a guffaw of laughter erupted among the men over something Nate had said, and no one heard her.

"She left early, complaining of a headache." Steve Fuller appeared to help her with the table. "I told her not to worry about you, that I'd take you home. I tried to find you to tell you, but Mrs. Foster said you were in the basement."

"Ah." She nodded, aware of Tom turning in their direction. She smiled brightly at Steve. "Thank you," she said. "I'd appreciate that."

Everyone left together, the store manager waving them off and thanking them for the liveliest evening she'd had in years.

They stood in a large group on the sidewalk in the fragrant early fall darkness. Nancy hugged Jo, Karma and Amy for all their efforts with the food, then hugged the men just because, she said, "There hasn't been a kinder or more handsome foursome of heroes since the Three Musketeers and d'Artagnan."

"Well!" Nate exclaimed. "That must mean we get to go wenching."

"No," Karma corrected him clearly, "it doesn't." She grabbed his arm and pulled him toward their car.

He waved a laughing good-night.

"Who needs him, anyway," Ryan said to Jave and Tom, and the three turned, as though prepared to go wenching on their own.

Jo caught Ryan.

"Aw, come on," Ryan grumbled. "I was just going to watch."

Jo hooked an arm around his waist and smiled into his eyes. "If you come home with me, you can actually participate."

"Ooh," he said, obviously lured away by the promise. He waved to his friends. "You'll have to carry on without me." And they turned in the direction of the side street.

Jave looked at Tom. "I guess it's just you and me."

Nancy smiled at Jave sweetly. "Guess what? It's just him. 'Night, Tom."

Jave shrugged helplessly as Nancy led him away.

Tom turned to Amy and Steve. "I don't suppose," he said to Steve, "that the high school principal could be caught wenching?"

Steve laughed. "Another time, maybe. Tonight I promised to take Amy home."

Tom nodded amiably, apparently unaffected by that news. After her experience with him in the basement, Amy couldn't help a certain annoyance.

It mounted when Tom smiled at her and said with a significance in his eyes only she would have interpreted, "Let me know about the leaded-glass window tomorrow, will you?" His expression was bland, but there was an I-told-you-so in his eyes.

Fifteen minutes later, Amy stood on her front porch in Steve Fuller's embrace, being kissed with tender care.

She looped her arms around his neck, wanting to give the experience a real chance, wanting to see, if she put her heart into it, if there could be something here.

His lips were tender but impassioned, his touch was gentle but competent. It was nice. It was really nice. But her heart didn't seem to be interested.

She guessed when he drew away that he'd read her reaction. His smile was wry and regretful.

"How long have you been in love with Nicholas?" he asked.

"Nicholas," she said, deliberately misunderstanding, "is married to one of my best friends."

He scolded her with a look. "You know which Nicholas I mean. I was told you two had broken up a couple of years ago."

She leaned back against her front door, her smile apologetic. "We did. It's over. I just...have too much on my mind for romance."

"Really." He braced a hand against the door and looked down at her doubtfully. "That must be why the two of you came up from the basement looking like you'd been necking in some hayloft."

Hayloft. Funny he should say that. She remembered sitting in her hayloft with Tom and feeling as though her entire life had just been dropped out a window, like a bale of hay.

"We'd been arguing," she said, rummaging in her purse for her key.

"Arguing doesn't put that look in your eye," he disputed quietly. "And he looks at me with direct hostility."

Amy took exception to that. "He's always been very polite to you."

He dropped his hand and put both in his pockets. "Yes, he has, but I get the feeling if I touched you in his presence, he'd rip my throat out."

Amy frowned. "Well, that's a lovely image to go to sleep on. Thanks for the ride home."

"Look." He stopped her before she could push the door open and smiled thinly in the dim porch light. "I wanted to know if there could be anything between us, and I got my answer.'' His smile widened slightly. ''There is something between us. It's Tom Nicholas.'' He leaned down and kissed her cheek. ''If you ever do decide it really is over between you, call me. Good night, Amy.''

''Good night.''

Amy waved as he drove away, then pushed her way into the empty house. It was shadowy and quiet, and she absorbed the stillness, knowing that in less than eight hours it would be chaos in this room.

She sank onto the sofa and put a hand to her heart, feeling chaos there, too. And Tom Nicholas was going to be working in her backyard for the next two months. Great. By the time the barn was ready for Kids & Co.'s expansion, she should be ready for an asylum.

Chapter Seven

GARRETT: Don't look at me. I didn't do it. I didn't even see it. I went into the bathroom to be by myself, then Kate followed me in and misinterpreted my intentions and stayed to help me do what I didn't really want to do in the first place. Anyway, what do you expect? You know how girls are. Chelsea and Malia must have ripped into it when our backs were turned. You should tell that kid to learn to put her things away.

MALIA: I helped, but it was Chelsea's idea. She's lusted after it ever since Darcy started bringing it. And, you know, considering she left it on the floor, you can't blame us for thinking she was through with it.

CHELSEA: Okay, it was me. But Beautiful Brenda couldn't breathe in that box! It was probably like being in jail. And then she got all these cool new clothes and she couldn't even put them on! Mom says we have to shake off the things that hold us back—and I think that includes the plastic wrapper from the store.

"Oh, no!"

Amy stood in the kitchen with Rodney, trying to

freeze a wad of gum out of his hair with an ice cube, and heard Kate's plaintive cry. Even considering Kate's tendency to drama, the sound sent a finger of dread along Amy's spine.

"What is it?" she shouted, still applying the cube to the gum.

There was a moment's hesitation. Amy felt a second finger of dread.

"You'd better come," Kate said in a weak voice Amy didn't like at all.

She sat Rodney in a kitchen chair and handed him the Baggie-wrapped ice cube. "Hold that to the gum, sweetie," she said, and hurried into the living room where the sight that met her eyes drew a heartfelt groan from deep inside her.

Three of the world's most beautiful toddlers sat in a circle surrounded by the most advanced educational toys and the most practical tried-and-true playthings money could buy—and what they'd chosen to play with was Darcy's "investment."

The plastic wrap had been efficiently ripped off of both the doll and the clothes. Tiny garments were strewn everywhere, the bridal veil had been ripped off Brenda's head, and her hair looked as though she'd seen *Alien* one too many times.

Chelsea held Brenda in her scrap of blankie and did not look willing to relinquish her.

Amy closed her eyes and wondered why she hadn't gone into something more simple—like the diplomatic corps in the Middle East.

"I'm sorry," Kate said, sounding close to tears. "Garrett went into the bathroom and sat on the potty chair, only he was still wearing everything, so I went to help him. The girls were playing nicely with the beads, and I hadn't noticed that Darcy left her Brenda when she and Truman and the Nicholas boys went outside to play." Kate ended with a sigh. "She's going to be so upset. I think it's a transference thing for her, you know. Oh, it's all my fault!"

Amy put an arm around Kate's shoulders, trying desperately to think of a solution. "It's all right. Who'd have ever thought Darcy would leave it behind?"

"This will ruin the whole afternoon for her," Kate said, wringing her hands. "The pumpkin patch won't be any fun for her when she sees what's happened to Brenda."

"Okay." Amy went into action. She scooped Chelsea into her arms and pointed to the rubble on the floor. "If we can get it all picked up, maybe she won't notice Brenda's missing until after we go to the pumpkin patch. Rodney!"

The boy came out of the kitchen holding the ice cube to his head. Then he spotted the bad-hair-day Brenda in Chelsea's arms and the clothes strewn all over the floor, and said feelingly, "Holy s---!"

"Rodney!" Amy scolded.

"I mean, darn!" he said apologetically. "But Darcy's going to kick a— I mean, butt, when she gets back!"

"We're not going to say anything to her about it until after we've been to the pumpkin patch," Amy said firmly. "Understand?"

He got down on his knees beside Kate and hurriedly gathered up clothes. He stopped to look up at her. "You mean we're going to lie?"

"No," Amy replied. "I mean, we're going to keep it to ourselves so that she can have fun this afternoon."

"What if she sees it's missing and tries to find it?"

"We'll hope she'll be too preoccupied with picking out pumpkins to notice."

He looked doubtful but helped Kate pick up the doll clothes, then looked for a second minuscule little shoe.

Amy took Chelsea into the nap room and tried to negotiate for the Brenda doll.

"I'm sorry, Chelsea," she said reasonably. "I know you want to play with it, but it isn't yours. You have to give it back." Amy took hold of Brenda and pulled.

Chelsea shrieked. "No! Mine! No!"

You listen to me, Amy Brown. Brenda has been suffocating in that box for weeks, and I couldn't stand it another moment. We're all mothers in this world, and the children are everybody's children. You wouldn't keep me in a box wrapped in plastic, would you? Well, I saw an injustice and I rectified it. Now she's mine!

"Chelsea, she isn't yours," Amy said patiently. "She belongs to Darcy. Some toys we can share, and others belong to the children who bring them." Amy pulled again.

Chelsea bellowed. "No! Chessy's! No!"

Don't preach to me about ownership! I've had my blankie stolen and flushed, my apple juice ripped off, and my binkie grabbed, and nobody made a fuss about that. Well, you did bring Lia's Uncle Tom to get my blankie, and I appreciate that. But if Darcy wants her Brenda back, tell her to have her mother hire one of the lawyers she works for and see if they don't consider Darcy an abusive parent!

Amy pulled the sturdy little fingers from around Brenda's throat and removed the doll. Chelsea screeched.

"I'm sorry, Chelsea," she said, hiding the doll in a dresser drawer and bouncing Chelsea in her arms to comfort her. "I know that was rotten, but Brenda isn't yours. Come on. We'll find something else for you to play with."

Don't think you're going to buy my silence with a handful of Cheerios or a Cabbage Patch doll. I want Brenda! And I'm going to make your life miserable until I get her! Put that away, I don't want... Mmm. What is it?

Amy probed Chelsea's pursed lips with a spoonful of strawberry ice cream. The toddler stopped screaming and sucked on the spoon, making a face over the cold, then opening her mouth for more.

Hey, what's she got? I want some!

Amy looked down to find Garrett hanging on to her leg, looking soulfully up at the spoon.

If he gets some, I want some!

Malia appeared, reaching up for the spoon. "Lia some!" she cried.

Order had been restored and all signs of Brenda hidden when Darcy and the boys came inside again.

"Okay, everybody get coats on," Amy said before Darcy had a moment to remember that she'd misplaced her "investment." "We're going to Dr. Foster's pumpkin patch."

Darcy, Rodney and Pete hurried to comply. Truman sat in a kitchen chair. Eddy stood beside him, hands in his pockets.

"We're not going," Truman said, pointing to Eddy, then himself. "It's stupid and embarrassing."

Amy handed Chelsea to Kate, who had collected the toddler's coats. The prospect of a trip had the little ones going to the door.

"Why is it stupid?" Amy asked. "You guys don't like the idea of Halloween and trick-or-treating?"

Truman fiddled with one of the rungs on the ladder-back chair, his large, already strong hands moving restlessly. "Yeah, but carving pumpkins is for girls."

"And picking 'em out," Eddy added, "is for babies."

The back door opened and Tom appeared. He opened his mouth to speak, but before he could state his business, Amy said briskly, "Really? Well, Tom's coming."

Tom blinked and started to speak again, but before he could, Truman demanded suspiciously, "He is?" Then, in-unison with Eddy, he turned to Tom. "You are?"

Amy sent a plea across the room with her eyes.

"Ah...yeah. I am," Tom said. The look he returned her begged for some clue about what he'd agreed to.

Truman appeared confused. "I thought going to a pumpkin patch was a girlie thing to do."

Amy saw in Tom's eyes that he grasped the issue. He remained in the doorway. His jeans and green-and-white flannel shirt were streaked with old paint and covered with fresh sawdust. She could smell the Douglas fir across the room.

Tom grinned. "Most guys like activities that include girls," he said to the boys. "And there's nothing girlie about a place that invites ghosts, bats and big hairy spiders, is there?"

Truman and Eddy looked at each other and appeared to reconsider.

"I'll dust myself off and change my shirt," Tom told Amy with an expression that suggested he'd expect to be repaid for this, "and be right back."

OVER THE LAST FEW WEEKS, Tom had spent enough time around Amy's house to know that one had to have nerves on a very low setting in order to cope. Children, it seemed, were always going full tilt at high volume.

He was somewhat used to that with his nephews and niece, but eight children, particularly in an excited mode, could deafen a man and make him crazy.

But Amy, who seemed to have difficulty with office jobs, moved among the children with a serenity that astounded him. She was usually carrying one child and had two others clamoring for her attention, with another shouting to her from another room, yet she somehow managed to give everyone the attention required and fill all needs.

And that was how it was at the pumpkin patch. The day was blustery, the afternoon sky threatening rain as they wandered through the large patch Nate and Karma had put in at Amy's urging. Wood smoke curled from the A-frame's chimney, and its pungent perfume filled the air.

Tom had Malia in his arms, and Truman and Eddy flanking him, still a little afraid of appearing less than masculine, as he wandered among the fat orange pumpkins strewn along curly, big-leaved vines.

Karma had come home from her office early to help, and Garrett ran to her when she came out to welcome them. She scooped him up and met Amy, who held on to Chelsea's hand.

Darcy, Pete and Rodney ran freely up and down the rows, stopping to inspect, dismiss, reconsider and wrap their arms around the pumpkins to judge size.

The children's laughter and excitement became infectious, and soon Truman and Eddy had gone off to explore and Tom was left to trail Malia, who had wriggled down and was conducting her own search for the perfect pumpkin.

It was an hour before decisions were made, pumpkins were cut from the vine, and the bottoms marked with the appropriate child's name. Tom and Truman loaded the pumpkins into Amy's van, then Karma served apple juice and doughnuts in her big country kitchen.

Tom decided as he drove back to Amy's with Truman and Eddy beside him, and Rodney and Pete in the jump seat behind him, that he wouldn't have missed the experience for the world. The boys had pleaded to ride with him while Amy and Kate drove back in Amy's van with Darcy, Chelsea and Malia. Garrett had stayed with his mother.

"You know," Truman said, "I didn't see one ghost, one bat or one hairy spider."

"They probably all went into hiding when we arrived," Tom said matter-of-factly. "I don't think any of them like noise."

"I think you tricked us into going," Eddy accused him with a grin as he leaned around Truman.

Tom glanced at him with an answering grin. "Did you have a good time?"

"Yeah."

"Did you feel like a girl when you carried your thirty-seven-pound pumpkin to the van?"

"No."

"Then, why are we talking about it?"

Truman studied him a moment, then said frankly, "You're kind of weird, you know?"

Tom laughed. "So I've been told."

"You hear about Darcy's Brenda doll?" Rodney asked.

"No." Tom glanced at him in the mirror. "What about it?"

"She left the box on the floor when she came out to

play with us, and Chelsea ripped it open and messed up the doll's hair. She had the clothes all over the place, and I had to help clean up.''

Tom imagined Darcy's distress and couldn't decide if having the doll forcibly removed from its box would have a good or bad effect on her.

''She doesn't know about it yet,'' Pete contributed. ''Amy didn't want to spoil the trip to the pumpkin patch. She's gonna tell her when we get back. Rodney had to promise to be quiet, then we all had to promise, too.''

Tom watched the road, thinking about Darcy's effort to keep the gift from her father in the pristine condition in which she'd received it. He remembered that he'd treated his life that way, that his strengths and his talents had been like a gift, tightly wrapped, contained. Then the fire had ripped off the wrapping and spilled out the contents and just like everything removed from its original package, things hadn't fit back in in the same way.

There were things that had to be folded to be put back in, things that hung out, things that didn't fit in at all.

''I mean, it's stupid when you think about it,'' Truman said. ''Carrying around a doll in a box. But she liked it that way. Things never stay the way you like them.''

Tom considered that an astute observation from the boy who'd lost his mother.

Rodney sighed. ''It was from her dad and she never gets to see him. That's why she did it.''

Eddy made a sympathetic face. ''She's pretty dorky sometimes, but I feel sorry for her.''

Pete sighed from the jump seat. ''Me and Eddy used

to feel real bad when our mom left. You know, the other mom. Before Nancy.''

Tom nodded, commiserating, and thinking that it was scary how perceptive these children were, but warming to see their genuine concern.

He got to the intersection, watched Amy make the left turn toward her home, and hesitated. He turned to his companions. ''Guys,'' he said. ''I have a plan.''

AMY WASHED THE PUMPKINS outside with the hose while Kate and Darcy kept the toddlers from getting involved. Then they carried the pumpkins into the kitchen, and Darcy disappeared into the living room.

Kate caught Amy's eye in distress. ''I should be the one to tell her,'' Kate said quietly. ''It's my fault.''

''It's nobody's fault,'' Amy insisted. ''You keep the babies busy and I'll tell her.''

She'd just spoken the words when Darcy came running back into the kitchen, eyes round and distressed. ''Amy?'' she asked. ''Have you seen Brenda? I didn't take her to the pumpkin patch, but I can't find her.''

''I know where she is,'' Amy said.

Darcy sighed with relief, then asked, ''Where? Where is she?''

Amy led Darcy to the nap room where she'd stashed the doll among the crib linens. She sat her on one of two single beds and sat beside her.

''I think you must have left her on the floor when you and the boys went outside to play,'' Amy said calmly. ''I'm afraid…she got out of the box.''

Darcy's eyes widened and then filled instantly with tears. ''Truman did it!''

''No. He was outside with you, remember? I didn't see what happened until Brenda was already out of the box, but I think it was Chelsea. You know she didn't do it on purpose. She's too little to know she was doing something wrong.'' Amy forced a cheerful smile. "But I think Brenda's fine.'' She opened the drawer and handed the doll with her rumpled hair to Darcy. "I'm sure if we comb her hair and put her veil back on, she'll be okay.''

Darcy took the doll from Amy and stared at her in horror. Then she watched with the same expression as Amy spread the clothes out on the bed.

"When I was a little girl,'' Amy said, desperate to erase the anguish from Darcy's face, "Brenda came with a wardrobe trunk for keeping her clothes in. I think my mom still has it in the attic where I used to live. I'll ask her to look for it, and we can put all Brenda's cl—''

Darcy's tears began to fall, and she ran a hand over the rumpled hair. "It was a investment!'' she said plaintively. She began to sob and held the doll to her. "My dad sent it!''

Amy held her and rocked her, at a complete loss over what to do for her. It was an offense against nature to expect a child to keep a toy in a box, but she imagined that Darcy had somehow confused the love she felt for the father she never saw with the gift he'd sent her, and wanted it forever protected in its wrapper. And it was also a way to help the mother she loved as well—or so her grandmother had made her believe.

"I think your dad would like it if you played with it,'' Amy said. "Your mom says she doesn't want you to save it and sell it. She *wants* you to play with it.''

"But she needs the money!''

"Honey, it'll be years before the doll is worth enough

to sell it. By then, you'll probably have a job and you can help your mom that way.''

''I wanted her in the box,'' she sobbed, while hugging the doll to her with a fervor that belied her words.

Amy had known that logic would be wasted on the child who had taken the complicated elements of her life and come to an understanding that worked for her, but she'd had to try.

''Well, we've still got the box.'' She pulled that, too, out of the drawer. ''Do you want to see if we can get it all back inside and put plastic wrap over it? Collectibles in their original wrapping are worth more, but you can still get money for them even if they're not. Brenda will still be protected.''

Darcy held the doll away from her, looked into her face and made the hard decision. ''Okay,'' she said.

The babies were holding their pumpkins and watching cartoons when Amy and Darcy came out of the nap room. Kate was picking up toys.

Amy frowned at her. ''Where are Tom and the boys?''

''Tom just called,'' Kate replied, arms filled with colorful plastic. ''He said they took a detour. They'll be back in half an hour.''

''Where did they go?''

Kate shrugged. ''He didn't say.''

Oh, good, Amy thought. Parents would be arriving in twenty minutes and she would have to explain that she didn't know where their children were, except that she'd let them drive off with the carpenter. Yes. That would be a fitting end to a trying day—and possibly her career.

"THERE'S MY DAD'S JEEP," Rodney said as Tom passed it and pulled into Amy's driveway.

Truman pointed to the silver Buick Regal in front of Jave's new white Volvo. "There's my dad's car, too."

"Okay." Tom backed out again and parked on the street. "We'd better leave them room to get out. Climb out on the sidewalk side, and don't dawdle, okay? Your dads are probably anxious to get you home."

The parents appeared less impatient than Tom expected when he followed the four boys into the house. Fuller sat on the sofa in conversation with Jo, who still wore her coat and had dressed Chelsea for outdoors.

Jave and Boomer were dutifully admiring Malia's pumpkin.

Amy stood in a corner with Mrs. Billings, who held a weeping Darcy in her arms. Amy looked across the room and flayed Tom with her eyes.

He groaned silently.

Truman, carrying the package, turned to make sure his friends were following. They stacked up behind him like a row of dominoes. Assured of their support, he led the way to Darcy and thrust the gift-wrapped box at her as though it were a weapon.

She sniffed and looked at it suspiciously, then at the boys.

Mrs. Billings smiled at Truman. "What's this?" she asked. When Truman stammered awkwardly, she looked to Amy for an explanation.

Amy spread her hands helplessly, the anger in her expression turning to confusion as she glanced at Tom.

"It's a present," Eddy said. "Open it, Darcy."

Darcy took the gift, carefully untaped the ends, then the back. As the paper fell away, she held up the Blue Grass Brenda. It had taken twenty minutes for four boys to agree on it when they couldn't find the ill-fated Beautiful Bride Brenda.

"You can save this one," Truman said, "and play with the one your dad sent."

"An' it's only three months older than the other one," Eddy reasoned, "so it should be worth almost as much when you're ready to sell it."

"The lady in the store looked it up," Rodney said, "and it's very collectible."

"And the horse," Pete added with sincere interest, "is really cool!"

It was difficult to tell if Darcy was more shocked by the gift, or by the gesture from the boys who usually loved to persecute her.

"You boys bought this yourselves?" Mrs. Billings asked.

"Well…" Truman pointed behind him to Tom. "We kicked in what we had, but Tom lent us the rest. And he drove us to the toy store. We…you know…" He shuffled nervously, looked to his friends for support, but they all looked the other way. "We knew," he finally finished on his own, "she'd feel bad about Brenda coming out of the box."

The woman looked about to burst into tears. Amy put an arm around her and she pulled herself together. "Well, that's about the nicest present Darcy's ever gotten," she said, hugging each boy in turn. "And it makes me very happy to know she has such good friends."

Darcy sniffed again, handed her mother the box and disappeared into the kitchen. She came back with the Brenda she'd carried around for months, only now she was out of her box and clutched in her arms.

"Don't forget her clothes," Amy said, retrieving a plastic grocery bag from the kitchen table. She handed it to Darcy's mother and walked her and Darcy to the door.

Ginger Billings turned and cast an embarrassed but smiling glance around the room. "Thank you all for your concern."

Jo stood, holding Chelsea by the hand. "I apologize again for my little vandal."

Ginger shook her head. "It's all right. Goodbye."

She called to Tom, who'd had about enough of the intimacy of the moment and was trying to slip out to the barn.

He stopped at the foot of the steps.

She walked down to him, Darcy behind her and Amy beside her. "You're the carpenter," she said.

"Right." He offered his hand. "Tom Nicholas."

She took it in a warm grip. "You made the pencil holder Darcy came home with the other day."

He tried to ward off gratitude. "A leftover block of four-by-four and a dozen passes with the drill."

She smiled. "But driving the boys to town and lending them the money to buy the doll was more than that. Thank you."

"They wanted to do something for her. I was just the wheels. Darcy's a great kid."

"I've always thought so. Thank you again."

"My pleasure."

Tom stood with Amy to wave off the Billingses, then finally made his escape.

Or so he thought. He looked up from hanging Sheetrock on the loft wall and found Jave standing behind him.

"What do I owe you?" Jave asked.

Tom picked up a couple of nails from the sawhorse

table at his side. "A little peace and quiet, respect, probably half a dozen apologies for various…"

"I mean," Jave interrupted, "for the boys' share of the doll."

"Nothing." Tom turned away from him to hammer in a nail. "It's a deal between me and the boys. They're going to help me with a couple of projects."

"You really think you're going to get work out of them?"

Tom turned back to him. "Sure. They promised. If you have any more questions, you'll have to save them because Amy's paying me by the hour, and it just cost her sixty bucks to take me to a pumpkin patch to convince the boys that it wasn't sissy stuff."

Jave grinned. It was that "I know you better than you know yourself" grin that always annoyed Tom. "And then you took it upon yourself to show them that kindness isn't for sissies, either."

"They wanted to do something for Darcy," Tom insisted. "I happened to have the Visa card. Now, get out of here before I'm forced to drywall right over you."

Jave didn't seem to feel threatened. "Thank you," he said. "It was good for them to see concern and compassion for someone else in someone they admire."

Tom put an arm around his shoulders, a score of warm and heartfelt responses on the tip of his tongue. But those things were hard for him. And he knew Jave knew it. So he walked him to the new stairs. "You're welcome," he said. "And I'm sure it would be good for them to see punctuality in you. So take them home before they miss dinner. Give my love to Nancy."

Jave spared him further discomfort with a knowing nod. "See you at Diantha's on Halloween."

"Right." Tom groaned. "Costumes."

Jave ran lightly down the steps. "Yes," he called back. "And you can't come as a carpenter."

Boomer walked into the barn as Jave left, Fuller right behind him.

Boomer had his wallet in hand. "We want to pay you for the…"

"No," Tom said, coming the rest of the way down the stairs. "It was a deal between the boys and me. They're going to work it off."

Fuller raised an eyebrow. "Truman?"

Boomer shook his head fatalistically. "Rodney's going to owe it all back to you in cuss fines."

Tom laughed and pushed away the bill Fuller tried to hand him. "Thanks, but the boys wanted to do it. They borrowed the money from me, and they should pay it back to me themselves, don't you think?"

Boomer studied him a moment, then pocketed his wallet. Fuller stuffed the bill back in his pocket.

"Well, hell. Thank you." Boomer reached a hand toward him.

Tom shook it. "You're welcome. Rodney's a nice kid."

Fuller took his hand, his expression half gratitude, half resentment. He was close to making that move on Amy, Tom guessed.

"Truman talks about you all the time," he said. "He's gone from wanting to be a rodeo rider to wanting to be a carpenter."

Tom nodded. "Good choice. Sawhorses are a lot easier to ride."

Fuller measured him with a steady look, then gave him a reluctant smile. "Thanks. I like knowing other people care about him."

All right, Tom thought. So he wasn't so bad.

The men left, and Tom was halfway up the stairs again when a feminine voice called his name. He turned to find Jo, a checkbook in her hand, delving into her purse, apparently for a pen.

"God!" Tom exclaimed, going down again to meet her. "What is wrong with everyone? It was a measly thirty bucks for a doll. That's all! It was a deal between the boys and me and we're going to square up."

Jo treated him to the smile that made her coffee bar the most popular watering hole in three counties. "But my daughter was responsible for..."

"The way I heard it, no one saw who did it. Chelsea just happened to be holding the evidence when it was discovered. I've seen both Malia and Garrett at work. Either of them is clever enough to do it and frame someone else."

She found a pen and looked around to find a place to sit and write the check.

Tom took the pen from her, dropped it into the huge satchel hanging over her shoulder, put an arm around her and walked her across the field. "You're not going to pay me for it. The boys' fathers, my brother included, seem to think it was a good object lesson for the boys, so we're letting the deal stand."

She frowned at him. "It was my understanding they were all coming back here to pay you their shares."

"I talked them out of it," he said.

"But I feel as though I should..."

"No," Tom said firmly. "I'm sure that's a word you've heard before. Ryan must use it on you all the time."

She laughed as they reached the walkway and he ushered her onto it. "He does, he just isn't usually able to make it stick."

Tom nodded, spotting Amy holding Chelsea and standing by Jo's van across the street. "Well, see, that's the difference between bankers and carpenters. Bankers get soft sitting behind a desk, so when their women challenge them, they're forced to back down. But we carpenters are throwing heavy stuff around all the time and building up our pecs and biceps, so that in a crunch, we can say no and mean it."

They stopped on the sidewalk, and she turned to him with a look so femininely superior that he found himself pitying Ryan. "One day, when you're married, and your wife and children have you wound around their little fingers, you'll remember that you said that and laugh at yourself."

"You think so."

"Yes." She reached up to kiss his cheek, then pat it affectionately. "But meanwhile, go ahead and live the fantasy. See you at Diantha's."

"Right." He waved when she reached the other side of the street, then loped back to the barn and thought that he could get the wall done in an hour if he wasn't interrupted again.

He realized that was a vain wish five minutes later when he heard footsteps on his new stairs. He was going to take the damn things down, he thought, as he turned to see who the new intruder was.

It was Amy. He remembered the look she'd given him in the house when he'd returned with the boys, and guessed she was going to chew him out for taking them to town without telling her first.

He dropped his hammer into the toolbox and gave up on the wall. He pulled up a sawhorse and gestured her toward another facing his.

She was carrying a small pumpkin, and she stood

holding it in her arms for a minute while she looked around, admiring the two walls that were finished.

"You're almost ready to paint up here!" she said, obviously pleased.

"I could have started in the afternoon, but I've had a lot of disruptions." He wiped his hands on a rag and tossed it into a trash box. Then he gave her his full attention, prepared to accept the reprimand without complaint.

"I have two things for you," she said, holding out the pumpkin. "This is just to remind you that you gave up your time for us—to prove to the boys that you're never too grown-up for fun traditions."

He was touched. The pumpkin was only a four or five pounder, but it was nicely rounded, without a scar, and had apparently been washed by a careful hand. The stem had a curl of vine still attached that made it aesthetically perfect.

"Without your mom there," she said, "there's probably nothing at home to remind you that it's Halloween."

It was hard for him to think of that as a bad thing, because Halloween meant Diantha's party, and that meant a costume. And Jave had just shot down the only idea he had.

She'd said she had two things for him, yet there was nothing else in her hands.

"The second thing," he guessed, "has to be a lecture about taking off with the kids without telling you where we were going. I'm sorry. I thought we'd be back before the parents arrived."

"I was embarrassed that I had to tell the parents that I didn't know where you'd taken the boys," she admitted. "But when they heard they were with you, no one seemed to mind particularly. And you did call. But it would be nice if you didn't do that again."

"I concluded that myself."

"Good. But that wasn't the second thing."

"It wasn't?"

"No." She stood. "Please put the pumpkin down."

All right. Apparently he was going to need his hands free. That sounded promising. He balanced the pumpkin on the sawhorse.

"Stand up."

He did, thinking this interruption was suddenly taking a very interesting turn.

She put her arms around his neck, pulled his head down and kissed him with a sweetness that hit him too deeply, too emphatically to allow passion to take over. Almost. That is, he knew by the spirit in which she offered the kiss that it shouldn't, so he held it down.

She was slow and sweet and thorough. Then she held him tightly and rested her forehead against his shoulder. "You and the boys made the whole incident work in Darcy's favor, when it could have just made her so unhappy. And if I'd bought her another doll, or if Jo had replaced it like she wanted to, it wouldn't have been the same. Now she can love the Brenda her father gave her, and save the one from her friends."

She drew back, and her eyes were brimming with emotion. "Only the gesture was so sweet, she might have as much trouble keeping that one wrapped up, too. It's hard not to handle something that's given to you with love. Thank you."

He had to clear his throat. "You're welcome."

She smiled suddenly, dropped her arms from him and reached into a pocket of her jeans. "I forgot. Actually, I had three things for you." She unfolded the list of supplies and charges he'd given her to look over the day before.

"Something wrong?" he asked.

"Yes." She handed him the list, then started for the stairs. She stopped at the top to look over her shoulder at him and smile. "You have to charge me for the leaded-glass window. You won fair and square. See you in the morning."

Chapter Eight

Things changed at Kids & Co. The difference wasn't enormous, or even dramatic, but Amy saw it and realized that she had to credit Tom for it.

Now when parents dropped off or picked up their children, though they were still in a hurry, they stopped long enough to exchange pleasantries with one another. Darcy and her mother made cookies for the other families as a thank-you for the doll, Boomer arranged for the older children to visit the longshoreman's hall and to watch a ship being loaded with logs.

Jo, insisting on making amends for Chelsea's vandalism, brought a sampler pack of coffees for Ginger Billings, and hot chocolate for Darcy. Ginger raved so much about the coffee to the other parents that regular stops at Coffee Country became a part of everyone's morning routine.

Boomer and Rodney were swearing less.

The children got along the way children always would, bickering continually while learning to coexist. But no one felt excluded anymore. Everyone was part of the fray.

The loft was almost finished. Tom had salvaged a railing with turned balusters from an old office building across the river in Washington, and installed it along the edge of the loft.

Amy wandered into the barn with Truman one night after all the other children were gone. His father had to remain at the school for an open house that night, and Truman was in Amy's care until around ten.

"Do not touch anything," Amy said firmly, seeing Tom's tools strewn around.

"Wow!" Truman knelt to admire the half of the railing that had been stained a warm oak color. The difference in appearance was remarkable. With walls and light, and the leaded-glass window installed where the hay doors were, it looked like an office—but one out of *Architectural Digest.*

"They're still wet," Tom cautioned Truman, then he glanced up from the bucket of stain to smile at Amy. "Hi. What's up?"

His manner hadn't been more than friendly since the night Amy had kissed him, and she wasn't sure what that meant—or what to do about it. Had he lost interest in her, she wondered, or was he waiting for her to make the next move? She couldn't be sure. With the volatility between them, anything more than friendly was chancy on several levels.

So, she'd been coasting, unwilling to risk the wrong move.

"I can't believe how wonderful the window looks," she said, going over to admire it. She turned back to give him a grin over their joke about it.

He caught her eyes but didn't seem to catch the joke. He turned his attention to Truman, who came to stand over his shoulder and watch him work.

Frustrated, Amy walked the length of the loft, pacing

off the distance. Someday, she might be able to afford carpeting.

"Twenty-six feet," Tom said, without looking up from the stain. "And eighteen across."

So he *was* paying attention to her.

"Sam called today from the Secondhand Barn," she said, coming to stand on Tom's other side. "He said he has a few pieces for me to look at that might be right for the office."

"Great." The can of stain was empty. He carried it to a plastic tarp set up across the loft where he had tools and cans of stain. He opened another with the tip of a screwdriver, then picked up a power drill with a stirring attachment on it and the loft was filled with a whirring noise for several seconds while he stirred the stain.

He turned off the drill, removed the attachment and wiped it off with a rag. He drew the last bit of stain out of the old can with his brush.

"You want to come with me?" she asked in a rush, before she could lose her nerve.

This was just what Tom had been waiting for—the smallest sign that there was still feeling for him behind the gratitude. The kiss a week ago had been wonderful, but not something he could react to with anything but friendship.

Of course, she might just want him along on a trip to buy furniture for his professional contribution.

"Sure," he said, trying not to imbue the acceptance with any excitement.

"I know you're expected at Jave's in the afternoon for a costume fitting for the party Thursday," she said. "So I won't keep you very long. I guess Jo commandeered some great stuff from the college's drama department."

Tom was less than enthusiastic about this. He wasn't anxious to see himself in plumes and lace—and even less anxious to appear in public in them.

"I'd rather be worked over with a staple gun," he said.

"It'll be fun," she insisted. "Everybody'll..." She glanced over his shoulder and went suddenly chalk white.

She pushed him aside and ran to the railing. He turned to see Truman holding on to it and walking along the outside of it, dangling over fifteen feet of empty space. Tom's heart leaped to his throat.

By the time he reached them, Amy had caught Truman's arms, but his weight was overbalancing her and she was leaning precariously over rather than drawing the boy back.

Tom caught Amy's upper body in one arm and pulled her back while catching Truman's arm in the other and drawing him toward him. The instant the boy was close enough, Tom reached for him with both hands and lifted him over the railing.

"What is wrong with you?" he barked at the boy.

Amy was between them in an instant, her voice high but quiet. "Tom..." she began.

He pushed her aside. Truman watched him, wide-eyed, his face pale.

Tom felt his heart now rocketing against his ribs and forced himself to calm down. "It's a scientific fact," he said more quietly, "that flesh and bone hitting concrete from a drop of fifteen feet results in sausage. You want to climb around, you do it on the monkey bars, not on my project. You got me?"

Truman swallowed. "Yeah," he said in a small voice.

Amy was giving him that mother-cat look again. "Truman, wait for me downstairs," she said, and waited for the boy to comply. Then she turned to Tom. "Sausage," she said with disapproval. She was still trembling herself, and he watched her put her hands in her jeans pockets, probably in the hope that he wouldn't notice. "That was a charming parable. You think that was the best way to handle that?"

"Last week alone," he said, keeping his voice down, "you found him hanging out your second story window, twelve feet up a Douglas fir on the edge of the woods and hiding in the UPS truck. So far, asking him sweetly not to do things isn't working."

"Intimidation is not a parenting skill!"

"Neither is permissiveness."

She folded her arms belligerently. "You know so much about it, of course, with all the children you have."

He went to pick up the new can of stain. "I've spent a lot of time with Eddy and Pete," he returned calmly, "double trouble in a spray can. There are times when reasoning gets me nowhere. The threat of bodily harm does."

She raised a haughty eyebrow. "You're expecting me to believe that you've actually employed *reason* on something?"

"I don't know if you could believe it," he retorted, "since you probably couldn't even *identify* reason if you found it in your playpen! Now. You're paying me twenty bucks an hour. You really want me to spend it arguing with you?"

She squared her shoulders, bristling. A corner of his mind not completely annoyed with her thought she looked delicious.

"Do you want to keep the job?" she asked.

It was clear the question was a threat. Annoyance became something deeper. "No," he said, "but I have a signed contract that says I have it until I'm finished. I believe it's hysterical-lady proof."

Had the power drill been between her and Tom rather than behind him, Amy would have ventilated him.

As it was, she didn't trust what he might do if she got within reach. So she stalked down the stairs and took Truman back to the house.

TOM PULLED ON HIS WORK jeans and a sweatshirt Saturday morning, thinking he'd take advantage of Amy's absence from home to get some work done. He hadn't seen her after she stormed out on him the night before, and he presumed the invitation to accompany her to Sam's was off.

He grabbed his jacket, opened his front door and discovered he was wrong. He was face-to-face with Amy.

She wore jeans, a denim jacket over a red turtleneck, and a pugnacious expression. Her hand was raised in a fist as though she'd been just about to knock.

"Good morning," she said. The greeting was grudging at best.

"Good morning," he replied in the same tone.

She looked away from him, then back at him, sighed and shifted her weight. "I happen to be a very reasonable woman," she said, as though their conversation of the evening before had not been interrupted by the night. "Except where you're concerned."

He folded his arms, patience strained. He wasn't anxious to fight this out all over again. But she'd made the admission. He should at least listen.

"I've noticed," he said. "What do you suppose accounts for that?"

"It's simple," she answered, her lips quirking as though a smile threatened. "You defy reason."

He rolled his eyes. "That's hardly a quote from the lips of Aristotle."

She laughed outright, hooked an arm in his and drew him down the stairs. "I'm sorry. I guess I was really mad at myself because I hadn't been watching Truman. I know how he is. I just try hard not to yell at the kids. Their mothers don't like that."

Tom had to admit she had a point there. Caring for someone else's children didn't afford you the same options available to you when you reacted to your own.

"I'm sorry, too," he admitted reluctantly. "My adrenaline was pumping. But you should talk to Fuller about him. That kid's got a death wish."

She nodded, her eyes grave with concern. "He's aware of the problem. He thinks part of it is Truman's age, and part of it has to be adjusting to the loss of his mother."

As meddlesome as his own mother was, Tom thought with an unconscious smile, she'd been there every time he'd turned to her throughout his life. He couldn't imagine what it would have been like to have lost her as a boy.

Amy drew a breath suddenly and shook her head. "It's Saturday. I just want to enjoy my freedom. Are you ready?"

He focused on her with a wolfish smile. "To enjoy your freedom?"

She pinched the arm she held. "To come with me to Sam's."

It was easy to put all his annoyance with her aside when she smiled at him with that intimate sweetness.

"Come on." He took her arm and led her to the passenger side of his truck. "We'll take this in case you like the stuff and we have to haul it home."

Amy loved it all. Sam, a burly, bearded man in bib overalls, led them to a back room where he had stashed a turn-of-the-century writing desk with a shallow riser that contained pigeonholes and drawers, and an old barrel-back chair that matched.

Amy sat in the chair and ran a hand over the desk.

"We've got oak filin' cabinets," Sam pointed out, indicating seven or eight four-drawer cabinets across the room, "a credenza and—" he pulled a tarp off something bulky in a corner "—a bookcase."

They made a deal for one of the file cabinets and all the other pieces.

Amy spotted the teapot on their way out. It was a mottled yellow and black with a small, lionlike figure serving as a knob on the lid.

She got down on her knees to inspect it, sitting on a coffee table.

Tom felt himself go weak at her expression. He found the piece ugly, but ran a reverent index finger over the shell-like fluting on the belly of the pot.

Amy knew very little about antiques and dealt mostly in simply used things. But this looked old and special.

"Staffordshire Agateware," Sam said. "About 1760. I checked my books. Lady who brought it in says it went to the colonies with a lady from London. That lady's granddaughter brought it west on a wagon train."

Tom leaned over Amy. "Got a lust for it?" he asked, his voice deep and quiet.

"I was thinking," she replied, "that it would make a great office teapot."

Sam, apparently recognizing vulnerability, moved in with more detail.

"Great-great-great-granddaughter brought it in. She said the lady who brought it west was coming to San Francisco to meet her husband, who was building a hotel. But he was killed when a beam slipped as they were putting it into place. She stayed, though, and used the building for an orphanage."

"Orphanage?" Amy looked up, feeling electricity in her fingertips. "She cared for children," she whispered to Tom.

For an instant they were locked together in the one-in-a-million chance that the pot clearly belonged to her.

Sam smiled over them. "Curious parallel here. She married one of the carpenters working on the building."

Tom looked up at Sam. "We'll take it," he said.

"Wait. How much?" Amy asked practically.

Sam looked apologetic. "It's in perfect condition. The book says..." He named a figure that was beyond Amy's already blown budget. She wanted so much to justify its purchase on the basis of fate, if nothing else, but she'd already spent a lot, and she still had to supply the downstairs of the barn with children's toys and more furniture—the whole point of the renovation.

"We'll take it," Tom repeated.

Amy got to her feet. "I can't," she said firmly. "I've already..."

"You write her up," Tom said to Sam, ignoring her protests, "and I'll start loading the truck. Is Jed here to help me today?"

Sam started toward the counter, tipping his head back and bellowing, "Je-e-ed!"

"Tom, I..." Amy began again.

"Consider it a gift from me," Tom said. "And if you don't like that idea, I'll give you the window back. So it just comes out of your already budgeted expenses."

"But Steve did..." She wanted to be honest without betraying a very nice man. "I mean, I don't know that you could call it a move, exactly, because he was just... I mean, I sort of...encouraged him."

She wasn't sure how she'd wanted Tom to react to that. She just knew it wasn't with a smile and a shrug and the philosophical "It's a free country" with which he did reply.

THEY LOOKED LIKE an illustration from Alexandre Dumas's *The Three Musketeers* come to life in Diantha Pennyman's den. Tom watched his friends, garbed in the Musketeers costumes Jo had borrowed from the college, and shook his head over their affability as they waited for their women, who were helping their hostess refill the buffet table.

It had become tradition to take a brief break at Diantha's annual Halloween party to make plans for the hospital's Christmas party for underprivileged children. Jave usually chaired the event, and all the principals he bullied into helping were present at Diantha's.

Jave talked with Nate and Ryan, his ostrich-plumed hat at a rakish angle, his hand resting negligently on the hilt of a sword, as though he really did know how to use one. His breeches were black and his jacket—or doublet, as Jo had called it—was deep red and trimmed with braid. Around his neck was a deep lace collar, and at his wrist, ruffled cuffs.

His companions were dressed similarly, all wearing

the black breeches and the boots with deep, turned-down cuffs, but Ryan's doublet was dark green, and Nate's gold.

Tom had strongly protested the lavender doublet that had been left for him.

Ryan held a musket at his side, the palm of his hand on the barrel.

Nate held his over his shoulder, as though he'd just returned from hunting quail, or whatever wildlife inhabited the French countryside.

The door burst open and the women finally arrived on a wave of laughter. They were dressed like ladies of the period, in gowns with boned bodices, long skirts and puffed sleeves that became skin-tight below the elbow. They wore the same hairstyle—the back caught up in a bun, the sides hanging in tight ringlets. They looked prim and starched and unlike their free-spirited selves.

Jo carried a tray, which she put down on the coffee table, then distributed paper plates.

The couples helped themselves to snacks, then paired off around the room, Karma in Nate's lap in a big chair, Nancy in a corner of the sofa, Jave on the arm of it beside her, Jo tucked into Ryan's arm at the other end.

Tom, expecting Amy to sit in the middle of the sofa, was surprised when she turned instead and came to join him on a balding brocade love seat by the window.

"Monsieur d'Artagnan," she said with a flirtatious smile. "May I join you?"

"By all means," he replied, returning her smile. "But watch the sword. I think I've been responsible for a few torn skirts this evening."

She widened eyes that were dramatically made up. "I suppose you'll be facing the guillotine."

He leaned toward her. ''I don't think it's been invented yet,'' he said under his voice.

She shrugged as though that made no difference. ''Then we'll have to throw you into the Seine.''

''But I'm a good swimmer.''

''We'll tie weights to your feet.''

He studied her with feigned concern. ''You're very bloodthirsty, *mademoiselle*.''

She fluttered both hands expressively. ''I'm French, *monsieur*. It's love or war with us.''

''And you've chosen war?''

She rested an elbow on his shoulder and, looking deeply into his eyes said, ''Actually, I've chosen love.''

It was the sudden silence in the room that alerted them. Tom and Amy turned away from each other to see their friends watching them, the men amused, the women interested.

''I asked,'' Jave said with exaggerated patience, ''if you can make those pencil holder things like you made for the kids. We want to use them for centerpieces at the hospital's Christmas party. Amy thinks they'd not only look good, they could be put to good use when people got them home.''

Tom had to force his mind into gear. It wanted to linger on Amy. He gave her a teasing frown. ''Thank you, Amy. I needed another project.''

She smiled brightly. ''The boys can help you to work off their debt.''

He closed his eyes in prayer as he considered that prospect. Then he opened them and nodded at Jave. ''Sure. I'll do it.''

''Good. The girls are on an Old French kick this year, so they're making angels and flowers out of French lace.''

"Ah...?" Tom raised his hand.

"Yeah?" Jave asked.

"Pardon me, but how will pencil holders fit into an Old French theme?"

"Easily," Amy replied. "We'll just put the angels and flowers and greenery on florist wire and tuck them into the holes. It'll look great."

Tom looked around the room to see if the idea seemed less than lucid to anyone else. Apparently it didn't.

"Okay," he acceded. "Angels in a pencil holder. That makes sense."

Amy smiled, undaunted. "Everything makes sense at Christmas." Then, to his complete surprise, she leaned toward him and kissed him lightly on the mouth. "Even you, Tom."

Their friends cheered and applauded.

Tom took their ribbing in stride. He'd been hanging back with Amy this week, hoping that giving her space would lighten the tension between them. She'd grumbled at him about the teapot all the way home last Saturday, but he'd noticed on Tuesday that it had a spot of honor in the middle of her hutch.

Tonight she seemed to have taken an aggressive approach to their relationship. It might be time for him to change his battle plan.

Tom's eyes promised payback, and Amy let herself accept that that pleased her. He'd been keeping his distance for days, and while there'd been a time when she'd thought she would appreciate that, she now knew she'd been wrong.

And since his kindness with Darcy, his quick thinking with Truman's high-wire act, his purchase of the teapot, and that damnable whatever it was about him that made her want and need him, she knew it was time to make *her* move—that was, if she hadn't discouraged him with her mercurial moods and her two-year-old grudge.

Amy panicked halfway through the party when she couldn't find Tom. Moments ago she'd seen him dancing with Jo, then Karma had cut in, and now he seemed to have disappeared.

The party had spilled out into all the other downstairs rooms, and she checked them all, wondering if he'd just gone looking for a comfortable place to sit out the tango now blaring from the disc player.

But he wasn't there. She slipped outside to see if he'd simply needed air. She encountered the two straw figures Diantha made every year and placed on her porch swing, jack-o'-lanterns on the stairs, and a harem dancer and a cowboy, late arrivals to the party. But no Tom.

Just her luck, she thought. She'd finally decided to do something positive about their relationship—and picked the moment he'd apparently decided to forget the whole thing.

She wandered down the steps and onto the gravel walk, a frosty moon lighting her way. The smell of wood smoke filled the air, along with the fresh and salty tang of Katherine's Bay on the other side of the road. She heard the lap of water, the stir of a light wind in the trees.

This town, she thought, opening her arms in an unconscious effort to embrace it, had given her everything she'd ever wanted in the way of friendships and a sense of purpose and belonging. But without Tom there was a bittersweetness about it.

Amy picked up her skirts, prepared to walk a little farther, when a call from the direction of the house stopped her.

"Aimée!"

She whirled, the very sound of Tom's voice filling her chest with a warmth that suddenly seemed to clarify everything. And he's used the French pronunciation of her name, which meant "beloved."

He came down the steps toward her, a tall, broad silhouette in his seventeenth-century clothes. In the darkness, the white plume of his hat fluttered, and his cape billowed out behind him as he came toward her.

The sword bumped against his leg, and the leather of his boots bit the gravel. She had the strangest sense of being lost in literary fiction.

"Monsieur?" she asked.

"Ladies are not permitted to wander the grounds at night unescorted," he said as he approached.

"But I set out to find you, sir." She looked up at him, trying to read his eyes in the shadows. "Were you hiding from me?"

"Not at all," he replied. "I brought in wood for the mistress of our…inn." He swept a lace-cuffed wrist toward Diantha's home, warmly lit against the dark. "When I returned, my comrades told me you'd gone out without an escort."

"My escort," she said, "was apparently busy seeing to the needs of another lady."

They stared at each other for a moment, a man and a woman in seventeenth-century dress under a harvest moon, hearing clearly everything that wasn't being said.

Tom put a hand to the hilt of his sword and shifted his weight. "My apologies, *mademoiselle,*" he said quietly. "You wished for an escort to take a walk in the dark?"

Amy wound her arms around his neck and reached up on tiptoe until her mouth was a fraction of an inch from his. "No, *monsieur*. I wish you would escort me home."

"Amy…"

"Please."

The fictional spell broken, the night became suddenly very real.

Tom ripped off the hat and wig and mustache. And the air of gentlemanly courtesy.

"No more theatrics, Amy," he warned. "I am so tired of dancing around the issue. D'Artagnan has left the building. Do you want Tom Nicholas to take you home?"

Amy kissed him slowly, dipping into his mouth with the tip of her tongue, nipping at his lip, kissing a path to his ear. "I want Tom Nicholas to make love with me tonight," she whispered.

Tom didn't give her time for second thoughts. He whipped the cape off and wrapped it around her. Then he lifted her into his arms, carried her to his truck and headed for her house.

"We should have told someone we were leaving," Amy said softly as she fumbled in her very twentieth-century purse for her key in the meager light of her front porch.

"Everyone will have figured it out," Tom assured her. "They know more about us than we do. Would it be easier for me to break a window?"

"Got it." She turned the key in the lock and pushed the door in, then waited for him to follow her inside and locked it behind him.

The instant she turned away from the door, he had her in his arms. He carried her upstairs to her bedroom, carefully skirting the table in the hallway. There was a new pot on it, holding the familiar eucalyptus.

A light she'd left on in the hall illuminated the foot of a four-poster with a crocheted spread and canopy.

He set her on her feet and smiled at their surroundings. "It's almost too bad we left d'Artagnan behind. He probably would have felt right at home here."

Amy pushed him lightly until he sat on the edge of the bed, then she turned her back to him and drew up his right leg to pull off the boot.

He planted his other boot against the seat of her skirt and pushed.

She turned back to him with a smile of surprise. "It amazes me that that works. You see that in movies all the time, and it seems so...I don't know..."

"Indelicate?" he suggested.

"Yes." She turned again and raised his other leg. She handled it carefully. This was the one that had been badly burned and that had given him so much trouble. To relieve any discomfort he might feel, she chattered on. "I mean, can you imagine being engaged in a dalliance for the first time, setting the scene in some romantic hunting lodge or something, and having the gentleman kick the lady halfway across the room in the process of removing his boots?"

"Believe it or not," he said, leaning back on his elbows and planting his boot very lightly on her, "I haven't given that much thought. But it is essential to get the boots off. I mean, how many ladies would want them on their lovely linens? Of course, there's the option of making love on the carpeting, or in the hayloft. Then he could leave his boots on."

She pulled off the second boot, then turned to him, laughing. "Do you suppose *that's* why love is made so often in haylofts?"

He sat up, caught her waist and brought her down

beside him. Then he knelt astride her, prepared to undress her. But there were no buttons or zippers that he could see.

"While you were considering the delicate problem of the gentleman's boot on the lady's derriere," he said, grinning down at her, "did you come to a solution for the gentleman eventually uncovering said derriere?"

She laughed again. "The top is laced up the back," she said. "And the skirt is separate."

She turned over, brushing the inside of his thigh and that part of him already aching for her. He lost his breath, his ability to joke.

He unlaced the top and found a bow at the back of her skirt that was easily untied. Bracing his hands on the mattress on either side of her, he slipped backward off the bed and pulled off the skirt and a pair of little silky slippers. Then she sat up and he helped her remove the top.

Her breasts rose beautifully out of a corset so tight that it made him wince just looking at it. Then his attention was caught by a pair of white undies that looked like bloomers with a slip attached.

"Petticoat breeches," she said, her voice sounding a little high.

His hand went to the front laces of the corset. "Let's get this instrument of torture off first."

"You undo the back laces," she said, turning her back to him. He got her out of it, then tipped her backward onto the bed and pulled off the fussy bloomers.

"So I guess the man who remained interested after all that," she said, her ivory body lying on the lace like some very artful pattern in it, "deserved the lady's charms."

The breath caught in his throat, and he felt his blood

thicken at the sight of her full, beautiful breasts, her narrow waist, the very feminine flare of hip and length of thigh. He felt awed and reverent all at once.

He groaned her name and leaned over her to plant a kiss at her throat.

They'd gotten this far before, he remembered, with the sense of that having been in another lifetime. Then she'd touched his bad leg, he'd gone a little crazy, they'd shouted at each other and he'd gathered up his clothes and stalked away.

But he was different now, and that made this all new. And he wanted to make up to her for the last time.

He pulled his belt and sword off and tossed them onto the floor. He was working competently at the tiny buttons on his doublet, until she put her hands to his waist to unfasten his breeches and he seemed to lose all co-ordination.

He regained it again when she knelt up on the bed and slipped her hands between his flesh and the out-of-character Joe Boxers he wore under the breeches and whispered, "Oh, Tom. I've waited so long for this."

In a moment they were naked in the middle of the bed. She had tossed the coverlet back and they lay on sheets that were soft against his skin—flannel, he guessed. The air was cool but he was at the point of combustion.

He tucked her into his right arm, and with his left hand he explored every rise and hollow of her body, every beautiful curve and every musky secret.

Her hands moved over him tenderly, but with a boldness that surprised and flattered him. He felt her breath against his shoulder, sometimes deep and content, sometimes coming in shallow little puffs, depending on where she touched.

Her fingertips ran over his ribs, into the indentation of his waist, then over his stomach. Then they detoured from where he wanted them to his leg—the bad one.

She stopped at the juncture of thigh and torso, just where the scars began, and turned her face to look into his eyes.

"I've loved you for a long time, Tom," she whispered. "And I've loved all of you—good leg, bad leg, good moods, bad moods...." She smiled and kissed his nipple. "Nothing about you is ugly to me. The scars on your leg are just a reminder that you were willing to risk your life for someone in danger. And your grief over Davey defines that part of you that wants to do more and be more than anyone ever expects of you."

She drew her hand up to wrap it around his waist as she lay her head on his chest. "And I want—all I ever wanted—was to be allowed in. Let me share what you feel, whatever it is. And let me love who you are, scars and all. All right?"

He almost didn't have the voice to answer. He had to swallow and accept that he would never belong to himself again. "All right," he said finally.

She braced herself to kiss his mouth, then pushed herself down his body until she could explore his leg with lips and fingertips.

Amy felt the hard ridges of scars from the top of his thigh to the soles of his foot. The part of her that knew his anguish and felt his pain wanted to scream with the image of the agony he'd experienced in that minute when his leg had been trapped under a burning wall.

She put her lips to the tracery of scars, repeating with kisses and the gentle strokes of her fingertips everything she'd told him earlier—that all of him was beautiful to her.

She breathed love words and kisses over his knee and down his shinbone, then up again. Then she kissed the firm length of his manhood.

Tom experienced the benediction of her healing kisses on his leg, then his heart jolted to a stop when she kissed his eager erection. In that split second the anguish of two long years was erased, and the future he'd thought was lost reappeared.

But his need was urgent, imminent. And he didn't want to lose her in this wondrous second chance.

He caught her shoulders and pulled her down beside him. She wrapped her arms around him, breasts straining against his chest. He reached gently inside her, gritting his teeth against his own need to take time to prepare her for him.

But she was ready, opening for him, straining up to him.

He entered her swiftly, deeply, and held there as she enfolded him with a little moan he might have interpreted as pain if she hadn't held so tightly to him, wrapped her legs around him and tightened on him like a tide-pool flower.

He groaned, too, with the exquisite pleasure.

Amy felt as though she'd gained a new dimension. While trapped between promise and pleasure, she waited, wrapped deliciously in his arms. She could feel every muscle in his body in contact with hers, every pore absorb his breath, felt the hair on his chest abrading the tips of her breasts and causing a conflagration at the waiting heart of her.

Tom moved gently out of her, then in again with possessive confidence. He withdrew and returned again and again until the tightening tension made her wild.

He thrust again as she rose to him and her world

ignited. Everything familiar flew apart, and everything she'd ever wished for came together. It was like rebirth, she thought, some quiet part of her brain still functioning in the explosion of sensation.

She trembled inside and out. Sparks raced along her veins toward a powder keg of feeling, but instead of destroying her, the flames seemed to race back to their source and build warmth there.

She felt like Venus rising out of the sea. Or like the woman whose teapot she owned must have felt when she turned around in the rubble of her old life and found the carpenter standing there.

Everything was new again.

THE TROUBLE BEGAN about 3:00 a.m. Amy sat in a robe in front of the fireplace and Tom lay propped on his elbow beside her in a pair of sweats he'd retrieved from his gym bag in the truck. They were sharing a sandwich she'd made and a bottle of merlot she'd received as a birthday gift months ago and never opened.

"I was thinking," Tom said, topping up their glasses with the wine, "that when the barn's finished, we could take the *Mud Hen* out for a week or so before we get caught up in the holiday confusion."

She sipped at her wine, loving the idea of a week alone with him. Reality, however, had to prevail. "That sounds wonderful." She passed a large slice of spicy pickle from her plate to his. "But I'm fixing up the barn because I have a waiting list of children."

He met her gaze and asked reasonably, "But they've been waiting all this time. Would one more week make that much difference?"

"Well..." It probably wouldn't, but the whole point of doing this from the beginning had been to make it a success, to serve as many families as wanted to use her services. "What about the children who come regularly now?"

"Couldn't they make other arrangements for a week?" he insisted quietly. "Three of them belong to Jave and Nancy, and they only come a couple of days. I imagine they could work something out. And certainly the others would understand your need for a week's break."

Amy was experiencing a mild sense of panic she didn't entirely understand. Kids & Co. had become her identity, it was the first thing she'd done entirely on her own, and it was succeeding beyond her expectations. And it would thrill her enormously to see it become bigger and better.

If this expansion proved profitable, she was considering opening a branch in Seaside, down the coast. For the first time in her life she could hold her head up among her successful family members. Granted, it wasn't a courtroom or Hollywood, but it was her own.

She tried to explain that to Tom.

He listened to her patiently, his expression growing more and more unreadable as she went on.

"Amy, we're talking about seven days," he said when she'd finally finished. "I know you have this need to compete with your sisters, but don't you want a life that isn't governed by them?"

She frowned, confused. "What do you mean? That's why I came to Heron Point."

"Amy, moving didn't do it." His tone was losing some of its quiet reasonableness. "You're still ruled by the need to do your sisters one better. Don't you want anything besides that? Don't you have some personal goals that don't involve familial revenge?"

"It isn't revenge," she disputed. "It's...I don't know. I guess I have to know that I measure up."

"To whom? All you have to be is who *you* are."

She stood impatiently and paced across the room. "You're very philosophical for someone who had to run away from his problems."

Tom sat up slowly, eyes darkening. "I went away to straighten myself out. I'd lived with guilt so long, I was no longer sure who I was without it. But I found out. Still me—not perfect, not awful, just me. And that's all I want from you—not some day-care mogul with branches in fifty states. Just Amy—who makes every little kid feel special."

She appreciated his simple assessment, but she had things to prove, and he had to understand that. "You told me you went away because you had to understand yourself before you could be anything to me. Well, I'm the same. I'm the new, improved Amy, and I have to know that I have no limits. Particularly any set by someone else."

He got to his feet but remained where he stood as she marched past him in her agitated pacing. Her shoulder brushed his. She felt his stiffness, his anger.

"What you're telling me," he assessed, "is that you're not making any concessions to me. If that's the case, then why is it so important to get inside me, to 'be allowed in' as you put it, if what I'm feeling doesn't matter to you?"

"I'm telling you," she corrected him, straining to make him understand, "that I want to build the day care and make it the best one around."

"You're not interested in a personal life beyond the occasional blanket waltz after a party, then?"

The question was asked lightly, diminishing the significance of all that had gone before during the night.

She wanted very much to hit him. Instead, she fixed him with a look of disdain. "I think this conversation is deteriorating beyond redemption. Don't get holier than thou with me about our relationship. It was second to what *you* needed two years ago."

He caught her arm and pulled her to him, his face set in tight, angry lines. "No. It was first, and that was why I left. But you don't seem to understand that no matter how often I say it, so I guess you're right. This conversation—just like this relationship—is going nowhere." The silence ticked as he dropped his hands from her and grabbed his keys from the coffee table. "I'll finish the job, and then I'm out of here. The best thing you can do for me in the interim is stay out of my way."

"That will be my pleasure!" she shouted after him as he slammed the front door behind him.

Chapter Nine

Amy rose Friday morning with a throbbing headache and the sense of oppression that always accompanied the first few waking moments of the day after a tragedy. But it wasn't a tragedy, she told herself bracingly. She'd survived before and she could do it again.

She glanced at the bedside clock and groaned. She was half an hour later than usual, and this was going to be a day that required she have all her wits about her.

She had all three September 23 babies for the entire weekend. Their fathers were in Portland for a workshop on new medical equipment—Jave and Nate representing the hospital, and Ryan as a member of the hospital board.

When Amy had heard their wives speculate dreamily over the opportunity to accompany them and do some early Christmas shopping, she volunteered to watch the babies free of charge, not as their day-care provider, but as their friend.

"But we wouldn't be back until Monday night," Nancy said, her protest halfhearted.

Amy had shrugged. "No problem."

But that had been before the argument with Tom had snapped her spirit in two.

All the after-school kids would be coming today, as well as several drop-ins. She and Kate would be tried to their limits.

The whine of a saw came from the direction of the barn, and an echoing cry tried to form inside her. But she pushed it away.

She was doing fine. She would continue to be fine.

She swung her legs out of bed and stepped down onto the carpet, prepared to sprint to the shower and jump into her clothes.

But her feet connected with something metallic and cold, and she looked down in surprise, wondering what it was.

There, still trapped in the leather-worked baldric that had strapped them to Tom's waist, were the sword and scabbard he'd discarded last night just before he'd made love to her.

She managed to step over it and head for the shower, but she sobbed all the way.

THERE WAS NOTHING like a house filled with children, she thought by the middle of the afternoon, to force a woman to rise to the occasion. She dispensed meals, hugs, cautions, Band-Aids, toys and treats with an efficiency that made even Kate take notice.

"What's with you today?" she asked while the babies napped in the afternoon. "You're like a madwoman, but a sort of…robotic one. Repressed anxiety? Unresolved anger? Unrequited love?"

Amy ignored her questions and handed her a fresh box of disposable diapers to put away. Nothing seemed to matter much except that the children's needs were seen to and that the whine continued from the direction of the barn.

She had a sudden fear that Tom might wander in for a glass of water or a cup of coffee as he'd gotten in the habit of doing, and that she would burst into tears.

She hadn't shed one since she'd come out of the shower, but she felt as though they were just behind her eyes, a sob waiting in her throat.

But as long as the saw was whining, she knew Tom was a safe distance away.

The after-school kids arrived in a rowdy mood, high, she guessed, on all the Halloween candy they'd devoured. It was also another rare sunny fall day, and they were pushing and shoving one another, obviously in an outdoor mood. They showed off for the drop-in kids, a brother and a sister who were Truman's and Rodney's ages, but far less rambunctious.

The girl was happy to play dolls with Darcy, though it took some explaining for her to understand why one of the dolls was still in its original box and had to remain there. But when Darcy gave her the other doll to play with, she didn't care.

The boy went out to play on the monkey bars with the others, then returned a while later and busied himself with Legos on the coffee table.

Mercifully, the babies slept on.

Amy had mopped up a glass of juice Darcy had spilled and was emptying her wet-dry vac when she suddenly noticed the silence. She went to the window over the kitchen sink and looked out at the monkey bars and found them empty.

She put the vac down and went to the back door and yanked it open. The slide was empty, there was no one on the teeter-totter, and the swings dangled in the afternoon breeze.

Amy shouted to Kate. "Have you seen the boys?"

Kate came around the corner of the kitchen. "They were on the monkey bars a few minutes ago." She looked over Amy's shoulder into the empty backyard. "I'll check out the front."

She hurried off and was back a moment later. "Not there," she said. "I know you've insisted that they not bother Tom, but you know how he invites them into the barn sometimes."

"Tom's truck left half an hour ago," Amy said. "He must have gone for supplies or to get something to eat." Then a horrible thought struck her. It was possible the boys had gone to the barn to investigate his tools without someone cautioning them not to touch this or that, not to press buttons or flip switches.

There was a cry from the nap room. One of the babies was awake. That meant they would all be up in a minute.

"I'm going to run out to the barn," Amy said. "Will you be all right alone for a few minutes?"

"Sure." Kate shooed her out the door. "I'll feed the little ones and they'll be fine. The other kids are all busy."

Amy ran across the field to the barn, unable to shake a sense of foreboding. She put it down to the grimness of her state of mind after her argument with Tom and told herself that the boys would be in the barn, simply eager to look over the tools.

But they weren't there. She looked upstairs, just to cover all bases, and felt a stab of fear when she didn't see them.

She couldn't imagine where they could have gone. They knew the woods were off-limits. But they were preadolescent boys, she reminded herself, a completely unpredictable species. And they were in a rowdy mood

today. It was entirely possible that they'd chosen to ignore the rules and go exploring.

She ran down the stairs and across the barn to the
door, where she was almost impaled by a length of
molding.

Tom shouted a warning and she darted aside.

"You didn't take the boys to the lumberyard with
you, did you?" she demanded anxiously.

It sounded like a sarcastic question, and she saw him
set the molding down and prepare to answer in the same
tone—and then he looked into her eyes and his expression changed.

"No," he replied. "Why? What's wrong?"

"They're missing," she said, pushing past him to
step outside. "I've looked everywhere. All that's left is
the woods, but they know they're not supposed to go
in. They were feeling their oats today, though, so they
might have decided to do it, anyway."

"Who's missing?"

"The four boys. Your nephews, and Rodney and Truman."

He rolled his eyes. "All right. I'll help you look."
He pointed to the trail right behind the barn. "You
know where the stream is just before you get to the
road?"

"Yes."

"You follow this trail to the stream. I'll take the one
that starts at the other edge of the woods. Deer come
out of there all the time, and they might have spotted
one and followed it in. I'll meet you at the stream."

Amy didn't wait to discuss it any longer. She walked
at a brisk pace, but stopped to listen every few minutes,
convinced that four boys between the ages of eight and
twelve could be neither invisible nor inaudible.

But she didn't see them, and she didn't hear a sound that didn't belong to the woods. Wings flapped, things scurried, insects buzzed—and there was that eerie sense of being watched by eyes that couldn't be seen.

She walked on, careful of her footing as roots rose out of the muddy path and ferns and vines reached out for her.

Tom felt like a boiling cauldron of anger, fear and regret.

Uppermost was fear. Reason told him that his nephews were capable and competent boys who usually knew better than to flout the rules. But Eddy was growing more adventurous with age, and Pete was determined to keep up with him. Truman was a wild card the equation didn't need, and Rodney, despite his propensity for swear words, was happy to go along with anyone on anything.

Tom prayed that it was simply adventure that had drawn them, and not one of the dozens of nameless evils that preyed on children—even in cozy little Heron Point.

His anger might have been explained as a normal response to a situation he couldn't control, but it had already been alive in him when he'd found Amy in the barn with that frightened look on her face.

Anger had been bristling in him since their argument in the early hours of the morning, but had been nicely fanned by the possibility that Eddy and Pete had taken off on a lark when their parents were a hundred miles away.

He really didn't understand the regret. It was just there. He didn't know why he should regret the loss of a woman who didn't particularly want to spend time with him—unless it was the memory of her making love with him last night like a woman obsessed.

He put emotions out of his mind and tried to concentrate on several sets of boy-sized footprints. They seemed to step all over one another, then move off the trail and into the trees. They were lost completely in the thick underbrush, so he stayed with the trail, eyes and ears scanning as he moved.

He was almost to the stream when he heard the sound of excited voices and a growl that didn't sound quite doglike. He recognized it instantly.

Raccoons fought over cat food left out overnight in his mother's neighborhood. They were beautiful creatures and generally harmless, but every once in a while there was one with an attitude.

And as Tom came upon the boys and Amy on the edge of the stream, he understood what had upset this particular raccoon. The odds were it was a female, and the small raccoon Amy held in her hands was its baby.

The mother raccoon was inches from her, teeth bared as it gave her its demon-from-hell growl. The boys fanned out around her, and Eddy was poking at the mother with a stick when it got too close. Amy was inspecting something on the baby raccoon's foot.

"Put it down!" Tom shouted at her as he came through the trees.

She glanced up at him, her eyes startled, but she continued to work on the small raccoon's foot.

The mother raccoon charged again, but Eddy beat it back. It parried with his stick on its hind legs, its teeth bared in a vicious snarl.

Tom, imagining the raccoon leaping onto Amy after its baby, cleared the few yards that still separated them, snatched the baby from her and tossed it low on the ground toward its mother. Mother and baby disappeared into the underbrush, the mother still snarling and scolding.

Tom turned to the boys and Amy, anger now definitely uppermost. Amy's face and Eddy's wrist were scratched, and Truman had scratches on both hands.

Eddy and Pete looked up at him, eyes wide and uncertain, then Eddy turned back to Amy. "Did you get it?" he asked.

She held up a two-inch length of blackberry stem with its vicious thorns.

The boys cheered and Amy grinned.

Tom felt on the brink of apoplexy.

"Eddy," he said deliberately, trying to control his voice, though he kept his hands on his hips to withstand the temptation to use them in a throttling motion. The only thing that truly prevented him was that he didn't know whose teeth to rattle first—the boys who'd obviously disobeyed the directive about the woods, or Amy, who'd stopped to do first aid on a baby raccoon while its mother charged her. "I'd like to know why you guys ignored Amy's rule about the woods."

Eddy swallowed. "You left," he said quickly, "and we went to the barn to look in at your stuff. Just to look!" he added on a defensive note when Tom's gaze narrowed on him. "We didn't touch anything. Then we saw the mother raccoon and two babies running across the field toward the woods. One of the babies was limping. So we went in after it."

"The woods are off-limits," Tom reminded him.

Truman frowned at him. "The baby was limping," he repeated Eddy's words.

"So we followed them," Eddy went on, giving Tom a judicious look. "Dad's a doctor. He'd understand."

Tom doubted it seriously. He'd seen Jave in action when the boys had behaved recklessly, and it wasn't for the fainthearted.

"You could have been hurt!" Tom said quietly but firmly. "I can't believe you boys haven't seen enough nature films to know that wild animal mothers don't stop to analyze if you're helping or hurting their babies. All they know is that you've got them and they want them back!" He turned to Amy. "And you had to hold it?"

She glared at him and opened her mouth to reply, but Truman came instantly to her defense. "I picked the baby up. She took it from me when the mother tried to jump at me."

"Then Eddy got the stick," Rodney said excitedly, "and held the damn thing off!" When Amy and Tom both turned to him he took a step back and amended more quietly, "Sorry. The darn thing."

"Yeah! It was so cool, Uncle Tom!" Pete added. "It coulda got an infection or something, but we saved it! Just like Dad or Uncle Nate!"

"You listen to me," he said, focusing on one boy, then the next, until he had the undivided attention of all four pairs of eyes. "You boys got really lucky that Amy found you in time, otherwise the raccoon could have really hurt you. You should not have come into the woods in the first place. Amy put it off-limits, and when you're here, she's the boss! In the second place, *never* pick up a wild animal, even if it looks cute and cuddly. Raccoons have long nails and strong teeth! And I don't think we have the problem in Oregon, but a lot of times they have rabies!"

"You have to get shots in the gut for that!" Rodney

said, as though the idea had serious appeal. "It hurts like hell! Heck, I mean!"

Eddy shook his head and told Tom defensively, "They don't do that anymore. There's a new way that isn't so bad."

Tom held his stare. "That's not the point, Eddy."

Eddy sighed. "I know. We just felt bad seeing the little guy limp." His eyes reminded Tom suddenly, startlingly, of Jave's. "Like when you used to limp. It was like I could feel it, even though it was on you and not on me."

For a moment Tom was speechless. And during that time he could feel Amy's gaze boring a hole into him. He ignored it.

"It's great that you guys wanted to help," he said finally. "But I think all your dads would be pretty upset. I think they would rather have you safe than the raccoon."

For the first time since he'd found Amy in the barn, Tom noticed that she hadn't stopped to put on a jacket, and that there was gooseflesh on her arms and she was trembling.

"Let's get back to the house," he said to the boys. Then he pulled off his denim jacket and held it open for Amy.

"I'm fine, thank you," she said stiffly, and tried to move past him.

He caught her arm and forced it into a sleeve. "Don't act like a brat in front of the boys," he said under his breath.

She jammed her arm into the other sleeve, pulled away from him and fell in line between Eddy and Rodney as they headed back up the trail. Pete followed her.

Truman kept pace with Tom.

"I think it would be all right with my dad," he said, looking up at Tom through the long blond hair falling over his eyes, "if something happened to me."

Edgy and irritable, Tom shook his head and turned his attention to the trail. "That's ridiculous, Truman. And you know it."

"No, it's true," the boy said seriously. "He tries to pretend, but I know he doesn't like me anymore."

"Truman…"

"My mom died because of me," Truman blurted out, his voice alarmingly matter-of-fact.

But when Tom stopped in his tracks and Truman looked up at him, Tom saw that his eyes had filled and his bottom lip trembled dangerously.

"Truman." Tom put his hands on his shoulders and leaned down to him. "That isn't true. You told me she had cancer."

He tried to speak, but a choked sob came out instead.

Then he drew a breath and tried again. "Because… she always used to say, 'Truman, someday you'll be the death of me.'" He shrugged a shoulder and a tear fell onto his dirty cheek. "And then I was."

Tom felt Truman's pain go right through him. He shook him gently, then said with all the conviction he could collect, "No, you were not. She died because sometimes cancer is big, bad stuff and even doctors with all the best medicines and treatment have trouble fighting it. It wasn't because of anything you did."

Truman dragged the sleeve of his flannel jacket across his eyes. "But maybe she got it 'cause she worried about the things I did."

"No. That can't happen, Truman. They're not always sure what makes somebody get it, but something your body can't fight gets inside it and takes over. But you can't get it from worry about somebody. Absolutely not.''

Truman considered that, then shook his head. ''But she said…''

''No. That's just an expression. When parents love their kids a lot, they tell them that so they'll stop doing things that worry them. You didn't do it. The cancer did.''

Truman thought about that, then frowned, apparently concentrating on the differences between how he'd thought things were and how they might be. ''Are you sure?'' he asked doubtfully.

''You know what I think we should do,'' Tom suggested, eager to hold on to the small advance he thought he was making here. ''My brother, Eddy and Pete's dad, is a radiologist. You know what that is?''

Truman nodded. ''He takes pictures of your guts.''

That was close enough. ''Right. I think you and your dad should go talk to him. He helps people who have cancer, and he can tell you how it works, that one person can't make another person get it. Okay? But he's in Portland for the weekend, so it'll have to be next week, okay?''

''Yeah,'' Truman said. ''We're all going on a Boy Scout camp-out. Rodney's dad is gonna take us all home with him tonight.''

''Right.'' When Tom had volunteered to keep the boys for the weekend, Jave had told him about the camp-out. ''Well, we'll talk to him about it when he comes back.''

Truman's eyes were still worried. ''Okay.''

''But until then,'' Tom said, holding the boy to him for a moment, ''you can be sure your dad loves you very much.''

"How do you know?"

"Amy told me."

That seemed to put the issue into a believable area for him. Because Amy said so.

Tom led him back to the house.

When they arrived, Boomer was there to pick up the boys, and Amy gave Tom another glare when he straggled in with Truman. She had the boys' camping gear stashed in the kitchen, and doubled-checked that they had everything before they left. Apparently she hadn't said anything about the raccoon.

The boys watched Tom apprehensively as he shook hands with Boomer and exchanged waterfront gossip. But he went out onto the front porch with Amy to wave them off without mentioning the raccoon incident.

Amy ripped into him the moment the car was out of the driveway.

"This is *my* day care!" she roared at him, pointing her finger at him, except that it had little impact because it barely protruded from the long sleeve of his jacket. "Don't you *ever* take over like that again!"

"You asked *me* for help," he retorted.

"I know you snarled because you were frightened for your nephews, but can't you ever correct children without jumping on them with both feet! They're not nails you hammer in until they're in place, they're boys who have malleable, impressionable, suggestible little minds that can be turned in the wrong direction so fast...."

That was true. Truman had just borne that out.

He caught the hand, or rather the sleeve with which she now jabbed him in the shoulder, and held it still. "Amy, those boys are smart and inquisitive. If you aren't more firm with them and don't make them accountable when they don't listen, they'll do themselves harm.''

"Can you really scold them," she demanded, ''for wanting to help an injured animal?''

"Yes!" he shouted back at her. ''Or didn't you see the mother snapping and snarling at you?''

Amy knew he was right, but she was so angry at him at the moment for so many different things—personal and professional—she felt obliged to stand against him, whatever the issue.

Then she noticed a subtle shift in his mood. His frown deepened. "Incidentally, are you aware that Truman considers himself responsible for his mother's death?''

Amy had to stare at him for a moment while she tried to comprehend the question. "What? How?''

"Apparently she used an unfortunate choice of words. She used to tell him he was going to be the death of her.'' Tom shook his head. ''My mother *always* said that to me. Only in Truman's case—she did die. And in his child's brain he thinks it means he *did* become the death of her. I think you should tell Fuller about it. He's probably not aware of it, either. I told Truman he should talk to Jave when he gets back. He'll be able to put it in terms that should put Truman's mind at ease.''

Then Tom's mood changed again, and he freed her hand and said with male arrogance, ''I don't see how you can in all conscience consider expanding to accept more children when you don't understand and can't control the ones you already have.''

Then he walked around the house and back to the barn.

Amy was torn between wanting to kill him and wanting to bludgeon herself. Poor Truman! She'd suspected that his grief over his mother was partially responsible for his recklessness, but she'd had no idea he blamed himself for her death. And she felt that she'd failed him, somehow, because he hadn't confided that to her.

She helped the babies play with big wooden puzzles while Darcy and the two walk-ins played Old Maid at the kitchen table. But her mind kept going first to Truman, then to the fact that she'd allowed the boys to slip away from her. It was easy for parents to comfort each other when children did reckless things by saying that they were quick, that even the most vigilant parent could miss a child's move toward potential danger.

But when that child was being watched by a child-care professional, there were no excuses that applied. Her job was to watch them at all times even more vigilantly than a parent would.

So in a sense, Tom was right. But she refused to even think about him. Love that had turned to anger was a corrosive thing, particularly when it came around a second time.

The walk-ins' mother arrived just before five. Amy was gratified when the children told their mother they'd love to come again.

"I'd like to come all the time!" the boy said with sudden animation. "The other guys got to see all the carpenter's power tools and saved a whole family of raccoons from a bear!"

When the boy began to talk, Amy closed her eyes, certain her new client-care provider relationship with their mother was about to go down the tubes. Fortunately, the exaggeration and bravado with which the story had apparently been told by the other boys ultimately saved her.

The children's mother smiled, apparently put the

story down to exaggeration and told the boy to put on his jacket. She paid Amy and promised her she would check her calendar and set a formal schedule for the rest of the month.

Amy privately applauded her lucky escape, and her foresight in renovating the barn. But that brought back thoughts of Tom, so she busied herself helping Darcy put the cards away.

Steve Fuller arrived a few moments later. Amy held the door open for him in surprise. "Did you forget that Truman was going away for the weekend?" she asked.

He laughed lightly. "Hardly. I just wanted to make sure the boys got off okay."

"Yes," she replied. "About half an hour ago. Come in. I'll pour you a cup of coffee. I'd like to talk to you about Truman."

Steve winced. "What did he do?"

She smiled and pointed him to the kitchen table. If Tom wasn't saying anything about the raccoon rescue, she wouldn't, either. "Let me put a tape in for Darcy and I'll be right there."

The babies were busy with a PlaySkool slide she kept in a corner of the living room. She could watch them easily from the kitchen table.

She poured Steve a cup of coffee and sat across from him with her own and told him what Tom had told her. He stared at her, just as she'd stared at Tom.

"But...it's just an expression!" he said. "She also used to tell *me* that all the time."

"Well, you know, kids are very literal. He'd probably like to know that she said the same thing to you."

"But, I..." He was clearly upset.

Amy patted his arm. "It's hard to know what's going on in a child's mind. Don't beat yourself up because you didn't see it. I didn't, either, and I'm supposed to be trained to do this. And he functions very well, he just has a propensity for danger that might diminish if he was sure you didn't blame him for anything. Tom suggested you take him to see Jave Nicholas. That he can explain to Truman that what he thinks happened is impossible.''

Steve closed his eyes and let his head fall back, a sound of anguish escaping him. ''God. I can't believe this.''

''What? What happened?'' Darcy's mother had let herself in as she often did when the noise level in the house was high and she didn't think her knock would be heard. She came to the table. ''Is something wrong with Truman?''

Steve had both hands over his face. Ginger sat down beside him and put a hand on his shoulder.

''Truman's all right,'' Amy said, getting up to pour another cup of coffee. ''He just…misunderstood something about his mother's death.''

Unsure how much Steve would want to reveal, Amy had answered Ginger carefully, then sat back in surprise when Ginger leaned toward Steve and asked quietly, ''Do you want to talk about it? There's nothing scarier than raising a child by yourself, is there?''

Steve lowered his hands and drew a deep breath. ''It makes me feel like a complete incompetent.''

Ginger nodded. ''Been there. In fact, I'm still there.'' She smiled at him. ''Darcy and I are going for pizza tonight. Since Truman's with the Scouts this weekend, you want to come with us? We can cry on each other's shoulder while Darcy plays video games.''

Steve blinked once, as though he wasn't certain he'd

comprehended the question. Then he nodded slowly. "Yes," he said finally. "Pizza sounds good."

They were gone in a matter of minutes. Amy watched Ginger drive off, Steve pulling onto the road behind her, and wondered if anyone else had ever considered that a day-care business could provide parent care and a dating service, as well.

"Okay, babies," she said, closing and locking the door. "It's just us for the whole weekend. What do you want to do?"

MALIA: Let's go to Darby's Dresses and try on clothes!

CHELSEA: Let's order Chinese takeout and watch *The Sound of Music!*

GARRETT: Bowling!

TOM COULDN'T IMAGINE where Amy was going with three two-year-olds, but he told himself he didn't care. She didn't want his help—even when she asked for it—so she could just fend for herself. She was the trained professional, anyway.

He was packing his truck two hours later when she returned, holding Garrett between her knees and Chelsea by the arm as she released Malia from her car seat.

Apparently just fed, they were even harder to keep tabs on than usual. But before they could scatter on her, she picked up Garrett, the explorer, anchored Malia by the hand because she was used to running with her brothers, and controlled Chelsea, the mellow one, with her voice.

She had them back in the house in a couple of minutes. He had to give her credit. He also regretted his remark earlier about being unable to control the kids she had. He'd known it wasn't fair when he'd said it, but he'd been mad as hell at her for other reasons, and it had been a convenient way to hurt her. He didn't like knowing he was capable of that.

He would apologize for it, but not tonight. He was still too angry.

He was back at eight in the morning, thinking that he might be able to handle the apology today. He'd slept well, done a couple dozen push-ups this morning, and had a Danish and a cup of coffee in a bag on the seat of the truck.

He'd resolved that things weren't going to come together for him and Amy, so he was going to put it behind him. The barn was going well. He'd finished the floor, installed the new windows and had wallboard up and mudded upstairs and down. One more week of slapping paint and he'd be on to new projects and new women.

He slammed on the brakes when he rounded the back corner of the house and encountered Amy, waving him to a stop. She looked a little rough this morning. Her jeans and shirt were soaked, and her hair tumbled over her eye. She looked as though her composure hung by a thread.

He rolled the window down as she ran around to the driver's side door.

"I'm sorry to stop you before you even get to park the truck," she said, her manner carefully distant. But he could see that desperation lay just under the surface. "The bathroom faucet came off in my hand. I managed to shut off the cutoff valve, but I'm not sure where to go from there. I tried to call a plumber, but all I've gotten so far are answering services. And there's a limit to how long I can go without hot water with three babies in the house.''

"Sure," he said, trying to respond with the same neutrality. He liked that she had to ask him for help, but he'd like it better if she acted a little more needy about it. "No problem." He climbed out of the truck, pulled his plumbing tools out of the back and followed her in through the back door.

Three babies in the playpen meant she'd had to keep them out of her hair. He patted heads, then went into the bathroom where a stack of wet towels attested to a mop-up operation.

"I'll get you a cup of coffee," she said.

"Thank you," he replied, setting to work.

Amy wasn't sure what was wrong with her, but she seemed to be enduring some kind of emotional degeneration. It was happening too slowly to qualify as a collapse, but it was happening.

Last night, when she'd brought the babies home from an excursion to a fast-food place where they'd gotten prizes with their meals, she'd had a revelation. She'd looked at the three beautiful little babies playing on the floor with their bendable animals and wondered if she would spend her entire life looking after someone else's children.

Well, she would, of course. That was the plan. But would she do it without ever having children of her own—children who wouldn't go home with someone else at the end of the day. Children who called her Mom rather than Amy.

And it had gotten slowly but progressively worse from there.

When she'd finally gotten all three babies asleep, she curled up in a corner of the sofa, intent on reading the current Diane Hankins thriller. But she was distracted by the silence.

Usually, she considered silence a blessed thing. But last night it had seemed to scream with loneliness. There were three babies in the next room, she told herself.

"But they're not yours," a hostile inner voice needled.

She'd finally gone to bed and stared at the ceiling for several hours as the feeling of not fitting in that she'd struggled against for so long and thought she'd finally defeated came back to haunt her.

She fought it off. It wasn't her fault that Tom had taken off and left her to find other things to do to make up for the void in her life. It wasn't her fault that the things she'd found to do had served their purpose and now she couldn't just chuck it all—even for a week— to take off with him on a lark.

It *was* her fault, however, that she'd let four little boys wander off into the woods. That she'd shouted at Tom for shouting at them. That she'd known she was wrong but resisted apologizing because she was hurt and angry and didn't want to make that concession.

It *was* her fault that no matter what happened between them, she couldn't seem to see her life without him in it. Even when it stared her emptily in the face as it did in the melancholy darkness of every early morning, she kept thinking about what it would be like if he were there beside her.

She'd finally turned into her pillow and cried herself to sleep. Then Chelsea had awakened, then Garrett, then Malia, and it had taken until almost 4:00 a.m. to get them all back to sleep.

After the long night, she'd gotten up, brushed her teeth and turned on the hot water, intending to put a soothing washcloth on her face, and the faucet had come off and drenched her with warm water in an instant.

And it was just after eight on Saturday morning.

She ran into the bedroom, peeled off her clothes and pulled on a robe, then went into the kitchen for the coffee she'd promised Tom.

She stopped in the bathroom doorway, momentarily paralyzed by the sight of his broad back in a white cotton T-shirt and his trim backside in well-worn jeans as he worked on the faucet with a wrench.

He glanced up into the mirror above the sink and caught her studying him, and she was reminded of their conversation that night in the loft when she'd made light of his warning that Steve intended to make a move on her by admitting that she'd eyed Steve's hips.

He raised an eyebrow.

She put his coffee cup down on the wide windowsill and left the room without a word.

By all indications, it was going to be a very long weekend.

She thought later that she'd had no idea precisely how long until there was a knock on the front door. She looked at the clock, wondering who it could be at this hour. Most of her close friends were out of town, and she'd made it clear to her client parents that having three two-year-olds until Monday evening would make it impossible for her to take any other children until Kate arrived on Monday morning.

She pulled the door open and felt her heart bolt, as though it was trying to hide behind her spinal column.

It wasn't her client parents at all—it was her *real* parents. And her two sisters and her brother-in-law.

She stared at them in stupefaction. They were all supposed to be thousands of miles away—her parents in New York, Peggy on a runway somewhere fashionable, and Jane and Beau winning courtroom battles in Boston. But they were here in Heron Point. On her doorstep. She prayed for death. Or at least unconsciousness.

Chapter Ten

Amy's mother hugged her, then passed her to her father, and she was transferred from one pair of arms to another until she reached her brother-in-law, who held out his hand. She wasn't offended. She'd seen him greet his own mother with a handshake.

"How are you, Amy?" her mother demanded, her lightly mascaraed, discerning blue eyes going over Amy diagnostically. They widened in horror over her appearance, then rested on her gaze with a look of concern. "It's been so long. I know it's rude to drop in, but *so* much is happening, and we were all just praying you'd be home. Is this...a bad time?"

"Oh, how can it be a bad time?" her father asked in the hale and hearty voice that always dismissed every suggestion of a problem with the insistence that it didn't exist. "Amy's our little ray of sunshine, aren't you, Amy?"

Amy found herself falling into the old pattern, forgetting that she was the new, improved Amy. Her father wanted a little ray of sunshine? She would give him a little ray of sunshine.

"Of course not." Amy opened the door wider. "Come in. Come in."

"What a…quaint old house," her mother said, walking into the living room strewn with toys.

Amy knew her mother didn't really mean it. Sabina Brown had lived too long in a Long Island mansion to appreciate a rundown old Victorian.

In a peacock blue flared knit dress and snakeskin pumps, she picked her way over a PlaySkool train and half the plastic population of Noah's ark, then stopped short at the sight of the playpen and its three inhabitants.

Her sisters followed, Peggy in a winter white bulky sweater, leggings and knee-high boots, her leggy model's body moving with grace and fluidity. Her blond hair was short and chic, her makeup flawless.

Jane, much smaller but just as perfect in a brisk, no-nonsense sort of way, wore a navy-and-white pantsuit, complete with white shirt and tie.

Her father and Beau wore designer suits she knew had probably been purchased from Barney's in New York and Louis's in Boston.

Her mother went into raptures. "Amy! You wrote and said you'd left the hospital and were embarking on a new adventure, but you didn't say what it was!"

"Oh, I…" Amy began.

Her mother turned to her suddenly, putting both hands to her heart and saying in a high whine, "You got married!"

Amy was momentarily distracted by an inability to determine how her mother had come to that conclusion. And before she could respond to it, Peggy said with a roll of her eyes, "Get real, Mom. Didn't you see the sign on the front lawn. It's a day-care center."

"But it's Saturday!" her mother argued.

"So?" Peggy went closer to the playpen to look down at the cherubic little faces looking up at her.

"Lots of people put their children in day care on Saturday. Hi, babies."

"But…" Her mother leaned down to study the babies closely. "These all look to be about the same age. And they're dressed exactly alike. Amy, you've given birth to *triplets?*"

Amy opened her mouth to explain, but Jane said, "Relax, Mom. She isn't married. We haven't been to a wedding, have we? And, anyway—" she patted Amy on the shoulder "—poor Amy is afraid of men."

Amy felt the quicksand of her childhood sucking at her feet. She struggled against it and entertained for just a moment the notion of pretending that these were her babies and that her husband was at work, or on some errand. If she'd been sure they'd only stopped by for an hour, she'd have tried to get away with it, just to see her sisters' looks of surprise.

But that kind of thing always fell apart on one, and she wasn't much of an actress.

Her mother, it seemed, was determined to believe the fantasy Amy couldn't voice.

"But they have the same color hair, except for the bald one. And they all have brown eyes."

Peggy sighed. "Amy's eyes are gray," she said.

"But *his* aren't."

Every head in the room turned toward Jane when she made that observation, then followed the line of her wide-eyed stare to the doorway into the hall where Tom stood, wiping his hands on a towel.

It occurred to Amy that he looked like every uptight woman's secret dream, standing there in white cotton straining across his shoulders, and old jeans clinging to every muscular curve of thigh and calf. His dark good looks stood in dramatic relief above the white shirt.

The casual competence with which he accomplished his task—and the subtly stiff manner he adopted around her as a matter of course—clung to him as he wiped his hands.

Amy's mother and sisters stared. Even Peggy looked back at Amy in disbelief, apparently assuming by the way he'd walked out of the back of the house that he was a love interest.

Her mother looked at the babies, then looked at him and gasped. The babies were all dark like Tom was, and because they were now very used to his presence, they reacted gleefully when he walked into the room. Amy watched in astonishment as her mother's imagination did the rest.

"Amy!" Sabina said on a strangled cry, still staring at Tom. "You...*did* it!"

Amy had no doubt what that unspecific exclamation meant. "You found a man," it said with respectful disbelief. "None of us believed you ever would." She might have been offended at the clear shock on everyone's face, but she was too busy enjoying their near-prostration.

"Amaryllis," her father said briskly. "I think you should introduce us."

"Yes, of course." Amy walked around the playpen toward Tom, enjoying her fantasy for the final few seconds of its life. Then she would introduce Tom to her family as the carpenter who was renovating the barn and explain how he happened to be in the house.

But their thrilled, astounded expressions and cries of admiration continued to fill her awareness, and she realized that for all the "Amy's!" that had been gasped, breathed and shouted, there hadn't been one "*poor*

Amy!'' Because they thought she was married to this man, and that she'd had his three children.

As she reached Tom, she found she just couldn't slough off her family's image of her as a winner—even if it was completely mistaken.

She hooked her arm in Tom's and gave him a look that was half plea, half threat, then turned to her family.

''Everyone, I'd like you to meet my husband, Tom Nicholas, and our children...'' She tugged him toward the playpen so that she could point at each baby as she ticked off their names. She felt the muscle in Tom's arm constrict, and sensed the sharp turn of his head, but she refused to look up at him. ''Malia, Chelsea and Garrett. Tom,'' she went on before anyone could interrupt her, ''I'd like you to meet my parents, Sabina and Nelson Brown. And my sisters, Peggy Brown and Jane Brown Jones, and her husband, Beau. You all get acquainted, and I'll put on another pot of coffee.''

Sabina flew into Tom's arms with a tearful cry, and Amy turned her back on the scene as everyone else converged on him with offers of shocked and belated congratulations. She hurried to the kitchen, her limbs shaking, her mind screaming, ''What are you *doing?*''

She had the coffee going and was microwaving muffins out of the freezer when Tom came into the kitchen.

She started to make a shushing gesture, knowing anything said in a regular tone of voice would be heard in the living room, but he caught her arm and yanked her out the back door. He stopped just outside with her and pulled the door to quietly.

''What *in the hell* do you think you're doing?'' He repeated her mind's question, but with typical male exaggeration.

She was already regretting the impulse, but it had felt so good, she had trouble feeling guilty about it.

"I know, I know," she said, raising both hands in a plea for understanding. "It was stupid and maybe even unforgivable, but I couldn't help it. They were so...shocked when they thought I'd found someone. And you strolled out looking like such a perfect specimen, that for the first time ever, they looked at me with respect. And I just couldn't trade that off for the truth...." She frowned up at him. "That you left me for two whole years and coped just fine without me. That we just can't get it together."

Tom gestured broadly in exasperation. "Amy! You just claimed a husband and children you don't have! These people aren't strangers, they're your family. How long do you think you can keep this up?"

"We probably won't have to for more than a few hours. They do this every couple of years. Somehow all their schedules coincide and they jet in someplace to get together, then they all come to see me because I'm the only one who can't afford to fly anywhere." She sighed ruefully. "We have lunch or dinner together, then they disperse once again, back to their busy lives." She shrugged a shoulder. "It shouldn't be too hard, but you don't owe me anything. If you don't want to cooperate, you don't have to. You can leave, and I'll tell them you had a job to go to or something."

"Or," he said, folding his arms, "I could simply go back inside and tell them the truth."

The thought that her family would be disappointed in her yet again still held all the old horrors. It was demoralizing to know that.

She nodded grimly. "Yes, you could."

He considered her a moment, and she felt her heart fall to her toes as he relished the idea.

"You decided to end a relationship with me," he said, "because you had to prove to yourself that you could be as successful as everyone else in your family. So, in all fairness, I should be able to sacrifice *you* in order to have what I want—which is absolutely no part of this!"

He bristled with anger, and she accepted that she was in all probability facing humiliation in front of her family, followed by alienation from them. It surprised her to feel alarmed by that possibility. She didn't understand them, couldn't relate to them, sometimes didn't like them, and was almost always annoyed by them. But they were her family.

Tom studied her woeful face and knew he couldn't do it. She deserved it, but he was pathetic in his concern for her. And he had overheard some of the conversation from the living room when he'd been wiping down the sink after finishing with the faucet.

He'd heard Peggy's slightly scornful teasing about Amy being afraid of men, and Jane's adamant refusal to even consider that she'd attracted one. If that was indeed a habitual reaction from her sisters, it was no wonder Amy wanted them to believe she was married.

"How do we explain that they weren't invited to the wedding?" he asked. "That you never even wrote and told them you were married? That they have grandchildren? A letter getting lost won't work in this day of cell phones and faxes."

She apparently interpreted his question as a suggestion that he might cooperate and appeared to be racking her brain for a solution. "They'll believe it. They're all generally too busy to keep in close touch except for birthdays and the occasional visit.''

He looked skeptical.

''We could say I was pregnant before we got married,'' she proposed eagerly, ''and was afraid they wouldn't approve?''

''And you wouldn't even have confided in a sister?''

''They don't confide, they compete,'' she said. ''I think they'll believe it.''

He drew a breath, sure he was going to hate himself for this before the two hours were over. ''Okay. But if it all falls apart, *you* have to explain everything. And I'm charging you retail for the leaded-glass window.''

Her eyes closed and she seemed to fall in on herself in relief. Then she opened her eyes and focused on him with a small smile. ''Thank you,'' she whispered. ''I won't forget this.''

She had that right. ''Damn straight you won't,'' he said, and pushed the back door open.

NOT ONLY DID Amy's family seem to swallow the story whole, they fell in love with Tom and the babies.

GARRETT: Hey, this guy's as good as my dad at swinging me around. I wonder how many G's I'm pulling? Who is he, anyway? How come they're acting like they like us so much?

CHELSEA: I wish I was flying. This lady's going to squeeze the life out of me. And she keeps staring at my face. I think it's because Amy's acting like she's our mother and Malia's uncle is our father. Why would they do that? I mean, I know our parents are gone and everything, but usually Amy just baby-sits for us, she doesn't become our mom. You don't think we've been sold, do you?

MALIA: Right. Like anybody, even Amy, would pay to take us. At least your lady seems to like you. Mine keeps staring at me like she's gonna cry. And the man next to her looks like he's afraid of me. I think this is like the Halloween party our parents went to where they pretend to be somebody else. Only this time they're doing it in their own clothes. I'm not sure what it's all about, but Amy will tell us when she has time. She always explains everything to us. Meanwhile, I like the attention. But I wish these two would smile!

AMY CLEARED AWAY plates, refilled coffee cups and smiled privately when Malia wriggled out of Jane's grasp and toddled to Tom, who was in conversation with Peggy.

The gesture looked so natural, it couldn't have been better if she'd staged it.

Her father sat on Tom's other side, also involved in their conversation while he dandled Garrett on his knee.

Her mother watched him with a pleased smile. Jane studied him with a kind of lambent lust. Amy's older sister had always been so controlled, so cool, that Amy had always wondered if there was any warmth inside her. She'd rarely exhibited it.

And the fact that she'd chosen to love a man who, despite a law firm partnership three years out of law school, had all the animation of a mannequin tended to confirm that she didn't.

But now Amy wondered. Had Jane secretly harbored a longing all this time for a big-shouldered man in a T-shirt?

And Peggy, who'd starred opposite Christian Slater, Alec Baldwin and Ethan Brennan, seemed fascinated with him.

Amy thought she might burst with a sense of success. In a couple of days, when they were all back home, she would write them and confess everything, absolving Tom of all responsibility. It was the coward's way out without a doubt, but she was simply enjoying these few hours too much to give them up.

Later, when Tom was finished with the barn and gone, and she was alone again with other people's children, she would live on the memory of this morning and the fact that for several hours she'd been Rich Amy. Really Rich Amy.

Then her mother dropped the bomb.

"Well, my goodness!" She fluttered slim-fingered hands, jewels glittering on each ring finger and pinkie. "In all the excitement, we forgot to tell you what we're doing here!"

"I thought it was just your every few years' visit," Amy said, a little sense of foreboding creeping into her flush of success.

"Peggy just finished doing a special show for Isaac Mizrahi and called to say she was coming home with an announcement!"

Amy kept smiling. "And that was?" She turned to Peggy, expecting her to explain, but she seemed not to be following the conversation. There was a pleat between her eyebrows as she watched the babies.

Sabina leaned toward Amy, flushed with excitement. "First of all, she's going to be in a movie with Brad Pitt!"

Amy reacted with appropriate astonishment. It was remarkable, when she thought about it. Her sister in a movie opposite one of the moment's prime sex symbols. But then Peggy had always been remarkable.

"Congratulations!" Amy said. "That's wonderful, Peggy."

Peggy seemed to bring the conversation back into focus. She smiled. "Thank you."

"It starts filming next week," her mother went on, "so she has to fly to Hawaii on Monday. And…" There was a sort of "da-da!" quality to her mother's pause. "She's getting married on Sunday! To Ethan Brennan! Isn't that so exciting! The hottest box-office draw in the last three years and our Peggy got him!"

Jane smiled. At least that was how Amy interpreted the little quirk of her bottom lip. "We're so happy for her," Jane said in a tone more suited to "and there were no survivors."

"Anyway…" her mother went on, letting Chelsea go when she started to fuss. The baby ran to Amy, who lifted her into her lap. "We called Jane and Beau's office and arranged to meet them at Logan Airport so we could charter a plane, come west and pick you up, then fly on to Seattle where Ethan's family is. Then Ethan's off to Toronto for filming while Peggy goes to Hawaii." She bobbed her elegant golden blond bun from side to side in a we-do-what-we-must gesture. "Gstaad would have been a more romantic setting, but *c'est la guerre.*"

Amy knew she'd heard all the facts, but all she could focus on at the moment was "pick you up, then fly on to Seattle."

"So." Nelson Brown took the plastic truck Garrett offered him. "You're not as footloose as we'd imagined. Can you come?"

Thank God, Amy thought instantly. An out.

"I'm so happy for you, Peggy," she said, reaching

out to touch her sister's hand. Then she gestured around the room to the three babies, now moving in three different directions. "But it isn't very easy for us to just pick up and…"

"Amy," Peggy said, holding on to her hand as she tried to withdraw it. "You've got to come. Please." There was something desperate in her eyes. Amy focused on it, certain she must be mistaken. Peggy had never needed her for anything, even as a child. And when they'd all grown up, she'd been openly scornful of Amy's little dreams.

"Darling, you can't deprive us of an opportunity to get to know our new son-in-law and grandbabies." Her mother looked severe. "Particularly considering we're being very civilized about the fact that you didn't even tell us about them."

She had her there. "But Tom has work…." she argued futilely, now even afraid to look in Tom's direction.

"Your mother's right," her father said. "You owe us that much."

It was on the tip of Amy's tongue to tell him that she didn't owe them anything, that all the time she and her sisters were growing up, the only accomplishments their parents had appreciated in their children had been Jane's scholastic ability and Peggy's beauty.

Amy's talents were making friends and being happy even when the situation didn't warrant it. But those accomplishments had been far too small to deserve their notice. And when she'd blossomed like a weed rather than a rose, tall and sturdy and plain, she'd become Poor Amy.

But Amy tried to suppress that whole line of thinking. In her child-care experience, she was learning that many people were gifted parents and as many were not. But what seemed common to most of them was that they did their best in a job that was demanding, relentless and terrifying.

Also—it was hard to fault them for their behavior when hers this morning was reprehensible. And she couldn't even think about trying to straighten it out now because then she would ruin Peggy's wedding. So she just had to go with it. She couldn't in all conscience be sanctimonious with them.

Peggy squeezed her hand again. "Please, Amy."

Amy squeezed back, at a loss to explain her younger sister's behavior. Her need seemed very genuine.

Amy turned to her parents. "Would you mind if Tom and I talk it over for a few minutes?" She stood and reached for Tom's hand, praying he wouldn't ignore it, or worse yet, slap it away and spill the truth.

"Of course not," her mother said. "Go ahead. We'll watch the babies. And Daddy and I are picking up all expenses, so that's something to figure into your considerations."

Tom caught her hand, but he did not allow her to lead him out, he led her, and at a pace that had her airborne by the time they reached her bedroom.

He pushed her in before him and leaned back against the door like a sentry after closing it.

"Tell me again," he challenged her, folding his arms, "how this shouldn't be too hard, how it'll only take two hours then they'll all disperse back to their—"

She rolled her eyes impatiently. "All right!" she shouted in a whisper. "I'm sorry! Every other time we've come together since my high school graduation, it's been for a few hours at a time. Except for Jane's wedding, and that was just one day long and there were hundreds of other people there.''

She fell onto the edge of the bed with a groan. ''Frankly, I have no idea what to do. If I tell them the truth, I ruin Peggy's wedding, and for some reason she seems so...I don't know...insecure, or something. She clung to my hand. She's never done that.''

She looked at him for understanding. He didn't seem willing to offer it. So she continued to explain.

''If we do go with them, we've got two major, *major* strikes against us.''

''Only two?''

She ignored his sarcasm and went on. ''We're traveling with three two-year-olds. And I really don't see us being able to pull off being married.''

''So you want to tell them?''

''No.''

''Then we'll have to pull it off.''

Amy was surprised to hear him concede that. She was sure it was the only way to go, but it amazed her that he was willing to consider it.

''Do you think you can? I mean, you'll actually have to talk to me as though I'm there,'' she said. ''Not like you're dealing with a hologram or a personal representative.''

She surprised herself with that remark. She hadn't realized she'd been sitting on that resentment until she blurted it out.

Tom, too, focused on her eyes as though there'd been a revelation in that little outburst.

''You act like a hologram,'' he retorted quietly, ''or as though you've sent in a stand-in. You say the words, you do the actions, but there's nothing behind it, nothing inside.''

She stood up angrily. "You didn't behave as though you felt that way the night of the party."

"That's because you were you the night of the party," he retorted. "It was when I suggested you leave your work to spend a little time with me that you suddenly sent in a double."

"You don't understand."

"No, I don't. Just like when I had to leave two years ago, you didn't understand. Apparently ours isn't a marriage made in heaven, despite our three little angels." He straightened away from the door and took hold of the knob. "Let's just do this. I can make it through Sunday night if you can. And try to look happier about it, or we're not going to fool anybody."

"Yeah, right," she said grimly, coming to the door, waiting for him to open it. "Like your approach to this would inspire love and joy in a woman."

"Well." He caught her arm and pulled her to him. "Let's see what I can do about that."

He lowered his head and opened his mouth over hers, giving her a kiss that swiftly cleared her mind of thought. He caught one hand in her hair and lowered the other to her hip and held her against him with it, stroking her, reminding her of all they'd had together that night, and all she'd missed since.

Then he raised his head and looked into her eyes. She knew they had to reflect the instant rush of desire that had raced through her.

He grinned with arrogant satisfaction. "That's better. Now, put a little soul into your performance, Amy. You can't send in a double for this one." He opened the door and pushed her through it.

THEY WERE IN SEATTLE for lunch.

GARRETT: The airplane was cool! I'm going to pilot a ship to Mars, you know. And when I'm done doing that,

I'm going to be president. Hey, look. There's a flying saucer on a stick.

MALIA: Jerk! That's the Space Needle. I think our hotel's around here someplace. We're going to be in a wedding! I heard that lady who thinks she's our grandma talking, and she says she's going to buy us matching outfits!

GARRETT: Oh, no! I'm not wearing an *outfit*. Those things end up having doodads all over them and I'll look like a girl. Nothing doing!

CHELSEA: Astronauts wear outfits. It's the same thing. It's just that this is a wedding. You'll end up looking very handsome.

GARRETT: You think so?

CHELSEA: Of course. How could you be anything else?

GARRETT: All right, then.

MALIA: Good one, Chelsea.

CHELSEA: I try.

SABINA HAD CALLED AHEAD to book the bridal suite of the Seattle Roxbury Arms.

A bellhop led them to the top floor and into an enormous living area filled with sofas and chairs and a large dining table. A small kitchen was set to one side and a glorious view of the city was visible through the large window on the other.

"The cribs are in this room," the bellhop said, leading Tom and Amy into the largest of the four rooms that radiated off the living area like spokes.

It was huge. Amy didn't know where they'd found three matching cribs, but they had, and they were arranged in a row at the foot of the room.

On the other end was a king-size bed and two end tables with stained glass reading lamps. A little sofa stood under a window that looked onto the city from another angle.

"The hotel has a full day-care facility if you need it," the bellhop said as Tom tipped him. The babies, set on their feet, took off in all directions. "Press 11 on the telephone. Thank you, sir."

Amy began pulling off the babies' coats and Tom squatted down to help her.

Sabina carried in a box of toys they'd brought along. "I guess the most efficient thing to do," she said, dusting off her hands, "is to have lunch, then we'll leave the men behind to watch the babies while we get our dresses. Ethan's parents will be meeting us in the restaurant for dinner at about the same time Ethan, himself, arrives from London where *he's* been filming. Don't you love it?"

Amy ignored that question because she had one of her own. "Dresses? But I brought…"

Her mother was shaking her head. "Just because we're doing this quickly is no reason not to do it right. And Ethan's parents and friends will be here. You and Jane will have matching dresses, and I'll be a stunning mother of the bride." She clasped her hands together in a near-swoon of anticipation. "Peggy's going to wear a dress she modeled for Isaac Mizrahi!"

Great, Amy thought. She and Jane in matching dresses, so everyone could see how delicate and chic Jane looked in hers, and how robust and out of place Amy appeared in the same thing.

Sabina smiled at Tom. "You brought along a suit?"

Amy had thought about that when they'd taken a precious hour to pack while her mother walked around the living room like a field marshal checking assault plans. Because of the nature of child care, Amy had enough changes of baby clothes on hand to make her fabrication appear real, but when it came to Tom, he had only the clothes on his back. She could not have explained away his going home and returning with a suitcase, so they'd opted to buy him a few things when they arrived.

"I don't own one," he lied with a charming smile. "But I saw a clothing store in the lobby. I'll find something."

Sabina seemed more intrigued than shocked that a man could live his life without a suit. "You charge it to the room and we'll take care of it." She patted Tom's cheek. "I'm sure none of Ethan's actor friends could be any more handsome than you are."

"Don't let it go to your head," Amy said to Tom under her breath as her mother left the room. She took something out of Garrett's hand, and discovered to her horror that it was a knob. "Oh, no. What is this from?"

GARRETT: Cool, huh? Right over there. That thing with the drawers against the wall. It just came right off. Don't you like it?

"Don't panic," Tom said, taking it from her and going to the dresser. "It screws right back in. No, Garrett. We have to put it back."

GARRETT: But it's mine! I found it and gave it to Amy! No! Give it back!

Tom pulled the screaming toddler into his arms, handed him back the drawer pull, then guided his hand into screwing it back in place.

Garrett abruptly stopped screaming, distracted by the small action. He had to unscrew it and replace it several more times. Tom stood by patiently, and Amy thought, not for the first time, how good he was with the babies. She shouldn't be surprised of course, he'd always been a big part of Eddy's and Pete's lives.

He grinned at Amy over his shoulder.

"Wait till I tell Nate the kid's showing signs of being a carpenter rather than a doctor," he said.

She smiled, sharing the joke with him. For a brief moment, it was sweet to share something, then Malia and Chelsea got into a tug-of-war over a roll of toilet paper Chelsea found in the bathroom, and Amy lost the moment's peace.

"YOU'RE GOING TO LEAVE *three* babies with Beau and me?" Amy's father asked in obvious concern over lunch. Three high chairs were distributed among the six adults seated around the coffee shop's largest table. Other diners were staring at Peggy. She was seldom recognized as an actress or a runway model, but was always noticed for her spectacular beauty.

"Tom will be in the men's shop right here in the lobby," Sabina said calmly, "and he'll be right back when he's finished. Won't you, dear?''

"I have briefs to review," Beau said. There was real panic in his serious hazel eyes.

"Oh, for heaven's sake!" Jane snapped at him. "You're an uncle! You can put work aside long enough to get acquainted with your nieces and nephew."

Everyone except Tom turned in surprise at Jane's uncharacteristic outburst.

Jane shifted uncomfortably and stabbed at a slice of sautéed vegetable with her fork. "I asked him not to bring work," she offered querulously by way of explanation.

"Darling," Sabina said quietly, leaning toward her. "We're in public."

Jane scraped her chair back, slapped her napkin down and said at the top of her voice, "I don't care if we're on the stage at Carnegie Hall! He works eighty hours a week and spends twenty of the other forty in the law library! The rest of the time I get to watch him sleep! I *asked* him not to bring work with him...."

Amy, seated beside Jane, caught her hand. She wasn't sure what her intentions were, but touch often worked with children who were too upset to be coherent.

Jane stopped her tirade and looked down at Amy in complete surprise. She glanced around at the other diners who'd stopped eating to stare at her, and fell into her chair with a sigh.

Embarrassed, Sabina fanned herself with a tent card from the middle of the table that advertised hors d'oeuvres.

Nelson smiled sympathetically at Jane while patting Sabina's shoulder. "Whatever's bothering you, baby," he said gently, "it'll be all right. Don't you worry."

Jane looked into Amy's eyes, and Amy saw there the same grimness she'd always felt when her father repeated his favorite platitude. It was the code that governed his life. *Don't worry*. However, he failed to back up that directive with any effort to relieve the source of concern.

Amy had learned early on that he would always love his daughters, but he was incapable of taking charge of anything to help them. Representatives had always run his business, and their mother had always run their home. All he'd ever had to do was tell everyone not to worry.

Amy rubbed gently up and down Jane's spine. Jane turned to her with another look of surprise and a whispered "thank you."

Chapter Eleven

Amy tried to zip herself into the sophisticated rose taffeta gown Peggy and Sabina had decided would look wonderful in the hotel's white-and-silver garden room where the wedding would take place.

"You'll look like a pair of roses," Sabina said. "A tea rose..." She smiled at small, slender Jane who didn't seem to be paying attention to business at all. "And a...a cabbage rose," she added for Amy after a panicky hesitation. "Those *must* have a more romantic name."

Amy had to laugh. "A cabbage by any other name..." she said, and shouldering the dress, headed off toward the dressing rooms while Peggy and Sabina moved on to mother-of-the-bride dresses.

Even a long-stemmed rose, she thought wryly, wouldn't be able to reach this zipper.

"Amy?"

The voice was small and sounded exasperated. It belonged to Jane in the next dressing room.

"Yes?" Amy replied.

"Could you come and help me?"

For a moment, Amy stood transfixed. That was a first.

Controlled, self-sufficient Jane was asking the cabbage rose for help?

Amy left her dressing room and rapped lightly on the louvered doors of Jane's.

Jane pulled it open and turned back to the mirror quickly, but not before Amy saw a tear well out of brimming blue eyes.

Amy tugged gently down on the fabric at the base of the zipper and drew the tab up over a delicate, crenulated spinal column. "Janie, are you all right?" she asked, taking a step to the side to look at her sister's reflection in the mirror.

The vivid color of the dress lent drama to her fine features and color to her milky complexion. She looked beautiful...and very sad.

Jane moved to get behind Amy and returned the favor, pulling up her zipper. "You look very beautiful," she said, stepping out from behind her so that they were both reflected in the mirror.

Amy studied the two images and felt a moment's debilitating shock. Jane was as beautiful as Peggy, but her petite proportions made her look like a porcelain doll, delicate and precious.

But she, Amy, looked...beautiful, too. She studied the face looking back at her and wondered what it was that had changed.

Feature by feature, she was far less dramatic in appearance, but she'd learned over the last few years to make the most of her silver-blond hair and gray eyes. And her hard work and determination showed, defining the contours of her mouth and chin.

Perhaps it was Kids & Co. She'd done it all on her own, it was successful, and it had all the promise of being even more so. If that was what she wanted. Maybe success affected looks.

Then she thought about Tom, and watched something subtle change in her expression.

It was pain, she thought wryly. Suffering. Loving Tom had put her through the proverbial mill. Then she felt a smile bubble up inside her and she accepted that she'd gotten as much love and laughter from him as distress. It was just that they weren't sure how to put it all together.

Her expression changed again, and for a moment, there was a strong family resemblance between herself and Jane. It was in the grimness of the set of the mouth, the melancholy in the eyes. Her problem, she knew, was that she felt something precious slipping away from her and didn't know how to hold on to it.

Was Jane's problem the same?

"Are you and Beau having...trouble?" she asked, then added quickly, "I know it's none of my business, and you don't have to answer me if you don't want to. I just hate to see you so...upset."

Jane sniffed and looked at Amy's reflection. "I can see that you do," she said, seeming genuinely puzzled. "I saw that in you at the restaurant. But I thought you never liked me."

Amy was at a loss for a moment, feeling as though the subject of sisterly affection was just too big for the confines of the dressing room. "Of course I like you. You're my sister."

"Yeah." Jane fussed with the flared sleeve distractedly. "But this isn't exactly the 'Brady Bunch,' is it? I mean, we don't support one another, we compete." She sighed and pulled at the band that held her platinum hair in a tight knot. "Mom wants us to be perfect, and

Dad wants us not to worry—so he won't have to. They don't care if you have a problem, as long as you don't show it.''

Amy experienced both relief and panic. Jane felt all the same things she felt—only Amy had suppressed them so long, she wasn't sure she wanted to deal with them now. So, she tried to sidestep to Jane's issues.

''So you *do* have a problem?''

Jane combed her hair with her fingers as another tear slid down her cheek. ''I think it's over between Beau and me. He does nothing but work. I mean, I married him because he was ambitious, but this is ridiculous. I think he uses it as a way of staying away from me.''

''Why would he want to do that?'' Amy asked logically. ''You're beautiful and brilliant. You have everything.''

''I'm also afraid of everything,'' Jane said with a sigh. And that little gesture seemed to open something inside her that she must have kept closed for a long time. Her tears began to fall more freely, and her bottom lip quivered. ''I'd be terrified of a man like your Tom.''

Amy blinked. Tom and terror were an impossible equation. Tom and murder—maybe.

''Whatever for?''

Jane burst into sobs. ''Because all I've ever gotten from Beau is gentle, respectful, he-following-my-lead kind of sex, and I'm sick of it! He *must* hate me—or feel nothing when he touches me, which is even worse!'' She wept brokenheartedly.

Amy drew her into her arms and felt as though the real world had disintegrated and she was living in some mirror world inhabited by the same people, but with personalities she no longer recognized.

''Beau's just not very…animated. In fact, I remember

when you called to tell me you were getting married, you said that you loved him because he was always temperate. He didn't run hot or cold.''

Jane tightened her grip on her as she continued to weep. ''God. I don't know what's happening to me. It isn't like me to whine and be dissatisfied.'' Amy found a box of tissue on a shelf and handed her one. ''Thank you. I used to be able to be the perfect doll with a brain that Mom created, but...I don't know. Maybe I'm getting a little older. Maybe my hormones are surging. But...''

She drew away from Amy and made an expressive gesture with her hands and the fluttering tissue. ''I *want* stuff. I want kisses that mean something, I want sex that's out of control, I want Beau to call me from the office and tell me that he has lascivious plans for me when he comes home. I want to be more important to him than his work.''

She pressed the tissue to her nose and sobbed again. When she stopped, she blurted, her voice frail, ''I want a baby!'' Then she began to sob anew.

Amy pushed her gently onto the seat built into the dressing room wall.

''*I* want you to take deep breaths,'' she said, stroking her sister's hair. ''And I don't want you to say a word until you stop choking. You stay right here. I have a bottle of water in my purse.''

Amy retrieved the bottle, uncapped it and gave it to Jane, playing for time. How did one advise a sister who felt as though her marriage was on the rocks because she was comparing it to hers—which really didn't exist?

''Beau won't hear of it,'' Jane said finally, her voice quieter, her breathing more normal, though tears con-

tinued to flow. "He says we have to get the house on
Back Bay before we have a baby."

"Because there'll be too many expenses afterward?"

Jane balled the tissue into her fist and sniffed. "I
guess. I don't know."

"You didn't ask?" Amy leaned against the opposite
wall and watched Jane shake her head. "Have you told
him how you feel about…sex being unsatisfactory?"

Jane shook her head again. "Should I have to? I
mean, if sex wasn't satisfying for you, don't you think
Tom would know it? Do you think he'd even let it happen?"

Amy remembered vividly his consummate care and
attention to her every gasp and sigh the night he'd made
love to her. Then she pushed that thought from her mind
before she became overloaded with her own concerns
and couldn't focus on Jane's. "We're all different,
Janie. I think before you chuck it all, you should sit him
down, tell him what you're feeling, and make him tell
you why he's working late and why he doesn't want a
baby. After watching him react to the news that he and
Dad were going to have to watch the babies this afternoon, I'd say he was afraid of them. But I think that's
pretty common, and that fear is usually dismissed by
spending a little time with one."

Jane sniffed again, seemed to consider her advice,
then rose slowly to her feet and studied her with something Amy couldn't remember ever seeing on her face
before—affection.

"Thank you, Amy," Jane said. She drew a breath
and she seemed to grow an inch, Amy thought. "I don't
know that any of that will work, but…I've felt so alone
in all this. But I don't feel that anymore." She smiled

with a little spark of sincere joy. "I never thought of you as being on my side."

"I didn't know you wanted me there."

"When I was trying to be Mom's perfect showpiece, I was such a snot. I think I felt like you didn't have a chance," she said, the brutal honesty tempered with a self-deprecating smile. "What I never saw was that Peggy and I were clones. You were an original."

Amy laughed. "Only because I was too large and too klutzy to be a clone. I really wanted to be. I just didn't have what it took. And I hated myself and resented all of you because of it for a long time."

"Until Tom?"

Amy thought about that. It was Tom's leaving that had made her get herself together. And his coming back that had left her in a shambles.

She was saved from having to answer when the sound of Peggy's and Sabina's voices drifted into the dressing rooms area.

"I hope this dress is as perfect as it appears on the hanger," Sabina was saying. "The diagonal cut on the bodice sort of reflects the cut of your dress, don't you think?"

"It's a pretty dress, Mom." Peggy sounded weary. "You try it on. I'll see how Amy and Jane are doing. Guys?"

"Right here." Amy and Jane moved out into the common area and the three-way mirror. Peggy looked into Jane's still pink-and-puffy face and glanced at Amy. "What's wrong?"

"Man trouble," Jane said, quickly dismissing her sister's question while she turned in front of the mirror. "Nothing that's going to spoil your wedding. What do you think? Do we look great?"

Jane and Amy posed, did a few theatrical turns, and
Peggy laughed. It occurred to Amy that she looked as
though the laugh was a relief, as though it had to struggle out of her past some great obstruction.

She didn't look like a happy bride at all.

"You look wonderful," she said, and came to put a
hand on each of them. Then she said in mild surprise,
"I've missed you."

Jane hugged her, then reached out to pull Amy into
their embrace. Amy, feeling as though she was moving
deeper and deeper into that mirror world, let them en-
fold her. But the sting of tears in her eyes was very real.

AMY WAS SO HAPPY to see Tom and the babies again.
She even went into his arms, not because she thought
it would make their relationship look authentic, but because…well, she wasn't sure. Her first thought was that
he provided balance in her life, but he didn't really.
He'd turned it upside down. Maybe it was just that he
seemed so sane and uncomplicated when compared with
her family.

She excused herself from the rest of the group and
led him into their room.

"How are the kids?" she asked, clinging to him.

"Fine," he replied. "Napping. Rough day?"

"Just…complicated. Maybe I'll take a nap myself."

He patted her back, and she thought the gesture had
the suggestion of apology. "No time," he said. "Ethan
called. He's here, and he and his family are meeting us
in the dining room in half an hour."

She groaned and leaned her head against his shoulder
with a thunk. "I don't know why I let you talk me into
this trip," she teased.

"It was because you always do what I ask," he replied in the same tone.

"Why don't you ask me to go home?" she suggested, still leaning on him.

"Now?" he asked, laughter in his voice. "After we've defrauded your family and kidnapped three babies? We're probably just getting to the good part."

She closed her eyes and sighed. "Well. As long as there's going to be a good part."

He was quiet, and she lifted her face to look at him, wondering what had squelched the playful mood, and encountered the look Jane admitted to being afraid of. It was hot and demanding and deliciously dangerous.

But Amy had not an instant's trepidation. She stretched up as he leaned down and their lips fused in a kiss that seemed to be about reunion, resurgence, regeneration.

His hands moved over her as hers explored him, and she thought it couldn't make sense to feel this passionately about someone with whom she knew she had no future. Unless it was that pretending they shared a future made it real enough to confuse their libidos.

A rap on the door broke the kiss but left them clinging to each other.

"We're due in the dining room in twenty-five minutes!" Sabina called cheerfully through the door. "Do try to look nice. Ethan's parents will be there. His dad's a surgeon," she added as an aside, "and Ethan's co-star from 'Cleveland Cops' is going to be his best man. He's here, too."

TOM DISLIKED Ethan Brennan on sight. He had no justification for it, except a gut feeling that would be difficult to explain to anyone else. But he'd gone into burn-

ing buildings with many men, and there were those you
trusted, and those you didn't.

It was as simple as that.

Brennan was tall and muscular, and though hotel security had to push back hordes of young people when
he and his friend left the limo for the hotel, Tom could
honestly say he'd never even seen a photo of him. Or
if he had, it hadn't meant much because he wasn't into
popular movies.

He had blond hair tied back in a short ponytail and
wore a wrinkled jacket over a silk shirt and a pair of
jeans. His appearance made Tom wonder what the fuss
had been about "looking nice."

His friend, Bill Channing, was of similar height and
build, but his hair was dark and buzz cut. According to
Sabina, they'd just made some kind of buddy movie
together, and they appeared to have held on to the big-
ger-than-life swagger probably common to men who
have the lines written for them and stunt-doubles to take
their risks.

But they were polite and affable, and Tom thought
the weird weekend might just have given him a skewed
outlook on everything.

Amy included. He wanted to kill Channing when he
was introduced to Amy and brought her hand to his lips.
But she yanked her hand away from him when he held
it too long. Channing blinked at her, as though unable
to believe his attentions were being scorned, and Tom
was satisfied.

Beau came to stand beside him. They'd watched a
49ers game together while Nelson slept and the babies
climbed all over them. Despite Beau's appearance of
having a frozen core, Tom had concluded that he was
all right.

"Big stuff," Beau said.

"So it seems."

Brennan pulled Peggy to him and security cleared their path through the hotel and into the dining room. Amy's family closed ranks behind them.

Tom was surprised that Brennan's parents were already seated at the large table. "Can't stand that crowd and fuss," the senior Brennan said, pulling out Sabina's chair. "And we had all the dinner rolls to ourselves. Julian Brennan. My wife, Dora."

Introductions were made all over again, and Tom found Amy studying Brennan over her menu as conversation buzzed around the table. He gathered from the set of her jaw that she didn't like him, either.

And he was beginning to see what her problem was with her parents—why she had the overwhelming need to prove something to herself and to them. They seemed to credit all their daughters only with how they looked, what they had, and what they'd achieved. There was none of the love for love's sake that abounded in his family. No unconditional devotion just because you were you.

No wonder she didn't understand him when he told her that all he wanted was her. She'd never been valued that way before. He needed a new tack.

MALIA: Hi! How was Ethan Brennan? Was he as gorgeous as he is in the movies? Did you mention my name? Tell him I'm available to do location work? Eddy says I'm cute enough to do commercials, but I think I'd prefer film.

CHELSEA: Hi! The lady from the hotel day care was very nice, but we thought it would be rude to be asleep when you came home 'cause we thought you'd want to tell us all about it! Did you bring back any leftovers?

GARRETT: About those outfits that grandma-person bought. I'm not wearing mine. Girls can wear little animals and flowers, but I'm into plaids and denim. And this hotel day-care lady tried to give me milk in a bottle! I tried to tell her I'm using a cup, but I guess we don't speak the same language. Could I have some now, please?

Amy and Tom were greeted by a frazzled sitter when the group arrived home. Everyone else said their good-nights and drifted off to their rooms, apparently reluctant to deal with three wide-awake two-year-olds at one in the morning. Amy could certainly understand.

And she was the one pretending to be the mom.

She left Tom in charge and went to the kitchen to fill Chelsea's and Malia's bottles and Garrett's two-handled cup with milk.

She came back to the bedroom to find the three tumbling on the mattress under Tom's supervision amid uproarious giggling. He looked up from their antics as she returned, and she saw him smiling with the infectious quality of their laughter.

It occurred to her that that ability was probably rare in a man at that hour.

Then Malia, a little more exuberant than the other two, tumbled a little too close to the edge. But good reflexes and a long reach allowed him to boost her back toward the middle of the bed.

They were having such a good time, Amy feared that relaxing them with bottles would be hopeless, at least for a while, but Chelsea came for hers greedily and settled down immediately into the crook of Amy's arm.

Amy leaned back against the head of the bed with a sigh while Tom tried to lure Malia to him with her bottle. But she was still too rambunctious. Garrett, however, was happy to take his cup.

Tom had pulled off his shoes and lay propped on an elbow across the foot of the bed so that Garrett could lean against him, but so that he could still guide Malia's tumbles.

"I didn't like him," Amy said, the niggle of worry that had bothered her throughout the evening coming forward with insistence.

Tom smoothed Garrett's hair. "I know. I didn't, either. But he's Peggy's choice."

Amy leaned her head back. "I can't help but wonder why."

"What do you mean? Didn't his mother say *People* magazine just voted him second sexiest man alive, or something?"

She made a face and rolled her eyes. "He might have something that comes across on the screen, but in person he seems so...disconnected or something. I got the feeling he found us all very boring and was wishing he was somewhere else." She pulled a corner of the bedspread up over Chelsea as the toddler's eyes began to close. "And I don't like the way he kisses Peggy."

Tom arched an eyebrow at that. "But apparently she does."

Amy made another face that made him smile. It involved a wrinkled nose and a curious downward twist to her mouth he guessed meant revulsion. "First of all, I don't think it's cool to kiss open-mouthed at the table or in front of your fiancée's family. And secondly, though he has all the mechanics of kissing down, he has none of the style.''

"Really?''

"Yes.'' She was distracted now, her eyes unfocused as she apparently thought back on the scene. "He could learn a lot from you.''

Then she seemed to realize what she'd said, and she pretended absorption in Chelsea. He was sure she was going to retract the statement, or at least qualify it. But she didn't. After a moment she relaxed and gave him a small smile.

"Don't look so surprised,'' she said, smoothing Chelsea's bald head. "You know you're a good kisser.''

He put a hand to his heart. "But I'm honored to know you think so, too. Whoa!'' That same hand reached out just in time to catch Malia as she tumbled dangerously close to Garrett's face. He pinned her in the crook of the arm on which he supported himself and offered her the bottle again. "If we don't get her to sleep, we're going to look pretty rough for the wedding.''

MALIA: Come on! It's still early! People come to Seattle for the nightlife—I heard it on TV. I don't want...oh, all right. But what a pair of rubes you two turned out to be.

Malia took her bottle and was soon rubbing her eyes and resisting their gradual drift closed.

Tom looked down at Garrett just in time to catch the cup as his little hand went slack around the handle. He transferred it to the hand that held Malia. Garrett's eyes popped open, but Tom pushed him gently down to the mattress and rubbed his back. He was back to sleep in a moment. Malia began to snore.

"I suppose we don't dare move," Tom said quietly, "or everyone's going to wake up again."

Amy nodded. "Let's just give them a few minutes." Her eyes went from baby to baby in that perpetual sweep he'd noticed at home. But this time, two of the babies were all entangled with him, so he received that watchful, analytical glance, as well.

He thought he saw something wistful in it. "What are you thinking?" he asked softly.

She sighed and gently pulled the bottle from Chelsea's little pursed lips. They continued to make a perfect circle, even after the bottle was removed.

"I was thinking that this is nice," she said. Her voice had a dreamy quality.

"What? Being awake at—" he checked his watch "—1:45 a.m.?"

"The peace," she corrected him with a scolding glance. Then she gave him a look that might have buckled his knees had he been upright. It was filled with need and confusion—and gratitude. "Did I ever thank you for agreeing to do this?"

"I figured it was implied," he answered.

"You should know it's appreciated. Thank you."

"You're welcome."

"Jane wants a baby." He was beginning to recognize a sudden shift in topic as her modus operandi when she was upset.

He grinned. "Well, we've got three."

She gave him that look again that was half laughter, half reprimand. "She wants to get pregnant. But she thinks her marriage is over."

"Why?"

"Because Beau spends most of his time at work."

"He's buying a house in some exclusive area of Boston."

Her eyes widened in surprise. "Back Bay. How do you know that?"

"He told me," Tom replied in a whisper as Garrett shifted position.

"I thought guys didn't have those kinds of discussions. Particularly with strangers."

He didn't understand the problem. "About houses?"

"About plans. Dreams."

"Well, it's a fact, not a dream, and when you've spent an entire afternoon side by side in combat with three babies, you're no longer strangers."

"Didn't my father help?"

"No. He told us not to worry, that the babies would be fine. Then he took a nap."

Amy frowned apologetically. "How did you find time to buy clothes?"

"I didn't want to leave Beau alone with all three, so I brought the girls with me, and a couple of the clerks helped keep an eye on them while I bought a suit. When we got back, Beau was doing fine with Garrett. I think he kind of got into it. He's really all right."

Amy gingerly swung her legs over the side of the bed and got to her feet without waking Chelsea. She put her into the crib, covered her and returned to the bed to scoop Garrett into her arms.

He protested sleepily, but she put him to her shoulder and he fell asleep again. When she eased him into the second crib, he didn't stir.

Tom held Malia to him and stood. She groaned, made a face, rubbed her eyes and fussed when he placed her in the crib. But he gave her her pacifier and patted her back, and she was asleep in a minute.

He and Amy collapsed against each other in congratulations. Then she went into the bathroom and he stripped down to T-shirt and briefs and climbed into bed.

She was back in a minute in a cotton nightgown and climbed in beside him, leaving a body's space between them.

He started to turn away from her, intent on diminishing the agony he knew was in store for him over the next few hours as they lay side by side without touching.

But she caught his shoulder and turned him toward her, pulling the blankets up over both their heads. For a blissful instant, he thought she was inviting him into her arms—but she wanted only to talk.

"What do you mean, the house is a fact?" she whispered under the acoustical confidence of the blankets.

He struggled for equilibrium in the wake of disappointment. "What house?"

She clicked her tongue. "The house you and Beau talked about."

"I *mean* that he's bought it."

"Why didn't he tell Jane?"

"Amy, how would I know that?"

"Well, you said you had a chummy chat."

"About a house, not about why he can't confide in his wife. Now, I'm sure you'll manage to look beautiful in the morning, anyway, but I spent all afternoon with the kids while you were shopping, and spent most of dinner listening to your mom and Mrs. Brennan try to out-name-drop each other. I'm beat."

He couldn't see her in the undercover darkness, but he got a distinct sense of hurt feelings.

"Of course," she whispered. "Good night." And she turned over, folding the blankets back again.

He felt a clutch of guilt and exasperation. "Amy," he said, and caught her shoulder, trying to turn her toward him. "I didn't mean to bark at you."

She resisted his efforts and kept her back to him. "It's all right," she whispered, but he could hear a sob in her voice. "I'm fine. Go to sleep."

It would be safer to do that, he knew, but his conscience wouldn't let him. He forced an arm under her and turned her bodily toward him, a little surprised but pleased when she offered no resistance.

"Is something bothering you," he asked quietly, and with amusement, "about your sister's marriage problems? I mean, we *are* lying, but your family thinks we're the ideal couple and that our babies are miracles of genetic engineering. I thought you'd be happy to have one up on her?"

He was further surprised when she dissolved into tears against him. He pulled the blankets up over their heads again to muffle the sound. In their little cocoon of woven cotton he simply held her and waited out the storm, blotting out all thought of how her softness felt against him, trying to ignore all awareness of her knee riding up and down his leg in distress.

"That's not my priority anymore," she admitted in a choked whisper as she tried to catch her breath. "We were helping each other into the dresses this afternoon in this teeny little dressing room and she started to cry."

She wept a little more, and she wasn't sure if it was in sympathy for her sister or for herself.

He continued to hold her close, ignoring the ravages to his own nervous system.

"She told me that they have dull sex," she went on,

her arm hooking unconsciously over his waist, wedging her body even closer to his and unconsciously assuring him that if the opportunity arose for *them* to have sex, it would not be dull. "And that she feels the same way about our family that I've always felt. Like she'd be left out in a minute if she wasn't beautiful and perfect. The only difference is that she was able to be, so she got stuck in it longer than I did."

Tom kissed her cheek in comfort. His family was so loving and supportive no matter how difficult or stupid or wrong you were that it hurt to imagine a young and vulnerable Amy without that kind of love.

"And all that time, she thought I didn't like her and didn't care about her...." She turned her face into his throat and added in a strained voice, "And I was thinking the same about her. So when we maybe could have helped each other, we were...I guess...busy saving ourselves."

She raised her head and looked down into his eyes. Her own were tear-filled and unhappy. "Isn't that awful?"

He brushed her hair back and tucked it behind her ear. "It is. But your mom's too superficial and your dad's too disconnected for it to be different. You didn't do anything wrong. And if you and Jane have started talking about it, you can probably reestablish a relationship."

"Yeah." She settled into his shoulder, that arm hooking chummily around him again. "I wish I could get Peggy to tell me what's wrong."

"You mean, besides the boyfriend?"

"I don't think she loves him. I don't think she even likes him."

"Then, why would she be marrying him? She certainly doesn't need the money or the publicity."

Amy nuzzled into him with a deep sigh. "I have no idea. And I'm too tired to think straight. But I'm glad you're here, Tom. I'm really glad you're here."

He closed his eyes and gritted his teeth as she threw a leg over him. "Yeah," he said, pulling the blankets down and taking a gulp of air. "Me, too."

Chapter Twelve

MALIA: Wow! Do we look great, or what? I understand the press will be here! Chelsea, this could be our chance to get a gig like the Olson twins.

CHELSEA: Lia, are you forgetting that we aren't *really* related? We're pretending to be triplets, but we don't look anything alike. I can't believe these people haven't noticed.

MALIA: We don't have to look alike. All we have to do is be cute and charming. We can do it. Well, I can do it.

GARRETT: Yeah, well you're doing it without me. I told you before this outfit was going to make me look like a girl, and I was right.

CHELSEA: Garrett, you look great.

GARRETT: You're just saying that because you don't like fuss. Well, brace yourself, because I'm about to make one. No! You're not putting that dorky tie on me! Where's my baseball jacket? Where's my...?

Garrett screeched as Amy sat with him in the suite's living room and tried to snap on the little blue-and-white polka-dot tie that matched the cummerbund on his one-piece white shirt and blue pants. The placket of the shirt was decorated with colorfully embroidered zoo animals.

The girls' outfits matched, except that they had flared skirts rather than pants.

Amy longed for Tom's helping hand, but he'd watched the babies while she showered, so he was still dressing.

"Can I help?" Beau appeared in an elegant blue-and-white pin-striped suit and a subdued tie. He gave Amy a cautious smile. "I got pretty good with him yesterday while Tom was out."

Amy recovered quickly from surprise. "Ah...yes. Please. He's just like his father. Hates to get dressed up."

That was true, she thought defensively. Nate hated formal occasions.

Garrett went to Beau's lap without complaint, but continued to resist when Amy tried to snap on the bow.

"A formal occasion calls for a tie, Garrett," Beau said reasonably, capturing the little hands that tried to interfere with Amy. "There are some rules you just can't get around. Although, I'm with you. A standard tie is so much less dandy."

Amy laughed with him at his joke, and that made Garrett laugh. While he was distracted, Amy snapped on the bow.

Before she could congratulate herself on her success, Peggy marched through in full wedding regalia, complete with veiled pillbox headpiece.

The dress had been lovingly tailored to her every

curve, and her long, slender legs made the handkerchief hemline sway as she went past. But Amy noticed that though the bridal dress and veil looked beautiful, the bride did not. She was pale and wounded-looking as she headed determinedly for the door.

"Peggy?" Jane, also dressed for the wedding in the gown that matched Amy's, came hurrying out of her bedroom. She had Malia in her arms. Chelsea had wandered in to visit Sabina and Nelson. "Do you want to borrow my pearl earrings? Peggy?"

Peggy opened the door and kept going as though she hadn't seen or heard anyone.

Amy caught Jane's eye and read the same concern she felt.

"Could you keep an eye on Garrett for a minute?" she asked Beau.

"Sure."

"And her, too?" Jane asked, and deposited Malia on his other knee without waiting for an answer.

Amy ran after Peggy and Jane followed.

Peggy stood in front of a door at the far end of the corridor. She was knocking incessantly on the door, demanding admission.

"Peggy, what...?" Amy began.

The door was yanked open before she could finish, and Ethan stood there in pajama bottoms, chest bare, hair tousled, and a look of blatant insolence on his face.

A young woman wrapped in a towel was visible behind him in the middle of the room.

Peggy was breathing heavily and her face was crumpling. "You promised me this wouldn't happen again," she said.

He put a hand to her arm. "Honey, I didn't..."

"I call you the morning of our wedding," she interrupted, "to tell you I love you, and a *woman* answers?"

Ethan sighed, as though the burden of explanation was beneath him. "She spent the night with Bill," he said. "You just jumped to conclusions."

Bill Channing also appeared behind Ethan, and Amy saw a look of surprised uncertainty cross Peggy's face.

Amy didn't believe him for a minute.

"I'd like to come inside," Peggy said firmly.

Ethan studied her with disdain. "That would be a violation of my privacy."

Peggy walked around him into the room. Amy and Jane followed.

"You're a *star,* Ethan," Peggy said, underlining the word with scorn. "You don't have any privacy." She found a closed door and threw it open. Another young woman with bright red hair lay in a large bed with the covers pulled up to her chin. There were enough clothes strewn around to suggest there'd been an animated foursome in the bed.

Peggy slammed the door closed and turned to face Ethan. The girl in the towel ran out the door.

Channing sat down at a table by the window, his face in his hands.

Ethan went to the coffeepot behind the bar and calmly poured a cup. "I warned you that I had difficulty being faithful," he said, striding back around the bar.

Peggy yanked off her veil. "Later, you said I'd made you change your mind. That you'd love me always."

He shrugged. "And I will. Only not exclusively."

Peggy flew at him, screaming, hitting, kicking. He screamed as hot coffee splashed on his chest.

Channing rose from the table to pull at Peggy as Amy

ran to try to pull the combatants apart. Ethan tried to push her aside and she pushed back.

She never was sure what happened next except that she was yanked away and the small fracas seemed to turn into a riot. Fists flew, men shouted and grunted, and every time she tried to look up from the sofa on which she'd been thrown to see what was happening, lights flashed, blinding her. She wondered idly if she'd sustained a concussion without noticing that she'd been hit. But that made no sense.

When order was finally established, Ethan and Channing were on the floor, out cold, and Tom and Beau stood over them, bruised and mussed, their suits in disarray.

Ethan's mother was in a chair, and Sabina fanned her with the room service menu.

Ethan's father knelt over his son. He glanced up, eyes dark and angry. "Which one of you hit him?" he asked of Tom and Beau.

"I did," Tom replied.

The man glanced toward the room where the young woman in the bed was clearly visible and now crying hysterically. He stood and extended his hand.

"My thanks," he said. "If you discounted my son's good looks, he'd be worthless. Unfortunately, he's able to make money on them. You should have broken his nose. That might have changed things."

"My intention wasn't to break anything," Tom replied quietly. "He pushed at my wife and I just jumped into the middle. My...brother-in-law came to help."

Amy heard his explanation with a crackling flare of excitement. It was adrenaline, she told herself.

Ethan's father shook Beau's hand, as well. "Bill Channing's the same caliber. I'll square things with hotel security. Come along, Dora.'' He took his wife's arm and pulled her from the sofa. She looked as though she might collapse at any moment.

Sabina was beside herself. ''I see no reason why we should be hasty here,'' she said, now fanning herself with the menu as she got to her feet. ''Perhaps Ethan has an explanation for...''

''He does have an explanation, Mother,'' Peggy said. ''They were four in a bed!''

''But the...'' Sabina pointed down, in the direction of the garden room where the wedding was scheduled to take place in a matter of minutes.

''The wedding's off, Mom,'' Peggy insisted. ''Face it. I apologize for embarrassing you, Mr. and Mrs. Brennan, but I can't...''

Julian Brennan took her in his arms for a moment. ''Of course you can't. Don't worry about us. Ethan's embarrassed us quite a few times in his life. I'll also explain to the hotel caterer. Most of the guests who aren't family were friends of ours, anyway. You don't even have to make an appearance downstairs if you don't want to.'' He smiled apologetically at the rest of the family. ''I'm sorry. I thought success might have taught him some humility. It does that for some people. But apparently not. I'm sure this is best all around. We enjoyed meeting you. I'm sure your beautiful daughter will find a man worthy of her.''

''Thank you.'' Sabina walked the Brennans to the door.

''But...Ethan.'' Dora pointed to her son, just beginning to stir on the carpet.

''I'm a doctor, darling. He's fine.'' Julian guided her firmly out the door.

Jane ushered everyone back to the bridal suite.

Amy caught Tom's arm. "Thank you for coming to our rescue," she whispered, smiling. "Technically, I guess women aren't supposed to want protectors anymore, but you dispensed with him more efficiently than I was doing."

He inclined his head modestly. "I had a little lapse into d'Artagnan. It was my pleasure."

Amy gasped suddenly. "The babies!" she cried, and ran on ahead, horrified that she hadn't given the triplets—God, now *she* was doing it!—the babies a thought since she'd left Garrett with Beau. But Beau was now behind her. Had her father been left with all three babies?

When Amy reached the suite, he was almost blithering, and all three babies were screaming.

GARRETT: Not only do you dress me up like some cutesy ad for toilet tissue, but then you *leave* me!

MALIA: He never even turned on the television!

CHELSEA: Did we miss the wedding? Did you bring me any cake?

Amy went straight to the refrigerator, knowing food would quell the noise. Tom picked up Malia, Peggy lifted Chelsea, unmindful of little shoes on the skirt of her wedding dress, and Jane watched in fascination as Beau scooped Garrett into his arms.

The screams of rage quieted to simple anger and, at the sight of string cheese, stopped altogether. Everyone converged on the sofas, babies distributed among them and eating greedily.

Amy watched her mother cry into a floral hanky, and

accepted with a new lease on reality that she was crying as much for the contacts she'd lost as for Peggy's unhappiness.

Her father was patting her mother's shoulder and telling her not to worry, that everything would be all right.

Her mother ignored him and wept on.

Jane kicked her shoes off and propped her feet on the coffee table with a distinct lack of the decorum that usually defined her. "Did I hear you tell that bum that he'd promised you 'it wouldn't happen *again?*'" she demanded of Peggy.

Peggy nodded.

"You mean he'd cheated on you already and you were still going to marry him?"

Peggy's response was to stare at her hands.

"Why?" Amy asked. "You're a beautiful model with the potential for a film career, and he's a classless idiot who treated you badly."

"But *People* magazine voted him…" Sabina began tearfully.

Jane turned to her with a murderous look and she subsided.

"I don't know." Peggy curled into her corner of the sofa and Amy thought she didn't look like a star at all. She looked frightened and alone. "Hollywood's different, you know? Being a celebrity you get caught up in the scene. And make-believe and reality get all twisted around. I guess I thought he was Joey Karminski, the Cleveland cop who was hard as nails but treated his girlfriend like a queen. And I was lonely. I mean, there are always a lot of people around me, but most of them care about how big the next offer is, not about me, particularly."

"Then, don't stay there," Amy said. "If you're not happy, you don't have to be there."

"But...she's about to become a star!" Sabina protested, the hanky pressed to her mouth.

"Why don't you come home with us?" Jane suggested. "If you don't like Boston, you can visit Amy and Tom and check out Heron Point."

Peggy looked from one sister to the other in amazement. "You know...I've lived my whole life thinking that you guys hated me because I was the youngest. I had no idea you even cared, much less that you'd come to my defense with Ethan." She focused on Tom and on Beau. "And the two of you. Thank you. I hope Denny Brewer doesn't ruin your lives."

"Denny Brewer?" Tom asked.

"The photographer for *Star Snaps*. He must have gotten wind of the wedding, somehow. I saw him in the doorway of Ethan's suite, shooting like crazy."

Tom turned to Amy. She read the message in his eyes very clearly. "We're dead."

Peggy drew a deep breath and smiled. It looked less Hollywood, Amy thought, and more genuine. "I think I might have married him, anyway," Peggy said, patting Amy's hand, "if I hadn't seen what a great life you and Tom have. I think it clarified my confusion over make-believe and reality. Tom's always there to help you with the babies, he always speaks to you with respect, and when he touches you—" she rubbed her arms as though to erase a bad memory "—it seems to be always tenderly. I want passion, of course, but I want to be treated like a woman, not a...an appliance."

Jane caught Amy's eye. Amy knew she was remembering their discussion in the dressing room. Then she turned to Beau seated beside her, still holding Garrett, and her face softened. She moved in closer. Apparently pleased, he looped an arm around her.

Her parents sat arm in arm on the love seat, obviously confused and upset.

Amy studied everyone else in the room before she finally turned to Tom. The guilt she'd been warding off since she'd first introduced Tom as her husband back in Heron Point now fell on her like a ton of bricks.

She had to believe her deception had brought about a good thing, but did the end justify the means in this case?

Tom's dark eyes met hers steadily and told her without words that he thought it was time to come clean.

"You're absolutely right," Amy said, taking Peggy's hand. "You deserve to be appreciated and treated well. But I have to tell you…something."

Peggy patted her hand and turned toward her, waiting. "What is it?"

Amy sensed everyone else's attention turn in her direction. She felt a new and very real fear.

This trip had taught her that she did love her parents, but as sensible and responsible human beings they were—as she'd always suspected—pretty hopeless.

But at the same time, she'd found something new in her relationships with her sisters. They hadn't learned to work together as children and to support and defend one another—but they seemed to be doing it now. Maybe blood was thicker than whatever tried to stand against it. She and Jane had closed ranks when they thought Peggy needed help.

It was curious, Amy thought in a still reasonable corner of her mind, that at the moment when she appeared to have the upper hand over her sisters—a moment she'd dreamed about since she was eight or nine—she was not only not going to lord it over them, she was about to admit to being the worst of them all.

"Tom and I aren't married," she said in a breathless rush.

Everyone stared at her, and there was a moment of absolute silence. Jane turned to Beau, then both turned to Amy and Tom in dual astonishment.

Sabina gasped, and Nelson, still not recovered from having been left with the babies, looked as though he was about to dissolve into a puddle of stress.

Peggy put her free hand to her mouth.

Amy felt curiously cut off from everyone—even Tom, because she could no longer pretend, even to herself, that they were in love.

Then she felt his hand on her shoulder. It squeezed gently. The action gave her courage.

She went on to try to explain how she'd always felt inadequate and outside of the family unit. "It was never that I didn't love you," she explained hastily. "But that I always felt like a misfit. A disappointment." She smiled at Jane. "You were always so beautiful and so smart." She squeezed Peggy's hand. "And you were such a personality from the very beginning. I always felt like a mistake."

Her parents were studying each other in puzzlement. Amy knew they would never understand, but she wanted her sisters to know how she felt. "Tom..." She laced her fingers in the hand he'd placed on her shoulder. "Tom is a carpenter who is renovating a barn on my property, and he'd come in yesterday morning to help me with a plumbing problem. When you all arrived without warning, I wanted you to think I was as happy and successful as you all were because I thought this was going to be one of your every-other-year, two-hour visits.'' She smiled at Tom. ''Tom went along with it because he's a good friend, and I'm sure he didn't want to embarrass me in front of you. When you invited us to come to Seattle, and we went into the bedroom to talk about it, he didn't want to lie to you, but I insisted.''

Her sisters still appeared speechless, but Beau asked logically, ''But the triplets…''

Amy laughed lightly, thinking that she was going to have some explaining to do when she got home.

''They're the babies of some friends of ours who are away for the weekend. I'm just baby-sitting for them.''

''But they love you and Tom,'' Sabina said.

Amy nodded. ''They come to my day care a couple of times a week, and Malia is really Tom's niece, and the other two babies belong to his good friends, so they're used to him.''

''I have to lie down,'' Sabina said. ''Nelson, darling, will you help me?''

It was just like her, Amy thought, to miss the real issue. She'd understood nothing Amy had tried to explain.

''Of course, dear. Now, don't worry about a thing.'' He took her arm and started to walk her to their room. ''Everything will be all right.''

Amy studied Peggy. ''You did the right thing in telling Ethan to take a hike, even though my marriage isn't real. I don't think you did it because of me, I think you did it because you know you're smart and talented and gorgeous, and that settling for anything less than love and fidelity from a man would be stupid.''

Peggy twisted her lips in wry denial. ''I think I did it because I knew I had backup. You and Janie were

right behind me, looking like a matched pair of aveng-
ing angels. It gave me courage.''

Jane came to sit on an edge of the coffee table facing
Amy and Peggy. "Good. And we're going to continue
to do that for you, even if we have to do it from opposite ends of the country. And you…'' She turned her
determined blue eyes on Amy. "You were just reacting
to the same insecurities Peggy and I have, so stop looking so guilty. If you hadn't come here with us…'' She
frowned and shook her head, her manner grave. "I
knew I had relatives, but I didn't really understand that
I had sisters until we all got together for this wedding."
She leaned forward to wrap them in her embrace. "And
this is what's important. We have one another."

Peggy looked a little anxiously in the direction of
their parents' bedroom. "I feel badly that Mom's so
disappointed."

Jane shook her. "Stop it. She doesn't get it. She
never did, she never will. That's not our fault. And Dad
sort of gets it, but he doesn't want to have to deal with
any difficulties, so he pretends they don't exist." She
hugged Amy again. "If you hadn't been there for me
to talk to in the dressing room yesterday afternoon, I
might have imploded. Thank you for that."

"You're welcome," Amy replied. "Thank you for
forgiving me for the lie."

Jane shook her head, denying that it had a negative
effect. "If it hadn't been for seeing you so happy—or
thinking you were—I wouldn't have talked to Beau like
you suggested and straightened everything out." She
smiled in his direction. Beau was now chasing all the
babies around the other sofa. The babies were giggling
hysterically.

She turned back to her sisters. "And if Peggy hadn't

seen you and Tom and realized life had something more
to offer than Ethan was willing to give her, she might
have married the bum. So, see? It all worked out for
the best.''

Jane leaned around Amy to smile at Tom—only to
discover that he was no longer there. The sound of water running turned all heads in the direction of the
kitchen. Tom was making a fresh pot of coffee, apparently deciding to leave the women to their rediscovery
of one another.

Jane frowned at his broad back, then at Amy.
''We've agreed that it doesn't matter that you tricked
us, but if you're trying to trick yourself into believing
you shouldn't be married to Tom Nicholas, you're making a big mistake.''

''You seem so comfortable together,'' Peggy said
quietly.

''We were involved once,'' Amy admitted. ''But
that's over.''

''Is it?'' Jane asked pointedly.

Amy rolled her eyes. ''Please don't worry about me.
I'll be fine.''

Jane shook her head at her. ''And who does *that*
sound like?''

AMY WANTED TO EXPLAIN to Tom that she was getting
a new perspective on her life, that her priorities had
shifted over the past few days, and she was beginning
to realize that she didn't have as much to prove as she
thought she did. At least, not to her family.

But there was no time. Peggy had to be at the airport
at four, and they had to leave for Heron Point that night
so that Amy would be at the day care in the morning.
The babies kept them busy during the brief flight,

then she'd said goodbye to her parents. Her mother had recovered somewhat, though Amy guessed it would be some time before she was herself again.

"I don't know where you get this about your being a disappointment," Sabina said, pulling Amy aside at the little Heron Point airport. "That's never been true. We just wanted you to be happy, that's all. And... usually we're happier when we *do* things, *have* things." Then she'd kissed her cheek and said, "Dear Amy." There was a little pity in the sound, but at least she hadn't called her "poor Amy."

Her father told her not to worry about a thing, that her mother would get over "the disappointment."

Amy congratulated herself on being mature enough to accept that she loved her parents and always would. She simply couldn't feel the respect for them that gave the child-parent bond the depth and texture Jave and Tom had for their mother, or Jo Jeffries for her dad. But she decided that was all right. She would take what she could get.

But when she hugged Jane goodbye, she felt the strength of new friendship there. And Beau hugged her with a new vitality and a subtle smile. It pleased Amy that she'd helped bring about a renewal of their love. She'd overheard them talking on the flight and Jane now knew that Beau had been working long hours to buy the house she'd admired and that he thought would make her happy. She'd told him that having his baby would make her happy, and he'd promised to do his utmost to see that she was pregnant by Christmas.

Amy wished she could make her own future look as good as Jane's did at that moment.

She was determined to talk to Tom when they got

back to the house, but the babies were fussy and Tom's pager beeped.

He returned the call from Amy's and discovered it was his mother calling from the airport. She'd gotten homesick and caught a last-minute flight home from Europe a week early and wondered if he could pick her up since she couldn't reach Jave.

"Sure, Mom," he said, holding one ear closed against the babies crying behind him. "But it'll take me a couple of hours to get there, so why don't you take the shuttle to the Howard Johnson's, book a room and get some rest if you can until I get there."

"Do I hear babies crying?" she asked hopefully. "Did you come home from Arizona with babies?"

He ran a hand over his face, not minding the two-hour drive to Portland to pick her up, but dreading the two-hour drive back under her interrogation.

"No, Mom," he replied. "I'm working at Amy's day care."

"But it's eleven o'clock on a Sunday night."

He closed his eyes. "It's a long story. I'll explain on the way home."

"Good." She imbued the simple word with great significance. "I'm anxious to see you, Tommy. I love you."

"I love you, too, Mom."

Amy heard the tenderness with which he spoke the words and felt a knot of anguish tighten inside her.

He'd never talked to *her* with that sweet indulgence. Of course, who could blame him?

And she agonized over the realization that he had to leave before she could tell him how she felt. It wasn't something she could blurt out just before he left to drive most of the trip on a dark and winding road.

"Mom's back," he said, hanging up the phone. "I'm going to go pick her up." He looked tired, she thought.

That was no surprise. The weekend had been difficult at best, and because she'd had him turning in a performance most of the time, and doing physical battle in her defense the rest of the time, it had to have been worse than that for him.

"I'll make you a thermos of coffee," she said, turning away to the kitchen.

He caught her arm. "No. I'm wide-awake. You going to be okay with the kids?"

"Sure." Words came to the tip of her tongue. Love words, questions, promises, pleas. But she couldn't turn any of them into sound.

He didn't really look at the moment as though he'd be glad to hear them. Perhaps tomorrow they could talk.

He squeezed her arm gently and left with a simple goodbye.

She wondered for hours afterward if that was what it had been. A simple goodbye.

TOM DROVE THROUGH the black night wondering if arriving home had changed everything. In Seattle she'd needed him, depended upon him, had been relieved to be rescued by him.

But they were back in Heron Point and the fantasy was over. No pretend marriage, no babies that belonged to somebody else. No need for d'Artagnan.

He'd seen a lot of things in her eyes that might have been his imagination—probably were because she hadn't given voice to them.

But then he hadn't realized until he'd met her parents how she must have felt when he'd left two years ago. All she seemed to get from them was artfully subtle rejection. She must have thought that was what she was getting from him.

Well. He was going to have to make it clear to her tomorrow how things were, then he guessed it was pretty much up to her.

It was a good thing he'd be driving home with his mother since he wouldn't be sleeping, anyway.

Chapter Thirteen

Amy noticed Monday morning that Heron Point had a new quality. Part of the difference was seasonal. The rains had come with a vengeance, and Kate reported when she arrived at work after stopping for doughnuts that there were honeycomb paper turkeys in all the shop windows downtown.

The children who came to Kids & Co. on the school bus brought turkeys they'd created at school, and one of the mothers brought a large Pilgrim puzzle. The children watched an afternoon special about the *Mayflower*.

But another part of the difference was that she used to be miserable at Thanksgiving, knowing that almost everyone else but she would be spending it with a loving family.

This year things were different. She wouldn't be able to spend the holiday with her sisters, but she knew they were out there, thinking about her, caring about her.

While she appreciated that, she couldn't help but wonder if that was all she would have. Tom had reported to work this morning without the greeting beep of his horn as he turned up the drive, and he hadn't made one single visit for a cup of coffee.

And she'd been too busy to go to him.

But on the good side—she was able to report to Rodney's father that he was going home without owing the cuss box a penny for that afternoon.

Boomer beamed.

Darcy and Truman, Amy noticed, seemed to have made a curious forward leap in their relationship. Rodney teased her about the Blue Grass Brenda, which was now also out of the box and looking mussy and loved, and Truman told him to stop it.

Rodney had been shocked.

"Just leave her alone," Truman said.

Amy didn't understand until Ginger Billings and Steve Fuller arrived together to pick up their children, and Amy saw that the Friday night pizza they'd been about to share before her own weekend became a three-act play must have developed into something else.

There was a glow in their eyes and the suggestion that Truman already had things figured out and was looking out for his "sister."

The six parents of Amy's "triplets" returned as planned about seven Monday evening to pick up their children. They brought Aggie Nicholas, Tom and Jave's mother, with them. Tom was working late on the barn.

Jave sat on the sofa with an excited Malia in his arms, and Nancy sat beside him, Pete pressing in between them and Eddy leaning in on her other side, showing her leaves he'd collected on the Boy Scout trip. Aggie, a plump, gray-haired woman in green sweats, had taken the room's only rocking chair and smiled at them from across the room. Amy remembered what a rocky beginning the couple had had and found herself smiling over the warm unit they'd become.

Chelsea climbed into the chair where Jo sat, Ryan sitting on the arm, and told her parents a long story that made no sense, but seemed to include a "plane." They, too, had struggled to find common ground when Ryan's wife, Jo's sister, had died. But they'd found it in Chelsea in the most rewarding way.

Nate and Karma sat cross-legged on the floor as Garrett showed them the book about turkeys one of the other mothers had brought. For a romance that had begun in the ER at Riverview Hospital, it looked very healthy to Amy.

Amy braced herself as Chelsea continued to talk about a plane. She was going to have to tell these people that she'd taken their children to Seattle. But she and Tom had agreed that no one had to know they'd pretended to be married and passed the children off as theirs.

She prayed she wouldn't lose them as clients. Though she'd agreed to baby-sit as a friend, and not as their day-care provider, absconding with their children with or without her professional hat on was not a commendable thing.

"Ah. I have something to tell you," she said.

She became immediately suspicious when all eyes met across the room, then turned to her.

They knew.

"That's good," Nate said with a smile that did not appear hostile, "because we'd like to talk to you, too."

Jave pulled out a cellular phone and stabbed out a number. "Tom," he said after a moment. "Yeah, we're here at Amy's. I saw the lights on in the barn and figured you were still there. Come to the house. We want to talk to you." He listened a moment. "Well, I don't know," he said. "*Is* everything fine?" He listened again. "Thanks, but you don't have to worry about picking up something for Mom for dinner because

Nancy and I picked her up on our way into town and brought her with us. Come and join us.'' He closed and pocketed the phone. ''He'll be right here,'' he told the group.

''You know that we took your children to Seattle,'' Amy said, pretty certain the matter was no longer in question. This had all the makings of a confrontation.

''Yes,'' Ryan replied, ''but let's wait for Tom. What do you say we call for pizza?''

There was an immediate discussion about number and toppings, then Nancy, Jo and Karma took over Amy's kitchen, setting the table with paper plates and making coffee.

Tom had taken a few minutes to clean up in the bathroom he'd added in the barn, and appeared at the back door looking startlingly handsome and just a little aggressive.

''My mother's here?'' he asked under his breath as Amy let him in.

Amy nodded in concern.

''They're upset about our taking the kids?''

''I think so,'' she replied, ''because I didn't get a chance to tell them. They seem to already know.''

''How?''

''No idea. They wanted to wait for you before we discussed it.''

He ran a hand over his face. ''You and your easy two hours.''

''I'm sorry.''

''I hope so.''

Everyone took a place at the table, except Pete and Eddy, who were allowed to watch television until the pizza arrived, and the babies, who were tricycling around the coffee table in the living room.

Tom went to hug his mother, then took the chair at the head table and remained standing, hands lightly on his hips as he greeted everyone. "Okay," he said. "It was a stupid thing for us to do and we apologize. Amy's back was to the wall with her family and she took her best shot. The kids had a great time, and they were never in any danger or even discomfort. Amy had her cell phone, so if you'd called, you'd have reached her. She did try to call you before we left to make sure you didn't mind our taking the kids, but you guys were in a workshop, and we thought paging you out would only panic you unnecessarily."

"Wait." Amy, seated at his right, stood and put a staying hand on his arm. "Tom was never in agreement. He objected from the beginning and resisted all along the way, but I had already made retreat impossible and so...he did the gentlemanly thing and came along."

Jave leaned back in his chair. "Gentlemanly? Really? Nate, check his vital signs."

Nate shook his head. "Don't have to. He's nuts. I can tell by looking at him."

Tom gave his brother, then his friend, a lethal glance. "Look. I laid out a couple of pretty big guys this weekend. Don't mess with me."

"Actually..." Jo unfolded a newspaper and placed it in the center of the table. "That's what we want to talk about. Although all this other stuff you've alluded to sounds pretty interesting, too. But this, first." She tapped her index finger on the front page of the paper. "What in the hell happened?"

Tom and Amy leaned over the table to study the front page of the *Star Snaps* tabloid. In a half-page photo in brilliant color, Tom held Amy with one arm and had just delivered a right cross to Ethan Brennan's face with his fist. Amy, in bridesmaid attire, looked shocked and had obviously just been taken from the other man's grasp. His hand was still curled around her arm, though his head was snapped back and his hair flew out behind him. His large, muscular chest was exposed and naked as he looked about to fall backward.

Beside him, Beau, with perfect boxing club form, had a fist in the stomach of Bill Channing, who was doubled over. Behind him, Jane, dressed just like Amy, had both hands over her face, her wide eyes filled with an avid excitement over the tips of her fingers.

Under the photo, the caption read, *People* Magazine's Second Sexiest Man Felled by World's Smoothest Right Cross. The photo credit belonged to the man Peggy had warned them about—Denny Brewer.

"Tell us," Nancy said, "that this was some scene in an operetta. I mean, you do all look like you were dressed for it. And where were our children at this time?"

Tom sat down with a groan.

Amy sat primly on the edge of her chair, determined to extricate him from the mess.

Carefully, painstakingly, she told the whole story— how she'd always felt like a misfit in her family, how the opportunity to show them a husband and family when they arrived unexpectedly was more of a temptation than she could withstand, and how what she'd expected to be an innocent few hours turned into the weekend from purgatory.

She explained about Ethan Brennan's boorish behavior and Peggy's eleventh-hour march to his room that had yielded a bedmate—three, in fact.

"Oh, my," Aggie said.

"But your babies were safe with my father the whole

time," Amy assured everyone. "Honestly. In fact, when my family discovered Tom and I weren't married, their biggest disappointment was that the babies weren't in the family. They even have wedding outfits now if you ever end up going to one."

"So you didn't get married while we were gone?" Jave asked. "This story—" he pointed to the paper "—says you're husband and wife."

Amy shook her head. "No, we're not married."

Aggie closed her eyes in a gesture of relief. "Well, that's good, because I'd have pummeled both of you if you'd gotten married without letting me plan everything."

Nancy smiled blandly at them. "We all want to help. What about a Christmas wedding?"

Amy blinked. "You're not upset that we took the babies to Seattle?"

The three couples looked at one another, then shook their heads.

"It would have been nice if you'd told us," Nancy said, "but we'd trust either of you with them at any time."

Karma grimaced. "But how was it dealing with triplets?"

Amy looked at them in disbelief. Was this all going to end peacefully, after all?

"It was great," Tom said before she could reply. "And do your thing with the Christmas wedding, Mom. As of this weekend, Amy and I are formally engaged."

Aggie and the women shrieked, the men cheered. Jave leveled a steady gaze on Tom, which he returned. Then Jave smiled and applauded with the rest. Aggie leaned over to hug her oldest son.

Amy was thunderstruck. She'd known that a peaceful

solution had been too much to hope for. She opened her mouth to correct Tom, because while that was what she wanted, they'd barely exchanged a word all day long. Then she remembered the moment when the tables had been turned and she'd wanted *his* cooperation. He'd given it without embarrassing her. But what was he *doing?*

The doorbell rang, announcing the arrival of the pizza, and there was a flurry of activity as Jo got the door. Karma went to pour soft drinks and Nancy distributed pizza.

Amy beckoned Tom. "Could I speak to you for a minute, please?" she asked sweetly.

"Of course." He grinned at his brother and his friends. "She's insatiable. She wants me all the time."

Guffaws trailed him as he followed her out the back door.

"What are you doing?" she demanded.

The night was cold and she folded her arms, shrinking into her big sweater. Inside, she was shuddering with emotions she didn't understand and was sure were unwarranted.

He leaned a shoulder against the back of the house, his expression visible in the light from the kitchen window. She found it difficult to read. It was hard, she thought, to profess love to a man when you couldn't tell what he was thinking.

"You think you're the only one who can lie through her teeth and expect cooperation?" he asked.

"But that was *my* family, and I thought they were only going to be in town for a couple of hours. These are our friends! And your mother and your brother!"

"Yes, I know." Laughter exploded inside the house and Tom turned toward it and smiled. When he looked back at her again, his expression had softened. "That's why we're going to have to keep it up for longer than a couple of hours."

There was an energy emanating from him that Amy didn't entirely understand. His pose was casual, his manner lazy, yet the air around him, between her and him, was alive with something....

"For how...long?" she asked on a whisper.

"Forty years," he replied quietly. "Fifty, if we're lucky." Then, without warning, he straightened away from the house, caught her arm and pulled her with him to the middle of the field, where he stopped under the big November moon.

The night was alive with sounds, and laughter came again from the house. The scent of fall and wood smoke wound around them.

Tom framed her face in his hands and looked down into her eyes, feeling as though he knew her very well without understanding her at all. He wouldn't have thought that possible.

"Are you going to help me?" he asked.

She looked back at him, and he saw her eyes well with tears. He felt a moment's panic, but then she wrapped her arms around his waist and fell against him. Now he was completely confused.

"I can't," she wept.

He experienced the cold, downward rush of dread. Oh, no. No.

Then she drew back to look at him, her lashes wet and spiked, but she was smiling.

"Because if you want me to lie," she said, "then I'd have to go back in there and tell them I *don't* love you."

He absorbed the words and thought he was about to go insane. Saying she *didn't* love him would be a lie?

Desperately needing his world righted, he took her arms and shook her lightly. "Say it directly, Amy!" he demanded.

The night wind circled them, lifting her hair, carrying her jasmine scent to his nostrils. "I love you, Tom," she whispered, then stood on tiptoe and kissed him with all the passion and fervor in her heart.

Amy was crushed in Tom's arms as he returned her kisses. He lifted her off the grass and swung her in a circle. Everything that had ever stood between them disintegrated, and all the feelings and dreams that had lingered on the edges of their lives awaiting a nourishing atmosphere rushed in to tighten their embrace.

"Amy, I love you," he said against her cheek. "I'm going to cherish you so that you'll forget the past and think only about what lies ahead of us."

"I'm sorry I closed the door on you two years ago," she said in a rush. "I was thinking about *me,* not about you and me...."

He silenced her with a kiss. "No, I should have made you understand, but it was easier to be wounded and angry. I was getting really good at that."

"And I want to spend a week on the *Mud Hen.*" She held him tighter, relishing the knowledge that after all this time he was finally hers. "Just give me enough time to warn my clients."

"We'll do it when the barn's finished," he suggested, kissing her hair. "Then you can reopen with a grand opening of the new building."

"Hey!" Jave's voice shouted from the back door. "You'd better come back and defend yourselves. We're planning Thanksgiving, and so far you two are bringing everything!"

Tom waved at Jave. "Be right there."

Amy started toward the house, but Tom pulled her back. He reached into the pocket of his shirt and slipped a marquis-cut diamond on the third finger of her left hand. Then he kissed it.

Amy stared at it, then held it up. Moonlight winked in it and illuminated a broad band filigreed in heart shapes.

She wrapped her arms around him, speechless with love and joy.

He held her close, his heart too full for words.

The back door opened again, and Jave shouted. "Step on it! Now you're hosting Christmas!"

Epilogue

BABY #1: What's all the noise?

BABY #2: They're singing Christmas carols. Nice, isn't it? Did you hear all those people and kids? We must have a big family and lots of friends.

BABY #1: Yeah. Lucky. I can't wait for her to tell him we're here. Then we'll get some of the attention all those bigger babies are getting.

BABY #2: She said she was going to tell him tonight— that we're going to be a Christmas present. But even she doesn't know there are two of us yet.

BABY #1: I bet they'd have liked us better if you were a boy, too.

BABY #2: No way. One boy and one girl is supposed to make a perfect family.

BABY #1: They sound pretty perfect. I like the way she laughs, and I like the sound of his voice.

BABY #2: I like it when he holds us all tight. Yep. There he is. Can you feel his arms around us?

BABY #1: Mmm. Yeah.

BABY #2: I think we got really lucky. Merry Christmas.

BABY #1: Yeah, Merry Christmas. Whoa. Somebody out there's off-key.

BABY #2: Sounds beautiful to me.

MAKE WAY FOR MOMMY

Prologue

This is what I know so far.

When I am born, I'm going to be called Chelsea Annabel, and I'm going to be special. That's because I have one father and two mothers. Other kids only get one.

We went to a hospital in Portland where they took stuff from my mother Cassie and Daddy to make me, then put it inside Aunt Jo.

Everyone was so excited when I began to grow that Aunt Jo started calling Cassie "Mama Cass," after a singer from the sixties in a group called the Mamas and the Papas. She plays their music all the time.

Mama Cass started calling her "Mama Jo," because it was taking the two of them to get me born.

Then there was an accident, and Mama Cass went to heaven. It's not bad for me, because I talk to her all the time, but Daddy and Mama Jo miss her a lot.

Mama Jo says when I'm born I won't belong to her anymore, I'll just be Daddy's. Sometimes she cries about it. I'm confused. I guess one mother can't just take the place of another.

It feels like we're going to work now. Mama Jo owns

a coffee bar, but she can't have any coffee, 'cause it isn't good for me.

We live upstairs over the bar, so it doesn't take us long to get there. Daddy lives in a condo.

It's starting to get hard to get comfortable in here. My feet are up around my neck. But Mama Jo says in another month, I'll have all the room I want, so in the meantime, will I please stay off her bladder?

Whoops! Are we falling? I think we're falling. Yup. There's the stair against my bottom.

And there's a word I haven't heard before.

Chapter One

Josanne Arceneau struck every one of the last eight steps with her bottom and landed in a sitting position in the tiny, dark hallway. Her heart pounded in fear as she remained still, waiting to feel evidence that she'd seriously hurt her unborn baby—or herself.

She heard the faint sound of laughter coming from her coffee shop on the other side of the wall, traffic passing on the street just beyond the door, the honk of a horn, the bark of a dog—the sound of her own panicked breathing.

But she felt no pain. She'd half expected it to rip across her abdomen as the baby protested this rough treatment and demanded immediate freedom. But it didn't happen. Except for a gash on her right forearm where she must have snagged a carpet nail, she didn't seem to be hurt.

She ran a hand soothingly over the large mound of her pregnancy. The baby had been active day and night lately, and she waited for a kick to reassure her that the child was unharmed. Silence pulsed around her, disturbed only by the subtle, faraway sounds. She felt no response against her hand.

Her heartbeat accelerated, and she fought back a

brand-new panic. Did lack of pain mean that the fall had caused a damage *deeper* than pain?

"Come on, Chelsea," she said, rubbing a little harder, more urgently. "Talk to Mama Jo. Are you okay?"

Nothing.

"Oh, Cassie…" Jo closed her eyes and called upon her sister as fear and grief tumbled together inside her. "You always fixed everything. Please let Chelsea be all right."

As Jo leaned a hand on the bottom stair to push herself to her knees, the door to the street flew open with a sudden jolt.

A tall shape was outlined against the late-August early-morning sunlight. It had broad shoulders, long arms braced in the doorway, and a tension about it she recognized easily. The scent of Polo blew into the hallway.

Jo looked up from her kneeling position, paradoxically relieved and distressed to see the father of her baby. He must have been next door in the shop for his morning double cappuccino and heard the thud.

"Ryan," she said, her voice strained with concern and lingering shock from the fall. "Hi."

He was on his knees beside her in an instant, one hand on her upper arm, the other on her swollen belly. Out of the backlit shadows, his angular face was taut with fear. "Did you fall?" he demanded.

She nodded, trying to drag in a breath. "Just the last few steps. I don't feel pain, but…I don't feel movement, either."

He held her gaze for one grim moment, then turned to look over his shoulder. Jo noticed for the first time all her regular customers gathered several deep in the open doorway.

"Call 911," he ordered calmly.

Devon, her white-aproned assistant, turned to comply.

"It's going to be all right, Jo." Diantha pushed her way to the front of the little crowd. She was a plump woman in her sixties, wearing a denim skirt and blouse adorned with silver-and-turquoise jewelry. Long gray hair was caught at the nape of her neck in a silver clip. "I charted your day. Aquarius is in your sign today— that's good for making love, and for making little children listen to you. Tell the baby she's fine, and she will be."

Ryan braced a forearm on his bent knee and turned to Diantha with impatience. Jo prudently forestalled whatever he would have said with a polite thank-you.

If only things were as simple as her neighbor in the health food store thought them to be. Diantha firmly believed that order in the universe meant order in one's daily life—if one simply complied with the astrological flow.

Jo concentrated on breathing regularly and remaining calm, hoping that would bring calm and comfortable conditions to the baby.

Ryan, his long-fingered hand splayed across her abdomen, probed for a kick, a roll, a movement of any kind. Jo willed the baby to move. But it didn't.

RYAN JEFFRIES felt Jo's slenderness in one hand and her almost-ripe pregnancy in the other. He refused to let himself panic when he felt no movement.

"The baby's all right," Jo said, her voice raspy and

trembling faintly. "I know she is. Cassie wouldn't let it be otherwise."

He resisted an impatient response. He wasn't in the mood for his sister-in-law's cosmically spiritual approach to things. He'd lost his wife, and he didn't believe she still existed, on the fringes of their lives somewhere, assisting with their destinies. She was gone. He felt the yawning blackness of her absence every moment of his life.

"She's not an angel, Jo," he said quietly, as he wrapped an arm around her back and eased her into a sitting position on the second stair from the bottom. "She's just gone. How do you feel?"

He caught a glimpse of hurt and disappointment in her eyes. Then she gave a small shiver. He pulled off his suit jacket and placed it around her.

She wore a long, thin dress in some floaty fabric that fell almost to her ankles, and light brown hiking boots over baggy socks. The soles of her boots were as thick as snow tires.

He'd always thought Jo had atrocious fashion sense, but that was all part and parcel of her generally off-the-wall personality. With her passion for nature and her relaxed approach to life and living, she was like some sixties hippie caught in a time warp. He despaired of ever being able to relate to her—which was not a healthy situation, when she carried his baby.

And she knew it, too. He saw it in the pale blue eyes that watched him from under a riot of curly blond hair. It was always outrageously styled. This morning it was caught up high on her head, the long curly ends left to fall to her eyelashes and just above her ears, like a fringe.

"You believe what you want," she said finally, with a sigh. "I'll believe what I want."

The little crowd parted, and Devon appeared, his lean young face pale with worry. "Ambulance is on its way."

"Thank you." With a dark look, Ryan stopped the young man from coming any closer.

Devon wiped his hands nervously on his apron. "Can I do anything?"

Ryan shook his head. "Just give her room to breathe."

Heron Point Medics was located three blocks from downtown, and the whine of its siren could already be heard as it raced toward Coffee Country. Devon ran out to flag down the ambulance, and the little crowd peeled back from the door to make room for the emergency medical technicians.

"TAKE A DEEP BREATH, Jo, and don't move." J. V. Nicholas, Riverview Hospital's radiologist, turned knobs and controls on the ultrasound machine, and it made a whirring noise as he took an impression.

HI, Mama Jo! Wow! Am I going to have hair like that?
Hi, Daddy!
I can't wait to get out of here and into somebody's arms. Things are getting pretty tight.
I'm okay. I can't kick anymore, because there isn't enough room in here, so I'll have to just wiggle.
What? Oh, sure. Mama Cass says "Hi."

"GOOD. Got it," Jave said. "Okay, Jo. That should do it."

He turned off the machine and flipped on the light.

He smiled at Jo, and at Ryan, who sat in a chair on the other side of the gurney. "Everything looks fine to me, but Dr. McNamara will want to check my pictures, of course. The baby was wriggling all over the place while we were photographing her."

Jo felt enormous relief. She even saw the set of Ryan's shoulders relax. Test after test had proven that Chelsea was unharmed by the fall.

"She might just have been surprised into stillness by the jolt," Jave said. "Or she might have dozed off. She's worked with you for eight months now behind the counter of Coffee Country. She probably thinks she can report to work on automatic pilot." Jave folded back the light blanket that covered her and helped her to a sitting position on the edge of the gurney. "I can't believe you showed up here without my caramel latte, though."

She grinned at him. "Thoughtless of me, I know. Come by when you get off, and you can have a double on the house."

"Thanks, but I've got a date with my brother, Tom, at the handball court. I don't want anything to slow me down."

He looked away as he spoke, an edge of tension in him. Jo wondered about it. He'd been at her first Lamaze class the previous week, as the coach of Nancy Malone, whom someone else in the class told her was the wife of a coastguardsman. She'd thought that curious, considering the intimacy required between a mother-to-be and her coach. She knew it was common for single women to bring women friends as coaches, or men friends with whom they shared a special bond. But she doubted that it was customary for married women whose husbands were away to bring single men.

"How's everything at the bank, Ryan?" Jave asked, disturbing her speculations. "I keep watching for an Overstocked on Fifty-Dollar Bills sale, but it never happens."

Ryan stood, relief that the baby was safe making him feel energized. He was even able to expel the tension with a light laugh. "Money's a precious commodity. No one ever has too much, not even banks. How's the boat coming?"

"Greatly improved. We no longer have a hole in the deck of the *Mud Hen.*"

"Sounds like a definite plus."

"I thought so. But my brother thought we should have left it and seen if the fish could find their way in without so much effort on our part. Excuse me." The phone rang, and Jave reached across his equipment to answer it.

Ryan helped Jo to her feet and across the room to the dressing cubicle. "I'll wait for you in the hallway," he said. "Then we're supposed to go back to McNamara's office."

"I can take it from here," she offered, "if you have to get back to work. I feel fine."

He studied her consideringly for a moment, then shook his head. She wasn't sure whether it meant that he didn't consider her sufficiently competent to "take it from here," or that he *wanted* to stay with her.

"I'll be in the hallway."

Jo closed the curtains of the cubicle behind her and rolled her eyes to heaven. Ryan was an enigma. But she was giddy with relief at the moment, and she decided it didn't matter. The baby was fine. That was the important thing.

A little thrill of excitement ran along her spine. One

more month, and Chelsea would be a living, breathing, squalling presence in her arms.

Relief was eclipsed for an instant by the realization that she wouldn't be in her arms for very long; she would then belong to Ryan. But she pushed that thought aside, knowing she'd find a way to deal with it. She would.

And for now, she had another month as Chelsea's mother. She rubbed the round protrusion affectionately and felt the baby squirm inside her. She smiled broadly. A month with Chelsea was a lot.

IT WAS MIDAFTERNOON when Jo and Ryan finally left the hospital with a clean bill of health for mother and baby.

They rode back to town in a taxi, because Ryan had ridden with Jo in the ambulance.

"Coffee Country, please," Jo said to the driver, a pretty young woman in a blue baseball cap with a picture of Elvis pinned to the front.

"Right." The woman turned on the meter and pulled away from the hospital's entrance.

"Scratch that," Ryan told her. "Take us to the Heron Point Condominiums, please."

Jo turned to him in surprise. "Your place? Why?"

"Because from now on," he replied, in a matter-of-fact tone that he hoped would discourage argument, "it's going to be your place, too."

Jo didn't stop to analyze why he felt the need to suggest that. She only knew she wouldn't let him. "The hell it will," she replied coolly. "Coffee Country, driver. Ignore this man. He's insane."

Ryan figured he should have known better. The tone had sometimes worked on Cassie, but only when she knew she could get her own way by subterfuge, rather than open argument. Jo knew nothing of such subtleties. With Jo, all-out war was the only option.

"The condo, driver," he said. "Ignore this woman. She hates Elvis."

The driver braked to a sudden stop at the road. Jo, in the process of putting on her seat belt, jerked forward. Ryan put a hand out to stop her.

The driver found Jo's gaze in the rearview mirror. "You don't like the King?"

Jo gave Ryan a lethal side-glance and smiled at the driver's reflection. "No, I don't. I'm sorry. I know it's un-American." Then, knowing she needed the woman's cooperation, she added placatingly, "But I liked his stamp. I even bought a firstday issue. Would you take us to Coffee—?"

Ryan put a hand on Jo's arm to silence her. "There are twenty steps up to your apartment," he said reasonably. "Today, you fell down eight of them. What if you'd fallen from the top? What if you'd fallen head-first, or sideways, or..."

"You," she pointed out, "live on the second floor."

"My building," he said, "has an elevator."

"Your condo is a long way from my business, and I don't have a car."

"The bank is a block away from your coffee bar. I'll drive you in every morning and pick you up at night."

She folded her arms stubbornly. Resting atop the bulk of her baby, they were almost under her chin. "I open at six. You start at nine."

His scolding glance chided her for trying to put one over on him. "*Devon* opens at six. You show up at eight or eight-thirty, and I often start early."

"Ryan," she said urgently, knowing she had to get

through to him, "it won't work. We can't live together.
It *won't work.*"

"You're repeating yourself," he said, then added
over the front seat, "The condo, driver."

"It *bears* repeating," she said forcefully, feeling
more than a little desperate. "Ryan, we don't like each
other. You think I'm an airhead, and I think you're a
stuffed shirt."

He acknowledged that with a nod. "But we're having
a baby together. Certainly that becomes the priority."

Jo was aware of the driver's wide eyes reflected in
the rearview mirror as she turned onto the Coast Road.

"But we—"

"Look," he said, the hand on her arm tightening,
"Can we save this for a more private moment?"

"No," Jo began, pulling away from him. "Public or
private, my feelings on the matter are—"

The taxi driver screeched to a halt, pitching both of
them forward, despite their belts. Then she made a wide
turn around a UPS truck that had stopped in front of an
auto-parts shop.

She smiled meekly in the mirror. "Sorry. Lost my
focus, there."

Jo leaned back in the seat and decided the driver was
too interested in their conversation to ensure the safety
of a trip to *any* destination.

"Fine," she said curtly, turning away from Ryan to
watch the very familiar passing scenery. "We'll go to
your place, but don't think I'm moving in with you.
Because I'm not."

Jo was no stranger to the condo. In the five years
Ryan and her sister were married, she had attended
many a holiday and family dinner there, and had often
visited on a whim with a pound of the hazelnut blend

Cassie loved, or a few ounces of the Spanish saffron whose price was exorbitantly high on the retail market.

In all that time, Jo and Ryan had simply tolerated each other. She'd known he considered her quirky and weird, and she'd always thought him stuffy. But they'd coexisted, because Cassie was the common denominator—petite, witty, optimistically determined Cassie, who'd been convinced there was a solution to every problem if one simply looked hard enough.

Ryan led Jo into the blue-and-gray clapboard building, punctuated by gables and cupolas, that rambled comfortably across Heron Point. He was silent in the elevator, then unlocked the door of number 27 and ushered her inside.

She hesitated, then drew in a deep breath and stepped into the large living room. She hadn't been here since she'd helped Ryan and her father sort through Cassie's things, right after the funeral, six months ago.

It was decorated in the shades of the river view beyond the windows—a cloudy, stormy blue, the gray of the herons that nested nearby, giving the point its name, the pristine white of the sea gulls that cavorted and called around the passing fishing boats.

Ryan pulled at his tie as he headed for the French doors and the small patio that hung out over the river. He pulled a caned chair away from the small glass table and gestured for her to sit. "Tea?" he asked. "Juice? Evian?"

"Evian, please," she replied, watching him a little nervously as he pulled off his jacket and tossed it at a chair. He'd always been very formal with her, and all their meetings since Cassie's death had been on neutral ground and conducted with civility and simple good manners—more like discussions of a business deal than an exchange of information regarding the pregnancy they had in common. He'd insisted on weekly reports on how she and the baby were doing.

But now that he'd removed the jacket, she could see the lean waist under his European-cut white shirt, the neat, taut hips in gray-and-white pinstripe, the shoulders that were formidable even without the jacket.

No. She looked away and simply listened while he opened the refrigerator door, reached into a cupboard, poured the imported water into a glass. She'd put this out of her mind for more than five years, and this was not the time to even let the thought form. God. She had to get out of here.

She pretended interest in the sailboarders taking advantage of the remnants of summer on the bay when Ryan brought her a tall glass. He put his own in the place opposite her and sat down.

He looked earnest and determined. She sought desperately to divert his attention.

"I've often wondered," she said, peering over the slatted railing, "if the right current could take you all the way to Hawaii on one of those sailboards."

She wasn't looking at him, but she could feel his gaze. She knew he saw through the ploy. "Well, maybe to Washington," he said.

"I guess I'd really rather go north, anyway. Sunny climes just aren't my thing." She chattered without turning away from the sailboarders. "I'd like to be where there are craggy mountains, lots of snow, cozy fires and moonless nights."

She heard the crackle of the cane chair as he leaned back in it. "Remember that you once broke a leg skiing," he said.

"Oh, I wouldn't ski. I'd sit by the fire, sipping Spanish coffee and writing moody poetry."

"You get drunk on one brandy. You'd have to write pretty fast."

He knew entirely too much about her. Jo turned back to him with obvious reluctance and met his quiet gaze. He studied her that way often, as though she interested but annoyed him. Which annoyed *her*. And it was time to confront the issue.

"Well, I can't go anywhere for another month, anyway," she said. "But that doesn't mean I'll be moving in here."

Ryan took her resistance calmly. He didn't intend to argue about it, because she thrived on that. She loved any opportunity to oppose him on anything. She'd always been that way. Cassie had insisted that her sister had never had a combative personality, that he alone inspired that reaction in her. And judging by how calmly and agreeably she dealt with friends, co-workers and customers, he could only believe it was true. He alone brought out this side of her.

But that was all right. She'd always made *him* edgy. They had bad chemistry.

But, for the next month, they had to find a way around their animosity. This baby was going to be born safely if it killed him. Cassie had been convinced there was a solution to every problem. He hoped she was right.

"A woman who is eight months along," he said, "should not be climbing all those stairs several times a day. It isn't safe. And I think at this stage of the pregnancy, you shouldn't be alone."

"At this stage of my pregnancy," Jo pointed out, "I shouldn't be upset, and you know that's what would happen if you and I cohabited. And it wouldn't be good for you, either. The best-run branch the bank has would suddenly be out of balance on a regular basis, or you'd be giving loans that had no chance of ever being repaid, and you'd end up unemployed.''

He shook his head over her simplified view of banking. ''I never let my domestic situation affect my work.''

She snickered. ''Because your domestic situation was always perfect.''

He raised an eyebrow. ''It was?''

She frowned. ''Wasn't it?''

He shrugged a shoulder. ''Depends on your definition of *perfect*. My life with Cassie was often wonderful, sometimes volatile, but always exciting. And, like many precious things, its value was in its *im*perfection. We were great together, but not because we never disagreed.''

Jo blinked in surprise. In five years, all Cassie had ever said about Ryan was that he was the most delicious husband any woman ever had. Then she would close her eyes and lift her shoulders in an ecstatic little gesture that isolated her with her thoughts and made Jo embarrassed to even wonder what was on her sister's mind.

Ryan stared at the glass he was toying with and smiled to himself. Then he refocused on Jo. ''So. We're two adults,'' he said finally. ''Certainly we can get along for a month, until Chelsea's born. I promise to do my part, if you'll do yours.''

Jo racked her brain for an excuse. She could not move in here. Her feelings would be too hard to hide, and then he'd *know*. It was hard enough to act nonchalant when he walked into the bar, or during their meetings about the baby.

"I think it's a bad idea," she said coolly, pushing her chair back and rising to her feet. But she didn't accomplish the maneuver with the grace and style she'd hoped would accompany it. She bumped the edge of the table with her stomach and dumped her water glass onto the floor, then backed away and knocked her chair into the rack of plants behind her.

She groaned as Ryan reached behind him on a small buffet table for napkins and dropped them onto the puddle. Then he came around to right the chair that had blocked her in the corner of the patio.

"Sorry," she said. "Thank you."

"You need a helping hand, Jo." His look said, *I told you so,* though those weren't precisely his words. "Before you kill yourself or destroy your surroundings."

The situation was getting desperate, she told herself. She had to get tough. When he took her hand to help her into the house, she pulled it away. He studied her in surprise for a moment, then stepped aside when she moved past him and went into the living room. The furniture was all plump and cushy, and she chose the only chair she felt reasonably sure she could still get out of—a Boston rocker.

"You don't like me," she said honestly. "That makes it impossible for us to live together, even for a month, even if we try to get along."

Ryan wandered into the house after her, but went to the window that looked out on the pilings below left over from a long-abandoned cannery. "*You* don't like *me,* but you agreed to carry the baby for Cassie and me anyway. My feelings wouldn't prevent me from seeing that you have all you need to be comfortable."

"Comfort," she said stubbornly, "isn't everything."

He turned away from the window to pace toward her. She sat in the rocker, looking a little like a flowered dumpling wearing snow tires. But there was something urgent in her eyes. He sat on the ottoman that belonged to the big chair opposite her.

"What do you mean?" he asked.

"I mean," she said, her voice a little high, as she rubbed her stomach, "that I have just four more weeks with Chelsea, and I want them to be…you know…" She groped for the right word and finally settled for "Intimate."

He spread his hands, confused by her reaction. "You're carrying the baby within your body. How much more intimacy do you require?"

Jo knew he would never understand. She'd sat in this very living room last Thanksgiving Day and listened to the plan Cassie had concocted that would allow her and Ryan to have a baby that was their very own creation, despite Cassie's inability to carry that life herself.

And Jo had agreed, because her sister was as precious to her as her own life—and because she'd loved her sister's husband from the moment Cassie brought him home to meet the family.

It had always been her secret, though her father had guessed it. And it would remain their secret into eternity.

She'd agreed to carry their baby as her gift of love to their life together. And had Cassie lived, she imagined, the prospect of handing this baby over to her would not have made the future look so bleak.

But Cassie was gone, and the configuration of their complex little family had changed considerably.

She saw Ryan's shoulders square and his eyes sharpen. "You aren't thinking about—?"

She forestalled him with a quelling look before emotion could overtake her. "Backing out?" she asked. "Of course not. We made a deal, and I'll fulfill my part. I just don't think I should have to give her up until it's time."

"Then you wouldn't want to do anything," he said quietly, "that would make you deliver early, like climbing too many stairs, and falling down them. If you stay here, you won't have that problem."

Jo opened her mouth to deny that was necessary, then remembered how close she'd come to just such a situation that morning. Certainly the baby was a more important consideration than her unrequited affection for the baby's father. Jo felt like some beleaguered character in an adventure movie, trapped in a room in which the walls were closing in, threatening to squash her.

She didn't want to live here, where *he* would be every spare moment. She didn't want to live with constant reminders of Cassie that would bring back that last day in vivid detail. But she didn't want to endanger the baby, either.

"So why don't you rest here this afternoon?" Ryan said. "I'll pack up your closet, and whatever else you think you'll need, and bring it back tonight. I checked with Devon while we were still at the hospital, and he said things were going fine. He's not taking this summer class for credit, so he just cut classes today." He glanced up at the oak-trimmed clock above the bar. "It's already almost three."

He was right, of course. She knew he didn't care about her, but he was genuinely concerned for the baby's safety. They did, at least, have that in common.

"Okay," she agreed. She would do this for Chelsea. But she had the most unsettling feeling that she was making a serious mistake.

GREAT! Mama Cass says she has wonderful memories of this place. I like it, too. Won't it be nice to have Daddy around all the time? Mama Jo?

Chapter Two

"The doctor's sure she's all right?" Devon, spooning a dollop of foamed milk into a demitasse of espresso, looked up at Ryan in concern. The mellow sounds of "California Dreamin'" came from the CD player on the shelf behind him.

Ryan nodded. "Positive." He suspected Devon was infatuated with Jo, despite the ten-year difference in their ages.

"That's great news. There you go, ma'am. Espresso macchiato." Devon handed the cup across the counter to a young woman in an elegant gray suit. "Tell her her regulars chipped in for this." He pointed to a tall green plant at the far end of the counter. "People have been stopping in all day to ask about her."

"Assure them that she's fine."

"Jeffries."

Ryan turned in the act of walking away. Devon met his gaze evenly, a mild challenge in his eyes. "Tell her I send my love," he said.

Ryan held his gaze an extra moment. "I will," he said finally. Then he turned to leave and found himself face-to-fingernail with Diantha.

"Didn't I tell you it would be all right?" she asked,

shaking her index finger at him. Silver bracelets jangled. "You didn't believe me. But I knew. I knew. Aquarius came onto the scene today."

He'd always thought Diantha Pennyman was a little shy of plumb, but she was a good businesswoman, and he knew for a fact that she had as hefty an IRA as could be found in Heron Point. Still, he doubted the stars could be credited for her business acumen. And though there'd been a time when they guided ships, he didn't think they could guide lives.

"I'm glad you were right, Diantha," he said, and tried to slip past her.

She sidestepped him into a corner, as all the other patrons went about their business.

"You know, you shouldn't smirk at the heavens," she said, her unsettlingly clear gray eyes boring into his. "Particularly since you're a man who'd do something as unorthodox as plant his seed in a test tube."

Ryan drew a breath for forbearance. "It was a petri dish."

"That's beside the point. You stepped out in faith and took a wild chance that a life would be created, then successfully nurtured to birth in a surrogate womb. That's a lot like believing in the stars."

Ryan shifted his weight. "We rather thought we were believing in God."

She raised both eyebrows. "Who do you think made and moves the stars?" She pinned him with her gaze an extra moment, then stepped aside and let him pass.

Ryan took the steps to Jo's apartment two at a time. The coffee bar always made him feel a little as though he'd dropped into that alien bar in *Star Wars*. The people there were not only unfamiliar, but downright weird.

Jo's apartment was a small one-bedroom with colorful, mismatched furniture, and the artwork of friends on the walls. He supposed it was charming, if one could be comfortable in such a small space.

In her bedroom was a brass bedstead he and Cassie had helped her carry up the stairs after a church rummage sale, and a circa-1950s dresser with rounded edges and large round pulls.

She'd told him that all her "pregnant" clothes were in the top drawer of the dresser and the right end of the closet. Her purple velour bathrobe was the dividing line. She had a suitcase under the bed.

Everything fit in the case, with room to spare. He'd noticed over the past months that she didn't have that many changes of clothes. He bought coffee at the bar every morning and midafternoon, as a way of checking on her and the progress of their baby. When he suggested lending her his credit card to buy clothes, she'd given him a look that might have withered a man less accustomed to the ire of people turned down for loans, or whose boats or cars he'd helped repossess.

He hadn't broached the subject again. But maybe he'd have to brave it now.

He took her contour pillow from the bed, and remembered to get her shoes. He frowned over them as he put them in a grocery bag. There was a pair of absolutely flat black slippers, some Birkenstock sandals, and another very worn pair of boots, similar to the ones she'd worn today.

He thought it was no wonder she'd fallen in those boots. The tread was enough to steady an elephant on ice. Once they hit the carpeting on the stairs, they'd probably stopped her cold.

Shaking his head, he took a last look around the

apartment, added water to a philodendron on a bookcase, then locked the door and headed for home.

Jo PUTTERED in the kitchen. And putter was all she could do with the meager contents of the refrigerator and cupboards. In the refrigerator, she found Evian water, milk, beer, a large bag of apples, and a pound of coffee, from her shop, that she mixed personally and called Eye-opener. It was a blend of French roast and Continental, and even the decaf was like a surge of adrenaline.

In the freezer was a bag of ice, a box of Häagen-Dazs bars, a loaf of bread, and a pound of almond-chocolate coffee she'd put in Cassie's Christmas stocking. Her sister had been wimpy about her brew.

In the cupboard was a half-empty jar of mixed nuts, a revolving spice rack, a box of herbal tea, a jar of peanut butter and a box of crackers. She guessed Ryan ate out most of the time.

She made a cup of herbal tea and looked for something to do to avoid thinking. The condo was spotless. She knew Ryan had a housekeeper, because he came to the shop half an hour early the two mornings a week that she cleaned.

Soap operas could be entertaining, but she had no idea what was happening on any one of them, and she hated talk shows.

The bedroom Ryan had told her to use was large and airy and also spotless, and decorated in mallard green, white and burgundy. She'd used it for one night just last year, when a pipe in her bathroom sprang a leak and flooded her apartment and part of her shop. She examined the room's view of the bridge that connected Heron Point to Washington, then stood uncertainly in the middle of the green-carpeted hallway, wondering whether to try to take a nap she didn't need, or to explore further.

The master bedroom was across the hall. She wondered idly if it was tidy behind the closed door, then dismissed the thought. It was none of her business.

Then she turned to the last door at the end of the hallway. Cassie had intended to make it the nursery. Certainly that *was* her business.

But she hesitated before turning the knob. Since Cassie had been gone, she and Ryan had somehow managed to keep the baby out of their relationship, even though it was the only reason for it. They met to talk about it, he accompanied her to her doctor's appointments, and they'd agreed that when the time came, he'd be her Lamaze coach, just as Cassie had intended to be.

And even though she carried the baby, she'd felt oddly removed from all that would happen to it after it was born and Ryan took over.

But walking into this room, seeing all he and Cassie had planned for it, would be like a glimpse into its future. It would put her on a different footing with Ryan, and she wasn't sure that was a good idea.

I THINK IT'S A GOOD IDEA. Let's look.

THEN SHE DECIDED that she didn't care if it was or not, she wanted to see it. And she was trading her final month of solitude with Chelsea for Ryan's peace of mind, so she was entitled.

She pushed the door open boldly, then stopped just inside the door with an ''Ah...'' of approval.

WHAT, Mama Jo? What do you see?

THE ROOM was painted white, and a deep border of animal characters in primary colors paraded just below the ceiling, along with musical instruments, balloons and stars on a string.

A bright red carpet covered the floor, and the furniture was coordinated with the paper and a ruffly valance above a bay window with miniblinds pulled up to reveal the river view. A window seat was covered in the same fabric, and Jo sat on it to take in the rest of the room.

Bookshelves already held books, and a colorful shelf of sturdy plastic squares held a pale brown musical bear she'd bought when they learned the pregnancy had taken, a package of diapers, a little fern in a lamb-shaped planter that her father had sent, and several other odds and ends already collected from friends and relatives.

There was a rocking horse in one corner, and a child-size blue upholstered chair in the other. Jo picked up the bear and turned its key. Brahms's "Lullaby" filled the silence.

MUSIC. Mama Cass says it's a bear, and that you *gave it to me. I can't wait to see it.*

ABOVE THE BOOKSHELF was a framed photograph of the three of them—Cassie, Ryan and her—on her sister's wedding day. Ryan, in a morning coat, had an arm around each of them. Cassie was laughing happily, veil flying out behind her, the cleft in her chin that Jo had always envied very prominent.

She, Jo, was smiling under a coronet of rosebuds. Had anyone else, she wondered, noticed the wistful look in her eyes?

She unconsciously rubbed Chelsea. "There we are, baby," she said aloud. "Your parents."

Jo smiled at that thought, but at the same moment, a

sob rose out of her that came from very deep inside and hurt abominably. Delight mingled with profound sadness.

She rubbed gently at the protuberance of Chelsea and accepted, not for the first time, how difficult it was going to be to give her up. Even knowing the baby was coming to this place of privilege and adoration.

Cassie would have smothered her with love, and she knew Ryan would, too, because she was part of Cassie.

"All Mama Jo is," she said, with a final pat for the baby and a toss of her head meant to dismiss any self-pity, "is the somewhat sophisticated paper bag that's holding you."

MAMA CASS *says without* you, *I wouldn't be here. She thinks you should talk to Daddy.*

JO STOOD, pushing against the seat to manage her bulk, and felt the seat flip up slightly as she let it go. Storage? she wondered. She peered inside and found it lined with cedar.

At the bottom of the fragrant space was a cloth bag with a drawstring. Jo recognized it as Cassie's sewing bag. Her sister had been an avid needleworker in her spare time, and had always carried projects back and forth to work at the bank or on Sunday drives.

Curious, Jo pulled out the bag. It was filled with finely spun yarn in soft baby colors—yellow, green, pink and blue. Only a dozen rows or so had been worked, in crochet, to produce about three inches of a baby blanket. A wooden hook dangled from the last stitch made in the middle of a row.

Jo pulled the work out to look at it more closely, and suddenly the perfect stitches in the barely begun project and the dangling hook seemed to exemplify for her Cassie's life and death, and she buried her face in the wool and wept.

RYAN HEARD THE SOUND the moment he opened the front door. It was soft and at the other end of the condo, but it struck at his heart like a blow.

He dropped the suitcase and the bag of shoes just inside the door, and the take-out food on the coffee table, and hurried down the hallway.

Jo was in the nursery. He should have guessed. It shouldn't annoy him that she'd looked in, but it did. This room was something he and Cassie had planned and begun together, and he'd finished it himself, with an almost ritualistic adherence to what his wife had wanted. It was absurd to consider Jo an intruder, and he wasn't sure that was the problem. But it seemed the more he missed Cassie, the more he resented her sister.

He was almost surprised to find Jo crying. She'd been so stoic at the funeral—as stoic as he was. They'd stood arm in arm—it was almost the only time in five years that they'd ever touched—and he'd felt her anger, as deep and roiling as his, and a grief that went deeper than any utterance could ever express.

He wished he could find that release somewhere. But feeling had clotted inside him, blocking any emotion from entering or leaving. He had to find a way to solve that, he knew, before the baby came.

He stepped into the room without a clue as to how to handle the situation. When Cassie cried, he'd simply wrapped her in a bear hug and held fast until she poured out what troubled her. But she'd loved him. She'd welcomed his caring bullying.

Jo simply tolerated him. But she was carrying his

baby, and this sobbing couldn't be good for either of them.

HI, Daddy. Mama Cass says do *something!*

"Jo?" He put a hand on her shoulder. It startled her into turning. Her cheeks were flushed and blotchy from crying, and her eyes, usually clear blue and skeptical when they focused on him, were naked with grief. For an instant, he felt the same curious kinship with her that he'd felt at Cassie's graveside. It was grim, he thought, that the only bridge between them was pain.

She sniffed and squared her shoulders the moment her eyes focused on him. "I'm sorry," she said, her voice raspy and low. "I shouldn't have come in. I shouldn't have snooped. But I found this, and..."

Ryan's eyes went to the strip of soft-colored wool in her hands. It was unfamiliar.

"What is it?" he asked.

Jo shook her head, wiping the back of her hand across one eye, the heel of her hand across the other. "I found it in the window seat. I guess..." She drew a breath for composure. "I guess Cassie started a baby blanket."

He remembered suddenly the day she'd bought the yarn, at a little shop across the river. They hadn't yet been sure the pregnancy would take, and she'd called the purchase an act of faith. He'd just accepted an office with the Downtown Merchants Association, and she'd said the project would keep her busy while he was at meetings. He hadn't known she'd started it.

He studied the small strip of fine stitches and fought an overwhelming sense of loss. Cassie's life had been like that—beautiful and barely begun, the ending of it like a dropped stitch in the fabric of time.

He took the yarn from Jo, stuffed it into the bag and dropped the whole into the window seat and let it close with a slam. It seemed to pull both of them together.

"I brought home Chinese," he said, leading the way out of the room, then closing the door firmly behind her.

She preceded him into the living room. "Good," she said, striving for emotional equilibrium. She found it, as usual with him, in half playful, half serious animosity. "I was afraid you'd be expecting me to cook. I did make coffee."

He gave her a wry glance as he picked up her things. "I've tasted your cooking. You can stick to making the coffee. I'll lay this on your bed, if you'll get plates and silverware."

"Right." Jo carried the bag of takeout to the table and went about her assigned task. Ryan was back in a moment, his suit and white shirt exchanged for khaki shorts and a short-sleeved white sweatshirt with First Coastal Bank emblazoned across the chest.

They passed cartons of pan-fried noodles, kung pao chicken, fried rice and fried shrimp in a continual circle as they talked and ate. She'd been afraid their first meal together would be uncomfortable, but he'd chosen to discuss the very practical subject of their schedules for the next month.

"So you'd like to be at work by eight-thirty Monday through Friday?" he asked.

"Tuesday through Saturday," she replied. "Devon does Mondays, because he has no classes, and I do Saturdays so he can have his weekends."

Ryan nodded, then remembered the boy's message. "He asked me to give you his love."

Jo was startled for just an instant. The thought of

Ryan delivering her anyone's love was enough to stir unwanted feelings. She felt just the suggestion of a blush rising at her throat, and fought it down with determined force of will.

"Devon's a buddy," she said, making a production of dipping a shrimp in duck sauce. "At nineteen, he's more sensitive than most mature men I know."

"And your regulars chipped in for a plant and card," Ryan went on. "I left it at the shop, because you spend so much of your time there, and I thought they'd probably enjoy seeing it on the counter when they come in."

Jo pretended surprise. "Also very sensitive. Mr. Jeffries, you surprise me."

"Really." He gave her an even glance as he dipped his shrimp in hot mustard. "You think all I do is foreclose on widows and orphans?"

"Oh, hardly. I know you have a reputation around town as the only banker who'll stake first-time entrepreneurs, single women in business, adventurous schemes that sound shaky to everyone else but that you see as potentially profitable."

Now he looked surprised. "Praise, from judgmental Jo? I must be misreading the message."

Jo rolled her eyes. "I know you're a fine, community-minded businessman. I'm just surprised you care about *my* business. I thought you considered it…flaky."

He gave her a noncommittal lift of his eyebrows over the rim of his cup.

Jo knew what it meant. She knew she should back away because the issue was potentially problematic, but she was often incapable of doing the diplomatic thing.

"It's me you consider flaky," she went on accusingly. "Because of Cassie, and the restaurant thing."

He inclined his head in a gesture that conceded her

point. "She wanted it badly. You didn't want to work that hard. But I never called you flaky."

Trouble loomed closer and closer. She ignored it. "How many restaurants do you think Heron Point can support?" she asked. "I've worked in restaurants. All Cassie'd ever done was cook for you and cater for a few friends. The reality of restaurant work is hours of preparation and hours of cleanup broken up by sixteen hours of backbreaking fetching, carrying and tension."

Ryan remembered how hard Cassie had tried to talk Jo into entering into a partnership with her, and how disappointed she'd been when her sister couldn't be persuaded to come around.

He waved a hand, as though to dismiss the issue, and reached for the carton of rice. "Like I said. You didn't want to work that hard."

"She didn't know what she'd be getting into."

He couldn't let that pass. He looked into her eyes. "Yes, she did. She'd researched well. The old warehouse on the waterfront was an ideal location, and her cooking and your management savvy would have brought every tourist in the Northwest."

"It would have taken a fortune to get started," she said thinly.

"Not true. She had the loan, and it wasn't even through me. The Bank of Heron Point believed it'd go, too."

Jo was out of arguments—except for the real one, the one she couldn't share. She hadn't wanted to go into partnership with her sister because the plan was that Ryan would host on evenings and weekends, and she'd doubted that what she felt for her brother-in-law would remain invisible in such close proximity.

It had hurt to hurt her sister, but she'd felt sure then

that she'd done the right thing. Now, as Ryan sat across the table from her, intelligent, loyal to Cassie, concerned for his baby—all the things she loved in him— she was still sure.

"It's a moot point now, isn't it?" she asked finally.

"You brought it up," he reminded her. Then he sighed, more than willing to put the unresolvable issue aside. "But, yes, it is. What else is on your schedule that we have to think about? You're involved in that Heron Point Has It project I'm chairing."

"Yes." She made herself concentrate on the subject. The plan for a communitywide commercial fair had generated a lot of excitement at the last association meeting, and was intended to show that everything the big city offered could be found in little Heron Point. All the restaurants and gourmet shops would offer food, gift shops would show samples of their wares, craftsmen would exhibit their work and be available for questions and consultation, community-service groups would distribute pamphlets and offer raffles and giveaways. "I have a couple of meetings with the restaurant cooperative's committee over the next two weeks."

He nodded. "I'll get you there. And I'll find some help to get you set up the day of the event on the chance Devon's tied up with school. I'm sure I'll be up to my ears in blown fuses and power outages. You know how the old fairgrounds building is."

It was strange, she thought, to realize that Chelsea would be almost two months old by the time the event was held. She could only wonder what her own situation would be then. The thought made her quarrelsome.

She shrugged a shoulder. "That'll be after Chelsea's born," she said. "You'll no longer be responsible for my welfare."

He frowned at her. "That's a coldhearted approach to this."

It was. But she knew that approach was the only one that would get her through. She pushed rice back and forth on her plate with the tip of her fork. "It was the deal we made in the beginning, remember. I carry the baby, then she's yours. I was welcome to be a doting aunt, but it would confuse a child to have three parents."

Ryan put his fork down quietly and leaned back in his chair, his dark eyes assessing her. She wished she could seal her mouth closed. One moment she made harsh promises to herself about remaining on the fringes of his life without a fuss, and the next she came off sounding like a shrew with self-esteem problems.

"I want her aunt to be a part of her life," he said.

"I know." She tried to sound amenable. "I just meant that you won't feel the same…duty…to Chelsea's *aunt* as you do to me now, while I'm carrying her."

She spoke the words with the utmost reasonableness, but Ryan heard all the unresolved issues underneath. Cassie had insisted there would be none. She and Jo, though as different as night and day, had been as close as it was possible for two sisters to be. She had complete faith in Jo's generosity, she'd told him. In her integrity, and in her love.

And it might all have worked as Cassie projected it would—if she had lived. But her death had changed everything. Now Jo would be giving this child to him, and not to her sister. And she didn't like him. That was bound to compromise her generosity.

He resisted the pull of panic.

"Do you want to talk about this?" he asked calmly.

She looked at him blandly, pretending to misunderstand. "About what?"

He was almost afraid to say the words, afraid they'd make her run. But he had to. It was what their lives were all about for the next month. "About giving me Chelsea."

There was a hard lump in Jo's throat. "There's nothing to talk about. I promised Cassie. And I promised you." She forced herself to smile. "All I meant was, that our relationship—yours and mine—will change. When Chelsea's here, you'll no longer have to worry about how I get to meetings, because I'll be back in my own apartment, living my own life. Will you pass the chicken, please?"

Jo ignored his pensive gaze and chattered on about anything and everything on her schedule that she could remember, and a few things she invented, in the hope of making him forget that little exchange.

They finally tidied up together, and she excused herself to retire to her room.

"I'll be ready to drive you at eight-fifteen," he called after her.

She turned at the head of the hallway. "Do you work on Saturday?"

"A couple of hours. But I'll be back to pick you up at five." His eyes roved her bulbous silhouette. "You're sure it's a good idea to be on your feet that long at this stage?"

"I'm doing okay so far," she said. "And I have a chair in the back I can use when it's quiet."

"All right. Your bathroom should be well stocked, and the TV-VCR remote is in the bedside-table drawer. But if you need anything, I'm right across the hall."

"Right. Thanks."

Jo put the few things in her suitcase away, then put the case itself in a corner of the cavernous closet. She read a chapter in the book she'd bought months ago on pregnancy and birth, she watched evening television, she tossed and turned and had trouble getting comfortable.

She was finally dozing off when the phone rang. The ringer was turned off in her room, but she heard it across the hall in Ryan's bedroom. Anyone who had ever run a business, she thought, trying to settle down again, was attuned to the sound of a telephone.

A knock on her bedroom door brought her up on her elbows. "Yes?" she asked.

Ryan's head peered around the door. "Did I wake you?"

She shook her head. "Something wrong?"

"No. But your father's on the phone. He got worried when he couldn't reach you at home, so he called me."

"Oh." She pushed herself up awkwardly. Ryan came to push her contour pillow aside and stuff the plump pillow she'd discarded behind her. Then he reached under her arms and pulled her up.

The contact left her breathless for an instant. Then he handed her the phone and walked away, apparently without noticing that there'd been nothing between his hands and her body but thin white cotton.

"Hello?" she said into the phone, her voice a little unsteady.

"Jo. Baby, are you all right?" Matthew Arcenau's voice came loudly and urgently over the cross-country connection. He taught American history at a rural Connecticut high school. He claimed the beautiful surroundings made for a perfect semiretirement. "Ryan says you fell."

"I'm fine," she assured him quickly, clearing her throat and repeating the declaration in a firm tone. "I'm fine. I've had every test possible, and the baby and I are both doing beautifully."

"Well, that's a relief." His tone quieted. Then there was a moment's hesitation. "I'm glad you're staying with Ryan. I was worried about you being all alone at this stage of the pregnancy."

"Oh, he's kept close tabs on me all along."

"I know. I just feel better knowing there's someone with you at night." She heard a smile in his voice. "You're the one who always needed a night-light."

Jo laughed lightly. "I've gotten over that, Dad."

"In some ways, maybe. You're not as tough as you're always trying to make us believe."

"Am too."

"Are not."

"Can you drink Turkish coffee?"

There was a pause, then a rumble of laughter. "It tastes like tobacco."

"Point proven. I'm tougher than you are. So, don't hassle me. How's school?"

"Great. I've got a good bunch of kids this year." He said that every year. "But I have a sub lined up, so I can visit when the baby comes. Ryan says it's all right with him. What do you think?"

"Um...that'd be good." It would be wonderful to see him, and it would be good to have her father's support then. She'd promised herself she wouldn't become maudlin about giving up the baby. But she doubted that anything about it would be easy. She was sure her father knew that.

"You're still...okay about everything?" he asked.

His voice was gentle, almost a whisper. "I mean, I'm sure if this is going to be too hard on you—"

"What?" she asked wryly, interrupting him. "I can decide not to have the baby?"

"Jo..."

"I have no choice, Dad." She sighed, remembering the colorful little strip of crochet. "I made a deal with Cassie. I have to follow through."

"Maybe...another solution will present itself," he said, with an innocence she had to applaud but ignore.

"Yeah." She laughed. "Maybe I'm carrying a hidden twin, and there'll be one for each of us."

NOPE. Nobody here but me.

THERE WAS a moment's silence, and then her father said briskly, "Well. I just wanted to be sure you were well. Keep me posted, and I'll keep in touch. I'll make reservations to be there around the twentieth. That all right?"

"Great." Her due date was September 23.

"Okay. Good night, baby. Let me talk to Ryan before I hang up."

"'Night, Dad." Jo shouted for Ryan to pick up the phone. The moment she heard him on the line, she hung up. She leaned back against the plump pillow, thinking that this deal with Cassie rated right up there with the time her sister had talked her into sneaking into the movie theater, when they were ten and eleven. They'd been chased by a vigilant usher, leapt from the ladies' room window, and ended up in the Dumpster of the pizzeria next door. They'd smelled like the Meaty Pizza Special for days.

Ten minutes later, Ryan peered around the door

again. He stopped there, saw that she'd reclaimed her pillow and gotten back down under the covers on her own.

"Everything all right?"

"Fine. Thank you. See you in the morning."

That remark had been meant to dismiss him. But he remained, somehow invading her space from across the room.

"How do you feel?" he asked.

She sighed. "Like the Meaty Pizza Special," she replied.

He raised an eyebrow. "The what?"

"Never mind. Private joke. Good night." That was less subtle.

Ryan got the point. With a shake of his head, he pulled the door closed behind him.

Chapter Three

Jo saw it all happening again. She was dreaming. Somehow, she knew that. But it was all as clear as the day it had really happened. And she didn't want to go through it again. She didn't.

She could stop it, she knew. All she had to do was resist. But it was getting harder and harder. Every time the dream came back, it took her a little farther.

She saw Cassie and herself, walking along a busy Portland street. They were shopping. Handled bags hung from their fingers, and their near arms were laced in each other's.

Cassie was ecstatic. "It worked!" She was laughing. "Can you believe it worked? We fertilized an egg and put it inside you and you're pregnant with *my* baby!"

Jo felt her own warmth and happiness as though she still inhabited that image in her dream. She heard her own delighted laughter. "I can't believe I can do something you can't. You and your faulty womb. Imagine it taking *three* people to make a baby."

Cassie smiled up at her. "I hope the baby gets all your good qualities while she's inside you. Your generosity, your fearlessness." She sobered suddenly. "I know everything about this isn't easy for you."

"It's a labor of love," Jo replied, her voice emphasizing the significant word in the hackneyed phrase, which had been sincerely spoken. "And when I'm *in* labor—" she laughed "—remind me that I said that."

It was going to happen now. She felt the horror coming, the dark, awful moment. She saw herself with her back turned, looking in a shop window, seeing the reflection of Cassie stepping out into the street as a big, dark car sped toward her. A sudden paralysis of her entire body made it impossible to do anything but watch. She screwed her eyes closed.

Then she felt pain in her leg. And that was strange, because that wasn't the way it had happened. It hadn't been her. It had been Cassie.

Wrenching pain in her right leg woke Jo out of her fitful sleep. Leg cramp. She'd had them before, but this one was a doozy. She tried to struggle out of bed to stand on it, forgetting where she was, and collided with the bedside table. She gasped and fell back again, groaning as the cramp tightened and the bulk of her stomach made it impossible to reach.

The overhead light went on, and Ryan stood there, barechested, in a pair of gray fleece shorts. A corner of her mind considered it amazing that she could awake, in pain, out of an emotional dream, and still notice her brother-in-law's physical assets. He had straight, strong legs, and a chest just meant to inspire security in a woman.

"What?" he asked, his eyes dark, as he hurried to the side of the bed. "Tell me you're not in labor."

"No." She grimaced as the pain tightened even further. "Leg cramp. And I can't stand up." She stretched a hand out toward him, desperate for help.

He caught it and pulled, arching that arm around his

neck as he got her on her feet. He wrapped his other arm around her back.

Jo felt the baby wriggle, adjusting to the change in position. Out of habit, she patted her with her free hand.

Ryan walked her back and forth at the foot of the bed as she worked the cramp out.

"Getting better?" he asked.

"Barely," she replied, still feeling the rocklike tension in her calf. "This one's a killer."

He paced her across the room. "You get them a lot?"

She slanted him a grin. "Part and parcel of the advanced stages of the third trimester."

She didn't realize she was perspiring until he stopped her when they reached the window and wiped his hand across her brow.

He looked solicitous, worried, and for the flash of an instant she felt the precious gift of a man's tender concern.

Ryan felt her warm, damp flesh under his hand and looked into her eyes, eyes made turbulent by distress. She hung from his neck, the bulk of her stomach bumping against him, and he was aware of having to make an effort to remain clinical. His instinct was to touch her in comfort, to soothe her. But this was Jo, who probably wouldn't welcome the gesture. Although she seemed grateful enough for his supporting strength.

As they paced back across the room, the baby moved inside her, and he felt it against him, a completely surprising and mystifying experience. It paralyzed him for an instant.

DADDY? Hi. What are we doing up?

JO SAW something change in his eyes, from serious concern to absorption, fascination. And she knew what it was. Over the months, despite their regular meetings and his presence at her appointments with her obstetrician, neither of them had been sufficiently comfortable with the other for him to touch her to feel the baby's movement.

That morning, when he did it instinctively, out of concern, the baby hadn't moved. Now it was wriggling steadily, apparently impatient with her pacing. And the way he supported her weight, her stomach was wedged against his waist.

She felt sudden sympathy for him. She knew how much he'd loved Cassie, and she was well aware of his grief. Still, she'd known Chelsea would be his the moment she was born, so it'd been hard to think of him as deprived.

It hadn't occurred to her that he was missing out on a large part of the expectant-father experience because he and she weren't intimate.

Without hesitating to think about it, she took the hand with which he held her arm around his neck and placed it high on her stomach, where a tiny fist or elbow waved impatiently. The gentle protrusion moved visibly across her stomach, under his fingertips.

Ryan's dark eyes reacted, then looked into hers with a brilliance that touched her. She smiled, sharing the moment.

"Diantha says that Librans are doers," she said, "and exert impressive physical energy. She predicts she'll like tennis, hiking and aerobics."

He laughed, It was a rich, deep sound in the brightly lit silence of the condo. "I suppose what we just felt was backhand practice."

I WAS JUST TRYING to find my thumb. Ah. There it is. 'Night.

"PROBABLY. I guess since I'm up, she thought she should be too."

They exchanged a smile, and then the atmosphere in the room shifted abruptly. Suddenly the baby wasn't the only element she was aware of in his touch. She felt every one of his fingertips through the cotton over her tender stomach, the warm but ironlike arm that still held her close, the strong, solid thigh that helped support her weight.

Old longing, suppressed in deference to his love for her sister, rose virulently out of the past. It came back, not as memory, but as reality. It pulsed with life, and beat like a little hammer at the base of her throat.

She saw Ryan's expression change, and quickly, guiltily, removed her hand from his.

Ryan felt the small jolt of sexual awareness with total surprise. Jo was his sister-in-law. She didn't like him. She annoyed him. She was reasonably pretty, though she dressed like an example of "What's Out." And she was eight months pregnant.

That was it, he thought, searching his mind for a reason for this niggle of feeling. It was some mistaken impulse from brain to body because of the lateness of the hour and the unique circumstances. He was confusing concern for her, as the host mother of his child, with interest.

And with that thought came a flood of memories of Cassie and everything she'd been to him, of her determination that they find a way to bear a child, of her absolute delirium when the doctor had confirmed that Jo was indeed carrying their baby.

Then guilt overrode everything else he felt. God. It had only been six months. What was wrong with him? He dropped his hand from Jo and stepped back so that he was supporting her only with a forearm clasping hers.

She looked away.

He cleared his throat. "Better?" he asked.

"Yes." The sudden distance he'd placed between them brought reality sharply into focus for Jo. She might feel lust, but Ryan still loved her sister, and probably always would.

She made her way back to the bed without hobbling. The cramp had relaxed somewhat, but an uncomfortable tightness remained. She wished she could reach it to rub it away.

But not every pain could be rubbed away. She'd learned that the hard way, a long time ago.

Ryan stood by to lend support if necessary, but she made it back into bed without help. He drew up the blankets, careful not to touch her, then crossed the room to turn off the light.

He left with a quiet "Good night."

JO CONFRONTED her reflection in the door of the microwave at seven-thirty the following morning. She pointed a butter knife at herself.

"You are not going to live with this theatrically tragic feeling of unrequited love throughout this child's life," she told herself. "He never even *noticed* you, except as an annoyance, and he's only sparing time for you now because you're carrying Chelsea. Your hormones are hysterical, and that instant of sexual awareness last night meant only that you're a jerk. The fat lady sang even before you met him, because he was already in love with Cassie. So *stop* it!''

RYAN PULLED a black-and-gray argyle sweater over his head, and looked out at the view of the river from his bedroom window. He still felt strangely shaken by what he'd felt the night before when helping Jo.

He'd analyzed the incident, if it could even be called that, and he understood what had happened. It was probably only natural that emotion over his first contact with Chelsea should sort of overlap onto the woman whose body sheltered her. That was all it was. No reason to panic. No reason to wallow in guilt. It meant nothing significant.

In fact, this unusual circumstance of having to share space with Jo was going to be a misery, unless both of them relaxed. He had to discuss that with her.

He was surprised to find her in the kitchen and the coffee brewing fragrantly when he walked in. She seemed to be muttering to the microwave, or to herself. She wore a long blue cotton skirt this morning, and a blue-and-black sweater that hung like a tarp to her knees. And those same fat-soled boots.

''Good morning,'' he said, noticing that she'd set two places at the table, with bowls and mugs.

She turned, her eyes wide and...guilty? ''Hi,'' she said. ''I was just...psyching myself up to face the day. You didn't hear me, did you?''

He reached into the drawer for spoons. ''No. Why? Did I miss something enlightening?''

The toast popped, and Jo concocted a story as she put them on a plate and buttered them, glancing at him as she worked. ''Not enlightening. Embarrassing. I always get myself going by telling myself that a dark, handsome stranger's going to walk into the shop to order a double cap and fall madly in love with me."

He smiled as he placed spoons on the table and reached to the counter for the napkin holder. "Anyone in particular?"

"No. A rock star, maybe, or a humanitarian."

He laughed. "A broad choice. But I thought you were a Heron Point flower, adapted to your environment. Would you be happy anywhere else?"

"Oh, I wouldn't leave. He'd abandon his past and stay here to help me with the shop."

"Ah." He took the plate of toast from her and placed it on the table. "You think a rock star or a humanitarian would want to stay here? I mean, would he want to stage a concert in the basement of the Methodist church? Or add on a wing to the one-room Heron Point Library?"

She met his gaze steadily. "For love of me, he'll do anything."

"Of course," Ryan said. "What was I thinking? What are the bowls for?"

She took a plate out of the refrigerator and handed it to him. It held a bright red-and-yellow Jonathan Delicious. Then she reached into the freezer for a paper-wrapped ice-cream bar. "Apple for you, Häagen-Dazs for me." She frowned. "I couldn't find cereal."

"Yes," he said, taking the plate from her with a skeptical frown. "We have to go grocery shopping. But how come I get the apple? You're the one we're supposed to keep healthy."

"My gums bleed easily." She smiled, obviously pleased with herself for having a legitimate reason to get the ice-cream bar. "Another bonus of the third trimester."

The day was overcast and cool, dark gray clouds hanging heavily over the purple gray hills on the Washington side of the river. They merged seamlessly with the dark gray water.

Downtown started quietly on Saturdays, and it was virtually deserted now, except for people coming and going from the bakery down the street.

Ryan pulled up in front of the coffee shop, then walked around the car to help Jo out. She took his hand, reminding herself that the gesture was nothing but a simple courtesy. When he held on to it, she realized he meant only to help her step from the street onto the sidewalk.

When he still didn't let her go, she felt her hand begin to tingle. She reminded herself firmly of this morning's speech into the microwave.

"Can I come in for a minute?" he asked.

She was now certain he had something on his mind, but she couldn't imagine what. Some alteration to their deal, perhaps? But why? He already had every advantage on his side.

"Of course," she said. She unlocked the shop, then locked the door again as the little bell above it tingled cheerfully. Out of habit, she went behind the counter. She noticed the tall ficus at the other end that must be the gift from the regulars, but she didn't move toward it. She had to know what Ryan had on his mind. He sat on one of four stools pulled up to the counter. Six tables-for-two took up the rest of the small space, and beyond the swinging doors in the back was a small meeting room.

Ryan wondered how to approach the subject of their situation for the next month. Then the antique coffee poster of an old Turkish proverb framed on the wall behind Jo's head caught his eye. He'd always liked it. And part of it related significantly to what he wanted to say.

He pointed to it, and Jo turned to look.

"'Coffee should be black as hell,'" he read, "'strong as death, and sweet as love.'"

Jo turned to him, her eyes perplexed, as she waited for him to explain.

"Strong as death, and sweet as love," he said again. He crossed his arms on the counter and focused on her, his expression grave. "You and I have to come to terms with spending the next month together."

She nodded faintly, certain that was true, but wondering precisely what he meant. She couldn't help the little sprig of hope that pushed through the acceptance inside her.

"Death is strong," he said. "We've both lost Cassie, and though you like to think she still exists on the fringes of our lives, affecting them somehow, she's physically gone. And we're left to finish what the three of us started together."

'SCUSE ME. *Make that* four *of us. I'm the star here, you know.*

JO NODDED AGAIN, her heartbeat picking up, her breath stalling somewhere in her throat.

"Love is sweet," he said.

Her heart kicked at her ribs. Or was it the baby? She waited.

"I think we've both put our love for Cassie into Chelsea. And we both want, more than anything, for her to be born healthy and happy."

"Yes."

"This month is critical for the baby, and for us."

Afraid to think or analyze, she simply listened.

"So we have to learn to be friends."

Friends.

"I think we should put aside all our preconceived notions of each other, and try to come to a new understanding. We need to cultivate harmony."

Harmony. The little shoot of hope inside her shriveled and died. She accepted that she'd been foolish to ever think it might flower into... Well.

So here they were again. He wanted to be friends, and she wanted to kill him.

But she, too, wanted harmony for Chelsea. She folded her arms. "Well, I made breakfast. The next move is yours."

His level gaze chided her for being flippant. "I'm not suggesting you do anything for me. But I'd like us to be able to relax around each other, to create a healthy atmosphere. Aren't babies supposed to be able to see and hear by the eighth month?"

I CAN SEE what's going on in here, but all I'm getting from out there is light. I can hear everything, though.

JO REGRETTED teasing about what was obviously an earnest proposal. She nodded. "Librans, particularly, according to Diantha. They love music, flowers and perfume. They like aesthetically pleasing surroundings."

Something softened in his eyes. "Then that should be our mission. A happy home for Chelsea's last four weeks of warm-up. Think we can do it?"

"Of course," she insisted brightly. But she added to herself that it wouldn't be easy.

"All right." He slid off the stool and offered his hand. "Peace."

She took it. "Friends," she agreed. She felt warmth and solidity in his grip, and that calmed her, despite the futility of her hopes and dreams.

She could do this. It would be good for Chelsea.

Ryan was convinced this was a good idea. Her hand felt small and fragile in his, reaffirming his decision to watch over her. Her blue eyes were curiously sad, despite her smile. He didn't understand that, but he was sure there was a lot about his sister-in-law he'd never understand.

"Pick you up at five," he said.

She nodded. "I'll be ready."

He left with a smile and a wave, and Jo turned on the CD player and went about the business of opening up shop, telling herself it was going to work. For a month, she could be his friend. His harmonious friend.

Then she took the change from the safe in the back, put it in the cash register, and found herself looking at the poster above it that Ryan had quoted.

He hadn't related the "black as hell" part of it to anything, she thought. But she did. That was what her future was going to look like, if she had to restrict all the love she felt for Ryan and Chelsea to that of a sister-in-law and an aunt.

Chapter Four

There was no other alternative, Jo decided. She had to ask Ryan for help. He probably wouldn't appreciate being awakened at seven-thirty on a Sunday morning, but her living here was his idea. He had to deal with the consequences.

She took her fleece jacket off the foot of the bed and went to his bedroom door. It was slightly ajar, and she peered around it, expecting to find him fast asleep in the opulent dark blue bedding.

Instead, she was completely surprised to see him seated at the foot of the neatly made bed, in shorts and a T-shirt, tying the laces of a running shoe. He looked up. His rich, dark hair was combed, his eyes were bright, his angular chin was shaved. She felt a pang of guilt over the bed she'd left rumpled, and the hair she'd simply brushed quickly and stuffed under a wool beret.

"Good morning," he said, coming to pull the door open farther. His eyes ran over her in assessment. "Everything all right?"

"Um…yes." She took a step backward, experiencing an unsettling sense of awareness as he pushed aside the door that separated them. He stood braced on long, strong legs. Muscular arms flexed as he studied her, hands on his hips.

"Get over it," she told herself firmly. "He wants you only to be harmonious and friendly." She smiled casually.

"You going for a jog?"

He shook his head. "I could never get into that. I'm going to the gym." His eyes roved her fleece jacket and her hat, then met her eyes with a frown. "Where are you going at this hour?"

"For a walk," she said. Then, bracing a hand against the molding, she held up one foot, on which a walking shoe rested, still untied. "But a curious thing happened during the night. Either the baby's doubled up and doing yoga, or she's grown suddenly. But I can no longer tie my shoes. Would you mind?"

I THINK WE GAINED A POUND. Must have been the ice-cream bar.

RYAN KNELT BEFORE HER without reply and braced her left foot on his bent knee. He tugged on the tongue of her shoe and straightened it before pulling the laces tight and making a neat bow. He pulled the ribbed hem of her gray sweatpants over the tops of her socks. He repeated the process with her right shoe, then rose smoothly to his feet to frown down at her.

"Walk?" he asked. "Outside?"

She looked at him a moment, wondering if this was a trick question. "Right," she replied finally. "Outside. Along the river and around the point. Why? Where do you usually walk?"

"I don't," he replied, going to the bedroom window to look out.

He snapped a cord and pulled the partially opened drapes all the way back. Fabric that matched the bedspread swirled fluidly and settled into neat columns on both sides of the window. Even from across the room, Jo could see the broad expanse of fog that obscured the river and the town that occupied its banks and the hills around it.

"It's cold and damp," he said, reaching to a bedside chair for a gray sweatshirt, which he pulled on. When his head emerged from the neck, he said briskly, "I'll drive you wherever you need to go. No point in your getting chilled."

Jo resisted a surge of annoyance. "Where I need to go," she said patiently, "is for a walk. To get exercise and see what's going on in the world."

He leaned down to snag the handles of a light brown leather gym bag and came toward her. "Not much to see in that fog. What did you want to do? Stop in at church? Get something from the bakery?"

He flipped off the light and turned her toward the hallway with a hand on her shoulder.

She held her smile firmly in place. "I want exercise. But if you want something from the bakery, I'll gladly pick it up on my walk." She preceded him through the living room to the condo's front door.

"Jo," he said, his tone suggesting that he would be reasonable only to a point. And that they were about to reach it. "You'll get chilled. You'll chill the baby. I don't want that."

Jo turned to him, no longer pretending to smile. She gave him the full impact of her most determined glare. "Let's get something straight, Jeffries," she said. "I've moved in here so that you can rest easy about the baby's well-being, because you are the baby's father. But you're not my husband, and you're not going to make me turn this child into some kind of hothouse flower to suit your antiseptic ideas about life.''

One hand on the doorknob, he raised an eyebrow. ''Anti—''

''Antiseptic!'' she repeated, enunciating carefully. ''You are welcome to go exercise indoors, breathing recycled, carbon-sanitized air while you pit your muscles against machinery.'' Aware suddenly that she'd raised her voice in her vehemence, she took pains to quiet it before going on. ''Chelsea and I, on the other hand, will breathe in fresh air, the perfume of flowers and grass and the river, while we get a cardiovascular workout by strolling under the trees, by the ducks, and over the bridge, with a view of the marina.''

Wow! I wish I could see *all that stuff.*

EXASPERATED, Ryan pointed toward the window, and the all-encompassing fog. ''You won't *see* anything.''

She shook her head against his claim. ''Of course I will. You can already see the sun behind it. The fog will be gone by the time I get to town. Now, will you please open the door and let me go?''

He considered her a moment. She was wearing sweat bottoms, one of her many tentlike sweaters, and a gray fleece jacket several inches shorter that didn't come close to closing over her stomach. Her hair was stuffed into a magenta wool beret that deepened the color of her cheeks and contributed to her waiflike appearance.

''No,'' he said, putting his bag down.

She focused on him pugnaciously, her hands on her hips. ''Look, Ryan...''

He couldn't help but grin. She looked like an A-frame on which someone had strung laundry.

"I'll come with you," he said. He pulled a pair of weight-training pants out of the bag and slipped them on.

She rolled her eyes. "Aw, come on, Ryan. We'll just spoil it for each other. You probably stop at every red light, even when there's no traffic, and I stop at every heron and just stare until I've had my fill. You'll just want to raise your heart rate, and I just want to feel the wind in my face." She grew suddenly grave. "You'll probably hyperventilate. You're not used to real air, you know. You might poison your system. You'd better stay with your plan and go to the gym."

He wouldn't give her the satisfaction of seeing him grin. He merely pushed her gently through the door into the carpeted hallway and locked the condo's door behind him.

"If I let you go out alone at this hour," he said, leading the way to the elevator, then turning to look at her, "in that getup, you'll get arrested for vagrancy."

"If I were sensitive to a yuppie's opinion of my appearance," she said, angling her chin, "that might hurt my feelings, because I've outgrown all my cool-weather clothes. But the truth is, it's hard to put your fashion trust in people who wear their labels on the *outside*." She pointed a short-nailed index finger at the label on the back of the neck of his sweatshirt, and then at the one on the waistband of his pants.

A melodic bell rang, and the elevator doors parted. He gestured her inside. "Funny. I offered you my credit card to go shopping, but you glared at me."

The car started down with a little jerk, and she caught

hold of the bar to steady herself. Instinctively braced against the movement, he took hold of her other arm.

She gave him a quick glance that he didn't understand, though he did note that it held mild accusation and vague disdain. Then the doors parted and she stepped off, pulling away from him and starting across the condo's lawn to the trail that led around the point.

The fog was thick and damp against his face, the air cool and pungent. He picked up his pace as she disappeared into the swirling stuff ahead.

He caught up with her and matched her smaller steps on the narrow, sandy trail, which was bordered by seagrass.

"What did that mean?" he asked.

She glanced up at him again, her expression bland. "The label thing? You have to admit it's a faddish—"

He shook his head. "I mean the look. Why were you offended by my offer to pay for your shopping? I know you're a self-sufficient businesswoman, I just thought you might appreciate a little help with the extras."

She jammed her hands into the pockets of her jacket. "You thought," she said quietly, "that you could make me look the way you'd like me to look—at least while I'm carrying your baby."

He kept pace beside her, with no outward appearance of temper, even as he thought that he'd never known a woman who could bring him as quickly to anger as she could.

"And how do I want you to look?" he asked challengingly.

She shrugged a shoulder as she walked on with a sure and steady stride. "I suppose like Cassie always looked. Like a Donna Karan model with a Victoria's Secret alter ego—the perfect combination of efficiency and simmering sex. Well, that isn't me.''

He would have agreed that was certainly true, but the subject seemed to make her strangely vulnerable, despite her honestly clinical discussion of it.

She heaved a sigh and said candidly, ''I was never the pretty one. I was the quirky one, so you'll just have to take me as I am.''

''You're very pretty,'' he told her. ''But since Cassie was pretty, too, you probably learned that being quirky got you more attention.''

She stopped in her tracks for a moment, her eyes wide, accusing—and faintly stricken. Then she started walking again, her gaze focused on the horizon, her pace picking up.

''We're straying from the subject,'' she said. ''I don't want you to buy me clothes.''

''That's fine. But I had no ulterior motive in offering you my credit card. Since we're not emotionally involved, it doesn't matter to me whether you look like a Donna Karan model, a Victoria's Secret alter ego, or a very large bag lady. I just thought you might be getting uncomfortable in your nonmaternity clothes, the closer you get to term.''

''That's thoughtful of you,'' she said, in a tone that betrayed her true sentiments, ''but I'm fine.''

''Good,'' he said coolly.

''Good,'' she replied. He was sure it was just to get the last word.

They followed the trail through the marina. Jave and Tom were at work on the *Mud Hen*. The boat, Jo saw, was an old cabin cruiser built in the early part of the century. It had a lapstrake hull and mahogany trim. Ryan detoured to say hello. Jo wandered after him.

"Hey!" Jave waved a paintbrush at them from the bow as they approached. He wore a torn sweatshirt that bore splotches of the white deck paint on his brush. "Want to come aboard?"

Ryan turned to Jo, who shook her head and smiled. "Thanks," she said to Jave, "but I don't fit on anything smaller than the *Queen Mary*. How's it going?"

At the same moment she asked, Tom surfaced from below decks, his clothes covered in the same paint Jave sported, wearing a painter's cap backward. Loud rock music came from below, and Tom gyrated outrageously to the sound as he brought Jave a canned soft drink.

Jo and Ryan exchanged amused glances. Tom had been a regular customer of Coffee Country since Jo had opened the shop, and he was still a fireman. Since the fire a year ago that had killed his friend and put him in the hospital, she'd empathized with his struggle to put the past behind him and start over as a carpenter and general craftsman.

Jave rolled his eyes. "I'd have had this boat seaworthy a week ago," he said, "if I'd been working by myself."

"Hi!" Tom's dance stopped abruptly when he noticed them, and he waved over the side. "Come on up. We've got mineral water and iced tea, too."

Ryan shook his head. "Thanks. We're just out for a walk. Saw Jave working and thought we'd say hi."

"We'll take you on a harbor tour when we get her going," Jave said. "Pretty soon." He inclined his head toward Tom. "Depends on how much help I get from Little Brother."

"Make your jokes," Tom said, with an air of superiority. "When it comes time to find the fish, you'll be begging for my help."

Jave frowned ruefully at Ryan. "Unfortunately, that's true."

Ryan shook his head. "Should have left the hole in the deck, so they could jump in on their own. Take care."

"Don't you think that's strange?" Jo asked under her breath as they walked back along the dock to the road. A water hose had been stretched across the planks, and Ryan took Jo's elbow to help her over it. "About Nancy Malone and Jave, I mean."

The trail now took a subtle but definite incline, and Jo, distracted by her thoughts, looped an arm through Ryan's for support. He noticed, but pretended not to.

"Strange in what way?" he asked.

"Well, Nancy's married," Jo said. "When we were at the hospital, the staff in OB was talking about how she's going to be the model mother for the opening festivities for the new birthing rooms."

Riverview Hospital's redesigned OB facility was a source of excitement in Heron Point. It included birthing rooms in which the expectant father, and whatever other family members and friends the mother approved, could remain with her during labor and birth. They were decorated like bedrooms out of *Better Homes and Gardens.*

The austere and lonely hospital room was a thing of the past—at least in OB.

He didn't understand the problem. "And?"

"And," she said, as though it ought to be obvious to him, "Jave is her Lamaze coach. That doesn't seem strange to you?"

"No," he replied.

"Why not?" she asked, obviously perplexed. "She's married, and her husband's friend is her Lamaze coach?

Come on. Women alone in their pregnancy usually choose another woman as their coach. Like Karma Endicott, the accountant, who comes with that girl from your bank.''

''Ah.'' He did, at least, know the young woman who worked at his bank. ''Roberta Dawson.''

''Right. You don't see her there with another man. Yet Nancy Malone comes with Jave.''

''If he's her husband's friend, chances are he's her friend, too.''

''But…'' She rubbed her swollen stomach. ''Delivery is an intimate thing.''

He nodded. ''And a personal one. And no time for prudery. If she's comfortable with him, that's what counts. So it shouldn't matter to anyone else.''

She angled him a rueful glance. ''Are you telling me to mind my business?''

He put a theatrical hand to his heart. ''Heaven forfend! I just don't think you should lose any sleep over it, if Nancy and Jave are comfortable with it.''

They'd crested the hill that led to town and turned onto paved sidewalk. Jo was apparently unaware that she still held his arm. He continued to pretend not to notice, thinking that it was curiously pleasant. He missed a lot of big, important intimacies since Cassie's death, but he missed many of the small things, too. Like the easy trust of her hand in his arm.

He wasn't mistaking Jo for Cassie, he knew, but he liked the feeling anyway. He recognized it as another small step toward healing. He knew he would never heal completely; he and Cassie had loved each other too much. But it was important for their baby that he make life's demanding adjustments.

He heaved a sigh as they walked on.

Jo looked up at him in mock concern. "I heard that," she said teasingly. "Getting winded? Doesn't your treadmill at the gym incline this steeply? Want to find a bench, so you can sit down and catch your breath?"

"Who," he asked, with a pointed glance at her hand, clutching his arm, "is holding on to whom?"

She studied it a moment in surprise, then withdrew it and put it in her pocket. "I was climbing for two," she said briskly. "But it's downhill from here. Didn't I tell you the sun would be out before we got to town?"

She pointed to the horizon formed by the hilltops of Washington, across the river, meeting a bright blue sky. The fog was now simply a gauzy ribbon clinging to the foothills. "You'd have missed this view at the gym."

"True." He had to concede that. In the six years he'd lived in Heron Point, he'd never seen it from this particular angle. He'd driven this way in the car, but then his attention had been focused on the road, watching for all the children and pets that lived in this old neighborhood and ran across without checking the traffic.

It was beautiful. Two lines of turn-of-the-century homes meandered down the hill toward the river in colorful splendor. Some were newly repainted, others charmingly faded, but all were fronted by the rich green grass always in evidence in rainy Oregon, even in early fall.

As they passed a yellow-and-white house, a Golden Retriever ran from the porch steps to the chain-link fence, tail wagging as she barked excitedly at Jo.

"Hi, Buttercup," Jo said, reaching over the fence so that she could scratch between the dog's ears. The bulk of the baby made the movement difficult, but Buttercup stood on her hind legs accommodatingly and whined in ecstasy at the attention. "This is Ryan. Ryan, meet Buttercup, former contender for field trials champion in Oregon, but now just a happy house dog.''

MAMA CASS says she was going to get me a puppy when I was born. Can we have one? Huh?

RYAN REACHED OVER the fence to stroke the dog, who butted her nose trustingly against his hand, and greeted his ministrations with the same whining delirium.

"Buttercup told you all this?" he asked Jo with a grin.

Jo laughed lightly. "Her master is a police officer who comes in for coffee every morning before his shift."

Ryan gave the dog a final pat, and they moved on. Buttercup followed them to the very edge of the fence, barking a protest at their departure.

"So, you're kind of like a bartender," he suggested, stopping at the curb as a late-model station wagon passed, filled with children wearing their Sunday best. "Listening to personal stories, probably giving advice?"

The curb was high, and he offered her his hand for balance as she stepped down.

"I'm a good listener," she said, "but I leave the advice to Diantha. At least she has astrology to back it up. Bill! Hi!"

They'd reached the other side of the street, and Ryan looked for the man or boy responsible for her greeting, but saw no one. Then he noticed a black tuxedo cat, sporting white markings that resembled a mustache and a bow tie. He was young, and approached Jo with a playful, stiff-legged prance.

"Hi, baby!" she said, trying to bend. Remembering

suddenly that she couldn't, she turned to Ryan with a smile of appeal. "Would you pet him for me? But don't touch his tail—he doesn't like that."

With a long-suffering groan, Ryan squatted down to stroke the cat, who studied him suspiciously for a moment, then rubbed obligingly against his knee.

A calico kitten scampered over from across the street and bumped her way in between the tuxedo and Ryan's hand.

A KITTEN WOULD BE OKAY. Could we have a kitten?

"CAMOUFLAGE!" Jo exclaimed. "How're you doing?" To Ryan, she added, "You can rub her anywhere. She loves attention. But watch yourself. She plays like a predator."

She'd just spoken the words when the purring kitten rolled onto her back, grabbed Ryan's hand in her front paws and ripped at it with her back feet.

Ryan tried to withdraw his hand with a spirited oath, and lifted it waist-high, only to find the kitten still attached, still attacking. Jo gently extricated Camouflage, who purred, then whopped her on the nose with a paw. Jo laughed and placed the kitten on the nearby gatepost.

Ryan studied the angry red scratches on his hand. "You didn't tell me we'd be walking through Wildlife Safari," he said, taking her elbow to pull her along. "How many more species will we be encountering before we get to town?"

She took his hand in hers and examined it. He experienced an instant's disassociation from the world around him. Her touch filled the moment—the softness of her fingertip, the light rasp of her index fingernail as she traced a scratch, the bump of her shoulder against his upper arm as she leaned close to him in her inspection.

"You'll live," she said finally, dropping his hand.

The magnified moment dissolved, and he put it out of his mind, striving for normalcy. She seemed completely unaffected. "Sure, but I'll be scarred," he said. "I suppose their masters are also customers of yours?"

"No, I just met them on my walk. Aren't they great?"

"And they told you their names?"

She gave him the scolding look the question deserved. "They wear tags. Anyway, I can't have pets in my apartment, and I wouldn't have one downtown, anyway. It's too dangerous. So I have to get my pet fix around here." She asked curiously, "Have you ever had a pet?"

He shook his head. "My parents both worked and didn't think it was fair to leave one alone. Then Cassie and I were in the same situation. And, frankly, I don't like the idea of having to set my schedule around a pet that has to be fed and let out, requiring me to be home at definite intervals, or preventing me from taking trips."

Jo stopped in her tracks and blinked up at him. "Ryan," she said. "That's precisely what the baby will do to your life."

They'd reached the edge of the downtown area, where the blocks of houses were replaced by small shops and other places of business. Bright sunlight bounced off store windows and the windshields of cars.

"Really," he said, with a dry glance at her, as they stopped at the traffic light at Heron Point's main intersection. "I thought I could just put her in my briefcase and take her to work with me. Or maybe drop her off at Coffee Country, and you could put her on a shelf till I get off.''

''She can hear everything, you know,'' she said in a scolding tone as the light changed to green. ''Sarcasm is not a nice thing to teach her.''

Ryan stepped off the curb. ''Neither is the notion that her father's a thoughtless jerk who hasn't made any plans for her care.''

''Have you?'' she asked in surprise.

He'd taken several steps across the street, and when he looked back and saw that she wasn't following, he went back to catch her hand and pull her after him. ''Of course I have. I told you I was going to call Mrs. Bennett about moving in when you go back to work.''

Mrs. Who? I don't think I'll like that. I want to go to work with Mama Jo. Mama, tell him.

JO TRAILED after him moodily, remembering that he had mentioned talking to Helen Bennett. She'd built an impressive reputation around town as an infant nanny. At sixty-two, she preferred small babies to toddlers that had to be chased and corralled.

It shouldn't surprise her that he'd actually done it. He was very responsible and reliable, especially where the baby was concerned. She simply found it unsettling that he'd arranged circumstances so that she would eventually be unnecessary—at least where Chelsea's daily care was concerned.

On the opposite side of the street, he stopped and looked down into her forlorn expression. ''You're the one,'' he reminded her in mild concern, ''who suggested Mrs. Bennett.''

''I know.'' She drew a deep breath and shook off the

pall of depression. She forced a smile. "That'll be perfect. Can you buy me a cup of tea and a brioche?"

Ryan studied the melancholy look in her eyes an extra moment, and then, since she'd initiated an abrupt change of subject, let the matter drop. "Ah...sure." He looked up the deserted street where the bakery was, and saw that it, like most of the shops downtown, was closed. "But where?"

"The bakery at the supermarket has them, and a table where we can sit."

They talked about nothing significant while they ate in the market, which was also deserted at this hour of a Sunday morning. Warm, sweet smells surrounded them, enclosing them in a cozy atmosphere directly at odds with how they felt in each other's company.

Ryan watched as Jo talked. She'd pulled off her beret, and a riot of curly blond hair fell to her shoulders and down her back, frizzy and rumpled and somehow completely captivating.

He'd never noticed before that the millions of tiny corkscrew curls appeared gilded where they caught the light, and made her look like something from a Botticelli painting. His eyes wandered over it, but he still caught every subtle little nuance in her voice.

She was telling him about a fundamentalist customer who'd gotten into an argument with Diantha, and though she spoke animatedly, he could hear that her enthusiasm was forced and fraudulent. There was an underlying sigh in her tone.

Jo knew she was babbling, but he was watching her with that casual attention that always made her feel he saw and understood more than he let on. And that he would eventually know more about her than she knew herself.

And there was so much she had to keep from him.

Even as that thought formed, a flush filled her cheeks and rose to her hairline. She cursed the honest nature that made it so difficult to hide what she felt.

She pulled at the neckline of her sweater and fanned herself with a napkin. "What was that you said about getting chilled?" she asked, deciding that if he was wondering what had brought on that rush of color the better part of valor would be to distract him by putting him on the defensive. "We'd both be more comfortable now in bathing suits." Then, glancing down at her rotund form, she added with a laugh, "Well, not necessarily glamorous, but more comfortable."

Ryan wondered about the blush. He couldn't imagine a reason for it, unless she truly was overheated. But then, he'd never understood her anyway, and he doubted that he ever would.

He was also confused by his feelings for her. At the moment, he was looking at her with new interest. In the somewhat normal sweater she wore, and with her hair tumbled but simply flowing free, and not in one of the bizarre styles she usually preferred, she was attractive. The very notion robbed him of logic.

He'd always considered her everything he stood against—disorderly, irreverent, liberal. But he seemed strangely unaware of those facts at the moment. He saw only that her cheeks were pink, her eyes were bright, her hair was wildly beautiful—and she was carrying his baby.

For an instant, the convoluted method of the baby's conception was forgotten, and he felt a very elemental attachment to the woman who was pregnant with his child.

That mellow mood lasted until Ryan realized he and

Jo were staring at each other—and that her blush had deepened. He downed his coffee.

"Ready?" he asked, slapping their empty paper cups together and tossing them at the wastebasket.

"Ah...yes." She studied him for one uncertain moment, then stood awkwardly, draping her fleece jacket over her arm. The air was charged, she noted, and she didn't know why. So she found stability in the antagonism that was their conversational currency.

"The next leg of our journey is uphill, you know," she warned him, gathering up their napkins and dropping them in the basket. "It's even harder on a full stomach. You want to hop a cab, and I'll meet you at the condo?"

Ryan felt himself relax. It was strange, he thought, that fighting with her was comfortable.

"Get real," he said. "I could carry you back and not even raise my heart rate."

"Ha!" She snorted. "I'd like to see *that* happen." Then she stopped his progress toward the door with a tug on the sleeve of his sweatshirt. "Can you buy a bag of day-old bread?"

He frowned. "Why?"

"So we can feed the sea gulls near the cannery."

He withdrew a fistful of change and held it open to her. "God. You mean there's more to Jo's Wild Kingdom?"

She shook her head at him as she took three quarters. "You're supposed to be in harmony with your surroundings, Jeffries."

"Yeah, well, usually my surroundings involve receipting machines and bank vaults. They don't require petting and feeding."

She asked the clerk for a bag of dried bread, then

turned back to him while she waited. "You've got to remember that machinery isn't life, Ryan. Life is people, nature." She sighed deeply and pretended that she bore the weight of a great burden. "I have *so* much to teach you, in such a short time."

Chapter Five

"Miss Arceneau! Josanne!"

Jo stopped in the middle of the hospital corridor and turned to find a tall young woman chasing her down. She carried a clipboard and was waving excitedly. Jo had seen her around the hospital on her regular visits, and assumed from her nonuniform garb that she was some sort of administrative personnel. She waited with a combination of interest and perplexity for the woman to reach her.

"Whew!" the woman exclaimed as she came to an awkward stop in front of Jo. She was tall and angularly built, dressed in a green cotton dress with too much lace. Her long hair was lank and silver-blond, though apparently some attempt had been made to curl it, and she wore little makeup. Clear-framed, frumpy glasses rested on a small, well-shaped nose. But she had a smile that lit her eyes and warmed Jo with its sincerity. "I'm Amy Brown, public relations director for the hospital. Thanks for waiting for me." She made a production of drawing a deep breath. "Jogging just isn't my thing, and as you can see, I'm not built for speed. May I have a few minutes of your time?"

"Of course." Jo allowed herself to be led to a small

office off the reception area at the back of the hospital. Ryan hadn't been able to accompany her to her appointment this morning, but had sent his assistant to drive her. She'd been headed for the pay phone to call for her ride back when Amy Brown intercepted her.

"Would you like some tea?" Amy asked. "Cocoa?"

Jo shook her head. "No, thank you."

Amy nodded, pointed Jo to a chair and took the one behind a small, orderly desk. "Then I'll get right to it. I'm sure you're aware of the hospital's new birthing rooms. We had something about it in the *Herald* just the other day."

Jo nodded. "Yes. I'm looking forward to using one."

Amy sat a little straighter, her eyes beaming. "That's precisely what I want to talk to you about. In order to 'launch' our birthing rooms, so to speak, we've planned to shower with gifts the first mother to use one of our rooms. We've gotten the merchants involved, and they've donated the most remarkable prizes for the first baby born there."

Jo nodded. "That was in the article. And Nancy Malone's your model mother, isn't she? She's in my Lamaze class."

Amy shook her head, her expression indulgently accepting. "She isn't anymore—our model mother, I mean. She's…abdicated."

Jo tried not to look too interested. She'd known there was something strange going on there. "Why," she asked, "would she do that?"

Amy thought about her reply for a moment, obviously picking and choosing her words carefully. "Well…it seems we sort of…were confused by her records, and presumed she was married."

Jo couldn't hide the interest now. "Isn't she?"

Amy shook her head. "She's divorced. That was no problem for us, of course. We'd have still been delighted to use her, but she... Well, it's all very complicated. But the upshot is, we need a new model mother." She smiled at Jo. "Would you consider taking on the role? You're due just about the same time Nancy is."

Jo couldn't decide which issue caught her interest more strongly—that Nancy Malone wasn't married and was therefore entitled to be seen all over town with Jave Nicholas, or that Amy Brown wanted *her* to assume the position of model mother.

She obviously had to explain a few things—and then she wanted a few things explained to her.

"I'm flattered, of course," Jo said, "but you're probably not aware that my circumstances are rather unique."

"I know you run Coffee Country, and that you're single," Amy said. "A completely outfitted nursery would be a real boost to your budget, wouldn't it?"

"It would," Jo answered, "if the baby were mine."

Amy's eyes widened. Then she leaned back in her chair, looking very much as though she required an explanation but, considering her quest for someone to take Nancy's place, didn't particularly want to hear it. She seemed to suspect it would rob her of her candidate.

Jo explained about Chelsea's unorthodox conception, then Cassie's accident. "My sister and brother-in-law had made all their plans for the nursery when we learned the pregnancy had taken," she said. "Then, when Cassie died, Ryan finished and furnished it down to the last detail." She smiled apologetically at Amy. "I'm sorry, I thought everyone in town knew the situation. And there isn't a thing we need."

Amy nodded ruefully. "I just moved to Heron Point

a couple of months ago. I guess I should have talked to Dr. Mac before approaching you, but I noticed you when you came into Emergency last week, and when Nancy withdrew, I thought you'd be perfect.'' She sighed, raising her hands in a gesture of defeat. ''I'm sorry I wasted your time. I hope I didn't…upset you, or anything.''

Jo pushed herself laboriously to her feet. ''Of course not. I'm sure you'll find another candidate. In fact,'' she added with sudden enthusiasm, ''my Lamaze class has several other couples, and a single woman who—''

Amy shook her head. ''I checked. The other couples are going to Portland for their deliveries, and Karma Endicott, the single woman, isn't due until the end of October.''

Jo smiled sympathetically. ''If you can't find another model mother, maybe you'll just have to delay the opening a month.''

Amy walked Jo to the door. ''Thanks. I was so sure this was a great idea, and that mothers would be pushing each other out of the way to get all the gifts for their babies.'' She shook her head, obviously mystified. ''But everyone's turning me down instead. Go figure the American consumer. Where are you parked? I'll walk you—''

They'd just stepped out into the hall when their conversation was interrupted by a man's impatient bellow.

''Josanne! God! You scared me to death. What are you doing in the PR office? Don't you ever take a direct route anywhere? You were supposed to call the bank when you were finished, so someone could pick you up. You don't call. So we call Dr. McNamara and he says you left the office an hour ago.''

Ryan, the sides of his conservative gray suit jacket

thrown back and braced there by the hands on his hips, frowned down at Jo, obviously displeased.

She resisted an annoyed reply, deciding he was making more than enough noise for a hospital corridor all by himself. Instead, she said politely, "Amy, I'd like you to meet my brother-in-law, Ryan Jeffries. Ryan, this is Amy Brown, the hospital's PR director."

Ryan dropped his annoyed-lordship posture and shook Amy's hand.

"I apologize," he said, with a glance at Jo that made it clear the apology did not extend to her. "When I couldn't find Jo, I got a little nervous. Particularly after her fall the other day. I thought—"

Amy smiled at him and shook her head. "I should apologize to you. I'm the one who stopped Jo on her way out and delayed her. So please don't shout at her. It was all my fault."

Ryan replied politely, but did not appear entirely appeased.

A short, square nurse with the air of a drill sergeant marched past. "Call Tom Nicholas," she said, without pausing in her steps. "And next time you leave your office unattended, take your beeper, and other people won't have to take your messages." She gave a curt nod in Ryan's direction. "Mr. Jeffries."

Ryan nodded back. "Nurse Beacham."

"Tom Nich—" Amy repeated, a shamelessly thrilled note in her voice. Color filled her cheeks, and she looked suddenly befuddled. She turned one way, and then the other, took a step, collided with her office door, then seemed to remember her guests and turned back again.

"Thank you for giving me your time, Miss Arceneau," she said to Jo, then added to Ryan, "And forgive me for frightening you." Her expression of professional concern was replaced suddenly by a glowing smile as she turned and stepped into her office and closed the door firmly behind her.

Jo looked up at Ryan, forgetting his irritation for a moment. "Tom Nicholas? Are they—?" She held up two crossed fingers, the gesture suggesting a relationship.

Ryan interrupted her. "I don't want to talk about Tom Nicholas," he said, taking hold of her arm and drawing her with him down the corridor. "I want to talk about why it never occurred to you to call, if you knew you were going to be late."

"Ryan," she said patiently, "I was heading for the phone when Amy stopped me." She explained briefly about the model mother-birthing room situation and Amy's offer of the position to her. "Of course, I had to refuse."

"And that took an hour?"

"No, it took about ten minutes. But I—"

"Then where the hell were you?"

She stopped at the glass doors to the outside to growl at him exasperatedly. "I spent a little time at the nursery window, all right? When the birthing rooms are in use, babies will stay with their mothers, and we oglers will have nothing more to look at. Anyway, I got to looking at all those pretty babies and thinking that in just under three weeks, ours will be—" She hesitated, then corrected herself. "I mean, *yours* will be here. It was a startling notion, so I kept staring and thinking about it. I guess I was longer than I realized."

Mama Cass says I'm cuter than any of them. And, Daddy? She says stop shouting.

RYAN'S TAUT FEATURES softened. He shifted his weight, then assumed that displeased-lordship stance again, though far less convincingly.

"Okay," he said quietly. "But I wish you'd remember that we're in this together, and that while you're carrying the baby and feeling great and taking walks in the fog and dawdling at your doctor's appointment, I'm watching everything from a worrisome distance. All I know is that you seem awfully small to be carrying this burden, that I'm worried every moment that something could go wrong with you or with the baby, and when you take off in your independent way I go mildly crazy."

That admission was a major concession to her, Jo knew. Far more vulnerability than she'd ever thought he'd admit. It put them on somewhat equal footing—a status she'd never imagined he'd accord her, given that the baby was half Cassie's, and she, Jo, was only there because of the unusual circumstances.

She smiled fractionally. "Mildly?" she asked, her tone challenging.

He let a smile slip. "Okay, wildly. So, have a heart, would you? Come on. I'll take you to lunch before I take you back to work."

"I'd love that. Can we go to Chez Pasta?"

"Wherever you like."

"Can we stop at Dairy Queen after for fat-free yogurt?"

"If you'd like that."

"Will you buy me the Jeep Cherokee I've been admiring at Lum's Auto Center?"

He had helped her into his red Volvo, and walked around to slip in behind the wheel. He cast her a cautionary glance. "You're pushing it, Jo."

She buckled her seat belt and laughed wickedly. "Your guilt reflex was working so well, I thought I'd go for it. You'll never guess what I learned from Amy."

He turned the key in the ignition and headed for the exit to the road. "What?"

"Nancy Malone isn't married, she's divorced. So that's why Jave Nicholas is her Lamaze coach."

He considered that a moment, then shook his head. "That doesn't necessarily follow."

"Sure it does. They must have a relationship. I bet that's why she gave up the model mother position. Because she wanted him more than she wanted the gifts."

Ryan turned onto the road, heading in the direction of Chez Pasta. "I think you're employing creative reasoning."

She shook her head pityingly. "It's all so obvious. But you're so left-brained. You don't believe anything that isn't substantiated by columns of figures or an audit. Want to make a small wager?"

He pulled up at a red light, and turned to look at her. She saw laughter in his eyes, and was pleased by it. "On what terms?" he asked.

"I'll bet you Nancy and Jave are married by the time she has her baby. If I win, you can buy me a new winter jacket. If *you* win…what do you want?"

He rested the inside of his wrist against the top of the steering wheel and thought.

"Remember my budget," she put in.

He nodded. "I'd rather go for some kind of service, anyway, so that you'd have to remember every time you did it that I was right and you were wrong."

"You're a pillar of nobility."

"I try." The light turned green, and he accelerated. "How about," he asked, giving her a quick, smug glance, "latte delivered to me at the bank every afternoon for a month?"

"But…you'd have to wait awhile for it," she pointed out seriously. "I mean, we won't know until her baby's born, and by then Chelsea will be, too, and I'll be home."

Ryan glanced at her again as they sped along the road that paralleled the river. "No problem," he said. "I can wait until you go back to work. As long as I collect."

When she went back to work, she thought, Mrs. Bennett would take over Chelsea's care, and she'd be relegated to aunt status.

"Yeah," she said quickly. "Right." She fidgeted and looked out the window.

"What is it?" he asked, with another worried look in her direction. "Don't tell me you're concerned that *I'm* getting the good end of the deal?"

She warned herself sternly to get it together. She laughed and backhanded his upper arm. "Of course not. Your end of the deal is already forfeit, anyway. I'm sure of it. They're in love. They'll be married by the time that baby comes. If I have dessert," she asked, "do I have to give up yogurt at the Dairy Queen?"

"BREATHE IN…" Serena Borders, the Lamaze-certified trainer, directed as she walked among the couples seated among pillows on the carpeted floor. "Then breathe out, concentrating on expelling every negative thought, every concern, every idea clamoring for your attention. Breathe out and relax. Empty your mind. Clear even your dreams away."

Jo lay in the spoon position, a pillow between her knees, trying to concentrate on the instructions. But Ryan, spooned behind her, was fidgeting.

She propped herself up on an elbow and turned to whisper to him while Serena paused to give Karma Endicott instruction. "What's the matter?"

"They're faulty directions," Ryan complained, though he held his position. "How can you listen to instructions and clear your mind? Your mind has to be busy to concentrate on what she's saying. And you have to think about breathing."

"No, you don't. It's instinctive."

He propped himself up on his elbow, too, to dispute that. "Well, normally it is, but when someone tells you how you should be doing it, then you have to think about it to do it right. So, you can't."

"Jeez, Jeffries," Jo whispered. "You make everything so hard. Just breathe and go with it. I can't believe emptying *your* mind would be such a big deal. And this is our third class. You should be into this by now." She turned and resumed her position.

He stared moodily at the back of her head. Her mass of curls was caught loosely at the nape of her neck, then seemed to explode from the tie like a spurt of gold rain.

He closed his eyes. He was tired of noticing her hair. But then he felt tired of everything today. He was tired of people with no money and no means of acquiring any wanting to borrow from the bank. He was tired of employees needing time off and forgetting to schedule it ahead of time. He was tired of careless errors and of slipshod double checks that missed them.

He pushed himself to a sitting position at the teacher's instruction and positioned himself behind Jo. He drew a breath, wishing the class was over and they could go home. He would retire to his room with a brandy and the *Wall Street Journal* and try to forget for a moment that he had no idea what the hell was happening to his life.

Eight months ago, it had stretched before him like a ribbon of promise—good position with the bank, beautiful, loving wife, baby on the way, however unconventionally.

Even after Cassie's death, he'd known precisely what he had to do—protect the baby they'd made together, by watching over Jo until Chelsea was born. Then he would love Chelsea and see that she had everything she wanted.

It had been so clear.

But he seemed to be losing that comfort level lately. The closer the time came to his baby's delivery, the less secure he felt about what had once seemed so simple.

He was going to be a father. A single father. And his child was a girl. He'd have Mrs. Bennett for a while, and Jo would be around to help, but ninety-nine percent of the responsibility for her happiness, her health, her sense of security, eventually even her image of herself as a woman—would be his. That was a daunting thought.

And then there was Jo. Their relationship was undergoing a subtle change. He couldn't quite define it, or even understand it in the most basic sense. He just knew it was making him nervous.

He'd never noticed her much before, except as an annoyance. Now he found himself aware of her most of the time. He guessed it was because she'd moved in with him. Proximity was bound to make them more conscious of each other.

But he had an unsettling feeling it was more than that. He didn't know what, and he wasn't sure why, and all he wanted to do was put it out of his mind. But they were in a Lamaze class, with its touchy-feely approach to delivery.

He understood its value. He'd even been the one to insist they take the class when Jo was reluctant—probably for the same reasons he was now. But today, particularly, it was making his life difficult.

"All right," Serena said. "Let's work on our full body massage."

Jo assumed the gently stretched position in a brisk and clinical manner, and prayed for the strength to hold herself aloof throughout the exercise. She could do it. All she had to do was concentrate.

Ryan was right, she thought as he placed a hand on her head according to Serena's directions. It was difficult to clear one's mind and concentrate at the same time.

Although, in an unexpected sense, it seemed to be working. As his hands moved from her head to her shoulders, she wasn't thinking, she was simply feeling.

His hands were long-fingered, and broad from little finger to thumb, and left a wide swath of sensation from the tip of her shoulder to the middle of her back. A tingle rippled along under her skin in the path of his fingertips, and she had to concentrate to prevent herself from fidgeting. Concentration prevented relaxation, but she stopped herself from moving by pretending she was stone. The trick served her purpose, but not Serena's.

"Jo Arceneau!" the trainer exclaimed, for all to hear. "You're like concrete!" But instead of being displeased, the woman turned to Ryan with a satisfied smile. "Coach," she said, "this is excellent training for you. Tensing up will be the mother's instinctive reaction to pain and fear and doubt. It's *your* job to remind her to relax, and to apply your hands to her body in a way that'll make her notice your touch over her own pain. Now, what have I taught you?''

Jo's body turned from stone to putty as Ryan dutifully proved that he'd paid attention. ''I apply sufficient pressure,'' he said, his thumbs on her spinal column, his fingertips rayed out toward her sides as he rubbed in a slow downward motion, ''to help her relax, always listening for her reaction. If she's distracted, I ask where she wants to be massaged, and let her dictate how lightly or how firmly.''

He reached the back of her waist, then his thumbs dipped down to the small of her back. ''I'm careful here, because this might relieve her pain, or cause it. So I listen for feedback.''

OH, right there, Daddy. Down. Over. A little to the right. Ahh...

SERENA LAUGHED. ''And sometimes you'll get that very explosively, if you've touched an area that causes more pain. But just remember that every cell in her being is at a heightened pitch, and she's just reacting at that level. So what must you do?''

Ryan stroked his way up her back again with firm but gentle confidence. ''I remain calm, keep my voice down, and try to fulfill her needs, whatever they are.''

''Excellent!'' Serena patted his shoulder. ''You're so good, I might lend you out to other mothers with less competent coaches.''

She walked away, and Ryan dropped his hands from Jo, surprised to find them less than steady. His heartbeat was erratic, too, and his breathing shallow. His brain, far from relaxed, was thinking how soft Jo felt for a woman who was generally angular and athletic. It was probably the pregnancy.

The moment Ryan's hands fell away from her, Jo felt the absence of his touch, as though a lack could be a tangible thing. Tension began to build in her again, and with it came the old guilt and confusion.

He didn't want to be doing this, she knew that. Oh, he wanted to study the Lamaze method for the sake of his baby's safety and ease of delivery, but he didn't want to have to coach her. He was doing it because he had to.

She had to remember that. No matter how comforting his touch, how exciting and promising, any further effects of it were entirely in her imagination.

Jo glanced around the room as Serena moved among her students, and saw Nancy Malone and Jave Nicholas laughing together and gazing into each other's eyes with a look of love that was unmistakable. She remembered her wager with Ryan. She was going to win that jacket.

Karma Endicott, the attractive accountant who stopped in regularly for house-blend tea but was always too busy to chat, was practicing breathing exercises with stern-faced concentration.

Easy for *her* to concentrate, Jo thought dryly. She had another woman as a coach, not a man with strong, distracting hands.

Groaning at her own foolishness, Jo struggled to her knees as Serena declared the class over. Ryan offered her his hands to help her to her feet, but she couldn't help staring at them for a moment, thinking how ironic it was. Those hands represented everything she wanted—except permanence. She had to keep reminding herself that she had only until the time Chelsea was born, and she had to be satisfied with that.

She placed her hands in his and glanced up at him as he smoothly pulled her upright. His dark eyes were unfocused, and his thoughts clearly miles away. Automatically he helped Jo with the old fleece jacket, and picked up their pillows and stacked them in the corner with the others.

"Hi, Mr. Jeffries," Roberta Dawson said. She was Karma Endicott's coach, and worked at the bank. "You were quite a star tonight. Can we line you up to help Karma if I lose my nerve?"

Ryan smiled politely. "No, thanks. I think I'll be good for one time only. And the closer it gets, the less sure I am about it."

Roberta agreed. "Me too. It seemed so easy—and so far away—at first. Now I'm tempted to be out of town when Karma's due."

Ryan nodded. "I know the feeling."

Jave tossed his and Nancy's pillows onto the pile. "You're both experiencing prenatal jitters. They have a sound medical basis. Relax, and everything will be fine."

"Ha!" Roberta said, with a teasingly scornful look at Jave. "Doctors! They think they know everything about medicine. This is terror, pure and simple." Then she winked. "See you next week. See you tomorrow, Mr. Jeffries."

"Ryan," Jave said, "I'd like to see you tomorrow, too. Do you have a small block of time in the afternoon?"

Ryan noted that Jave looked beyond him as he spoke, to Nancy, who was in earnest conversation with Serena. He was smiling unconsciously, his usually steady expression disgustingly besotted. Ryan saw his chances of winning the bet slip considerably.

"Sure," he replied. "I'm back from lunch at two o'clock. Would that work for you?"

"Great. My whole afternoon's clear."

Ryan was quiet on the drive home, but Jo thought little about it. In the two weeks she'd lived with him, she'd learned he wasn't one to make small talk comfortably.

But by the time they stepped off the elevator in the condo's hallway, she knew he was experiencing more than a simple unwillingness to chatter. He seemed angry.

He reached into his pants pockets for his keys. Jo saw his frown deepen as he reached into his other pants pocket, then patted the pockets of his jacket.

"Would you open the door, please?" he asked, with stiff courtesy. "I don't seem to have my keys."

Jo sensed trouble. "I'm sorry," she said. "I don't have my keys with me. Maybe you—"

"What do you mean, you don't have them with you?" he demanded, still furiously patting pockets.

She wasn't in the mood for this. She didn't know what his problem was, but her back hurt, her head hurt, and her libido was in a confused and sorry state. All she wanted was to go to bed and watch "Murphy Brown" reruns.

"I mean," she said, her patience strained, "that I do not have my key with me. I don't know how to clarify that any further."

"I had two made for you," he reminded crossly.

She shifted her weight. So did the baby. "I know. But one's at the shop, and the other's in my tote bag. Maybe you—"

"Why," he asked, interrupting her, "would you not carry one with you?"

"Because," she said, in the same annoyed tone he used, "I was going to be with *you*. I thought, foolishly, it seems, that you would know where *yours* was!"

They glared at one another for a moment, he leaning a forearm against the doorway molding in complete exasperation, she with her feet squarely planted to relieve her sore back.

"Interesting," he said finally, his voice now quietly angry, "that the same woman who can be so independent in some ways refuses to take responsibility for herself in others."

Anger rose in her like heat up a chimney. "We're no longer talking keys, are we?" She forced herself to speak quietly, knowing Mrs. Drummond across the hall probably had her ear to her door. "I'm getting a little tired of arguing the restaurant deal. I...didn't... want...to do it!" She enunciated emphatically. "This is a free country, you know. I know Cassie wanted it, and I'm sorry I disappointed her, but I came through in the end, didn't I?!" Despite her resolve, she forgot Mrs. Drummond across the hall and spoke in an increasingly louder tone.

"Jo..." he began quietly, cautioningly.

She pointed to her protruding belly. "I made it possible for you and Cassie to have your baby!" she shouted. "I know you wish I'd been hit instead of Cassie, but unfortunately I—"

He put one hand to the back of her head and one over her mouth. He leaned over her until they were nose-to-nose and then he said sternly, "Stop it now."

Two tears slid down her cheeks and onto his hand. She nodded quickly, horrified that she'd spoken the thought aloud.

He dropped the hand over her mouth, but the one in

Make Way for Mommy

her hair clamped at the nape of her neck, and he said in a low growl, "Don't you *ever* say that." He drew a breath that sounded as though it hurt, then added, "I'd give anything to have her back—anything but someone else's life. Except, maybe, my own."

Jo felt as though her world had exploded at that admission. She'd certainly entertained the thought for months, but she couldn't believe she'd spoken it aloud. She felt naked and exposed, yet vaguely comforted by his vehement and unmistakably honest denial of her claim.

"I'm sorry," she whispered.

"I hope so," he said. Then in a curiously tender gesture, given the circumstances, he pulled her head to his chest for a moment and held her there while he heaved a ragged sigh.

She finally drew away, a light warming in her breast. She sniffed and cleared her throat. "Maybe your…ah, your keys fell out in the car," she said. "I remember in class you took them out of your pants pocket and put them in your jacket. Maybe…maybe they fell out when you tossed your coat in the back."

He considered that a moment, then turned back to the elevator. "Wait right here."

The moment he stepped onto the car, Jo sagged against the wall, exhausted, spent. She stood without thinking, feeling strangely composed of pain and promise throbbing in every little corner of her being.

MAMA JO? Mama Cass says stop being a twit. Can we go to bed? All that breathing made me sleepy.

RYAN WAS BACK in a matter of minutes, his expression still moody and tense. But he held up his house keys as he stepped off the elevator. "You were right," he said.

"Why don't you keep them on the same ring?" she asked.

"Too bulky, with all my bank keys," he replied. "This way I can put them in separate pockets."

He unlocked the door and stepped aside to let her in. The condo was quiet and cool, the dusk over the river visible from the living room window.

"All that relaxation is exhausting," Jo said, turning immediately in the direction of the bedrooms. She felt as though she were standing on the high end of a teeter-totter. "I'm going to go to bed early, maybe watch TV for a little while."

He seemed relieved. "Me too. Want me to bring you a cup of tea before I turn in?"

She shook her head. "Thanks, but I don't need a thing. See you at breakfast."

"Good night," he said.

She smiled and disappeared into the hallway.

Ryan made himself a cup of cocoa and poured a generous measure of brandy in it. He stepped out onto the patio with it, and scanned the familiar view without seeing it.

He knew why he'd accused her of refusing to accept responsibility. He'd been angry at her, and he'd wanted to hurt her in some way. That was uncharacteristic of him, but then, so was confusion—and that was all he felt at the moment.

The Lamaze class had been even harder than usual tonight. He'd absorbed the instructions, but he'd been conscious every moment of Jo's full, round body under his hand.

Her bone structure felt very fragile, yet every curve of her was full and ripe with the impending delivery.

If it was simple lust he'd felt, it might be more understandable. He'd been celibate since Cassie's death.

But his awareness of Jo's body was more complex than sexual deprivation. It was as though she were becoming for him the personification of woman. She seemed delicate but strong, swollen with the baby, yet curiously graceful, high-strung sometimes, then serenely competent at others.

She was all the enigmas, all the mysteries, all the ambivalence, that was female. And he found himself inextricably drawn toward her, like every sane man in the world attracted by what he knew to be illogical.

It didn't make sense. He hated things that didn't add up. But there it was. He'd tried to reason those feelings away for several days now, but tonight, when he lost his temper, had been proof.

He examined his alternatives as he sipped the doctored cocoa. He decided he had only one. He would ignore the whole thing and hope it went away.

Even as the thought formed, he knew it to be cowardly, but he was in no shape for heroics tonight. He was lonely, confused, depressed and exhausted. And any other course of action would probably horrify Jo, hammer him with guilt, and ruin the friendly relationship they were trying so hard to build. He couldn't risk that.

His mind replayed her distraught declaration, and he winced against it. He was horrified that she could think the thing, horrified that he might have done anything to nurture such a thought.

He put his cup in the sink, then went to rap on her bedroom door with a new resolve.

There was an instant's silence. Then she called, "Yes? Come in."

He pushed the door open, but stood firmly on the threshold. "You all right?" he asked.

She was reading, and looked at him over the book balanced on the hill of her stomach. She seemed subdued, vaguely wary. "I'm fine," she said. Her foot moved under the bedcovers. "I'm sorry I shouted at you."

He leaned a hand on the doorknob and put his other in his pants pocket. "I verbally attacked you. You had every right to shout. Jo…"

He considered his words carefully. There was a lot between them—divergent interests and personalities, the awkwardness of their situation, their shared grief, and a weird confusion that seemed to be taking on a life of its own. But there was one point on which he wanted her to be clear.

"I swear to you," he said gravely, "that it has never crossed my mind that you should have died instead of Cassie."

She smiled gently. "Poor Ryan," she said, leaning her head back against her propped up pillows. "Cassie and I put you in quite a fix, didn't we? We thought we'd set up the perfect situation, and then, when fate stepped in, you were destined to lose. If the poor old man having a heart attack behind the wheel of that car had hit me, you'd have lost your baby." She shook her head with the fatal acceptance of someone faced with God's supremacy. "Some choice. Your wife or your child."

He hadn't intended to step into the room. But he was determined to make his point, and he couldn't do it from the doorway. He went to sit on the edge of her bed.

"First of all," he said, "since Cassie died, I've felt as though my life's been broken in two. But I don't feel like a victim of fate. I had Cassie. She loved me. It was far too short, but it was mine and it will always be mine."

Tears brimmed in her eyes. He took her hand, his throat tight with emotion, as he went on.

"I don't think I can count myself a loser. I feel very, very lucky that you and the baby are fine."

Jo squeezed his hand. She'd loved Cassie, too, and valued every moment they shared as sisters and friends. Her memories were warm, and many were filled with laughter. It was difficult to feel abandoned when she still carried her love and her baby.

But, God, how she wished she were more to Ryan than simply the surrogate pregnant with his child. Before Cassie and Ryan were married, when he used to join them for holiday dinners, she would taunt and verbally tease him to cover what she truly felt. Then conversation would swell around the table and she would remain quiet and simply watch him—pretending that Cassie was out of the picture, that he'd come to dinner with her family because he loved *her,* Jo.

She would imagine living a suburban life, buying a station wagon, going to school functions and chauffeuring children who were blond like her, but with Ryan's defined features and dark eyes.

Then Cassie would laugh about something with that hearty abandon that had always made everyone turn in her direction, and she, Jo, would look up to see Ryan smiling at Cassie with that look in his eyes that made Jo know for certain his love could never belong to anyone else.

She sighed and pulled her hand away. "I forgot to

be *harmonious* tonight," she said, giving special emphasis to the word. "I guess Lamaze class wore me out. I'll do better tomorrow."

Ryan stood. He'd said what he wanted to say, but he wasn't sure he'd gotten through. That worried him, but she looked tired. He suddenly felt very old.

"Sleep well. Did you have your banana today to ward off the leg cramps?"

Jo smiled, that small policing gesture making her feel that things were approaching normalcy. "Yes, I did. You sleep well, too. I'm making pancakes in the morning."

"Oh, no!" he said, without pausing to monitor his reaction. Then he saw her raised eyebrow and added quickly, "I mean…really? Are you sure? Wouldn't you rather sleep in, and I'll…"

"Diantha gave me a foolproof recipe," she insisted, knowing now that things *were* back to normal. She felt herself relax. "Using rice flour, Egg Beaters, and fruit juice concentrate."

I'LL SLEEP IN, thanks.

"OH…" he said feebly. "Good. Well. I'd better let you rest up, if you're going to tackle cooking."

"You might be pleasantly surprised," she told him challengingly as he walked to the door.

He smiled blandly. "Hey. I'm an optimist. Good night."

Jo watched him walk through the door and close it behind him. She smiled with the bittersweet thought that he was a far more interesting man than even she'd imagined.

SHE HAD the Cassie dream again. She saw everything repeated in slow motion, saw the sweater that had claimed her attention in the shop window, the reflected image of Cassie stepping off the curb and the big car on a collision course with her. She felt the terror again, the paralysis.

She awoke panting and perspiring. She listened for some indication that she'd disturbed Ryan, but the house was quiet.

She lay back, rubbing the baby. She felt her move under her hand. She patted her, telling her everything would be all right—and prayed that she was right.

I DON'T LIKE THAT DREAM, Mama Jo. And Mama Cass says put that memory away and everything will be all right.

Chapter Six

"What do you think?" Jo asked.

Ryan chewed the rubber disk which had little flavor other than extreme sweetness, and wished he had an alternative to swallowing. He hated the thought of the latexlike mixture in his mouth moving into his digestive system and becoming a part of his body.

But Jo was standing over him with a raised spatula and an expectant expression—he pardoned himself for the involuntary pun—and he gave serious thought to his personal safety if he was to tell the truth.

Her hair was piled high on her head, curly golden ends dangling from a green ribbon. She wore a long white sweater over a green skirt, and an apron hung from her neck, the ties, too short to meet around her considerable girth, dangling uselessly at her sides.

He had no choice. He swallowed. He guessed it must be what swallowing a balloon felt like.

"It's very filling," he said diplomatically, trying desperately not to taste.

Her soft blue eyes widened with distress. "Diantha said it was foolproof!"

He glanced at the plate of pancakes that lay before him, looking very much like small, round carpet samples. The texture of the rice flour even gave some of them a sixties-shag look.

"Well…" He took a quick sip of coffee. The woman did make the world's best coffee. "It's overcast and rainy today. Isn't the barometer supposed to affect cooking?"

"I think that's baking," she said. She took the fork from the side of his plate, speared three layers of pancake covered with butter and syrup, and put it in her mouth. She chewed contemplatively, but then her expression changed abruptly to one of distaste.

He handed her his napkin. She put it to her mouth, then turned away to the trash can concealed under the sink and tossed the bite away.

She brought a carton of milk and a box of granola to the table. "You should have told me they tasted like leather," she said scoldingly, going back to the cupboard for bowls and spoons.

"I was thinking filleted bungee cords," he said.

She giggled and sat opposite him, pulling a cup of tea toward her. "I don't know what made me think I should try to cook, anyway. Must be some kind of nesting frenzy, or something."

He laughed lightly. "It helps to know one's limitations. The baby's afghan is coming along well."

It was. She brought the project back and forth to work, and it had grown to about half its final size. The intricate pattern in pastel rainbow colors was familiar now, after dozens of repetitions, and she was confident she would have it finished by the time the baby arrived.

"And you do make great coffee," he added, pouring granola into her bowl, then into his.

She dabbed desultorily at the granules with her spoon. "I don't want to have limitations."

He passed her the milk. "Limitations are a fact of life."

She poured a small amount, then passed it back.

She hated to accept it, but she knew that to be true—particularly in her case and in her present circumstances. The thought depressed her. "Well," she said with a sigh, "as long as I'm not required to like it."

"I don't think so."

"Good." She pushed her bowl away with sudden ill temper and prepared to stand. "I think I'll pass on breakfast and have a bagel at work."

He leveled a dark, even gaze on her. "Uh-uh. You need the milk, and the food value in the grains. A bagel won't do the same thing for you."

He was right, but she didn't have to like that, either. She pulled the bowl back toward her and gave him a rebellious glance. "I'm doing it because you're right, not because you said so."

Ryan, spoon poised over his bowl, tried to make sense of that remark and failed. He decided he didn't have to understand it, as long as she ate the cereal.

"YOU'RE KIDDING." Ryan studied Jave Nicholas, who was sitting in one of the upholstered chairs in the small conversation area in his office, and wondered why he was surprised. He'd guessed as much last night at the Lamaze class. "*When* did you get married?"

Jave looked smugly self-satisfied. "Last weekend. And let me tell you, it was no small feat."

Ryan nodded. He had shed his suit coat and Jave had a jeans-clad leg hooked over the side of the chair. "We all thought she was married to a—"

"I know. A coastguardsman." Jave shook his head, as though that falsehood had caused him considerable trouble. "She'd just moved from New York after an unpleasant divorce, when Amy Brown at the hospital got this idea about the birthing room extravaganza."

Ryan nodded, remembering the afternoon she'd tried to talk Jo into taking Nancy's place.

"She saw Nancy's records from New York, and they indicated a husband. She presumed Nancy still had him, and that she'd be the perfect all-American mom for the project. When Nancy saw all the gifts she'd be getting for the baby, she knew that it was far more than she could ever provide the baby alone, so she agreed to do it, and let Amy go on thinking she did have a husband. She explained his absence by saying he was away on a Coast Guard cutter on a security cruise."

Ryan grinned. "When'd you figure it out?"

"Almost right away," Jave replied. "But she insisted I was mistaken. When I had her dead to rights—when the cutter put into Long Beach, California, for repairs and she didn't know it—she finally came clean. But her first marriage had been so bad, it took me a long time to convince her that marriage to me would be different."

"And how do your boys feel about a new mother and a new baby?"

Jave shrugged a shoulder. "I'm sure we won't always be like an episode of the 'Brady Bunch,' but the boys love Nancy, and they're excited about the prospect of a new baby. At least until she starts keeping them up nights and breaking their toys."

"So, you know it's a girl?"

"Yep. Yours, too. We're going to have a lot to learn. Me with my boys, and you being a complete novice."

Ryan rolled his eyes. "I've got a nanny lined up until

the baby starts walking. I'm sure I'm in for a lot of character-building experiences.''

"Kids are great. You'll love it." Then he drew a deep breath, and his eyes filled with empathy. Ryan had come to know that those gestures usually preceded an expression of sympathy. "I'm sorry Cassie isn't here to hold her baby."

Ryan fought the old knot in his throat, the anger that surged without warning. "Well. Jo insists she's watching over us—like some kind of guardian angel, or something."

Jave smiled. "Jo's a gift to mankind. You're lucky to have her for a sister-in-law. I imagine it isn't every woman who'd be willing to carry her sister's baby." He sobered suddenly. "And it'll be doubly hard for her to give the baby up with Cassie gone."

Ryan handed Jave a folder that contained trust-account paperwork. "She doesn't have to give her up completely," he said, resisting an instinctively defensive feeling. "I mean, she's still the child's aunt."

"I know." Jave tapped the folder against his other hand. "But she's carried the baby all this time. I've seen it before. It'll be more difficult for her to hand the baby over to someone else than she ever imagined, and I'm sure far more difficult than *you* ever imagined it could be for her. And with Cassie gone, she's lost that unique tie. You might remarry one day."

"No," Ryan said.

"You think that now."

"No," Ryan said again. "And Jo's okay with this. We've talked about it."

Jave stood and offered his hand. "Good. Well, I'm just warning you that women become pretty irrational about their offspring. So you'll take care of Malia's trust fund for me?''

Ryan shook his hand and walked him to the door. ''With her new trust account, your little daughter will be as well set up as your boys. Take care. Don't forget that promise of a harbor tour when the *Mud Hen*'s operational.''

''Right.''

Ryan watched Jave stride through the bank and out the door toward his GMC, parked across the side street. His mind, already cluttered with memories of his argument with Jo and the unsettling acceptance in her eyes that had resulted, was now overburdened by Jave's remarks.

It'll be more difficult for her to hand the baby over to someone else than she ever imagined—and I'm sure far more difficult than you *ever imagined it could be for her.*

When Jo became pregnant, the gifts of modern medical science had seemed like such a boon to their lives. Now that fate had interceded and the dynamics had changed, it appeared to be turning into another situation that was bound to produce a loser—Josanne. Maybe the message was, he thought, that it wasn't safe to manipulate the hand life dealt you.

A headache forming between his eyes, Ryan looked over the quiet bank, then went back into his office and checked his calendar. He had no appointments after Jave. He called his assistant manager to tell her he was taking a few hours off, then grabbed his jacket off the oak rack near the window and left the bank.

''IF SHE'S BORN on your due date,'' Diantha said, sitting at the far end of the counter in Coffee Country, ''she's going to be a finicky eater, and probably develop food allergies.''

Her index finger in the handle of a short glass mug, she sipped at a mocha and leafed through ten or twelve notebook-size pages stapled together. ''But she'll be nurturing. Hospitable, compassionate, even philanthropic. She'll treat everyone as part of her family.''

Jo sat on a stool behind the counter, her chin in her hand as she watched her friend read the chart she'd produced.

Diantha turned a page. ''She'll have a keen intellect, and a—''

''She gets that from me,'' Jo interjected.

Diantha looked at her over the rim of her glasses. ''She gets it,'' she replied, ''from natal Mercury in Scorpio.''

''Of course.''

''Her mental powers will not be bogged down by sentiment.''

''That,'' Jo said with a grin, ''she gets from her father.''

Diantha put the sheets down and brought her cup to her lips. Silver bangles moved musically at her wrists. ''How're things with you and Ryan?''

Jo raised an eyebrow, pretending surprise that Diantha would ask, when everyone knew they were simply in-laws—though in-laws in a curious position. But she knew she wasn't fooling anyone. She wasn't sure where Diantha got her intuitive powers—from the stars or from some innate ability to read minds—but she saw far more clearly into people than anyone Jo knew.

''We're coexisting,'' Jo replied, taking a sip from the long-neglected cup of raspberry-and-rosehip tea at her elbow. ''That's all we're required to do.''

"Mmm…" Diantha put her cup down. She met Jo's gaze evenly. "When are you going to ask him to marry you?"

"What?" Jo shrieked. Color flooded her face, and Tom Nicholas, reading the newspaper at a small table at the front of the room, looked up.

"If the gossip is that good," he said, with a grin at the women, "I want in on it."

Jo laughed lightly. "Di's telling shocking stories. Go back to your stock quotes."

He looked offended. "I'm reading the comics," he said. "So if you're not going to share, could you at least keep it down?"

Jo turned back to Diantha and whispered indignantly, *"What* are you talking about?"

"As if you didn't know," Diantha whispered back. "You love him. You're carrying his baby—not in the traditional meaning of the term, granted, but the fact remains. He's frustrated by his attraction to you. Seems to—"

"He is?" Jo asked, stiffening suddenly on the stool.

Diantha nodded. "Seems to me you're holding all the cards."

Jo looked doubtful. "How do you know?"

Diantha sipped her coffee. "I read the stars."

"I mean *really* how do you know?"

Diantha frowned at her. "You mean I spent all morning preparing a chart for you, and you're a nonbeliever?"

Jo bobbed her head from side to side uncertainly. "Let's just say I'm intrigued but skeptical." Then she looked her in the eye. "What makes you think he's attracted to me?"

"He takes care of you," Diantha replied. "Do you

really think that before you moved in with him he came in here every morning and every afternoon just for coffee?''

''He didn't?''

''Of course not. He was checking on you.''

''He was checking,'' Jo told her, ''on his baby.''

Diantha narrowed her eyes and focused on the coffee menu behind Jo's head. ''I don't think so. I think he's drawn to you—and he's not sure why, or even if it's a good thing.''

Jo listened to her friend in complete surprise and consternation. ''I... You.., I don't *think* so.''

Diantha folded her arms on the counter and leaned earnestly toward Jo. ''I *do*. Cassie will always be with the two of you, but in subtle, possibly even unconscious ways, you're both beginning to realize that having a baby is about *life*—and that can't help but put death in the background, even the death of someone you both loved so much. And that clears the way for...'' She shrugged and smiled. ''For whatever the two of you will allow to happen.''

MAMA CASS SAYS give Diantha a free mocha.

''I THOUGHT the stars dictated what happened,'' Jo said challengingly.

Diantha nodded with confidence. ''I believe they affect events. But how events affect us is our own decision.''

Jo leaned toward her and said quietly, ''You're getting batty in your middle years, Pennyman.''

Diantha laughed throatily and patted her cheek. ''Who else would keep company with you? So here.'' She pushed her cup aside and thrust the sheaf of papers at her. "Get acquainted with this profile of your child, and—"

"She's not *my* child." Jo said, bracing her hands at her back as she shifted her weight carefully off the stool. "She's Ryan's."

Diantha repeated her earlier words significantly. "How events affect us is up to us."

"Heavy," Ryan said. "Is this a private philosophical discussion, or can anyone join in?"

Jo and Diantha turned in surprise as Ryan took the stool next to the one Diantha occupied.

"Now what would a mercenary banker," Diantha said dryly as she picked up her wallet and keys, "know about philosophy?"

He pulled at his tie. "We lend money. You don't think that requires a philosophical outlook?"

"Good point." She laughed and slapped his shoulder.

"Don't let them fool you," Tom called from his corner. "They've been telling dirty stories and shrieking."

Ryan turned to Jo with feigned shock. "Miss Arceneau. I'm horrified."

She waved a careless hand. "We were just gossiping." Then she turned quickly away before he could see in her eyes precisely who they'd discussed—and what. "Ready for your afternoon latte?"

"'Bye, all," Diantha called as she headed for the door. "Tom, I've got that Vitamin E cream you asked about."

"Great." He folded the newspaper and replaced it on a shelf covered with other newspapers and magazines, then followed Diantha out the door, with a parting wave for Jo and Ryan.

The door closed behind them, and silence settled over the coffee bar.

"No latte," Ryan said to Jo.

She turned from the refrigerator, an eyebrow raised. "Juice? Mineral water?"

He shrugged off his suit coat and placed it on the stool beside him, then pulled off his tie. "No. I was wondering if you could get away this afternoon."

She blinked, startled by the suggestion. She glanced up at the clock. "Devon's due in about fifteen minutes," she said. "But why?"

He raised his hand in a gesture of helpless resignation. "Because you won the bet."

"What bet?" she asked, then remembered. "You're kidding!" She squealed, suddenly all smiles, and came to stand just opposite him at the counter. "Nancy and Jave are getting married?"

"Already did it. Last weekend. Just the family." He considered her thrilled expression. "I didn't realize you were such a proponent of matrimony. In fact, you've turned down two proposals since I've known you."

She rolled her eyes. "A redneck and a Republican. Please."

"Ah, yes." He grinned and folded his arms on the counter. "You're looking for a rock star or a philanthropist. I keep forgetting."

"Chelsea's going to be a philanthropist, according to Diantha." Jo ran her thumb along the edge of the small stack of pages and handed it to him. "She ran her chart with this new software she just bought. She claims the baby will also be a finicky eater and very intelligent."

Ryan gave her a skeptical smile, but lifted the top page of the chart. "Aren't all babies finicky eaters?"

"I wasn't. I loved spinach and asparagus when I was a child."

Ryan concentrated on the page, then marked a line

with his index finger and read aloud. "Once she forms an opinion, she will stick to it stubbornly." He glanced up with a wince of concern that Jo found charmingly disarming. "That doesn't sound good for me."

Jo laughed, instinctively covering his hand with hers. "If it's any comfort, I was glancing through the chart and saw something about great charm and personal attractiveness. It's in one of those First House paragraphs."

The instant Jo felt Ryan's knuckles against the soft pads of her fingertips, the warmth of his skin against her sensitive palm, she saw his eyes fly up to hers, startlingly dark and deep.

But they contained no annoyance at the intimacy, she noticed, no suggestion that she'd intruded where she didn't belong. Mesmerized by that acceptance, she stared into his eyes.

The bell over the door tinkled merrily as it opened, admitting three women juggling bags and bundles and laughing loudly.

Jo drew her hand away quickly, and was surprised when Ryan smiled at the guilty action.

"You...ah, you look that over," she stammered, wiping her hands on her apron as she backed away from him, toward her customers. "Devon should be here any minute."

Jo's hands were shaking as she pulled out cups for three Borgias. Everything inside her was trembling, too. She had the strangest feeling that, for reasons she couldn't imagine, some barrier had been removed from between them.

She didn't know what it meant, and couldn't guess what it portended—she simply liked the way it felt. She hummed softly to herself as she reached for the orange syrup.

Chapter Seven

"Actually, this isn't a very practical idea," Jo said, hanging back as Ryan led the way toward a small cluster of stores two blocks away from Coffee Country. "I'm only going to be pregnant for two more weeks. It'd be silly to buy a jacket now."

She knew he was headed for Darby's, an exclusive women's clothing store she'd avoided since wandering in to look it over one day and discovering that a scarf she admired was over a hundred dollars.

"I mean, you were only going to get free lattes for a month," she said. "And everything in here is astronomically priced."

"Free lattes *delivered*." He grinned over the distinction. "That doubles the value to a busy man."

She remained rooted in place when he opened the shop's elegant stained-glass doors. "A busy man," she said, "doesn't take a woman shopping in the middle of the afternoon."

He remembered suddenly the impulse of guilt and confusion that had led him from the bank.

"There are moments in life," he said, "that defy order and duty."

Her eyes widened. "Wow. You *do* have a philosophical bent."

"I have my moments." He opened the door wider. "Let's go."

She remained where she was, peering uncertainly into the fragrant, moodily lit rose-and-green interior. "We should be at a wilderness outfitter's, shopping for a tent or a tarp."

He rolled his eyes and caught her hand. "How you do go on. I thought we could get you one of those fling-coat things." He made an awkward sweeping gesture with one hand, while pulling the door closed with the other.

Jo narrowed her eyes in confusion. "Fling things?" she repeated.

"You remember," he said, taking her elbow and pulling her toward a clerk. "It's narrow at the top and kind of floats out widely at the bottom. Cassie had a gray one she wore all the time. If you got one of those, it'd fit you now, and *after* Chelsea's born."

Jo remembered Cassie's coat, but she had no idea what the style was called.

"A swing coat!" Lauren, the clerk, proclaimed after Ryan's unself-conscious description. The young woman was so perfectly made up, groomed and dressed that Jo fought an impulse to poke her, to see if she reacted.

Lauren cast an assessing glance over Jo's impossible proportions and nodded. "A good idea. We have a fine selection. Follow me."

Ryan and Jo fell into step behind her as she led the way through the elegant shop, like Napoleon leading the French army over the Alps.

Ryan, an arm hooked around Jo's shoulders as though he were afraid she might try to escape, smiled smugly.

"I told you I knew what I was talking about," he said under his breath.

"Oh, right," she answered in a teasing whisper. "You called it a 'fling' coat."

"Fling, swing," he said, dismissing his misnomer. "I knew it related to some sexual indiscretion."

She laughed aloud. She couldn't help it. She'd never seen him in quite this kind of a mood. He was always polite, and often kind, but he'd never been so deliberately amenable before. He seemed to have set out this afternoon not only to buy her a coat, but to be charming.

She should resist him, she thought. This kind of coziness between them wasn't safe.

But Lauren claimed her attention when they reached the coat department, and for the next half hour she was completely distracted as Lauren helped her in and out of every pattern of swing coat on the racks.

Ryan waited patiently in a pink brocade chair, her tote bag, her beret and her old fleece jacket at his feet.

She looked wonderful in neon colors, Ryan decided, and wondered if that was why she usually chose them. He was sure if that was true, her choice was unconscious, because nothing about her style of dress was intended to flatter her person in any way.

It was probably more likely that she loved brightness in color, as she did in everything else about her life. Everything she did seemed to be just a step beyond what everyone else preferred. It was as though, he thought with sudden insight, she pushed everything to its limit to make a statement of recklessness or courage.

"That one," he said, when Lauren helped her into an electric blue coat with a mandarin collar, softly molded shoulders, crown-shaped gold buttons and yards of wool that floated softly down at the sides and back to just around her knees.

I LIKE THIS ONE, too. It's very soft. And it makes it even warmer in here. Now, if only there was more room!

HER PROTRUDING STOMACH hiked the front up several inches, but she looked stunning in it all the same.

He went to stand beside the clerk, eyeing Jo critically.

"He's right," Lauren said. "That's the one. Look at what it does to your eyes."

Jo looked at herself in the mirror. "All it's supposed to do is keep me warm."

Lauren looked horrified at the notion that a woman's clothing should be simply functional. She came to stand behind Jo, to fuss with the collar and smooth the shoulders.

"That's a barbaric idea," she said with a sudden smile. To that point, her manner had been as glossy as her appearance. "Clothes reflect the woman inside." She reached down to the thick forest green carpet to pick up Jo's magenta beret and twirl it on her finger. "I thought a woman who wears a beret would know that. I believe everything you put on your body, consciously or unconsciously, says, 'This is me.' We think we're holding all our little secrets so closely, but our bodies and our instincts betray us. Deep down, we want to share who and what we *really* are. I think we do that with what we wear."

Jo looked at her in openmouthed surprise. This beautiful Barbie-woman was the last person from whom she'd have expected such deep thought.

The woman apparently read her thoughts, because she gave her a so-there tilt of her chin.

Jo looked back at her reflection, a little unsettled. The coat was beautiful, and hung in elegant lines, despite the intrusion of her pregnancy. And the color did seem to darken her eyes and brighten the color in her cheeks.

She'd brushed her hair and tied it up in a knot before leaving the shop, and it looked unusually tidy—almost stylish. The idea alarmed her. She'd always gone out of her way to flout conventional style, in favor of her own personal expression of it.

Was this what Lauren meant? she wondered. Did she like this coat because somewhere inside her was a woman who wanted to look chic and elegant, rather than free and comfortable?

She dismissed that thought as the product of weariness and the continual confusion Ryan caused in her, and brought the issue back to what a coat should be all about.

Was it warm?

It was.

Did it reach across her stomach?

It did.

Would she be able to wear it after she delivered Chelsea?

She would.

She lifted the right sleeve in search of the price tag. Her eyes widened at the three digits, and she started to unbutton it.

"We'll take it," Ryan said, then raised a hand to silence Jo's attempt to protest.

Lauren, still holding the beret, held it up and studied it critically. "Maybe we should find you a hat to coordinate with the coat?"

Jo took the hat from her with a firm shake of her head. "Thanks, but I like this one."

"Come on," Ryan coaxed. "Just have a look. Those colors don't go together, do they?"

Jo placed the hat on her head at a rakish angle. "Cassie gave it to me. It goes with everything."

Ryan looked to Lauren questioningly.

She studied Jo closely, smiled, then raised her arms in a gesture of helplessness. "When a woman's comfortable with the way she looks, *everything* works— even electric blue and magenta."

Jo made a face at Ryan as Lauren walked to the gazebolike area in the middle of the shop where the counter was located.

"I could be warm," she whispered, "for a third the price of this coat."

"But you couldn't look as beautiful," he said with smiling gallantry. "Lauren?" He turned his attention to the clerk, who looked up from lining a box with tissue. "Perfume?"

"Perfume?" Jo repeated. "Ryan, perfume is not going to keep me warm on a..."

Her protest trailed off as Ryan followed Lauren across the shop.

Jo remained at the counter. She watched Lauren and Ryan engage in a brief conversation. Then Lauren uncapped a bottle, spritzed it on her wrist, and held up the slender, graceful line of it to Ryan's nose.

He dipped his head to sniff. Jo felt deep, hot emotion, and recognized it immediately for what it was—jealousy. Fortunately, that also allowed her to chide herself for being stupid, and to come to her senses.

That wrist-to-the-nose process was repeated several more times, with other fragrances, and the two finally came back to the counter with two bottles.

"Floral or musky?" Ryan asked.

"I never wear perfume," she said frankly, with an apologetic glance at Lauren.

"Diantha said," he reminded her, "that the baby would be sensitive to smells. She'll be closest to yours."

Jo took a blue-and-silver bottle from him. "And I smell like French roast coffee." Because she was wearing long sleeves, she spritzed the contents on the inside of her left hand. Then she held her fingertips to her nose. The scent was floral, a little stronger on the side of gardenias.

Ryan took that bottle from her and gave her the other. She sprayed it on her right hand. That fragrance was deeply, sumptuously heavy.

"The floral," Jo said, handing the bottle back.

Lauren took them. "Are you sure? Rendezvous—" she held up the musky fragrance "—is heavy-duty stuff."

Ryan took both of Jo's hands in his and lifted them toward his face as he leaned down to intercept first one fragrance, then the other. The backs of her hands were cradled in his much larger palms, and his strong fingertips closed around her hands to keep them still.

Jo felt the air catch in her throat, her heartbeat stutter. She stood quietly under his touch, her entire being absorbing the sensation of being the subject of his complete attention.

He turned to Lauren and gently shook Jo's left hand. "This one."

Lauren went back to the display for a boxed perfume. "The floral it is," she said.

They left the shop, Ryan carrying the green-and-rose box that contained Jo's coat, Jo carrying her perfume in a decorated gift bag. The shopping had tired her, and she took Ryan's arm as they walked slowly back toward the bank parking lot.

"Worn-out?" he asked.

She nodded and rotated her shoulders. "A little. My back hurts all the time now."

They stopped at the light, and he put a hand to the small of her back and gently rubbed while they waited.

She couldn't help a little moan of relief when her tense muscles loosened a little. "What could I pay you," she asked with a little laugh, "to do that continually for the next two weeks?"

He grinned. "The service comes free with Lamaze coaching. Serena is always reminding us that coaching starts long before labor. Do you like cabbage?"

"Ah…" Jo required a moment to switch her thoughts from his comforting reassurance to his completely unrelated question. "Yes. I love cabbage," she finally replied, with a puzzled glance up at him. The light changed, and they walked across the street. "Why?"

"Would you like stuffed cabbage for dinner? You can wait in the car while I pick up what we need."

MAMA CASS says say no—*fast!*

SHE STOPPED in her tracks in the middle of the sidewalk in pleased anticipation. Stuffed cabbage was one of her favorite meals.

"I'd love it!" she said. "My mother used to make it, but Cassie didn't like it, so we didn't have it that often. Isn't it an awful lot of trouble?"

He shook his head and pulled her along toward the car. "It'll be worth it. Cassie obviously never fixed them, but my Polish grandmother made the best *golabki* in the whole world. You're in for a treat, Josanne."

He helped her into the car, and she waited in a little cocoon of mellow warmth for him to slip in beside her and drive her home.

WHITE SHIRTSLEEVES rolled up to his elbows, and wearing a blue-and-white-striped "Cordon Bleu" apron, Ryan expertly blanched and separated cabbage leaves, mixed a filling of hamburger, rice, egg and seasonings, and sat beside Jo at the table, sharing the duty of neatly rolling the cabbage leaves around the filling.

"How long will they have to bake?" Jo asked, placing a roll next to a row of others in the long pan between them.

"Almost an hour," he replied. "Why? Will you need an hors d'oeuvre?"

She looked hopeful. "Like what?"

He cast her a knowing glance. "Mini bagel pizzas. Pepperoni."

She stared at him. Another of her favorite things. "I *love* those!"

"I know," he said dryly. "When Cassie bought a package to see if she could improve upon them with her own recipe, you ate them all before she was able to analyze them. Remember?"

She did. She concentrated on making precise corners on her cabbage roll. "I'd just spent all day at the children's fair at the park. You spend twelve hours with a pack of five-to-eight-year-olds wanting you to read to them and paint their faces and see if *you* don't crave carbohydrates."

He folded the sides of a cabbage leaf around the filling placed at the top, gave it one tuck to keep the filling in place, then completed the roll with one long sweep of his hand. "I imagine I'll have the opportunity one day in the not-too-distant future." He placed that roll in the pan, then went to the kitchen to pull a flat box out of the freezer.

I, Jo thought, will probably not. I'll be running a coffeehouse somewhere in Alaska, because I will no longer be able to stand being near both of you and not loving you as I want to. I'll wind down toward spinsterhood with an old dog, a passel of cats, and clothes even more bizarre than I wear now. Except for my blue swing coat. I'll always feel different when I wear it.

"Speaking of community events," Ryan said, closing the door on the microwave and setting the timer, "does the county carry its own insurance on the fairgrounds, or does the host of the event have to provide it?"

She came out of her cheerless thoughts to concentrate on the moment.

"For Heron Point Has It, you mean?" She placed a dollop of filling at the top of the last cabbage leaf. "The downtown association carries its own. You don't have to worry about it."

"That's a relief. Something to drink with this?"

"Tea, please."

"What's Coffee Country going to be serving?" he asked conversationally as he took plates and cups down from the cupboard.

Jo watched him move skillfully around the kitchen, his long-muscled biceps flexing as he pulled the oven door open. "Um...you know. All the things we serve. Biscotti, shortbread, scones..."

"Mmm... Sounds good." He came back to the table to take the pan of cabbage rolls from her, and saw that one roll remained unfinished—the one she'd been working on while watching him. He raised a questioning eyebrow. "You waiting for that one to roll itself?"

"Ha, ha," she said, and quickly finished it and placed it in the pan.

"Good work," he said, taking it to the oven. "Why don't you sit in the recliner, and I'll bring you your hors d'oeuvres as soon as they're done."

Jo couldn't stand it another moment. "Are you softening me up to tell me something unpleasant?" she asked.

He closed the oven door on the baking pan and set the timer. Then he turned to her, hands resting loosely on his hips. "You needed a coat that closed, the perfume was really for the baby, and we have to eat. There's nothing here to make you suspicious."

Jo shook her head, denying his denial. "Not so. You took off in the middle of the afternoon, spent far too much money, bought a fragrance that was even more than I'd have paid for the *coat,* and now—" she waved a hand in the direction of the kitchen surrounding him "—all of this."

She saw just a trace of discomfort pass over his expression. It was barely visible, but she was finely attuned to every nuance in their curious relationship.

"All right," he said finally. He leaned a hip against the counter and folded his arms. "I...was thinking about you today..."

He paused, obviously thinking over what he intended to say.

Jo felt every life-sustaining function in her body slow dangerously. Every nerve ending trembled, waiting. *I was thinking about you today.*

"What..." she asked softly, "did you think about?"

"How generous it was for you to do this for me and Cassie," he replied. His voice was quiet and sincere. The kitchen was harshly lit, but beyond, the living room lay in the long shadows of early evening. He sighed and met her eyes. "How hard it's been for you with Cassie gone."

She couldn't deny that, but her entire being was focused on what she hoped he was about to say. *Maybe there's a solution here we haven't considered, Jo. When we try, we get on fairly well together. Why don't we—?*

"I love this baby," she said, her voice husky with feeling, "as much as you do."

He came back to the table to take the chair he'd vacated earlier. "I know. That's why I wanted to…"

Every thought in her head fled. Her heart pounded, her blood raced, her breath threatened to strangle her.

"To what?" she breathed.

He placed his hand over hers on the table. She turned hers to catch his fingers, a charge of power running up her arm, straight to her heart.

"To try to let you know that I appreciate you. That I want to keep you warm and comfortable. To try to pay you back for all you've—"

Despite the bulk of the baby, Jo shot up out of the chair as though she were her old size-eight self once again.

"Pay me back?" she asked, in a dangerously quiet voice. Then she repeated again, in utter disbelief, "Pay me *back?*"

Somewhere deep inside, she knew this was simply a matter of semantics. But her emotions weren't deep inside at all. They were right on the surface, throbbing for release, bursting through, powered by longing and pain and profound disappointment.

She had not wanted to hear that these wonderful few hours had been intended to pay her back for anything.

She'd wanted to know that they were the beginning of something new, and for no reason at all.

Ryan understood he was in trouble the instant he saw her light blue eyes turn to the color of lead.

"I've told you over and over," she said, in a voice he didn't even recognize as hers, "that I agreed to have this baby because Cassie wanted it more than anything in the world. And that's the spirit in which I'm seeing it through. Her love for you started this baby, and my love for *her,* and now for Chelsea, is bringing it to life." She was fairly trembling with fury.

"Do you think for one moment," she demanded, "that *anything*—particularly a coat and a bottle of perfume— could ever repay me for the feelings invested in this baby?"

Ryan was totally surprised by her reaction. What he'd intended to express was diametrically opposed to what she'd apparently heard. He felt himself slip back into the familiar morass of their inability to communicate— only this time, even after their wonderful afternoon, there was nothing comfortable about it.

"Jo..." he began, reaching for her wrist. "I meant—"

"I know what you meant," she said, snatching her wrist away. "You just don't want to be beholden to me for anything when she's born, so that when you don't need *me* anymore, she'll be all yours!"

She turned on her heel and waddled from the room. She stormed into her bedroom and flung the door closed behind her. Instead of slamming, it made a hollow thunking sound. She turned to see that it had struck Ryan's hand. He'd followed her.

He slammed it behind him, and they stood together

in the dark room, which was lit only by the glow of a halogen light from the condo's parking area.

He jabbed a finger at her shoulder. "You're wrong, Josanne," he said, in a breathless tone that betrayed temper barely controlled. "I had no ulterior motives, except to let you know that I care. But you have to throw it off by pretending it isn't good enough, or that it isn't offered with the degree of perfection you deem necessary. Well, I don't pretend to know what motivates you, but over the years I've begun to see a pattern. Is it that you don't know what to do with admiration when you get it, or that you don't think you deserve it?"

"Get out of my room," she ordered in a deadly whisper.

He ignored her. "Something's responsible for the bizarre getups and your acidic manner. You're trying to keep men away from you, aren't you? In fact, I could conclude that you're trying to push me farther and farther away from you, so that when I'm not looking you can run off with the baby."

This time she physically pushed him. He didn't even budge. "You say one more word—" she choked on a sob "—and I *will* run!"

"Don't try it, Jo," he warned. "You'll never get past me."

He reached behind him and yanked the door open, then slammed it again and was gone.

COME ON, *Mama Jo. You can't run. You can barely walk. And that kind of talk upsets me. And when I get upset, I get restless, and you don't want that to happen in this tight spot.*

Chapter Eight

Heron Point—possibly even the entire world, as far as Jo could see—was shrouded in fog. The annual fall pattern of low fog that burned off by midmorning had firmly established itself.

Jo turned away from her bedroom window and pulled her coat on over stirrup pants and a sweater. The weather seemed to parallel her life—except that for the past three days, she'd known no sunny afternoons.

Since her fight with Ryan, they'd barely spoken. He'd driven her to work and picked her up, and she'd made breakfast and cleaned up after he prepared dinner—but they'd done everything in silence.

And she never had eaten the cabbage rolls. She hadn't come out of her room for dinner that night, but she'd tried to sneak one in the early hours of the morning and been unable to find them. They hadn't been in the refrigerator or the freezer, or the trash. She'd settled for peanut butter on a celery stick instead, in bitter disappointment.

She knew she'd been horrible, but so had he. Of course, she'd been worse. And she'd started it.

She'd never been one who found it impossible to apologize for being wrong. It had always seemed as important a function of pride as accepting praise for being right.

But she kept remembering him cradling her hands in his as he leaned over them to sniff the perfume. She remembered him telling her she looked beautiful in the coat. She remembered his laborious preparations for the cabbage rolls that had virtually disappeared without ever being tasted—by her, anyway.

And he'd done all that to "pay her back." In retrospect she could admit that he'd meant nothing dishonorable. She'd become so upset because what she'd *wanted* to hear him say was "I'm falling in love with you."

She'd tried a dozen times since then to tell him she was sorry, but every time she approached, he turned away. She was sure it was more than coincidence.

She wrote a note that said she was going for a walk before breakfast and taped it to his bedroom door. Then she pulled on her beret and headed out.

She stood in the hallway and pressed the button for the elevator. After a moment, the up signal flashed, the bell rang, and the doors parted—revealing Ryan in jeans and a distressed-leather jacket, holding a small bag of groceries. He hadn't shaved, she noticed, and he looked sexily dangerous. A tingling vibration communicated itself from him to her.

His grim expression changed to one of surprise, then angry suspicion. He stepped off the elevator and blocked her path onto it. "Where are you going?" he asked.

Her only intention had been to take a walk, but confronted with his open suspicion, she felt her face flush and knew she must look as though she'd just cleared out his bank account and intended to take his car and his baby as far away as possible.

"I...ah, I..."

He caught her arm and pulled her back toward the condo. "I told you you wouldn't get past me," he said, maintaining a grip on her arm as he put the grocery bag on the floor and reached into his jacket pocket for his key.

"This is ridiculous!" Jo said, anger curiously absent from her reactions to his faulty conclusion. She was very tired of being at odds with him. "I was going for a walk," she said reasonably. "I do this all the time, remember? That is, I used to, until Hulk Jeffries became my bodyguard. I even left a note on your bedroom door. Go check, if you don't believe me. Go..."

Mrs. Drummond's apartment door opened suddenly, and she appeared in blue velour robe and slipper socks to reach for *The Oregonian* on her floor mat. Her jet black curls were standing upright, like rows of question marks. She looked embarrassed, and reached up to smooth them.

Then she said, with sudden enthusiasm, "Mr. Jeffries,

I've never enjoyed a meal as much as I enjoyed those cabbage rolls. Thank you so much! I even had my sister over for dinner last night, and I still have another two or three meals in the freezer."

He smiled and nodded. "Glad you enjoyed them." Then he turned the key in the lock, pushed the door open, reached for the grocery bag and hauled Jo inside.

She rolled her eyes and leaned wearily against the closed door. She pointed toward the bedroom. "Go look. I left a note."

"The note wouldn't prove anything," he said. "Just

that you could say you were doing one thing when you were really doing another.''

Exasperated, she held her arms out at her sides. ''Where could I go in this condition—on foot? Do you want to check my pockets for your car keys?''

He dismissed that notion as impossible. ''I had the car with me.''

''And where did *you* go?'' she asked, beginning to unbutton her coat, figuring the walk was out after all. ''You didn't even leave me a note, and you don't see me accusing you of…of abandonment.''

''I went to the bakery,'' he said, passing her the grocery bag. The suspicion had left his expression, and he now simply looked tired.

She peered inside the bag. It contained brioches from the supermarket's bakery. She looked up at him, wondering if what she held in her hands was an olive branch.

MAMA JO? Mama Cass says you got lucky with the cabbage rolls. Take the bakery buns and make peace. You were wrong, anyway.

HIS NEXT WORDS answered the question. ''I'm sorry about the other night,'' he said, hands in his pockets. ''I had no right to…make those judgments.''

She shrugged a shoulder. ''I'm sorry, too. It was my fault for attacking you. I know that isn't what you meant.''

They looked at each other, each almost afraid to go on and risk the sudden truce. Jo finally pulled her coat off and turned toward the kitchen. ''I'll put on the coffee and make some tea.''

He rubbed his stubbly jaw. "I have to shave," he said.

"Oh, don't" was on the tip of her tongue, but she bit it back. Instead, she said, "Go ahead." Then she couldn't resist taunting him. "Unless you're afraid I'll make my escape while you're gone, and you'd be more comfortable if I came into the bathroom with you?"

He gave her a look that acknowledged the taunt, then slid down to take in her generous proportions. "Thanks, but you wouldn't fit in the bathroom. I figure the brioches will keep you here until I get back."

She turned away to the kitchen. "Only if I eat yours, too."

IT HAD BEGUN. Ryan wrapped an arm around Jo's shoulders as they left Dr. McNamara's office after her weekly visit, and walked out to the car. He felt both exultant and terrified.

According to the obstetrician, Jo had experienced lightening and engagement—medical terms that meant the baby had "dropped" and that her head was in position and about to begin the gradual trip down, though actual birth could still be a week or more away.

MAMA JO? Are you using gravity boots?

SHE WAS REMARKABLY CALM at the moment—even serene. But he knew that situation could change in an instant. They'd lived in relative peace in the four days since their brioche breakfast, but her wild and abrupt changes of mood kept him alert. He never knew from one moment to the next whether he would have to comfort a sobbing woman, or laugh with one who was delivering one-liners about her size.

To his surprise, she wrapped an arm around his waist and looked up at him with a smile that was empathetic. "Scared?" she asked.

"Profoundly," he replied with a brief laugh. "You?"

She nodded. "Yes. But I'm excited, too. I can't believe we're on the brink of finally seeing what Chelsea looks like."

"Jo! Hi!" Jo and Ryan turned to see Amy Brown hurrying across the parking lot toward the hospital. She was flushed with excitement. "Guess what?"

Jo did. "You got your model mother?"

"Yes!" Amy shrieked. "Coast Guard family. Just moved here a month ago. She's very excited, and I'm thrilled to death! She's just been admitted, so I want to be around for the grand finale."

"Wonderful!" Jo patted her hand. "Well done."

Amy's beeper went off, and she rolled her eyes, switched her purse to her other arm so that she could reach it, then frowned as she read the digital display.

"Yeah?" she mumbled to herself. "Well, you can just wait until I'm good and ready."

"What?" Jo asked.

Amy looked up at her, as though surprised she was still there. "What? Oh, nothing. Just mumbling to myself. So, you're about to do your thing, too, aren't you?"

Jo nodded. "All the right things are happening. My due date's a week from today." Then she shooed Amy toward the building. "Don't let us keep you. I know you don't want to miss anything. Good luck."

"Right." Amy waved as she started off. "See you next week. You take care of her, Mr. Jeffries."

"That I will," he promised.

"I wonder who that call was from," Jo asked as

Ryan unlocked the passenger side door of the Volvo. "She didn't seem particularly thrilled by it."

"Tom Nicholas, maybe?" Ryan suggested, lifting her feet for her and putting them into the car. This had become a ritual over the past few days.

Jo turned to him with a frown. "Why do you say that?"

"Just a guess. She had a message from him the last time we saw her, remember?"

"That's right. Do you think they've had a falling-out? The last time he called her, she was so excited, she was barely coherent."

He nodded, slipping in behind the wheel. "I remember. Well, you know how love is," he said.

"No," she replied candidly. "I don't. How is it?"

He met her eyes. "Wonderful, difficult, happy, sad, tragic, funny, enervating, debilitating—everything that exists in this world, and its direct opposite."

She frowned at that explanation, seriously interested. "And how do the two of you ever get anywhere?"

"Ah...well..." He stared through the windshield. "You don't really have to *get* anywhere. You just have to *be,* and love sort of generates its own propulsion. And you really have very little control over where it takes you. All you have to do is sustain each other along the way."

She turned slightly toward him, fascinated by his description. "How did a practical, organized man like yourself even *want* to enter into a...a...situation so unstructured?"

He folded his hands at the top of the steering wheel. "Again, it's not like you have a choice. Had I been asked by anyone, I'd have declined. But Cassie came to work at the bank, and from the moment I saw her, I knew I had no personal future without her.''

Mama Cass says to hug Daddy.

CASSIE. Jo felt no resentment that her sister's name had come up. After all, she, Jo, had asked Ryan about love, and the love of his life had been Cassie. He had no other reference point.

And she was carrying Cassie's baby. It didn't matter that she had sheltered and nurtured its body for nine months, that she'd grown to love it with everything she was and more. When Chelsea finally made her appearance a week or so from now, she would be half Ryan and half Cassie. And Jo's job would be done.

The sudden, desperate loss she felt made a fist of emotion in the pit of her stomach.

''I'm exhausted,'' she said, in a carefully neutral voice. ''Can we go home instead of going to lunch?''

Ryan put his key in the ignition, frowning in sudden concern. ''Right away.''

At home, he tried to put her to bed, but she insisted on lying on the recliner. ''It's easier to get out of,'' she said as he placed a sunflower-patterned cotton throw over her. ''And could you get my crochet bag before you go back to work?'' As he headed down the corridor, she called after him, ''I think I left it on the floor beside my bed.''

Ryan found it immediately and took it to her. The bag was now stuffed, the project almost three feet long. She'd worked on it faithfully on breaks at work and in the evenings. He always felt an odd twinge when he saw it. Cassie had begun it, and Jo was finishing it. Just as they'd done with Chelsea. It amazed and touched him what women would do for one another.

He microwaved a cup of tea for her and placed it on the lamp table at her elbow.

"Anything else?" he asked cheerfully.

Something about the look in her eyes made him force a carefree mood. She smiled pleasantly, and she had that same air of serenity about her, but it had a quality of fatal acceptance in it that he didn't trust. It had come over her, he remembered, when he mentioned Cassie.

She shook her head. "Nope. Got everything. Thanks. You want me to put potatoes in the oven for dinner, or anything?" She smiled grimly. "I'll even remember to poke holes in them this time."

He laughed lightly. "Thanks, but I'll bring home takeout. Chinese? Italian? Mexican?"

"How about—" she thought with great concentration "—that bow-tie pasta salad from Chez Pasta, and the Macho Nacho appetizer from the bar?"

He leaned over the chair to make sure he'd understood her. "Bow-tie salad and nachos?"

"Yeah."

"And…you're going to have them together?"

She didn't seem to see a problem. "Yeah. And could you pick up cannolis for dessert?"

He felt his stomach roil. "Sure."

"Thanks," she said quietly.

Her hair was down in a wild mass around her shoulders, and her cheeks were pink with weariness. Her eyes were bright, her skin was flawless, her fingers were long and slender on the blanket. Under it, his baby mounded like a little Everest.

He felt drawn to her like the sea to the shore, as

though God himself had ordained this movement at the moment of Creation.

Before he could second-guess the impulse, he closed the gap between them and kissed her mouth.

Jo's heartbeat rose into her throat as she read the intention in the dark eyes focused on her lips. She parted them, startled, at the same moment that he claimed them. But all she felt was the tender warmth of his mouth for what was but a brief instant—but one that played over in her mind for the hours he was gone, as though that kiss had taken an eternity.

She ate half of everything he brought home, including half of *his* cannoli. And each of them studiously avoided any mention of the kiss. When they'd finished eating, she asked brightly, "You want to go for a walk?"

He looked up from wiping off the table. She closed the door on the dishwasher and the few utensils they'd used.

"At night?" he asked.

She frowned. "This isn't Central Park, Ryan, it's Heron Point. I thought we'd just walk along the river a little way."

"You said you walked to see things," he reminded. "You can't see anything at night."

"At night you walk to *smell* things."

He tossed the sponge at the sink and looked doubtful. "What kind of things?"

"I'll show you." She took his arm and pushed him toward the coat closet. "Come on. I've got to work off some of this." She patted her watermelon stomach.

He grinned. "Good idea, but it won't work. You still have to give birth to it."

She rolled her eyes. "You know what I mean."

GET 2 BOOKS FREE!

To get your 2 free books, affix this peel-off sticker to the reply card and mail it today!

MIRA® Books, The Brightest Stars in Fiction, presents

The Best of the Best™

Superb collector's editions of the very best novels by some of today's best-known authors!

★ **FREE BOOKS!** To introduce you to "The Best of the Best" we'll send you 2 books ABSOLUTELY FREE!

★ **FREE GIFT!** Get an exciting mystery gift FREE!

★ **BEST BOOKS!** "The Best of the Best" brings you the best books by some of today's most popular authors!

GET 2

HOW TO GET YOUR
2 FREE BOOKS AND FREE GIFT!

1. Peel off the MIRA sticker on the front cover. Place it in the space provided at right. This automatically entitles you to receive two free books and an exciting mystery gift.

2. Send back this card and you'll get 2 "The Best of the Best™" novels. These books have a combined cover price of $11.00 or more in the U.S. and $13.00 or more in Canada, but they are yours to keep absolutely FREE!

3. There's <u>no</u> catch. You're under <u>no</u> obligation to buy anything. We charge nothing – ZERO – for your first shipment. And you don't have to make any minimum number of purchases – not even one!

4. We call this line "The Best of the Best" because each month you'll receive the best books by some of today's hottest authors. These authors show up time and time again on all the major bestseller lists and their books sell out as soon as they hit the stores. You'll like the convenience of getting them delivered to your home at our special discount prices . . . and you'll love your *Heart to Heart* subscriber newsletter featuring author news, horoscopes, recipes, book reviews and much more!

5. We hope that after receiving your free books you'll want to remain a subscriber. But the choice is yours – to continue or cancel, anytime at all! So why not take us up on our invitation, with no risk of any kind. You'll be glad you did!

6. And remember...we'll send you a mystery gift ABSOLUTELY FREE just for giving "The Best of the Best" a try.

SPECIAL FREE GIFT!

We'll send you a fabulous surprise gift, absolutely FREE, simply for accepting our no-risk offer!

Visit us online at
www.mirabooks.com

® and TM are trademarks of Harlequin Enterprises Limited.

BOOKS FREE!

Hurry!

Return this card promptly to GET 2 FREE BOOKS & A FREE GIFT!

◀ DETACH AND MAIL CARD TODAY! ▶

The Best of the Best™

Affix
peel-off
MIRA
sticker here

YES! Please send me the 2 FREE "The Best of the Best" novels and FREE gift for which I qualify. I understand that I am under no obligation to purchase anything further, as explained on the opposite page.

(P-BB3-01)

385 MDL C6PQ   185 MDL C6PP

NAME   (PLEASE PRINT CLEARLY)

ADDRESS

APT.#   CITY

STATE/PROV.   ZIP/POSTAL CODE

Offer limited to one per household and not valid to current subscribers of "The Best of the Best." All orders subject to approval. Books received may vary.
©1995 MIRA BOOKS

The Best of the Best™ — Here's How it Works:

Accepting your 2 free books and gift places you under no obligation to buy anything. You may keep the books and gift and return the shipping statement marked "cancel." If you do not cancel, about a month later we will send you 4 additional novels and bill you just $4.24 each in the U.S., or $4.74 each in Canada, plus 25¢ shipping & handling per book and applicable taxes if any.* That's the complete price and — compared to cover prices of $5.50 or more each in the U.S. and $6.50 or more each in Canada — it's quite a bargain! You may cancel at any time, but if you choose to continue, every month we'll send you 4 more books, which you may either purchase at the discount price or return to us and cancel your subscription.

*Terms and prices subject to change without notice. Sales tax applicable in N.Y. Canadian residents will be charged applicable provincial taxes and GST.

If offer card is missing write to: The Best of the Best, 3010 Walden Ave., P.O. Box 1867, Buffalo, NY 14240-1867

BUSINESS REPLY MAIL
FIRST-CLASS MAIL   PERMIT NO. 717   BUFFALO, NY

POSTAGE WILL BE PAID BY ADDRESSEE

**THE BEST OF THE BEST
3010 WALDEN AVE
PO BOX 1867
BUFFALO NY 14240-9952**

NO POSTAGE
NECESSARY
IF MAILED
IN THE
UNITED STATES

He laughed and handed her her coat and beret.

The fog that was in place every morning when they looked out the condo window was already lying over the water like a length of thick gauze. Foghorns blared from the channel where ships sailed upriver to Portland, and sometimes anchored, waiting for a berth at the port.

Jo and Ryan walked along the well-lit dock arm in arm, drawn together by a force neither understood or tried to explain. It was like the kiss neither understood nor regretted.

They stopped about a quarter mile from the condo and leaned their forearms on the railing.

"This is so stimulating," Ryan said in teasing tones of feigned boredom. Fog covered everything, and there truly was nothing to see.

Jo reached a hand up and covered his eyes. "What do you smell?"

"Why are you covering my eyes?" he asked. "I can't see anything."

"Because you're distracted," she said, "by the fact that there's nothing to see. Concentrate on the smells."

"Okay." He sighed, let himself concentrate for just a moment on the cool softness of her hand against his cheekbones and the bridge of his nose, then worked on answering her question. "Ah...salt water, diesel oil, creosote..."

Jo murmured, "God, you're stubborn," and turned his face in the direction of the mouth of the river. "Breathe deeply," she instructed.

He complied. And then he got it—lungfuls of some indescribable natural perfume that must have drifted on the air and rolled with the ocean into the river to come to this place and this point in time with this particular combination of fragrances.

"Oh," he said on a breath, trying to filter and separate the components. "I smell Bangkok," he said, "the Serengeti, some Alpine meadow, and a..." He sniffed, catching a whiff of something sweet. "Paris, I think," he said. "A bakery on the rue de Rivoli."

She dropped her hand from his eyes and giggled. The fog seemed to act as soundproofing, and kept the musical sound lingering at his ear.

"What a nose," she said admiringly. "That was pretty specific. Why the rue de Rivoli?"

"When I was in college," he said, "I did my junior year in Paris. A friend and I went there for croissants every morning." He smiled down at her. "You think the brioches at the market's bakery are delicious? You should have tasted those. Anyway...the aroma would wake us up, it was so wonderful. But so far, I've done all the work. What do you smell?"

They leaned shoulder to shoulder on the railing, enclosed in their misty world. Water lapped against the invisible pilings, and a foghorn warned against trespassing too close.

"Well, frankly, I've never broken it down that way," Jo admitted. "I've just always thought of it as... invitation. Promise. The fragrance of tomorrow."

"So, you want to travel?" he asked.

"No." Her denial was quick. "Not an invitation to visit the source of all those exotic fragrances, but the invitation to accept that they're out there, and the promise that the world is a wide and exciting place."

He looked down at the face at his shoulder. "A world that you don't want to see?"

She shrugged a shoulder. "Not at the moment, anyway. I guess it's weird to feel excited just *knowing* what's out there."

He put an arm around her shoulder. "It isn't weird. It's a sort of Joian philosophy."

She laughed and looped an arm around his waist. She looked up at the sky, but it was hidden by the fog.

He followed her gaze. "Looking for a star to wish on?"

"No." She leaned her head back in the hollow of his shoulder. "I was looking for Chelsea. Some people believe babies are stars before they're born."

IT ISN'T TRUE. We just like to be stars after we're born. I can't wait.

"NO KIDDING." He was a little surprised to find himself straining to peer through the fog. But the sky was virtually invisible. "Is she the North Star, do you think?"

She laughed lightly. "Probably. I imagine her as big and boisterous."

"Incidentally, your father called the bank today to ask if I still had my Volvo, and what the dimensions of the trunk were."

She blinked. "What's he bringing?"

"He wouldn't say. I can only conclude it's big." He squeezed her shoulder. "Are there any more smell tests, or can we go home now?"

They stood arm in arm, and she was leaning into him. He supported her weight easily, casually. Several hours ago, he had kissed her. Yet there was nothing different about him that she could see to indicate that they had blundered onto new ground. She felt it, though she didn't understand it, and she wanted him to feel it, too.

"No," she replied, "but there is a taste test."

He raised an eyebrow. "After pasta salad, nachos and cannolis?"

She ignored that. "It also involves closing your eyes."

"Jo…"

"Do it, Ryan, or I'll send you out for anchovies and orange juice at 2:00 a.m."

With a groan, he closed his eyes.

The obstruction of the baby prevented her from getting close enough to stand on tiptoe and reach his lips with hers. So she put a hand to the back of his neck and tipped his head down toward her.

His eyes opened, and she saw a quick surprise in them, then an admission that it had to be, an acceptance that it was inevitable. He didn't take the initiative from her, but he didn't resist, either.

Jo put her mouth to his, felt his interest and attention, and tried to put into the gesture all the emotion that was blossoming up inside her. *I love you,* she told him with the artful attention of her lips. *I've loved you for so long. There's something here, Ryan. Can't you see it? Can't you feel it?*

She looped her arms around his neck, drawing him closer. *I know we're opposites, but we're finding ways to deal with that, aren't we? I think we could be happy.*

His response was tentative for just an instant, but then she felt her emotion ignite his, and he crushed her to him, Chelsea squirming between them.

HAVE I MENTIONED that it's already very tight in here?

HE KNEW there were a dozen reasons why this shouldn't happen—he'd been widowed only seven months, this was his sister-in-law, the woman who carried the baby he'd made with his dead wife, the woman who was 360 degrees different from himself. Well, maybe that wasn't true anymore. Living and giving had seemed to lessen the distance between them considerably.

And she was warm, generous, funny, and touchingly brave. Something in her called to him, and something in him was eager to respond.

It occurred to him to wonder if that was love. He'd experienced it once, but loss made it seem like an eternity ago. Jo put her lips to his ear at that moment, and he lost whatever fragile grip he'd had on thought. So he simply went with what he felt.

Desire erupted in him like steam from a geyser. He kissed her hair, her eyes, her cheeks, her jaw. He nipped at her earlobe, and when she uttered a little cry of pleasure, he raised her face in his hands and plundered her mouth.

Jo was giddy with ecstasy. He felt it. He knew! Then she became giddy from lack of air and pushed at his chest, wresting her lips from his with a little laugh that drifted around them in the fog. She leaned her forehead against his throat and laughed lightly. "The baby needs oxygen," she said breathlessly.

GASP!

THE BABY. Ryan felt it wriggling against his own abdomen—alive, and eager, probably, to escape the confined space of the womb and join the world. Cassie's baby.

He felt Jo in his arms, warm and laughing, her breath against his throat, and felt quite literally as though the past and the present were trying to tear him in two.

He'd been so careful all this time, resisting his attraction to Jo, sure it was all wrapped up in the pregnancy. But in the midst of this kiss, he'd almost forgotten the baby—until it moved against him. And even now, when memories of Cassie intruded, he found it difficult to open his arms and set Jo free.

But she took the responsibility from him. As she stepped backward, out of his embrace, he looked down into her eyes and saw the laughter wiped away. Pain had replaced it.

He took hold of her arms as she tried to move away. "Don't look like that," he pleaded. "I wanted that kiss as much as you did."

Her lips took on a wry twist as she looked deeply into his eyes. "Yes," she said quietly, mockingly. "I can see that. You look utterly miserable. Let's go home."

"No." He pulled her back when she tried to turn. The night was damp and cold, and he moved his hands from her arms to tie the top button of her coat. He couldn't analyze what he felt, but he didn't want her to think he felt nothing. "We're not in a simple relationship here," he said reasonably. "I've been…attracted to you since I moved you in with me, but I want to understand what's at the heart of it."

"The heart," she pointed out quietly, "usually generates love."

He framed her face in his hands, his brow furrowed. "Jo, surrogate motherhood between sisters generates *confusion* for the widower of the one, who is also the father of the other's baby! No matter how I add it up, someone gets subtracted! I need time to think about this."

DADDY. Mama Cass says she's already gone. She wants you to think of you and me. Please snuggle up against me again. That was nice.

SHE SUBSIDED, knowing he was right. She wanted it to be simple, because what she felt was so clear. But it wasn't simple—particularly not for him.

"You're right," she said. "I'm sorry."

"Don't be sorry." He put an arm around her and started back slowly toward the condominium. "Just be patient."

Patient, Jo thought as the foghorn bleated its lonely call. She had a week left before Chelsea was born. And she'd come to love the baby and her father so much that she couldn't imagine living on the periphery of their lives after the birth. She was beginning to understand that she would have to be as important to them as they were to her, or she couldn't stay. She would be gone.

Patience—at least more than a week's worth—was not an option.

"WELL, my God, Jo!" Matthew Arceneau, tall and bony and professorial, with shaggy white hair and a beard, leaned down to try to wrap his daughter in his arms. "You look as though you're about to fly away."

Jo turned to one side to make it possible to get closer, and reached her arms around his neck. "This approach usually works best." She laughed as he kissed her cheek soundly. "I'm far too leaden to fly away, believe me. I'll probably hatch a T-Rex or something. It's so good to see you, Daddy."

Hi, Grandpa! Mama Cass says to tell you she loves you. And she sends love from Grandma, too.

THEY STOOD in the tiny terminal at the Coast Guard air station at Heron Point, which rented an airstrip to the commercial short-hop carrier that had flown Matthew in from Portland.

Ryan excused himself to collect his father-in-law's bags, but Matthew caught his arm. "You'll need my help," he said, pushing Jo gently to the terminal's single bank of green vinyl chairs. "We'll be right back, Joey."

"How is she doing?" Matthew asked Ryan as they went to the small, warm office at the back of the terminal where luggage was placed in the middle of the floor to await collection.

"The doctor says she's healthy," he replied, avoiding the man's eyes, reading the implication in the question. Matt Arceneau had been his father-in-law for six years, and Ryan was well aware of his fierce love and loyalty for his daughters, and the deceptively charming mailed fist that was behind all his efforts to do what was best for them. "And the baby's great. He doesn't foresee any problems. Which bags?"

"All my stuff has a Continental flag sticker on it," Matthew replied, pointing to one blue tweed garment bag in a far corner, and another, smaller leather bag on the opposite side. He headed for an item that rose from the middle of the sea of luggage like the *Queen Mary*— except the queen was a lion.

Ryan stopped with his hand on the garment bag and watched in amazement as Matthew picked up the stuffed toy, which must have sat five feet tall, and gingerly made his way back out again.

Both bags in hand, Ryan met him near the door. "What *is* that?"

Matthew grinned, stroking the elaborate mane. "My granddaughter's first stuffed toy." Then he sobered again. "But, how *is* Jo?"

Ryan sighed and gave up trying to hedge. "She's serene, in charge, efficient and eager one moment, then tearful and worried the next."

Matthew nodded. "Well, that's pretty par, as I recall. Hormones in a flap, you know. All part and parcel of the process. The day before her mother delivered her, she hit me with a tent stake in the middle of the outdoor department at Sears. Thought I shouldn't be looking at sporting goods when she was shopping for a nightgown to take to the hospital where she was going to have *my* baby."

Ryan laughed. "I didn't realize being a father was so dangerous."

Matt looked him in the eye and shook his head. "Being a father is wonderful. It's being a husband that's dangerous. Don't you remember?"

Ryan tried to think back, but the details of being married to Cassie seemed as though they'd happened a lifetime ago, to someone else. He was surprised to discover that, when waiting for the baby kept the essence of his life with her so near.

Ryan shook his head. "I remember mostly that we laughed a lot, loved each other madly, and that she was always concocting schemes I was sure would never work out. But she was convinced there was a solution to every problem, if you wanted something badly enough. And, somehow, she always found one."

Matthew smiled a little sadly, apparently also remembering that quality in his daughter. "So, how are *you* coping, Ryan?" he asked. "Are you ready to be a single father?"

He didn't hesitate. "Of course. That's the hand I've been dealt." He turned back to the terminal, gesturing

Matthew to follow. "Come on. Jo will be wondering what's happened to us."

"Maybe," Matthew muttered quietly as he fell into step behind him, "you should pick up another card."

Jo looked up from the magazine she was perusing as Ryan and her father approached. She took one look at the giant lion and shrieked, "Simba!"

Ryan raised an eyebrow. "You've met before?"

"He's the Lion King!" she cried, reaching up for the toy. Her father placed it on the floor before her. It stood taller than she did. "Oh, Daddy..." She smoothed the fuzzy orange mane with her hands, then ran a fingertip down the length of its nose. "Chelsea will love it!"

"Okay, let's go," Ryan said. "We've got reservations at Chez Pasta for seven o'clock."

Matthew picked up the lion. Jo smiled from her chair. "I'd like to, but I can't."

Ryan frowned. "Why not?"

She looked around surreptitiously, then admitted under her breath, "Because I'm stuck."

Ryan rolled his eyes and put the bags down, exchanging a grin with Matthew, who stepped back with the lion.

"Well, don't be upset with me," she said, raising her arms as Ryan squatted down to assess her position. "Daddy's the one who suggested I sit here. On my own, I'd have concluded that a wraparound waiting-area chair was not a good choice, but I was trying to be cooperative."

Matthew snickered. "Ha! For twenty-nine years of her life, she's a hellion. *Now* she chooses to cooperate."

Ryan gently forced his fingers in between her stomach and the kidney-shaped table arm attached to the chair. "Okay, slip sideways," he instructed.

DADDY, you're bending my foot.

SHE LOOKED AT HIM as though he were insane. "Ryan, I don't even move *forward* very well anymore."

"Jo..." His tone held amusement and mild impatience. Then he placed his other arm around the back of her waist to pull. "Put your arm around my neck. If I miss my ravioli with sausage, I won't let you forget it."

She inched sideways, tried to slip out, but the three chairs attached to the one in which she sat rose with it.

She sat back with a sigh, her arm still hooked around his neck. Their noses were an inch apart. "There isn't much I *want* to forget," she whispered for his ears alone.

His dark eyes held hers for an instant, and she thought she saw a smile there. Then, realizing they were beginning to collect an audience, Ryan inched her backward a little farther, pushed a little harder on her stomach and instructed a young boy observing with a Tootsie Pop in his mouth to sit in the next chair.

"Okay, now," he said. The boy sat, Ryan pulled, Jo pushed, and she was free. Their small audience applauded. Jo bowed.

THANK YOU. Thank you.

"WELL, that was entertaining," Matthew said as they headed for the car. "And people think small towns are no fun. That would never happen at Logan Airport."

Ryan opened the trunk. "If Jo were there, it might."

It wasn't until later that night, when her father was asleep on the hideaway bed in the living room and Ryan looked in on her before turning in, that Jo noticed his hand.

He was about to close her door with it when she noticed the rough, bloodred scrapes on his first three fingers from knuckle to knuckle. She remembered his hand slipping between her and the chair arm at the airport terminal.

"Your hand..." she said, coming to him to examine it. She wore a tentlike bright blue cotton gown, and her hair was piled on top of her head after her shower.

He enjoyed her solicitousness, but dismissed the problem with a wave of his free hand. "It's fine."

She ignored his denial and, maintaining her grip on him, drew him into her bathroom. She reached into the medicine cabinet, remembering that she'd seen a tube of Neosporin and a box of Band-Aids. He leaned a hip on the counter and let her work on him.

She was barefoot, and they were eye-to-eye, though she seemed studiously to be avoiding his gaze. He found himself wanting to look into her eyes, wanting to see that warmth and excitement there, that fascination with and enthusiasm for everything, which was so uniquely her.

Cassie had loved life and everything in it—and had always been determined to scoop it all into her experience and coax it into providing her what she wanted.

Jo seemed to enjoy it without needing to control it, and he found himself admiring the way she moved from day to day, thrilled by the unexpected, relishing the surprises.

He was beginning to think that after a month in her company he was learning something.

DADDY, Mama Cass says we're all entitled to a different approach.

JO WAS FIDGETING. She'd bandaged all three fingers, and there was nothing left to do but put the Band-Aids away, but she hated to spoil this moment of domestic intimacy. She liked being closed with him in the bathroom. She could pretend she was brushing her hair and he was shaving as they prepared for an evening on the town, a baby-sitter in the next room with Chelsea. That was fantasy, of course, but it didn't seem to matter. Her whole life this past year had been one enlightening or shattering event after another. She was anxious to deal in a little dreamy escape.

So when Ryan took the box of Band-Aids from her hands, put it aside, then wrapped his arms around her and pulled her close, she thought for a moment that she was simply getting really good at this—that her imagination had virtual-reality capability.

Then she felt the warmth of his hands roving her back, the strength of his shoulder against her cheek, his lips in her hair. It was really happening.

But she'd learned a little since the other night, in the fog on the pier. She simply held him and said nothing, letting all she felt build up inside, letting all she longed for remain unspoken.

It was best that way. She didn't know what to ask of him, anyway. As much as she loved him, she had a better understanding of his love for Cassie. She knew it lived in him still, deep and strong, and she wouldn't have taken a moment of it away from him, even if it meant she could take its place.

The baby squirmed, and she swore she felt its head

move, pressing against her pelvic floor. She stiffened in
discomfort and uttered a little cry.

Ryan took her weight and put a hand on the baby.
"What?" he demanded.

YOU'RE SQUISHING ME. My big toe is in my ear!

SHE SHOOK HER HEAD and laughed softly, drawing a
breath. "Nothing, really. Just movement. But the way
she's placed now, I can feel every turn of her head."

He relaxed somewhat, sharply reminded of what lay
ahead of them. He lifted her into his arms, carried her
to her bedroom and placed her in the middle of her
blankets. "You're sure you're all right?"

"Positive," she assured him. "Don't worry. It was
just a twinge."

"Okay. Good night."

"Good night."

He stood in her doorway a moment, looking at her
lying on her side in the virginal single bed, and thought
how lonely she looked there, and how unfair it was that
she wasn't in some wide four-poster with the man of
her dreams and a baby that would be all hers.

But, this baby was all *his*. And that was what decided
him.

He went back to her bed, tossed the blankets aside
as she gasped in surprise and confusion, picked her up
again and carried her to his king-size bed.

"Don't panic," he said, settling her in on the inside
and pulling the covers up over her. "I have no designs
on your virtue, just your comfort and your safety. I
don't want you in there alone if you need something in
the middle of the night."

"But..." She pointed toward the living room, where her father slept.

"I know," he said, going to the light switch to turn it off, and closing the door. "If we find ourselves having to explain it to him, I'll worry about it then. Right now, I need you near me."

Jo snuggled into the pillow where he'd placed her, thinking that if he expected an argument from her on that score, he'd be waiting a long time.

"Good night, Ryan," she said.

There was an instant's surprised silence, and then she heard him move to his side of the bed and sit on it to pull off his shoes. "Good night, Jo," he replied.

IF DADDY WANTS US near him, why is he all the way over there?

Chapter Nine

Matthew did laundry, prepared and froze several casseroles for use after they brought the baby home, and accompanied Jo on her walks, though Ryan left them the Volvo and rode in to work with his assistant manager.

Matthew met Buttercup, Bill and Camouflage, and then he and Jo stopped in at Coffee Country, where Devon had everything under complete control.

Jo seated her father at the counter with a mochaccino and went into the back room to put together what she knew would be the last deposit before the baby came. She had to keep busy. Even her father's conversation couldn't distract her from memories of waking up in the dark hours of early morning, curled against Ryan's chest, his arms loosely wrapped around her as he slept.

The first night she spent in his bed, she'd managed to stay on her side, but last night she'd had the Cassie dream again. She had a vague recollection of having recoiled from it—and of reaching for the warm harbor of Ryan's arms. She remembered his body curved around hers, his strong voice in the darkness telling her quietly that she'd been dreaming and to go back to sleep.

When she'd awakened again, he was gone. He'd told her father he had an early meeting with the district manager, who was visiting from Seattle.

The coffee bar had made a lot of money in the few days she'd been home, she noticed, feeling a curious sensation of dispensability. Devon, experienced and charming, had done a fine job of keeping everything tidy and efficient.

If she did decide to walk away from all this when Chelsea was born, it seemed she wouldn't even be missed.

For the past two days, she'd worried over bouts of false labor and considered her options. Spending the nights in Ryan's bed, though all they'd done was sleep, had given her a glimpse of all she could have—if she could just help Ryan see it. Maybe it would be worth the painful distance of being simply his sister-in-law for a while, simply Chelsea's aunt—if it meant that in the end she could have both of them.

But she vacillated, one moment joyfully hopeful that it could happen, and the next cynically certain that it was all in her imagination, that Ryan's concern was just for Chelsea, and that once the baby was born, she, Jo, would be out of the picture. Maybe she should call Lisa, her college roommate who now lived in Port Townsend, on Puget Sound, and see how she would feel about company for a few weeks. If Ryan decided he didn't need her, she didn't think she could stay in Heron Point.

She was a bundle of nerves. Even her father had commented on the walk downtown that she was like grease on a griddle. She would kill, she thought, for a cup of espresso. It was one of the first things she intended to have the moment Chelsea was delivered.

When Jo emerged from the back room, it was to find

her father and Diantha in urgent conversation, the woman holding Matthew's hand palm up as she ran her index finger along one of its lines.

"Oh, a very long lifeline," Jo heard Diantha say as she approached the table. "Late eighties would be my guess. And when a robust man like yourself takes care of himself—" Jo noted in amazement that Diantha's cheeks were pink, and her voice was low and husky "—he can enjoy *all* life has to offer well into his early nineties."

Matthew, chin leaning on his free hand, said feelingly, "Now there's a dream come true."

Since neither person had yet noticed her presence, Jo went to Devon, asked him to make Matthew and Diantha another round, and walked the half block to the bank to see if Ryan wanted to join them for lunch.

It would steady her to see him, she thought. She'd come to rely on him a great deal in the past month. And she felt slightly neglected because he'd gone off to work that morning without saying goodbye.

Roberta Dawson smiled her apologies. "I'm afraid he's already left for lunch about an hour ago with the western-district CEO and his entourage."

"Oh." Jo tried to hide her disappointment. "Don't bother to tell him I stopped in. I imagine it's pretty tense for all of you to have management checking on you."

Roberta shook her head. "They're not after us, this time. They're just interested in Mr. Jeffries."

"Oh?"

She lowered her voice. "It's that Los Angeles thing. You know."

Jo sat in the chair beside Roberta's desk, her senses on the alert. She lowered her own voice. "No, I don't. What Los Angeles thing?"

Jo saw the sudden concern in Roberta's eyes. "He didn't tell you?" she asked, sitting back in her chair, as though to put a distance between them. "Maybe I shouldn't have..."

Jo smiled widely and pooh-poohed that notion with a casual wave of her hand. "Don't be silly. My father's just arrived from Connecticut for the birth of the baby, and we've hardly had time to talk." She made her tone friendly, but injected it with a touch of an imperious right to know. "Now, what about Los Angeles?"

"Well..." Roberta appeared reluctant to reveal the news. "It's about the...promotion."

"Oh, that." Jo had no idea what promotion, but was simply trying to generate confidence. For the moment, she wasn't thinking about what it could mean to her, hoping only to decipher what it meant, period. "They're...they're serious about it, are they?"

Roberta relaxed. "Apparently. It sounds as though they're going to really make it worth your while to move there."

The words struck Jo like a blow, but her only outward reaction was an instinctive covering of her baby with a protective arm.

"That's what you get," Roberta said, "for being with the most imaginative and practical banker in the entire West Coast division." She grinned proudly. "Those were the words of the CEO himself. I heard that when I took coffee into their meeting this morning. From Coffee Country," she added. "Which they enjoyed enormously, by the way."

Jo drew a breath and asked calmly, "Did they say when this will come about?"

"Not until after Christmas."

"Oh, good. Well..." She felt very much as though

she'd been nailed to the chair, but she pushed herself to her feet, with more determination than grace, Roberta steadying her arm those last few inches when she had to let go of the desk. "Thank you, Roberta. You've been very enlightening."

Roberta looked worried again as she walked Jo to the door. "You *are* going with him, aren't you?" she asked. "I mean, we all thought, with your sis—" she stopped abruptly, then began again "—with Mrs. Jeffries gone, that you and he would... I mean, there's the baby..."

Jo nodded and smiled sadly, feeling everything that had been positive inside her during the past two complicated days being choked off from its sustenance and dying. "Sort of defies a solution, doesn't it? 'Bye, Roberta. And please don't tell him I was here. I'm sure...he'll want to tell me himself."

She could imagine what he would say as she walked back to the coffee bar to pick up her father. "See you, Jo. Chelsea and I are off to L.A. You don't want to come, do you?" Or maybe "Moving to Los Angeles, Jo. Thank you for giving birth to Cassie's and my child and stepping graciously out of the way. I'll keep in touch."

"Joey," Matthew pleaded as she pulled him from the shop and toward the taxi stand in front of the supermarket. "What's the matter? Are you all right? Is it labor?"

"No," she said, with an edge to her voice that made him give her a second look as he helped her in beside the driver. "It's a lust for blood. Get in, Daddy, so we can get home."

Matthew climbed into the back of the cab and studied the back of his daughter's head with concern. The last time he'd seen that look in her eye, she'd been thirteen and Cassie had "borrowed" her baby-sitting money to bankroll a pie-baking business of her own. Cassie had sported a shiner for a week.

It wasn't the money, Jo had confided to him then, it was the deceit in someone she'd trusted.

"He's moving to Los Angeles!" Jo stormed across the living room, through the dining room and into the kitchen. She filled the teakettle and banged it down on the stove. "Just like that! After Christmas."

Matthew followed her into the kitchen, his arms folded, his brow furrowed. "What?" he asked. "Who told you?"

"Roberta Dawson, at the bank. He was having lunch with the bigwigs from the district. They're promoting him because he's imaginative and efficient. He's sneaky, too, but they probably don't know that." She yanked a tin from the countertop and struggled with the hinged lid. Matthew moved forward to take it from her. He flipped the lid with his thumbs, then offered it to her. She pulled a tea bag out and slammed the tin on the counter. It vibrated like a cymbal. "I suppose he'd have told me before he started packing. Or maybe not. Maybe he'd have left me a note: 'Bye, Aunt Jo. Thanks for everything, but we'll be fine without you now.'"

"Jo." Matthew wandered after her as she marched into Ryan's bedroom and yanked her crocheting bag off the chair. "Honey, don't jump to conclusions until you hear his side."

She gave him a pitying look and marched past him, back toward the door. "He apparently has no intention of telling me. And *I* have no intention of asking."

MAMA JO? Does that make sense? I'm standing on my head, so things aren't always very clear to me, but shouldn't you ask? I mean—isn't it important?

AT THE DOOR, she caught a whiff of Ryan's herbal scent clinging to the robe he'd left over a chair. Tears rose in her throat and collected there, hot and pointed and painful.

She had a mental flash of waking in the night and finding herself surrounded by his arms and his scent. She'd built an imaginary future for herself based on those few moments that reality had just ground to powder.

Well. She'd been prepared to lose so that he could have everything Cassie had wanted him to have, because she'd promised Cassie. But it was standard practice, even in banking, that dishonesty negated any signature or any pledge.

"You have to listen to his side," Matthew insisted. "It's only fair."

Jo went back into the kitchen in answer to the kettle's shrill call. "Fair, shmair. He lied."

"He didn't lie, he just didn't say anything. Maybe he was picking his moment. Can I have second dunk on that tea bag?"

Jo took down another cup and poured water over the bag for a second cup. "Really? And what could he possibly be waiting for? For a moment when I'm more pregnant, more stressed, more hormonally hysterical?"

Matthew waited for her to put the kettle down, then took her arm and pulled her toward the recliner. "Sit down, and *calm* down. If you go into labor while I'm alone with you, you're grounded! Now, here—wrap up in this." He brought her the cotton throw, then went into the kitchen for her cup. He sat in the chair opposite her with his own cup.

"Now think about it," he said. "He's been taking good care of you, hasn't he?"

"He's been taking good care of Chelsea."

He considered that a moment, then conceded the point. "But he brought you into his bed, didn't he?" he asked with a candor that surprised her.

"Because he wanted to make sure the baby was safe."

"Maybe he just wanted to hold you."

"I don't think so."

"Because you've never been able to give anyone the benefit of the doubt." He looked into her face without flinching at her wounded expression. "I'm sorry, but it's true. You're brutally demanding of the people in your life. Cassie was demanding of the *things,* but you're demanding of the people. Not only do they have to do all the things you think they should do, but their motives have to be noble, as well. So, let him explain. Maybe he didn't want to startle or upset you at this stage of the pregnancy. Maybe," he suggested, narrowing his gaze on her, "he was going to ask you to go with him."

She knew that wasn't true. Ryan knew how she felt. He would have told her if he intended to take her along.

She sat quietly, wanting her father to stop talking so she could analyze the plan forming in her mind. It was radical and selfish, but the situation was radical, and she was sick to death of being generous. And she had not made a fine art of pregnancy so that this child could be raised in congested, smog-and-crime-ridden Los Angeles.

She crocheted while Matthew read, a plot brewing under her studiously calm surface.

It was early evening when her father stood and stretched and went for his jacket. "I promised to pick up Ryan tonight. That woman he's been riding with had to leave early for her son's football game. I'll leave a little early and pick up some of those brioches for breakfast tomorrow."

He leaned down to kiss her forehead, and she hugged him tightly.

"Think about what you want to ask him," he advised gently, "without name-calling or accusations, and I'll make myself scarce in the shower."

The moment he was out the door, Jo packed a small bag and called the cab company. This was a rotten thing to do to her father, who'd traveled all this way to be with her at the baby's birth, but it was the only solution she could think of for the baby.

No, Mama Jo. I don't want to leave Daddy. Mama Cass says it isn't a good idea. And I'm going to want out of here pretty soon.

THE CABDRIVER was the young woman with the Elvis button on her cap. She smiled at Jo a little nervously, her eyes focusing on the enormous jut of her stomach. "How's it going? You aren't going to have that in my cab, are you?"

Jo shook her head. "No. If all goes well, I'm having it in Port Townsend."

The cabbie frowned. "I don't have to drive you there, do I? That's two hundred miles away."

"No," Jo replied, watching the road in concern for the Volvo's headlights. But all the traffic was passing right by the condo's turnoff. "Just to the car rental agency."

"So, you two had a good day?" Ryan asked. He'd driven back, and Matthew studied his profile for signs of guilt as he pulled into the condo's covered parking area.

Matthew slipped off his seat belt and unlocked the doors. "Yes. Jo tried to get you to join us for lunch, but you were already gone."

Ryan nodded as he pushed his door open. "Yeah. District brass was here. They insisted on the steak house outside of town, because someone at their hotel had recommended it. It was good, but I kept dozing off at my desk this afternoon."

"Heavy food?" Matthew asked casually as Ryan set the car alarm and started toward the door to the condo. "Or are you having trouble sleeping?"

Ryan wasn't certain whether the question was genuine solicitousness, or a subtle way to make him comment on the sleeping arrangements.

"Every time Jo moves during the night," he said, prepared to defend the situation if necessary, "I wake up, wondering if it's time."

To his surprise, Matthew smiled reminiscingly. "I remember what that was like. Especially the first time. I was a basket case. Cassie was a week overdue."

Ryan unlocked the door, let Matthew inside, then pulled it to again. They walked to the elevators. "If Jo's a week late," Ryan said, "I think I'll need counseling, possibly even incarceration."

They rode up to the quiet floor and stepped off. "What's for dinner?" Ryan asked Matthew.

"Baked chicken," Matthew replied, thinking if the

man was guilty of something, he must also be amoral. He seemed completely unaffected by it. "Rice. Carrots."

"Hmmm…" Ryan made an appreciative sound as he turned his key in the lock of their apartment door. "You wouldn't want to stay forever, would you?"

Ryan knew something was wrong the moment he stepped inside. It was too quiet. Her old tape player was usually playing the Mamas and the Papas when he arrived home. He knew the sequence by heart. "Dedicated to the One I Love," "My Girl," "Creeque Alley." And Jo was sitting in the recliner, working on the baby blanket, or setting the table, and playfully harassing her father about getting dinner ready because she was starving.

But there was no one in the kitchen, or in the recliner, and there wasn't a sound.

Of course, Matthew had come to pick him up. That was it. Maybe she'd decided to lie down, or take a shower.

"Jo?" he called. He started toward the bedroom at a walk, telling himself she would be there, supine on the bed, her stomach bulging like a little mountain, her hair fanned out on the pillow like sunlight.

When she wasn't there, he took two hasty steps to the bathroom, then strode anxiously across the hall to the guest room. Not there.

"Jo!" he shouted. He shoved open the door to the nursery, and found everything just as it had been since he'd completed the room three months ago—bright, pristine, waiting.

He turned, panic bubbling up inside him, and saw Matthew standing in the nursery doorway.

Ryan pushed past him and checked the coat closet.

The blue coat and her beret were gone, as well as the tote bag that went everywhere with her.

"Her coat's gone!" Ryan shouted, meeting Matthew in the hallway. He didn't want to consider what that could mean.

"Simba's gone, too," Matthew said, a hand on his forehead. "And that package of things for bringing the baby home from the hospital."

Ryan felt a fury so terrible, he was afraid to speak for a moment. She'd done it. She'd run off with his baby, after all those promises that she wouldn't, after luring him into a sense of complacency with her smile and her natural ways. And all the time she'd been perpetrating a deceit.

"You should have told her," Matthew said quietly.

"Told her what?" Ryan was hardly aware of having asked the question, and was paying little attention to the answer. He was calculating times. If she'd been here when Matthew left, and he'd been gone only forty-five minutes, she couldn't have gotten far. Then he heard Matthew say, "Los Angeles."

He refocused his attention on his father-in-law. "What?" he demanded.

"She knows about you moving to Los Angeles," Matthew said. "Someone at the bank told her about your lunch with the district managers today."

"What do you mean? When?"

"When she went to ask you to join us for lunch today."

Ryan closed his eyes and groaned. "Oh, no. No."

"You should have told her."

Ryan didn't bother to argue. He headed for the door at a run, pulling his keys out of his pocket. Matthew followed.

He went to Coffee Country. Devon was closing up, and he looked concerned when he asked if he'd seen Jo.

"No, I haven't," he replied. "Haven't you?"

Ryan was in no mood. "If I had, would I be here?" he asked crossly, going into the back room to look. It was empty.

"I don't know," Devon answered, in the same tone. "Would you? You'd think a man would know how to keep track of the woman who's carrying his baby."

Ryan had Devon's shirt collar in his fist in an instant, but Matthew interceded. "Is there any way this is going to find Jo?" he asked reasonably.

"Jo," Ryan said to Devon in a deadly tone, "is my business, not yours."

Devon pulled Ryan's hand away from his throat. "Then why don't you know where she is?"

Ryan gave him a lethal look, then went to the other entrance and loped up the steps to her old apartment. It was dark, everything in it just as he'd left it the day he moved her into his place. A hole burned in his gut. Where was she?

He looked up Diantha's number in the book and called her from the apartment. She hadn't seen Jo or heard from her, and she was full of worried questions. Ryan promised to get back to her when he found Jo.

"She wouldn't have left town, would she?" Ryan asked Matthew. "Tomorrow's her due date, for God's sake. She wouldn't leave her doctor the day before she was to deliver, would she?"

Matthew would have preferred to believe she had more sense, but he knew her better than that. And he'd seen how angry and hurt she was.

"Is there a car rental agency in this town?" Matthew

asked. "A bus station? She can't fly in her condition, can she?"

"Ah, yeah..." The tall, thin man locking up the car rental agency office remembered her. He held both hands way out in front of him. "Pregnant out to here?"

"That's her," Ryan said. "What did you rent her?"

He shook his head. "Nothing. She had no major credit card. You've got to have a—"

Ryan cut him off. "Right. Did she tell you where she was going?"

He started to shake his head, then remembered. "She said something about not needing a major credit card to take a bus."

Ryan repeated his story to the man behind the counter at the Greyhound office, behind the library.

"Yeah, I remember her," he said. He held both hands out in front of him. "Ten months pregnant?"

Ryan nodded wearily. "That's her. Where did she go?"

He shrugged. "Nowhere. We don't have a run north until tomorrow afternoon."

"Did she happen to say where she was going next?" Matthew asked.

He smiled wryly. "She said it was no wonder the diesel-guzzling airlines ruled the travel industry. They, at least, kept a daily schedule. I told her she'd missed our daily Seattle run, but she didn't seem to want to listen."

Ryan thanked him and raced for the airport. As he floored the accelerator, he concentrated on her being there. He didn't want to think about how far away from him she could get by air. Of course, this airline went only to Portland or Seattle, but from there—she could get anywhere.

The ticket clerk, a middle-aged woman with platinum hair and a wide smile said, "Oh, yes, I remember her. Very, very pregnant, and very, very angry when I told her a woman as far along as she was couldn't fly without written approval from her doctor."

Ryan felt relief—but just for an instant. "Did she say where she was going?"

The woman shook her head. "By that point," she said, "she was no longer speaking to me."

Ryan and Matthew sat in the car in the parking lot and stared out the windshield.

"I can't think of anything else to do," Ryan said, "but drive up and down the streets, check the hotels, maybe even the hospital."

Matthew nodded. "Take me back to the condo, and I'll make the calls while you drive around. I'll call you on that cellular thing if I learn anything, and you can call me if you find her."

Ryan turned the key in the ignition, thinking it was a weak and flimsy plan at best, but he could think of nothing better. He felt as though all light had deserted him.

He drove Matthew back to the condominium, turned the car off so that he could take the condo's outer door key off his ring to give it to his father-in-law. And that was when he saw her in the path of his headlights, sitting on the bench in the small landscaped area between the parking lot and the condominium. Simba sat beside her, taller than she was. She was crying.

Chapter Ten

Ryan was almost afraid to move, afraid she would take fright and run away. Then he was distracted from her woeful face by her considerable dimensions, and realized with gallows humor that she couldn't run anywhere. But he still employed caution.

"I'll go make coffee or something," Matthew said. He picked his way through the shrubbery, leaned over Jo and kissed her cheek. She kissed him back, they shared a brief murmured exchange, then Matthew disappeared into the building.

Ryan went to sit beside her. She was no longer sobbing, but tears continued to flow freely. He offered her his handkerchief. The air smelled of wood smoke and river water.

She gave him a suspicious look from under spiked lashes, then took it from him and dabbed at her eyes.

"Do you know," she asked, her tone tearful but quarrelsome, "that a pregnant woman can't leave this town? I think that's a form of discrimination the ACLU should look into."

He leaned an elbow on the back of the bench. She still looked as though she might bolt at any moment. In the glow from the floodlights behind the condo, he

Make Way for Mommy

could see that her cheeks and nose were red, while every other inch of her that was visible seemed particularly pale. He wanted to touch her, but didn't dare.

"I know," he said calmly. "We traced your path from Ace Auto Rentals to Greyhound to the airport. How'd you get back home?"

She gave him a look that was less angry than frank. "This is your home, Ryan, not mine. My home is an apartment over the coffee bar."

He acknowledged the distinction with a nod, thinking privately that they'd fight that out later. "Then why are you here, and not at the apartment?"

"Because...all my stuff is here." She looked away from him when she replied. "And I left my keys when I thought I wasn't coming back. I came here in a cab."

"So, you came back because you want me to let you in so you can collect your things?"

She looked back at him then, her tear-filled eyes somehow managing to blaze. "I came back to tell you that even though I can't get away with Chelsea—" her voice was strained, but she forced the words out "—you're not going to raise her in Los Angeles."

He studied her quivering bottom lip for a moment, then replied quietly, "No, I'm not."

She swallowed and frowned. "What do you mean? You're moving."

"No," he repeated. "I'm not."

She pointed in the general direction of the bank. "But Roberta said..."

"That I'd been offered a promotion that involved moving to Los Angeles."

She spread both hands, frustrated and perplexed. "Well, that means... "

"That I was offered a promotion," he said patiently,

"which I accepted, but only after we cut a deal. I'll have to travel to Los Angeles once a month, but I...am...not...moving there."

She stared at him for several seconds. She fell back heavily against the slats of the bench. "Oh," she said.

When he was searching for her, Ryan had been alternately furious that she would take off on him without one word of warning and terrified that she would succeed in getting away. Now that he knew she was safe, all the things that *could* have happened to a woman in her condition still left him with conflicting emotions.

"Is that all you have to say?" he asked coolly, "after scaring me to death, and walking out on your father when he came over three thousand miles to be with you? Where in the hell were you going, when your due date's tomorrow?"

Her eyes were still wide and pained. The knowledge that he wasn't leaving had provided some relief, but apparently not all she needed. Somehow, that annoyed him further.

"I was going to visit my friend Lisa, in Port Townsend," she replied. Then she asked, her voice raspy, "Why did you decide to stay in Heron Point?"

"Because I want to raise Chelsea here," he replied, his tone aggressive, "among nice people who have time for each other and for things that count. What? You didn't think I had a grip on what's important for a baby?"

Jo, an arm hooked around Simba, burst into noisy sobs. Ryan watched her in mystified fascination. Hormonal hysteria, Matthew had called it. That must be what this was. She didn't seem able to find comfort in anything he said. And he was trying. Considering that a part of him wanted to scream at her and shake her, he was really trying.

Jo was horrified to hear herself choking and gasping. She'd always hated women who cried when they should be making sense, but she seemed powerless over her own emotions.

Tonight had begun as an escape from what she'd thought was Ryan's decision to raise the baby in a giant, bad-smelling, crime-infested city. But as the evening wore on and she grew more and more desperate, she'd realized what was really at the heart of her attempt to escape. And she had to explain it to him. She wasn't sure she was up to it.

"Jo," he said gently. She felt his arm come around her shoulders. That only served to make her cry harder. But she still had to tell him.

"Ryan." She sat up and pulled herself together. She sniffed and wiped her nose and sniffed again. "I...have to tell you something."

"Fine. But why don't we go inside, where it's warm?" he suggested.

She shook her head. "No. I have to do it now. While I have the courage."

He leaned back again, an arm along the bench behind her. She could see in his eyes that he suspected. But, curiously, she saw no anger there. That confused her.

"All right," he said. "Tell me."

She raised her eyes to a dark, starry heaven—it was free of fog for the first time in weeks—and silently asked Cassie's forgiveness.

MAMA CASS says forget that and do it! Do it!

SHE HAD TO DRAW A BREATH to swallow her cowardice. "I've told myself..." she began in a raspy voice

"…over and over during the last few months, that…that Chelsea isn't mine…" She paused to draw another breath, and a sob rose in her throat. She willed herself not to succumb to tears again. "But my heart doesn't believe it. Ryan, I love her so much. I've lived for her. I'm…I'm her mother."

She held the handkerchief to her mouth, as though it could hold back the roiling emotions inside her, the groveling pleas on the tip of her tongue.

Ryan's eyes remained dark and quiet. Now that the words were spoken, she expected temper to flare there, accusations to remind her brutally that she'd known and accepted the conditions from the beginning.

But there was still no anger. Just a quiet acceptance that stunned and baffled her.

Ryan had somehow known all along, he thought, that it would come to this. It was contrary to nature to expect a woman to carry a baby for nine months, then willingly turn it over to someone else to raise.

And he'd lived with Jo for a month. He knew just how much love and attention and cherishing she'd invested in this baby. He knew how she talked to Chelsea, and read to her and sang to her—how she'd walk into the nursery when she thought he wasn't watching, and go to the crib and run her hands over the colorful bedding, or turn the musical mobile attached to it, imagining the baby there.

He'd watched her work on the crocheted blanket night after night, smiling unconsciously, humming a lullaby.

He knew Chelsea wasn't his alone.

"All right," he said.

Jo heard the words, but for a moment she could not imbue them with meaning. Then she was sure she'd misunderstood them.

"What?" she breathed.

He wrapped his arms around her and pulled her close. "I said, all right. You *are* Chelsea's mother."

Jo heard *those* words and knew she'd gone insane. She felt his arms tenderly, comfortingly enfolding her, and looked up into his eyes to see understanding there.

This was less than she'd dreamed, but far more than she'd ever truly hoped for.

"But...what'll we do?"

"The world is full of unorthodox families today," he said, holding her closer as a sharp night wind wove around them, then moved on to make the evergreens whisper. "We'll just stay together and raise her as the two parents who love her. For now, I think that's all the plan we need."

She looked up at him again in disbelief. "Can you do that?" she asked. "I mean, that's pretty... progressive for a conservative like you."

He smiled. To Jo, who only moments ago had felt like a drowning sailor, that smile was the beacon that would guide her home. "Yes," he said, with a philosophical tilt of his head. "I can. Love eventually makes liberals of us all, don't you think? And I love this baby. Come on. Let's go in."

ALL RIGHT! *We're going to* stay *together. Mama Cass says...well, she can't say anything. She's crying.*

Ah...Mama Jo. About the space in here...

As RYAN LED HER INSIDE, Jo felt showered with blessings, bathed in the kindness of a generous God, though she was very aware that Ryan had said he loved the baby, not her. But the same love that had turned conservative Ryan Jeffries into a liberal had turned peaceloving Jo Arceneau into a warrior. All I need is time,

Lord, she prayed, and I'll turn him into a screaming radical!

"How does everyone feel about omelets?" Matthew asked when they'd shed hats and coats and stood in the condo's living room. "It's a little late for a big meal."

Ryan glanced at the clock. It was 8:45. It occurred to him that the past two and a half hours had been among the longest of his life. Now a curious peace had settled over him.

That was due, he guessed, to the strange serenity that had overtaken Jo. She was looking at him as though he were somehow divine. He rather liked it, though he knew it was generated entirely, or at least mostly, by her desire to stay with the baby.

But one seldom had the upper hand with her. He intended to make the most of it.

She smiled at Matthew, wrapped her arms around him and told her she loved him.

"I love you, too, you incorrigible brat," he said. "See if I ever come and visit you again."

She kissed his cheek. "You didn't come to see me, you came to be one of the first to see Chelsea Annabel, and you know it. No omelet for me, please. Thanks, though."

"Tea?" he called after her as she waddled toward the bedroom.

"No, thank you," she called back sweetly.

Ryan followed her into the room. She had shaken out the baby afghan, and was inspecting it.

"When did you eat last?" he asked, determined that she wasn't going to let her health slide in the final stretch. He'd been more than lucky to get her back tonight safe and sound. He wasn't going to let anything happen to her now.

She held the blanket to her and gave him that adoring

look over the top of it. "I bought some cheese crackers from a vending machine at the airport."

He closed his eyes and shook his head. "And Chelsea's supposed to do her windup on cheese crackers?"

She smiled widely, shook the blanket out again and let it float down on the bed. The delicate colors were soft against the dark blue of his quilt. She had done a beautiful job.

"Actually, I think she's beyond her windup, and stealing third." Then she turned to him with a husky laugh. "Or am I mixing metaphors? I mean, I know they're both baseball, but windup indicates pitching, and stealing third suggests…"

He suddenly realized what she was saying. He caught her arm. "Are you telling me you're in labor?" he demanded.

She nodded. "Pretty sure. At first I thought it was just false labor again, but I had a pretty good one on the bench, waiting for you to come home."

He felt suddenly frantic, and pushed her toward the chair. "Well, why didn't you say something? We have to get you—"

She shook her head, smiling that serene smile. "I think we have plenty of time. They're pretty far apart."

"How far?"

"What time is it?" she asked.

He knelt in front of her. "You mean, you're having one *now?*"

IT'S GETTING DARK and weird in here. Things are moving. Is this it? Is it my birthday?

"UH-HUH. What time is it?"

"Oh, God." He couldn't think. It was only when she

repeated the question that intelligence overrode emotion. He pulled off his watch. "It's 8:51."

She patted his shoulder and breathed out. "Good," she said after a moment. "Twenty minutes since the last one. This is just latent labor. I'm already packed for the hospital, so I'll probably have a couple of hours to make fringe."

Ryan blinked at her. She'd taken charge of her body, as Serena had directed, but she seemed also to have completely lost her *mind*.

"Fringe?" he asked.

She dipped her knees to reach into the crochet bag on the bed and pulled out a skein of yarn. She dipped her knees again and groped inside for something she couldn't seem to find. "Fringe," she replied. "For Chelsea's blanket. Shouldn't you be writing down the time of that contraction, so we sound like we know what we're doing when we call Dr. Mac?"

"Ah...right." Ryan opened the bedside-table drawer, where there was always a yellow pad for working into the night, and logged the time. "We won't tell him you're making fringe. He might decide childbirth has sent you over the edge. What in the hell are you looking for?"

"My fringe measure," she replied. "I cut it out just the other day."

Ryan took the bag away from her, and rummaged through it for her. "What does it look like? God, I can't believe I'm about to become a father and I'm groping in a bag for a fringe measurer."

Jo pushed him into the chair. "Daddy!" she shouted. "Would you bring Ryan a cup of coffee?" To Ryan she said, "Get it together, Jeffries. I'm going to need you."

"Right," he said. He drew a steadying breath. Then

he caught her eye and gave her a wry grin. "I think I'd have been all right if you hadn't started talking about fringe."

She pointed to the bag in his lap. "It's just a square of cardboard. You wind yarn around it to measure the length of the fringe."

He frowned as he dug in the bag. "I thought fringe was loose?"

"It is. You wind the yarn over and over the cardboard. Then, when it's taken all it can hold, you cut one end, then you have a lap full of long strands of yarn doubled over to make fringe."

He tried to picture it and couldn't. But he did find the piece of cardboard. You'd have thought by Jo's reaction that he'd found a precious stone. He studied her wide smile and thought the blanket had become a symbol for her—a taking over of something Cassie had started. And her job was almost finished. Or just begun, depending on how you looked at it.

So they were in this together now, he realized with a gripping fist of fear in the pit of his stomach. So far, except for his initial contribution of sperm in a laboratory, Jo had done all the work concerning Chelsea. Now he had to see her through labor and birth. He felt both valuable and desperate to escape.

Matthew appeared with a steaming mug of coffee. His eyes went to Ryan, in the chair with Jo's needlework bag, and Jo, walking around the room and humming while winding yarn around a square of cardboard.

He smiled warily at Ryan. "Are we on 'America's Funniest Home Videos?'"

Ryan stood, put the bag on the bed and accepted the coffee gratefully. "We're having a baby," he said, toasting his father-in-law with his cup. "But we're making fringe first."

"What?"

"Never mind." Ryan turned him back toward the kitchen. "You'd better eat something. It's going to be a long night."

ALL RIGHT. He was getting the hang of this. Of course, it was about time he did. It had been almost eight hours, and they were now in transitional labor.

"Coming again," he warned Jo as he watched the fetal heart monitor register the beginning of another contraction. He firmed his grip on her hand and started breathing with her as she stiffened, grimaced, and finally emitted a primitive, eerie sound of pain.

Her nails dug into his knuckles, but he was more aware of her pain than of his, of keeping her breathing through the contraction to gain her at least the small measure of relief that provided.

"Going, going..." he said, watching the monitor. "Better?"

She sighed, her face flushed and wet with perspiration. He dabbed a wet towel on her cheeks and kissed her hand. "You are doing so great," he told her, amazed at what she'd endured during the long night.

Matthew, unable to bear the sight of his daughter in pain, was wandering the halls and bringing back gossip and reports. He'd come back shortly after midnight to tell them Jave and Nancy Nicholas had had their girl. Six pounds, eleven ounces. "Malia Rose," he'd said. Then he'd frowned. "Are there no Margarets or Elizabeths anymore?"

Jo had laughed. "This is a new generation of women, Dad. They're going to bring prosperity and peace and make men happier than they've ever been."

Matthew had exchanged a smile with him. "Tall order for anyone to fill."

Jo held on to his hand and breathed shallowly, obviously exhausted. He reminded her to take deep breaths, to try to relax.

MAMA JO, I'm coming, I promise. I'm just having trouble with the door!

"MY FEET ARE COLD," she complained.

"Okay. We'll take care of that." Pleased to be handed a problem he could do something about, Ryan went to her overnight bag for the knee socks they'd packed. He freed the blankets, found her feet and tugged the socks on. Just in time for another contraction.

He hurried back to her side to catch her hand and breathe with her through it. She finally fell back against the pillow with a dispirited groan.

"I think its time to choke me with my fringe, Ryan," she murmured.

He smoothed her hair back. "Actually, your dad took the blanket with him to the cafeteria. He's supposed to be working on it."

She smiled weakly. "I'll bet he's watching the sports channel and charming the nurses, and our baby's blanket will be bald."

Our baby. Even as Ryan smiled over her whimsical remark, those two words struck at the very heart of him. He'd accepted from a personal perspective that the baby wasn't his alone, but he hadn't considered what it would mean to share responsibility for a life with another person. With a woman. With Jo.

It was drawing them into an intimacy even deeper than what they'd shared when she was simply carrying Chelsea. They'd be cohabiting, planning together, reaching mutual decisions—pouring their love into the same child.

Was he ready for that?

As he contemplated the thought, Jo went into another contraction. He squeezed her hand, breathing with her, reminding her not to push, and decided that it didn't matter if he was ready or not. It was about to happen.

"Well, the baby will probably be bald, too," he said lightly as she came out of the contraction. "They'll match."

CHELSEA ANNABEL began to appear just before 10:00 a.m. on September 23.

"Bald as a billiard ball," Dr. McNamara said teasingly from his position at the foot of the bed. The blanket and its lack of fringe on two sides had been the joke that eased pain and tension for the last hour as Jo proceeded from labor to delivery. "You'll need fringe on the other side of that blanket. But we need the rest of her, Jo. Push her out."

Ryan supported Jo's back as she held her knees and pushed. Her hair now hung in damp spirals, and he couldn't imagine where she would be able to find another particle of strength with which to expel the baby.

HURRY, Mama Jo! It's so tight in here my head is pointed!

SHE LEANED BACK against Ryan's arm, panting.

Jo felt as though her entire world was ruled by grave exhaustion and excruciating pain. It was a revelation to learn that this kind of misery existed.

There would be a baby at the end of this ordeal, but at this moment, her pain seemed eternal, and it was impossible to consider a result, because a result suggested an end, and this had been going on forever.

She'd been such an innocent, she thought, when she agreed to do this for Cassie.

She realized in a state of near delirium that she hadn't thought about her sister since she'd gone into labor. This had all been so personal—so *hers*.

And Ryan had been a rock. Ryan was going to let her be Chelsea's mother. His hand felt so solid in hers. She clutched it, trying to absorb strength.

"Come on, Jo," he said gently in her ear. "One more push and we'll have her. One more."

She grasped her knees, trying to force the thought from her brain to the baby. Out. Out. Out.

She pushed long and hard. Words of encouragement came from Dr. Mac, and from Ryan, who supported her back and alternately praised and cajoled and bullied.

"I love you."

In the midst of all the excitement and activity around her, though she felt the mind-bending relief of the baby leaving her body, though for an instant everything swam and whirled around her with the cessation of strain, she heard every single one of the three words as clearly as though the room had been otherwise silent.

"What?" she whispered, not even sure who'd spoken. "What did you say?"

Then Dr. McNamara handed her a squalling mass with a bald head and a pruny little face, and her mind was swept clean by adoration of her daughter.

YOU DIDN'T TELL ME it would be this cold! Where's the warm water? Where's the food? Where's my thumb?

"MY...God," Ryan whispered in wonder, leaning over her. "Chelsea."

His voice held the same note of reverence she felt.

His large hand cupped the tiny head, and the baby moved against it, still screaming.

Then his index finger went to the barest suggestion of a cleft in the tiny chin. Jo noticed it, and tears sprang to her eyes. "Cassie's chin," she whispered.

She heard Ryan swallow, and then he stroked her arm and kissed her temple. "Your voice," he told her. *His* voice was choked and tight.

She turned to him, feeling Cassie's absence, but too filled with joy that Chelsea was here and safe for grief to even hurt. "She's beautiful," she whispered. "We did a good job."

He leaned his head against hers. "Yes, we did."

Then the nurse reclaimed the baby to take her footprint and weigh her.

"Eight pounds," she called from across the room, then added with emphasis, "and *eleven* ounces!"

Jo groaned and laughed. "Is that all?"

The nurse looked over her shoulder to smile at Ryan. "We have to tidy Jo up now, take a few stitches. Why don't you take a break for about an hour?"

Ryan stood, easing Jo back against the pillows, his expression wry. "Sounds like you're in for even more fun. I owe you big. I'll be back in an hour."

Jo caught his hand. Her eyes brimmed with tears. "Cassie was here, Ryan," she whispered. "She didn't miss it."

He leaned down to put his cheek to hers, and she felt the tension in him, one single quake of emotion. She wrapped her arm around his neck and held on.

"It's going to be all right," she promised. "We can do this."

He kissed her cheek and straightened, his eyes turbulent, but his face calm. "Right. See you in an hour."

Ryan felt as though his body and his mind might fly

apart. It didn't seem possible that anyone could host the conflicting emotions he felt and survive.

Chelsea was here. Beautiful. Perfect. He felt a happiness and a relief so profound it was startling.

But Cassie wasn't here. Cassie, who had wanted Chelsea so badly, who'd come up with male and female names the night they learned Jo was indeed pregnant, who'd made elaborate nursery plans, elaborate life plans, she'd never been able to carry out.

His pain was as deep as his joy was high.

But he wasn't what mattered here. He had to get it together.

He met Jave Nicholas at the coffeemaker in the waiting room. He offered his hand and a congratulatory smile. "Jo's father was cruising the hall for news and told us about your baby. Good work."

Jave shook his hand. "Thank you. I heard Jo had been admitted. You taking a break?"

Ryan nodded. "A well-deserved one. Chelsea was just born about five minutes ago."

"All right!" Jave poured him a cup of coffee. "Congratulations to *you!* What'd she weigh?"

"Eight pounds, eleven ounces."

"Bigger than ours," Jave said, then added competitively, "But ours has hair."

Ryan grinned. "Got me there. Bald. Very bald."

"How's Jo?"

"Exhausted, but fine, all in all." He took a sip of coffee and closed his eyes as the near-boiling caffeine hit the vicinity of his chest and went down in a hot, restorative stream. "God, that's good. Nancy okay?"

Jave nodded. "Hard to imagine what a woman can go through and come out smiling. I'd have been demanding drugs during latent labor."

Ryan nodded. "And insisting on adoption as a means of acquiring future children."

"Amen." Jave downed the last of his coffee, crumpled the cup and tossed it in the plastic container under the table. He studied Ryan a moment, as though considering whether or not to ask the question on his mind.

Ryan saved him the trouble. "We're going to stay together and raise the baby."

Jave still looked as though he had a question.

"To share parenting duties," Ryan added, thinking that sometimes it was difficult to have friends who cared about you. It made them nosy.

"And that's all?"

"Yeah."

Jave shook his head at him. "I'm glad you take care of my money, and not my personal life. That'll never work, buddy. Nothing generates as much emotion, as much need to communicate, as much temper between parents, as children. You generate all that between a man and a woman who are just sharing space, and you know what results, don't you?"

"I'm sure you're going to tell me."

"Sex."

Ryan rolled his eyes. "Cassie's only been gone—"

"You're a single man with a woman and a child needing you, depending upon you." Jave clapped him on the shoulder. "You'll have to go into hiding if you want to keep your heart out of it."

"Did I hear someone mention sex?" A tall, fair-haired man, white lab coat unbuttoned at the throat, peered into the waiting room. "Nicholas!" he exclaimed, laughing. "I should have known it was you. You passing out cigars? We got word in ER about an hour ago."

Jave waved him into the room. "Hey, Nate. Congratulate another new father. Nate Foster, Ryan Jeffries, father of a bald little girl.''

Nate came to shake Ryan's hand. ''Sounds like my type. I drive a Jag convertible, and they're not always asking you to put the top up so they don't mess their hair. I suppose you already have rules about her dating older men.''

''I'm sure he has some about her dating doctors,'' Jave said. ''Aren't you supposed to be going away or something?''

Nate nodded, glancing up at the clock. ''Another couple of hours, then I'm off for four weeks in western Canada.'' He rolled his eyes. ''And God, do I need it. Almost thirty days of communing with nature, listening to the birds, eating fish I've caught myself in some sylvan stream.'' He smiled wickedly from one man to the other. ''Sleeping under the stars. Or at least with a tent flap open to the stars. You two, on the other hand, will probably get very little sleep for the next month. Or the next several years. But I wouldn't be the one to make a point of my own good fortune.''

''Someday,'' Jave warned, ''you'll be walking the floor with a colicky baby.''

Nate shook his head determinedly. ''Not me. You stay away from women with marriage on their minds and you don't get into that kind of trouble.''

Ryan turned to Jave. ''What do you think? Headfirst in the coffeepot, or a wild ride down the stairs in a housekeeping bucket?''

Jave regarded Nate with a wry twist of his lips. ''First one, then the other. I hope you get a tick in your sleeping bag.''

''A pregnant tick,'' Ryan added.

Nate pretended indignation. ''Well, it was nice to meet you, too. Geez. Stop by to offer a friendly hello, a little good cheer, and who appreciates you? No one.'' He looked at the clock again and groaned. ''Gotta go.'' He backed toward the door, suddenly serious. ''It really was nice to meet you,'' he said to Ryan. To Jave he added, ''And give Nancy my best.''

Ryan frowned wryly at the now empty doorway. ''I think I was probably that smug once.''

Jave shook his head. ''Best emergency room doctor I've ever seen, but he always passes the kids in ER on to someone else. He doesn't like to work on them. Has an aversion to kids in all forms.''

Ryan found that surprising in a man who'd seemed so good-natured. ''Why?''

Jave shrugged a shoulder. ''No idea. He's also very private. Well...'' He offered his hand again. ''This is my third, so I can tell you, your life will never be the same after this moment. So, take care. In a couple of weeks, when our lives settle down again, we'll cruise on the *Mud Hen.*''

Ryan nodded. ''I'll look forward to it.'' Then he went to find his father-in-law.

Chapter Eleven

Jo went two weeks without sleep—or at least that was how it felt. Her eyes burned, everything in her and on her ached, but she couldn't ever remember being as happy as when she held Chelsea to her breast and watched her suckle. The depth of her emotion was as exhausting as the endless cycle of feeding, changing and walking the floor.

Even Ryan didn't seem to exist for her. She knew he was around mornings and evenings, somewhere on the nebulous fringes of her life, but there was never time to find him.

She remembered hearing the words "I love you" at the moment she delivered, knew they had to be Ryan's words. But he hadn't said them again.

She concluded the words had been spoken in the drama of the moment and had since been regretted.

She'd moved out of his room and back into her own, and she felt a little as though she were living alone.

"She cries an awful lot," Jo said worriedly to her father as she paced across the kitchen, bouncing the screaming baby at her shoulder.

WELL, my tummy hurts, and it's not as warm out here as it was in there, and it's all so…big!

MATTHEW, putting lunch dishes in the dishwasher, looked up to say cheerfully, "She's probably tired of looking at you. The doctor said she's fine, she's not allergic to anything. But you never let anyone else hold her. She's probably thinking, "Oh, no! Is that broad with the bloodshot eyes the only person in my life?""

Jo gave her father a scolding frown. "I'm just trying to do everything right."

"Doing everything right," he said, "would include letting her know she has a father and a grandfather. But you barely let us near her. I hear Ryan try to help you with her during the night, but you won't let him."

She stiffened at the unfair accusation. "He has to get up in the morning and go to work. I'm trying to help him get some sleep."

"You're trying," Matthew said, "to keep her to yourself."

"That's not fair."

"It's still true."

She sighed dispiritedly. "Cassie would have done this perfectly."

Matthew closed the door on the dishwasher and considered her. "I think we need to have a father-daughter talk. Bundle up the baby. I'll get our coats."

"But...it's cold," she protested.

"You need fresh air. Come on." He shooed her toward the nursery. "Get cracking. Wrap that bald blanket around her."

The still fringeless side of Chelsea's blanket remained their family joke. But her father didn't look as though he were kidding.

He was carrying the baby in a bright red belly pack Diantha had brought over when Jo came home from the hospital. He wore it unself-consciously, even strutted a little in it, as they walked along the road toward the marina.

Chelsea slept, her still bright pink face at peace, little bow mouth open and almost all that was visible under the pink-and-white knitted hat that matched the quilted snowsuit she wore. Matthew's hands clasped around the baby, held the crocheted blanket to her.

The day was crisp and cold, and an early frost had many of the trees of the hill already turning gold and copper.

"I think," Matthew said as they strolled along at a relaxed pace, "that you have to get some perspective here."

Jo, hands in the pockets of her blue coat, looked up at the tufty white clouds against the bright blue sky. "I have perspective. I'm a mother now. I have a lot to do. I'll get the hang of it."

"Jo, you already have the hang of it. But no one expects you to be Wonder Woman—even Cassie. Raising a child should be a shared experience from the very beginning. You're pushing Ryan away."

She stopped in indignation. "I'm not."

He, too, stopped, unconsciously patting the sleeping baby. "You are. And I know why."

She eyed him warily. "Really?"

"Not because you don't need him. You do. I see it in your eyes every time you look at him."

She folded her arms and demanded in a bored tone, "Then why?"

He looked her in the eye. "Because you don't want him to see you being less than perfect—less than you think Cassie would be in the same situation."

Jo decided that denial would be futile. For a man

raising two teenage daughters, he'd understood them uncannily well. He apparently hadn't lost the knack.

She walked on. He followed.

"She was always prettier and smarter," Jo said matter-of-factly. "All I could do to be noticed was be braver, more heroic. That's why I agreed to have her baby. On one level, of course, it was because I loved her. But on another it was because I thought it was heroic. And I thought heroism was a step up from pretty and smart. Now, I'm not so sure. I feel inadequate and terrified."

"Don't you think all new mothers feel that way?"

"Cassie wouldn't have," she said with a sigh. "Cassie always had everything under control."

"Yeah, well…life isn't about taking control," Matthew said. "It's about working with what you're given, about making harmony—not necessarily order—out of all of our misfortunes and successes. You used to know how to do that."

"Daddy." They'd reached the marina, and Jo stopped to looked down at the irregular line of boats, their glass and chrome winking in the sunlight. She turned to her father. "I have a brand-new baby, whose father has agreed to let me be her mother, though in truth, she's no biological part of me. We've agreed to spend the next twenty or so years of our lives raising her together while sharing space in a home, but not a bed. And over both of us is the memory of the wife and sister we both adored. Finding harmony there would be a trick for Houdini."

He put an arm around her shoulders and smiled. "Well, if it was easy, it would be fiction. It isn't. It's life." He squeezed. "So just be you and go after what you want."

She looked up at him, not certain what he meant, surprised by what he *might* mean.

He nodded. "That's right. We all loved Cassie. But for the sake of this baby, the two of you have to move on without her. She's gone."

Jo put an index finger to the tiny cleft in the baby's chin. Her voice was heavy. "She's not, though, Daddy. She's in this baby. Every time Ryan looks at her, he sees Cassie."

"And that's just fine, honey, as long as when he looks at you," he said significantly, "he sees you."

RYAN CAME AWAKE at the sound of Chelsea's screech. He got out of bed, as he always did, and went to the nursery door. But this time there was no Jo bustling across the hall, looking urgent and desperate, telling him to go back to bed, that she'd take care of it.

He'd always willingly obliged her, because he knew every time she looked at him she was remembering that he'd told her he loved her. And he wasn't anxious to confront or try to explain what he felt. He was in love with two women, one who'd passed away, and one who was very much alive, and he had no idea what to do about it.

He peered into Jo's room and saw her lying on her stomach, clearly in a deep, exhausted sleep. He pulled her door closed.

In the glow of a Lion King night-light, he went to the crib and leaned over the little bundle of arms and legs, uncovered and moving with robotic stiffness. He replaced the soft quilt Chelsea had kicked off and lifted her into his arms.

The feeling of the warm, wiggling body against him was still new enough to make everything else recede for a moment while he experienced the wonder of it. And—giving him an everlasting sense of accomplishment and near divinity—the baby stopped crying.

He tilted her back in his hand to look into her face, and found her looking right back at him. Jo's book, which he'd been reading whenever he found it out of her hands, said babies saw only in black and white. Since he was dark-featured, he decided his daughter was probably getting a fairly accurate picture of him. He smiled.

HI, Daddy! I was wondering where you were.

"HI, Snooks," he said. "What's the problem? Hungry?"

WHAT HAVE WE GOT?

"WET?"

YES, I am.

"YEAH? Well, we know what to do about that." He went to the changing table and put her down. She reached up for him with arms and legs, as though she were a little monkey and he the mother monkey—or the tree. The Moro reflex. He'd read about that, too. The primal urge to remain connected.

"I haven't actually *done* this before, you understand," he said, reaching under the table for a cotton diaper. They'd been given several packages of disposables, but Jo had hidden those at the back of the closet for emergencies that somehow superseded environmental awareness. "But I've seen it done several times, and

Jo has these all folded and specially prepped with liners.''

Chelsea watched him with grave, bug-eyed interest.

DON'T FORGET the wiper thing, and the powder.

"OKAY. Off with the old." He tossed the liner away and put the diaper into a covered bucket filled with sudsy water that Jo had against the wall. He wiped and powdered her. "On with the new." He struggled a little with the pins as the baby squirmed.

WATCH IT WITH THOSE, Daddy!

THE DIAPER finally in place, Ryan admired the perfect, doll-like little legs protruding from the bulky mass of cotton fabric. He caught one gently in each hand, his fingers covering it from toe to torso, and marveled at them—knobby little knees, tiny little toes, minuscule toenails.

But Chelsea apparently resented the restriction, and began to bellow.

I WANT OUT OF THIS ROOM. I want to be carried around, sung to, rocked. And what did you say we had to eat?

"ALL RIGHT, all right," he said, lifting her up again and putting her against his chest. She rooted at this throat. "Your mother doesn't like to be held down, either. Well, actually, neither did your other mother. You probably don't even know you've already had two, do you?"

YES, I do. Mama Cass told me all about it. She says to touch you and tell you that she loves you.

RYAN FELT the tiny flailing hand hit his cheek. He caught it and kissed it. "I love you, too, Snooks. Come on. We'll talk about it over a midnight snack."

Ryan held the baby to him in one large hand, and took the bottle of expressed breast milk from the refrigerator. He ran it under warm water, then cradled Chelsea in his arm and teased her lips with the nipple. She complained about the change in position, until she realized it meant milk. Then she sucked happily, grunting and gurgling.

He stroked her cheek with his index knuckle and watched her tiny fist flail the air.

"So—you had a mother whose name was Cassie. Cassandra, really, but she never let anybody call her that. She said it was pretentious. Anyway…she worked very hard to bring you here." The little fist flailed. He considered it her way of encouraging him to go on with his story.

YES, I know her. She says I'm the best thing she's ever done—next to marrying you.

"SHE COULDN'T CARRY YOU, so she gave you to your aunt Jo to take care of until you could be born." He carried the baby to the sofa, put his feet on the coffee table and stretched out. Chelsea lay contentedly on his chest, still guzzling milk. "Then, almost right after that… there was an accident…"

DADDY, I know all this. You don't have to…

HIS THROAT TIGHTENED and he kissed the top of the baby's head. Grief welled up in him, but for the first time in months, he found something easing it; the warm bundle lying atop him.

''This is the hard part,'' he explained. He heard the tight sound of his own voice in the living room, which was lit only by the light over the stove in the kitchen. He swallowed and went on. ''There was an accident,'' he said again, ''and your mother Cassie died. But you were lucky, because you were growing inside Jo, who was taking really good care of you. And somewhere along the way, Jo changed from your aunt to your mother.''

The baby drew away from the bottle finally, squirming and fussing. Ryan set the bottle aside, put the baby to his shoulder and patted her back. ''I know this is all very complicated, but I think you should know how much...how much love went into bringing you into this world. And how much love greeted you when you arrived. Your grandfather—that white-haired man with the beard who leaned over your crib and made ridiculous noises...''

YEAH. I love that!

''HE CAME all the way across the country just to see you. He's gone home now, but he stopped by the bank before he left and put money into a special account so that when it's time for you to go to college, there'll be enough to send you to Harvard. There'll be time to talk about that later, but that's what you're faced with everywhere you turn, Snookie. Love. Lots of it. It'll be good for you. A little complicated for me, but good for you.''

Chelsea burped.

"Good," Ryan said, continuing to pat. "I'm glad you appreciate it. I don't have to tell you, I suppose, how much your mother Jo loves you. Every time you peep, she comes running. I have to get up in the middle of the night to spend time with you. I think she's even forgotten *I'm* here. Not that I want to steal your thunder or anything, but I was kind of getting to like those adoring looks across the room after I told her we could share you. Once, I think I even caught a lustful glance in the bedroom mirror when she thought I was asleep. Or maybe I imagined it. My life seems so damned complicated these days. Whoa. Forget you heard that. *Damn* isn't for ladies. I know it's a sexist attitude, but I don't like it when ladies swear.

"Would you like a puppy?"

YEAH. A big one, with lots of babies!

"YOUR CONDO AGREEMENT doesn't allow pets, does it?" Jo, in her purple velour robe, put a knee on the sofa and curled up beside him. She put a hand to the baby's head, as though she couldn't be that close and not touch her. "And anyway, you might want to approach her about it when she's *awake.*"

"Hmmm…" he said, wondering how much Jo had heard. "And I thought I had her complete attention."

"When I came in, you were telling her ladies shouldn't swear." She gave him a smile that was sweetly indulgent. It relieved him. It seemed the love dilemma could just slide for a while. "She probably figured she didn't have to pay attention to that for at least a year and a half. She won't be talking until then." Then she frowned apologetically. "I'm sorry I didn't hear her. Why don't you go back to bed? I'll put her down."

He shook his head. "This is my responsibility, as well as yours. You have to let me help you."

Jo smiled around a yawn. "I know. My father chewed me out about that. I'm sorry. I was just... You know. Trying to be perfect."

"I'm sure no one's requiring that of you," he said quietly. "Even Chelsea."

Seated beside him on the comfy sofa in the nearly dark living room with their baby on his chest, understanding that perfection was *not* required of her, Jo felt both mellow and deliriously happy. "Were you serious about the puppy?" she asked.

He looked around the beautifully appointed but small living room. "Yes. It's time to start thinking about a yard with a sandbox, a dog to protect Chelsea, room to run." He smiled at her companionably. "And you need more room to spread out than that bedroom gives you."

He caught her eye as he said that. She wondered if there was a message there for her, then decided it was simply wishful thinking. She didn't need space. All she wanted was to be invited into his. But until he understood that, all she could do was agree. "That would be nice."

"I'll keep my eyes open," he said. "River view, or something on the edge of the woods?"

"I love the river view." She yawned again. He hooked an arm around her and pulled her head down to his shoulder.

She tried to take the gesture calmly, not to betray delight. But she couldn't resist snuggling in. "But the nursery's so perfect here."

"True," he said. "But we'll just put all her great stuff in the new one. We can even paint it the same way, reinstall the carpet."

A house, she thought greedily. Ryan and the baby and me in a *house*. Like a kaleidoscopic glimpse into the future, she foresaw birthday parties, Christmas trees, badminton games, tree houses, barbecues, snowmen. She shuddered with excitement.

Ryan, misinterpreting the gesture, pulled the afghan off the back of the sofa and draped it over her one-handed. "Better?"

She took advantage of his misunderstanding to snuggle farther into him. "Mmm..." she said. And as his arm closed firmly around her shoulder, it was her last coherent thought.

"I CAN'T BELIEVE," Diantha said, cooing into the baby carrier that held Chelsea in a quilted pink blanket, "that she's almost six weeks old. It seems like you just had her. I'm glad you decided against hiring Mrs. Bennett, dear soul that she is, and are looking after the baby yourself. Watch Chelsea's eyes follow my bracelets."

Jo, between customers, leaned on the counter beside her daughter and marveled at how she'd grown. She'd gained more than two pounds, was awake and watching her more often, and responded to the sound of her voice. But she seemed to save her smiles for Ryan, who liked to lie in the middle of the floor on his back and use her like a free weight. At those times, she would open her mouth wide, and gurgles of delight would fill the room.

Tom Nicholas, in coveralls and a baseball cap, burst into the bar.

"The usual," he said, reaching to the counter for the paper, then spotting the baby. Smiling, he came to stand beside Diantha and made funny faces at Chelsea.

Chelsea flailed her arms. She definitely had a thing for men, Jo accepted.

Then the counter filled with newcomers, and Jo left Chelsea to the attentions of her admirers.

Ryan came in several moments later, and went straight to the spot where the carrier usually stood, at the end of the counter. Jo watched him raise an eyebrow when he saw that the carrier was there but the baby wasn't. He looked up at her with a frown.

She pointed to the corner of the shop, where Jave and Nancy Nicholas sat, *each* holding a baby. They were standing the babies face-to-face, obviously introducing them. The two of them studied each other curiously— Malia looking horrified, Chelsea grinning broadly, pink gums exposed. Tom sat on the other side of the table, laughing at their expressions.

"Hi, Baldy!"
"Hi, yourself! Where'd you get that wig?"

Jave and Nancy waved, and Ryan waved back. "Another month of all this attention," he said to Jo as he straddled a stool, "and we won't be able to do anything with her."

Jo began to prepare his latte.

"I need it to go," he said quickly, when she poured a shot of espresso into a tall glass. "Busy afternoon."

"Okay." *Another* busy afternoon? She was aware that her tone was mildly testy as she poured the espresso from the glass into a paper cup. But this was the way they'd been dealing with each other for the past week. Not only had he not repeated his love words, but after several weeks of their coexisting in relative peace, their relationship had taken an unpleasant turn.

Ryan had been tense and she'd been edgy, and they'd engaged in some artful needling. She suspected their house-hunting had precipitated it, though she wasn't certain. But something was keeping Ryan away from her for longer periods. Chelsea managed to snag his attention during the night with a cry from the nursery that invariably brought him to her, his deep voice rumbling quietly in the darkness.

Jo contributed to the tension between them by pretending nothing was wrong. It annoyed him, and she knew it. She found that satisfying.

"It's supposed to be impossible to spoil babies at this stage," she said over her shoulder. "More attention is just more sensory impressions for her to absorb and store. Jave and Nancy have invited us for Thanksgiving."

"That's nice," he said. But his tone didn't match the words. He annoyed *her* by saying one thing when he clearly meant another. "But I was thinking we'd go away for that weekend."

She raised an eyebrow as she turned back to the counter and dolloped foamed milk onto the top of the concoction. "Really. Where?"

"I don't know. Down the coast. East to Bend."

She dropped a stirring straw into the drink. "Who gets to keep the baby?"

He frowned. "What do you mean? We'll bring her with us."

"But whose room does she stay in? Your room or mine? Will we have a connecting door, so whoever doesn't have her will have easy access to her? Or will one of us have to leave his or her room in the dark to visit the baby in the middle of the night?" She fired the questions at him with a sudden vitriol that surprised her, as well as him.

He studied her, eyes narrowed. She turned quickly

away, afraid the cause of that little outburst would be as obvious to him as it suddenly was to her.

Ryan stood and took the paper cup in one tense but steady hand. A foul mood had been ripening in him all day, and he was in no position to deal with hers. He decided to ignore it.

"Did you remember the Heron Point Has It meeting tonight?" he asked briskly.

"Merchants have been calling us day and night," she replied evenly, wiping off the espresso machine. "How could I forget?"

He let that, too, pass. "What do you want to do about dinner?" he asked.

She turned to him, an eyebrow raised, the cleaning rag crumpled in her hand. "Eat it, perhaps?"

He grasped his temper with both hands. "Before or after the meeting?"

"*You're* the cook."

"*That's* why I'm asking."

Her expression seemed to crumple for a moment. Then she stiffened and slapped the rag on the counter. "Your call," she said. "I'll do whatever."

"Thank you," he said, his tone suggesting she'd done nothing to earn gratitude.

He stopped at the Nicholases's table on the way out, put his cup down and took his daughter from Jave. He dipped his index finger into the foamed milk and put it to her mouth. She sucked it greedily.

Hi, Daddy! Yum. I'm cuter than her, don't you think? She has all that ugly hair.

"MALIA AND CHELSEA have agreed to have a slumber party in July 2009," Nancy said. "Chelsea has to bring the potato chips.''

Ryan had to rouse himself out of his dark mood to deal with her cheerful silliness. ''Who's chaperoning this gig?''

''Jave and I will be there, of course. Because now there are boys on the horizon. You know, potential slumber-party crashers.''

When he looked surprised, she explained with a broad smile, ''Remember Karma Endicott, from our Lamaze class?''

''Oh, right.'' He began to put it together. ''She had a boy a month early, on the same day our two were born. And Roberta Dawson was out of town. The only one of us coaches who truly did get to escape.''

Nancy nuzzled Malia, who flailed her arms and legs in appreciation. ''You have to admit it was all worth it.''

Ryan looked down into his daughter's interested gaze and had to admit that it was. But that didn't stop him from thinking he wasn't sure the same was true of her mother.

He kissed Chelsea's cheek and handed her back to Jave. ''When they start talking elopements, put her back in the carrier, would you?'' He chucked Malia under the chin and went back to the bank.

Chapter Twelve

"You're speeding." Jo delivered the accusation calmly, then glanced over her shoulder at the infant seat in the back of the car, in which Chelsea snored happily, unaware of the ripe hostility in the front.

"I'm not speeding," Ryan replied, a ragged edge to his quiet voice. "I have the car under complete control." He wished he could say the same for himself.

Jo tossed her head. He saw the gesture out of the corner of his eyes. She'd worn her hair loose to the Heron Point Has It meeting, and it billowed around her like a spiraled halo.

"That's your answer for everything, isn't it?" she asked.

"What?"

"Control. *Complete* control. Even at meetings."

He made a scornful sound. "So that's it. You were out of order, Josanne. Marsh was still talking."

"Out of order!" she shouted. "It wasn't Parliament, Jeffries! It was a simple downtown association meeting!"

"In which you were out of order."

He slowed to turn onto the road that led to the condos. If Chelsea hadn't been in the car, he thought, he'd have loved to take that corner at full speed and see how Jo liked that.

"You!" Jo said, jabbing him in the shoulder, "are the one who's out of order. Your head is out of order. Your heart is out of order! Your whole damn body..." she suggested hotly in the darkness as they pulled into the covered parking area, "...is probably out of order!"

Silence dropped over them like a blanket. The tension that had governed their lives for the past six or seven days was now a living thing between them—palpable, audible, almost visible.

She reached into the back for the baby, but he brushed her aside, untying the straps and holding Chelsea to him as he stepped backward out of the car. He left Jo to carry the diaper bag and blankets. He marched ahead, unlocked the door and held it silently while she marched through, chin at a defiant angle.

As they waited for the elevator, he kept his eyes determinedly from the short, formfitting blue-and-gold sweater she wore over her favorite long denim skirt. Combined with the graceful lace-up granny boots she wore, it made for a stylish version of the thrown-together look she usually preferred. Everyone had told her tonight how wonderful she looked.

He'd noticed, too. But, though she'd had smiles and glowing baby reports for everyone else, she'd had only sniping and sarcasm for him. When she disrupted the meeting by insisting that none of the booths use foam cups and containers because of their nonbiodegradability, he'd taken a certain satisfaction as chairman of the meeting in insisting that she be quiet until the floor was opened for discussion.

Then, when she'd finally had her say, he'd been more than happy to tell her that the chair had already foreseen that issue and obtained paper receptacles for all involved.

She'd thanked him politely, if stiffly, and folded gracefully into her chair. But there'd been murder in her eye.

He'd been more than happy to confront it.

And if she was going to impugn the competence of his brain, his heart *and* his body, he would happily settle the question for her. On all counts.

In the apartment, he put the baby in her crib, and breathed a sigh of relief when she wriggled and grunted, but never opened her eyes.

I'M NOT SPEAKING to either of you until you stop shouting. Good night.

HE PULLED the nursery door partially closed, and went in search of Jo. She was not in the kitchen or the living room, and he was damn sure she wasn't in his bedroom. And her bedroom door was closed. He pushed it open, and found her sitting on the side of the bed, pulling off her boots.

"Come out here," he ordered, and went into the living room to wait for her to comply.

She did. She walked in in her stockinged feet, arms folded, expression superior, almost pitying. She stopped within a yard of him.

"What?" she asked.

He had pulled off his suit coat and tie. He now stood in the middle of the living room, unbuttoning the French cuffs of his white shirt. "There seems to be a question," he said, "about my ability to function on several levels."

Jo looked heavenward. "This is so sophomoric of you, Ryan."

"I don't think so," he said, folding back the cuff on his left sleeve. "When I suggested you were out of order at the meeting, you called me on it. You weren't happy until Diantha read from *Robert's Rules of Order*." He rolled up the other sleeve. "And you just called me 'out of order.'"

Despite her outward appearance of boredom, Jo watched the tensile grace of his movements in bemused fascination. She had no idea what he was up to. She could only judge by the vague combination of unease and excitement brewing inside her that it was going to be trouble. And that was something she already had in abundance.

She pretended disinterest. "But there are no *Robert's Rules* for the kind of order you're out of."

Sleeves rolled up, he rested his hands on his hips. "Then we'll just have to work it out ourselves—won't we?"

She was tempted to run for it, but she'd endured childbirth not too long ago. She felt cocky. "And how do you suggest we do that?" She knew it was a loaded question, but she asked it anyway.

He took two steps toward her and closed the distance between them. They would touch now, if either one of them reached out.

"Well, we'll take the accusations one at a time," he said quietly. "You suggested my brain isn't functioning." He shrugged a shoulder with almost good-natured amusement. "While I prefer to behave modestly, I'm forced to point out that I'm the manager of a bank, and that I've just been given a prestigious promotion."

"True," she conceded, her arms folded so tightly she

wondered if they might break off. They seemed to be all that stood between her and Ryan. When she breathed out, she could feel the cotton of his shirtsleeve against her elbow. She found it difficult to pretend disdain when tension and lust were about to strangle her. "But...a high I.Q. doesn't necessarily...indicate intelligence and common sense."

To her surprise, he agreed. "You're a prime example of that. You're concerned about all the world's causes, but you don't know what's going on under your very own nose."

Her hands were suddenly fisted on her hips. "What do you—?"

He cut her off. "But we're talking about me, aren't we?"

He moved, and she resisted the instinct to shrink away. But instead of touching her, he simply walked slowly around her, like some predator toying with his prey. Again his shirtsleeve brushed the tip of her elbow. She stood her ground, her heartbeat tripping out of control. She felt his breath against her ear as he spoke.

"You said my heart was out of order." He bumped her other elbow, then came around to stand directly in front of her. A breeze could not have fit between them. "I remind you that I have many friends, and a baby daughter who now recognizes me and shrieks with delight every time I touch her." He paused. She prayed for her next breath. "Would someone without a heart," he asked, "elicit that kind of reaction?"

She opened her mouth to reply, but could make no sound. His eyes locked on hers. There seemed to be no breath in her lungs.

He shifted his weight. His cotton brushed against her wool.

''And then you said,'' he reminded with feigned confusion, ''that my body was out of order. What did you mean by that, specifically?''

The words crowded to the tip of her tongue. *I meant that I adore you, that all I can remember when I go to bed is what it was like for those few days to sleep in your arms, and all my dreams are full of images of the two of us making love. I meant that I know your body reacts to mine, but it doesn't seem to reduce you to the same frustration I feel. You're so controlled. You can feel need and desire, but it doesn't force you to reach for me the way I want to reach for you.*

But she couldn't speak.

Then he raised a long-fingered hand in front of her face. ''Do you think there's something wrong with my hands?'' he asked softly, at the same moment he touched the side of her face. She closed her eyes and swallowed as he ran his fingertips along her jaw to her chin, then gently down her throat until he reached the neckline of her sweater.

Then he finally took that fractional step that brought them body to body, and she found herself in his embrace. Her eyes flew open.

''Perhaps you think my arms don't function,'' he said, tightening them around her so that there was little doubt. Her breasts flattened against the solid wall of him, and she shuddered with the relief of it, and the subtle agony. Corded muscle held her in place.

''Or my legs?'' At that he braced a foot on the ottoman and dipped her backward over his bent knee, as though they were in the middle of some sophisticated tango. She uttered a strangled little cry and gripped his upper arms. The thigh against her back was like oak.

And then she finally saw it in his eyes—passion that

ran as deep as hers, desire billowing out of control. Naked need. Maybe he couldn't repeat the words she wanted to hear, but he felt them.

And that was all it took to ignite those smoking emotions in her. She loosened her grip on his arms and slid her hands up to his shoulders and around his neck. She locked her fingers together and pulled his face down to hers.

"Well, if your legs work," she said softly, "you'd better run while you can."

Ryan had watched the expression on her face change from anger, to wariness, to languid desire—and he finally understood what had raged between them this past week. Words of love, once spoken, could not be allowed to slide. They demanded recognition. And action.

He'd thought he couldn't or shouldn't love a woman so soon after Cassie's death, but the new life they shared in his daughter had turned his focus, out of necessity, from what he'd lost to what he held. Chelsea. Josanne.

And this was more than frustration. It was newfound passion. Desire finally free of confusion. This was right. This was what he wanted.

"Watch," he whispered against her mouth, "how well they work." He straightened, lifting her into his arms, and carried her into his bedroom.

Jo tightened her grip on him, unable to believe this was happening. She looked into his eyes when he stopped at the edge of the bed. "Ryan," she whispered, hating herself for needing to give him a way out. "Are you sure?"

He rubbed his chin against her cheekbone. "Are you?" he asked in sudden concern. "It's just been six weeks since you had Chelsea."

She kissed his jaw, touched by his concern, fueled by his willingness to think twice. "Dr. Mac said it was all right." She tightened her grip further and nipped his ear. "I think he knows…I love you."

He set her on her feet, his smile white in the darkness. "I love you," he said, then opened his mouth over hers as his hands reached up under the hem of her sweater to lift it up.

He paused as his fingertips touched a warm, firm breast encased in silky fabric. He felt a strangely primal reaction, a need to feel in his palm the instrument of his child's nourishment and his woman's beauty.

She helped him pull the sweater off, and he reached around her to unhook the nursing bra. He took the full globes carefully in his hands, the strong nipple against his palm. They were warm and heavy, and he heard a small, shuddering sigh escape her.

"Tender?" he asked, stroking a thumb gently across the tip.

She put her hands to his waist and leaned into him for balance, his touch weakening her spine, almost buckling her knees. "No," she said on a little laugh. "Wonderful. I warn you, though. When I'm not pregnant or nursing, I have a very unimpressive chest. You, on the other hand…" She reached up to pull at the buttons of his shirt. Under it was a crisp white T-shirt that she pulled out of his pants.

He dropped his hands from her to shrug out of the shirt and pull off the T-shirt. She ran exploratory fingertips up his muscled torso, through the wiry dark hair covering his pecs, to the impressively wide line of his shoulders.

"…are magnificent," she said.

He kissed her. "That might be mildly overstated,"

he said, slipping his fingers into the elastic waistband of her skirt. "But thank you."

His fingertip met silk, and he reached into another elastic band and found yet more silk. His hands explored inside the last elastic band and found silk again—but this time it was the silk of flesh.

Jo felt his warm, strong hands touch her hipbone, then move around to her bottom and cup her possessively. She kissed his collarbone and whispered his name.

He drew the layers of clothing over her hips and down her thighs until she could step out of them. Then he tossed skirt, slip and panties aside.

She unbuckled his belt and unbuttoned and unzipped his pants. Ryan closed his eyes as her hands explored as his had done. The tips of her fingernails traced a line over his buttocks, and down the backs of his legs, as she pulled down on his slacks and briefs.

He sat on the edge of the bed to kick them off, then wrapped an arm around her waist and pulled her to the mattress with him.

"The least discomfort," he said, holding her to him as he pushed them to the middle of the bed, "and I want you to stop me."

"I'll be fine," she assured him, fascinated at the realization that she now sat astride him, when there'd been such antagonism between them for so long. Somehow, by some miracle, that had all disappeared, and here was this wildly beating passion that had their fingers linked—as though they had been linked through time and eternity.

She leaned down to kiss his chest, and he held her shoulders away from him so that he could look into her eyes.

"I mean it, Jo," he said. "You have no idea how you'll feel. The book says it could be…"

She melted with tenderness. Every step along the way in this pregnancy, he'd known almost as much about it as she did, because he'd read her book. Before she moved in with him, he'd borrowed it, and since they'd been living together, she would come upon him reading it when she'd thought him busy with something else.

"Do you have to do everything," she asked teasingly, nipping his chin, "by the book?"

"Jo…"

"I will be fine." She kissed a line across his collarbone, then from shoulder to shoulder. "But if you don't stop worrying," she warned, "*I* might hurt *you*—on purpose."

"Joey, I want…" he began, intending to be stern with her.

But she was moving back down his body, stringing kisses along the center of him, and he couldn't remember what he'd wanted an instant ago. He felt her fingertips over his hipbones, in the concavity of his stomach, along the length of his maleness. And when he was sure that would kill him, he felt the ends of her hair like strands of silk following her touch—over his hipbones, in the concavity of his stomach, along the length of his maleness. All he wanted now was to be inside her.

She rose over him and guided him, her artful fingers negating all his efforts to move slowly. She swayed atop him like a flower in the breeze. He braced her hands with his, moving his hips with hers as they traced the circle that defined so much of life—man, woman, eternity.

Jo felt no pain, only ecstasy. She, too, had read that

chapter of the book and had been sure the pleasure would far outweigh the possible pain. But even she had had no idea.

She felt as though heaven had opened to her and showered her with its secrets. This was love—not simply lovemaking, but love-giving, a sharing beyond anything she'd ever known or understood. And sharing it with Ryan gave her life meaning—even apart from her identity as Chelsea's mother, and her own personal pride in herself as a woman.

Then all lofty thought about what love meant was absorbed in the onslaught of physical sensation. The artful circling of him beneath her; the tantalizing beginning, the swelling approach of fulfillment that taunted nearer and nearer. And finally the explosion, the delicious gift of climax that tumbled over and over her, making her body quake with its power.

Ryan felt her fingernails in his knuckles and remembered another moment, on the brink of Chelsea's birth, when she'd dug her nails into him and cried out. Now, as she clung to him with that same desperate need for him, he erupted inside her, all pleasure and revelation, and thought that at this moment she'd given birth again—this time to him.

THEY LAY wrapped in each other's arms, one side of the blankets they'd never turned down pulled over them. Jo had never known such happiness.

"I take it back." She burrowed her nose sleepily into his throat.

"What's that?" he asked lazily, twining one of her spiraled curls around his fingertip. He felt a deep-down joy that radiated to every hidden corner of his being.

She sighed and kissed the underside of his chin. "You're definitely *not* out of order."

His soft laugh was rich and self-satisfied. "*Robert's Rules* was wrong about you, too. Geez."

She leaned her head back to look into his eyes. "I love you. Did I ever get to say that?"

He kissed the tip of her nose. "You can say it again. Repeat it often."

She nibbled at his lips, murmuring, "I love you. I love you."

They were settling down again, arms and legs entangled, when a demanding cry came from the nursery. They groaned together. Then Ryan laughed. "I'll get her."

Jo caught his arm. "Bring her back to bed. I'll feed her here."

Ryan, propped up against the pillows, held Jo and Chelsea in his arms while the baby ate, noisily, greedily.

Jo was delirious with the pleasure of Ryan's arms around her and the healthy, pink-cheeked baby they'd worked so hard to bring to life.

MAMA CASS?

"It's all right, darling. I'm supposed to be forgotten. Keep eating."

RYAN TIED the strings at the throat of his Dracula cape and studied his reflection in the bathroom mirror with a disgruntled frown. In front of him, Jo, in a ruffly pink silk organza top, applied a beauty mark just below her bottom lip with an eyebrow pencil.

"Dracula is so trite," Ryan said, putting a hand to the hair she'd slicked back for him and making a face.

Jo, who'd been listening to his grumblings since

she'd brought the costumes home the day before, straightened to study her makeup. "It was all the costume shop had left," she said absently. "And since Chelsea and I went all the way to Longview for them, I should think you'd be grateful." She pressed her lips together and patted down the pile of gold curls atop her head. She tugged her sleeves off her shoulders and studied her reflection critically. "And since Anne Rice brought the vampire Lestat on the scene," she went on, glancing up at Ryan's reflection, "vampires are anything but trite. Show me some teeth."

He frowned doubtfully at her assurances and said, with stubborn insistence, "I am *not* putting on false fangs."

She turned to him, the bottom half of her clad only in ruffly pantalets. She'd left off the hoop and skirts that would have taken up the entire space in the bathroom.

"You've got to get into the spirit of this," she said, looping her arms around his neck. It had only been three days, and she still couldn't believe she had the right to touch him. A sensation like an electric current ran from him to her. "It's going to be fun. Jave and Nancy are going to be there. And I think Tom's bringing Amy."

"Are they on again?" Ryan asked absently, leaning down to nibble on Jo's neck. She smelled like flowers and felt like love, and he was suddenly very aware of all the things they could be doing at home tonight instead of going to Diantha's.

"He...ah...is trying to remain friends with her. But she..." Jo hunched her shoulder as Ryan kissed one of the cords of her neck and pleasure raced along her nerve endings. "Ryan," she protested breathlessly. "Don't start..."

"I'm just trying to get into character," he argued

softly, raising his head to give her a swift kiss before moving to the other side of her neck. "You don't want me to arrive at the party in costume, but inexperienced in my seductive vampire wiles, do you? What were you going to say about Amy?"

"She…um…she wants a more…more serious relationship. Ryan…"

"Hmm?" His lips had moved to the swell of her breast above the deep neckline of her ruffly top. And his hand cupped her cotton-clad bottom. She leaned weakly against him, forgetting they were already late for the party.

"We're supposed to be getting ready…"

"I am," he said. It was clear he didn't mean for the party.

Jo heard a baby sound from the front room.

MOM! Daddy! Where are you? Who's the old lady with the peppermint breath?

JO PUSHED on Ryan's shoulders with sudden determination. She had to draw a breath before she could speak. "Mrs. Bennett is in the front room with Chelsea," she whispered.

He groaned against her throat, then reluctantly lifted his head. His eyes were dark with banked passion. "Okay," he said, a grin forming on his lips. "But when we get back from the party, I'm going to make you a vampire, too."

Joy billowed in her at the possessive look in his eyes. She kissed him soundly. "Don't worry," she said. "I'm already yours."

"AH…" Jo and Ryan stopped halfway up the walk to Diantha's home on the hill overlooking Heron Point, and watched a figure burst from the front door and run down the steps. It was completely dressed in a pale color that shone eerily in the moonlight—pants, long top, a hat that covered the head completely, and a mask pulled off and hanging down. "Do you see a white ninja?" Ryan asked Jo quietly, "Or am I finally going under from sleep deprivation?"

Jo peered through the darkness at the figure, now only several yards from them. "I think...that's the hospital's surgery garb," she said, pulling Ryan back with her as the figure continued to approach, moving quickly.

"Amy, wait!" The door burst open again, and a man in a bearskin and a Viking helmet erupted from the pandemonium of laughter and loud conversation inside the house.

When the other figure kept moving, the Viking shouted in a roar, "Amaryllis Brown! Stop this minute!"

"It's Amy," Jo whispered. "And Tom."

Ryan covered her mouth as Amy stopped just a yard away from them, the shadows and her own obvious preoccupation making her unaware of their presence in the shelter of the rhododendron.

"YOU'RE BEING CHILDISH!" Tom shouted as he loped down the walk, stopping a foot from Amy. He pulled off his helmet. Under it was a scraggly blond wig, and he pulled that off, too. "I can't come to the hospital dinner, because I'm in the middle of putting a new roof on Nancy's beach house. I explained that."

"Oh, right," Amy said, her usual sunny disposition replaced by angry cynicism. "And you're going to be doing that at night."

There was an instant's silence. "Yes," he said defensively. "I am. The winter rains are about to—"

"Oh, save it!" she shouted at him. "You aren't coming because you're afraid it might mean we're becoming important to one another, and you're not about to let that happen!"

"Amy…"

"I know you have emotional scars from the fire that killed your friend and ended your career," she said, lowering her voice but not the level of her anger, "and if you want to hold on to them until you're an old man, that's fine. But I have my own problems. And among them is the need to be loved by someone, even though I'm tall and awkward and plain."

Ryan saw Tom straighten, with an expression that seemed to indicate genuine puzzlement. "You're not—" he began.

But Amy wasn't finished. "You're entitled to wallow in your feelings of guilt, and to be shy about your burned leg, and your wounded psyche. But those feelings put me on the outside of our relationship, and that's not where I want to be. Goodbye, Tom."

He grabbed for her arm, but she yanked it away and ran toward the long row of cars parked along the sidewalk.

Tom said a four-letter word, tossed the helmet and wig, and took off in the other direction.

Jo put a hand to her lips. "Poor Amy," she murmured sympathetically.

Ryan drew her up the walk toward the house. "Poor Amy?" he repeated in surprise. He'd helped Tom sell the *River Lady,* consolidate his bills, get a loan to begin his life over again. He knew what he'd been through. "Poor Tom. He's been to hell and back—almost literally. She's not going to get anywhere by hammering at him.''

Jo let the matter drop, unwilling to point out that that was what had finally placed them in the position of lovers. She'd simply refused to give up on him, to let him belong only to Cassie, even though she was gone.

Jave Nicholas stood in the doorway when they reached it. He was dressed as a pirate, complete with phony beard and mustache, a cutlass dangling at his hip. He was frowning in the direction Tom had gone.

Nancy appeared at his shoulder in a red silk skirt slit up to the thigh, fishnet stockings, a cameo on a strip of black velvet around her neck and a gaudy plume in her hair.

''Maybe you should go after him,'' she said worriedly to Jave.

He shook his head. ''He'd only bite my head off, too.''

''Want me to go?'' Ryan asked, half-seriously. ''I'm qualified to bite back.''

Jave turned to him and laughed, pulling him inside the house. ''Get in here. He'll be fine. He's got to work it out himself.'' He bowed to Jo as he offered her a hand over the threshold. ''Good evening, Miss Scarlett. Just think of me as a blockade-runner from an earlier time.'' He drew her into the party.

Nancy hooked an arm through Ryan's. ''So, Count,'' she said, ''buy you a drink? We have B negative on tap.''

Chapter Thirteen

"It's a shame women aren't wearing those anymore," Ryan said as Jo carefully folded the organza skirt back into a box nested with tissue paper on the foot of the bed. He lay across the coverlet in a brown terry robe, his head propped on his hand as he watched her.

She glanced up from folding the top of the dress into the tissue. "You mean hoops and big skirts?"

He reached out to catch her wrist and pull her down on top of him. His hands ran over the ruffles covering her bottom. "No, I mean these drawers. The ruffles move in a very enticing manner when you move."

Lust flared in her instantly. She could feel his sturdy chest beneath her, his strong arms around her, his thigh raised between hers where his foot was braced on the bed. There was nowhere she would rather be. This morning they'd put down earnest money on a three-story Victorian on a knoll overlooking the river. She was so happy it hurt.

She laughed as she nuzzled his throat. "So, you mean you'd like me to keep them on?"

He nipped her ear punitively. "No, I don't mean that at all. But I think I'd like a picture of you in them that

I could pull out of my desk on tedious afternoons at the bank.''

He tried to slip his hand inside the waistband and discovered he couldn't. "No elastic in those days?" he asked.

"I think they had it, but it wasn't in common use," she replied, moving his hand to the bow she'd tied at the side. "They used strings instead."

He turned to lay her down on the coverlet. One deft yank unfastened the bow.

"It seems if a gentleman wanted to seduce a lady," he observed, tugging the ruffly pantalets down, "he had to tug on more than her *heart*strings."

She sat up to push his robe off and pull him back to her. "All you'd have to do," she said, stroking a fingertip over his lips, "is flash your pearly teeth. So, if I understand the lore, by morning I'll be a vampire, too?"

He nodded gravely. "And we'll live for all eternity."

"Do we have to bite the baby?"

He gave that a moment's thought. "I don't think so. She probably inherits immortality from me."

Jo leaned up on an elbow. "Are you sure? Now that I think about it, I've never read about vampire babies. Do they even—?"

Ryan rolled his eyes and kissed her into silence. "You used to be the one," he said finally, divesting her of the camisole and nonauthentic bra she'd worn under it, "who was fanciful and didn't care about detail, and I was the pragmatist."

Thought slipped away as his hand closed over her breast. "Love," she whispered, "blurs the lines that divide."

She was right, he thought, as he felt the sole of her foot slip up and down his leg, her hands explore his back, her fingernails leave a tantalizing trail of sensation.

Each of them had changed, and what separated them in action and philosophy seemed so much less important than what connected them.

He held her against him, lips to lips, breasts to chest, eager maleness to waiting femininity.

Jo opened for him like a flower, and enclosed him with all the love and hope she felt in their closeness, in their daughter, in their future.

Feeling spiraled out of control inside her. Ryan thrust deeper, and they climaxed together, lives and destinies entangled.

"Ryan!" she cried in a whisper.

"Cassie!" he breathed against her shoulder. "Oh, Cassie."

Complete stillness fell upon the bedroom.

In the silence, Jo heard the name like a shout in her brain—and felt her life shudder to a stop.

Ryan heard the echo of his own voice and closed his eyes in disbelief. No. He hadn't said that.

Jo stiffened in his arms, and he tightened his embrace instinctively, turning so that she lay in his arms. "Don't," he said urgently. "I'm sorry. It was a slip of the tongue. I was…it was all so perfect that for a minute I was…" He backed away from the words he'd been about to speak, afraid she'd misunderstand. "Jo, I'm sorry. I didn't mistake you for her. I swear I didn't."

Jo felt as though a train had run over her, as though everything inside her was crushed and broken.

But she loved him enough, she wanted a life with him enough, to listen to her brain telling her over and over that it had simply been a slip of the tongue. It hadn't meant that when he made love to her he thought of Cassie. It hadn't.

She wrapped her arms around his neck. "Of course not," she said, with a conviction she thought sounded genuine. She kissed his throat and snuggled closer. "It's all right. Don't think about it anymore."

"Jo…" he began. But the baby cried, and she wriggled out of his arms to go to her.

He caught her wrist and tried to pull her back. "Jo, listen to me."

She smiled but pulled her hand firmly away. "Go to sleep. I'll feed Chelsea and be right back."

She walked out of the room and closed the door. Ryan fell back against the pillow with a groan, his arm tracing the empty expanse of bed beside him, He had a feeling that, however innocently, he'd made a fatal mistake.

IT WAS A PERFECT DAY for boating. The *Mud Hen,* newly refurbished, sailed amid the soft swells of the Columbia River, with far more dignity then her namesake.

"I wanted to change the name," Jave said to Ryan as he guided the small craft up the channel. They passed two braying, glossy harbor seals lying on a buoy, a lone heron majestically perched on a piling, and a host of cormorants ranged on a long-abandoned dock, several of them with wings outstretched. He pointed a finger at Tom, who lounged against the boat's cabin with a can of cola in his hand. "But Little Brother thought it gave her character. Character. Do you believe it?"

"No, I don't," Ryan replied, more to elicit a response from Tom than because he agreed—the same reason, he was sure, Jave had raised the subject. Tom had been morose and withdrawn all morning—and the reason was below decks with Jo and Nancy, making sandwiches. "I wouldn't try to raid the coast in it, or anything. Somehow, I don't think the *Mud Hen*—" he repeated the name loudly, teasingly, in Tom's direction "—would raise terror in the hearts of the common folk."

When Tom didn't even turn in his direction, he frowned at Jave.

Ryan had been surprised to see that Amy had been invited to join their company, considering how her evening with Tom had ended just a week ago. But he understood that women were inveterate cupids, and Nancy, apparently, was one of the most optimistic. But Tom and Amy hadn't spoken to each other since each's initial shock at finding the other in the boating party.

That had resulted in an old-fashioned gender separation that had kept the women in the galley and the men at the wheel.

Ryan was frankly relieved. Jo had been terminally sweet and cheerful since the night he'd called her Cassie, and he was beginning to feel as though he were living with a doll rather than a woman.

It was all his fault. He understood that. But in an effort to pretend her feelings *weren't* hurt, Jo was behaving with all the sincerity of a Stepford wife. She conversed charmingly, she made love eagerly, she sat close to him and touched him. But there was an air of staginess about it that was getting on his nerves.

All his attempts to talk about it were smilingly rebuffed, because the baby needed something, or because she had to carry out some chore relating to the Heron Point Has It event the following week. He didn't know what to do about it.

Ryan turned to lean against the rail and watch the bright green coastline of Washington go by. He was surprised when Tom suddenly came to lean beside him.

"There's no point," Tom said with a sigh, "inviting a woman into your life, when you don't even have your life together yet." Then he turned to Ryan with a level gaze. "Is there?" he asked. "We all know your situation. Your lady's smiling, but she looks a little too desperate for me to believe that all's well with the two of you."

"Jeez, Tom," Jave said, turning the small boat into a wooded harbor. "Why don't you hit him with a sledgehammer?"

Tom clapped Ryan's shoulder in a sort of philosophical apology. "I was just making a point. I don't think he's the one to get on my case about Amy."

Ryan raised an eyebrow. "I don't recall saying a word."

"You don't have to." He inclined his head in Jave's direction. "You pontifical types who know what's best for everyone don't even have to open your mouths. Your manner radiates disapproval."

"No one disapproves of *you*," Jave said, pulling down the bill of his cap as bright sunlight embroidered the water of the bay. "We disapprove of your self-protective cowardice."

Ryan turned to Jave. "Jeez, Jave," he said, echoing his friend's own words. "Why don't you just hit him with a sledgehammer?"

NANCY OFFERED Amy a tissue. Jo sat beside her, an arm around her shoulders in the galley's tiny nook. Malia and Chelsea sat in their carriers, both lulled to sleep by the movement of the boat.

"I'm sorry," Nancy said. "In retrospect, I can see it was stupid, but when I called you yesterday and failed to mention that Tom was coming along, I thought I was just helping you two communicate." Her voice lowered regretfully. "I guess I didn't realize it was so...over."

Amy's face crumpled again, for the fifth time in the past half hour, and Jo tightened her grip on her.

"The worst part is—" she was weeping now "—he's a great guy. Except for that unwillingness to share what hurts."

Nancy arranged sandwiches on a plate. "I reacted that way after my first marriage," she said. "I gave Jave a terrible time. Remember?"

Amy nodded.

"But he didn't give up on me."

Amy sniffed and drew a deep breath. "Well, he probably had more self-confidence than I do. As the ugly duckling in a beautiful, intelligent bevy of Brown women, I'm just barely holding my head above water. I don't think I'm strong enough to keep us both afloat. It has to be over, or we'll both drown."

Nancy smiled. "Lots of seagoing metaphors, there.

Maybe it's time to take this picnic ashore and get some fresh air. Jo and I will stay between you and Tom. Don't worry.''

As the three couples ate with artificially boisterous good cheer, Jo considered her situation with Ryan in a new and unsettling light.

She had forced Ryan into this relationship. There had been clear signs of interest in her on his part, but he'd obviously needed more time, more distance from everything he'd shared with Cassie. But she'd seen a glimmer of opportunity, and she'd pushed.

But she remembered their lovemaking, their quiet moments with Chelsea, the insignificant, unremarkable everydayness of the past few weeks of their lives and found it hard to believe that it wasn't what God intended. She was so happy with him. He'd seemed so happy with her. Until he'd called her by her sister's name.

A simple mistake? She tried to think so. She wanted him to believe she thought so. But the more time wore on, the more deeply it hurt to remember that, during one of the most personal moments of a woman's life, she'd been mistaken for another. For Cassie, who'd always had everything she, Jo, wanted. And apparently still did.

CASSIE WAS BACK. Jo bumped into her on the street in downtown Portland, while she was pushing Chelsea in a stroller. They were all moving in slow motion through a glittering fog. Jo ran to her, her mouth open in silent shock, her arms open to welcome her back to life.

"Cassie!" she heard herself exclaim. Then she

crushed her in her arms. "God, Cassie, I've missed you!"

"Jo!" Cassie greeted her with the warmth and affection they'd always shared. She hooked her free arm in hers and laughing, led the way down the street.

Jo was aware of overwhelming joy, tempered only slightly with a vague sense of disbelief. Cassie was back. It couldn't be, but it was. They were arm in arm, pushing the baby together, the way they'd dreamed it would be, in the beginning, over that Thanksgiving weekend.

They walked together in happy conversation, the baby gurgling and flailing her arms. Then the fog dissipated and the scene became sharply, terrifyingly familiar.

"I know all of this won't be easy for you," Cassie said.

Jo saw herself laugh. "I'm doing it as a labor of love," she replied. "And when I'm *in* labor, remind me that I said that."

Then they stopped at the street corner to cross. Jo watched in horror as she saw herself turn to look at a marigold-colored sweater in a shop window. She willed herself to turn, to reach for Cassie to stop her from crossing. She heard herself groan, knowing she would experience that agonizing paralysis, that sense of impending horror swelling even as she was frozen in that moment in time.

But this time was different. She watched herself turn away, saw herself cover the distance that separated them in several long steps taken in slow motion. Then she saw herself snatch the baby from Cassie and watch without uttering a word of warning as she stepped into the street.

The sound of brakes screeching mingled with her scream. The high-pitched sound filled her ears, dominated her reality, went on and on and on.

RYAN SHOOK HER and shouted her name. The quality of her scream filled the room with her anguish, and deepened his desperation to wake her.

"Josanne!" he shouted as he pulled her up into a sitting position. He accompanied her name with one solid single shake. "Wake *up!*"

She came to with a start, the scream waning to an ever smaller sound that, conversely, conveyed an ever deeper pain.

He still held her arms and looked into her eyes, trying to help her come out of the nightmare. "It's over," he said. "You're awake. It's me, Jo. You're okay."

She finally focused on him, and he saw recognition there, awareness of where she was. Her hair tumbled past her shoulders in wild and curly disarray, and her blue eyes looked into his with an expression he couldn't read—except to know that it didn't look at all like relief.

Then her mouth contorted, and she fell against him with a sob.

"Jo…" he murmured softly, leaning against the pillows and pulling her into his arms. She wrapped hers around his bare middle and held on with a desperation that concerned him.

He glanced at the clock. Almost five. They'd made love just hours ago, and she'd been eager and responsive, if still a little remote, as though only part of her were engaged in the act. Afterward, he'd tried to coax her into conversation, to talk about the boating trip and the situation with Tom and Amy. When she simply shrugged over their relationship, he'd brought up the house they were buying, but her answers had been monosyllabic, and she'd finally fallen asleep against him.

He pulled the blankets over her bare shoulders and wrapped his arms around her to hold them in place. Apparently whatever was bothering her, whatever was creating a gulf between them, had worked on her subconscious while she slept.

He tightened his grip on her, hating to see her in pain, but privately grateful that now he had something he could deal with. He waited for her sobs to quiet.

Jo held Ryan tightly and forced herself to confront the truth. She could not have Ryan and Chelsea. The dream had just told her that she'd stolen them from Cassie. She hadn't been responsible for Cassie's death, of course, but she'd stepped in eagerly to benefit from it. And it wasn't that simple.

She felt Ryan's lips against her temple. "Tell me about it," he said gently.

She remained still, her cheek against the solid warmth of his shoulder, her arms wrapped around him. She closed her eyes to commit the moment to memory. It would have to last her a long time. She knew what she had to do.

"I dreamed about Cassie," she said, her voice heavy with tears. "We were walking down the street in Portland, and she had Chelsea."

Ryan felt his own emotions roil at the memories of that day. He hadn't been with them. They'd parted company to shop separately, and made plans to meet for lunch. He'd waited for them for more than an hour before a policeman sent by Jo finally came searching for him and explained about the accident.

He remembered the overpowering rage, the need to destroy things, to scream his horrible grief. Then, finally, he'd understood the overwhelming enormity of his loss, and everything inside him had died.

Pain scraped at him now, but it was for the woman in his arms and not for himself. In the intervening time, she'd eased his loss and given him his daughter—something new and wonderful.

"Go on," he said encouragingly.

She shook her head against him. "No. It'll hurt you."

He rubbed her shoulder. "I can take it."

"It's about…the accident."

"I'm listening."

Jo told him everything. She told him about the paralysis that always overtook her during the dream, and how this time it had been different. Her voice a strained whisper, she told him about snatching the baby from Cassie and watching her cross the street.

Then she pulled out of his arms and sat alone on her side of the bed, the blankets clutched to her. "Do you see what it means?" she asked, staring into the darkness.

"Yes," he said, putting a hand to her back. It felt fragile to his touch. "You saved Cassie's baby."

She turned to him, her eyes glistening sadness in the shadows. "I *took* Cassie's baby," she said. "I tried to take you."

He understood with sudden insight what was troubling her. "No," he said, leaning forward to look into her eyes. "We *gave* you the baby to carry for us." He put a hand to her face. "And I give you my love willingly. You haven't *taken* anything from me."

She held his hand to her, turned her face to kiss its palm, then put it away from her. "I rushed you, Ryan. I have you all confused. You just think you need me because of the baby, and because you miss Cassie."

He stood angrily, snatching his robe off the foot of the bed and putting it on. She was upset, he told himself. Distraught, even. He had to remain calm. But he didn't feel calm.

"You know me better than that," he said from the foot of the bed. "I don't use anyone for my purposes. I was going to hire Mrs. Bennett to take care of Chelsea, remember? And I do miss Cassie. I will probably always miss her. But I *love* you!"

She listened, but she remained stiffly unyielding, knees pulled up under her chin, her arms wrapped around them.

"It won't work between us," she said.

He didn't want to hear that. "Not if you don't think it will."

She uttered a protracted sigh. "I wanted to slip into Cassie's place."

"You made your own place."

Jo wanted to believe that—but he'd made love to her and called her Cassie. And she couldn't blame him, because she'd pushed him into a relationship before he was ready.

"I think the trouble is," she said with sudden acceptance, "that Cassie and I are occupying the same place.

And that isn't healthy for you or me. I think I have to go.''

She pushed the blankets aside and got to her feet. Ryan couldn't move. ''What do you mean?'' he demanded.

She gave him that distant Stepford-wife smile and went to the closet. He'd moved her clothes from the guest room just a week or so ago. ''Why don't we talk about it later? You have to be at the fairgrounds in an hour, and I have to load Devon's truck with my supplies for the fair.''

''Oh, no.'' He caught her arm as she tried to walk past him toward the bathroom, a skirt and sweater over her arm. ''You're not going to bring up separation, then tell me we'll talk about it later. We'll talk about it now. You're not going anywhere.''

She shook her head and raised one hand to smooth her hair. It defied the action, springing up in wild abandon, like the personification of the woman herself.

''First of all,'' she said, with a sudden control he found frightening, ''it isn't separation. We're not married. We're just living together to share the duties of raising a baby.''

''Bull.''

''Okay, it got physical, and that confused us. But it wasn't love.''

''It *is* love,'' he insisted.

She sighed patiently. ''Ryan, we could argue yes-it-is-no-it-isn't all day long, but what would it prove?''

''That one of us has to win the other over,'' he said.

''All right,'' she granted. ''Then let's talk about this later, when we have time.''

As though on cue, Chelsea announced with a screech that she was awake. Jo pushed her clothes into Ryan's arms and smiled faintly. "I guess you get first go at the shower. Would you lay those on the bed for me?"

Jo rocked as she fed Chelsea, and listened to the sound of the shower. Tears streamed down her face, and she let them, telling herself there would be plenty of time later to be strong.

MAMA CASS says she doesn't like what you're thinking. And you're getting tears on me.

RYAN PULLED UP in front of Coffee Country and saw that Devon was already there, loading boxes into a black Chevy pickup. Chelsea, in her infant seat, dozed in the back of the Volvo.

"When I drop her at Mrs. Bennett's," he said as Jo opened the passenger side door, "I'm going to ask her if she'll keep her until later tonight. I'm making reservations at Chez Pasta, and we're going to talk."

She smiled. There was no point in arguing. "All right," she said. Then, because she knew she would need to remember it later, she leaned across the seat and kissed him quickly. At least that was her intention.

But he cupped the back of her head in his hand and held her there while he prolonged the kiss, deepened it artfully with the tip of his tongue, then released her.

"Think about that today," he said, "and tell me that anything about the last few months we've shared suggests that we don't belong together for the rest of our lives."

Jo looked into his eyes and memorized everything

about him that she loved. Then she opened the car door and stepped out.

"Bye," she said, then reached into the back to touch the baby's foot. Pain radiated everywhere inside her. "Bye, baby," she whispered, and closed the car door.

Ryan drove away with a tap on the horn, and Jo quite literally felt her heart sink.

Devon opened the coffee bar's door. "Hey, Jose," he said. "you want the coffee candies, too, or just—?" He stopped in surprise as she raced past him into the bar, her eyes glazed with pain and spilling tears.

FOR THE FIRST TWO HOURS of the commercial fair, Ryan didn't have a moment to think. He had to deal with a pop machine that poured carbonated water and no syrup; the vintage clothing exhibitor who wanted to be moved from beside the Rotary Club's sausage-and-onions booth, pleading that everything lace had probably already been ruined by the smell; and an electrical outlet at the back of the building that was smoking.

By the time he'd called an electrician and the pop vendor who'd supplied the machine, and moved Frothy Fashions next to an herbalist, he was desperate for a cup of coffee.

He was about to head for Jo's booth when Tom Nicholas brought him a double espresso.

"Here you go, big guy," he said. "You look stressed."

Ryan smiled thinly. "Generally, banks are a lot quieter than this, and money problems are easier to solve."

Tom nodded. "I suppose so. Either you have it or you don't. Simple."

"Something like that."

"Ah…" Tom pointed to a booth in the far corner. "Riverview Hospital's in a dark spot," he said, with studied nonchalance, as he indicated the absence of an overhead fluorescent there. "You think you could find a trouble light or something she could just hook on the top of the booth?"

"I'll see what I can do." Ryan studied him suspiciously. "Did Amy ask you to ask me?"

He shook his head. "We're not speaking. I overheard her talking about it when I walked by." Tom raised his cup to him. "Thanks. Better get back to my booth."

Were relationships in general impossible, Ryan wondered, or just those among himself and his friends?

He headed toward the front door to check the morning receipts.

By noon, the Heron Point Has It commercial fair had admitted four times the visitors they'd expected, and many exhibitors had approached Ryan about signing up to participate the following year.

Only Diantha glared at him, over the crowds of people studying her natural, organically grown products. He was used to that from her and almost didn't give it a second thought.

It was early afternoon before he had a moment to himself. He headed for the Coffee Country booth to see if Jo had managed to have anything for lunch besides her own fare. He found Devon behind the counter.

"Where's Jo?" he asked.

Devon glanced up at him while restocking a pedestal plate with scones. "Taking a break. Booth-hopping, I think."

Ryan might have accepted that and walked away, had he not caught the hatred in Devon's eyes. He knew the young man had always disliked him, but he'd never seen quite that degree of condemnation in him before. It reminded him with sudden sharpness of the look he'd gotten from Diantha.

Connected with the conversation he and Jo had had early that morning, those looks brought to mind a thought too ugly to consider. No. She wouldn't have.

"She say what booth?" he asked, his calm tone edged with grim suspicion.

Devon glared up at him again. "Why don't you just look around?"

Ryan's calm evaporated. He grabbed Devon by his shirt collar and pulled him toward him so that their noses almost met over the counter.

"I've *been* around all morning. I haven't seen her. I thought she was here. Where is she?"

Devon hesitated for an instant, but it was long enough for Ryan to know that something was wrong, and that Devon had been sworn to silence.

He tightened his grip. "Where," he demanded, his voice deadly quiet, "did she go?"

"I don't know," Devon replied. The anger in his eyes subsided slightly. It wasn't fear, Ryan saw, but general concern for Jo. "I told her it was stupid."

Ryan freed him out of self-protection. He was sure fury had made lethal weapons of his hands.

Ryan ran across the building and sideways down a narrow aisle until he reached Diantha's booth. He cut into her conversation with a customer.

"Where's Jo?" he demanded. "And don't bother telling me you don't know."

She raised a judgmental eyebrow. She excused herself to the customer, then said to Ryan, "She was perfect for you, you know."

"I know!" he shouted at her. The customer whose conversation he'd interrupted backed out of the booth. He lowered his voice. "Diantha, I know. I told her that. But she didn't believe me. Where is she? Please."

She considered him a moment, then sighed and folded her arms. "She went to Connecticut."

He stared at her in disbelief. "Connecticut," he repeated flatly.

Her manner softened, her voice quieted. "To her father."

"For how long?"

She looked apologetic. "She asked me if I wanted to buy Coffee Country."

Ryan forgot that he had a reputation for control. He ran to find Tom Nicholas, grabbed his arm, and brought him with him to the parking lot.

"I have to leave," he said. "I think all the major crises are handled. The high school drama club has agreed to clean up as a fund-raiser. So all you have to do is lock up after everybody's gone." He handed him a key as they reached his car. "I know it'll cost you a few hours and I'm sorry to take advantage, but I've got to—"

Tom cut him off. "Of course I'll do it. Just tell me nothing's wrong with Jo or the baby."

The baby.

Ryan forced himself to refocus his attention one more

moment. "Jo's left," he said. "I've got to get her back."

"All right." Tom backed away. "Go. But drive carefully."

The baby!

Ryan tried to dial Mrs. Bennett on his cellular phone as he raced the Volvo toward her little duplex behind the Methodist church. But her line was busy. He closed the phone in frustration and tossed it aside.

Had Jo taken the baby? No wonder she'd given him so little argument about talking the problem out tonight. She'd had an escape plan. And she'd probably taken his daughter.

By the time he reached Mrs. Bennett's, anger and desperation were so entangled inside him that he could barely see. He took the porch steps two at a time and banged loudly on her door. And he didn't stop until the old woman pulled it open.

"Mr. Jeffries," she said in concerned surprise. "Is something wrong?" She held Chelsea in her arms, wrapped in the blanket with the fringe on only three sides.

Ryan heard a strangled sound come from his throat, and then he reached for his daughter. She stared at him, big-eyed, and it was all he could do not to burst into tears.

DADDY! I'm so glad you're back. Mama Cass says Mama Jo left for...

HE HELD HER AGAINST HIM and buried his nose in her blanket. He had to pull himself together.

"I'm sorry, Mrs. Bennett," he said after a moment. Holding the baby with one arm, he reached into his breast pocket with the other and handed the sitter twice her usual rate. "Everything's... Plans have changed," he said. "I'll take Chelsea with me now."

She looked surprised, then reached behind the door and handed him the diaper bag. "Well, of course that's fine, but I thought you and Jo had a hot date tonight."

He'd thought so, too. He smiled his thanks and held Chelsea tightly to him as he walked back to the car.

He drove home, glancing often in the rearview mirror at the baby, who made loud, high-pitched, happy noises from her infant seat.

DADDY! You're gonna go get Mama Jo, right? Daddy?

CHELSEA WAS ASLEEP when he reached the condo, but he couldn't make himself put her down. The fear that she'd been taken was still too new, too complete. He balanced her against his shoulder as he went to the kitchen and dialed Matthew's number. His answering machine picked up. He left a message.

Then he sat down in the recliner, the baby a comforting weight in his arms, and accepted the feeling of devastation. Jo had left him. But she hadn't taken the baby. Knowing how much she loved Chelsea, he saw it as a gesture of how much she loved *him*.

Of course, she'd made that clear over and over during the past few months. What she hadn't understood was how much he loved her. This morning, all his efforts had fallen on stubborn ears.

He didn't know what else to say.

Chapter Fourteen

Matthew Arceneau held his weeping daughter in his arms. He had no idea how to help her. Deep sobs had racked her since he'd picked her up at the airport an hour ago and brought her home to his farmhouse at the edge of a wood.

She'd told him about Ryan thinking he'd fallen in love with her, then calling her Cassie while they made love. Then she told him about the dream in which she'd snatched the baby from her sister, then done nothing to stop her from walking out in front of the car.

"It's foolish," he said, "to change the entire direction of your life because of a dream."

She finally pushed out of his arms, ran a hand over the hair she'd tied back in a braid and sniffed. "It explained everything to me, Dad," she said, sitting up and dabbing at her red nose with a crumpled tissue. "I thought I could just step into the situation as Chelsea's mother and Ryan's love, because I'd always loved him, and deep down I guess I thought it was my right. But you can't force love on someone. They'll love whomever they want to love."

Matthew watched her ball the tissue into an impossibly small piece, then reach behind him for the box and place it on the sofa cushion between them.

"You said he explained to you why he called you Cassie. That sounds logical to me. That..." he said, smiling fondly at her, "and the fact that it isn't impossible for a man to love the woman he's lost and still love the woman who's vital and beside him and helping him find his way again. It isn't that he loves her memory more than he loves you, it's that he loves you both. Is that so awful?"

"I don't know." She snatched up a new tissue, her brow furrowed, her eyes focused on her memories of the dream. "Why did I take the baby from her, but not stop her from crossing the street?" she asked. "All the other times I was paralyzed, but this time I wasn't. This time I could have stopped her." She looked into Matthew's eyes, fresh tears brimming. "I wonder if it means—?"

He'd read her mind since she was a child. He read it now. "That you wanted her out of the picture so you could have Ryan and Chelsea?" He blurted out the words so that she could hear them for the nonsense they were. "No. Absolutely not. When Cassie was here, you never betrayed your feelings about Ryan. Neither of them ever suspected. But with her gone, you did what a heart filled with love is supposed to do—you tried to give it. You haven't stolen anything from Cassie, Jo. Cassie's gone."

Jo took one more tissue, blew her nose, then drew a deep breath and sat forward.

"It's better this way," she said, trying to think of something other than the ache in her arms to hold Chelsea, the ache in her breasts to feed her, the ache in her heart where her love for Ryan would always be. "It just wasn't meant to be, from the beginning. He's always belonged to her. Now he has his baby, and he can find someone to love on his own, without encouragement from a prejudiced party."

She smiled affectionately at her father. "Thanks for letting me stay for a few days. I'll start job-hunting first thing in the morning, then I'll get an apartment and be out of your hair."

"Stay as long as you like," he said. He let the subject of Ryan drop. She'd made up her mind, and arguing with her would be futile until she was ready to listen. "It's not like I have a parade of women through here and need my privacy."

"I'm sure the fault's not on your side." Jo stood and gathered up their pottery mugs on the coffee table. "Diantha was pretty taken with you."

He smiled. "I liked her, too. She might visit me next summer."

Jo raised an eyebrow. "She didn't tell me."

He took the cups from her and gave her a look of paternal superiority. "You don't know everything, you know. Why don't you go put your things away, and I'll call for a pizza? Oh, wait." He sobered suddenly. "Ryan's left four messages," he said. "I have to return his call. What do you want me to tell him?"

That I love him, she thought. *That I will always love him.* But she drew a breath and said, "That I arrived safely and am fine, and that I send my best." She had to swallow before she added the next. And even then her voice came out thin and hollow. "And ask him how Chelsea is."

"What if he wants to talk to you?"

"Tell him I'm asleep."

"That won't solve the problem. He'll just call again tomorrow."

"It solves the problem for today. And right now I can only handle a day at a time."

"I'M SORRY, Ryan." Matthew's reasonable, professorial voice came quietly across the phone line. "But she won't talk to you. She's...convinced it's over."

Ryan closed his eyes against the words, then opened them again, telling himself that he didn't have to lend the words any credence.

"I'm booked on a flight out in the morning," he said. "And tell her not to try to hide. That I'll just keep looking until I find her."

"Give her a little time," Matthew cautioned.

Ryan swore. "Time isn't going to change anything, Matt. She thinks I'm confusing love for Cassie with love for her."

"She told me. Look. You've both had such a difficult year. Why don't you just let her be for a few weeks? Let her think things through."

Ryan uttered a scornful sound. "You know her," he said. "She thinks that she's right about everything. Do you really think time will change her mind?"

Matthew hesitated.

Ryan hadn't expected him to lie, but seeing that possibility now as his last hope, he wished he would.

"No," Matthew said finally. "But there's probably

a way to bring that about, if we could just come up with it.''

"Like what?"

"I don't know. Think. Meanwhile, I'll pray. I'm supposed to ask how Chelsea is.''

"How does she think she is?" Ryan demanded angrily. He held the phone away from his ear so that Matthew could hear the squalling from the nursery. "She's fussy. She knows something's wrong. She's gotten nothing but bottled milk all day. Tell her Chelsea's very, very unhappy, because she misses her mother.''

"I'll tell her.''

"Thanks, Matt.''

Ryan hung up the telephone and hurried to the nursery to pick up the baby. She continued to cry for a moment, then quieted as he walked with her into the kitchen to run a bottle of store-bought formula under the hot water.

THAT stuff again? You mean she isn't back yet? I want you to know I'm very upset. I want my mother!

"IT's GOING to be all right," he assured Chelsea as he settled her in the crook of his arm and gave her the bottle. He paced the room with her, too restless himself to sit.

"Your mama Jo's just confused," he said, stroking a thumb over the warm and very bald little head.

The small pink scalp reminded him of their jokes about the bald blanket, and that reminded him of all the hours Jo had put into finishing it—and how it remained unfinished yet, like the resolution of their relationship.

Well, there had to be a solution. Cassie had believed there was a solution to everything.

And there in the middle of his dark apartment, with the baby dozing off in his arms and the lights on the guiding buoys visible from his window, it came to him.

He stopped pacing and stood still—the power and the possibilities of it playing out in his mind.

It could work. Or he could lose everything.

But he didn't have to think twice. Jo's love was all-or-nothing stakes.

JO HAD SPENT THE DAY on the sofa with an ice pack on her head. Her brave resolution to go job hunting in the morning hadn't taken into account the physical results of a broken heart.

She'd awakened with a pounding headache from a night of crying, acute nausea from six pieces of green pepper-and-pepperoni pizza in a stomach that hadn't seen food in sixteen hours, and a general misery that made stepping out of the house impossible.

Her father had walked her to the sofa, covered her with a blanket, brought her a pot of tea and the TV remote and gone off to school.

She pushed the blanket aside and sat up gingerly. She gave her head a few minutes to stop thumping and spinning, then stood, holding on to the back of the sofa, and made her way carefully to the kitchen.

Her father would be home soon. She should have something ready for dinner.

She opened a cupboard, and found nothing that reminded her of home, but suddenly she saw in her mind's eye the day several months ago when Ryan had moved her into his condo and she'd browsed through the cupboards. She put a hand to her heart, where pain throbbed.

She leaned against the countertop, weak from the emptiness of a future without Ryan and Chelsea. All the hope she'd once had in every moment of every day had been ground to dust by loneliness. And she'd been gone less than twenty-four hours. She couldn't imagine how this would hurt a month from now. Or a year.

The thought was too horrible to contemplate. She found canned soup and sandwich makings, and was about to tackle the task of preparing them when the doorbell rang.

She turned slowly to look at the door, dread in her heart. Oh, no! Her father told her Ryan had planned to fly out to Connecticut, but that he had talked him out of it. What if he'd changed his mind? What if he'd come anyway, determined to bully her into coming back to Heron Point?

She felt a moment's sunburst of excitement at the thought. God, how she missed him! How wonderful it would be to wrap her arms around him, to feel him holding her!

Excitement dissipated as she accepted that she would only have to send him back alone. He didn't belong to her.

The doorbell sounded again, and she braced herself to walk across the room and answer it. If she ignored it, and it was Ryan, he would only wait until her father came home, and she would be forced to confront him anyway.

As the doorbell rang a third time, she put her hand on the knob and pulled the door open.

It was dark outside, but her visitors were brightly lit by the old coach lantern on the porch.

She stared in openmouthed shock at the baby. "Chelsea!" she gasped, grabbing the baby to her. She was dressed completely in white wool, a ruffly cap framing her pudgy pink face. She gave Jo an openmouthed smile, little hands flailing the air. The infamous blanket was wrapped around her.

"Oh, baby!"

MAMA JO! Thank goodness! But this still isn't right. Daddy's still at the other place.

JO CRUSHED Chelsea against her, feeling the little mouth already rooting at her neck. The baby's warmth and freshly powdered smell brightened the deep-down darkness that filled her being.

Then she noticed the woman who'd been carrying Chelsea.

"Diantha!" she said, in complete amazement. "What are you doing here?"

Diantha, in a natural suede jacket with fringed collar and cuffs, smiled wryly. "Well, it's a cinch the baby wasn't going to get here on her own. So, here I am. I always wanted to belong to an escort service, but this isn't precisely how I imagined it." She turned to wave off the cab idling at the curb. "Thank you!"

"But…" Jo continued to stare at her in perplexity.

Diantha pointed beyond Jo, to the cozy-looking living room. "Could we talk about this inside?"

"Oh! Of course." She stepped aside, pausing to nuzzle Chelsea while Diantha picked up an overnight bag and went past her into the house.

Jo closed the door, her mind darting in a hundred different directions as she tried to make sense of Diantha's turning up on her doorstep with Chelsea. How had Diantha gotten the baby away from Ryan? Why had she wanted to?

Diantha stopped in the middle of the living room and looked around with a smile. "Traditional, but very nice." Then her expression altered subtly, and her color rose. "Where's your father?"

"Still at school. He's due home soon. Diantha, I don't understand."

Diantha nodded and reached down to push aside the blanket on the sofa, then sat down. "Been a couch potato today, have we?" she asked. Then she took a good look at Jo as she sat beside her with the baby, and smiled sympathetically. "Ryan sent me." she added.

Jo placed Chelsea on the sofa cushion between them and began to remove her hat and snowsuit. "What?" she asked in surprise. "Why? Why would he do that?"

Diantha shook her head as she reached into her coat pocket for a rattle that she shook over the baby's head to distract her while Jo fussed with her clothes.

MAMA CASS says it's because he… Oooh! I like that. Can I have it?

"I'M JUST HERE to escort the baby," Diantha said. "I'm going back tomorrow."

Jo wrapped the blanket around Chelsea and cradled

her in her arms. She felt such happiness at the sight of her, but concern, too, over what her presence meant.

"Why," Jo asked patiently, "did Ryan ask you to bring her here?" She tensed suddenly as a possible answer occurred to her. "Is something wrong? Is he all right?"

Diantha unfastened the buttons of her coat. "No," she said, "I wouldn't say he's all right." She angled Jo a bland, wide-eyed glance as she shrugged out of her coat. "Maybe you haven't heard, but the woman he loves walked out on him without warning and moved across the country."

"Diantha."

"I know. You mean physically. Yes, he's fine. There is nothing wrong." She delved into her purse and produced a small, square envelope. The name Jo was printed on it in neat block letters. "He asked me to give this to you, and to tell you to read it when you have a quiet, private moment."

Jo accepted the envelope. It was thick and cream-colored, and was engraved with Ryan's return address. Once *her* address. Heron Point Condominiums, number 27.

Emotion frothed inside her. What had he done? She looked up at Diantha, what should have been a joyful turn of events somehow making her terribly sad. "But he wanted her so badly," she said, mystified. "He loves her so much."

Diantha patted her shoulder, her manner distinctly maternal. "And what does that tell you, my little thick-headed double Aquarius?"

Jo frowned at her friend. She knew being a double

Aquarius meant that Aquarius was not only her astrological sign, but her rising sign as well—the sign that had passed over the eastern horizon when she was born and consequently exercised great influence. But how that related now, Jo had no idea.

Apparently reading her mind, Diantha explained simply, "You're eccentric, and you think deeply, and because of that you think you know everything. But you don't. So think again. Think hard."

Matthew walked in while Jo was still staring at Diantha. He was almost as shocked as Jo had been to see his two new guests. He tossed coat and briefcase aside and came to scoop his granddaughter from Jo's lap.

"And how is my precious Pumpkin?" he asked, dangling her over his head. She shrieked at him. "And what are you doing here?"

PUMPKIN? Those fat orange things? Malia Rose's grandfather calls her Angel.

HE PULLED HER into his arms, took the bottle Diantha handed him and sat opposite them in a platform recliner.

"Diantha, it's wonderful to see you, but what on earth is going on?"

Diantha explained while Jo took down another can of soup and made sandwiches. Her friend and her father talked through dinner, and afterward, while Jo tidied up and played with the baby. Her father was animated and witty. Diantha's eyes sparkled.

"How's Coffee Country?" Jo asked. Diantha answered succinctly that Devon, bored with school, was happy to work it full-time until she could hire someone to share the hours. Then she turned to Matthew and resumed their conversation.

Jo carried the baby to the spare bedroom she'd used the night before, mentally calculating all the things she would need to make the baby comfortable. First priority was a crib.

Having the baby would affect all her plans about working, and probably about renting an apartment. She would have to find a rental house, somewhere that accepted children. And she would have to look into child care.

She told herself she was excited. But she wasn't. She was thrilled to have the baby—it felt as though some vital part of her that had been severed the morning before had been painlessly replaced. Well—not precisely painlessly. Because she did feel pain. It just wasn't her own. It was Ryan's.

She couldn't imagine why he'd sent Chelsea to her. She knew how much he loved his daughter, how he played with her with genuine delight, how he gave her her bottle with the utmost tenderness and fascination, how he watched her sleep, a proud smile on his lips.

She remembered how empty she, Jo, had felt last night, when an entire continent separated her from Ryan and the baby. She could imagine how he felt at this moment. She glanced at the clock. Almost 8:00 p.m.

It would be almost five in Heron Point. Ryan would just be leaving the bank, in the darkness of the late-fall evening. He would smell the river and wood smoke as he walked to his car, and he would hear the lonely bellow of the sea lions. And he would know that when he got to the condominium, there would be no one there.

Her eyes brimmed and her throat burned with unshed tears.

Jo put on the light on the bedside table, placed the now sleeping baby beside her on the coverlet, propped a pillow up against the headboard and leaned back to read Ryan's note. It was block-printed, like her name on the envelope.

Hi, Jo,
Spoke to your father last night, and he told me you arrived safely in Connecticut. I wanted to come out and talk to you, but he said you would prefer I didn't, so I've sent you all my love instead. The thought of you alone without your baby hurt me even more than my own pain. So I've asked Diantha to take Chelsea to you. I've sent on Simba and the rest of her things express mail, so they should be arriving within forty-eight hours. Take care of both of you. The work is not very skilled, but Bert showed me how to finish the fringe on Chelsea's blanket, so rest easy. Your circle's complete.
Ryan

Jo sat absolutely still, as pain and joy and a dozen other emotions she couldn't quite isolate or identify swelled inside her.

She reached down to inspect the fringe on the blanket Cassie had begun, that she'd almost finished, that her father had taken to the cafeteria to work on while she was in labor—and saw that the fringe had been finished on the bald end of it. It was pulled through evenly and with care—but a sob of happiness escaped her when she saw that it was on backward. She ran to the living room for the cordless phone.

RYAN WAS LATE for work. Very late. He took a last sip of tasteless coffee and glanced at the kitchen clock. It was almost eleven. There'd been no word from Jo, though Diantha had called very late last night to tell him that Jo had been ecstatic at the sight of Chelsea. That news had provided all the comfort he knew the situation could provide him. And that was fine. He'd known the chance he was taking when he sent Chelsea to Connecticut.

But it was one thing to do the noble and heroic thing, and quite another to live with it. He hadn't even gone to bed last night, knowing he wouldn't sleep. He'd prowled the dark apartment, the silence ringing loudly in his ears.

He'd gone into the nursery and touched all the things Jo and Chelsea had touched just a few days before, and sworn that he felt their impressions on it, smelled the lingering fragrance of baby powder and Jo's gardenia scent.

He'd known grief before, but that had resulted from a life God had taken from him. But this grief seemed to run even deeper and hurt even more, because Jo and Chelsea were alive and well—he simply couldn't have them. And that was a torture he'd have to live with. He just didn't know how he was going to do it.

He'd showered and shaved hours ago, he just didn't want to leave the condo, where the essence of them still lingered. He didn't even have to concentrate to see Jo sitting in a corner of the sofa, the baby at her breast, a smile on her lips as she hummed a Mamas and the Papas tune.

But he forced himself to put the coffee down, put on his jacket, and go to the door. Jo and Chelsea would be happy together. He had to find comfort in that and get on with his life.

He stepped out into the hall, locked the condo door behind him and pushed the button for the elevator.

He'd tackle some big project today, he decided. He'd review an impossible loan application, or work on that tangled checking account that no one at the branch seemed able to reconcile. That should keep his mind occupied so that he could get through the day. The night was too grim to even consider at this point.

The down bell rang, and the elevator doors parted.

Ryan took a step forward to get on—and everything inside him jolted to a halt. Air clogged in his lungs, blood ebbed in his veins, and his brain refused to function.

I'm seeing Jo in her blue swing coat and her magenta beret, and Chelsea in the white snowsuit and bonnet I put on her to send her to Connecticut.

He blinked. They were still there. And beside them with the diaper bag and a small suitcase was the cabbie with the Elvis button on her hat.

"Ryan! Oh, Ryan!" Jo wept as she flew into his arms, stepping on his foot, cutting off his air, the baby's cries as she was pressed between them threatening to shatter his ear drums.

I'M TIRED OF THE PLANE! I'm tired of us not being together! I want it to be just like this, all three of us—

*and I'm not going to stop screaming until someone tells
me that's the way it's going to be!*

THEY WERE very much flesh and blood, he decided in
a kind of disbelieving stupor. And they were back.

Jo, her free arm still in a stranglehold around his
neck, her left foot still squarely on his right one, the
baby still screaming, kissed his cheek, his jaw, his chin,
then his lips.

"I love you," she said, her mouth just centimeters
from his as her eyes, drunk with love, seemed to devour
his face. "And you love *me!*" Her grip tightened on
him even further. "You sent me the *baby!*" she whispered, a sob in the sound. "You would have let me
have Chelsea!"

Ryan kissed her soundly, feeling as though a star had
exploded inside his being. All-or-nothing bets were hard
on the nerves, but God, when they paid off...

"She's ours," he said, pulling the beret off her and
taking a handful of her hair. "And you're mine. Do you
understand that? Do you finally understand that?"

"Yes. Ryan, yes!"

Ryan kissed her again. Then she pulled out of his
arms when the baby suddenly stopped crying.

"Are you okay, Chelsea, baby?" Jo asked.

*SNIFF. Yes, thank you. That's better. Mama Cass says
she has to go now. She's going to trust the two of you
to be happy together and to make me happy. Did you
hear me? What do you have to say?*

RYAN, an arm around Jo, leaned down to kiss the baby's
forehead. "Everything's all right now, Chelsea," he

said.

Jo leaned into his shoulder. He enclosed both of them in his embrace.

"I'm sure this is the way Cassie would want it," Jo whispered.

"Maybe she knows," Ryan said. "I'm sure if she does, she's happy."

CASSIE, on her way home and no longer needing a spokesman, touched Ryan's cheek and Jo's hair.

"Who," she asked, "do you think gave you the idea to send Jo the baby?"

RYAN NOTICED the cabdriver still standing there, smiling at them. She'd put the bags down.

"Sorry." He laughed, reaching into his breast pocket for his wallet. "You probably haven't been—"

"No." She held both hands out in front of her in a gesture of refusal, her smile widening. At Ryan's look of surprise, she gestured from him to Jo and the baby. "Hey. Love me tender. This one's on me."

Ryan caught her hand and pressed a bill in it. "Then here's a tip. Thank you."

"You're welcome."

Ryan took the baby from Jo, then put an arm around her and turned her toward the apartment.

BYE, Mama Cass. I'll take it from here. Don't worry. I love you.

THE CABBIE turned at the sound of the elevator's bell. The doors parted.

An elegant older woman with a mesh shopping bag smiled at the cabbie. "Going up?"

CASSIE WATCHED her family walk into their home. "I love you, too, baby," she whispered. "I love you all." Then she heaved a sigh of relief, and swept past the cabbie, calling, "Hold the elevator!"

MERRY CHRISTMAS,
MOMMY

Prologue

Mother? What happened? Sounded like someone dropped a piano on the car. Are we all right?

Um...Mother? I think you're breathing too fast. And you're pushing on me awfully hard. You explained to me how this was going to work, but don't we still have three weeks to go?

Who was that? Where are all those voices coming from? What are the "jaws of life"? I don't like the sound of that. I'm willing to be born if you're sure this is the right time, but I'd hoped to be brought into the world by something that sounds more friendly.

Mother?

Okay. I don't like this. You're not answering me. I can feel your hand on me, but it isn't moving. You're hurt—I know it. Well, I'm staying right here until someone tells me that you're fine and will be there to welcome me.

I mean, we've planned this carefully. Labor was going to be induced on October the fourteenth, I was going to arrive with a minimum of fuss, we were going to enjoy a quiet night in the hospital, then spend the rest of our lives together doing tax returns, payroll reports,

*financial statements and all those other things that keep
Endicott Accounting in business.*

*So don't expect cooperation from me. See there? I'm
crossing my arms. Just try to get me out of here and
see what happens. If I don't hear your voice, I'm not
coming.*

Chapter One

"Okay, I'm calm," Karma Endicott told herself in an even tone calculated to be convincing. "I'm calm. I think my left arm's broken, but that's okay—I'm right-handed. I'll be fine. I feel the baby moving. That's good. We're both fine. Good. I'm calm. I'm fine."

But the sound of her own voice didn't blunt the sound of rending metal, as she'd hoped it would. The giant pliers being wielded by several firemen were making sheet metal out of the Geo Metro on which she'd just made her last payment. And she couldn't help it. Her accountant's brain was calculating the loss, even with the insurance replacement. And she would just bet the rusty red pickup that had run the stop sign didn't even *have* insurance.

"That doesn't matter," she told herself as the driver's-side door was ripped off. "The baby's fine, I'm— Oh, God!"

A cramp tightened her abdomen in a grip that made her think the jaws of life at work outside the car had grabbed her by mistake. It was hard and lasted a long moment.

"No," she said, rubbing at the rigid mound of her stomach. "Baby, don't do this. It isn't time. We have the Butler Logging payroll due, and Mr. Fielding from Fielding Enterprises is coming in this afternoon for a personnel benefits consulta— Ah!''

"Hi.'' A young man with earnest blue eyes and a medical bag appeared where the door had been and pushed the steering wheel to its farthest position. "Labor?'' he asked as he leaned over her and checked for injuries.

"Broken arm, I think,'' she said, wincing as he touched it and pain seemed to consume her entire body.

MOM! Thank God! I'm sorry, I'm not really ready to do this, either, but it seems to be happening anyway. The walls are closing in here!

"GOOD DIAGNOSIS,'' the medical technician said, turning to shout over his shoulder for a splint. He glanced into her eyes with a smile as he cut the sleeve of her white silk shirt away. "Want to work for us? You seem to be good at this. Are you having labor pains?''

"No,'' she said as the pain in her abdomen subsided. "I'm not due until October 14, when Dr. McNamara intends to induce labor, and I refuse to give birth a moment sooner.''

A second young man handed him a contraption that he fitted gently along her arm.

Under a glaze of pain, she watched the people clustered around her car. A police officer talking to a middle-aged man in coveralls, who pointed to the red truck another officer was pushing to the side of the street, firemen clearing away their equipment, bystanders trying to peer through her windshield as they stood beyond the flares placed on the asphalt.

She felt as though she were watching a scene from a

TV show like "Cops." This couldn't be happening to her. She'd planned so carefully from the beginning—the right moment in her life, the right sperm bank, a sperm harvest with a high possibility of producing a girl, the right obstetrician in the right hospital.

She refused to let it all go bad on her now.

"Uh-oh," the medical tech said. He was running his hands carefully along her legs and ankles.

Her eyes flew to his as he looked up at her, that same friendly smile in place. "What?" she demanded.

"Your water's broken," he said. "You *are* in labor, ma'am." He turned to his partner. "Tell ER we've got an MVA coming in with a hot baby."

The sound of sirens as the ambulance sped Karma toward the hospital deepened her sense of unreality. She never got hurt, she seldom got sick. Emergencies were unheard-of in her life because she was a planner. She hated last-minute surprises. Eighteen years with Daisy Dawn and Mountain Man had taught her more than she wanted to know about the spontaneity of life on the road without roots or destination. She'd loved her parents, but she'd promised herself she'd never live that way again.

And here she was, a victim of chance, speeding toward the hospital with a "hot baby." There was no justice.

"CAN YOU MEET THAT ONE, Nate?" Jackie Palmrose, Riverview Hospital's emergency room doctor on the day shift, peered around the curtains surrounding bed four and pointed in the general direction of the sound of a wailing siren.

Nathan Foster, just getting off the night shift, had

already changed clothes and was shouldering a brown leather backpack.

He threatened her with a glance as the whoop of the siren grew deafening and finally stopped abruptly in front of the emergency room doors.

"As of ten minutes ago," he said, "I'm on vacation. The Canadian wilderness is calling my name." But he dropped his pack.

She shrugged, her expression blandly innocent under an irregular fringe of blond hair. "Sorry. This chest pain has us all tied up. That's a motor vehicle accident with a hot baby out there. Medic called it in while you were changing. You know how it's done. All we do is turn her over to OB."

Joanie, the nurse, peered around the dividing curtain on the other side and grinned at him. "We know how much you like babies."

"Go ahead," he said, moving toward the door. "Be cute." He lowered his voice as he pointed to the curtain. "You know that's a bad gallbladder and not a heart attack."

"But it's the administrator," she whispered back. "And he thinks he's having a heart attack. We want him to see us doing everything right."

"Fine. You can both forget the maple candy you asked for, *and* the bachelor Mounties."

"Just one Mountie?" Jackie whispered loudly as he opened the doors and stepped outside. "Joanie and I'll share him!"

Nate met the gurney. It held a very pregnant young woman with a tight knot of dark hair and big gold earrings. Her left forearm was in a splint. Pushing the rolling cot was his favorite pair of EMTs. Baldwin had taken a year off medical school to earn money to go back. He was capable and accurate and calm. Prentice was less experienced, but smart, if good-naturedly naive. He blushed purple at the nurses' teasing, and took the doctors' friendly abuse as a sort of rite of passage.

"We're having a baby," Baldwin said as they helped push the gurney into the ER. "You better get OB down here, or you're going to be delivering it." He grinned. "And we all know how much you like babies."

"If I want abuse," Nate said, "I've got Jackie and Joanie."

He leaned over the woman with his stethoscope. Her eyes were closed and her delicate features were taut with concentration as she breathed through a contraction. She grimaced and reached a slender hand out of the blanket, as though searching for something to hold on to.

He put his hand in hers, and she ground his knuckles together with more efficiency than Sugar Ray Leonard could have. He had to make a conscious effort not to wince. Baldwin and Prentice would have enjoyed it too much.

The woman opened her eyes. They were chocolate brown and filled with pain.

"Will you call Bert?" she asked, her voice breathless.

"Your husband?" Nate asked.

She shook her head. "My Lamaze coach. Roberta Dawson, at First Coastal Bank."

He nodded. "I'll get someone right on it. Dr. McNamara's on his way. Just hold on."

"I'm willing." She gave him a faint smile, but a tear slid from her eye down into her hair. "But the baby has other ideas. And she's three weeks early."

He squeezed the hand he held. "That shouldn't be a problem. Try to relax. You're in good hands now."

Her hand tightened on his again. "You don't understand. The nursery isn't finished. I was going to do that next week, after quarterly reports. I only have one box of diapers, no food in the freezer…"

"You'll have time to worry about that later," he said gently, thinking as she crushed his hand that it was a good thing he hadn't chosen to become a surgeon. "Right now, concentrate on relaxing so that this baby can make his big entrance."

"It should be a girl," she said. "I asked for a sperm harvest with a higher possibility of being female."

He blinked at her. "Say what?"

But Jackie called to him before he could make sense of that revelation. "Dr. Mac wants to know if we can bring Miss Endicott over. The arm will have to wait until after the baby."

"We'll take her," Baldwin said. He grinned at Nate. "Get going on your Calgary odyssey. And don't forget our maple candies."

Nate nodded to Jackie, then smiled down at the woman on the gurney. "These guys are going to take you to OB, and I'm going to call your coach—"

KARMA FELT her grip on him tighten. She couldn't have explained it, but she had some deep and powerful need to link their fingers inextricably, to keep him with her. He was tall, with longish blond hair, cheerful blue eyes and a wide-open smile. His grip was the only security in her world at the moment.

She could deal with any crisis, as long as she was prepared. But this was more than a simple crisis. This was—this was her baby's *life*. And it was coming into being three weeks early. Her plans weren't in place. Her schedule was decimated. She was terrified.

Admitting that, of course, was out of the question. She simply held on.

Nate tried to withdraw from her grip and couldn't—at least not without losing everything above the second knuckle.

Baldwin saw the woman's death grip and glanced at him with amusement curiously mingled with sympathy.

"Why don't I walk you over?" Nate suggested. He looked up to find Jackie nearby, also looking amused. Jackie was never sympathetic. "Would you call Roberta Dawson at First Coastal Bank? She's the patient's Lamaze coach. See if she can get down here."

"Of course." Jackie grinned widely and turned to the phone.

Baldwin pulled, Prentice pushed and Karma rolled toward OB, feeling as though her well-ordered existence was about to tumble out of control, like a piece of space debris.

All that could prevent that from happening was the solidity of the hand she held. It seemed to ground her somehow, prevent her from falling all the way down into the fear that yawned beyond the edge of the gurney.

"Well, isn't this a busy baby day." A nurse, who looked alarmingly military, met them at the juncture of the corridors. The EMTs wished Karma luck and left, and the nurse pushed her into a room that claimed her attention, despite her pain and anxiety.

It was lavender and blue, with flowered wallpaper and a coordinated print on the bedspread and curtains. She noticed oak details, and what appeared to be a parquet floor. Was she delirious already?

"This is one of our new birthing rooms," the nurse

said, throwing the covers back and lining the gurney up right beside the bed. "Got two others like it. What do you think? Would you believe they're all in use today? Delivered two girls already this morning. This makes a veritable baby boom in little old Heron Point. Okay, let's get you in the bed."

Nate freed his hand to lift her from the gurney to the bed, with its delivery room refinements. He straightened, thinking he was free at last. But she dropped her arm from around his neck, slid it down his arm and reclaimed his hand.

The nurse fluffed her pillows, pulled her blankets up and gave her a maternal smile that belied her military bearing. "I'll tell Dr. Mac you're here."

"Ah—Beachie?" Nate called after the nurse's retreating figure. "Would you call ER and see if Jackie got through to Miss Endicott's Lamaze coach?"

"Right." She started out the door, then leaned back in to grin knowingly at him. "Afraid of ending up in the baby business yourself, Dr. Foster?"

His answering frown only made her laugh as she pulled the door closed behind her.

The patient gripped his hand as another contraction tightened her abdomen. Nate pulled the chair up to the side of the bed, resigned to being stand-in moral support until her coach arrived.

"Ah...okay," he said, trying to remember the little he knew about labor. It was ER policy to turn all such patients over to OB immediately. "You're supposed to be breathing, not tightening up like that. Come on. Short, shallow breaths—you know how. Puff, puff, puff—just like a steam engine."

"Yeah...I forgot." Karma complied with three proper breaths, then drew in and expelled a lengthy one when the contraction faded away. "Thanks." She turned her head to look at him, and winced when one of the pins in the bun at the back of her head poked her scalp.

"Another contraction already?" Nate asked anxiously.

"No." She even smiled. "My hair hurts."

"Oh." Nate considered that a great relief. He'd had the horrible feeling that they'd advanced to the delivery phase without warning. He stood to lean over her and work at the knot of hair at the back of her head until it was free. He dropped three pins on the small table and combed his fingers through the thick coil of hair. It fell over his arm like warm silk. The sensation seemed to run along under his skin, right straight to his heart.

He sat down again, his other hand still crushed in hers. She was watching him, curiosity covering the pain in her dark eyes. "Why does everyone tease you about babies?" she asked. "Don't you like them?"

He shrugged a shoulder, glancing at the door, wishing her coach would arrive. "I like children fine," he replied. "I just don't like to work on them. Or even help deliver them."

That seemed to surprise her. "Why?"

"Well...they're vulnerable," he replied, deciding that a surface answer was all that was necessary. "Because they're so small. It makes our job harder. I'd rather work on burly loggers or aerobics instructors." He tacked on that last part on a jocular note. Then, wanting to redirect the conversation, he asked, "What's your first name, Ms. Endicott?"

"Karma," she replied, then frowned. "Did I hear someone say you were going on vacation?"

He nodded. "Soon as I'm out of here. I'm going camping for four weeks in Canada."

She grimaced. "I'd hate that. I need electricity and a comfortable mattress. I'd like to see Canada, but from a hotel window."

Now he winced. "That'd be like watching a movie of Canada. Might as well stay home and turn on the VCR."

She nodded. "I spend a lot of evenings that way. Uh-oh."

"Another one?"

"Uh-huh."

MOTHER! Could you send down a map? I thought this looked like the only logical road, but I seem to be at a dead end!

"BREATHE. Breathe." He demonstrated, and she copied his huffing, holding tightly to his hand as the contraction crested, then passed.

She sank back against the pillow, already tired, though she knew this was just the beginning. That very thought brought the ever-threatening fear closer. She turned to him to have something else to think about.

"Your name is...Nathaniel?"

"Nathan," he corrected. "Nathan Robert Foster."

"M.D.?"

"Right."

"Married?"

"Wrong."

"Me either," she said. "All the men *I* found interesting were married, and many of the men who found *me* interesting were also married. So, I decided to have

a baby on my own.'' She looked into his eyes. "I went
to a sperm bank. Do you think that's awful?''

"I think," he replied diplomatically, "that you have
charge of your own life."

Her gaze narrowed on him. "You *do* think it's awful."

He shook his head. "I think it's an option I wouldn't
choose. But I can't hold you to my rules."

"I wanted to share my life with someone," she said,
unconsciously rubbing across his knuckles with her
thumb. "There's a lot about life I really love, and I
thought it would be neat to give that to someone else."
She sighed, the loneliness and frustration of the past few
years crowding in on her as she held that sturdy hand.
"But I couldn't find the right man. And I didn't want
to settle for the wrong one. So, I thought I'd just skip
that step, and have the baby."

That sounded a little antiseptic to him, but then, he'd
never wanted a baby. At least not since Jimmy Cam-
eron.

He smiled. "Some people consider that the most important step—or, at least, the most memorable."

She smiled back. "With the right man, I'm sure it is.
With the wrong one, I can't think of anything to recommend it. So we settled for the invisible man."

"A handsome professional in good health?"

"Precisely. And he read Walt Whitman. That was
what decided me. Uh-oh."

Nate, who was leaning forward, elbows on his knees,
sat up alertly. He breathed with her through the contraction, then sat back in relief when it was over and
Beacham peered around the door.

"Roberta Dawson," she reported apologetically, "is

in Seattle at a district meeting. I guess she hadn't counted on you delivering three weeks early.''

Karma closed her eyes, and groaned. She'd completely forgotten that Bert was leaving this morning for a special week-long training session. Was this Murphy's Law at work, or what?

Well, she could do this without Bert. She intended to raise the baby alone; she could certainly have it alone.

But the pain was so much more frightening than she'd anticipated. And the suddenness of it all, the lack of time to prepare, to plan....

Nate saw a tear slip out of her eye and into her hair. He tightened his grip on her hand.

''You're going to be fine,'' he assured her. ''I know this is just dinky little Heron Point, but by some stroke of providence, we have the best collection of medical people here, bar none, and Mac's the best of those.''

She sniffed and nodded. ''I know. I'm not usually such a wimp. I just hate to be...unprepared.''

''You're not unprepared,'' he said bracingly. ''You have the baby and we have the doctor. It doesn't require anything else. You heard Beachie. We've already had two baby girls today.''

''Did you help with those, too?''

''No. One of the fathers is a friend of mine, and the other was a friend of his. I met them at the coffeepot right after the second baby was born. One had hair, and the other one was bald, but pretty big.'' He grinned. ''The babies, not the fathers.''

''Well, girls like to be showy.'' She spoke airily, but he could see that she was demoralized by her friend's absence.

And he was too much the doctor to walk away.

''I'll coach you through,'' he said, taking a tissue

from the bedside table and handing it to her. He could leave on vacation tomorrow morning. No big deal.

Something flared in her eyes—happiness, or perhaps relief—but then she said quietly, "But, you're on vacation."

"I'll leave tomorrow morning." He grinned teasingly. "Provided you don't have one of those interminable labors."

She sighed and squeezed his hand. "I'm usually very efficient. I'm an accountant, you know. Never a moment or a penny wasted."

"All right." He smiled up at Nurse Beacham. "Ice chips for the lady, waitress," he said, "and make mine a double espresso."

Chapter Two

"Okay," Dr. McNamara said from his stool at the foot of the bed. "This push is going to do it, Karma. Give it all you've got."

Karma wanted to tell him she'd done that over an hour ago. She had no courage, no strength, left. But this had all been her idea. It wasn't the result of uncontrollable passion, or a romantic accident. She had planned it all herself. Except that she'd intended to have all her deadlines met, the nursery ready, everything in place for this momentous development in her life.

But fate had changed that, and no complaint or resistance could reverse the march of events. The baby was here. She had to welcome it home.

From somewhere inside herself, she had to find the strength. It was just such a surprise to discover that she wasn't the paragon of strength she'd imagined herself to be. She'd gotten through the past two hours on the courage of the ER doctor she'd literally dragged into OB with her. Had she really done that? Mortification tried to make itself felt, but there simply wasn't room for it amid the pain, panic and desperation.

All right, she told herself, pacing her breathing, getting ready. Maybe it's there, and I just don't realize it is. Maybe it'll surprise me. Maybe it'll come through for me, after all.

"That's it," Nathan Robert Foster's voice said calmly in her ear. She sat propped up against the angled head of the bed, and he stood beside her, leaning over her, one arm wrapped around her back. For an instant, everything else in the room receded, and it was just the two of them in the tight circle his arm around her created. "Build up everything you've got. This is it. Little Lady Endicott makes her debut at—" he glanced up at the clock "—12:21 p.m. Come on, Karma. A deep breath, and push! Push!"

OKAY, stand back! Out of the way! Coming through!

KARMA LEANED into the arm wrapped around her and gave the push everything she had left, and everything she was able to steal from her commandeered coach.

The world went red with pain and tension for one interminable moment, and then she heard Dr. McNamara's cry of triumph and her own body's exhalation of relief.

"And here she… Whoops."

"Whoops?" Nate straightened and looked over Karma's knees to the doctor. "What do you mean, whoops? Tell me you didn't drop her, Mac."

"Ah…no. Karma, you know that theory the sperm bank sold you about sperm being harvested at a certain time guaranteeing gender?" Dr. McNamara, his mask pulled down to reveal his wide smile, came around the bed to hand her the screaming baby. It was a boy.

She gasped in surprise. "I was so sure he was a girl." She hadn't even considered boys' names.

GIRL? Who're you calling a girl? Do I look like a girl? Well, that's a fine greeting, I must say. After what I've just been through to get here. Someone had better make this up to me—and fast.

KARMA took the screeching baby in her arms and absorbed the surprise of his gender, along with his physical perfection and apparent good health. She felt great pride, and nothing that even remotely resembled disappointment.

"You are," she whispered, putting her cheek to his, "the most beautiful thing I've ever seen."

WELL. Hmm. Okay, then.

"HE'S ALL RIGHT?" she asked in disbelief. "The accident didn't hurt him?"

Dr. McNamara shook his head. "He looks perfect to me. Let's clean him up and weigh him in."

Karma relinquished the baby reluctantly. "He looks all right," she said to Nate as the doctor took the baby to the scale on a table across the room. "Don't you think he looks all right?"

"He's beautiful." Nate helped her ease back against the pillows. She was pale, her hair damp at her forehead and temples. Her eyes were turbulent, and her smile was a little uncertain.

"How's your arm?" Nate asked, still holding her good hand.

"Starting to hurt," she admitted with a light laugh. "The good part about labor is that you don't notice other pain."

He smoothed the damp hair off her forehead. "I'll

let them finish up here, then they're going to set your arm. I'll see you afterward.''

''Thank you for staying.'' Her voice was thready, weary, and her eyes were focused intently on him. ''You...kept the fear away.''

Nate put his other hand over hers. ''I'm glad I was here. I'll stick around until you wake up, to make sure everything's all right.''

Karma shook her head. ''I want you to go on your vacation. When you're sleeping under the stars, think of me and the baby. We'll be remembering how kind you were.''

''No,'' he insisted. ''I'll see you later.''

''If the baby's all right,'' she replied with a smile, ''I'll be perfect.''

Dr. McNamara returned to the bed, the baby in his arms. ''He weighs six pounds, twelve ounces. And had you carried him another three weeks, he'd have come out tall enough to play basketball.''

Karma noted that the baby now wore a plastic bracelet. A similar one was placed on her good wrist. ''Just so we don't give you to the wrong baby,'' the nurse said.

Nate frowned teasingly. ''This is the hospital's most inefficient department.''

Karma raised her good arm. ''Can I have him back now?''

Dr. McNamara shook his head. ''Sorry. We still have several rude things to do to you, and Dr. Dade, the pediatrician, has to give him a few tests.''

Karma groaned and grumbled at the doctor as he handed the baby to another nurse. ''You go through all this to have a baby, and nobody lets you hold him.''

Nate rubbed her shoulder. "You tell 'em. I'll see you in a while."

She fixed him with a stern look. "Go," she said firmly, "on vacation." Then she waved, her dark eyes holding his for one extra moment.

Nate strode down the hallway, torn between a compulsion to run out of the hospital and race north in his car and an equally strong need to have a heart-to-heart with Mac, to stay within hailing distance, should Karma Endicott need him, and to look over her chart himself.

He was supposed to be on vacation, but suddenly that was the farthest thing from his mind.

He caught a whiff of coffee from the OB waiting room as he passed. Caffeine. That was what he needed. He detoured into the room and filled a paper cup and went to the window. It looked out onto the east parking lot. The big mountain ash across the street was just beginning to change color, its combs of green leaves tipped with gold, its branches heavy with clusters of bright red berries.

God. He'd just coached a woman through childbirth. He wasn't shaking. He was too good a doctor for that. But everything inside him was going at warp speed. It was just an adrenaline rush. He knew that. But deep inside him, beyond all the physical mechanisms he knew and understood, something else was happening.

He stood still, sipped caffeine and tried to analyze it. It took only a moment's thought to realize that he understood what it wasn't better than he understood what it was.

It was more than concern. He was a dedicated ER doctor; he knew all about concern. He felt it for all his patients, even the drunks who were ill or injured because of their own weakness, the women who drank with them, went home with them and invariably ended up in the hospital as victims of abuse, the druggies who claimed excruciating back pain that required a prescription for Demerol. He could see past their circumstances to the pain inside them that wouldn't be diminished by anything at his disposal.

He knew this was different, because he could treat all of them to the best of his ability, then walk away. He couldn't do that today. He wanted to, but he didn't seem to be able to.

He kept remembering a slender hand gripping his with a strength that astonished him, frightened and pain-filled dark eyes in a delicate face studiously set in calm lines. He remembered those same eyes following him as he'd walked to the door.

He felt as though a large hand had taken hold of his rib cage and squeezed.

"Nate."

Nate turned away from the window at the greeting. The voice belonged to J. V. Nicholas, Riverview Hospital's radiologist, and the friend he'd told Karma about whose wife had had a girl that morning—the one with the hair.

"You're still here?" Jave grinned as he poured coffee into a paper cup. "I thought you'd be on the other side of Seattle by now, on your way to the wilderness."

Nate had a little difficulty surfacing from his mental images of Karma. He smiled distractedly and sipped from his cup. "Ah...had a patient at the last minute with...complications."

Jave sat on the black vinyl sofa near the window. "The OB with the broken arm?"

Nate turned back to him again, frowning. "Your wife

had a baby here today. You're supposed to be here as a civilian.''

"You know a doctor is never a civilian." Jave angled one ankle over the other knee. He grinned. "Our inherent nobility prevents that. I happened to wander through ER while Nancy was sleeping and heard about the traffic accident and the hot baby." Jave looked into his eyes, his expression bland. "I thought you didn't like babies."

Nate knew what he was doing. Jave was everybody's big brother. Well, he didn't want or need one. His attitude about children was not a psychological problem, it was a conscious decision reached through a compilation of data and personal experience.

"Don't start with me," he said with friendly firmness. "I like babies, I just don't want one. I happened to get involved with this patient before the baby arrived."

"Involved?"

"The mother was alone, and I stayed to help."

"Ah." Jave nodded, resting his cup on his knee. "Watch yourself. That's how I married Nancy."

Nate laughed mirthlessly. Everyone in the hospital knew Jave's story. As the divorced father of two, he'd fallen under the spell of a single mother with premature labor who'd been sent to radiology for an ultrasound.

Nate had never been entirely sure what had happened—he found hospital gossip interesting only to a point, and that point didn't include his friends. The next thing he knew, Nancy and Jave had been married. That had been several weeks ago.

"I think," Nate said, "that you were more... vulnerable to a woman's charms than I am."

Jave raised an eyebrow. "Really."

"Yes," he replied, ignoring the amusement in his friend's eyes. "You had boys who needed a mother. You...you need a woman."

Jave's eyebrow lowered to meet the other in a frown. "Why do I need a woman more than you do?"

"You have a neat mom. You had a wife." When Jave's frown deepened at that, he added quickly, "Well, it had been good before she ran off. You're used to having women around you. I was raised in military schools."

"And you could probably never get a date."

"And I could never get a date," Nate agreed, then studied his fingernails with a falsely modest air, "because women are intimidated by my wit and my charm."

"Yeah, right. So why is it that Karma wasn't intimidated by your wit and charm? I understand she had a death grip on you when Baldwin and Prentice tried to take her from ER to OB."

Nate shrugged a shoulder. "I was there. Had *you* been there, she probably would have clung to you. How do you know her name?"

"She was in Nancy's Lamaze class. Anyway, that's not the way Jackie tells it. Or Beachie. They say it could have gotten very complicated if you hadn't been there to keep Karma going."

Nate dismissed the praise. "We connected. She needed help and I was there."

Jave gave him a considering smile, downed his coffee and got to his feet. "That's the epitaph of many a brave bachelor, Nate. 'She needed help and I was there. We connected.'" He tossed his cup at the basket in the corner. "So, you're off to Canada now?"

No. He wasn't. "Ah...soon," he said.

Jave clapped him on the shoulder and went to the door. Nurse Beacham stood there with a clipboard.

"Beachie," Jave said, putting an arm around the nurses' shoulders. "What's up? Looking for me?"

The short, square woman batted her lashes theatrically. "I've been looking for you all my life, Doctor."

He dipped her backward over his arm. "But it can't be, Medora," he said, his voice assuming a deep and dramatic soap-opera-doctor quality. "Because you're married to the famous heart surgeon Lefty Ventricle, and I'm dying of salmonella."

Nurse Beacham put the back of her wrist to her forehead. "If only someone had told me there's no such thing as *chicken* tartare."

"It's all right, my darling. I know you didn't do it on purpose."

"But I did, my darling. Because you're standing between me and the only man I want at this moment—Dr. Foster."

Jave straightened, the very picture of the wounded lover. "Medora…"

Nate approached them. "Beachie, this is so sudden."

She smiled blandly. "I know. I was hit by a car while sleepwalking, and now I have amnesia." She turned to Jave. "We need to be alone."

He placed a hand over his heart. "You're fickle, Medora." To Nate, he added, "Call me if you need help."

The door closed behind Jave, and Nate turned to the nurse with a teasing smile. "Where'll we go, Beachie? The supply closet? The nurses' locker room?"

Beacham put a hand to his chest and pushed him onto the sofa, then sat beside him. "I need assurance of your discretion, Dr. Foster."

"Beachie…" He leaned away from her with a wary look. "You're starting to scare me."

She rolled her eyes. "Dr. Foster, I do not crave your body. Although the nurses all think it's pretty buff. I want your advice on what to do about Miss Endicott."

"What do you mean?" he asked, stiffening in his seat. "What's happened?"

"Nothing," she assured him. "We're going to keep her for a couple of days because of her arm, but when we release her, she'll be going home to no one, with a useless arm and a brand-new baby who'll have her thoroughly exhausted in twenty-four hours. I want to have a health-care nurse look in on her, but she refuses. She insists she'll manage just fine. That's because she's never taken care of a newborn before."

"Arrange for a nurse anyway," Nate said. "Tell her she doesn't have a choice."

Beacham shook her head at him. "She does have a choice, Doctor. This is America. You were with her all through labor. I thought she might have mentioned a relative or a friend or someone we could call on to help her cope when she gets home."

He thought back. It was absurd, but they'd talked politics, music, movies, food—and they'd cheerfully disagreed on every point. But they'd never talked people. He'd gotten the impression she didn't have any family. And her only close friend—the one who was supposed to be her Lamaze coach—worked full-time, and was away for a week, anyway.

He drew a breath to tell her he didn't think Karma Endicott had anyone—then decided maybe she did.

"I'll get back to you," he said.

KARMA did not want an outsider intruding upon her first days with her baby. And nothing at home was organized. Another person, even someone intending to help, would just be in the way.

No. She would manage. With her arm set, she felt almost human again. She was terrified, but she would manage. She turned to the bassinet beside her bed and was relieved to see that her son slept soundly.

It would help if she could decide upon a name. She'd fed him only three times, but she knew he resented her calling him "baby." He was supposed to have a title that was uniquely his—a label, for lack of a better word, that told the world what he was about.

She closed the book of baby names she'd been studying and allowed her mind to focus on the man who'd seen her through labor. Nathan. That was what she would name her son if she could be sure she'd never see the ER doctor again. But Heron Point was a small town. Sooner or later they'd meet downtown, or at a party, and recall the very unusual morning they'd spent together once in a Riverview Hospital birthing room. And he would be bound to ask politely, "Did you finally settle on a name?"

She couldn't say, "I named him Nathan after you, because you're the only man I've ever met whose name, I felt, should live beyond him."

He might mistake it for a romantic gesture. And that wasn't it at all. She simply admired him.

"Karma?" Her name was whispered from the door by a figure in a flowered robe.

"Nancy?" she asked, thinking she recognized the woman from her Lamaze class who'd married the radiologist. She was writing a murder mystery; people had been talking about it at the coffee bar downtown.

There were two little boys with her, one on either side, holding her hands.

Karma sat up in bed and gestured to them to come in. "What a nice surprise," she said, genuinely pleased to see her. "Nate...Dr. Foster...told me two little girls were born today. Was one of them yours?"

Nancy nodded. "She's beautiful. We're so proud."

"Was your little girl the bald one," Karma asked, "or the one with all the hair?"

"The one with the hair."

She smiled down at the boys. "These are my boys," she said, holding up the hand of the older one. "Eddy, and Pete." She smiled down at the smaller one. "We've been checking out everybody's babies. Jo Arceneau had hers today, too, you know. The bald one."

"All right!" Karma laughed. "A very large little girl, I understand."

"She's *huge!*" Pete said.

Eddy poked his younger brother. "Pete's going to marry her when he grows up."

"No way!" Pete protested loudly. "I'm going to be a pitcher and make lots of money and I won't go out with girls 'cause they're yucky!"

Nancy shushed him gently while smiling an apology at Karma. "We have to keep our voices down so we don't wake the baby. May we look, Karma?"

"Of course."

Nancy and the boys tiptoed to the bassinet. The boys looked in, clearly fascinated.

"It's a boy, isn't it?" Nancy asked.

Karma nodded.

"What's his name?" Pete wanted to know.

Karma held up her book. "I haven't decided yet. I was expecting him to be a girl."

Pete came to lean importantly by her bedside. "My dad does ultrasounds, so you can tell if it's a girl or a boy before it's borned."

She nodded. "I had two of those. And sometimes you can't tell for sure."

The older boy rolled his eyes. "He's too young to understand that the baby isn't always laying where you can tell."

Nancy ruffled his hair. "Why don't you take Pete to meet Grandma and Willie in the cafeteria?"

The boys went off, the little one resisting the older one's efforts to keep him at his side.

"Stay with Eddy, Pete!" Nancy called after them.

She turned back to Karma, wincing. "I'm new at being a mother," she said. "And I don't just mean the baby. Those are my husband's boys, and... Well, I guess you know we just got married a couple of weeks ago."

Karma studied her in wonder. "Where do you get the guts? I'm terrified of that little baby. I can't imagine going home with a baby *and* two beautiful but probably smart and lively little boys. I'd be paralyzed with fear."

Nancy laughed. "They move too fast for you to remain paralyzed very long. I'm sure in a couple of days we'll both feel like old pros."

Karma couldn't imagine that. "I have one box of diapers, a crib, and that's absolutely it. I thought I had another three weeks to prepare."

Nancy smiled sympathetically. "A procrastinator? That's me, too."

Karma shook her head. "No. I'm usually very organized. But the time I had set aside to finish the nursery was the two weeks before delivery. I had a couple of big projects at work I wanted to finish first."

Nancy frowned at Karma's broken arm. "I don't think you're going to run an adding machine, hold a baby, and feed it, too, all with your good arm."

Karma shrugged philosophically. "I'm going to have to."

"Well..." Nancy yawned. "I work at home, so maybe we can get together once in a while so we don't go crazy. Or I can watch your baby so you can get some rest, or get some work done."

Karma smiled gratefully. "That would be great. And I could watch yours so you and your husband can have some time alone. I'm sure privacy will be at a premium for you for a while."

Nancy nodded and yawned again. "I'll hold you to that. I've got to get back to bed. I keep thinking I'm feeling stronger, then I practically fall asleep on my feet."

"*There* you are." Jave Nicholas appeared in the doorway, and came to take Nancy by the arm. He smiled at Karma over her head. "Congratulations. The boys tell me you have a beautiful son."

She agreed. "I'm willing to take all the credit. You're just in time. Nancy's about to fall asleep standing up."

He shook his head over his wife's wanderings and swung her carefully into his arms. Nancy waved at Karma over his shoulder as Jave carried her back to her room.

Karma watched them go, a wistful smile on her face. Yes. That would have been nice. A loving husband to coddle her and help her through the next difficult few weeks...months...years... But that hadn't been in the scheme of things, so she'd chosen an alternative. There was no point in thinking of what might have been.

She had wanted a child and now she had him and he

was beautiful and healthy and everything she could have hoped for. And she wouldn't have to consider anyone else's opinion when she made decisions regarding him.

She could handle this. She could. She leaned into her pillow and closed her eyes, trying to organize the first few days in her mind, and promptly fell asleep.

IT WAS DUSK when she awoke. The baby remained asleep, her arm throbbed only minimally, and she felt a curious sense of comfort. She'd given birth to a perfect, whole baby boy, and that seemed like such a miracle.

She didn't let her mind move to going home with him. That would only cause her to panic, and she didn't want to do that now. She wanted to enjoy this nice mellow moment and stretch it out as long as possible.

Then she turned her head to look for the water pitcher—and saw Nate Foster sitting in the chair beside her bed, reading her baby names book. He looked as though he'd showered and changed. He wore a simple khaki-colored sweater over beige cords. Her reaction was equal parts interest and concern.

"I thought I told you to go to Canada," she said, pushing the button that controlled her bed so that the back lifted her to a sitting position.

He met her eyes over the top of the book. "You're used to having things the way you want them, aren't you?"

She smiled thinly. "Not precisely. I'm always trying for it, but everyone else usually has other ideas. Like you."

He looked down at the book. "Well, I'm going eventually. What about Dillon? It's Irish-French for 'like a lion.'"

"No. Too fancy."

He flipped a few pages. "Okay. Here. Mac. A Scottish or Irish surname prefix used as a given name. Just like Dr. McNamara, only as a given name, not a nickname."

She shook her head. "Too clever."

He looked surprised. "I thought the fact that you're using a baby names book meant you wanted something clever. I mean, you don't need a book for Bill, Bob and Mike."

"True. But it has to be just right."

"What about naming him after a man you admire?"

She shrugged simply. "I haven't admired many." Except you, she thought, but she kept that to herself.

He studied her closely. "Not even your father?" He'd seldom seen his father, but he'd admired him. It hadn't been his father's fault that fate entrusted him with the care of a child he had no idea what to do with.

"My father's name," she said with a grim smile, "was Mountain Man. Do you really want to do that to a helpless child?"

"Ah…" He narrowed an eye, certain he'd misheard her. "Mountain Man?"

"Yes. It had been Jeffrey Jamison Endicott, but he and my mother had such a revelation one sunny morning in the sixties, while camping at Big Sur in their VW bus, that he had it legally changed to Mountain Man. My mother's name was Daisy Dawn."

"Mercy."

"Yeah. I guess Karma isn't so bad, considering what they could have named me."

"They're…gone?" he asked cautiously.

She stiffened a little and nodded. "An auto accident a couple of years ago at Big Sur. In their bus that did zero to forty in five minutes.'' A sudden wince negated the joke. ''An oncoming truck hit ice, then hit them.''

''I'm sorry,'' he said.

She lifted a shoulder. ''They were very in touch with the life force of the universe. And they always wanted to go together. Okay,'' she said, her tone changing. She pointed to the book he held. ''I did see a name I like. What do you think of Garrett?''

He considered that a moment.

''It means 'spear-strong,''' she said. ''Too warlike?''

YAWN. I like it. Long as you don't call me Garry. Sigh. I'll be glad when I learn to turn over. I have a kink in my neck.

''GARRETT,'' he repeated. ''I'm a peaceful soul, myself, but yeah, I like it. Middle name?''

''Joseph. The ultimate father, since he doesn't really have his own. Garrett Joseph.'' She smiled, warming to the sound.

Nate smiled, because she did. ''Has my vote.'' Then he decided to broach the subject he'd come to discuss.

''Why won't you let the hospital arrange for a home health nurse to give you a hand?'' He asked the question abruptly, hoping to catch her off guard.

''Because I want to do this myself,'' she said reasonably. ''I'll be fine.''

So, she was *on* guard again. Her vulnerability had evaporated with the arrival of the baby.

''You have one arm in a sling, Karma,'' he pointed out. ''And with the other one you'll spend most of your time holding the baby. How do you intend to manage feeding, changing, cooking?''

"I'm sure I'll manage," she insisted. "I'm very organized and systematic."

That thought seemed to comfort her, but he saw it as trouble. He was a bachelor, but he'd spent enough time with married friends to know that sanity in a busy household required a tendency toward lunacy and a taste for chaos.

"Will you know enough," he asked, putting the book aside, "to call someone for help if you decide you need it?"

She folded her arms. She noticed absently how easy it was to do now that her stomach was gone.

"I grew up," she said, "in that Volkswagen bus, with two adults and an older brother. There was hardly room to change our minds, much less our clothes. Which was probably a good thing, since we didn't have many in the first place. When we could afford gas, we traveled around looking for work. Sometimes food was a day-to-day thing. I *hated* living that way, but my parents and my brother were happy as larks."

Nate wasn't sure how this related to her refusal to allow a nurse into her home, but he listened patiently as she went on.

"To this day, my nightmares consist of having anyone other than me in my house, and having empty cupboards." She shrugged self-deprecatingly. "I know I probably need a shrink, but that's the way it is. I have my life precisely the way I want it, and that's the way I intend to keep it."

"But you've purposefully chosen," he said, "to add another body to your household." He pointed to the bassinet and the sleeping baby. "How does that fit?"

"This is someone I've planned for," she explained

simply. "Someone who'll take up very little space for a long time. Someone I've already learned to love."

Nate studied her worriedly. "You know," he said finally, "I don't have firsthand experience with this, but anybody with children can tell you that babies take up a lot more space than is filled by their size. Their needs and demands require a lot of elbow room."

"I," she said firmly, "will manage."

"Where's your brother?" he asked.

She rolled her eyes. "In a commune in Baja. We send each other birthday and Christmas cards, but he's a little too out there for me, and I'm much too establishment for him."

"What's *his* name?" Nate asked.

She shook her head, smiling. "Aspen." Then she held her hand out toward him. "Thank you for all you've done. I don't think I'd have made it through labor without you. But now you have to take off on your vacation, and I have to get on with my baby and my life."

Nate stood and took her hand. "All right. But do you plan to live the next sixty years like that? With your cupboards full and your heart empty?"

Karma looked into his eyes and felt them draw her to him as if with a physical pull. She had to yank her hand away to break the connection. She smiled bravely. "Have a wonderful trip. Drive safely."

He recognized a brush-off when he heard it, but her big dark eyes told a completely different story. He wondered if she even knew how badly she needed someone.

Well. This was best. His own life was chaotic, and he liked it that way. He didn't need to worry about a quirky woman with a baby, who would grow up to be a toddler eager to explore and vulnerable to all the world's dangers. He didn't have the nerves for it.

"Goodbye," he said. And because they'd shared something unique and special, and because those dark eyes held such a curious longing, he brought the hand he held to his lips and kissed it.

Her lips parted in surprise. Her eyes widened and softened.

He went to the bassinet and looked down at the sleeping baby. Garrett Joseph was full-cheeked, with a light dusting of dark hair on his head. His tiny fists opened and closed and his tiny bow mouth worked as though he were anticipating his next meal.

"Goodbye, Garrett," he said, touching a tiny foot through the blanket. "Welcome to the world."

Then he left the room.

THANKS. Where you going? Hey!

KARMA reached a hand out to the bassinet as Garrett shrieked with displeasure.

Chapter Three

Karma had never heard any baby—human or animal—make such a noise in her life. It had come at the end of a thirty-minute screech, and was somewhere between a choke and a gurgle. She had no idea what it meant. She knew only that it sounded fatal. Heart pounding, lips forming an anxious prayer—"Please, please, please!"—she sat him up, and he stared at her silently for one long moment. His blue-black eyes were wide and weirdly serious.

Her rocketing heartbeat slowed. Thank God. Maybe he wasn't dying, after all.

Without warning, he screwed up his rash-covered little face and began to screech again. At 11:30 p.m. on a day that had seemed forty-eight hours long, she was ready to give Garret Joseph Endicott back to the Gypsies.

I'VE CHANGED MY MIND. I want back inside. I don't like *it here!*

SHE'D never entirely understood that old saying about giving a baby "back to the Gypsies." She'd always assumed it was a whimsical statement because Gypsies seemed like a magical and whimsical people.

But on day six of her baby's life—her third day at home with him—she saw it all so clearly. Gypsies kept no birth certificates, no social security numbers, no official records of any kind. Theoretically, one could give them a baby with whom one had failed miserably, and the terrible failure could never be traced.

"Garrett, please," she groaned, putting him to her shoulder and walking the floor of her small living room with him. "I'm doing the best I can. It isn't time to eat, you've been changed, rocked, walked. What *is* it?"

He screamed an indecipherable response.

MY LIP HURTS, I have gas, I'm sleepy, and that thing on your arm digs into my ribs every time you feed or hold me! Where's that straw thing I used to have in my stomach that connected me to my food? I want it back!

A BATH! Karma struck on the idea as though it had been divinely inspired. She'd resisted bathing Garrett because it seemed too difficult with one good arm and she was doing fine with a washcloth, but if she was very careful, it might quiet him. And she was desperate.

She let him scream in his crib for a few minutes while she filled the baby's tub with water carefully run to the right temperature. Then she undressed Garrett and carried his taut and screaming little body and poised it over the tub.

He became suddenly like a little helicopter, arms and legs swinging like wild rotors. His head and shoulders slipped right off her cast and into the water, and his face and chest were submerged.

She screamed and lifted him out. For a moment, he simply looked at her.

WATER! That was fun! Reminded me of the old days, before you pushed me out into this cold, uncomfortable place. Well, where is it? Where's my water?

GARRETT'S momentary silence ended abruptly with a loud, indignant wail that settled into the steady screeching that was about to make rubber of Karma's brain.

It was nearly midnight. If she called the emergency room one more time, they'd think she was insane. If she called Dr. Mac, he'd conclude she was incompetent and probably call Children's Services to take the baby away from her.

She considered calling Nancy Nicholas, then remembered that she had two little boys besides the baby, and if she was sleeping now, she well deserved to.

She thought longingly of Nate Foster and wondered where he was now. In his sleeping bag, probably, under some Canadian maple on the bank of a beautiful stream. She allowed herself to wonder what it would be like to be curled beside him, if she were not the rigid, orderly woman fate and life in the Volkswagen bus had made her.

Then Garrett's screeching forced her to deal with the matter at hand. She trudged wearily to the refrigerator for a bottle of formula.

The melodic sound of her doorbell stopped her in the act of closing the refrigerator door. She placed the bottle on the counter and went to the front door, thinking grimly that it was probably a neighbor, calling to complain of the incessant noise.

She didn't bother with the peephole, but simply

pulled the door open, a ready apology on the tip of her tongue.

But it wasn't a neighbor—it was Nate Foster. She stared at him in openmouthed surprise.

KARMA WAS A MESS. Nate stood under the porch light, studying her as she gaped at him. She was pale, her dark eyes were red rimmed from lack of sleep, and the delicate skin under them was bluish. Her mouth, free of lipstick, was dry and puckered, and her dark hair was caught back in a disheveled ponytail.

She wore a pink robe and an air of utter exhaustion. Her broken arm was out of the sling, as though she'd been trying to use it like the other.

Against her shoulder, Garrett screamed like a banshee.

THERE YOU ARE! Where've you been? She's pretty and everything, but she's not doing this very well, and I'd like to lodge a complaint!

"WHAT ARE YOU DOING HERE?" she asked as she stepped back to let him in. "I thought you were…"

He nodded, wincing against the baby's piercing cries. "I was. But I couldn't leave. Car trouble. I've got a loaner while it's being worked on, but I don't think it'd make it to the edge of town, much less Canada. I was coming back from a poker game and saw your lights on. I remembered your address from your chart." He grinned. "One hundred Second Street. I thought I'd check to see if everything was all right."

Her lips turned up in an obviously forced smile. "Everything's fine," she said. Then her bottom lip began to quiver. He took the baby from her as she dissolved into gulping sobs.

He took a look around and headed for the kitchen and the baby bottle on the countertop. He ran hot water into a pan and placed the bottle in it. "You were just about to feed him?" he asked.

She nodded, following him as he sat at the kitchen table and held the baby up in front of him.

"But it won't quiet him," she warned. "It's not time for him to eat, and he's been changed, everything, but he won't stop crying. Of course, I'm sure it didn't help that I dumped him on his head in his bathwater..."

He looked up at her at that. Tears streamed down her face, and she looked as though she hadn't slept since she'd left the hospital. He propped his foot against the chair at a right angle to him and pushed it away from the table. "Sit down," he said.

She did.

He turned his attention to the baby. "Whoa," he said. "You look pretty rough, buddy." There was a blister on Garrett's upper lip, as well as a triangular red mark between his eyes, and his face was covered with milia, tiny white pimples caused by the working of the sebaceous glands. He looked almost as bad as his mother.

"The blister's from sucking," she said tearfully, "and the rash will go away. But I've already called the ER twice today, and I just noticed the red mark on his forehead this afternoon. It doesn't seem to hurt him."

Nate grinned at her and pulled the baby into his shoulder, where he continued to scream. "We call that a 'stork bite,'" he said. "There's a collection of tiny capillaries there, and his skin's so transparent at this age that they show right through. It'll disappear. It's nothing."

He stood and went for the bottle, then returned to his chair, tucked the baby into his arm and offered him the nipple. His movements were economical and confident. Garrett began to eat greedily. The room became blessedly quiet, except for the rapid sucking sounds.

Karma slumped back against her chair dispiritedly. "Tell me what I'm doing wrong."

PLEASE. We don't have that much time.

NATE SHOOK HIS HEAD, glancing up at her. "Well, apparently he thought it *was* time to eat. Or it could be that you're just not a guy," he said teasingly. "Your biceps are flimsy. Garrett's got a lot of aches and pains at the moment, I imagine, and he wants to feel secure."

Karma watched them jealously. Trust her to be one of the fractional percentage of women to use a sperm bank and turn out the kind of child who truly needed a father in the picture.

"Well, all he's got are my flimsy biceps," she said, her tone quarrelsome. "He's going to have to get used to them."

"He will," Nate assured her. "These first few weeks are hard enough for mothers who have fathers to help them, or some other kind of support system. I imagine for a single woman with a broken arm it's been hell."

She could have pretended otherwise, but knew it would be fruitless. "I didn't expect to be so terrified of him. He's so fragile. And he makes the most frightening noises. I was sure he was dying several times today." She frowned. "How come you're so good at this? I know you're a doctor, but you admitted that you give all the cases involving children to someone else."

He shrugged. "I don't know. It's one of life's little

ironies, I guess. I did my stint in OB and pediatrics in medical school, just like everybody else. I liked it. Kids seem to like me.''

She sat up, interested in his life story. ''Why is that ironical? You told me when I was in labor that you don't like to treat children because they're so vulnerable. Is it just…too hard to see them in pain?''

He sighed and stretched his legs out, crossing his feet at the ankles. His leather tennies, she noted, were enormous.

''Yes,'' he admitted, smoothing Garrett's furrowed brow with the tip of his forefinger. Then he looked up at her, and she saw that it was more than that. That something personal had brought him to that decision. ''But it's even harder to watch them die. I know, I know. A doctor is supposed to adjust to that, and I had—at least as much as you can when you care about people.''

His concentration seemed to drift for a moment. Karma got up to get two colas out of the refrigerator, then came back to the table. She popped the top on his and handed it to him.

''Thank you.'' His long fingers closed over it and brought it to his mouth. ''Good stuff,'' he said after a long swallow. ''Poker's dry work.''

He put the can aside and leaned back in his chair. Garrett had almost finished the bottle. ''Anyway…I was an EMT for several summers while going to medical school, and we got a call one Saturday morning about a child who had something in his throat and couldn't breathe.''

Karma wrapped her arms around herself as she listened. After less than a week with Garrett, she could easily imagine the terror of that child's mother.

"It was the ideal situation. The mother had called right away. They were only blocks away. We thought it was going to be easy. To open an airway, you just put a tube down the throat and feed in air."

His eyes, blue and solemn, stared at the past. "But the object in his throat was a big chunk of soft, fresh bread, and every time we pushed the tube down, the bread clogged it. We'd dig it out, but that took precious time, so we started cutting the ends off and feeding it in again, but we couldn't get through it. We lost him. He wasn't quite two."

Karma felt his horror, his frustration and his grief. All she could think of to say sounded trite. "I'm sure you did everything you could."

His eyes focused on her suddenly. "We did. It isn't that I blamed myself. But I'll never forget his mother, screaming that it was only bread. How could something as harmless as a slice of bread have killed her child? And it was right then and there that I decided I didn't ever want a child's life dependent upon me for protection."

She certainly understood his reluctance, but every parent in the world was up against the same daunting challenge.

"But imagine," she said, "if someone had been afraid to raise *you*. You wouldn't be here."

Garrett pulled back from the bottle, and Nate raised him to his shoulder and patted his back. He gave Karma a wry grin. "Someone was. My mother passed away when I was seven, and my father sent me to military school."

Karma's eyes widened. He seemed like anything but the product of a regimented life-style. "Why?" she asked.

"He didn't know what to do with me," he replied, with a shrug that said he'd accepted the fact long ago. "He worked on Wall Street. Checked out at forty-four with a massive heart attack."

"I'm sorry," she said, then remembered clearly the moment he'd said those same words to her, when she told him about her parents. They had more in common than it appeared.

Garrett burped.

Nate laughed. "A fitting punctuation to a life story. What are you going to do about a car?"

She shifted in her chair, adjusting to the change of subject. "Heron Point Auto is one of my clients. I'm getting a used Volvo."

He nodded. "Good car. Do you have a rocking chair?"

"Yes," she said, pointing toward the living room, which was in darkness. "In here." She led the way to a Boston rocker Bert had refinished for her and to which she'd attached a green-and-pink cushion and back.

"Great," he said, easing into it, still patting the baby. "I'll see if I can get him to sleep while you take a hot shower and try to rest for a few hours."

The notion was certainly tempting, but Karma found herself reluctant to agree. Her labor had forced them into an unnatural intimacy, but in truth they barely knew each other.

"I couldn't—" she began to protest.

"Sure you can. Go, before I change my mind." When she continued to hesitate, he grinned. "I promise not to ravish you in your sleep. I like to do that when a woman's awake."

She gave him a reproachful twist of her lips, but it

didn't distract him from her blush. She saw his eyes go to her flushed cheeks, then to her eyes.

"Okay." He shifted the baby when he began to fuss. "I don't blame you for being concerned. But I assure you I can be a model of gentlemanly decorum."

She folded her arms. "You *are,* or you *can* be?"

He'd opened his mouth to reply when a strange beep came from the jacket he'd dropped over a chair when he came in.

Karma went to get it and handed it to him. He dug a cellular phone out of his pocket and answered it.

Karma heard a high female voice.

Nate glanced at Karma, guilt and amusement in his eyes as he laughed lightly. "Hi, Emmie. No, I'm not going to make it to the club tonight."

Karma sat on the arm of the sofa and shamelessly listened. She heard a lot of loud music and rapid conversation, though she couldn't distinguish the words.

Nate listened. The baby fussed. There was sudden silence on the other end of the line. Then Karma heard clearly, "What was that?"

Nate stood, the baby stretched across his forearm, his broad hand supporting the small torso, the little head nestling against his upper arm. "That was a baby," he said, pacing the living room. "No, smartie. He belongs to a friend. No, you'll have to party without me. Yeah, me, too. Say hi to everybody. Bye."

He flipped the phone so that it folded, then handed it back to Karma. "Would you put that back for me, please?" He looked into her carefully neutral expression and said, "And in answer to your question, I *am* a gentleman. I spent too long in a military environment not to revere the American flag and women everywhere."

She looked back at him innocently. "Emmie, particularly?"

He seemed intrigued that she approached the subject. "She worked in personnel at Riverview. Does a mean mambo."

She blinked. "I didn't know anyone mamboed in Heron Point."

He patted Garrett's back and earned another burp. "Good boy," he told him. To Karma, he said, "That's what you miss when you organize your life *not* to include the Scupper Tavern's Cuban night. Are you going to go take a shower and get some sleep, or do I have to get forceful about it?"

"I thought you were a gentleman," she challenged.

His smile was both sweet and dangerous. "A gentleman looks out for a lady," he said. "By whatever means are required. Will you go?"

A hot shower and a few hours' sleep were more than she could resist. But she had to get something straight.

"I...I'm very grateful for all you've done," she said, turning the end of the belt of her robe around her index finger. "But I like my life uncluttered."

He nodded, still patting the baby, who was now asleep. "So you said," he replied.

That didn't seem to get through. She tried again. "I mean that..."

He nodded again, forestalling her. "I know what you mean. I'm not to misconstrue this acceptance of my help as an indication of sexual interest."

She sighed, frustrated with his annoying way of distilling the facts.

She folded her arms, slightly discomfited. She was usually too prepared, too organized, to ever feel perplexed. It irritated her. "Yes," she said frankly. "That's what I mean."

"Not to worry." His assurance was amiable and heartfelt. "You're not in my plan, either. I was just being a friend."

"All right." She smiled gratefully. "Then I'll take advantage of that offer, and have a shower. I'll nap for an hour, then maybe you can still catch Emmie and mambo."

Karma walked away, turning back at the hallway to thank him again. But she found him watching her, a decidedly predatory look in his eye, a feral smile on his lips.

A sudden fluster replaced her gratitude, and she headed for the shower, her heart beating uncomfortably fast.

Chapter Four

Karma felt sunlight on her face, and she smelled bacon. The high-heeled shoe on her right foot pinched her big toe.

Though she was just beginning to surface from sleep to wakefulness, she understood that the sensations weren't real. They were remnants of a dream that had been filled with color and music and a man who had danced her around and around an opulent ballroom.

Eyes still closed, she smiled, stretched her arms, then turned on her side and curled into her pillow, trying to recapture the dream for a few more moments.

But the sound of a baby crying was a discordant note, and the ballroom cleared. Even the man in whose arms she'd danced the night away slipped out of her grasp and disappeared.

She snuggled deeper into the pillow, trying to call everyone back.

''Karma!'' a man's voice shouted.

''There you are,'' she said in a pleased and sultry voice, turning around and around in search of the man who'd spoken. ''Just one more dance? Where are you?''

''Right here.''

''Where?''

She couldn't find him, but his voice was close. He had to be within reach. She stretched out a hand. "One more dance?"

She felt his warm, strong hand close around hers and draw her near.

But what had happened to the music? The silence woke her.

Karma opened her eyes with a start. There *was* sunlight on her face. She *did* smell bacon cooking. Her big toe *was* being pinched, but not by a dancing shoe.

Nate Foster held it between the thumb and forefinger of his left hand. Her baby lay in his right.

She studied the sight of her toe in his hand for a stupefied moment.

"Sorry." He released it, grinning. "I had to wake you, and on the chance you didn't remember I was here, I didn't want to terrify you by getting too close."

"Oh, my God," she said with a surprised gasp. She wondered distractedly if her life would ever return to normal after her premature delivery. "What time is it?" She picked up the bedside clock, then put it down with a faint shriek when she read 9:12 a.m.

The events of the previous night began to come back to her. Nate had appeared when she was at her wit's end with the baby. He'd fed him, and quieted him, and sent her to take a shower and a nap.

That had been almost nine hours ago!

Color flooded her face. "I'm *so* sorry!" she said, throwing the covers aside and leaping out of bed—only to realize that all she wore were the panties and sports bra she'd worn under her robe the night before. As her color deepened, she resisted the impulse to press her knees together and cross her arms over her breasts.

Instead, she reached to the foot of the bed, where

she'd left the robe, but her broken arm made putting it on difficult. Nate came to hold it up for her while she groped for the sleeve. Then the best she could do was hold it closed.

Thoroughly rattled, she apologized again. "I don't know what happened! One moment I was too tired to sleep, and the next I—"

"Please," he said with a smile. Was it mocking her, or was that simply her imagination? "Stop apologizing. Brighton Construction wants to know if they should bring their payroll information over."

"They called?"

"They're on the phone right now."

"Oh, my God!" She ran to the kitchen to pick up the wall phone.

"Miss Endicott?" Alicia Brighton, the beautiful and efficient office manager and wife of the owner, sounded impatient. Karma had never met her, only seen her photo in the women's section of the paper. She was always bestowing something or being awarded something. "I understand you've had your baby prematurely," she said, her tone patronizing, "and I imagine you'll need time to get your life in order. Why don't we take our payroll to..."

"I'll expect your payroll this morning," Karma said. Her voice sounded husky with sleep, but she hoped the woman would mistake it for a professional tone. "I have a remarkably beautiful son, but it's business as usual at Endicott Accounting."

There was a surprised silence on the other end of the line. "But, you've just had a baby."

Which I have to support, Karma thought. But aloud she said, "I have a bassinet in my office, and life goes on."

There was a small laugh on the other end of the line. "Are you in for a surprise..." Then, in a more serious tone: "And we can have the payroll by the tenth?"

Fifty-six employees on different pay scales, different insurance rates, with quirky deductions and always, always, a dozen last-minute changes. Ah... "Absolutely," she replied. "I have everything on disk. Just bring me your September hours and I'm ready to go."

"Thank you."

Karma hung up the phone, wondering how she was going to keep her promise, and came face-to-face with Nate Foster and the reminder that a strange man had just spent the night in her house.

At his speculative smile, she closed her eyes and tried to pull herself together. Big deal. So the man had spent the night with her. He hadn't even been in the same room. And only days ago he'd sat with her through four grueling hours of labor and delivery. At this point, he knew her pretty well—physically *and* emotionally.

She opened her eyes again to thank him with some semblance of decorum—and saw that he seemed to find her dither interesting. His blue gaze ran over her in a lazy appraisal, stopping with distracting suddenness on her hair.

It must look like a hay bale after a wind, she thought, remembering that she'd ripped out the rubber band that held the ponytail. She put a hand to it and felt the disarray. She never strove for a glamorous appearance, but she was usually well-groomed and carefully dressed.

Last night she'd been too desperate to care how she looked. This morning—with him looking fresh and fit in an Oregon Ducks sweatshirt and jeans—she cared a lot.

And her imperfections always made her touchy.

"*Gentlemen,*" she said, reminding him with a tilt of her eyebrow that he'd claimed to be one the night before, "don't stare."

"Of course they do," he replied, "when the lady is seductively tousled."

Seductively tousled. She repeated the words to herself as she glanced at her reflection in the window over the sink. He must have more imagination than she did; she thought she just looked messy.

"Gentlemen also don't patronize," she said, taking Garrett from him. She was thrilled when the baby didn't scream. He stared at her, his little mouth opening as though he were convinced she had a bottle hidden somewhere on her person. She nuzzled him, and kissed his silky cheek.

HI, Mother! He's cool. He rubbed my back while we watched the news, and we danced in the kitchen while we cooked. He says he's going to introduce me to some babes.

"LADIES," Nate countered, taking the belt that dangled around her waist and tying it, "don't throw sincere compliments back in a gentleman's face. And while we're standing here arguing my credibility, your bacon and eggs are drying up." He pushed her gently toward the kitchen table.

He removed two plates of bacon and eggs from the oven. The eggs were gently over easy, the bacon was crisp and dry, the toast was golden.

Karma stared, still trying to adjust to having had his hands at the belt of her robe. Her mother hadn't been much of a cook, and space had been at a premium in the bus. Most hot meals had been cooked outside, and only if the weather allowed. Breakfast had usually been cereal.

Much as she hated those memories, she rarely cooked for herself these days, because she was simply too busy. But she knew that would have to change when Garrett began eating solid food.

She felt her mouth water. When she looked down and saw that her son had gone to sleep, she thought she'd died and gone to heaven. She hadn't had a peaceful meal since she'd brought him home.

"I'll just put him down," she said, going to the bassinet in the dining room, which she'd turned into an office. He didn't stir.

She went back to the kitchen and took her place, feeling suddenly guilty for being annoyed with Nate over *her* appearance. It wasn't even logical. And she *usually* was. She put it down to hormonal chaos after childbirth, and settled down to enjoy her bounty.

When she'd polished off her breakfast, Nate brought another round of toast and topped off her coffee. "Have you thought about hiring a nanny?" he asked, taking his chair again. His grin had an element she mistrusted.

"Can't afford one," she replied.

"Yes," he said. "You can."

She glanced at him suspiciously as she spread strawberry jam on a slice of toast. "How would I do that?"

"I'd work for free."

She'd taken a sip of coffee, and she choked on it.

"I can't go anywhere until my car's out of the shop," he explained, pushing away from the table so that he could angle one leg over the other. "And I've been bored at home."

Nate concentrated on pushing his plate aside so that she wouldn't see he was lying. There was nothing

wrong with his car, and he'd never been bored a moment in his life. But he couldn't tell her the truth about
why he was making this proposal, because he didn't
know why. As he kept telling everyone, he liked babies,
he just generally refused to take care of them. He also
didn't like women who were distant and suspicious—
as she was being now.

She'd just put up a barrier between them, as she'd
done that night in the hospital. She was probably certain
he was suggesting some lascivious alliance. The knowledge charged his sense of humor.

"So, what are you suggesting?" she asked coolly, an
eyebrow raised, her shoulders stiffly set. "That you live
in?"

He leaned toward her over his cup and met her judicious brown eyes with a practiced leer.

"Right," he replied softly, silkily. "Then we could
chuck the accounting business, open a call-girl operation and have wild sex ourselves on a daily basis."

He saw the condemnation in her eyes change to indignation, then reluctantly to amusement as she read the
humor in his.

"Aren't we clever this morning...." she observed.

"That's what you get," he said with a judicious look
of his own, "for presuming the worst. I was going to
make the perfectly civil suggestion that I spend a few
hours here with the baby in the afternoons so that you
can get some work done."

He looked back at her as she studied him, probably
for signs of duplicity.

"You don't like to be around babies," she reminded
him.

"Yeah, well..." He stacked up their dishes. "This
one and I are sort of bonding. And by the time he's old

enough to be a danger to himself, I'll be back to work and he can give someone else an ulcer or a heart attack.''

She followed him to the counter. ''I don't understand. What's in it for you?''

He put the dishes in the sink and frowned down at her as she pulled open the dishwasher. ''Does there have to be something in it for me?''

''There's always a debit and a credit,'' she said.

He rolled his eyes and turned on the hot-water faucet. ''Life is not a business ledger, Karma.''

''The world is set up,'' she insisted, ''so that everything is balanced by something else. For every action there's a reaction. What's debited one place has to be credited someplace else.''

He rinsed their dishes and utensils, then turned off the water. She took them from him and placed them in the rack, then closed the door.

''Doctors,'' he said, ''are less inclined than accountants to fix a cost on everything. There are exceptions, of course, but most of us do what has to be done, and worry about the cost—to the patient, and to ourselves—later.''

She folded her arms and leaned a hip on the counter. ''That's because of health insurance. For us, there's no such thing as 'loss insurance.' We have to keep the books balanced.''

Nate shook his head at her. ''So, you're saying you won't let me help you by spending a few hours here in the afternoon, unless I insist on payment of some kind? That your emotional books will be out of balance?''

She thought that over, and wasn't sure that was what she'd intended. He went on. ''Fine. So, let's retain the part of the plan where you and I have wild sex on a daily basis.''

Karma sought escape from the thoughts that suggestion provoked by giving him a dose of his own medicine. ''As charming as that sounds,'' she replied, ''I've just delivered a baby. I'm out of commission in that regard for a good six weeks.''

''Oh, gee,'' he said with bland surprise, ''how could a doctor like me have forgotten that?'' He narrowed his gaze on her, his scolding tone underlining his words. ''Unless my intentions *were* nonsexual. What about if you fixed me dinner before I left in the evening? Or is that too much bookkeeping? I mean, are there separate entries for meats and fish? Do you break down vegetables into green, yellow, tubers, cruci—''

''Oh, shut up,'' Karma said, torn between annoyance and amusement. She frankly felt a small degree of pleasure at his suggestion. She loved to cook. She seldom did, though, because it wasn't very satisfying to cook for one.

She looked into his blue eyes as she considered, and saw an element of danger there. It wasn't necessarily aimed at her, it simply existed in the depths of his eyes. He was carefree and flirtatious. He liked to mambo with a woman named Emmie.

No, she thought resolutely. It wasn't a good idea. She *would* need help with the baby, but it would be safer to find some reliable older woman, or a day care that took infants.

Whoever heard of a nanny—even a part-time one— who was a handsome man in his prime? And a doctor, at that? It wasn't logical. And she didn't trust anything that wasn't.

She opened her mouth to answer, but was interrupted by the ringing of his cellular phone directly behind her.

Nate, at the sofa where he'd left his jacket, called out to her, "Would you answer that, please?"

Karma raised the flexible antenna and pressed Phone. "Hello?"

There was an instant's silence. Then a husky feminine voice asked abruptly, "Who's this?"

The mambo queen? Karma wondered. Something about the demanding tone annoyed her. "Hillary's House of Harlots," she replied. "Who's this?"

Nate, shrugging into his jacket, snatched the phone from her with an expression that was half grin, half scolding frown. He found it interesting that the sweet courage in her that had appealed to him had a sharper, less predictable side.

"Hello," he said. There was an excited exclamation on the other end of the line. "That was Hillary herself," he replied with a punitive glance at Karma.

Karma dropped a curtsy as she passed him to wipe off the table.

"No," he said after another spate of excited conversation from the caller. "A friend. A very nice young woman I met at the hospital. I came to help with her baby." He listened for a moment. Then he shifted his weight, looking mildly impatient. "Yes, it is early." He listened again and then said evenly, "Yes, I did spend the night."

Karma looked up from her task, waiting for him to explain. But there was a stubbornness about his square-shouldered stance that told her he didn't intend to.

There was silence on the other end of the line. Then Karma heard the voice again. It was quieter now.

Nate glanced at the clock. "Hold on a minute, please,

Hadley.'' He held a hand over the mouthpiece and smiled at Karma. ''Am I employed?''

Karma was tempted, and that alarmed her. She couldn't have done without him when Garrett was born, but now he presented a complication she didn't need when she had a life to reorganize.

''Thank you, but no,'' she said. ''I'll manage.''

He studied her long enough that she almost changed her mind. ''You're sure?'' he asked.

The very fact that she wasn't made her tell him she was. ''Yes. I am.''

Without apparent disappointment, he turned his attention back to the woman on the phone. ''How about if I pick you up in fifteen minutes?''

After what must have been an affirmative reply, he pressed the End button and pocketed the phone.

''Was that the mambo queen?'' Karma asked, tossing the sponge at the sink.

He shook his head. ''Hadley. She's an outdoorswoman. We had a date to climb Camel Mountain today.''

''Is Hadley a first or a last name?''

''First. Hadley Brooks.''

Karma walked him to the door. They stopped on the foyer rug and turned to face each other. ''Shouldn't you have explained about spending the night?'' she asked. ''Just to ease her mind. She sounded upset.''

He shrugged a shoulder. ''I'm a free agent, and so is she. We hike together. That's it.''

Karma had a feeling that wasn't the way Hiking Hadley wanted it. ''Does she know about the mambo queen?''

Nate folded his arms and smiled down at her. ''I

don't know. For someone who's afraid to have me around, you're very interested in my social life.''

She raised an eyebrow. ''Afraid?'' she questioned imperiously.

''Deny it,'' he said challengingly. ''You're terrified of me. That's why you won't accept my help with the baby.''

She rolled her eyes heavenward—mostly so that he couldn't look into them. ''Terrified?'' She laughed. ''You're the gentlest man I've ever met, and I acquired that information under rather intimate conditions. Why would I be terrified of you?''

He caught her chin between his thumb and forefinger. His bright blue eyes looked into her dark ones, and she felt a tremor somewhere deep inside.

''Because you know that isn't all there is to me. And you're afraid you'll find something else you like.'' Then he leaned down and kissed her quickly, chastely, on the lips. ''See you.''

Karma stood for a full twenty seconds, eyes closed, heart fluttering, lips tingling. Then she marched to the computer and brought up Brighton Construction's file.

Nate Foster was absolutely right and there was no point in pretending he wasn't. She *was* afraid of becoming any more interested in him than she already was. She had a business and a baby, and that was all any woman in her right mind should tackle at any given time.

A husband, of course, was different. That, presumably, was a known quantity. But a boyfriend, a beau, a...an other—significant or otherwise—was a questionable factor. And she liked sure things.

''YOU MEAN,'' Tom Nicholas repeated slowly, carefully, ''that you decided *not* to spend four weeks in the

Canadian wilderness with no one to answer to but yourself because of a…a woman? One you'd just met?''

Nate stood several feet away from Tom, who was
spreading redwood stain on the railing of the deck he'd
just built onto the back of Nate's two-story A-frame at
the edge of Eaton's Woods.

''Yeah,'' Nate replied. ''You think that's out of character?''

Tom gave him a grinning glance as he continued to
work. ''You *have* no character. You keep more relationships going at one time than 'The Love Connection.' So, what's this all about?''

Nate thought about it a moment and shrugged. He
waved the coffee mug he held in a wide arc. ''Beats
me. She was delivering early, her Lamaze coach was
out of town, I was there…''

Tom gave him a frowning glance this time as he
shooed him backward and swept the brush farther along
the railing. ''Karma Endicott, my tax accountant. Nancy
told me she had her baby. You hate babies.''

''I don't *hate* babies,'' Nate said defensively, ''I just
don't like to take care of them.''

''Then you don't want to get serious about a woman
with one.''

''No,'' he said distractedly. ''Of course not.''

''So…consider yourself lucky.''

Nate knew he should do just that. He'd changed his
mind several times before finally going to check on
Karma and Garrett that night. Then he'd offered to help
with the baby only because she looked so tired, so surprised by the enormity of her new responsibilities.

They'd struck a rapport during the birth of her baby
that had brought him closer to her than he'd been to

anyone since his mother had died. He hadn't realized how much he'd missed that heart-to-heart connection until he felt it again. He wanted it back with a desperation that astonished him.

But he'd wanted a lot of things in his life he hadn't allowed himself to have because he knew they weren't good for him. Like the Porsche. And the yacht that had once belonged to a first baseman for the Boston Red Sox. And the harlequin Great Dane puppy.

The Porsche would have encouraged speed, but it was important in life to enjoy the passing scenery. The boat would have encouraged indolence, and a body needed exercise to remain fit. And the puppy would have been left alone much of the time, and that would have reminded him of his childhood. And he wouldn't have inflicted that on a dog.

No. He shouldn't pursue Karma Endicott, no matter how interesting or appealing he found her. That would encourage him to open up to the possibilities—and most of his feelings were in a vault.

"Move it, or get it stained Ripe Redwood," Tom warned as he advanced with the brush.

Nate backed up a few paces. "What about you and Amy Brown?" Nate asked, needing to divert himself from the futility of his own romantic interests. "Saw the two of you at Chez Pasta a week or so ago. What does Riverview Hospital's PR director see in you?"

Nate wished instantly that he'd used more care in picking his words. He was kidding, of course, but since the fire that had taken the life of Tom's friend, and put Tom himself in the hospital for several long months, his friend considered himself a diminished man. That had been almost two years ago, and he was taking the long road back.

Not that Tom ever spoke of it. But his brother, Jave, the radiologist, who'd warned him that his bachelor days might be numbered, sometimes shared his concerns with Nate, who'd been on duty the night of the fire. Tom had been brought in by his fellow firemen, smoke-blackened and blistered, with fourth-degree burns on his right leg.

"What everyone sees, of course," he replied as he pushed him farther back. His glance was filled with the wry humor that had gotten him through physical and emotional therapy and the birth of a new career in carpentry. "Wit, intelligence, charm, good humor, impeccably good ju—"

Nate interrupted him. "Please. My stomach's a little delicate."

"Big surprise. What did you and Miss Big Biceps have for lunch on your hike? Pinecones and bark dust?"

"Clever. If you had a little respect for your body, it wouldn't look quite so much like a Dodge truck."

"That's muscle." Tom had reached the end of the railing, and he turned back to check over his work.

"I thought we were talking about Amy."

"You asked a question and I answered it. What more is there to talk about?"

"When did you two start going out? Do you plan to see her again? What do—"

"Whoa, whoa!" Tom capped the can of stain and put the brush in a bucket of turpentine in the big wooden toolbox in the corner. "Did my mother hire you to spy on me?"

No, Jave had put him up to it, but Nate wasn't about to tell him that.

"Just curious. Everybody at the hospital loves Amy.

And since no one likes you, we're naturally concerned.''

Tom's eyes surveyed the finished deck. ''I bust my butt to finish this for you so you can sit on it in October and watch the leaves turn, and you want to talk women and harangue me?''

Nate clapped him on the shoulder. ''Good job, Tom. For which you're being well paid, I might add. The lady was looking at you with adoration in her eyes, and as your friend, I just want to know what it's all about. I mean, should I be planning a bachelor party, here? Should I send my tux to the cleaners? Should I—''

''You should mind your own business,'' Tom said amiably. ''And the next time my brother tells you to try to get something out of me because I'm not sharing with him, either, tell him where to go.''

Nate was not surprised Tom had seen through the plan. Espionage was not one of his skills.

''I can't do that. He's a department head. Just tell me you and Amy will be seeing each other again, so I can report back to Jave, and there'll be peace and harmony all around.''

Tom drew a breath for patience and collected his gear in the toolbox. ''I am *not* seeing Amy again.''

Nate could see that he was pushing the bounds of privacy. He'd intended that, of course, but he also knew he couldn't expect Tom to like it.

''Why not?'' Nate asked, following with the can of stain as Tom headed down the steps and across the driveway to his truck.

Tom set the toolbox on the ground and lowered the tailgate. ''Because I...I don't know.'' He put the toolbox in the bed of the truck and turned to take the can from Nate. ''I guess I'm just not ready.''

"For what?" Nate asked brutally. "For her to see your leg?"

Nate gave him a lethal look and lifted the tailgate into place.

"Or aren't you ready," Nate went on, "to admit to yourself that it wasn't your fault, that you did what you thought was the right thing and your friend died anyway because that's life and it often stinks? You could be happy if you could let yourself admit that. Is that what you're not ready for?"

Tom walked around to the driver's-side door. Nate followed intrepidly. Tom yanked the door open and glared at him. "I thought Singleton was Riverview's shrink."

"I did my psych internship," Nate said. "I can try out my skills if I want to."

Tom shook his head. "Try it out on somebody who has faith in your diagnosis."

Nate caught his arm and stopped him from climbing into the cab of the truck. "I'm right," he said quietly, steadily. "And you know it. You've been carrying that night on your back for almost two years, like some sort of penance. Let it go. You aren't responsible."

"I'll bill you for the deck," Tom said, shaking off Nate's hand and climbing up into the seat. He pulled the door closed with a slam and glared down at his friend as he turned the key in the ignition and jerked the truck into reverse.

"The advice," Nate shouted after him as he screeched backward out of the driveway, "was free of charge!"

He watched the truck disappear in a swirl of fallen leaves and wondered what the hell he thought he was doing psychoanalyzing Tom, when he'd canceled a long-awaited vacation on a moment's notice, and couldn't shake the mental image of a woman with dark hair and eyes and a squally little baby covered with a rash. Seemed his own sanity was suspect.

"OH, Karma! Oh, God, I'm *so* sorry. I can't believe you delivered early! I mean, I *prayed* I'd get out of being your Lamaze coach, but I never dreamed it'd really happen!"

Karma held her living room door open and stood aside as a young woman with blunt-cut brown hair and emphatic blue eyes stumbled inside, arms loaded with packages. She dropped everything on the sofa, then turned to take Karma in her embrace.

"You *know* I'm kidding. I really wanted to help you through this." She stood back and stopped talking for a minute to frown at Karma's arm. "You had to have a bone set *and* deliver a baby? Was it awful? You look like it was."

Karma laughed lightly. "You'll have to try it yourself sometime. There's nothing else quite like it." She pushed her friend onto the sofa. "I'll get you some coffee."

Roberta Dawson caught Karma's arm. "I don't have time—I'm on a lunch break. But I brought a few things for the baby, and something for you. Where is he? Can I see him?"

"Try and stop me from showing him off." Karma gestured to Bert to follow her into the bedroom, where a night-light illuminated the baby sleeping like a cherub in the crib beside her bed.

"Karma, he has measles!" Bert whispered as she leaned over the crib's padded rail.

Karma stroked the tiny head with her fingertips. "It's

just a rash. It'll go away.'' The sight of her son sleeping peacefully filled Karma with a satisfaction that went deeper than anything she'd ever known. ''Isn't he beautiful?''

''Oh, yes.'' Bert put the tip of her index finger to his tiny hand. ''Good work, Karma. You didn't even need me.''

''Well, you were off being Miss Career Woman. I had to cope without you.''

Bert straightened to grin at her. ''I understand,'' she said softly, ''that you bullied the studly Dr. Foster into taking my place.''

Karma rolled her eyes and led the way out of the room. She pulled the door halfway closed. ''I can't believe you've been home all of about twelve hours and you already know that.''

Bert smiled smugly as she fell onto the sofa beside her packages. ''There's a candy striper at the hospital whose older sister works with me. She told me this morning. Everyone's interested, you know. This is a small town, and you can't expect something like a sperm-bank pregnancy to go undiscussed. Particularly when the delivery involves the handsome emergency room doctor who delayed his vacation to see you through labor, then completely changed his mind about going.''

''Jeez! He had car trouble. It's in the shop.'' Then Karma analyzed Bert's statement. ''Am I being watched?''

Bert nodded. ''Of course. Oh, not literally spied on. But I'm sure you're being observed. Everyone wants to know how it's going to turn out.''

''Turn out?'' Karma frowned. ''It *has* turned out. I've *had* the baby. That's the outcome I wanted.''

Bert shook her head pityingly. "Karma, this is small-town America. It hasn't 'turned out' until they know what happens to you romantically."

Karma blinked, stunned. "Why would anyone care?"

"Because they like you. Because, although you're just a little more reserved than the average Heron Pointer, you've earned a reputation since you reduced Diantha Pennyman's tax debt and helped her invest her money. She tells anyone who'll listen how good you are. You contribute to community projects, *and* you always look nice. If a little..." She stopped and waggled her hand descriptively. "You know."

Karma looked down at her cotton slacks and sweatshirt. "A little what?" she asked. "I have a new baby."

Bert shook her head. "I don't mean those. Actually, they're an improvement. But your work clothes are... stodgy."

"They're professional."

"They're gray and blue and tailored. When you head for work, you look like somebody's lawyer."

Karma sighed dispiritedly. "Fine. Is your lunch break over yet? I don't think I can take much more of this friendly visit."

Bert glanced at her watch and smiled. "I'm afraid you have me for ten more minutes. So—are you seeing the doctor?"

Karma decided she could play the same game. "As a matter of fact, he spent the night earlier this week."

Bert's eyes widened, then narrowed. "What?" she asked flatly.

"He spent the night," Karma repeated, studying her fingernails. "With stodgy little old me."

"Oh, no." Bert's voice portended doom.

Karma straightened indignantly. "What do you mean, *no?* He did."

"You couldn't have…" Bert waggled two fingers together in a gesture Karma interpreted as suggesting a joining.

"No, we didn't. I did just deliver a baby, after all. Why? Does the idea seem impossible to you? That the handsome doctor could be attracted to stodgy old me?"

Bert frowned, obviously confused. "Well, nothing's *impossible,* but I thought you'd decided there isn't a man worth having, and Dr. Foster has a reputation for…um, my mother used to call it 'playing the field.' Be careful. You're kind of an innocent."

Karma put a hand to her eyes. "Bert. I'm twenty-seven, I have a business, and I have a baby. I know a little more than you think I do. And anyway, Nate just came to see how I was doing and stayed to watch the baby so I could take a shower and have a nap. He was here all night because I was exhausted and didn't wake up until nine the following morning. He performed a kindness. That's all it was. I tried to make it sound like something else just to rattle you, because *you* seem to think I'm a sexual nonentity."

"No, I don't." Bert reached for one of the packages she'd brought. "I just know you're afraid of men."

"I am *not* afraid," Karma told her emphatically, wondering what on earth she'd done to give everyone that impression. "Why does everyone say that?"

"Karma, your baby was fathered by a sperm bank."

"Because I wanted a baby and I was single. I didn't know any man I considered worthy to be my baby's father."

"Don't you ever wonder about the sperm donor? Particularly now that the baby's here?"

Karma didn't even have to think about her answer. "No. The very nature of the process confirms that he'd just as soon remain anonymous. And as far as I'm concerned, the baby's *mine*. And he's all I want."

"What about when he begins to wonder where his daddy is?"

Karma had considered that a concern since the moment she'd decided to use the sperm bank. And now that Garrett was a living, breathing reality, she wondered even more often how he would react to the way he'd been conceived. But he was here and he was wonderful, and she had far more immediate concerns to cope with.

"You know," she said, fixing Bert with a firm gaze, "if you'd been there when he was born and experienced the miracle of it all with me, you wouldn't be asking so many questions. You'd just accept him for the wonder that he is and let tomorrow take care of itself."

Bert stared back at her in surprise. "I only asked because you've *never* been one to let tomorrow take care of itself." She smiled suddenly. "Maybe the baby's changing you already. Well. I've got to get back to work." She stood, and pushed Karma back down when she would have followed her. "I'll let myself out. I'll call you about dinner one night this week. I have to check my calendar at the office. I'll bring something over, if it's too hard for you to get out."

Karma smiled at her from the sofa. "Thanks, Bert. That would be wonderful. I am getting a little tired of my own company."

Bert blew her a kiss and was gone.

Karma pulled the lid off the box and found a small card on top of the folded tissue.

Thought you might need something to make you feel glamorous after the very unglamorous work of producing a baby. Love, Bert.

Karma parted the tissue and found a turquoise silk slacks set with a big shirt top and full trouser legs. She made a soft sound of approval, knowing it would feel wonderful on.

Another package contained a one-piece suit for Garrett with ducks on it and a blue polka-dot tie that matched the romper pants. The last held a musical plush bear that played a lullaby.

Garrett loved it. Karma watched his eyes search for it as she cradled him in her arm to feed him. She'd placed the bear on the arm of the sofa and sat in the corner close to it.

HEY, I like that. Where did it come from? I used to look like that once—hair all over. 'Course, I wasn't out yet. I can't make music, though. You don't think I'm slow, do you?

SHE FELT curiously selfish, enjoying this moment all by herself. She wished there was someone she could turn to to say, "Do you see that? Isn't he cute?"

But there wasn't, and that was the way she'd wanted it. It was a new world, filled with single-parent families. But, staring at her beautiful baby, she couldn't help but wish he had someone else to admire him, too.

"You know what?" Karma said aloud to Garrett. "We are going to be the happiest mother-and-son team since...since...oh, what's her name? In *So Big*. I know you've never heard of that. It was written by Edna Ferber, and it's about a mother and son who keep their land against impossible odds when the father dies. And they work so well together that eventually they build a great empire.

"We're not going to do that, exactly, because it's hard to build an accounting empire unless you're H & R Block, and taxes really aren't my favorite part of the whole thing. But I'm just trying to tell you we're going to be fine. I think I'm over the blues, or whatever that was that made me melt all over Nate Foster when he came, and everything's going to be great for us. I'm sure of it.''

ME, TOO, Mother. But I do like him. He can hold me in one hand. Can't we invite him back?

Chapter Five

Karma awoke the following morning to the sound of the baby screaming—and to an emotional relapse.

She patted Garrett while she paced the kitchen, waiting for the milk to warm. She felt blue and hopeless, and the portion of the payroll she'd managed to work on last evening while Garrett slept seemed so small a part of the overall project. She had to finish it in the promised time to maintain her professional credibility.

What had she been thinking? Whatever had made her think she could maintain a business *and* raise a baby?

I'M VERY HUNGRY, *Mother. How long is this going to take? My rash itches, and I* really *wish I could have one of Nate's massages.*

GARRETT QUIETED after taking his formula in the company of the musical bear. Getting herself ready with one good arm took Karma until midmorning.

Garrett on her shoulder, she went to check the mailbox, hoping for sweepstakes winnings, or the appearance of a misdirected Mary Poppins.

The box contained neither, but she gasped at what she did find.

A bouquet of red roses protruded from the mailbox attached to the front of the house. There were no distracting ferns or baby's breath—just a dozen brilliant crimson, just-opening roses wrapped in florist's paper and sticking out of the old black box.

''Oh...'' Karma heard her own whispered, protracted exclamation. The beauty of the surprise made her heart thump, then her entire body soften as though she'd been patted on the head or stroked. ''Look, Garrett. Roses!''

She transferred Garrett to her wrapped arm and pulled the roses out of the box. She held them to her nose, then to the baby's. He stopped crying and flailed a hand.

''Can you smell them?'' she asked.

Wow! I bet it's a pretty color. Can I have one?

KARMA held the stems away from him, feeling the thorns through the paper. ''They're red, Garrett. Aren't they wonderful?''

UH-HUH. Yes. I bet he *left them.*

KARMA SUSPECTED Nate was responsible for this whiff of heaven.

She looked up and down the street, wondering if her benefactor had waited for her reaction. But she saw no one. Most of the cars in the neighborhood were gone, their owners off to work. All she saw was the battered blue truck her neighbor used to haul wood for his woodstove.

''Well. We'll take these inside,'' she told Garrett, ''and call Nate and see if he did leave them.'' She felt curiously excited, and was surprised to discover she was pleased to have an excuse to call him.

Karma looked up the number and placed Garrett in his carrier on the counter. She played with his tiny hand while waiting for Nate to pick up.

"Hi. You've reached Nate Foster," his voice said cheerfully. "I'm out. Leave a message after the beep and I'll call you back."

"What do you think, Garrett?" Karma asked the baby while the series of beeps played musically. "Should we leave a message?"

YES. Isn't that the polite thing to do? Tell him I said hi.

"POWER-PUNCH, please, Devon," Nate said to the young man behind the counter at Coffee Country, Heron Point's premier coffee bar. "With amaretto cream. And can I use the phone? I won't be long."

"Sure." Devon handed him a cordless phone. "Take the back table. I'll bring your coffee."

"Thanks. How's Jo? I hear she had a girl."

"Well…the baby's fine," Devon replied, his expression wry. "But she's caught in that weird situation, you know. Surrogate for her sister, her sister dies…and she's left to deal with the baby and the banker-father."

Nate raised an eyebrow at Devon's tone. "What do you mean? Ryan Jeffries is all right. I know him."

Devon shrugged and reached for a mug with the coffee bar's logo on it. "He acts like he owns her."

"Maybe he's just acting like he owns the baby. It is his."

Devon put the mug under the hot pot labeled Power-punch. "I guess. None of my business, anyway."

Nate stabbed out his number and wondered if Heron Point had always had so many unorthodox relationships and so many babies, or if he just happened to notice them because he'd been somewhat involved in one. Baby, that is. Relationships weren't really his forte— except friendships.

It occurred to him to wonder why he'd left a dozen roses in Karma's mailbox, if that was true, but he dismissed the thought. Analysis took all the pleasure out of spontaneity.

His answering machine picked up, and he pressed the keys to enter his remote access code and listened to his messages play back.

"Hi, Nate. Alexa. The reception I told you about for the Chilean sculptor is tonight. I heard your car's in the shop and you're still in town. Want to go? Let me know. I'll pick you up."

A beep ended the message.

"Nate, it's Emmie. Tango tournament at the Scupper. *Tell* me you'll be there. If I have to dance with Robert Botsford, you're a dead man. Thought you deserved a warning."

Nate smiled and waited through the beep.

"This is Hadley. Low tide tonight. Want to go clamming? Call me."

Devon brought his coffee. Nate thanked him and handed him a bill. He sat back and sipped at his coffee.

"Nate?" The voice was quiet and hesitant, and brought Nate instantly upright in his chair. He held the cup away as its contents sloshed onto the table. He heard baby sounds in the background. "Ah... Hi. This is Karma Endicott. Did you...I was wondering if you...left roses in my mailbox?" There was a pause. "If you did, thank you. They turned my day around. If you didn't...thank you again for everything else you've done. Garrett says hi. Bye."

"Yes!" Nate said in a quiet, triumphant whisper as

he stabbed out Karma's number, then dropped napkins on the puddle of coffee.

KARMA SAT at the computer with Garrett in a front pack, lolling contentedly against her, eyes looking up at her with flattering fascination. She had a handle on the Brighton Construction payroll—even though she could only hold it in one hand—and she was now making encouraging headway. It was lucky, she thought, that the number pad on her computer required only the right hand.

She'd placed the roses on a table at her elbow, and their fragrance enfolded her as she worked.

She was amazed by how positive they made her feel. She wondered if it was their color, their fragrance, or the simple fact that someone had thought about her, that had boosted her morale and helped her out of her hormonal slump.

The phone rang, and she reached for it absently as she reviewed the figures on the screen. She guessed it was Bert, calling to suggest a night for dinner.

"Hello?"

"Hillary's House of Harlots?" Nate asked.

Karma felt herself smile. She also experienced a sudden shortness of breath. "Yes, it is. You sound healthy. Hadley didn't push you off the mountain for having spent the night with me?" She closed her eyes and put a hand over her mouth when she heard her own words.

Nate heard her involuntary intake of breath and grinned. "No. She did try to walk me to death, though. I'm a foot shorter than the last time you saw me."

"Aw... I have a dozen more roses than the last time you saw me. Did you leave them?"

"I did," he replied. "I figured you probably already

had enough letters and bills. Your message said they turned your day around. Were you having a problem?''

"Probably postnatal depression. I thought it was a myth, or that work would keep it at bay. But..." She sighed, putting a fingertip to a silky red petal. "It seems to be very real. One moment I'm thrilled at the possibilities of my new world. And the next, I'm overwhelmed by my responsibilities.''

"I think that's a pretty typical reaction to childbirth— even for women who have help. You're sure there's nothing I can do?''

It would be so easy to say yes. She was managing to get *some* work done, but she'd have to accomplish a lot more before she could feel that Endicott Accounting was really back in business. In fact, Garrett was beginning to stir and fuss. That was all it took to make mincemeat of her productivity.

And she *wanted* to do this alone. This attraction to Nate Foster was probably the result of her body's hormonal riot since she'd given birth, and she couldn't change plans in midstream because of it.

"Thank you," she made herself say. "But I have Garrett in a front pack, and I got a little work done today. I just have to learn to cope.''

"Why," he asked quietly, "do you have to learn to cope *alone?*''

"Because I am alone," she said.

"By design, not by destiny.''

Karma gripped the phone, momentarily without an argument. "Does it matter?" she asked finally.

Of course it did, but he doubted there was any point in arguing that now. He tried another tack.

"So, if I understand things correctly, every debit requires a credit. Am I right?''

She sensed a trap, but she couldn't deny the facts. "That's right."

"Then, if I debited roses in your mailbox, you're required to credit my dinner table with your presence."

"Ah…" Karma considered that curious accounting maneuver with excitement and trepidation. She'd love it, but she couldn't afford to love it too much. "The currency is a little fuzzy, but I think that's two debits. A debit is a placement, a credit is a removal."

"Piece of cake," Nate said. "We credit your house and debit my dinner table."

She had to laugh. It was all so absurd.

"I appreciate the invitation," she said, "but I haven't really lined up a sitter yet, not that I'd want to leave Garrett this soon any…"

"That's what diaper bags, infant seats and those nifty wooden high chairs that can be turned upside down to hold them are for. Chez Pasta has them. I'll pick you and Garrett up at seven."

"But—"

The line was dead. Karma smiled at the squirmy baby. "Well," she said. "We have a dinner date."

I'M PLEASED ABOUT THAT. What'll we wear? I have that new outfit. The ducks are a little frivolous, but the bow tie is a sophisticated touch.

"HI. Are you… Whoa!" Nate stopped just inside the door, with a hand to his heart. He'd never seen Karma wearing makeup and with her hair combed. The sight of her stopped him in his tracks.

She was gorgeous. Her long, dark hair was straight as rainfall, and swung past her shoulders like a shimmering jet curtain. Thin bangs skimmed naturally dark eyebrows over thickly lashed brown eyes. Her cheeks were pink, her lips a darker shade of cherry.

She wore a pants outfit in a turquoise color that at first glance disappointed him. It was oversize, and though he knew the look to be fashionable, he shared most males' preference for the also-fashionable snug mini.

Then she crossed the room, beckoning to him to follow, and he saw that the voluminous silk moved seductively around her, flatteringly molding itself to her curves, draping tauntingly into the hollows. The color darkened her eyes and brightened her cheeks. Even the bulk of her wrapped arm in the left sleeve did nothing to diminish the impact. His breath caught in his throat. He had to clear it to speak.

"You don't look like an accountant," he said.

Karma felt every tendency toward common sense she possessed warn her to tell him she'd changed her mind.

Nate wore a simple pair of jeans with a white shirt, open at the throat, and a black linen blazer. His golden brown hair was side-parted and combed into order, a small wave at the side already resisting his good grooming.

She watched his blue eyes look her over—and approve what they saw with a masculine tilt of his eyebrow that spoke volumes. She knew she was in emotional danger. The self-protective instinct to tell him that she'd changed her mind, that Garrett felt feverish, was very strong.

But the impulse to face danger head-on was even stronger. And she couldn't quite believe that, because she'd never been a thrill seeker. She'd always avoided the unknown, the ungovernable, knowing they would only wreak havoc upon her orderly existence.

Childbirth has done this to me, she thought absently, as he took the step that brought them within touching distance. Having a baby has made me crazy.

He cupped her head in his hand and lowered his until their noses touched. "I *have* to kiss you," he said.

He smelled like the ocean on a windy day. "Well, if you *have* to…"

Karma felt his other hand slip around her waist, warm and strong and confidently competent. It held her against him as his mouth closed over hers, slowly, tenderly, expressively.

She counted her heartbeats, because they were so loud—and because counting was what she did. Then she lost count and got confused. Her heart beat fast, and everything else inside her seemed also to develop a pulse.

Mild panic began to develop. She pushed gently at his shoulder.

Nate drew away at the first sign of resistance, frankly surprised he'd gotten that far. Not that he was calculating his advance, but he knew how reluctant she was to let a man get close. He wondered if he did indeed have some appeal for her, or if she simply wasn't as reluctant as she thought she was. He considered it his masculine duty to find out.

"You look gorgeous when you're not in labor," he said with a grin. "Where's Garrett?"

Karma went to the overstuffed chair on which she'd placed the infant carrier. Garrett, all bundled up in a quilted baby blanket in shades of blue, gurgled at him and made wide, uncoordinated gestures with his hands.

HELLO! How've you been? I missed you. I hear we're going to dinner. That's great. I'll have what you're having.

"WE CAN'T STAY very late," Karma said, pausing to lock the door as Nate waited for her on the top step. "I'm working on the Brighton Construction payroll. I have only three more days to get it to them."

"Karma," he said gently, chidingly, holding the carrier in one hand and reaching the other toward her to help her down the steps. "You know what happened to Cinderella when constraints were placed upon her evening."

"Cinderella didn't have a baby."

"Only because no one troubled to write the sequel."

Chapter Six

"Oh! A brand-new baby!" Two waitresses greeted Nate and Karma as the host saw them to a table by a window. The young women placed one of the wooden high chairs Nate had talked about upside down at the side of the table and placed the infant carrier on it. "Aren't you just adorable?" they cooed over Garrett.

Hi! Yes, I guess I am kind of cute. Or maybe it's the tie. I'll have whatever Nate's having.

A BAND OF FOG invaded the sunny evening, clouding the sunset and enfolding the dusk like a tulle scarf. The lights that marked the ship channel were visible, their glow magnified by the prismatic effect of the fog. Karma watched the serene view as Nate tried to show her how to roll pasta onto her fork.

She turned her attention to him. "Is this a skill one would *want* to perfect?" she teased.

He seemed surprised that she'd asked. "We have contests in the hospital cafeteria. Try it."

She did, then shook her head over her awkward efforts. "Aren't you supposed to do it on a spoon? Maybe that would be easier."

"No," he said in disgust. "Spoons are for sissies. Just pin your fork to the plate and turn it."

Karma tried again. Several strands of pasta flew off her plate, and the rest refused to adhere to her fork. She dropped it in disgust.

"I give up. I don't have one drop of Italian blood in me. It's probably ethnically impossible for me to do this. Did you have an Italian grandparent, or something?"

"Roommate in college," he said, holding up his fork to show her, with a superior glance, an expertly rolled ball of pasta. "Antonio D'Oro. Loved opera. Got all the girls."

"*All* the girls?" she questioned, resigned to cutting her pasta into manageable pieces. "Is he the one who taught you your charm with the ladies who mambo and mountain climb?"

"Somewhat," Nate admitted with a grin. "At the heart of my success is the fact that I like them. And most women—most people—just want to be liked."

"But in romance," she said cautiously, "isn't it awkward to…like…a lot of women? I mean, what happens when the mambo queen meets Hiking Hadley?"

He shook his head, sprinkling more Parmesan on his pasta. "Nothing. They're not serious. And neither am I."

"You mean," she asked with a puzzled frown, "they want to be liked, but not seriously? How can that be?"

He thought about that a moment and shrugged a shoulder. "Well, Emmie's just a happy free agent. Alexa, too, I think. Hadley would like to get serious, maybe. But she's seeing an anthropology professor, too. She'll have to get serious with him."

Karma stabbed a bite of red pepper. "Alexa? That's a new one on me."

"Sorry. She's my cultural connection. Loves galleries and museums and theater openings."

"I didn't realize there were that many in Heron Point."

"A few. But she lives down the coast, and spends a lot of time in Portland. She's a decorator."

Karma leaned her chin on her fist and studied him. "How many more are there? And how do you keep them all straight?"

"Ah…" He narrowed one eye as he appeared to calculate. "Maris is a lawyer who also happens to be a weekend sailor, and Barb's a reporter for the *Herald*. Loves to go to movies and talk politics. They're all interesting and good company. We just fit into each other's schedules when we can. They all know I see other women, and I hold no claims on them."

"And you don't feel special about any particular one?"

He made a straight-line gesture with his fork that Karma interpreted as a no. "We all know it's just for the moment, and that's comfortable for all of us."

She shook her head, still confused. "Why would it be comfortable," she asked, "to not be special? To just be one of five or six?"

He frowned at her. "Maybe they consider it preferable to being alone. You may prefer solitude, but not every woman does."

"But too much company," she argued reasonably, "is not much different from too little. I mean—it ends up the same, doesn't it? When you're finished being temporary—you're alone again."

Nate examined the logic of that and decided he didn't

want to touch it. "Can we talk about something else?" he asked. "Tell me about your business. About your plans." She smiled suddenly. She glanced at the baby, found him still fast asleep, and reached for a breadstick. She snapped it in half and offered Nate a piece.

He was sure the gesture was unconscious, but he enjoyed it all the same.

"I'd love to have an office one day," she said, her eyes losing focus as she thought about it. "Outside my home, I mean. And I know just where."

"Where?"

"In the Chambers Office Building, fronting the park. I can't afford the rent yet, but someday. There's an upstairs office with a skylight." She lifted her shoulders in a gesture of happy anticipation that made him smile.

"Is there room for a crib?"

She shook her head. "I'll probably have to hire a nanny when I get to that point." She reached out to touch Garrett's sleeping form. "I love him to pieces, but he's already very vocal. I don't think I'd get very much done with him around." She grinned at him. "And *you'll* be back to work by then."

"There's an older woman in town who takes care of babies," he said, searching his brain to try to remember the name. "Jo Arceneau at Coffee Country was going to use her, but she changed her mind. She could give you some details about her."

Karma nodded. "I'm determined to try to cope for a month, then I'm going to have to get serious about work again. Is Jo back to running her business already?"

"No. Devon's spelling her for a while."

"Right. The student." She smiled speculatively. "I think he has a thing for her. I mean, I don't know either of them very well, but I've seen him watch her, and I think he has more than business on his mind. But then, I think the baby's father does, too. In our Lamaze classes, he always seemed so intense when he touched her.''

Nate laughed lightly. ''There are a lot of convoluted relationships in our little town.''

Karma laughed, too. ''And *you* have most of them.'' She put her coffee cup to her lips as he stopped chewing a bite of his breadstick to give her a scolding glance.

KARMA WAS DETERMINED not to invite Nate inside, but the phone was ringing when she unlocked the door, and Garrett, frustrated because the comforting motion of the car had stopped, was screaming at the top of his lungs.

''Get the phone,'' Nate said. ''I've got the baby.''

It was Bert. ''Where have you *been?*'' she demanded. ''I was beginning to get worried. If you didn't answer this time, I was going to come over there with the police!''

''To dinner,'' Karma replied calmly, aware of Nate taking Garrett out of the carrier and pacing across the living room with him. She turned her back to him.

There was a surprised silence on the other end of the line. ''With whom?''

''Nate Foster.'' Karma strove to sound nonchalant. ''And he's here. Can I call you back?''

''Is he staying the night again?''

''Bert…''

''All right, call me back.''

''My friend Bert,'' Karma explained to Nate from the kitchen, where she ran a bottle of milk under warm water. ''She was worried because I wasn't home.''

Nate came toward her, the plump, fussy baby held in one arm against the preppy elegance of his blazer.

That picture of him had been imprinted on her mind since the time he'd shown up at midnight to check on her. She loved the one-handed confidence with which he held Garrett, his manner relaxed despite the baby's cries.

Well, if I were a doctor, she thought wryly, I could be relaxed, too, instead of thinking my baby's always at death's door.

He leaned back against the counter beside her, holding Garrett right up to his face and looking into his big-eyed stare. The baby stopped crying.

OKAY, okay. I like you, too. But if you leave again, I'm going to be upset.

"So, what's the problem, buddy?" Nate asked. "Or are you trying to establish a nightly routine of mental anguish for your mom?"

WE WENT TO DINNER, and I clearly remember ordering whatever you were having. But nobody brought me anything.

"IT ISN'T OUR FAULT you slept through dinner," Nate said. Garrett's brow furrowed as he concentrated on his face. His little mouth worked into an O. "But we appreciate it. You gave us time to talk."

Nate reached a hand out for the bottle. Karma handed it to him, thinking that she shouldn't. She should thank him politely for a lovely dinner and explain that she had to be up early to deliver the payroll.

But there was that pleasure in watching him with the baby. There was something artful and touching in the long, lean muscles wrapped around the helpless little bundle, the big hand that could cover Garrett from ankle to chin.

She was surprised by the emotion it stirred in her, the little niggling of pain she felt at the thought that this was simply a momentary thing, that the man Garrett studied in fascination didn't really belong here.

Nate looked up from feeding the baby and surprised a look of... He wasn't sure what it was. There was a wistful smile on her lips, and a paradoxical combination of pleasure and sadness in her eyes.

It confused and unsettled him. He liked to think he understood women. He was always honest with them, and he appreciated it when they were honest with him.

Karma had told him she wanted to be alone. He'd suspected that wasn't as true as she thought it was, but that look in her eyes seemed to confirm his suspicion. She looked very much as though she wanted...him.

But *he* didn't want that. Did he? At least not in that way. He'd have enjoyed seeing desire in her eyes. But need? That was something else again.

Still, he felt an excitement he couldn't understand. He should be feeling panic.

Karma took the baby from him and ignored Garrett's loud protest.

I WANT him. How many times do I have to... Oh, what's that? Food. Okay.

KARMA BOUNCED HIM in her good arm, her injured one holding the bottle. He began to suck greedily again.

"Thank you, Nate," she said. "I enjoyed dinner very much. And I'll keep practicing that spaghetti roll."

Nate noticed a curious finality in her tone. The panic he should have felt a moment ago, he felt now.

"What are you doing tomorrow?" he asked.

"I'm working on Brighton's payroll," she said briskly, "then I might call Jo Arceneau about the sitter."

"I'll bring dinner over tomorrow night," he said.

That sounded wonderful. But she knew better than to believe it could be. "No. That wouldn't work."

He raised an eyebrow. "Dinner wouldn't work?"

She frowned at him. "You know what I mean. *We* wouldn't work. You're content with just-for-the-moment relationships, and I now have a baby to think about. I can't do anything just for the moment. So I'm going to follow my original instinct."

He studied her evenly, then asked, "To remain alone, you mean?"

She angled her chin. It was her decision. "Yes."

He nodded as though he understood. But something about the jut of *his* chin told her it wasn't going to be so simple.

"Well, that's certainly the easy way out," he said.

She shifted the baby's weight and asked coolly, "Easy way out of what?"

"Whatever's going on between us."

"Nothing," she replied, "is going on between us. I'm just...longing for *cozy* things I can't have." She gave the adjective a disparaging emphasis. "Because my hormones are in a tizzy. And, let's face it—" she looked him in the eye "—you're just looking for a woman to fill the sixth night of the week, and I don't think I'd like a class-action relationship."

"I explained that none of the ladies is serious about me, or me about them."

"So, presumably, I'd be expected to see you on that same basis. No."

He folded his arms. "Well, if you're intent on remaining alone, doesn't that suit your purposes?"

Hmm. She chose to sidestep his logic. "I'll be too busy for recreational dating."

He smiled. He couldn't help it. He saw that it annoyed her, and took a certain satisfaction in the fact. "Recreational dating," he repeated. "What a phrase. What do you call the kind of dating that's serious mate hunting? Acquisitions associating? Marriage marketing?"

She glared at him. "Maybe it's time you said goodnight."

He held his ground. "First I want to know what kind of 'cozy' things your hormones are longing for."

He thought for a moment that the question would unsettle her and give him the upper hand.

It did, but for just an instant. She looked vulnerable and desperate. Then she squared her shoulders and fixed him with a steady gaze. "A father for Garrett," she said candidly. "But you don't want to raise anybody's children, remember? Do you really think we have anything more to discuss?"

He thought there was probably volumes, but he was a little unsettled himself at the moment, and he didn't know what the hell to make of her.

He held his ground. "A father for Garrett," he pointed out, "would result in a husband for you. Have you thought about that? Or is there some fancy accounting here I'm unaware of?"

Her shoulders slumped visibly. Garrett began to fuss, and she put him up to her good shoulder. "I said I longed for it. I didn't say I thought I could have it. Please, Nate—"

"All right." He went to the door. She followed and

stood aside as he opened it. He turned to look down at her. "I'm leaving. But the minute I have you figured out, I'm coming back."

She smiled grimly, thinking that should take some time. She didn't understand herself. "Goodbye, Nate," she said. "Thanks for everything."

He took hold of her shoulders suddenly, apparently changing his mind about leaving. He pulled her close.

WHAT'S GOING ON, Mother? That feels good. It reminds me of the first time I saw you. He had his arms around us then, too.

"So, according to your double-entry bookkeeping system," he began. Karma rolled her eyes, knowing he was about to use his creative logic to try to undermine hers once again. "You were debited with dinner, so I should be credited with something."

"You can be given credit," she said smugly, "for an aggravatingly persistent nature."

He gave her a reproachful smile. "I mean credited as in an accounting sense."

"No. You see, *I* was debited with roses," she explained patiently, "and we debited *you* with my presence at dinner." She shook her head at him with concern. "You're just not getting the hang of this, are you? If I credit you, I have to take something from you. Remember? I explained this all to you yester—"

He cut her off with a nod. "I understand. I *want* you to take something from me."

Her brow furrowed. "What?"

He maintained a blandly innocent expression. "A kiss."

She looked back at him a full ten seconds, then expelled a nervous little breath. "Nate, I don't—"

"You said the world turns on it," he insisted. "A debit requires a credit. An action somewhere generates a reaction some—"

"All *right!*" She stopped him with a sharp tone of voice that was directly at odds with the trembling, melting feeling inside her. "Do you think you can keep your mouth closed that long?"

He looked dismayed, though there was amusement in his eyes. "If that's the kind of kiss you want to take. But I was rather hoping…"

She closed her eyes to summon up patience. And to help her resist the impulse to laugh. "I mean, can you be quiet that long?"

"I promise to try."

"Good. Are you ready?"

"Oh, yes."

He freed her hand, letting both of his fall to his sides. She took that as a sign that the initiative was hers.

She knew this was major trouble, but she'd be damned if she'd let him think she was afraid of this contact, as he'd suggested several days before. As Bert had suggested.

It occurred to her that, deep down, she had to prove it to herself. She had to give it everything she had.

Nate awaited her touch with a heart that had flatlined in anticipation. One more moment of waiting, and some cardiologist would have to crack his chest and massage his heart by hand. Garrett gurgled. Nate took him from her.

Karma raised her hand to the side of his head and combed her fingertips through the short hair there. He felt every pad of every finger against his scalp. Sensation rippled all the way down his spinal column. He struggled to keep his free hand still.

Her fingers explored his hair, slipped slowly down the nape of his neck, then tugged, encouraging him to lower his head.

He watched her eyes as he complied, and saw that they were focused on his mouth. The effort to remain passive became monumental.

Her lips were parted—in concentration, he guessed, rather than in passion. But he parted his on the chance that he was wrong.

He was.

The first touch of her mouth to his seemed to ignite something inside her that changed the contact from a game of one-upmanship to a deadly-serious communication.

Her lips were warm and pliant, and her tongue traced his for an instant in a cautious exploration. Then it delved inside, as though caution were the last thing on her mind.

And that was when he lost restraint.

Karma wasn't sure what was happening to her, except that for the second time ever in her recollection, she was following a path she knew to be dangerous. It was little comfort that he'd also been responsible for the first time.

She could have kept the kiss simple. She should have. But his mouth was warm and mobile and so deliciously tender that she had to know more. It was as though she found herself in some dark and velvety place that beckoned her deeper.

She felt his hand splayed between her shoulder blades, then in her hair, holding her close as his tongue toyed with hers. The earth spun out of control, and she clutched at his shoulder, the baby between her and him.

Nate's hand moved down to her back and roved over her hip, confident and possessive. She heard her own little groan against his mouth.

Garrett screeched—loudly.

HELLO. Does anyone remember I'm here? I'm happy that you're *happy, but I believe I have a hand jammed between two of Nate's ribs. Mother?*

KARMA DREW BACK and took the baby from Nate, horrified that, for an instant, her needs and not Garrett's had been uppermost in her mind.

"Oh, baby," she said apologetically, holding him up to study his puckered little face. "Are you all right? Did I hurt you?"

JUST MY FEELINGS. Can we eat now?

NATE WATCHED her fuss with the baby, and tried to calm his rampant libido. So. He was right. She'd convinced her brain that she wanted to be alone with her baby, but her body had other ideas. He suspected her heart did, too.

But she smiled at him with every appearance of control. "Well, there we are. Debit dinner, credit kiss. We're square. Goodbye, Nate."

He studied her—her face flushed, her hair rumpled from his hand, Garrett wriggling fussily at her shoulder—and decided that goodbye was the only solution. They were a powder keg and he was a lit match. The obvious result of their union would not be healthy for either of them.

The strange thing was that, though he knew that to be true, at some basic level where he made all serious decisions, he didn't seem to care.

He simply smiled and reached a hand to Garrett's back. "See you," he said, and walked out the door.

Garrett began screaming immediately.

No. I want Nate to stay. Where's he going? Call him back.

WITH A GROAN, Karma closed and locked the door, accepting that she was probably in for another sleepless night. But she'd done the right thing. She was sure of it.

"Do *YOU* THINK I did the right thing?" Karma leaned over Garrett, who had just been diapered and changed. He was inspecting a bright orange cloth toy shaped like a pumpkin. "You know, I *thought* I had, but—" she looked around surreptitiously "—I wouldn't admit this to just anyone, but I've missed him. I know you have, too."

Garrett hit her in the face with the pumpkin. She took that for an affirmative.

"But maybe I did do the right thing, because we said goodbye almost three weeks ago, and he hasn't called."

MOTHER. Goodbye means you're going away. That's why he hasn't called. You could call him. He has that phone thing that he carries with him. What is this, anyway? Do I eat it?

"WELL, we're doing fine, aren't we?" Karma lifted Garrett and placed him in the swing she'd put near the

computer. "I'm picking up more work all the time, and
I've even figured out how to do it with you around, you
little noise machine, and with me having only one good
hand to work with. I still haven't figured out how to
work sleep into the equation, but you have to start sleeping nights sometime. *Tell* me you're going to be sleeping nights sometime."

*BUT I LOVE IT when I wake up and it's dark and lonely
and I see your face over my crib.*

"WELL, look, Garrett. I want to talk to you about Friday
night. See, I've been invited to Diantha's party." Karma
sat at the computer and spoke to her son as she called
up Davis Dentistry on the screen.

*OH, good. A party. I like those. Is this Diantha person
bringing pizza like Aunt Bert does?*

"IT'S NOT THE KIND where friends come over and we
all curl up on the sofa and watch you be cute. I'm going
out to this one, and you're going to stay here with Aunt
Bert. You know how much she loves babies."

*THEN LET HER stay with one. Maybe one of those dorky
girls that are always at Coffee Country when we go in
there. I want to go to the party.*

"I WON'T BE GONE for very long, but I probably should
go, because I spend so much time with you that I feel
as though I'm losing all my social skills. Not that I was
ever very good at them, anyway. And not that you're
not stimulating company, but I need adults, you know.
People who will talk to me. And this is a Halloween

party. That's why we have a jack-o'-lantern on the kitchen table, and smiling paper ghosts taped to the windows. Next year I'll take you trick-or-treating. But this year you have to stay home.''

OH. So all this effort I'm making to carry on a conversation isn't appreciated. Well, that's fine. Go to your party. I'll stay home with Aunt Bert and tell her all about my day and see if she isn't fascinated. Don't think twice about me. I'll just mind my own business in this thing that bounces me around while that obnoxious music plays over and over.

KARMA WATCHED GARRETT happily occupied in the swing, and felt as though she were finally getting somewhere as a mother and as an accountant. Experience lent her a certain facility with him that was providing her comfort and excitement and reinforcing her conviction that having a baby had been a good idea.

She simply skipped over in her mind the idea of the baby having a father. It was too confusing and upsetting to contemplate, and she felt as though she'd reclaimed control of her life and her situation.

The baby was thriving, and the business was getting healthier every day. She was reestablishing organization, and she took satisfaction in that sense of having everything in her life in its proper place.

She smiled at Garrett. ''I was so smart to have you,'' she said. ''And I was smart to say goodbye to Nate Foster.''

DON'T TRY TO CHARM ME. I'm not speaking to you.

''ALL RIGHT. I want to know how you got your figure back in five short weeks. In that flapper dress, you look about a size three! You even look wonderful with your arm in a cast!''

A dancehall girl wearing theatrical makeup, a dime-size beauty mark on her cheek and a smile that looked vaguely familiar forced a cup of punch into Karma's hand and backed her into a corner. ''What are you using? A fat-free diet? The 'Buns of Steel' video? A shake for breakfast and lunch and a sensible meal for dinner?''

Karma peered at the painted face. ''Nancy?''

''Yes. Why? Have the six pounds I've gained made it impossible to tell?''

''Will you *stop* with the six pounds!'' A tall blond Southern belle appeared at Nancy's shoulder. She swatted her arm with her folded fan. ''No one is aware of it but you. You look wonderful.'' She shook her head at Nancy, then turned her attention to Karma. ''Hi. Remember me? Jo Arceneau, from Coffee Country and Serena Borders's Lamaze class?''

''Yes, of course.'' Karma smiled. ''Congratulations on your daughter. Life with a baby is certainly a revelation, isn't it?''

Jo laughed. ''Really. Who'd have guessed we could get by with so little sleep, and so little confidence in what we're doing.''

''I was clever enough to marry a man who already had two children of his own,'' Nancy said with a teasingly superior air. ''His experience was invaluable.''

Jo didn't seem to see the advantage. ''But for the past five weeks, you've been coping with a new baby *and* two small boys. That can't have been fun.''

Nancy smiled, her eyes filled with warmth. ''It's been wonderful.''

Jo frowned at Karma. ''She's entirely too cheerful.

Do you have any bad news with which we could douse her good humor? Diantha! Great party!''

A bejeweled Gypsy, gray hair wound into a bun into which she'd placed tiny flowers, hurried by in a flurry of colorful skirts. "Hi, everyone!" Diantha said. "Eat lots, and don't worry—the stars promise svelte bodies for all."

Jo elbowed Nancy. "Hear that?"

As Diantha bustled away, a vampire appeared in their midst with the swirl of a black silk cape. It fluttered about Jo as he wrapped an arm around her.

She smiled up at him, then at her companions. "You all know the count. Ryan, remember Karma Endicott from our Lamaze class?"

"Of course." He smiled and offered his free hand. "How's the baby?"

"Growing," she said vaguely, studying his face. "You have no fangs, Count."

"He keeps them in a glass on the bedside table," Jo said with a laugh.

He raised his cape to cover her mouth. "It's ethnic," he said with an exaggeratedly cultured accent. "My family's from southern Transylvania. There's a strong Bulgarian influence. No fangs."

Jo pulled his hand down. "Just a lot of 'bull.'" She laughed heartily at her own joke, then looked around the silent group. "Bull—get it? *Bul*garia. Just a lot of bull."

Ryan Jeffries grabbed the arm of a passing pirate and pulled him into their midst. "Hey, Blackbeard. Do you have a plank Jo could walk?"

Karma recognized Jave Nicholas under the woolly beard and mustache. His coat was made of a colorful brocade, and he carried a plumed hat. He managed somehow to look handsomely piratical, despite the phony accessories.

"What's her offense?" he asked.

"Bad jokes," Nancy replied.

"I regret," he said, "that my plank remains in the harbor with my ship."

Nancy put a hand to her hip in a gesture of displeasure. "Well, what a silly place to keep it."

"I do, however," he said, giving Nancy a quelling glance, "know a gentleman who *can* see that she suffers for her misdeeds." He looked around the crowded room, apparently spotted his quarry, and beckoned. "Over here, Officer!"

A policeman appeared in full blue uniform, leather belt creaking at his waist. "Trouble, matey?" he asked.

Karma's heart lurched as the man's bright blue eyes met hers. They didn't register surprise, though she was sure *hers* did.

"Matey?" Jave repeated, apparently taking issue with the name. "I'm the scourge of the seas. The terror of the Barbary Coast."

Nate nodded. "Sorry. Is there a problem, Mr. Scourge, sir?"

Jave fluffed the lace at his sleeves. "That's better. This young woman—" he indicated Jo "—has offended her companions with bad jokes."

"My," Nate said, unhooking the handcuffs from his belt. "Comedic crime. That's a felony. Come along, young lady."

He reached out so suddenly, so smoothly, that Karma didn't see trouble coming. But the next moment, there was a handcuff around her wrist.

"But, it's Jo who…"

"I'm sure the bad joke," he said in explanation to

the foursome that watched him prepare to take away what they considered the wrong perpetrator, ''was due to *this* woman's bad influence. We must fight crime at its source.''

''Ah...'' Karma tried to protest, but the music and laughter were very loud, and she was being led away by the second half of the handcuffs, which was now closed around Nate's wrist.

Chapter Seven

"You have the right to remain silent," Nate advised Karma as he pulled her out onto Diantha's front porch and closed the door behind them. He led her to a cushioned wicker love seat, then saw that it was occupied by a life-size scarecrow holding a pumpkin.

He changed direction and headed for the railing that ran the length of the porch. He leaned a hip on it where the porch column connected, and braced a foot on the railing. That allowed him to pull Karma right up against him.

She found his sudden nearness almost paralyzing. In the weak porch light, his blue eyes, now on a level with hers, looked dark and intense, despite the amusement she saw there, and his white-toothed smile seemed wolfishly dangerous. His fresh-scented cologne mingled with the salty, autumnal fragrance of the night. Her heart raced. Her pulse thumped. Everything else inside her waited.

"You have the right to remain silent," he repeated softly, his free arm snaking around her waist. "But I wouldn't recommend it."

"Why not?" she asked in a whisper.

"Because I want the whole truth, and nothing but the truth."

"About what?"

His arm tightened, and she felt every soft curve of her body in contact with every muscled plane of his.

"About whether or not you missed me."

Impulse told her to melt against him and tell him the truth. She'd thought about him often. Relived their dinner over and over. Dreamed of him holding Garrett, holding her. Missed him terribly.

But common sense reminded her that, apart from those inexplicable feelings, she was coping fine without him.

"I thought about you," she admitted, trying to wedge a little space between them. Feeling his muscled warmth against her was making it difficult to think. But he didn't loosen his grip, and she quickly discovered that wriggling was a mistake. They were far too close to move *anything* without serious consequences. "I don't imagine you missed me, with Emmie, Hadley, Alexa, Maris and Barb to keep you company these past three weeks."

He shook his head, his eyes roving her features with frowning concentration. "I haven't seen them. You look lovely, but you look tired. Not sleeping?"

"How come you haven't seen them?" she asked. She tugged on her right arm, which he had cuffed to his left. "Nobody who has a baby gets any sleep. And I've been working a lot. Business is picking up."

He lifted his wrist to accommodate her movements. "I'm glad about your business, but don't ruin your health. I haven't seen my ladies because I was on vacation. What *are* you doing with that arm?"

If she raised her arm, his hand lay against her breast.

If she lowered it, her hand lay against the inside of his thigh. She couldn't help fidgeting.

"Well…it's just awkward," she said. "One arm in a cast, and the other in a handcuff. Can't you unlock us?"

"No," he replied, clearly without giving the matter any consideration. "But maybe I can make you more comfortable." He turned her around so that her back was to him, and pulled her against his body. His cuffed arm circled her waist. "Better?" he asked, his breath a soft tickle against her ear.

"Sort of," she replied breathlessly. His legs cradled her body, and she felt both deliciously comfortable and as though she were about to fall off an emotional cliff. "So you finally went to Canada?"

"Yes, I did."

"And you had a great time?"

"No, I didn't."

"You didn't?" She turned her head in surprise. She stopped just short of turning her body, remembering that she'd probably dump them both off the railing. "I thought you wanted solitude in the wilderness, you and nature and a panful of trout."

"That was before I met you," he said, planting a kiss just behind her ear. "That was when I was a happy bachelor looking for adventure."

His words and his actions were elevating her blood pressure. "Aren't you…anymore?"

"I don't know," he replied honestly. "I'm confused." He nipped the lobe of her ear. "And it's all your fault. Yours and Garrett's. I went away finally because you were driving me crazy. I thought the solitude would allow me to clear my mind and just *be* for a couple of weeks. But…"

He sighed. His breath ran along the cord of her neck and made her shiver.

"Cold?" he asked, holding her closer, wrapping his other arm around her, too.

"I'm fine," she said softly, her voice strained. "But what?"

"Well...you know what's wrong with solitude?"

"What?"

"It encourages you to think. And all I could think of was you. So I spent a weekend at a campsite, where there were other people, but that was worse."

"Why?"

"It was filled with families. Men with women, couples with babies, children with grandparents, all kinds of cross-generational groups having a wonderful time together."

"And that's bad?"

"If you're trying to convince yourself that that isn't what you want, it is."

"So, you came home."

"No." He leaned forward and put his cheek to hers. "I stayed and observed—jealously."

Because of their position, she was forced to lean back against him or topple them both forward. "Why jealously?"

"Because," he said moodily, thoughtfully, "I never had that. Well, I guess I did while my mother was alive, when I was small enough to forget the details of what it was like to live in a family, but not too small to retain the longing to have it again. I went to military school at seven, then to college, then to medical school, then into residency at a Portland hospital. My memories consist primarily of meals at a cafeteria table, nights in a dormitory, and people who moved in and out of my life but never stayed. I remember a father who was simply an acquaintance.''

Karma turned her head to look into his eyes. She saw the sadness of his last statement there. She kissed his cheek. There was nothing sexual in the gesture, though only moments earlier the air had been charged with sexuality. She offered pure and simple comfort. That was why he loved chaos, she thought. It filled the emptiness.

''I'm sorry,'' she said. ''That's what you get for getting involved with my labor.. You should have gone to Canada the day your vacation started.''

He pulled her back so that they remained cheek to cheek, and he laughed. ''As I recall, you had a death grip on me. Anyway…'' His tone had changed. He'd put memories aside. ''I discovered that I missed you a hell of a lot. And Garrett, too. And if you don't agree to spend some time with me, I'll have to lock you up and throw the key away.''

She frowned at his logic. ''If you locked me up, you wouldn't be able to see me anyway.''

He nipped at her ear. ''You're so innocent. I'd lock you up at *my* place, and throw away the key.''

''Oh, of course.''

''I have an A-frame at the edge of Eaton's Woods. Tom Nicholas…'' He stopped abruptly and raised a questioning eyebrow. ''You know Tom?''

She nodded. ''I do his taxes, and I run into him once in a while at Coffee Country.''

Nate went on. ''He's a good carpenter. Just put a deck on for me. My house is rustic and warm, and generally stays pretty tidy, because I don't get to spend that much time there. I think you'd like it.''

''It sounds wonderful,'' she admitted. ''But much as I might enjoy being locked up there, it wouldn't be very good for my business. I think I'll just invite you to dinner once in a while instead."

He tipped her chin back and kissed her throat. "I love a cooperative prisoner."

"Hey, do you two want—" Ryan stepped out onto the porch. The breeze caught his cape and swirled it around him. He peered into the weak light. "Aren't I supposed to be doing that? Nibbling on necks is *my* prerogative."

"Ryan!" Jo caught his arm and tried to pull him back inside. "I don't think they'd have come out onto the porch if they wanted you gawking at them."

"What's happening?" Jave's bearded face peered out behind Jo's.

"Where?" Nancy squeezed between him and Jo.

Nate let his head fall back against the column with a thunk. "Life in a small town. You can't even take your girl onto the porch without everyone coming out to watch."

"Your girl?" Nancy asked, then added, with delight in her voice, "Really?" She turned to Jo. "Isn't that nice?"

"It's great," Jo agreed, trying to push everyone back inside. But they resisted. "So wouldn't it be nice if we gave them a little privacy?"

"No," Jave said. "We're about to have a quick meeting about the hospital's Christmas party, and we need Nate. He's the one who can fix everything."

"Jeez," Nate grumbled. "Is it that time again?"

"What time?" Jo asked Nancy.

Nancy deferred to Jave with a wave of her hand.

"The hospital throws a big party," he explained, "for all the underprivileged children in the county. We collect used toys for weeks, and repair and paint them so that every child gets a present." He smiled blandly at the group collected on the porch. "I'm chairman this year, so I'm enlisting all of you to help. So be prepared. From now until Christmas, your homes are going to become repositories for other people's junk, which you will have to rejuvenate into works of art." Jave grinned at Nate. "Much as I hate to credit Dr. Foster with any talent at all, he's the one who can always get the most decrepit toy to work. So I'm afraid you'll have to continue this rendezvous after the meeting. Duty calls."

"Does it not strike you as strange," Nate asked, steadying Karma on her feet as he lowered his own foot from the railing, "that we're having a meeting about a Christmas party while dressed for Halloween?"

Ryan shrugged. "It might, if this group had any standard for normalcy. But it includes you and Jave. Need I say more?"

"You're lucky it does, Ryan," Jave said, opening the front door and ushering everyone inside. "Because you're going to *need* a doctor. Everyone into Diantha's office."

"OKAY." Jave was seated behind Diantha's desk, where their hostess had left soft drinks and nibbles before hurrying back to her other guests. He studied the list he'd made on a yellow pad during the meeting. "Nancy's in charge of decorations, Jo is taking care of goodies with help from Diantha, I'm going to do press releases about the project and contact service groups, Ryan will arrange to have the bank used as a downtown collection site, and of course we'll use the hospital, too. Nate will repair toys that don't work, and we'll all pitch in to paint them and spruce up whatever's donated." He looked from face to face. "We're all agreed?"

''Agreed,'' they said in unison.

Jave grinned wryly. ''Tom will be helping, of course, but most of you witnessed his row with Amy earlier this evening, so neither of them is available at the moment.''

The group exchanged sympathetic glances.

''You didn't assign Karma anything,'' Nancy noted. ''I'm sure she wants to help.''

Jave turned to Karma.

''I do,'' she said. ''I'll make a cash contribution.''

Nate and Karma sat together in a battered love seat. He'd removed the handcuffs.

She almost regretted the fact.

''You don't really think you're going to get off that easy, do you?'' Nate asked.

''I have to,'' she insisted. ''The end of the year is a very busy time for me.''

He frowned at her. ''But it's going to be Garrett's first Christmas. You have to get in the spirit of this do. You can't do that by making a *cash contribution*.'' He repeated her words with obvious displeasure.

''Oh, come on,'' Karma said. ''Christmas 'spirit' is that warm, fuzzy euphoria generated by the merchant community to make the consumer spend. Christmas should be a time for spiritual reflection and renewal.''

''And in that spirit,'' Nate said, ''you're going to give *money?*''

Karma waited for someone in the group to support her position. But they appeared to be watching the by-play with interest.

''I'm *busy,*'' she pleaded reasonably. ''I don't have *time* for grand holiday preparations. And I doubt seriously that Garrett will notice.''

''Of course he will,'' Jo insisted. ''He's a Libra.

Chelsea's natal chart could apply to him or to Malia. They're eccentric children. They love fuss and are very aware of color and fragrance and sound. Karma.'' She fixed her with a serious stare. "You have to *make* time for Christmas.''

"You do.'' Nancy supported Jo's position. "Pete and Eddy are already starting to talk about it. And it's not commercialization to them. It's…love and magic.''

"And it's not just for children,'' Jave said. "I have a wonderful time at Christmas. My mother cooks and bakes things she's been making since *I* was a kid, we loosen up, fill the house with gaudy stuff, shop for all the things we've convinced the kids Santa might not be able to find, just so we can see their ecstasy on Christmas morning.''

Nancy went to stand behind him and wrap her arms around him. He crossed his hands over hers. "You don't want to deprive yourself of that.''

"I have to get my business going,'' Karma said feebly.

"Find a way to compromise,'' Ryan suggested, wrapping an arm around Jo and holding her closer. "Jo and I will sit for you a couple of nights so you can take some time to decorate or go shopping.''

She smiled, determined to apply her tried-and-true practices, even though she now had a baby in her life.

"I appreciate that, thank you. But I have the next few months planned, and, at the moment, the best I can do for your project is a cash contribution.''

Jave nodded in concession. "Okay, we'll take it. Ryan's going to set up an account at the bank for other donors who'd like to do the same.''

"Other *Scrooges*,'' Nate whispered in her ear as the meeting broke up. "I'm not giving up on you, Karma

Endicott. Your attitude is reprehensible. Come on. I'll work on you while we're dancing.''

Diantha's living and dining rooms adjoined, and she'd pushed all the furnishings to the edges of the room to accommodate the couples swaying to the music from a CD player.

''Good grief,'' Karma complained as he drew her into the middle of the crowd and wrapped both arms around her. ''I'm not something you can 'work on,' like a broken bone. I suppose all that Christmas stuff is all right if you have time for it. I do believe what it's all about, I just don't see why everyone has to crowd the season with sentimentality to feel as though they've celebrated it.''

''So, you don't send cards?'' he asked, pulling her closer to him as a flamboyant older gentleman dipped his lady with a wide flourish.

She shook her head. ''I include a greeting and a wish for a prosperous New Year with my December statements.''

He rolled his eyes heavenward.

She did the same. ''I suppose you send flocked cards covered with animals in earmuffs singing Christmas carols.''

''No.'' He sounded offended. ''I always look for a magi motif. I like the notion that they wanted to know what was happening, and set off to investigate, willing to take as long and go as far as necessary.'' He grinned. ''Not unlike the mission I've assigned myself of getting *you* into the Christmas spirit.''

''Nate,'' she said patiently, ''can't you just accept me as I am?''

He shook his head. ''Not that part of you. I helped

bring Garrett into this world. I'm not going to abandon him to a mother who doesn't have time for Christmas.''

The party was still going strong when Karma and Nate left, shortly after eleven.

''You don't have to leave,'' Karma told Nate. ''I drove here.''

''I'll follow you home,'' he insisted.

''I had a wonderful time,'' Karma told Diantha, ''but I promised my friend who's baby-sitting that I'd be home by eleven-thirty. She has to go to work in the morning.''

Diantha hugged her, her Gypsy jewelry clicking musically. ''I'm so glad you could come. Now you've got to try to get out more. You Capricorns have to learn to take life a little less seriously.''

Nate pulled up behind Karma in her driveway and got out of his car to walk her to the door. She looked back at his red Jaguar, which was illuminated by a streetlight.

''Wow,'' she said. ''So, that's the famous car that kept you from going on vacation, even after I loosened my death grip on you.''

He'd almost forgotten the story about his car being in for repairs. ''Right,'' he said. ''Good as new now.''

''You want to see Garrett?'' she asked. ''You won't believe how much he's grown.''

''Yes. Please.'' He followed her to the door. It was opened wide by a dark-haired young woman in jeans and a sweatshirt who looked at him with open suspicion.

''Nate, this is the famous Roberta Dawson,'' Karma said, tossing her coat and purse at a chair. ''Bert, meet Dr. Nathan Foster, who performed *your* coaching duties when I delivered Garrett.''

"Really." She offered her hand.

Nate shook it, getting the distinct impression that she didn't like him.

"I know Hadley Brooks," she said. "And Barb Wagner. *And* Alexa Winfield. Is that your entire lineup?"

"Bert!" Karma stopped in her tracks on her way to the bedroom to check on Garrett. "Wha—?"

"It's all right," Nate said, interrupting. "Go check on Garrett. I can take care of myself. As a matter of fact, Miss Dawson, I've also spent some time with Emily Drake and Maris Fuller. If you consider friends a *lineup*." He repeated her word with distaste.

"I just thought you should know that someone was counting. So Karma's number six." She picked up her purse and a paperback novel from the coffee table. "I suppose even God rested on the seventh day."

"Actually, they're all number one," he said quietly. "I value my friends. And I see you value yours."

She looked him over a moment, obviously confused by that last remark. "Karma has a life plan," she said, pointing the book at him. "It's a stupid plan that involves devoting her entire life to her child and her work, and leaving nothing for herself, but I'd hate to see it disturbed for her by someone who has no intention of replacing it with something better."

Karma came back into the room with Garrett in her arms. He looked wide-awake.

Nate reached for him, and Garrett allowed himself to be handed off without complaint. He studied Nate with wide-eyed interest, his hands waving, his legs, in the blanket, kicking.

"Hi, guy!" Nate said, lifting him high, then bringing him down close to his face. "He must have doubled his weight!"

WELL, she keeps feeding me. Every time I ask for some-thing, she puts that bottle in my mouth. How've you been?

KARMA CAME to stand beside Nate, leaning her face close to his shoulder so that she, too, could smile up at the baby. "He's over ten pounds now. Aren't you, chubs?"

THAT'S WHAT the doctor said. But I think he had his thumb on the scale.

GARRETT SMILED WIDELY, deliberately.

"Look at that!" Nate exclaimed.

Karma nodded. "He's been doing that for a couple of days. Tell me you've ever seen a cuter baby."

Nate brought him down again and settled him in his arm. "Well, Jave and Ryan might take issue with that, but then, you know, they've got girls. It takes a *guy* to really know how to turn on the charm."

"Isn't that the truth?" Bert said with a significant glance at him. She slung her purse over her shoulder and headed for the front door. "I'll call you, Karma. Lovely to meet you, Dr. Foster."

"Miss Dawson," Nate called, trailing behind Karma as she followed Bert to the door.

Bert stopped and turned to him, an eyebrow raised in an unspoken question.

"You have nothing to worry about," he said.

"Why?" Karma looked from one to the other. "What is she worried about?"

"Your plan," Nate replied, catching the baby's fin-gers between his lips.

"My plan?" Karma frowned at Bert.

Bert fixed Nate with a threatening stare. "See that I

don't,'' she said, blew the baby a kiss, and walked out the door.

Nate handed Karma the baby.

"I don't get it," she said.

"She thinks," he explained, reaching into his pocket for his keys, "that I intend to lure you out of your organized outline for life, then desert you for another member of my harem, leaving you wounded and vulnerable."

Karma laughed lightly. "I do *her* taxes because she keeps all her records in a Darby's Dresses box, and she worries about *me* being able to control my future?"

"I imagine she's just being a good friend."

"Did you explain to her that that was all you were doing with the other five ladies?"

The question sounded ingenuous, and there was no sign of teasing in her eyes. But he was beginning to know her better than to trust her innocent expression.

"I don't think she'd have believed it—just as you don't. So I'll say good-night. You said something about inviting me to dinner?"

"I have to work through the weekend. How about Monday night?"

"Perfect. I don't go back to work until Wednesday."

"Still the night shift?"

"I prefer it. Or I used to."

Karma didn't want to touch that. "Seven o'clock. With any luck, I'll have Garrett down by then. He slept six hours the other night, and when I woke up, I thought he'd gone into a coma, or been kidnapped, or something. I couldn't believe it."

GEE, Mother. I thought you'd be pleased.

HE LAUGHED and patted the baby's back. "Good night. See you Monday." He stopped at the door, turned and found her right behind him. God, she was beautiful, he thought, letting his eyes wander up the plume in her flapper headband. It made him smile. "Let your mind think about Christmas, okay? Come on. Jave's going to need all of our support, and money's just not going to cut it."

"He seemed to think it would do," she pointed out.

Nate shook his head. "He was just being nice." Then, because he couldn't resist the impulse, he leaned down and kissed her lightly on the lips. "Good night. Sweet dreams."

Garrett started crying when the door closed behind him.

"Garrett, come on," Karma pleaded, heading for the kitchen. "I could use a quiet night tonight, okay?"

I GAVE YOU ONE the other night, and you thought I was sick! Why does Nate always have to leave? Why can't he stay here like he did that other time? I slept on his chest. I really liked that. And in the morning we danced around the kitchen while he cooked. You don't dance. I mean, you feel nice and soft in the morning and you smell really good, but you never dance. Where does he go, anyway?

Chapter Eight

"What is all that?"

Karma held the door open for Nate, who carried a very large open box. It appeared to be heavy, and things stuck out of it that Karma couldn't identify. Until Nate set the box down and placed several of the strangely curved things on the floor.

"Train tracks," Nate explained. "Ryan just dropped this off. Apparently something's wrong with the caboose."

Karma laughed. "I know a few people to whom that diagnosis would apply. Would you mind keeping an eye on Garrett while I put the finishing touches on dinner?"

"'Course not. Where is he?"

Karma brought the carrier out of the kitchen. "If you spread the blanket on the floor, he's happy to lie on his stomach and watch you."

"Okay, bro." Nate did as Karma suggested, then constructed the tracks around him. "We're going to check out this thing and see what's wrong with it, so some little boy can find it under the tree on Christmas morning. So *you* can be part of the hospital's holiday project, even if your mother doesn't want to be."

"I heard that," Karma said from the other side of

the bar that separated the kitchen from the living room. In an alcove in the corner, a round table was set for two. "You can't turn him against me. He loves me as I am."

SURE I DO, but you don't want to help with Christmas? Come on, Mom. I have to. I mean, He knows who I am. We knew each other even before I got to know you. He'll expect me at His birthday party.

KARMA CHECKED the game hens and considered them browned to perfection. The dressing and the wild rice were fragrant and ready, and the vegetables were perfect—crisp but not crunchy. She removed biscuits from the oven and placed them in a pale green linen napkin in a basket and put them on the table.

"I'll make up our plates in the kitchen, if you don't mind," she called to him. "The table's a little small to set everything on."

"Great," he replied over the sound of a small, ailing motor revving. "I'm so used to eating cafeteria-style, that having a plate I don't have to fill will be a nice change."

Karma gave him extra-large helpings of everything. She'd always thought her childhood had challenged a child's coping skills, but at least it hadn't been lonely. Her parents had been eccentric and embarrassing, but they'd been *there*.

"Wine with dinner, or coffee?"

"What kind of wine?"

"A bottle of white zin I got for my birthday last year."

There was a moment's silence. She peered around the bar to where he lay on his stomach on the floor, examining the underside of the tiny caboose. He looked up at her.

"Don't you want to save it for a special occasion?" he asked.

She grinned. "Isn't this an occasion? My son gets to see his first electric train, a caboose gets a new life, you get a plate you don't have to fill, and I get to cook."

He looked surprised. "You *like* to cook?"

"Yes. Why?"

He shrugged a shoulder. "Well, it doesn't seem like an organized undertaking. I mean, cooking's sometimes unpredictable, isn't it?"

She dismissed that notion with a wave of her hand and disappeared again behind the bar. "I guess it is for those 'a pinch of this, beat it till it's done' kind of cooks. I follow recipes religiously. I *make* it organized."

"Of course," he said.

Karma poured the wine and placed their plates on the table. "You two ready?" she asked.

Nate appeared at the table, Garrett clutching the front of his shirt in a tight little fist. She pried it open and took Garrett, placing him in the carrier, on a third chair that she wedged between the wall and the table.

WHAT ARE WE HAVING? I want some. I can gum it. Or are you just going to presume, as usual, that because I can't hold a fork, I don't want any?

NATE KNEW he would hereafter consider sometime during that dinner as the moment he began to fall in love. It would take time to *be* in love, he knew; for him, the sharing of deep emotion was a slow and gradual process. But everything was changing.

This—whatever it was—with Karma was no longer a game, a diversion that might or might not become something more. It was. He'd been snared.

And it wasn't the food, although it was delicious. It was her face across the table, the long discussion about movies, music, Heron Point gossip, childhood stories, personal prejudices.

They agreed on some things and disagreed on others, but sharing them was funny and sad and intimate—and he couldn't remember ever being so comfortable and so on edge at the same time.

"I can't believe," she said with a laugh, "that you had a Flintstones sweatshirt, too. They let you wear that in military school?"

"I wore it to bed—" he grinned "—where I read *Tropic of Cancer* under the covers."

Karma studied him, her chin on her fist. "Now there's a picture. A boy in a Flintstones sweatshirt reading Henry Miller."

He inclined his head modestly. "I did my best to defy labels. I'll bet you did, too."

She frowned, thinking. "I was always *trying* to be conventional, because my parents weren't. I guess it's the old thing of wanting to be whatever it is you aren't. Except that I really wanted out of that bus." She looked around her at the somewhat confining dimensions of her little house. "One day I'll have a two-story house with a big yard, but for now, this is so much better than those days. I…"

She stopped herself, shaking her head, as though changing her mind about what she'd been about to say. She began to stack dishes.

Nate caught her hand and held it to the table. "What?" he asked gently.

She shrugged, embarrassed. "I'm sure you don't want to hear my personal discoveries. I mean, you didn't come here to—"

"I came here," he told her, "to figure out why I can't get you out of my mind. Please. Say it."

For a moment, Karma didn't know whether she was more unsettled by his admission or by what she was finally able to admit to herself. She drew a breath. She knew she could trust him with what she felt.

She shrugged a shoulder, her hand still caught in his. "It's not such a big thing, but…it was hard, you know, to love my parents, yet hate the way they lived. Inside, they were truly all love for each other, and mankind, and the earth. But we lived on top of one another, in conditions that made it difficult for *me* to feel those things. I was always angry—needing space, needing privacy." She sighed. "Just needing something else. Sometimes…" She hesitated and swallowed, then admitted with a rasp in her voice, "I regret that. I wish I'd been kinder, less demanding. I think they were generous with what they had to give. I just sometimes felt that their respect for the globe could be applied on a smaller scale to our family."

Nate pushed her wineglass toward her. "I know. Every time I went home from school, I'd behave like a monster, trying to make my father react. He was always kind, never raised his voice, and I was desperate for some sort of genuine response. But I think he truly didn't know what to do with me, figured he was supposed to love me, and that that meant taking whatever I threw his way. By the time I figured that out, he'd passed away and it was too late for both of us."

Karma turned her hand in his and squeezed it. "I'm sorry. I know it leaves a hole where all your happy childhood memories should be. I guess it's human nature to remember only what we've been deprived of. But I'm sure it'll make you a wonderful father when you can come to accept having children in your life. You'll know what they need, because you understand what you needed and didn't get."

She tried to pull free of his hand to get dessert, but he tightened his grip on her. He used it to pull her toward him and draw her into his lap.

She knew she should put up some resistance, but she couldn't think of one good reason why. She could think of no one she'd rather be with at this moment—or any time in the future. There were several unresolved issues between them, but she loved it when he kissed her, lived on memories of him when they were apart, and was perfectly willing to sacrifice common sense to have him kiss her again.

That alone, she thought, was big trouble. But some things in life were simply worth the risk.

The night he'd taken her to dinner, he'd allowed her the initiative in the kiss, but this time was different. This time, the moment he had her in his arms, he took complete control of the encounter.

He cradled her tenderly, tipping her sideways into his arm, tucking her legs up against him and holding her with an arm wrapped her thighs.

She looped her arms around his neck, thinking absently that she could sit that way forever, in his protective, possessive embrace.

He opened his mouth over hers, and she tightened her grip on him, desire flaring between them like a flame given air. His tongue delved deeply, and she teased it, warred with it, then planted kisses along his jaw and at his ear as his lips roved along her throat to the open collar of her shirt.

He raised his head to claim her mouth again, and she met it eagerly, returning kiss for kiss. Her hands moved over his shoulders, feeling strong muscle and rigid bone under the wool of his sweater.

She felt his hand wander up the back of her thigh, into her skirt, and made herself push away and gasp for breath.

He sat her up, resting his forehead against her shoulder while he, too, drew a deep, steadying breath.

"Mud...pie," she said in a ragged whisper.

He raised his head to frown at her. "What?"

She pointed a finger toward the refrigerator. "Mud pie. For dessert. In the refrigerator."

He grinned dryly, holding on to her hand as she pushed herself to her feet. "Maybe I should get in the refrigerator."

"You're supposed to be fixing a train," she reminded him, kissing his knuckles, then pulling her hand free. "I'll get dessert."

"Right."

He had the train running in fifteen minutes. Karma, sitting beside Nate on the floor, watched the HO-gauge train circle the track. It hummed as it neatly made all the curves. Garrett, sound asleep in the carrier on the floor beside them, was unaware of Nate's success.

"Good for you," Karma said. "You deserve another piece of mud pie."

"Oh, no." Nate shook his head adamantly and leaned back on an elbow. "It was wonderful, but I'm stuffed. I'm not sure I'll marry you, after all."

He was teasing; Karma knew that. But she had to concentrate not to betray a reaction. A good thing, she decided, since she didn't know what it would be, anyway.

"Really." She leaned on her hand, tucking her legs sideways. "I didn't know you were considering it."

"Well, I've always kept a good distance from the marriageable female," he said gravely, "but I had a change of heart when I tasted your cooking."

"Thank you, I think."

"But then—" he waggled his index finger at her suspiciously "—I realized it could be a control tool."

She grinned. "You mean the power to withhold dessert?"

"No. I mean, if you made a man fat enough, he'd become too sluggardly to argue with you. He'd relax into a comfortable stupor. Like the one I'm feeling right now."

Karma let her eyes wander over his athletic leanness and found the notion laughable.

"You mean if I said something quarrelsome, you'd let it pass?"

"Probably."

She leaned over him and whispered near his ear, "The contemporary celebration of Christmas is a plot of the downtown merchants."

She was shocked the next moment, when she lay on her back on the carpet and he knelt astride her, pinning her good hand above her head.

"Ah!" she cried, laughing and struggling at the same time. "You said you wouldn't…"

He firmed his grip on her. "I'm not arguing, am I?"

"Well, not verbally, but…"

"I don't believe you were specific about that. And for a lady who likes to spell out the details…"

"Well, if you're going to *get* specific, none of this

applies anyway, because for one thing, you're not my husband, and for another, you're not fat. So, what do you say to that?''

''I say I'd like to hear you take it back.''

''What?''

''The Christmas crack.''

''Never.''

''Then I'm afraid I have to take appropriate action.''

Karma felt excitement running along her nerve endings like a jolt of electricity. He was so near, so deliciously dangerous, but the only threat he seemed to pose was pleasure.

''And what would that be?'' she asked challengingly.

He thought a moment. ''I think this requires a two-part retribution. First, you owe me a kiss for taking rude advantage of my honest admission.''

She rolled her eyes. ''You were accusing *me* of having ulterior motives for being a good cook.'' She barely suppressed a smile. ''But, very well—if you're going to whine, you may have your kiss.''

''Thank you.'' Still pinning her hand, he leaned down to claim it. It was tender, but long and slow. When he finally raised his head, she felt intoxicated with his masculinity.

''Part two,'' he said, changing his grip to clasp her hands and pull her to her feet, ''is an eye for an eye—so to speak.''

''What?''

He reached into the box that had held the pieces of train track and retrieved a rag doll that was missing an eye and a foot, and was wearing an apron with a dark stain. He handed it to her.

''Neither of the other ladies in our group can sew. Can you?''

She hugged it to her instinctively. "My goodness. She looks like she's been through a lot."

He smiled. "Ryan said she was donated by a little girl who had loved her, and wanted to give her to another child to enjoy. The little girl's mother apologized for the state it was in, and told him privately that he could toss it away after they left. But we decided there's probably a lot of love attached to it, and that some other little girl will feel it. What do you think?"

She looked at the doll, then at him, her eyes large and limpid. Her mouth took on a suspicious twist. "I think you're an insidious manipulator."

He smiled innocently. "Thanks. I like you, too. I'll help you clean—"

The beep of his cellular phone interrupted him. He reached into the cardboard box for it, frowning at Karma. "My answering service is supposed to pick up everything tonight but hospital calls. Excuse me. Hello? Hi, Joanie. What—?"

He glanced at Karma with an expression she couldn't quite define, but chose to interpret as guilt.

"Hi, Hadley," he said with mild surprise.

Or was it feigned surprise? Karma wondered. I am not feeling jealousy, she told herself firmly as she went into the kitchen to clean up. So he carries his cellular phone with him so his girls know where to find him. So what? So he kisses me as though I provided him with something vital to his survival. He hasn't promised me anything he hasn't promised them. I'm not jealous.

And what does it matter, anyway? I'm attracted to his charm and his sexuality, neither of which is a quality that will change my mind about men. I don't want one. I don't want him. I'm just reacting to loneliness and a starving libido.

''A simple fracture?'' she heard him ask. ''Yes. Well, sixty-three isn't that old, Hadley, and she's a strong lady. Who's setting it? No, no need to worry. He's very good. Hadley, calm down. You're not going to be any good to her or to yourself if...'' He sighed. ''Yes. Sure. I'll meet you in the waiting room.''

Karma turned away from the sink, wiping her hands on a towel, when he came into the kitchen, flipping the phone closed.

''I'm sorry,'' he said. ''Hadley just took her mother into emergency with a broken leg. Seems she had pretty poor form in the bowling lanes. Fell down and broke her femur.''

''And Hadley needs you.'' Karma walked around him to the guest closet, where she'd hung his jacket.

She tried to help him into it, so that she could stay behind him and avoid his eyes, but he took the jacket from her and lifted her chin with his forefinger. ''I'm just being a friend. Her mother's a neat lady.''

Karma already felt guilty that she resented his defection. She didn't want him to compound it by being understanding.

''You aren't required to explain,'' she said, then added, in a tone that negated her noble words, ''If I still had a mother and she'd broken her leg, I'm sure you'd 'be a friend' and come and comfort me.''

''Karma.'' His tone was scolding.

''Nathan,'' she said in the same tone. ''Go. I understand that it will probably comfort Hadley's mother to see you. But even though you can be comfortable seeing six different women, you have to understand that there is not a cell of polygamous tendency in me.''

He smiled. Jealousy. That was a step in the right direction.

He reached out to take her in his arms. She side-stepped him. "No. No special privileges for you, until there are special privileges for me."

"Karma..." he said again.

"Nathan," she repeated, "you kiss me, then you run to her. Of course, you probably kiss her, too."

"I'm running," he said, his manner mildly impatient, "to her mother. I explained that I—"

"I know. That you love us all as friends. But you kiss me like a lover..." she was so surprised that she'd said the thought aloud that she paused for a moment, swallowed, then went on "...and I think you're going to have to organize your priorities if this is going to go on."

Now he was annoyed. He didn't like having his motives questioned, particularly by a woman who was seldom clear about her own.

"Is that so?" he asked. "And what are your priorities? Business expansion, bigger house, and a baby—precious as he is—that you got from a sperm bank. You don't even have time for Christmas!"

Infuriated, Karma yanked the door open. "Goodbye, Nate," she said stiffly.

"Goodbye, Karma" was his cool reply. "Please don't throw away the train when you're *organizing* things. I'll come back for it."

"Don't bother," she said. "I'll mail it to you!" And she slammed the door after him.

HE DID NOT COME BACK for the train. It had been almost a week.

Karma vacillated between hating herself for her self-ishness one moment and being convinced she'd been right to upbraid him the next. She wondered how Hadley's mother had come through. And just how long Nate had stayed around to comfort Hadley. He might still be doing it, for all she knew.

Work kept her very busy, and it was now habit to lay Garrett on a blanket on the overstuffed chair beside her while she was on the computer. He arched, turned, twisted and kicked until he finally exhausted himself and went to sleep. He seemed to learn something new every day.

I CAN'T WAIT until I can use the computer. I like the pie charts and the graphs. How's Nate? Did he come over? Did I sleep through it?

KARMA GAINED two new clients, Garrett slept through the night once again, but kept her up three nights running, just, she was sure, so that she wouldn't grow overconfident.

And she repaired the rag doll. She gave it two new black button eyes, and replaced both legs with a muslin fabric that matched the arms. Feeling artistic, she added a striped fabric at the bottom for socks, made a pair of Mary Janes out of felt and topped the skirt with a lace apron. And while she was at it she replaced the red yarn hair with a curly yarn that made her look as though she'd just had a perm.

When she was finished with it, she placed it near her computer and found that it made her smile. She wondered if she were going crazy, or if she *did* feel the love in it? She hoped it would affect its new "mother" just that way.

But Nate hadn't come to retrieve it, or the train. She considered calling him, then rejected the idea. She could imagine him receiving a call from her on his cellular phone while he was with Hadley or Barb, and found the idea distasteful. So she packaged up the train and did what she'd told him she'd do. She took it to the post office and mailed it to him one blustery mid-November day. She held on to the doll, telling herself she wanted to add a bow to the hair.

She went from the post office to Coffee Country for a change of scenery.

She found Devon behind the counter, and ordered a cappuccino. Nancy and a young blond woman sat at a table in the corner, poring over items spread out before them. Beside them, in a playpen lined with blankets, lay a beautiful baby.

"Karma, hi!" Nancy beckoned to her to join them. "Will you look at Garrett?" She stretched her arms up for him as Karma drew near. "Hi, handsome!" She kissed his cheek. "Have I got a couple of girls for you!"

"Is this Malia?" Karma asked, remembering vaguely that the day she delivered, Nate had mentioned that Nancy's baby had thick dark hair. She lay on her tummy, "swimming" with busy arms and legs. She wore pink corduroys and a long-sleeved cotton shirt with pink bunnies on it. In her spiky dark hair was a pink bandeau.

Karma took an empty chair, suddenly cheered by Nancy's company. Though she noticed quickly that she and her companion seemed far from cheerful themselves.

"Do you know Amy Brown?" Nancy asked, indicating the young woman seated across from her in a red sweater with tiny white hearts on it and a ruffle trimming the neck and arms.

"Ah...no." Karma smiled at her. The first thing that

caught her attention was how unflattering the fussy sweater was on her sturdy, angular frame. The second was that her warm smile distracted one from noticing anything else.

"She's the PR director at the hospital. Remember that special series of articles on the birthing rooms at Riverview?"

"Yes. They're what made me decide to have my baby here instead of in Portland. Not that I had much to say about it, when he arrived three weeks early."

Amy nodded appreciatively. "That's *precisely* what we were trying to do with the birthing rooms. I'm happy to meet you."

"We'd like your opinion," Nancy said. "On these Christmas decorations." Then she looked at her severely. "And I don't want to hear any of that bilge you were handing out at the Halloween party about not having time for Christmas. Can I put Garrett in with Malia?"

"You can try," she said. "He hasn't met other babies yet."

I DON'T KNOW ABOUT THIS. I know I've seen her before, but we've never actually touched. I know she's a girl. I believe they're inferior, right? I mean, is that supposed to be hair? Aren't there any other guys? Mother!

"I'M RIGHT HERE, sweetie." Karma waved at Garrett, who lay on his stomach, looking suspiciously at Malia. "It's all right. Ask her for a date. I think she likes you. Now." Karma turned her attention to the snowflakes, stars and trumpeting angels spread out on the table.

Devon brought her cappuccino in a glass cup. It wore a tall head of foamed milk.

"What do you think?" Nancy asked. Karma heard forced cheer in her voice. "Pete and Eddy and I made the snowflakes and the stars. Amy made the angels.

"Actually, Tom cut the stars out with his jigsaw," Nancy said. "And the boys and I painted them." The last few words were spoken weakly as Nancy and Amy exchanged a grim glance.

"What is it?" Karma asked candidly. "I can see something's wrong." Then it occurred to her, as she glanced at Devon, behind the counter. "Where's Jo?"

Nancy put a napkin to her nose, her mouth trembling. "Gone," she said.

Karma turned to Amy. "Gone where?"

Amy sighed. "To Connecticut. For good."

"What? You mean she and Ryan have—?"

Amy shook her head. "She went alone."

"Wait." Karma tried to pull together what she knew about Jo Arceneau. "But isn't the baby Ryan's? I mean, I know she acted as surrogate for her sister and Ryan, but she can't take Chelsea to—"

"She didn't," Nancy said, sniffing. "She left her with Ryan."

"But...she loves her." Karma felt a clutch in her stomach at the thought of Jo without her baby. The night of the Halloween party, everyone had laughed at her portfolio of photographs.

Nancy nodded, fresh tears springing up. "That's why Ryan sent Chelsea to Connecticut with Diantha. Did you notice the health food store was closed?"

Karma was having difficulty keeping up with events. "But *Ryan* loves Chelsea."

Nancy sniffed again. "He loves both of them, so he wants them to be together."

"I don't understand," Karma admitted. "Why did she leave?"

Nancy shrugged. "Doubts, confusion. You know how love is. And then, there's poor Amy here, who's thinking about moving to New York after the New Year because my brother-in-law is being such a jerk."

Karma turned sympathetically to Amy. "I'm sorry," she said. "I can relate, though. Men are a menace to our mental health."

It was ironic, she thought, that she'd come here looking for distraction from her problems and an infusion of good cheer.

GARRETT: A menace? Us?
Malia: Yes. You make us crazy.
Garrett: I thought you came that way. What's this? I want it.
Malia: Mom! He's got my pacifier!

"YOU TWO get along," Nancy said to the babies. Then she turned to her companions. "Okay. We're going to put all that aside and do what we have to do here, because those poor children need a Christmas party, whether or not we're in good spirits." She picked up a snowflake and handed it to Karma. "These are made from foam sheets. The fairgrounds where we're having the party is huge, though, and it'll take hundreds of them to really look festive."

Karma held it up. The lightness of the material made it spin and look very much like an oversize version of the real thing. "I think it's wonderful."

"Good. I thought we could hang those from the rafters. The stars can go on the walls in a random pattern...." She placed two on the wall beside the booth and leaned back to look at them. "They should look pretty under the light. And the angels..." She reached for one to hand it to Karma.

Karma noted that it had been drawn with style and artistically painted. Glitter had been sprinkled on the gown that trailed behind it. It appeared to be about a foot and a half long.

"I think we'll put some over the stage," Nancy said. "And where Santa will be sitting." She smiled winningly at Amy. "That means you'll have to make about a dozen."

Amy nodded. "What do you think about making the gowns different colors?"

Nancy nodded. "Good. And the glitter will look great overhead." She frowned, then smiled determinedly. "Jo and Diantha were going to make cookies and other goodies, and as an act of faith, we're going to pretend that's going to happen. Oh, and another piece of good news. You know April, the candy striper at the hospital?"

"Yes," Amy said. Karma nodded, remembering her, too. "Well, she and her mom have volunteered their services to watch our babies the day of the party."

There was a squeal from the playpen.

MALIA: I'm staying with my brothers. They love to have me around.
Garrett: No one's leaving me behind. They're talking about cookies. And didn't somebody mention Santa Claus?

NANCY FOLDED HER ARMS and looked at Karma. "We need some little things for teenage girls and mothers. I think we've got older boys and fathers covered, because the ladies of Saint James's Church have been knitting hats and scarves all year long. Isn't that great?''

Amy and Karma nodded dutifully.

''But we need some little gifts for girls and women. I know you're busy, but can you think of anything you can do that we can help with that would be appropriate?''

Karma saw it in her mind's eye the moment Nancy began to describe what was needed. And she remembered with sudden clarity the ingredients required and the wonderful fragrance produced.

''I can make a cinnamon bear ornament,'' she heard herself say, ''that's pretty simple, looks cute and smells heavenly.'' She stopped, unable to believe she'd volunteered that information.

''*You* can make them?'' Nancy asked.

No. She didn't have the time. She had a business to run, and a new baby, and she didn't believe in all this…

''Sure.'' That was her voice again. ''Jo…'' The mention of her name cast a brief pall over their enthusiasm. Karma tried again. ''Jo carries cinnamon. I can get it right here. Sure,'' she said again to convince herself. ''I'll provide the ladies' gifts.''

Nancy looked around surreptitiously. ''What if it puts you in the…'' She lowered her voice. Karma and Amy leaned closer to hear. ''…in the *Christmas spirit?*''

Karma swatted her arm. ''Very funny. I'm perfectly capable of making ornaments without catching the bug.''

Amy patted her shoulder consolingly. ''I hate to tell you this, but the way you volunteered those bears, you've already got it.''

Karma sat back and looked at her companions accusingly. "If I'm infected, I want you to know I hold you both responsible."

Nancy scooped her stars and snowflakes into a tote bag. "How's Nate doing? Is he feeling any better?"

Karma blinked. "What do you mean?"

"He got food poisoning." Nancy seemed surprised that she didn't know. "I'm sorry, I thought you guys were seeing each other."

"Well…" she said with a wry twist to her smile, "I'm never quite sure how that's going. How sick is he?"

Amy snickered commiseratingly. "I know just what you mean." Then she frowned seriously. "He's been off work for three days. Got something bad at a birthday lunch for Joanie."

"Jave and Tom have been checking on him," Nancy said, "but neither of them has that much time. That first night, he was really bad, Tom wanted to stay with him, but I guess he's a terrible patient. He wouldn't let him. I think he even threw something at him."

Consumed with guilt for having thought the worst about him, Karma bought two pounds of cinnamon, scooped Garrett out of the playpen and headed for the supermarket.

There she bought applesauce, the other ingredient in the cinnamon bears, a stewing chicken and a package of noodles, Jell-O, the ingredients for custard, and several other things she thought Nate might like. Then she called the answering service that picked up her calls when she was out and told them she'd be away for the rest of the afternoon.

She strapped Garrett into his car seat, then turned the Volvo in the direction of Eaton's Woods.

Chapter Nine

Karma had never seen a more beautiful setting for a home. Nate's A-frame sat in a clearing on the very edge of Eaton's Woods. Fir trees and mountain ash clustered around the rustic structure, creating a carpet of dry combs of golden leaves and clusters of red berries that crunched under her tires as she pulled up behind Nate's Jaguar.

Several steps led up to a front porch, where a rough twig sofa and chairs were grouped around a low table. Window boxes were filled with ornamental flowering cabbage.

"Okay, Garrett," she said, lifting him out of the back of the car and into the carrier. "We're going to visit Nate and see if he needs anything."

ALL RIGHT! I'll bet he's missed me.

THE AIR was chilly and damp, the sky overcast with heavy dark clouds. She tucked the baby's blue quilt in tightly and made her way up the steps with the carrier, then went back for the bag of groceries.

She rapped lightly and waited. There was no answer. She peered through loosely woven curtains and saw a stone fireplace, heavy furniture in a rich green—but no movement of any kind.

He had to be home, if his car was here. But if he was ill, he might be sleeping. Or he might simply be too ill to get to his feet.

Concern growing inside her at that possibility, she tried the door. It was locked. She left the groceries, but picked up the carrier and walked around to check the back.

The new deck he'd told her about ran the entire length of the back of the house. She climbed the stairs at the side and discovered a picnic table with a collection of pumpkins on it.

Karma tried the latch on the French doors and was surprised but pleased when it gave. She pulled the door open, stopping when the left side squeaked mournfully. She turned sideways and slipped inside, afraid of waking Nate.

She couldn't help the *ooh* of envy that escaped her when she found herself in a kind of sitting room decorated in shades of green and beige. One wall was brick, one was all books, and the others were decorated with old logging photographs and memorabilia.

She tiptoed through the room toward a doorway, wondering if it would lead her to Nate's bedroom. She stopped on the threshold and peered around it.

WATCH OUT, Mother!

"ALL RIGHT, freeze!" a raspy male voice shouted, right beside her.

She turned, her heart leaping into her throat at the sight of a putter swinging directly toward her head.

She screamed and ducked and closed her eyes. But nothing struck her.

"Karma?" that same voice asked in frail surprise.

She opened her eyes to see Nate in ratty gray sweat bottoms, still holding the putter in midswing. He lowered it with a thunk, as though holding it required great effort. She saw beads of perspiration standing out on his forehead. His face was pale under several days' growth of beard. She noticed, however, that his broad shoulders and muscular chest seemed unaffected by his illness. He looked terrible, but somehow the sight of him was wonderful. She didn't bother to analyze that.

She smiled. "Are you finished? May I play through?"

Nate wondered if he was hallucinating. He felt like hell, and he could barely lift his eyelids, much less the putter he'd taken up against what he thought was an intruder. The effort must have caved in what was left of his ability to reason.

But he thought he saw Karma standing there—looking fresh and scrumptious in gray slacks and a fuzzy pink high-necked sweater. Her hair was caught at the side of her head in a straight, gleaming ponytail.

Weak from lack of food and sleep, he frowned at the image, wondering if it was real. Had he heard her voice?

Then she touched his cheek, her hand soft and cool, and what little reserve of strength he'd mustered to protect his home deserted him. He leaned a shoulder against the wall and felt himself begin to slide down it.

"No, don't do that!" she cried. She quickly placed something on the floor, then slipped an arm between him and the wall. "Nate, don't fall! If you do, I'll never get you up again. I've only got one good arm, remember?"

Her face was inches from his. He tried to focus on her, but he couldn't steady the picture. "Go away," he said. "I'm fine."

"Yeah." She held on to him with remarkable strength. "You look fine. Okay, are you listening to me?"

"Can't help it," he said, leaning limply against her. "You're shouting in my ear."

"Sorry," she said. "I'm panicky. I don't want you to fall on the floor. But if you take three steps sideways, you can fall onto the bed. Can you do that?"

"Three...steps?" he asked in disbelief. "I don't think so."

"Sure you can," she insisted. "Here. You're still holding the putter. Just lean on it, and on me. And we'll take three steps. Just three. Come on. You can do it."

He felt her wedge her shoulder under his arm, pull his arm around her shoulders. He tried to resist but, for the moment, at least, she was stronger than he was.

"Come on, Nate. One..." She stepped away from the wall, taking him with her. The room reeled. He leaned heavily on the putter and lurched forward.

"Two, three!" she said as they landed together on the bed.

He felt the soft mattress take his weight, and the relief was so enormous for a moment that he couldn't bear the thought of moving.

"Well, that was a little faster than I'd planned," she said with a laugh, "but whatever works." She pushed against him.

He felt her arm under him, her body fitted to his side, her leg hitched over him. He wanted nothing to disturb that intimacy, but she seemed very determined. She pushed at his shoulder and pulled her arm out from under him. He regretted that.

But the next moment, her arm was under his and she was coaxing him backward, up to the pillows. He pushed himself along with the little reserve of strength he had left and landed lifelessly in the cradle of her body. He smiled to himself. That was nice. But again she managed to get free.

Then he felt her hand around his ankle, lifting his leg onto the bed. She did the same with the other, then pulled the blankets up over him.

Now that he didn't have to spare the energy to remain upright, he was able to focus. That ponytail dangled forward toward his face as she leaned over him. Her large brown eyes were soft with concern, and her smile was tender.

"Can you keep anything down?" she asked.

He managed to hook an arm around her and hold her to him. The ponytail fell onto his face. She laughed against his cheek, then pushed herself away from him by wedging her cast between them.

"Let me rephrase. Can you hold *food* down?"

"Don't know," he said. "Haven't tried for days."

"Okay." She sounded suddenly brisk. "We'll try you out on fruit gelatin. If that works, you can have soup tonight."

"Tonight?" he asked. She was smoothing his blankets, tucking them in. "You're coming back?"

She patted his head. "Not exactly. Rest. I'll have the gelatin ready in a few minutes."

NATE AWOKE to the sounds of a baby crying. It was night, and here on the edge of the woods there was very little light from town. Blackness surrounded him, but he tried to sit up, tried to make sense of the sound of a baby crying in his house in the middle of the night.

Then he remembered. Karma had been here. He was aware that he felt a little better, just a little stronger. He'd had Jell-O. Then he'd had chicken noodle soup. It had been delicious after several days of nothing.

The crying stopped, and he heard a soft, crooning voice. Karma? Was she still here?

That question was answered for him a moment later when his bedroom door creaked open and he felt her presence in the room. The scent of magnolias came to him first, then the scent of baby powder as she leaned over him and placed a hand on his forehead. It was warm, and it moved to his cheek.

He caught it there and placed his own hand against it. "Why are you still here?" he whispered.

"I'm just being a friend," she whispered back.

He remembered the words from their disagreement the night he'd left her to go to Hadley's mother. He squeezed her hand punitively. "This is beyond the call of friendship. *I* didn't stay the night with Hadley."

"Maybe you're not as good a friend as I am."

Nate felt something wriggle against his body. He put a hand out and felt Garrett's foot dangling from Karma's arms. "Garrett," he said softly. "How are ya, buddy?"

FINE. I like it here. Are you ever going to get out of there and play with me? We're making stuff in the kitchen. It smells great, but it's not to eat. Want to come and see? It's the middle of the night, and she doesn't even mind that I'm up!

"HE'S FINE. If you don't mind..." her voice took on a suddenly casual tone "... we're going to hang around tonight and see how you are in the morning."

"What time is it, anyway?"

"Just after eleven."

He tried to focus on her in the darkness. He saw the light color of the baby's blanket, the porcelain of her face, the gleam of her eyes. "What about your work?"

"I went home for my laptop," she replied. "I'm working on it when Garrett's asleep. When he's awake and deigns to allow me time, I'm making Christmas ornaments. Nancy and Amy have coerced me into helping out for the party. The ornaments are best made in a kitchen, and yours is bigger than mine, so it's easier to do them here. Do you mind?"

"Of course not. But...I hate to disrupt your life. I mean, I'm not in danger of death, or anything."

She made a very disdainful, very feminine sound. "And you call yourself a doctor. You aren't strong enough to get up and get food, and until you feed that six-feet-something of stubborn pride, you're not going to get better."

She tried to pull away but he kept a grip on her hand. "And where did you get your M.D.?"

"I have common sense," she said. He wondered if she knew she was rubbing her thumb across his knuckles. "I don't need a degree. Go back to sleep. Toast and soft-boiled eggs for breakfast."

"Can't wait," he said. But he brought the palm of her hand to his lips and kissed it. "Thank you," he said.

"You're welcome," she replied. Her voice was barely audible. "Good night." She pulled against him again, and this time he thought it safer for both of them to let her go.

"Night, sport."

NIGHT, Nate.

PLACIDO DOMINGO'S VOICE boomed from the radio, though Karma had it turned down very low. It was 4:00 a.m. She'd settled Garrett in the travelall she'd brought back with the laptop. It opened into a bed and fit on the sofa in the shadowy living room.

But she had raging insomnia and was into cinnamon bear production big-time. Two dozen of the ornaments sat on a cookie sheet to dry, redolent of the cinnamon and applesauce that were their basic components. The bears were made of eight little balls formed in the flat of the hand, a bigger one for the stomach, four smaller ones for arms and legs, and two smaller still for ears. A small loop of wire made them ready to hang.

The eyes were made with the indentation of a pen or pencil tip. When the bears were dry, they would be dressed with a thin ribbon tied into a bow.

Seeing the little army of bears, Karma was reminded sharply of the many dozens her mother had made every Christmas. She recalled how much she'd loved helping with them as a child, how wonderful the cinnamon had made the bus smell, how much fun it had been to park the bus in a friend's driveway over the holidays and to remain in the same spot for several weeks.

She'd loved that the most. There'd been playgrounds, backyard swing sets, basketball hoops, dime stores and candy shops. Her allowance had been minimal, but it had been so much fun to look at all the toys and other niceties the bus lacked that she didn't mind being unable to spend.

Until she'd become a teenager. Then she'd hated everything about the life—the constant moving, the day-to-day uncertainty, the curious picture her parents made, her mother in her long, bright dress, her father in his beard and coveralls.

It wouldn't have been so bad, she'd always thought, if they were shy and reticent people. But they'd been loud and cheerful, eager to talk to anyone, always full of funny stories and outrageously sunny philosophy. She'd wanted to die.

Then, thanks to a caring teacher, she'd gone away to college and discovered a wonderful new world of comfort and order and stability. Though exuberant in her new lifestyle, she'd discovered that she missed her parents' cheer in this more sober environment. But they'd have been miserable in a conventional setting, and she would never go back to life on the road. And the accident had taken them.

She smiled as she thought of them, then felt a salty tear on her lip. She swiped at her eyes and uttered a little laugh, then dabbed at her mouth with a paper towel.

Twenty-four perfectly formed little bears looked at her from the cookie sheet, reminding her that she'd gotten more from her childhood than she sometimes thought. And that there had once been a time when she'd enjoyed the warmth of Christmas.

One perfectly formed little baby reminded her that the future was bright with promise, if she took the best of what she remembered and coupled it with the best of what she'd learned. Then she would put all of it into protecting and caring for the son who would be her reach into infinity.

Karma set the bears aside to dry, tidied the kitchen,

then covered the rest of the dough and put it in the refrigerator. Garrett slept on.

Karma looked out the window and found that the autumn sky was still dark at 5:00 a.m. She curled up on the sofa with her coat over her shoulders, and decided to nap for a couple of hours, until Nate was ready for breakfast.

She closed her eyes and found herself wondering what life would be like confined with Nate on a bus. The palm of her hand tickled, and she remembered the touch of his lips, there in the darkness of his bedroom. She closed her hand tightly and fell asleep.

"ARE YOU AWAKE?"

Nate heard the voice and surfaced from sleep long enough to assign it an owner. It wasn't Karma. He lost interest and slipped back into the downy comfort of his pillow.

"Nate." The whisper was accompanied by a jab in his shoulder.

He grumbled a complaint.

Then he smelled coffee. The aroma was strong and rich and he could feel the heat coming from it. For the first time in days, it didn't make his stomach roil. He felt himself salivate for it.

He opened an eye and saw Tom Nicholas kneeling beside his bed, passing an open paper cup of coffee under his nose.

"Is that for me?" he asked. His voice sounded thick, and not quite conscious.

Tom held up a bag. "And there's a cranberry scone to go with it. Are you awake?"

Nate wanted to push himself up, but he wasn't sure

he had the necessary reserves of strength. So he took a minute to simply consider it. "I'm trying to be."

Tom put the coffee and bag on the bedside table and went to the doorway and peered out. Then he came back and said under his breath, "You know, I don't want to alarm you, but there's a beautiful brunette asleep on your sofa. And she has a baby. Are you listening to me?"

Nate nodded into his pillow. "Beautiful brunette. Sofa. Baby."

"What's Karma Endicott doing there?"

"You said she was sleeping."

"Okay, that's it."

Nate heard the crunch of paper as Tom grabbed the bag and cup and prepared to leave.

"I'm out of here. Next time you need someone to nurse you through the plague, call my brother."

"Okay. Okay." Nate pushed himself to a sitting position and winced against the daylight. "I'm up. I didn't call you, you came despite all my protests, and it was bad chicken salad, not the plague...though it did feel fatal."

"Whatever you say. What about Karma and the baby on the sofa? Is this your wild past come home to roost?"

Nate opened his eyes a little wider. So he hadn't dreamed last night. She'd been here. "That's my nurse," he said, pushing himself shakily to his feet.

Tom reached out to steady him when the last few inches became difficult. "Where are the square white shoes and the Stalinesque manner?"

Nate grinned and turned in the direction of the bathroom.

"Well, I only brought two coffees," Tom said. "Maybe I should put on a pot."

"Help yourself. I need a shower. Don't wake her."

"Afraid she'll prefer me to you?"

Nate gave him a not-a-chance look. "Please. She's a very discerning woman."

KARMA *did* seem to be enjoying Tom's company, Nate noticed twenty minutes later, when he walked into the kitchen, freshly showered and wearing jeans and a red-and-gray plaid flannel shirt. She was placing scones and cups of coffee on a tray, and he was giving Garrett his bottle. Dark jealousy rampaged through Nate's chest. He drew a steadying breath. He knew the emotion was unwarranted, but it was virulent all the same.

"Hi!" Karma noticed him with obvious pleasure and came toward him to take his arm in her good one and help him toward a stool. He gave Tom a superior look over his shoulder. "Are you sure you should be up?" she asked.

"I'm sure," he said. "And I think I can handle coffee and a scone."

She looked at him doubtfully. "I don't know. You just started eating real food yesterday."

He was touched by her concern, and confounded by the knowledge that she'd stayed all night and slept on the sofa. And he felt all kinds of other things he wasn't strong enough to do anything about this morning. But this afternoon might be another story.

"As I recall," he argued, letting his eyes betray what he was thinking, "we decided during the night that you have the common sense, but I have the medical degree."

Her cheeks grew pink and her eyes grew languid. He

felt his pulse pick up and knew it had nothing to do with a relapse.

Her eyes held his and told him in no uncertain terms that her thoughts were following his. Then she seemed to remember Tom's presence and turned her attention back to the tray.

Nate went to take Garrett from Tom. "Hi, big guy. What's new with you? Gained another pound this week, didn't you?"

I DON'T SEE HOW. *All I get's milk, and you guys get all the good things. Like what's that triangle thing with the little red stuff in it? Can I have a bite? With butter. Nobody ever gives me butter.*

"YOU'RE going to be on people food in no time," he said, teasing Garrett's lips with the nipple of the bottle. "But for now, this is your cocktail, buddy."

Tom took the tray from Karma, and they gathered around the farm-style table in the middle of the room.

"I'll take him so you can enjoy your scone," Karma said, trying to do just that.

Nate pushed her hand away. "I'm fine. He probably needs a little guy company. It's too bad he has to be exposed to the likes of Tom at such a tender age, but life is hard."

Tom shook his head at Karma. "That's the thanks I get for helping him through the fever crisis."

Nate rolled his eyes. "There was no fever crisis. You turned my electric blanket up too high and almost roasted me." Nate passed Karma the butter. "Never let a carpenter nurse you. They tend to repair things with nails and glue."

Tom made a face at him. "I'm good enough to cut out stars for the Christmas party."

"I saw them," Karma said, passing the butter on to Tom. "I was at Coffee Country yesterday, and Nancy and Amy were firming up their plans for decorations." She frowned suddenly at Nate. "Did you hear that Jo moved to Connecticut?"

Before Nate could comment, Tom said cheerfully, "No, she's back. Just this morning. Nancy told me."

Karma raised her good arm in the air. "All right! Nancy believed she'd come home."

Tom grinned. "She should write romances, instead of murder mysteries."

"Anyway," Karma said, wondering if there was something she could do about Amy's floundering romance, "your stars are beautiful, Tom. Have you seen Nancy's snowflakes?"

He nodded. "Was there this morning. She and the boys are still cutting them out."

Karma glanced conspiratorially under her lashes at Nate. "Have you seen Amy's angels?" she asked Tom.

It took him a moment to answer. "Ah…just the prototype."

She nodded enthusiastically. "It's beautifully done. I didn't think she was looking very well, though."

Tom's gaze sharpened on her. "Why not?"

Nate pretended interest in his coffee.

Karma shrugged a shoulder and broke off a tip of her scone. "She looks… I don't know. Wistful. Even heartbroken. She was talking about moving to New York to be with her sister."

Tom looked stricken for a moment, but then he took a sip of coffee and sat back in his chair. "Might be good for her. I'm not sure she's enjoying her work at the hospital.''

"I think she likes it fine," Nate said. "I think something else is bothering her."

Tom met his steady gaze head-on. Nate didn't flinch. The implication that Tom himself was Amy's problem was plainly visible on his face. Tom finally excused himself and grabbed his jacket off the back of his chair.

"It was a pleasure meeting you, Karma," he said politely. Then he turned to Nate with a far less congenial expression. "And you—I hope you *do* have a fever crisis."

Nate smiled amiably. "I'll see you to the door."

Tom marched to his truck, which was parked behind Karma's Volvo. Nate followed intrepidly.

"My life," Tom said, stopping at the driver's-side door to growl at his friend, "is not your business."

"I beg your pardon," Nate replied, "but it is. You're going to blow off this relationship, because it's easier to hurt than to get better."

Tom spread his hands in a gesture of utter frustration. "How in the hell would you know?"

"I do," Nate said calmly. "And if you were just ruining your life, I'd think, 'Hey. There are enough of us around who love you to do our best to see you through.' But you're ruining hers, too. And she doesn't have the kind of understanding support you have."

"At least," Tom said quietly, angrily, "I'm not afraid of babies."

Tom accepted that barb with equanimity. "You'll notice there's one in my kitchen right now. I'm trying to learn to deal with *my* fears. You should do the same." He slapped Tom on the shoulder. "Thanks for the coffee and scones."

Tom shrugged him off. "Go to hell."

Nate waved and headed back to the house. "See you there."

He found Karma standing just inside the doorway, the baby asleep in her arms. She'd obviously been eavesdropping. She smiled wryly. "You think maybe we were too subtle?"

He wrapped an arm around her and drew her inside. "He'll come to his senses. I have faith in his intelligence. But what I really want to know is, *is* there a subtle message in the fact that you heard I was ill, hurried to my aid, tucked me up in bed, fed me, and stayed the night to watch over me?"

He led her toward the kitchen as he spoke. He took the baby from her and shushed him when he stirred. He placed him in the carrier, then drew Karma into his arms.

Aw, come on. I spend so much time in this thing, it's growing onto my backside. Could we go somewhere? Do something? I like it when we walk around. Or when we're all in the car.

"You know," Nate said, his eyes looking deeply into her eyes, "a man could think you were being more than a friend."

"I was." She wrapped her good arm around his neck and met his gaze boldly, letting him see the truth as she knew it. "I was being a friend and a nurse," she added teasingly.

"A nurse who stayed the night."

"On the sofa."

He held her tighter, his eyes smoldering. "Well, let's do that the right way tonight. Or, why wait till tonight?"

Nate swept her up in his arms before she could protest.

"Put me down," Karma said, laughing. "You've just been out of bed an hour after four days of... Ah!"

He reeled, with an attack of dizziness, she guessed, and strode forward to drop her in a sitting position on the counter. He leaned his upper body against hers weakly as he laughed in self-deprecation.

"Maybe we should wait until tomorrow night," he said, then raised his head to add weakly, hopefully, "Unless you're the type of woman who likes to be in charge?"

She kissed his forehead. "Oh, I do. But I have work to do, and you have to rest. I imagine they'll expect you back at the hospital soon."

With a surge of energy that surprised her, he wrapped his hands around her thighs and pulled them around his hips until there was no space between their bodies, until they shared a single heartbeat.

She sobered, shaken by the power of her desire for him and his for her. Caution seemed insignificant in the face of it.

"It's about to happen, you know," he said, his turbulent blue eyes on a level with her wide brown gaze. "We're about to become lovers."

"We have to know more..." Her voice was a frail whisper as she felt every one of his fingertips against her thighs, even through the fabric of her slacks. Sensation rippled up every vertebra.

"I adore you," he said softly, his lips a millimeter from hers. "What else is there to know?"

She couldn't think, couldn't reason. She dropped her forehead against his shoulder and simply held him.

They leaned into each other for a few moments. Then

Nate's voice, filled with soft amusement, said suddenly, "Why, Karma Endicott."

She lifted her head. "What?"

He pointed to the tray of cinnamon bears drying in the corner of his counter. "What are those?"

"Ornaments," she replied. "I told you about them last night, remember?"

They studied each other quietly for a moment, each indulging a personal memory of those few minutes in the darkness.

He grinned. Her heart thumped in response.

"For the party?" he asked.

She nodded. "Nancy said—"

He interrupted her, his smile indulgent. "Karma. You've caught the Christmas spirit."

"No, I haven't," she answered quickly. "I was bullied into this."

"Karma." His scolding tone suggested she was lying. "They look as though they were made with care and attention."

"I do *everything* with care and attention," she said. "That has nothing…"

"Mmm…" he said, focusing on her lips. "I like the sound of that."

He took a gentle fistful of her hair, pulled her closer, and kissed her soundly. She clung to his shoulder with her good arm, feeling her temperature rise, her heartbeat quicken to the point of explosion, her limbs turn to jelly.

Nate knew he was losing all reason. He wanted this woman with a desperation that made him forget that he hadn't wanted a wife, that he hadn't wanted children.

All he knew with any certainty was that he wanted *her*. Her ardent lips along his jaw, her small hand exploring his back, her knees tightening around him in what he hoped was a physical reaction to what her mind was imagining—all drove him to the brink of frustrated madness.

Then, almost simultaneously, two jarring sounds forced him to free her. The phone rang, and the baby cried.

With a groan of reluctant acceptance, Nate lifted Karma off the counter and set her on her feet. He went to the telephone.

MOTHER, where are you? Why does this always happen? I rest my eyes for a few minutes and everyone disappears! Are we going out? Can I have one of those little brown things that smell so good? Where's Nate? I want Nate.

KARMA picked up her son and held him against her, grateful that he'd awakened and forced her back to reality. One more moment of Nate's persuasion, and she'd have forgotten that a few things remained unresolved between them.

He hung up the phone and turned to her, a wry quirk to his smile.

"Hadley?" she asked. "Barb?"

"Joanie," he replied.

She stopped and frowned. "Is that a new one?" With the hand that held Garrett, she pointed to her purse, on the back of a kitchen chair. "Would you put that on my shoulder?"

He obliged her, then pinched her chin. "No. She's an ER nurse. Flu's going around the hospital, and there's no one to cover for me tonight, so I guess I'm back on duty.''

Karma felt both disappointed and grateful for the reprieve. She wanted to be with him more than she wanted anything. But the squalling bundle in her arms reminded her that she had more than her own needs to consider.

She sighed and smiled thinly. ''You really need a few more days' rest.''

He took her face in his hands and leaned down to kiss her gently. ''I'll be fine. Let me take Garrett while you get your jacket. Hey, buddy. What's all the fuss about?''

ARE YOU COMING WITH US? Did you eat all those triangle things? I'm sleepy. We were up working most of the night, you know, and something's not right with my mother, I can feel it. She's nervous, or worried, or something. Please come with us. She smiles more when you're around.

''CAN I LEAVE THE BEARS to dry a few days?'' Karma asked. ''I'm afraid they'll get jostled in the back of the car.''

''Of course,'' he said. ''That means you'll have to come back for them.''

She looked around her at the cozy, rustic environment and nodded. ''This is a wonderful house. Coming back would be no hardship.''

He was happy to hear that. He followed her to the car with Garrett in a football hold in one arm and the carrier dangling from his other hand. Garrett complained loudly when he placed him in the car seat.

I WANT YOU to come with us!

"COME ON, buddy," Nate coaxed futilely, checking straps and buckles. "Be good for your mom. She's had a long night."

I WAS THERE part of the time, too, you know. I want you to come with us!

KARMA SIGHED in resignation as Nate closed the car door for her. She opened her window. "He has a fit every time you and I part company. I hope you realize this means I'm in for another day of not being able to concentrate on the computer, and another sleepless night."

He leaned into the open window to kiss her lingeringly. "You can make more bears," he said softly, then kissed her again. "And we'll have to think about a solution that'll make us all happy."

She raised an eyebrow doubtfully. "Is there one?"

"Christmas," he said, "is the season of miracles."

"It won't even be Thanksgiving," she pointed out, "for another week."

He looked at her sternly. "I will not believe you're hopeless. I will turn you into a believer."

She kissed him. "I believe in you. Is that enough?"

He was touched out of all proportion by the simple declaration. "It's a damned good start," he said, then backed away, while he still could. He ducked down to wave. "I'll probably be working long hours, but I'll call when I can."

Karma blew him a kiss and backed out of the driveway, Garrett screaming in the back seat.

NOBODY KISSED ME! I wanted him to come with us! How come I always have to sit back here all alone? I can't move in this thing. I like it better on the floor, where I can get some action going.

Are you listening to me? I wanted him to come with us!

KARMA found Garrett's screaming, purple face in the rearview mirror and smiled at him. ''I know, sweetie. I'm going to miss him, too. I know you think he belongs to us because he's been around from the moment you arrived, but he isn't really ours. And you have to understand that. I'd like it to be different—and it might. But it might not. You have to be ready for that. Okay?''

OF COURSE NOT! I want him!

Chapter Ten

"Karma. Hi, it's me."

"Nate, hi!" Karma needed no more identification than the sound of his voice on the telephone. Her lack of concentration over the past few days was only partly due to Garrett's continuous screaming. Loneliness was also responsible. She thought about Nate continuously.

"Did you get my message?" he asked.

She had. He'd called to tell her he was working back-to-back shifts, and that he missed her. When she called back, he'd had a patient and been unable to come to the phone.

"Yes," she replied, wondering if she should tell him she hadn't erased it, that she'd played it over and over just to hear his voice. "How are you feeling?"

"I'm completely recovered," he said. "I had a forty-year-old man going into cardiac arrest just as I was walking in the door that first night back. And things haven't slowed down since. How's Garrett?"

She groaned. "I imagine Attila the Hun was probably a better baby than he's been the past few days. I can't seem to make him happy."

ARE YOU TALKING TO HIM? Tell him to come home! I want him now!

"CAN YOU hear him screaming?" she asked. "The little darling's decided he hates me. Nancy has volunteered to take him for me for a few hours this afternoon so I can get some shopping done without driving everyone else out of the store. I don't suppose you'll be having a coffee break about that time?"

Nate would rather have been able to say yes to that question than win the lottery. But just the knowledge that she'd asked it helped blunt the disappointment.

"I'd kill to be able to say yes," he said wearily, "but that would only contribute to my work load. We've got a rent-a-doc from Portland, and he's great, but I hate to leave him alone."

There was an instant's silence. "A rent-a-doc?"

He laughed. "We use a staffing agency in Portland that provides us with doctors when we're shorthanded. They have a more formal name, but that's what we call them. It's sort of like a temp service, only they're medical people."

"What a world," she said, marveling that such a thing existed. "Well, I guess I'll just have to think about you when I stop at Coffee Country, and pretend you're sitting across the table."

She heard a smile in his voice. "And I'll think of you when I snitch the waiting room's coffee. Did Nancy tell you about Thanksgiving?"

"No."

"We're invited for dinner. I managed to get the afternoon off, but I have to go in at midnight. I'll pick you up at two, but we'll have to use your car. Mine doesn't have room for Garrett's car seat."

She felt a stir of excitement. She'd envisioned a lonely meal of turkey roll and Rice-a-Roni, with Nate working and Bert going to her parents' in Seattle.

"That would be fine, but are you sure Garrett and I are invited?"

"Yes, she was very specific. She said bring your ladylove." There was a velvet pause. "That's you."

A little shiver ran the length of her body. "How dare you tell me that," she scolded weakly, "over the telephone!"

"I'll reiterate," he promised, his voice rich and quiet, "when I pick you up Thursday. Wear that suit you wore the night I took you to dinner."

His name was shouted with loud urgency somewhere in the background.

"Gotta go," he said. "Kiss Garrett for me. I'll take care of you myself on Thursday."

Karma hung up the phone, putting a hand to her palpitating heart. Then she picked up her screaming son and rocked him from side to side.

She kissed his cheek. "That's from Nate, baby," she said, so thrilled by the phone call that she almost didn't notice that Garrett remained unappeased.

WELL, how come he couldn't deliver it himself? Where is he, anyway? I want him here! And isn't it time for milk?

"WHAT IN THE HELL did you say to Tom?" Jave asked Nate. He stood behind him at the candy machine in the hospital's deserted cafeteria. It was 2:00 a.m., and Jave had been called in to replace one of his technicians, who'd gone home ill.

Nate took a chocolate bar out of the chute and stepped aside. "I told him he'd rather be in pain than get over what happened," he replied, his brow furrowed. "Brutal, I know, but I'm getting desperate. I told him he could ruin his life, but he had no right to ruin Amy's.''

Jave put two quarters into the machine and pulled the lever for salsa-flavored corn chips. ''Did you tell him I asked you to spy on him?''

''No.'' They walked side by side to a round table in a corner. ''He figured it out for himself.''

Jave ripped the bag open as he fell into a chair. ''Thanks a lot. You were supposed to learn everything so shrewdly that he didn't suspect, so that if it worked I could be the hero. Now, I'm the villain. See if I engage your services again.''

Nate leaned his head back against the wall. He was so tired he felt as though his bones were made of paper. He bit off a third of the candy bar and chewed.

''Well,'' he said after he swallowed, ''I'd let you dismiss me, but I care too much. What are we going to do about him?''

Jave popped a red chip into his mouth and shook his head. ''He's that close to coming around.'' He held his thumb and index finger an inch apart. ''But it's more than putting the pain behind him, it's consigning his friend and the fire department to the past. And he can't do it until he can absolve himself of the blame.''

''Everything's so damned complicated,'' Nate grumbled moodily. ''Even things that shouldn't be.''

Jave grinned. ''Like love?''

Nate closed his eyes and sighed. ''I haven't even slept with Karma, and I love her so much it makes me crazy.''

Jave laughed softly. ''Been there. Done that.''

Nate opened his eyes, but it required effort. ''And you and Nancy are happy now?''

''Deliriously.''

"No lie?"

"No lie. I understand Karma's making Christmas ornaments for the party. Nancy thought they were wonderful."

"Yeah. Cinnamon bears. They're all over my kitchen. I'm in trouble, Jave."

Jave pretended surprise. "I thought you hadn't slept together yet."

Nate tossed his empty candy wrapper at him. "Not that kind of trouble. I think about her all the time. I love her baby."

"Uh-oh."

"I know. I'd make a nervous-Nellie father."

"Cheer up. Maybe she won't have you."

Nate smiled wearily. "You always know the right thing to say."

"Dr. Foster to the ER, stat!" an urgent voice called on the intercom. Nate remained still for one second, gathering his forces. "I'm going to have my name changed," he threatened. Then he stood, slapped Jave on the shoulder and loped for the door.

"How about Dr. Nervous Nellie?" Jave called after him.

KARMA DIDN'T HAVE TIME to say hello. She opened her front door at two o'clock Thursday afternoon and was swept up into a pair of arms so eager she barely identified their owner before they crushed her to him.

But she now knew Nate, she thought, with a power that went beyond the five senses. There was a connection between them that didn't require sight or sound or touch. She could be blindfolded now, she thought, and know him the moment he drew near.

But she was very glad she wasn't deprived of her

standard senses when she held on fiercely to his strong shoulders, when she smelled his herbal cologne, tasted his eager mouth, saw the love in his eyes, and heard him say in deadly earnest, "I love you, Karma. I *love* you. And, God, I've missed you."

Karma leaned against him and let the love words bathe her in their warmth. They made up for the loneliness of the past week—even for the loneliness of a lifetime.

She felt suddenly as though the sun had been turned on directly over her head.

"I love you, too," she said, hugging him tighter. "Do we really have all afternoon and evening?"

Pride, satisfaction, awe—all roiled in Nate's chest like some wonderful storm. She loved him. Well. He'd wanted to hear that admission more than anything, but there'd been moments when he doubted it could ever happen. He was humbled by the fact of it, and gave himself a moment to savor it.

"We do," he said finally, setting her on her feet and closing the door behind him. He laced his fingers in hers again and swept them downward so that they were body to body. Then he stood back in surprise and held up the two hands he held. The left one no longer sported a cast.

"All right!" he said, running his fingertips gently into her sleeve. "When did this happen? How does it feel?"

"Yesterday," she replied. "And it feels wonderful. Good as new. And it certainly simplifies my life."

He kissed her hand, then wrapped her arm around his neck. "Want to forget the dinner and stay home?" he asked with a waggle of his eyebrows. "See what else you can do with it?"

She nuzzled his cheek. "We can't. I'm bringing the pies. Besides..." She raised her head to smile into his eyes. "It's Thanksgiving. And we have so much to be thankful for."

The look in her eyes was a caress. Nate felt it everywhere.

She took his hand and pulled him into the kitchen, where Garrett, in his carrier on the kitchen table, shrieked angrily.

"I wanted to show you what I've been working on," she shouted above the baby's cries, "but I think you'd better pay attention to him first."

Nate lifted Garrett out of the blankets and held him over his head. The baby stopped screaming, but looked far from pleased. His large dark eyes threatened a new eruption of displeasure.

"What's happening, dude?" Nate asked, playing him like a trombone. "We're going to dinner. You're wearing a spiffy new outfit, and your mom and I are in love. What could possibly be wrong?"

WHERE HAVE YOU BEEN? I've been calling you for days! This suit is dorky! Would you go out with something that has snaps on the legs and a sailor collar? Where's my bow tie? Mother has no sense of style, where I'm concerned, and those girls are going to be there. I bet they'll have a lot to say about my suit.

You and Mother are what?

NATE PULLED HIM to his shoulder and patted his back. "It's okay," he said. "Just relax. Everything's going to be fine." He stopped in surprise at the sight of the small kitchen, cluttered with Christmas decorations in various stages of preparation. "Whoa! Did you and your mom do all this?"

He pointed to a group of flat Christmas shapes that looked as though they'd been made of candle wax.

"What are those?" he asked, then sniffed the air. He smelled clover.

"They're made of beeswax," she said, "in a candy mold." She pointed to the half-dozen bare wreaths that hung on cabinet knobs. "Those are made from the grapevines behind Jave's house. Nancy let me cut them the other day, when she watched Garrett."

He studied the circular and elliptical shapes. "How did you make them malleable?"

"You soak them in warm water in the bathtub. Amy's going to decorate them for the fairground doors. Oh. And before I forget to return this to you..." She took the rag doll from her computer desk and handed it to him. "Here she is. All well again. And you thought *you* were the one with the medical degree."

She gave him a teasingly superior look as she made to walk past him to the guest closet.

He caught her arm and pulled her to him, Garrett crushed between them.

ALL RIGHT. *This is more like it. Now, see? If you stuck around, we could do this all the time.*

"YOU'D BETTER PACK some things for the baby," Nate said as he nuzzled Karma's ear. Then he straightened to look into her eyes. His bore a message that she understood clearly. "Because I'm taking you home with me after the party."

She framed his face in her hands and kissed him. "Yes," she said.

NANCY'S DOOR was opened by an older woman wearing a white sweatshirt with a giant sunflower on it. She had wiry gray hair and a serious expression.

"Yes?" she asked gravely.

"Hi, Aggie," Nate said warmly. He stood behind Karma, with Garrett in his arms. "Happy Thanksgiving."

She looked from him to Karma. "You're here for dinner?"

"Yes."

"Show me your passes."

Karma saw the humor in the woman's wink at Nate and held up the pie in her left hand. "Pumpkin custard," she said, then held up the other. "Apple. We decided against mince."

The woman smiled broadly. "Good decision. Welcome. You must be Karma. I'm Aggie, Jave and Tom's mother. Since I'm the only mother-in-law here, I feel called upon to be difficult. The good cheer at this party is so thick, I thought some balance was required. Come in, come in."

The two boys who'd been with Nancy when she stopped in Karma's room at the hospital took their coats.

"You know Eddy and Pete?" Nate asked Karma.

She nodded. "Garrett and I met them right after he was born."

"Wow!" Pete said of Garrett. "Look at how big he's gotten. Malia isn't that big."

"Chelsea is, though," Eddy said. "She's a real porker. It's so weird that all three babies were born on the same day, in the same place."

"They all wanted to try the hospital's new birthing rooms," Jave said. In a white sweater and slim jeans, he strode toward them, carrying two glasses of wine. "Welcome. Come on. We're all in the kitchen. Nancy and Jo are cooking together." He winced, then added under his breath, "Mom insists she won't set foot in the kitchen, because this is Nancy's show, so we may have to send out for pizza. I just want you to be fore-warned."

Karma handed him the pies. "It's just wonderful to be here. Thank you for inviting me."

Jave smiled at her before turning in the direction of the kitchen. "I'm glad you were free. I understand you've caught the Christmas spirit. I saw one of your bears."

"No, I haven't," Karma said. "What I caught was some bullying from Nancy. That's all."

"Really." He didn't seem convinced. "Hey, guys," he called to the occupants of the kitchen. "Look who's here."

Jo and Nancy stood over an open oven in which a very white turkey sat in a roasting pan. Ryan Jeffries and Tom Nicholas sat at the table, peeling potatoes.

Everyone looked up with cheerful greetings. Tom booed at Nate, then pointed to the chair beside him with a fractional smile. "Park it. You can do the green beans. And you're not going to get out of it by holding a baby."

"Here." Aggie appeared beside Nate. "Give him to me." She pointed to the edge of the room, where a playpen held Malia and Chelsea. "Let's see what kind of a ladies' man he is."

MALIA: *Hi. Did you mug a sailor for that suit?*
Garrett: *Don't start with me. Where'd you buy your hair?*

Chelsea: Hey! What's the matter with you two? Our parents are having a party. Try to get along.
Malia: Yeah? Well, watch your binky. He's a thief!

KARMA WENT to join Jo and Nancy. She gave Jo a heartfelt hug.

"Shouldn't the bird be browning by now?" Nancy asked worriedly. She wore a jeweled black sweater over white stirrup pants, and over them—as an apron, Karma guessed—was a pale green hospital coat.

Jo shrugged an elegant shoulder in a blue silk blouse. A barbecue apron protected a long, matching skirt. She fairly glowed. "Well...white meat is supposed to be healthier, isn't it?"

Nancy looked up at her with a frown. "White meat *inside,* not outside."

"Did you put butter on it?" Karma asked. "Have you been basting?"

"The butter keeps falling off," Nancy said, "and burns in the bottom of the pan."

Karma bit back a smile. "Do you have cheesecloth?" she asked.

Nancy turned to Jave, who was placing a colander of green beans in front of Nate. "Honey, do we—?"

"Bottom drawer, right side," Aggie called before Nancy could finish the question. She'd positioned a rocking chair near the playpen, and she had one eye on the babies and one on the television.

The boys had taken their places with the men and were making faces as they peeled carrots and turnips.

"A small pan to melt butter in?" Karma asked.

"Right." Nancy handed Karma a small saucepan and a cube of butter, then wrapped a colorful cobbler apron around her. She grinned at Jo. "I love a take-charge woman, don't you? Even if she doesn't have the Christmas spirit."

"Don't hassle me." Karma laughed. "It's too early for the Christmas spirit."

Jo shook her head. "Mine starts when the first leaf falls and doesn't quit till the middle of January." Then she frowned worriedly as Karma cut off a length of cheesecloth and placed it in the pan with the butter. "Oh, God. She's going to cook cheesecloth."

Nancy looked over Karma's shoulder. "Maybe she's making cheese*cake?*"

Karma blinked worriedly at one woman, then the other. "It frightens me that you two are feeding children."

Jo shook her head. "Ryan cooks at our house. And the baby's still taking milk."

"Aggie cooks for us," Nancy admitted. "But I insisted she wouldn't have to lift a finger today."

Karma pushed her sleeves up. "Well, we're all lucky you invited me. We're going to cover this anemic bird and hope it isn't too late." She carried the pan, along with the cheesecloth soaked in melted butter, to the open oven door. She lifted the cheesecloth with a fork and opened it out over the turkey, then poured the butter left in the bottom of the pan over the top of the cloth.

"That'll give it some juice to work on, and pretty soon we'll have something to baste with. Tinfoil?"

Nancy handed it to her. She fitted it over the bird, pushed the rack in with a hotpad and closed the door. "Do you have a baster?"

"Second utensil drawer to the right," Aggie called.

Nancy found it. "Baste every half hour. Can I do anything else?"

Jo eyed her respectfully. "Can you make gravy?"

"Sure."

"Without a *can* of gravy?" Nancy asked.

"Yes. We'll have to wait for juice from the bird. Did you save the giblets?"

"Now how did *you* rate a woman who can cook?" Ryan asked Nate as he plopped a peeled potato into the pan of water that stood on the table between him and Tom.

"Who cares?" Jave said. "It looks like dinner is saved."

Nate looked up at the counter, where Karma was moving comfortably, laughingly, between Nancy and Jo, and felt a curious warmth inside him that he identified as domestic happiness. God. It was happening. He'd been so sure he'd be the only holdout in his circle of friends. And here he was, in the midst of their married and child-rearing circle and feeling very much as though he belonged.

Karma turned away from the counter to look toward the playpen, then caught his eye when she turned back. She winked at him. He winked back. He was lost.

GARRETT: *That's* my *mother. The one that's cooking.*
Malia: *Mine's wearing Daddy's hospital coat. And that's him in the white sweater.*
Chelsea: *Mine's the one peeling potatoes with Malia's uncle. Where's yours?*
Garrett: *The one in the black turtleneck.*
Malia: *He's not your father. He has to live with you to be your father. The one in the black turtleneck lives in the woods. Daddy and I took him soup and stuff when he was sick. And Mom and I went to your mother's house, and it's not the same place. He's not your daddy. You don't have one.*

Garrett: He is, too. He was there the day I got here.
He comes over all the time.
Chelsea: To be your daddy, he has to stay over. Every-
body knows that.
Malia: Yeah. And I still think that's a silly suit.

A SCREECH erupted from the playpen, followed immediately by a long, mournful wail.

Aggie lifted Garrett out of the playpen and tried to
rock him, but he continued to scream.

"Oh, that's temper," she said with a laugh. "What
did you girls say to him?"

Karma, chopping giblets, put the knife aside and began to dry her hands.

But Nate stood. "I'll get him," he said. "You keep
the food going." He took Garrett from Aggie and held
him to his shoulder. The baby settled there with quieter,
calmer sobs.

DID YOU HEAR THAT? They said you're not mine! How
come? Why not? If they have a dad, why don't I?
They're probably wrong, aren't they? Aren't you my
dad?

"WHAT'S THE MATTER, buddy? Didn't lunch agree with
you?" Nate walked into the dining room, pacing with
Garrett as he patted his back and tried to quiet him.
He'd always been a tearful baby, but he sounded particularly unhappy now.

"It's all right, you know," he said, walking to the
window with him and holding him so that he could look
out. "Can you see that? Trees that are red and gold.
Cozy neighborhood houses with chimneys smoking and

turkeys cooking. This is the life. You've got it made. You get to sleep curled up to your mom.''

BUT I DON'T HAVE A DAD!

"AND YOU KNOW WHAT? Tonight, you're going to have to start sharing her with me. She's not going to belong just to you anymore. She's going to be mine, too. And I'm going to be hers.''

THEN…does that make you mine?

"THIS IS kind of a big move for me," Nate went on, easing Garrett into a sitting position on his arm. "I didn't think I'd ever be able to get serious about a woman and a baby. But your mom's very special—and so are you. So, you promise me you're not going to make me crazy with worry? Hang upside down from monkey bars, and stuff like that?''

I DON'T KNOW. You promise me you're going to stay?

"I CAN'T BELIEVE," Tom said, his eyes glazed with satiety, "how delicious that was. I fully expected you to poison us, Nancy.''

Nancy smiled blandly at her brother-in-law. "Thank you, Tom. Actually, you have Karma to thank for the success of our Thanksgiving feast. And, of course, all of you who peeled spuds and vegetables.''

"She can make gravy," Jo marveled, "without a *can*.''

Ryan patted Jo's back supportively. "It's all right, darling. You did make good coffee.''

She smiled proudly. "I did, didn't I? Well, I can cut

pie, too. So if you gentlemen want to settle yourselves in front of the football game with one or the other of the Christmas projects, I'll bring pie and coffee along in a few minutes.''

Karma began to stack plates, and Nancy slapped her hand. ''No. Your work is done. You relax while I clean up.''

''*I'll* clean up,'' Aggie volunteered, ''with Pete and Eddy's help, while you feed the baby.''

Both boys groaned.

''Santa's watching, guys,'' Tom reminded.

''Then maybe you should help them,'' Jave suggested, ''because you have a lot to do to get off the naughty and onto the nice list. In fact, in only a month's time, I doubt that you could—''

''Who asked you?'' Tom demanded. ''Did anyone ask you? Come on, guys. We'll show your father how this is done with style and efficiency.''

''Ha!'' Nate carried the platter, with its almost bare turkey carcass, to the kitchen counter. ''For efficiency to result, you would have to be absent.''

Ryan followed with two empty bowls. ''Or at least tied to a chair.''

Tom glared at them, then put an arm around each of his nephews. ''The moral here, guys, is that you can't help being stuck with your brother, but you should exercise great care in picking your friends.''

Nate and Ryan stayed to help, taking every opportunity to harass Tom. Aggie loaded dishes into the dishwasher with experienced speed, then filled the sink with sudsy water for the roaster and the outsize pots and pans.

''Those should soak for a little while,'' she said,

shooing men and boys out of the kitchen. "Thank you for your help. Go have your pie and watch the game."

"You'll notice that your *good* son," Tom said exaggeratedly, indicating Jave's absence, "didn't stay to help."

Aggie patted his cheek. "I know, but he made the dressing and brought the extra chairs in from the garage while you were on the computer with the boys, playing Zork."

Eddy smiled up at him sympathetically. "I guess you should pick your mother carefully, too, huh, Unc?"

Tom sighed. "That's a little more difficult to do."

Pete shook his head. "It wasn't for us. We picked Nancy."

Nancy appeared just in time to hear the pleasure with which her stepson spoke the words. She wrapped her arms around him and hugged him. "Thank you. That was the best thing anybody ever did for me. Did anyone save me a piece of pie?"

"No pie," Jo said severely, passing her by with a dessert plate in each hand, "until you pick a Christmas project and settle down in front of the television. We don't want you tracking crumbs all over the place."

Nancy frowned at her. "Jo, this is my house."

"I know, but I promised to clean up afterward, and I'd rather not be faced with a mess. Pumpkin or apple? You can help me cut out snowflakes."

Jave and Ryan and the boys settled on a tarp on the carpet with stars cut out of pine and a can of yellow paint.

Jo and Nancy lay on the floor, a board between them, a stack of foam sheets, and two snowflake patterns. Malia lay on a blanket on the floor beside her mother, fast asleep.

Aggie sat in the rocking chair, with Chelsea in one arm and Garrett in the other.

CHELSEA: *I love this time when they need to rest, so they rock us to have an excuse.*
Garrett: *Yeah. Cool.*

NATE, faced with a coffee table covered with stars and a jar of glitter, looked around for support from Karma. But she was nowhere in sight. He went into the kitchen and found Tom leaning pensively in a corner of the counter. "Have you seen Karma?" he asked.

Tom looked almost surprised to see him there, as though he'd been far away in thought. "Huh? Ah, yeah. She went outside."

"Outside?" Nate repeated in surprise. It was cold, and threatening rain. "Why?"

Tom focused on him. "Who can explain why women do what they do? You do what you think they want, but you aren't doing it right, or your motives aren't right. Go figure."

Nate was torn for a moment between wondering where Karma had gone and wanting to be available to his friend's suddenly communicative mood. Sure Karma was in no danger, he leaned a hip on the counter beside Tom.

"We're talking about Amy?" he asked carefully.

Tom nodded. "She thinks a part of me is closed off to her."

Nate reached to the coffeepot beside them and poured two cups. He was going to need caffeine for this.

"Is it?" he asked, handing Tom a cup.

Tom sighed deeply and looked down into the dark

brew. "I don't know. I guess it's true. I guess part of me is closed off even from *me.*"

"Why? Because you think you're so bad?"

Tom looked up at him. His eyes, Nate saw, were haunted. "I left a friend alone, and he died."

Nate knew the whole story. "You left him," he said quietly, "because you thought you heard someone calling for help."

"We didn't find anybody. The building was surrounded by police and firemen. No one could have gotten out unnoticed."

"I imagine a building on fire is full of strange and eerie sounds."

"But I left him, for something that wasn't there."

"Tom," Nate said gently, reasonably, "you and your friend were victims of an accident. You lived and he didn't. It's nobody's fault, it was just the way it happened. If you don't accept that and move on, you'll survive, but you'll be as dead as Davey."

Tom closed his eyes and rubbed his forehead. "My mind knows that. It just can't make it settle inside, you know?" He ran a hand over his chest, as though something hurt there. "Nancy thinks I should go see Davey's parents." He opened his eyes again and smiled faintly. "They were great. I spent a few weekends with them when Davey and I went hunting."

"Why don't you? Maybe it'll help."

"Maybe." He sighed and took a long pull on his coffee cup.

"And maybe if you explain to Amy how you feel, *she* won't feel closed off."

"I've told her some of it," he said, then downed the rest of the coffee in a gulp. "But I wouldn't let her see my leg."

Nate frowned. "She asked to?"

"No." Tom put the cup on the counter with great care. "We were…making love, and I wanted the lights out. She agreed, but then she wanted to…touch my leg, and I wouldn't let her."

"Tom—"

"I know. I have it all figured out. I hate myself inside, so I hate myself outside. Besides which, the leg's ugly."

Nate put an arm around his shoulders. "Sometimes, Tom, you are such a lunatic that it amazes me you look so normal. I guarantee you she will not find it ugly, but you've already got that figured out. You have to come to that peace with yourself. So, for God's sake, do it. You're making Nate and me crazy with worry."

There was a sudden crash from outside, and a high-pitched scream. Nate recognized the sound instantly. Karma!

He ran out the back door, Tom following, and found Karma sitting astride the lower branches of a mountain ash in the middle of Jave's neat, square lawn. She held tightly to an upper branch.

On the grass was a collapsed ladder and a large basket, out of which spilled a big clump of moss.

"What are you doing?" Nate demanded, righting the ladder. Tom held it steady while Nate climbed halfway up. "You don't strike me as the tree-climbing type."

Karma frowned down at him. "I'm not tree climbing," she explained, "I'm moss collecting. And the pursuit happens to involve climbing trees."

"See?" Tom offered to Nate from below. "With that kind of reasoning, who can ever figure out what women are doing?"

Nate was too concerned to be amused. He held his

hand out to her. "We'll split hairs when you get down from there. Come on."

Karma took his hand and reached gingerly for the second step from the top with one of her simple black flats. His hand lent her sufficient balance and confidence to let go of the branch and step out with her other foot.

Bent almost double, she grabbed the top of the ladder in both hands and paused a moment to steady herself.

Nate leaped to the grass and waited until she was within reach, then swung her to the ground. He confronted her immediately. "What in the hell did you think you were doing? Where did you get the ladder?"

"Jave lent it to me." She held out the hem of the old gray sweater that covered her elegant suit. "Along with his sweater."

Nate turned to Tom. "Jave lent it to her," he said, in a tone that suggested he'd lent her a nuclear device.

Tom nodded with appropriate disgust. "The man's a swine."

Karma was surprised and a little amused by Nate's obvious annoyance. She was also touched and maybe even thrilled. He'd been afraid for her. No one had ever worried about her in that way.

She reached down for the clump of moss she'd collected and held it up to him. "Technically, I think it's a lichen, but we call it moss."

Tom folded the ladder with a grin at Nate. "I'll just leave you to your botany lesson. If it turns to biology, call me."

Nate studied Karma impatiently. She forced herself to withhold a smile. "This is moss," she explained gravely, "that I intend to use to decorate flowerpots for table centerpieces for the party. In big cities, you can buy it in flower or craft shops. The only place to get it in Heron Point is from a tree.''

He considered her. Though his expression didn't change, she thought she could see his irritation thinning.

''So you climb a tree,'' he said impatiently, ''in that beautiful outfit, with no one around to help you, with an arm that's been out of a cast all of twenty-four hours…''

''No,'' she replied. ''I climbed the *ladder*. I only got into the tree when the ladder fell.'' She put a hand back to a tear she'd felt when she snagged the seat of her slacks on a burl. ''I think I did ruin the outfit, though.''

Nate pulled her to him and investigated the tear with a gentle pass of his hand over her left hip. The breath clogged in her throat.

''Well, that's too bad,'' he said, freeing her only far enough that he could look down into her face. ''I really liked this suit on you.''

''But I ruined it in the interest of the Christmas party.'' She smiled winningly. ''That should absolve me of guilt.''

He studied her, but granted her no absolution. ''So, now you're making Christmas centerpieces?'' he asked.

''Yes,'' she replied.

''So…then…you've caught the Christmas spirit.''

''Well, I wouldn't say that. I just got a little caught up in Nancy and Jo's enthu—''

''Admit that you've caught the Christmas spirit,'' he warned, ''or I'm going to kiss you.''

''I haven't,'' she insisted. ''But Jave needs all this stuff prepared, and Nancy and Jo can't possibly—''

He followed through on his threat with satisfying thoroughness. He kissed her long and hard, and she felt limp when he'd finished.

He shook his head over her. "You're going to be a lot of work, Karma Endicott."

She dropped hers against his shoulder. "But you're going to love every minute of it, Nathan Foster," she promised.

Chapter Eleven

Goodbyes were noisy, filled with hugs and handshakes and plans for the next get-together to assess the status of the gifts and decorations, the first weekend in December.

Nate honked as they drove away, Garrett sound asleep in the back.

The night was dark, the streets deserted except for an occasional taxi or police car. Light blazed from the windows of homes snugly closed against the outside world. It was a family night.

Karma felt her heartbeat accelerate. Nate had promised to take her home with him tonight. Did he still intend to, or had he thought it over and changed his mind, remembering that there were other women in his life, less demanding than she was?

But he turned toward the road to the woods. Her senses responded, so heightened that she swore she could feel the movement of her blood in her veins.

By the time he pulled into the driveway, she could feel every separate cell functioning, every breath drawn in and expelled. Life was suddenly drama. She was about to make love with Nate.

For the first time in her recollection, time was something to savor and explore. It seemed to pass in slow motion as she watched Nate reach into the back seat for Garrett. She'd come to love the sight of her baby against his shoulder, the way he could hold him protectively with one long hand, and still use the other dexterously to lock and close the car door, then reach out for her and pull her into his arm.

Karma wrapped her arm around Nate's back, placed the other hand on her son, and felt the unity of their alliance, three separate parts of one cohesive whole. It brought tears to her throat and to her eyes.

"What?" Nate asked worriedly.

She hugged him fiercely. "It just feels so wonderful. The three of us. Does it feel wonderful to you?"

He kissed her upturned mouth. "That's too small a word for what I feel." Then he handed her his keys. "Give me the diaper bag and the carrier, and you open the door."

The house was dark and cold and smelled deliciously of its woodsy surroundings.

"Careful where you step," he warned. "There's a rocking horse with a bad runner somewhere in the middle of the—"

There was a thump and a little cry as Karma collided with it.

"Room," he finished apologetically as he flipped on the light. "Sorry."

"My fault. I got cocky," she said. "I thought I knew my way to the kitchen in the dark. My goodness! Where did all this come from?"

Karma looked around her at the array of toys spread out on every flat surface. On the floor were large items—the rocking horse on its side, a tricycle with a flat tire and a broken basket, a child's table-and-chair set badly in need of repainting.

"Donations are coming from everywhere. Tom's supposed to pick up the table and chairs and the rocking horse when he has time. The other things Jave and Ryan and I are going to work on."

On the sofa, the chairs, the coffee table, was a vast and motley collection of cars, trucks, dolls, tea sets, books, puzzles, games, and large boxes with odds and ends in them.

Nate was moving through the house, urging her to follow.

When he didn't head for the bedroom, as she expected, she thought he was going to the kitchen. But he passed the kitchen and started up the circular stairway. She hadn't investigated the second level when she spent the night nursing him.

"What's up here?" she asked, trailing several steps behind him.

He stopped to wait for her to catch up. "My bedroom," he said.

"I thought it was down there." She pointed over the railing to the room where she'd found him when he was ill.

He shook his head. "That's a guest room. I slept there for a few days because I felt like hell and it was easier than coming up here. Come on."

The loft bedroom and bath took up the entire second level. Tom had finished the walls and floors with planking he'd rescued from a scuttled dinner-cruise boat in Portland.

Old maps had been easy to find, and he'd bought a painting of a square-rigger at a hospital-auxiliary art auction. Aggie, interested in the project, had found a ship's lamp and a writing desk at Sam's Secondhand Barn.

The colorful quilt on the bed had been his grandmother's, and he had a sampler above the bed that *her* mother had done. All Things Bloom With Love, it read.

A stone fireplace like the one downstairs took up most of the opposite wall.

Karma stopped in the middle of the room and looked around, her eyes rapt, a soft smile forming on her mouth.

"What a beautiful room," she finally whispered. Then she turned to him, a curiously amused suspicion in her eyes. "Did Alexa help you? Isn't she the decorator?"

He placed the sleeping baby carefully in the middle of the bed, then went to wrap her tightly in his arms. "No. Tom and Aggie helped me. Forget my ladies, okay? There's only room for you in my life now. You fill my dreams, my thoughts, my plans."

Karma sighed against him. "You're everything I ever wanted."

Nate found that incredible, but refused to question his good fortune. He pulled her gently away from him. "You find a comfortable place for the baby while I build a fire."

He took her coat and hung it with his jacket in the closet.

Karma settled Garrett in his carrier and placed it on an overstuffed chair a safe distance from the fireplace. He'd had a big day, and he slept deeply, contentedly.

She went to kneel beside Nate as he patiently fed kindling to the frail beginnings of a fire.

There was something primitive about the action, something so different from her orderly world that she felt disoriented, vaguely out of step with life as she knew it.

She was trembling inside. She had to share a truth with him that she hoped wouldn't change anything, but she had to admit that it could. She opened her mouth to form the words. The single syllable "I..." came out just before courage stalled somewhere in her chest.

Nate looked over his shoulder at her as he leaned two logs against each other over the burning kindling. "Yes?" he said.

She opened her mouth to try again, but he had to turn his attention back to the fire as one of the logs caught. He added more kindling and leaned a third log against the other two.

In a moment, the fire was burning merrily, and he pulled an iron screen decorated with the pattern of a sailing ship across the hearth. He turned to her, a forearm balanced on his upraised knee, his smile warm and interested. "Now, what did you say?"

She stared at him, lips parted, knowing she owed him the truth, in all fairness, but knowing also how desperately unhappy she would be if it changed anything—if it changed tonight.

He looked into her eyes, and his interested smile turned into a look of gentle concern. He grinned suddenly. "Are you nervous?" He put a hand to the side of her face and stroked his thumb gently over her cheekbone. "It's okay. So am I."

She leaned forward to kiss his cheek, falling more deeply in love with him because of that admission. It made it easier to be honest. She leaned back to look him in the eye.

"I'm more than nervous. I'm...a virgin." She hitched a shoulder in sudden embarrassment. "Sort of."

Nate stared at her in astonishment for a moment, then dropped his raised knee and sat back on his heels.

"A what?" he asked.

She nodded, as though to assure him that he hadn't misunderstood her. "A virgin," she repeated. Then, with a nervous wave of her hand, she tacked on, "Well, you know—technically."

He narrowed one eye. "Technically?"

Karma nodded, her cheeks pink. "Well, I've had a baby, but I explained all that. The sperm bank and everything. It was a surgical procedure. Other than that..." She raised that shoulder again. "Technically...this is my first time."

Nate had calmness down to a science. And he was grateful, because this was the last thing he'd expected her to say. A virgin? Karma, whose baby he'd helped deliver, was a virgin? The woman he'd been dreaming all day of making love to all night...was a virgin?

He felt awe, amazement, the pressure of responsibility.

Karma saw the turbulence in his eyes and felt her own particular panic. "I only mention it," she said, swallowing, "because I...will probably be..." She made an open-handed, helpless gesture. "You know...less skilled than you probably...expected."

He scolded her with a look. "All I expected," he said quietly, "was a woman as eager to be with me as I am to be with her."

She wanted to wrap her arms around him, but she kept their knee-to-knee distance, still uncertain of his reaction.

"I *am* eager to be with you," she said, her voice thick with longing. "No man has ever been as important to me as you are. I'd saved up all my love, and when

I didn't think I'd find anybody, I went to the sperm bank for Garrett. But now…'' Tears welled up in her eyes, and she rose on her knees to frame his face in her hands. ''Now I wish I'd waited a year so that he was yours.''

''Oh, Karma,'' he groaned, kneeling, too, to take her in his arms. Every concern he felt fled, because love was guiding him—the love she offered, and the love he returned. ''I was there when he drew his first breath. And I'll be here from now on. That's what fatherhood's about—take it from someone who knows.''

She wrapped her arms around him and held. ''Thank you.'' She kissed his throat, his chin, his mouth, then looked into his eyes and tried to explain their curious circumstances. ''I usually resist doing anything I'm not good at. I study the subject, analyze the data, consider my approach from all angles.'' She smiled ruefully. ''You can't really do that with sex and treat it with the reverence it deserves.''

He couldn't help but smile. Not simply because he knew something she didn't—a fact that delighted him on some basic level—but also because she was trusting him to take her where she'd never been. Because she loved him.

All the love and tenderness he felt for her tripled.

He tipped her face up and kissed her. ''Stay right here,'' he said. ''I'll bring a blanket and pillows.''

He went to a closet across the room and returned with a down comforter that he spread on the floor, a little distance from the fire. She moved aside to help him, then caught the pillows one by one as he tossed them from the bed.

Before joining her, he went to the chair where she'd placed Garrett in his carrier and peered down at him.

"Sound asleep," he reported as he came to kneel with her in the middle of the thick comforter.

She opened her arms to him, wanting to hold him, wanting to be held, to relish the wonder of this choice.

"Are you warm enough?" he asked, running his broad hand up and down her spine. "Maybe we should wait a little while and give the fire time to—"

She smiled up at him. "I don't want to wait another moment. Lead on, and I'll do my best to follow."

Nate felt sure he could drown in the look of love in her eyes and never even make an effort to surface again. But he had things to teach her.

"All right." He held her away from him, just enough to allow him access to the top button of her shirt. "First of all, we're both wearing entirely too many clothes."

He unfastened just a few buttons, and the silky, over-size garment fell off her to puddle at her knees on the blanket.

Her ivory skin glowed in the firelight, her small breasts, in a scrap of vanilla lace, distracting Nate in his task of undressing her.

He unfastened the simple hook at the front of her bra and slipped it off her shoulders. Then he cradled her in his arms and tipped her backward so that she lay on the blanket. He kissed each pert little globe and enjoyed her ragged sigh of pleasure.

He dipped his fingertips inside the waistband of her silky slacks and pulled them down. A strip of lace that matched the bra came with them.

She was slender and delicately built, a small waist flaring only slightly to gently rounded hips and long, graceful legs.

Nate tossed the clothes aside and braced his hands on the blanket on either side of her waist to grin at her.

"It's too bad you ruined that outfit, but you look magnificent without it."

She smiled shyly and reached up to unbutton his shirt. "*Magnificent* is probably a little strong. I know that it applies to you, though," she said, her task finally completed.

He smiled and frowned simultaneously. "You've never seen me…naked. Have you?"

"Not exactly," she admitted, liking the vaguely worried look on his face. "I've seen you bare chested. Remember when you were sick and tried to bean me with the putter?"

"Oh, yeah." He knelt up to pull the shirt off, then yanked a snowy white T-shirt over his head. He leaned over her again to kiss her. "I'm afraid I don't remember what I was wearing—or not wearing. You were very lucky I was weak, or you might have found yourself somewhere in the park, or on the roof of Columbia Chocolates, downtown."

She smiled. "Not too terrible a fate." She put her hands to his chest and sat up, continuing to push him backward as she rose onto her knees and forced him to lie back. She knelt astride him and unbuckled his belt.

As an afterthought, she turned to look behind her, and noticed that he still wore his shoes. "Uh-oh," she said. "I think I've broken the pattern of graceful disrobing."

"Not a problem," he said, toeing off the shoes. "Loafers. You're a fine student. Gifted, even. Do continue."

Nate watched the top of her glossy dark head as she concentrated on unfastening his belt and the zipper of his pants. He could die a happy man now, he thought, with the memory of Karma eager to undress him.

Then he felt her fingertips against the flesh at his hipbone as she reached inside his slacks to pull them down. Air caught in his lungs. His brain was starved for oxygen, he was sure, but it didn't matter. It seemed no longer connected to his body, anyway.

Though he was a man used to making rapid-fire decisions and following them with quick, decisive action, he couldn't form one coherent thought.

He braced up on his elbows as Karma pulled the fabric down his legs and off, then watched her eyes peruse his body with smiling interest before she came back up to sit beside his waist and drape her upper body over his.

She ran a fingertip over his bottom lip, her expression suddenly serious. "And you're as beautiful *inside,* as well, aren't you?" she asked on a whisper. "How did I get so lucky?"

"Karma." His voice caressed her name, even as he turned onto his side and pulled her beside him. He held her to him and swept a hand along every silken hill and hollow of her.

Her small hands explored every inch of him, her innocence an erotic counterpoint to her bold touch. She smoothed a path along his back one moment, then stroked his hip the next, pitching him to the brink of madness.

She nestled against him with a sigh of pleasure, of rightness. He wrapped his body around hers, thinking that already he couldn't remember what it had been like when she wasn't in his arms.

Karma felt as though her entire world had been distilled into the warmth of Nate's arms. And the tightness of his embrace seemed to enlarge her world, rather than diminish it.

It gave life a density she'd never understood before.

Nate stroked the length of her thigh, then up again, this time along the sensitive inside. She bent her knee to accommodate him, and turned her face into his throat when he dipped a finger gently inside her.

It was an intimacy she'd never accorded anyone before, and it was a revelation to her how right she'd been to be so discriminating. As he found that pearl of sensitivity and caressed it, it was as if a light went on inside her. Feelings seemed to acquire substance. Pleasure was in the texture of his touch. Love had a face.

And she saw it above hers, burnished by the firelight, as her body, even her soul, seemed to be caught in some exotic, languid orbit she was powerless to resist. Then it seemed to tighten, and the world began to spin, drawing her deeply toward the heart of its mysteries.

Then it fragmented with the sudden explosion of pleasure as wave after wave of sensation rolled over her. She looped her arms around Nate's neck and held on, whispering his name.

Nate felt her pleasure as if it were his own. Given the recent birth of her baby, and her admission of virginity, he was willing to be satisfied with that.

But she was touching him, urging him to move atop her.

"Karma…"

She took a firm hold of his shoulders. Her dark eyes were determined in the undulating light. "That was absolutely…" She smiled. "Well, there is no word. But I don't want just pleasure. I want *you*."

That decimated every argument he could present—except one.

"It'll probably be uncomfortable for you," he warned.

She nodded. "*Wanting* you is uncomfortable." Then she lifted herself against him and kissed him forcefully. "Please?"

Nate entered her carefully, and when she made no complaint, he thrust more deeply, absorbing her small gasp against his shoulder.

"I'm fine," she assured him when he raised himself off her. She wrapped her arms around his neck and pulled him resolutely down to her. "I'm fine. Make love to me."

Her eagerness for him, and the wonderful rightness of being enclosed by her body, filled him with a profound tenderness, as well as a passion that he had under control—just.

He began to move inside her, alert for the smallest sign or sound of discomfort. But she looked up at him with lazy eyes, her dark hair like an inky cloud on the blanket. She smiled lovingly at him, and then her brow furrowed and she arched her back, uttering an indeterminate little sound.

Then he felt her body shudder around his, and his control disintegrated. They trembled together in the dancing light.

Karma continued to cling to him when they'd collapsed together and he'd pulled the other half of the blanket over them. She could think of nothing to say that could begin to express what she felt.

She'd known making love with him would change her world, but she hadn't realized it would change *her*.

All the angles in life seemed to have softened, and all the careful compartments in which she'd kept emotions and dreams had disappeared. Orderliness had been replaced by a chaotic tangle that held surprises that startled her, and muddled many of the truths she'd long believed in.

Amid the delicious pleasure, a little bud of fear began to grow inside her.

"I wish you'd say something," Nate encouraged worriedly, stroking her hair spread out on his shoulder.

She kissed his collarbone, wondering if *he* felt changed.

"I feel different," she admitted breathlessly. "I want to mix the colors in my closet, take the dividers out of my desk drawers, maybe even tear a page out of my phone book and throw it away."

He laughed. "I'd take that slowly. You might implode."

"I know. It's a little scary." She needed desperately to analyze it, to understand it. "I guess I feel…" She didn't know what she felt. She couldn't think clearly, and that alone was alarming.

On one level, making love with Nate made everything warm and wonderful. On another, it had shaken her grip on life as she knew it, as she'd worked so hard to build it. *That* was terrifying.

Nate brushed the hair from her face, his eyes dark with concern. "What is it?" he asked.

It was ironic, she thought, that the very man responsible for this feeling of being lost, adrift, was all she could hold on to as she struggled to right her world.

"Nothing," she whispered, resting her head in the hollow of his shoulder.

"Everything's going to be all right," he whispered, pulling the blanket up around her and stroking her hair. "I promise."

She hoped he was right.

Chapter Twelve

"I thought you were so tired, you *had* to have breakfast in bed!" Karma, whipping eggs and milk for omelets, shouted teasingly toward the noise in the living room.

In the four days since Thanksgiving, they'd fallen into the habit of making love when Nate came home in the morning, and following that with breakfast.

She knew she was courting danger with this relationship, but she'd convinced herself she could indulge it, as long as she promised nothing, surrendered nothing.

And being in his arms at night, and across the table from him when he came home from the hospital in the morning, filled her with such physical satisfaction that it was easy to dismiss the threat to her professional peace of mind.

"Just because you worked all night," she went on, "and made love to me twice, you think you should be waited on. Well, one of the times doesn't count. We did that underwater, and that reduces physical exer— Aaah!"

Karma screamed at the unexpected sight of Tom Nicholas standing in the kitchen doorway, a large cardboard box in his arms, a baseball cap on backward.

He appeared as shocked as she did. Not that that was

any surprise. How often did one find a woman wearing a long apron over a T-shirt and flannel boxer shorts. He looked around himself, as though wondering if he was in the wrong house. Seeing that he wasn't, he stammered apologetically.

"Karma, I'm sorry! I'm...ah... Where's Nate? I was supposed to drop this off and pick up some...some wooden...toys."

Karma held a hand to her thumping heart. "It's okay. I just didn't hear you come in. Ah—Nate just got home a little bit ago." She smiled and turned back to her task, embarrassed that he'd overheard her teasing remark. "You'll find him—"

"Right here." Nate appeared in the doorway beside Tom. He had Garrett against his shoulder and a wry smile on his lips. "Morning. Broke in to steal my valuables?"

Tom put the box down and glowered at him. "I came to give you these, and pick up the other stuff. Sorry. I thought you wouldn't be home yet, so I let myself in. I didn't know...you and Karma... I mean, only four days ago you were grumbling at her for climbing trees. You know, you could tell me these things."

Nate snickered. "Like you're so free with *your* life's details."

Tom ignored that and asked, with genuine awe, "Underwater?"

Nate ignored *him* and glanced across the kitchen at Karma. "Did he scare you to death?"

She waved a tea towel dismissively. "Not enough that I can't fix him an omelet, too. Cheese and sausage."

"Thanks," Tom said, smiling at her and shaking his

head. "I'm meeting Ryan and Jo at nine. Promised to help them move."

"Oh, that's right." Nate ran a hand over his face. "I'll sleep for a few hours, then come and help you guys finish up this afternoon."

"Good deal. I'll just take the rocking horse and the table and chairs and be on my way." He began to move away, then stopped. "Oh. Nancy asked me to tell you that we're all going to the tree farm next weekend to pick up the tree for the party. I'm borrowing a flatbed from Heron Point Hardware. We're meeting at Coffee Country Sunday at eight, and Aggie's watching the babies. That okay, Karma?"

"Sounds great."

Nate helped Tom by carrying two small chairs back-to-back in one hand. Tom leaped into the back of his truck and took them from him. He asked once again with a grin, "Underwater?"

Nate rolled his eyes. "Bathtub, blockhead."

"Oooh..."

Nate turned serious. "You're doing all right with that leg."

Tom indicated the cold but sunny weather. "Feels pretty good when it isn't raining."

"Anybody looked at it for you lately?" Nate asked.

Tom turned to respond, obviously presuming it had been a professional question. Then Nate saw him realize that it had been personal and referred to his refusal to let Amy touch it. He expected Tom to react defensively.

To his surprise, Tom leaped out of the truck, chucked Garrett under the chin and pointed to the house. "With a pair of legs like that waiting in your kitchen, I can't imagine why you're worried about mine. See ya."

HEY. Where you going with that horse?

NATE CARRIED GARRETT back into the kitchen, and leaned over Karma to kiss her neck while she poured sausage and cheese onto the egg mixture in the pan. It smelled heavenly, and so did she.

CAN I HAVE SOME OF THAT? Maybe a little of that orange stuff you guys have every morning. I'm getting a little tired of the milk.

NATE LOOKED DOWN at Garrett, who gave him a wide smile. He held the baby up so that Karma could see him. "I think he likes it here. He was smiling. Come on, buddy. Do it again. Smile." He tickled his chin.

OKAY, there's your smile. But for that I expect some of that stuff in the pan.

KARMA SMILED over his delight. "Who wouldn't love this house? Who wouldn't love you?" She kissed his chin, then made a face. "Is this night shift a forever thing?"

He shrugged. "I've always preferred it. I had nothing else to do, and most of the other staff have families." His eyes rested on her, the look in them suddenly significant. He caught the back of her neck and pulled her to him. "Why? Do you miss me at night?"

"Horribly. But that's life, I guess. I'll just have to suffer."

He reached around her to turn off the heat under the pan. He braced an arm against the counter to hold her there, and stilled her protests about breakfast with a kiss.

"Actually," he said when he raised his head, "you *don't* have to suffer."

She brightened. "I don't? You mean you can change shifts?"

He inclined his head, the gesture noncommittal. "I'm trying, but it'll probably take a while. Jackie Palmrose, the ER doctor on day shift, may be moving. In which case the day-shift slot would be open. Her husband is considering taking a job in Portland after the first of the year. But it's nothing definite yet."

She frowned, confused. "Then…why don't I have to suffer?"

"Well, there's a treatment for your condition," he explained, watching her eyes.

She studied him suspiciously. "What?"

"A kind of patch," he said, reaching into his pocket. "You know—like the insulin patch for diabetics, and the patch to combat seasickness that you wear on your skin to dis—"

She nodded. "Yes, I know. But how does that—?"

He put Garrett into her right arm, and took her left hand. "Now, this has to be worn on the third finger," he said, slipping on the simple half-carat marquise-cut diamond. "And my love will be with you, even when I'm not."

He heard her gasp, saw her eyes widen and soften with love as she looked from the ring to him. Then, to his complete surprise, fear rose out of her expression and, right beside it, a misery he couldn't begin to understand.

She lowered her eyes, her mouth working unsteadily. She rubbed an index finger over the brilliant surface of the diamond, then pulled the ring off.

She handed it back to him, her eyes brimming with tears.

MOTHER! What are you doing?

"I CAN'T," she whispered. "I want to, but I can't."

He was astonished. He'd thought marriage was what she'd wanted all along. He felt an odd disorientation.

"Why not?" he demanded.

She tried to push against his chest, but he stood firm, still blocking her with a hand on the counter.

"Nate, please—"

"You're not going anywhere," he said with dark resolve, "until I understand this. I thought we loved each other."

She looked into his eyes, her own bleak and confused. "We do. I *love* you."

"But you don't want to marry me."

"I do," she said, "but I can't."

This was going in circles, getting nowhere. "Why," he asked, his voice rising, "can't you?"

She gestured around the kitchen, which was strewn with Christmas projects, toward the living room, where toys had been collecting for weeks, and tried to speak, but didn't seem able to.

He had to interpret that himself. "You mean the mess? You can't marry me because the house is messy?"

She shook her head quickly. "No," she said, her voice strained. "Because this is how you make me feel *inside*."

He stared at her, desperately hoping to understand what she was telling him. "I make you feel…messy?"

Her voice was tight with tears. "You make me feel

chaotic, out of control, stacked up—like I haven't a clue where I'm going, or what's going to happen next. And I can't sort anything out.''

He took a step back from her. ''That isn't me, Karma. That's *life*. You've just been watching it all these years. Now you're living it.''

''Maybe,'' she conceded, ''but it doesn't change the fact that I feel that way.'' The confusion she felt was exaggerated by his nearness, and she took advantage of the step he'd taken backward to slip around him. ''And what kind of a wife would I be, when I don't know where I'm going?''

He turned impatiently and folded his arms. ''I thought that was clear. Expand your business. Live for Garrett.''

She gave him an accusing glare as she paced around the table, still wearing the apron over a pair of his boxers. Garrett, in her arms, looked mystified. ''My point exactly,'' she said. ''That was always so clear in my mind. Now it's not. I can't remember what I want.''

That was the first positive thing he'd heard her say. It was flimsy, but he was convinced it was positive.

''Maybe,'' he suggested, watching her come around the table toward him, ''that's because what you want is changing.''

She stopped two yards from him, her chin at a stubborn angle.

''I have worked long and hard,'' she said, ''to get my life on track. Having Garrett early disorganized everything, but I was just getting a grip on things again. I don't want to lose that.''

He frowned at her, shaking his head. ''Karma, I want for you what you want for you.''

She gave him a disbelieving look. ''Oh, right. This

morning I told you I was getting serious about renting office space, and what did you do?''

He remembered clearly. It had been wonderful. ''I kissed you and began…''

She put a hand out in a "stop" gesture. ''*I* remember what you did. I'm just trying to make another point. You distract me from what I've always wanted. You make me forget how important it is to plan, to get your priorities in order, to remember your long-range goals.''

''That's because,'' he pointed out gently, ''you always forget to live the moment. And don't try to tell me you didn't enjoy this morning as much as I did.''

''I wouldn't.'' Karma resented the suggestion that she might. ''I *told* you I love you. I just need more time to get my work done. More focus on…on…'' She couldn't even concentrate sharply enough on what she wanted to tell him it was.

''I'm sorry,'' she said finally. ''Maybe Garrett and I should go home.''

NATE! Did you hear that?

HE CAME toward her consideringly, hands loosely on his hips, the long, lean body she now knew intimately moving with easy grace. ''Do you want to go?''

The last thing she wanted to do was leave, but she'd thrown commitment back in his face. What could either of them do after that?

''No,'' she admitted. ''I love you. I just need…less playtime and more worktime.''

''All right.'' He stopped just inches from her, his eyes dark and grave. ''We'll try that. It should prove which one of us has the better angle on how to run a relationship.''

He took the baby from her. Garrett went without complaint.

"Garrett and I will finish fixing breakfast," he said.

"I can—"

He drew away when she tried to take Garrett back. "Just consider that sitting room in the back your office. I'll make a point of watching Garrett more often when I'm home, and I won't touch you unless you ask."

That didn't sound healthy to her. "Nate, I..."

He pushed her gently out of the kitchen. "Go on. I promised to help move Jo and Ryan this afternoon, so you'd better make use of the time."

"But you won't get any sleep before you go back to work tonight."

He smiled at her as he tossed away the omelet and prepared to start over. "Then we won't have to worry about my feeling amorous, will we?"

THEY LIVED like a pair of amiable friends. Karma hated it, but she refused to admit that Nate had a point.

He watched Garrett mornings so that she could work, then slept afternoons, while she concentrated on the Christmas projects, if the baby's mood allowed. They ate dinner in fraternal politeness, then Nate went to work. She thought about him much of the night.

He never seemed inclined to make time for them, and she, perversely, refused to complain.

All around them, the Christmas season blossomed. The house was filled with toys. Those in the living room had been repaired and painted, those in the spare bedroom awaited the caring hands of whoever had time to work on them.

Jave and his boys and Ryan came over once a week to collect a boxful to take home and work on, then returned the repaired ones and filled the box again. Karma marveled at their generosity and their good humor.

Tom repaired everything wooden, and had made a dozen trucks out of pine, with wheels and steering wheels that turned. Jave and Nate and Ryan had inspected them in Tom's absence and praised the carpentry and the care that had gone into them. Then they had worried over his situation with Amy.

Karma went to the toy shop downtown to pick up presents for Garrett, Chelsea, and all of Jave and Nancy's children. Fir swags of greenery and small white lights were draped on every Heron Point storefront, every light pole, and across every intersection.

Store windows were filled with sparkling decorations and sumptuous gifts, the bakery showed off gingerbread houses and pressed cookies in Christmas motifs, and shoppers and excited children were already clogging the sidewalks. Rain fell instead of snow, but it was Oregon, and everyone expected it and had long ago learned to live with it.

Umbrellas bloomed like poinsettias all around town.

If Karma called a client, she was treated to the sound of Christmas carols when she was put on hold.

She remembered that, last year, it had annoyed her. This year, she rather enjoyed it, though she and Nate were like ships in the night. She so missed the warm camaraderie they'd enjoyed before he proposed.

But Garrett seemed pleased with his surroundings and the time he spent with Nate. He ate well, slept for longer periods, smiled continually, and grew.

It rained buckets on their Christmas-tree safari Sunday. Karma stopped in her tracks when she saw Amy in the group collected at Coffee Country for breakfast. The shop was closed for regular business.

"Amy!" she gasped.

She'd worked with her and Jo on decorations several afternoons at Nancy's and thought she had the dearest heart, the sweetest smile, but the worst fashion sense, of any woman she'd ever met.

But today, her tall, well-proportioned figure was dressed in snug jeans into which she'd tucked a white turtleneck covered by a red-and-blue plaid flannel shirt.

Her hair, which had always been long and lank, had been trimmed to just below her ears and hung in a glossy bell shape, parted on the side and slipping seductively over one eye.

She wore light makeup and a confidence Karma had never seen in her before.

Nate, who'd been talking to Tom as they walked in together, slammed into Karma's back. He moved away quickly, as though the contact had hurt him.

Karma's glance scolded him for making so much of it.

He responded with a blink of bland innocence. Then he noticed Amy. "Jeez. Amy? Is that you?" He pretended to peer closer.

She laughed and nodded. "Thank you. That's very flattering," she said. "I'm glad you all approve of the new me." She smiled at the group, who applauded and whistled. "I decided I couldn't go to New York a frump, so I went to Portland for a makeover. Hi, Tom."

The tension in the air was palpable, as everyone awaited the meeting of these two who simply could not get their relationship together. Karma hoped Nate hadn't made it obvious to everyone that they weren't the only ones having difficulty.

Amy smiled charmingly at Tom, and behaved as though he were Jave, or Nate, or Ryan—just another of her male friends.

Karma wondered if Nate had given her lessons.

"You can have my seat," Amy said to Tom. "I've got a few things to do at the hospital, so I'll meet you all at the tree farm."

Tom hadn't said a word since he'd walked in the door, and he continued to watch her, speechless, as she walked out to her car.

The men looked confused. The women exchanged knowing looks. Tom seemed to have gone into a coma. Jave pushed him into a chair and handed him a cup of coffee.

IT LOOKED, Karma thought, as though the tree were being selected by ducks and derelicts. The tree farm provided a few hooded yellow slickers that were distributed to the women. The men, dressed to haul the tree, wore their oldest clothes. They moved through the evenly planted forest shouting eagerly to one another when a possibility was spotted.

They gathered for a consultation, then dispersed again, looking for one that was taller, fatter, more even.

Karma finally found the perfect tree alone on a slope in the middle of a field. "Look!" she breathed to Jo, almost as though she were afraid it would move away if she spoke too loudly. "I wonder if we could have that one?"

It was a noble fir about twelve feet high, beautifully proportioned and majestic in its solitude.

Jo beckoned Nancy and Amy, who were debating the qualities of a smaller, less spectacular tree at the edge of the lot.

"Oh, that's *it!*" Nancy said.

"Oh, definitely," Amy agreed. "But can we have it? It isn't in with the cultivated ones."

Jo put her little fingers to her lips and whistled shrilly. The men, dispersed throughout the forest, turned to look. "Come on!" she shouted. "We found it!"

Everyone gathered around it, like a group of eccentric druids. The men seemed to consider Tom the final authority.

He walked around it, the shoulders of his lined denim jacket drenched through, rain dripping from his hair into his eyes.

Karma noticed Amy's study of his spiked eyelashes, then her quick glance away when he nodded and turned to the group. "Looks perfect to me. Call Mr. Widdoes."

Mr. Widdoes was the tree farmer, who made a point of sitting back before his fire while shoppers selected their tree. He was happy to trek out with his saw when the tree was chosen, but the buyer had to haul it away.

Nate called him on his cellular phone and explained the location of the tree they'd selected.

"We can have it," Nate reported as he closed the phone and lowered the antenna. "He'll come and cut if for us, but we have to haul it down the hill."

Tom nodded. "I brought tarps and rope. Somebody want to come with me and help me bring them up here?"

"I vote we send the women," Jave said.

Ryan agreed. "I second that. All those in favor?"

Three male hands went up.

As the other women began to protest, Karma folded her arms. "You gentlemen seem to be missing the fact that you're outnumbered, and therefore outvoted."

Ryan frowned. "We're four to four. The best you can hope for is a tie."

She shook her head. "Tom has to go to unlock the toolbox on the flatbed, so he's not a vote. All those in favor of the *men* going to get the tarps and rope, say aye."

Four female hands went up.

"Pardon me, but *you*," Nate said to Karma, "have missed something important here. Tom can simply hand one of you the key."

Amy stepped away from the knot of women and confronted Tom, her expression faintly smiling. "Really?" she asked. "I'll bet I could talk him out of it."

Tom was both shocked by her willingness to tease him, considering their circumstances, and apparently concerned, judging by the way he studied her face, about just what form of persuasion she intended to use.

He folded his arms, prepared to stand firm. "I'll bet you can't."

Amy dropped her hood back, stretched her arms forward to reach beyond the confinement of her vinyl sleeves, and wrapped her arms around his neck.

While the rain came down in sheets, she kissed him with a fervor and a determination that made Jave and Ryan look at one another. Nate shifted his weight.

The women gaped silently.

The kiss went on.

Karma watched enviously. She missed the physical side of her relationship with Nate with an intensity that was almost pain. But she knew what he was doing by keeping his distance, and she refused to acknowledge that it affected her. Life did need order. It did have to be taken seriously. And if he seemed intent on proving that the extra time for it could only be taken away from time in bed, then so be it. She could hold out as long as he could.

She caught his eye across the crowd and knew he was reading her mind. She held his gaze boldly, then looked away when Jave moved.

He snatched the keys from Tom's lifeless fingers at Amy's back, and grinned at his companions. "Since none of us has brought diving gear, we'd better go for the tarp and ropes before we all drown."

The women applauded the decision, then made themselves scarce when Tom and Amy finally pulled apart.

NATE DIRECTED Jave, Ryan and Tom as they hauled the tree onto his back deck. It wouldn't be decorated until the night before the party, which was scheduled for the eighteenth of December. Then they joined the women inside to celebrate their success with Karma's homemade chili, corn bread and salad.

Jo had found *It's A Wonderful Life* on television. She and Ryan and Jave and Nancy occupied either end of the sofa in cozy twosomes.

Amy sat by the fire, buffing her hair with a towel, and Tom sat on the floor with a dump truck from the bottomless pile of toys to be fixed.

"I don't get it," Nate said quietly to Karma in the kitchen. "I thought Amy and Tom resolved their problem at the tree farm. But they still don't seem to be speaking."

She sprinkled more chili powder into the pan. "Men. You miss all the subtleties. I think that kiss was intended to show him what he'd be missing if he let her go to New York." She looked up, her own expression now blandly innocent. "You're telling me you're not acquainted with the tactic?"

"Tactic?" he inquired.

She gave him a look that openly doubted his need to question. *"Tac-tic."* She enunciated the word. "As in a campaign launched to defeat an opponent. Hotpad, please."

He handed her the quilted square. "Are we opponents?"

"Thank you. That seems to be the position you've taken."

He pretended confusion. "By providing you with what you claimed was missing?"

"By withholding," she said judiciously, wrapping the pot holder around the handle of the pan, "what should never have been at issue in the first place."

"Sex."

"Lovemaking."

"But you put it at issue." He held a pottery bowl steady as she poured the chili into it. "You said it distracted you from work."

"No, I..."

"Nate!" Ryan called from the living room. "Leave her alone! You're holding up dinner."

Karma threatened Nate with a glance as she hefted the bowl. "To be continued at a later date."

"Why not tonight?"

"Because I have a headache."

GARRETT: It looks beautiful, Mom. But how come we can't keep any of this neat stuff? I know you said it's for less fortunate children, but the rest of us need stuff, too, you know. Is there anything to eat?
Malia: Don't you ever think of anything but food?

Garrett: Yeah. Got your binky?
Chelsea: Come on, you two. It's Christmas. Santa's watching, remember?

KARMA FOLLOWED Nancy, Jo and Amy as they looked over the fairgrounds in its holiday splendor, and simply stared, amazed by what their efforts had brought about.

Picnic tables with red-and-green paper covers filled the room, a wide aisle cleared in the middle where the children would walk up to see Santa.

Tom's wooden stars, painted yellow and adorned with glitter, were hung in a random pattern all over the walls and caught the overhead light like the Milky Way.

Snowflakes and angels hung from the ceiling on fishing line, turning and dancing on the air, their beauty genuine enough to mimic the real thing.

Every table was decorated with her moss-trimmed flowerpots filled with votive candles. They filled the room with the fragrances of bayberry, cinnamon and vanilla.

But the real wonder was the treasure trove of toys locked in the office, every one beautifully wrapped and identified by age and gender with a tag. Jave, Ryan and Tom had been up most nights for the past week in Nate's living room repairing and painting the last of the toys.

Karma had paced the floor with Garrett, who was in an insomniac phase, and poured coffee and made a final batch of cinnamon bears.

"We did it," Jo said in wonder, her eyes roving the room as she smiled. Chelsea lay fast asleep in her arms. "Did you ever think we'd finally see it all come together?"

"Yes," Nancy replied, patting Malia's back as the

baby groped for the tie on her sweatshirt. "Despite our quirks, we're a remarkably efficient team."

Across the room, the men were putting the finishing touches on the tree. The doctors and nurses had provided the ornaments and lights, and one of Amy's angels had been placed at the top of the tree and touched the ceiling.

"Okay!" Nate, atop the ladder, shouted to Ryan, who'd moved toward the back door. "Kill the lights!"

The room went dark, and everyone in the room *aah*ed in unison.

The tree was a pillar of light and color in the darkness. The wooden stars picked up its light and glittered like a falling sky. The angels and snowflakes also collected its light and sparkled as they turned on invisible strings.

Amy uttered a quiet little gasp of distress. "I…have to go," she said, her voice frail in the darkness. "See you guys tomorrow at the party."

"Amy?" Nancy followed her as far as the door, then turned back to Jo and Karma. "Already gone. I swear, if that brother-in-law of mine doesn't come around, and soon, he's getting a fat lip for Christmas. And speaking of which, Karma…" She lowered her voice. "Is something wrong between you and Nate? You're so… polite."

Jo leaned closer to hear as Karma smiled wryly. "He proposed," Karma said.

Nancy asked in puzzlement, "And that's bad?"

Karma sighed and shifted Garrett to her other arm. "No, of course not. But we have…different approaches to life. I've worked so hard to get my business going, to make plans. But loving Nate has…" She sighed, as though the admission was hard. "It's made me think about more babies, more time at home. More Christmas parties!''

''Is that so terrible?'' Jo asked.

''Love is…sort of…dissolving what I want. Or used to want.''

''Is it fair to blame Nate for that?'' Nancy asked.

Jo pushed her long blond mane aside and patted Chelsea's back. ''I know it's not politically correct,'' she said, lowering her voice as the men approached them, laughing over something that earned Nate a playful shove, ''to talk about women compromising anything in a relationship, but with the right man, you get back a lot for whatever you give up. Trust me.''

The group dispersed quickly, Jave and Nancy leaving to pick up the boys, and Jo and Ryan hurrying off to relieve Devon at Coffee Country. All the downtown merchants were open late for Christmas shopping.

''Do you want to stop and eat on the way home, so you don't have to cook?'' Nate asked as they walked out to the parking lot. He pulled keys out of his pocket. They were driving Karma's Volvo, rather than his Jaguar, because of the infant seat.

She made a sudden decision. ''Let's pick something up,'' she said briskly, snatching the keys from him and handing him the baby. ''It'll save time.''

YEAH, let's pick something up. But make it soft. My throat's starting to hurt.

''FOR WHAT?'' he asked as she unlocked the passenger-side door.

She held his gaze for a moment, then walked around to the driver's side. ''You'll see,'' she said across the roof of the car.

Nate was grateful he had steady nerves, because there was something dangerous about Karma tonight that he'd never seen before. It was as though she were driven by some demon even she didn't understand.

She was considerably beyond the speed limit when they reached Burgers, Burgers and turned into the drive-through lane with competence but a shrill squeal of tires. They rocked to a stop at the menu. She ordered without consulting him.

Nate looked over his shoulder to check on Garrett and found him smiling.

COOL! Are we trying out for the Indy?

NATE GUESSED they hit fifty in the ten yards from the menu to the window. He had no idea how fast they were going on the road home, but he watched the side mirror for signs of a flashing red light.

It was the most fun he'd had since the day he'd proposed. Their careful neutrality was coming to an end. He felt his pulse pick up as he braced for the confrontation.

It came after they ate in relative silence and she put Garrett to bed in the back office.

Nate had built a fire and was making coffee, thinking it might lubricate what was bound to be a difficult discussion.

But she took the basket of the coffeemaker out of his hands, put it aside, and pulled him by the arm into the living room.

"Fair is fair," she said cryptically. "Take your shirt off."

He heard the words, but couldn't put them together in a sensible formation. *Fair is fair—take your shirt off?*

"Pardon me?" he said.

"Never mind," she growled impatiently. "I'll do it." She unbuttoned his shirt and pulled it out of his pants. Her eyes collided briefly with his as she operated with an unnerving determination. "I'm going to make love to you. If you have any objections, speak now."

"Do we have time for this?" he asked. He knew he was pushing it, but he'd never seen her this out of control. He couldn't help going for it. "Don't you have a profit-and-loss statement to produce for—?"

The shirt unbuttoned, she pushed it off his shoulders. He pulled his arms out obligingly and let it fall.

"I'll do it after," she said, her eyes snapping at him.

He felt a fleeting scrape of her fingernails as she pulled his T-shirt up. She had to strain on tiptoe, body to body with him, to get it off. Selfishly, he did nothing to help her. He was sure all his vitals were off the chart.

She tossed the T-shirt away, then pulled off her sweater and dropped it on the pile.

He held on to his control with his fingernails.

"That's fine," he said in a carefully removed tone. "We can make it quick."

She unhooked the front closure of her bra and dropped it, then put her fingertips inside the waistband of his jeans.

He felt his stomach muscles kick against her hand.

"We're going to take it slowly," she said, leaning against him so that he felt her breasts flatten against his stomach, the impression of their berry tips creating a memory he thought he would carry forever. "And you're going to regret withholding sex to teach me that work isn't everything."

He held his hands away from her, closing his eyes as she planted kisses across his pectoral muscles. "So far," he said in a thready voice, "I'd be hard put to...regret anything."

She unbuckled his belt. "But I'm not finished yet," she said softly. "Come with me."

She tugged him toward the sofa, unzipped his jeans, then pushed him backward onto the cushions, removed his shoes and tugged the jeans and briefs off.

He had to struggle not to move as she placed a pillow under his head. She kicked off her shoes, then wriggled slowly out of her slacks and panties.

By the time she'd finished and he saw every delicious curve of her enhanced by the firelight, he was beyond control. He grabbed her wrist and pulled her down astride him.

"I was trying to show you," he said, his hands running greedily over her back and hips, "that there *has* to be time for love and play. That even successful labors mean nothing to a soul that can't have fun."

She smiled suddenly, blindingly. "You were right."

He smiled, too. "Well. I love it when you see things my way."

"But our lives do need a little more structure."

"No, they don't." He grinned wickedly. "But do make me regret my high-handed methods. I like the way it's going so far."

"You're so bad," she said, leaning over him with purposeful intent.

He wrapped his arms around her in welcome. "I work at it."

Chapter Thirteen

"I thought this place was beautiful last night," Karma said to Nate as they did a last perusal of the room to make sure everything was going smoothly. "But it's even more beautiful swarming with children."

Parents occupied the tables, talking and laughing, and examining the gifts left at each table. But the children fairly hummed with excitement, their little bodies fidgeting on the benches as they watched the man and woman wandering up and down the aisle, strumming and singing Christmas carols.

Denise DiBenedetto and Willie Brock, Nancy's mother and stepfather, country singers who'd just finished a southwestern tour in time for the holidays, had insisted on being part of the festivities. They'd even painted stars and cut out snowflakes.

"This project is always very satisfying," Nate said, pointing toward the clock drawing very close to twelve noon. "But it was even more so this year..." He put an arm around her shoulders and pulled her close to kiss her temple. "Because I got to do it with you."

She smiled at him, drunk with the love she felt for him. Last night hadn't solved everything, but at least they'd agreed to disagree peacefully. "You're just self-satisfied because you made me a believer in Christmas.''

He kissed her again. ''That, too. Did you call April and her mom?''

Karma nodded. April and her mother were watching ''the three fussketeers,'' as the babies were now known among the group. ''She said Garrett slept this morning and was a little cranky, but he went back to sleep after she fed him. I hope that's just a cold.''

''That's what it looks like,'' Nate said. ''And he's just had his checkup. Any pediatrician's office is a hotbed of germs, no matter how much they sterilize. Come on. We'd better get ready.''

Nate pulled her toward the curtain behind the big chair, borrowed from the mayor, where Santa would sit to distribute gifts.

Their group had laughed over their bigamous Santa, who would require two Mrs. Santas to help him—Aggie in a long red dress and apron for the line of girls, and Diantha in a long flowered skirt and blouse and wire-rimmed spectacles for the line of boys. The sexist arrangement was the best they could come up with to help in the sorting and arrangement of presents.

''But the first kid who bad-mouths my outfit,'' Aggie threatened, ''gets nothing for Christmas.''

The role of Santa had been assumed by Jo's father, Matt Arceneau, who'd come from Connecticut to spend Christmas with Jo and Ryan. He'd needed a lot of padding to fulfill the physical requirements of the role, but he came equipped with a twinkle in his eye and the kind disposition of a man who gave to children. Karma had not been surprised to learn that he taught American history in a Connecticut high school.

When Riverview Hospital's chief of staff went to the

microphone to announce that Santa was ready to distribute toys, pandemonium broke loose.

It took hours to see that every child had the right toy. Karma and Nancy lined up gifts by age on the girls' side, and Nate and Jave did the same on the boys'.

Karma had kept her eye on the square package, wrapped in red and silver Santas, that contained the rag doll that she would always think of as the beginning of her life change. She'd peered through the curtain to see it given to a sturdily built little towhead in a clean but well-worn denim pinafore over a white blouse. She'd had scuffed brown shoes and an eager look in her eye. Karma hoped she wouldn't be disappointed.

By the time each child had a toy, the noise level, even in the huge room, was deafening. But, considering the noise was mostly composed of laughter and cries of delight, no one minded. Parents and those children not completely consumed with their toys went through a buffet table laden with Jo's and Diantha's cookies, and coffee and punch.

Karma used Nate's cellular phone to call April's mother, but found the line busy. Desperate for caffeine after those grueling few hours, she worked her way through the crowd to the table where Jo and Ryan held forth behind tons of cookies and a mountain-high stack of paper plates.

Jo slipped her a cup, pointing behind her to a little boy lovingly clutching one of Tom's wooden trucks in one arm and a Santa cookie in the other. The frosting was all over the child's face.

"I think we're a success," Jo said.

"Have you seen Amy?" Karma asked, groaning with pleasure as the coffee hit her taste buds, then started a warm path to her stomach.

Jo passed a plate to a little girl in braids and indicated the door with her chin. "She's had to schmooze with the press all afternoon. They've taken scores of pictures. I'll bet next year we get lots more help on this thing."

"And where's Tom?"

Jo pursed her lips and shrugged her shoulders. "Never showed up."

Karma stepped aside as a pair of giggling girls rushed past her. "What?"

Jo shrugged. "I don't know the details. I guess he left town for a few days."

"At Christmas? On the day of the party?"

"He called Nancy and said he'd be home for our party Christmas Eve. About that, would you mind bringing pies again? Same kinds?"

"Sure." As the line at the food table grew longer, Karma moved away, with no purpose in particular except to savor what was left of their event.

She couldn't help a small twinge of sadness in the midst of all the excitement. There'd been such fun for her in working with Jo and Nancy and Amy, who'd become her friends, and with Jave and Ryan and Tom, for whom she'd developed a fondness almost as dear.

Because of Nate and Garrett, she'd experienced the love and spirit of Christmas as she never had before.

Karma wandered up the side aisle, content that the afternoon was an unqualified success, and that all the hours spent tracing, cutting, pasting, gluing, painting, mixing and baking had been transformed into the happiness of several hundred little children.

Then, out of the corner of her eye, Karma caught a flash of blond hair and turned to see the little girl in the denim pinafore sitting cross-legged in the middle of a table pushed against the wall to clear a path to the back door. In her arms, in a death grip, was the rag doll. Karma felt tears burn her throat and her eyes. The rag doll would be loved.

The little girl looked up and saw her and turned the doll to face her. "Look," she said. "I got a baby!"

Karma went to sit on the edge of her table. "Well, she's very pretty. Have you given her a name?"

"My mother says Noelle would be nice, because that means Christmas." She hugged the doll to her again. "But I'm going to call her Kathy."

Karma smiled, hoping this bright little girl would find her way out of difficulty and to happiness and success.

"He isn't real, you know," the little girl said, pointing toward Santa, who was now wandering down the aisle, talking to children and parents. "That's just a man inside."

Karma felt compelled to challenge her worldly knowledge. "If he isn't Santa, where did he get so many presents?"

"People fix them up for us." She seemed delighted by the idea. "There's no Santas, just people."

"I see. Well, do you mind that your baby isn't new?"

The little girl looked surprised at the question. "No," she replied with all apparent honesty. "I'm not new, either. I'm five."

Karma hugged her; she couldn't help herself. Then she looked up to see Nate coming toward her.

"Hi," she said, pulling him toward the table. "This is Kathy..." She pointed to the doll in the little girl's arms and saw understanding in Nate's eyes as he glanced at her. "And this is her new mother."

"Hello," Nate said to the little girl. "I'm happy to meet you. And that's a very pretty baby Santa gave you."

Karma glanced at him quickly with a shake of her head, but she was too late to save him.

"Santa isn't real," the little girl said seriously. "He just pretends. People give him the stuff to give to us."

Nate raised an eyebrow in surprise. "Are you sure?"

She nodded. "Yeah. Mom said. The hospital people do this. It's not like a trick or anything, they do it to be nice, and the little babies like Santa, so I guess he's okay. But he isn't real. Only the hospital people are real. There's my mom."

She pointed to a young woman in jeans and a fleece jacket trying to hold on to one little boy pulling against her while buttoning a second one into a raincoat.

"I have to go," she said.

Nate lifted her to the floor. She smiled back at them before running to her mother. "Merry Christmas," she said.

Nate took Karma's face in his hands and brushed her tears away with his thumbs. "I'd say your rag baby is in very competent hands."

EVERYONE went for pizza after cleanup, but Karma begged off, concerned about Garrett.

"Why don't you go with them?" she asked Nate. "I'm sure Jave would bring you home."

He began to shake his head even before she'd finished. "As though I'd enjoy it without you. Come on. We'll get Garrett and have sandwiches when we get home."

Karma hugged him. "Thank you. What a day! I can't wait to get home."

Nate smiled as he negotiated the dark country road that led to April's family's farmhouse. Karma was anxious to go home—to his home, to the rustic retreat that he'd built as a bachelor palace and which *she'd* filled with cinnamon bears, drying moss, an accounting business and a baby.

Not precisely what he'd planned for himself, but he couldn't imagine being happier than he was at this moment. Unless he was married to her.

"You heard that Tom left town?" she asked.

He nodded, turning his brights on. "My guess is that he's gone to see the Porters. Jave thinks so, too. He told Nancy he'd be back by Christmas Eve."

A week and three days. Karma felt a rush of excitement—followed by that little niggling of fear that she guessed was the curse of every God-fearing cynic. Happiness always made you look over your shoulder and wonder what rain cloud might be following you.

Karma smiled against it, thinking she felt strong enough to take on anything. She didn't expect the challenge to be accepted so soon.

She knew something was wrong the moment a wide-eyed April let her into the quietly lit house. The sound of a baby's cries came from somewhere inside the house, but there was a labored sound to it, a curious rasp that raised gooseflesh on Karma's scalp.

She ran through the house in the direction of the sound, past Malia and Chelsea, asleep on a blanket on the sofa, Nate and April behind her. She found April's mother in the small bathroom, holding Garrett partially upright in her hands. She'd turned on the hot water in the shower as a kind of vaporizer.

"Thank God you're here," the woman said. Her face was pale, and her eyes were wide with worry.

Karma tried to take him from her, but Nate pushed her hands aside and took him, laying him on the flat of one arm, Garrett's head resting in his hand. He held the baby's jaw down and peered inside. Garrett whimpered pitifully. He sounded to Karma as though he were breathing his last.

"I was about to call an ambulance," April's mother said. "I don't think this is just a cold. He was doing fine this morning, but when he woke up this afternoon, he seemed suddenly worse. And there's that whistle in his breath. Then he's gotten much worse this evening. I called the fairgrounds, but you'd already left. I'm sorry."

Karma fought the impulse to rip the baby from Nate's arms and hold him to her. "What is it?" she demanded. "What's wrong?"

He shook his head. "I'm not sure. But it's no cold. Something's blocking his airway. Here, hold on to him and keep his head up." He went into the other room to call an ambulance.

"I think it's epiglottitis," he said to the dispatcher. "There's a stridor in his breath and the epiglottis is swollen."

The dispatcher sounded distressed herself. "Dr. Foster, our teams are both out. One's at a traffic accident at the other end of the county, and one's on a broken-hip call at the nursing home."

Nate swore, punched the phone off, and hurried back into the bathroom to take Karma by the arm. "Come on," he said. "We're going to the hospital."

Nate felt perspiration break out on his body as they ran to the car. He helped Karma in with Garrett, then ran around and started the car even before he closed his door. His hands weren't shaking; they never shook. But everything else inside him was the consistency of pudding.

Keep it together, he told himself firmly. *You've got to keep it together.*

Karma felt suddenly as though *she* couldn't breathe, as though *she* had a fever. Every labored little breath seemed to rip her own throat. She found herself breathing deeply, as though that could make Garrett do the same.

"Nate…" she said worriedly as the motor sparked to life.

Nate raced down the dark lane while calling the hospital on his cellular phone.

"I'm coming in with a three-month-old on the brink of respiratory arrest," he said. "I suspect epiglottitis." He listened a moment, then put the phone to the steering wheel just long enough to use both hands to turn onto the road. "Yeah," he said into the phone. "His doctor's Dade. Right. Garrett Endicott."

The brakes screeched and the tires squealed as Nate negotiated another turn. Gravel spewed in all directions.

"Nate, he sounds awful!" Karma said, barely fighting off panic.

"Sit him up against your arm a little higher," he said, flooring the accelerator. "Ten minutes. We'll be there in ten minutes."

Nate heard the baby's broken gasp for breath and felt dread, like a cold finger, hit every one of his vertebrae. Garrett didn't have ten minutes.

Nine minutes. He could be there in nine minutes. Then they could intubate him, give him antibiotics…

Old memories filled the darkness surrounding the car, rose around him like threatening specters—a baby gasping, purpling, dying under his hands. Clogged tubing, a mother crying.

He raced around a car, caused another coming from

the other direction to screech onto the shoulder, moved back into his lane and prayed, *Please, don't make me have to do this. Please. I don't want to do this.*

Seven minutes.

Six minutes.

Garrett tried to drag in air in one noisy rasp that stopped in the middle like a broken note. Then Karma screamed.

"Nate, he isn't breathing. I don't think he's breathing!"

Damn it! I said I didn't want to do this! Nate jerked the car off the road and down into the darkened parking lot of the mooring basin.

"Get in the back with him," he ordered Karma while he reached into the glove compartment for his flashlight, into his pocket for the knife on his key ring.

She didn't question him, but did as he asked. The pen in his pocket was the stick variety, and he reached over the back seat to hand her her purse.

"Do you have a pen?" he demanded, getting out of the front seat and kneeling down in the confining space in the back. There was barely room to move back here. He wouldn't be able to do this!

He steadied himself as best he could and turned the light on Garrett's face. He was turning blue.

Karma produced a pen. Another stick. He swore, panic threatening to overtake him. Then he noticed the narrow white-paper-wrapped drinking straw protruding from the pocket of a vinyl organizer on the back of the driver's seat. He thanked heaven for Karma's compulsion for tidiness.

He snatched it out, ripped the paper off and cut it to about three inches long with his knife.

Using the barrel of a pen for an airway had become

such a cliché anyway, he thought absently to distract himself from what he had to do. He'd seen it on "M*A*S*H," he'd seen it on one of those live-action cop shows, he remembered vividly the illustration of it in his emergency medicine text. But he didn't want to do it!

"Now hold this on his throat," he said, handing her the light.

He felt for the cricoid notch. On an adult, it was a small indentation between two ridges of cartilage. On a child, it was a minute space just above the vocal cords that only an experienced touch could find. And he'd always resisted working on children.

He tried to block out Karma's soft weeping and his own terror and remember his anatomy. Then he found it, almost nothing more than a suggestion of space in the tiny throat.

His heartbeat thudding in his ears, he positioned the sharp blade of his pocketknife precisely where he would make the incision.

"Nate!" Karma whispered, one fist going to her mouth when she realized what he was about to do, the other hand placed protectively over her baby.

He ignored her anguish. He ignored his own. He prayed for the steadiness for which he was well-known when there wasn't a child involved—when this child wasn't involved.

He tried prayer one more time. *All right, if you're going to make me do this, you damn well better stand by me!* It occurred to him that the style was poor, but the sincerity was certainly there.

Everything inside him trembling, though his hand was steady as a rock, he made the small incision. With great care, he separated skin and tissue with his thumb and forefinger, and didn't even register Karma's sob.

He held his hand out to her. "The straw."

She put it in his hand, and he inserted it into the incision. A whoosh of breath came through it almost immediately.

"All right!" he shouted. Then he pushed at Karma as he held the straw in place. "You have to drive. Go!"

Joanie, the rent-a-doc, McNamara and Dade met them in the parking lot. Mac and Dade took Garrett right up to surgery, and Nate sat with Karma in the waiting room. She lay curled against him, alternately sobbing and praying. His mind was blank.

"Epiglottitis," Dade reported cheerfully a miraculously short time later, as he sat down on the other side of Karma. "Nate was right. Comes on almost without warning, usually the result of the flu. Can be fatal if you're a long way from a hospital—unless you happen to be riding with an emergency room doctor. Good work, Nate. Neat little cricothyrotomy. Bitch to do on babies."

Karma sat up and sniffed. "You mean he's going to be all right?"

Dade nodded. "We'll have to keep him a few days, get some antibiotics into him. Can you stay?"

"Yes, of course."

Karma felt as though she'd been reborn. Watching Garrett choke had been like death, and watching Nate make the incision in her son's throat had been like being pitched into hell. But hearing that her baby would be fine was like coming alive again on a sunny morning.

"I'll arrange for a bed for you, Karma," Dade said. "Nate, go get a drink. You look like hell."

As the doctor left, Karma wrapped her arms around

Nate's neck and sobbed again, but this time she wept with happiness. "Oh, Nate. He's going to be all right. You saved him! You saved him!"

Her delirium ran so high that it was long moments before she became aware of Nate's unresponsiveness. Then she drew away apologetically, knowing he loved Garrett as much as she did, certain he was simply experiencing delayed terror now that the crisis was over. And suddenly she knew beyond a doubt that nothing short of marriage could contain her love for him.

"You saved Garrett's life," she told him, leaning forward to kiss his lips. "He's fine. He's going to be fine."

But he sat there stiffly, his eyes unfocused, his hands in his lap. He finally forced himself to meet her eyes and smile. He knew the result was thin. "Right," he said. "You go stay with him, and I'll check in with you in the morning."

And that was when the new terror hit her. That was when she felt as though she had died a second time.

"Check in with me?" she asked in a flat tone.

She saw him try to force a smile. "I meant I'll come and see you."

"Nate, I don't..." she began, prepared to confront whatever this problem was.

But he shook his head. "Tomorrow we'll talk ab—"

He tried to push off the vinyl sofa, but she held him down with a hand on his shoulder. "No. I want you to tell me what you're thinking."

That was the last thing he intended to do. He stood and pulled her with him. "Come on. We'll find out where they're putting him, and I—"

She caught his arm and pulled him to a stop as he headed for the door. "This is your nightmare realized, isn't it? This is why you didn't want to fall in love, why you didn't want to be a parent.''

Nate put a hand to his eyes, feeling as though the last two hours had been two weeks long. "Do we really have to do this now?"

"Yes," she insisted brutally. "Garrett is in a hospital bed, and I want to know if he's going to have you in his life tomorrow."

There were moments when he admired her ability to lay the truth bare. This wasn't one of them.

He tried to dig deep down where the truth was and find a way to make her understand it. "I can't tell you what it felt like to cut on him," he said. His voice was low, as though he'd blown some kind of personal fuse. "That fragile flesh, that tiny space..." he gasped, the memory a pain.

"Nate," she said, tears in her voice and in her eyes. "You saved his *life*." She swallowed and cleared her throat. Her voice came out stronger, fuller. "You knew what to do, because you're a doctor. You have the advantage over so many other parents. If I were in love with another accountant," she said, her voice rising, "my son would be dead now!"

Nate shook his head. "Maybe if he were a little bigger, a little older..."

She laughed mirthlessly. "Nate, if he were bigger, he'd be riding his bike downhill with no hands. If he were older, he'd be driving!"

Nate refused to accept her logic. Somewhere between the beginning of the incision he'd made in Garrett's throat and the end, he'd known he couldn't deal with having a child, after all.

He shook his head, his heart like an anchor in his chest. "Karma, I love you. And I love him. But I can't do this. Maybe you were right all along. I'm not sure this will work."

Cold dread filled her being. This couldn't be. Not now that she finally understood that she *wanted* to belong to him, wanted to make him exclusively hers—legally, spiritually, in any and every way she could seal the bargain. "What?" she asked flatly.

"I got lucky tonight," he said, "but it could just as well have ended badly. Believe me, I know. Would you have still loved me then?"

She uttered a sound of angry exasperation. "Nate, I love you more than my own life, and I think you're the kindest, most caring, smartest, most wonderful man I've ever met. But I *don't* think you're God! I adore the skill in you that saved Garrett's life, but do you think I'd have blamed you if he'd died?"

He couldn't reason anymore. He didn't even want to think. He needed to fall down somewhere and sleep for a week.

"I don't know," he said. "I only know I can deal with being responsible for an adult's life, but I don't want to be responsible for a child's."

Karma thought that was pretty clear. But she wasn't going to make it easy for him. He had to say it. "So, you want out?"

He looked at her, misery in every line of his body. "Be honest," he said. "Aren't *you* afraid to invest your love in something you can lose without warning?"

Karma let herself admit that it was over. It hurt like hell, but she imagined it would for a long time. "It seems," she said, snatching her purse off the sofa, "that I've already done that." She stalked out of the room.

"LOOK AT HIM," Bert cooed, leaning over the crib to hold both of Garrett's hands. He made wild noises and

smiled, showing her his gums. "You'd never guess
there'd been anything wrong with him. He's turning
into such a cutie. And what a grip!"

*WAIT till I'm ready to pitch! I feel so much better! But
where's Nate? Is he coming over soon? When do we
eat?*

KARMA LEANED beside her, amazed at her son's recu-
perative powers. Only three days after that horrifying
ordeal, he was bright eyed and pink cheeked, and
looked suddenly longer, bigger. She guessed it was her
own relief that was "enlarging" him, but whatever it
was, she took comfort in it. He was all she had left.

It was strange, she thought, that just three months
ago, before the automobile accident that brought on labor, he'd been all she had, and she'd looked forward
with excited anticipation to their lives together. She'd
envisioned working with him beside her, walks on
sunny days, and books to read and games to play when
it rained. She'd seen long, lazy evenings when they
would learn about each other and plan his future.

Now both of them knew that would never be enough.
They'd have been happy together, but their lives
wouldn't have had that dimension of surprise, curiously
coupled with security, that Nate gave them.

There wouldn't be as much laughter. There would be
no broken toys awaiting repair and cluttering the house
for months before Christmas, no one striding through
the house with Garrett in a football hold, no one leaving
roses in her mailbox. The sob she held back burned in
her chest.

"What are you going to do now?" Bert asked gently

as Karma turned on the new musical mobile Bert had brought Garrett.

"The same thing I did before," Karma replied. "I've acquired a lot of new clients, and the first of the year is a very busy time for me. Mrs. Bennett's going to come over half days so I can work hard and get enough money together to rent a work space. We're going to be fine."

Colorful little fabric animals danced in a circle to the tinkling music, and Garrett's eyes grew big as he watched. He waved his arms and kicked his feet. He was changing, Karma thought, feeling both maternal excitement and personal loss. Nate wasn't here to see him.

Wow! Those are cool! Thanks, Aunt Bert. The music's a little tinny, though. Nate plays The Three Tenors. *Now, that's music. Why are those animals out of my reach?*

SHE LED BERT to the living room, trying to turn her thoughts in another direction.

"I really appreciate you picking us up at the hospital this morning."

Bert dismissed her gratitude with a shake of her head. "My pleasure. Ryan told me to take as long as I needed to make sure you were okay. He said to tell you Nancy and Jo will bring your dinner by tonight."

Well, she wasn't *so* alone, she told herself bracingly. She had wonderful friends. "That's great. But *I'm* not an invalid. I'll be fine. You go back to work."

Bert looked into her eyes and said gently, "Maybe Nate will have second thoughts. You know, men hate being afraid, and I'll bet that just scared the bejeebers out of him because he loves Garrett so much. He loves

you so much. I mean, having to do that procedure on a
tiny baby in the back of a car in the dark! With a pocketknife!''

Karma put a hand on Bert's arm to stop her. She felt
woozy at the memory, recalled the stark terror of watching her baby turn blue and knowing that a knife at his
throat was the only thing that would save him.

''Oh, I'm sorry.'' Bert pushed her into a chair. ''I'll
put a pot of coffee on before I go. You want me to call
for Chinese takeout? A pizza?'' She peered out at her
from the kitchen, a grin on her lips. ''A half gallon of
rum-raisin ice cream?''

Karma frowned at her. ''No one delivers ice cream.''

''Yes, they do,'' Bert said. ''I've had it done a couple
of times. Once when the loan manager dumped me for
the gift shop lady with the big... deposits.'' She waggled her eyebrows. ''And once when my mother told
me I *wasn't* adopted. What's your favorite flavor?''

''Chocolate—white-chocolate chunk.''

''Good choice. I'll make the call.''

NATE AWOKE to a loud rap on his front door. He didn't
bother with a robe, but raced downstairs in his under-
wear to answer it.

He prayed that it was Karma. And he prayed that it
wasn't. He hadn't resolved the baby problem in his own
mind, but he was gradually dying of loneliness without
her and Garrett.

The morning after the nightmare procedure on the
side of the road, he'd gone to the hospital to see them.
Karma had been calmly polite. Garrett had lain weakly
amid tubes and blankets. It had been a grisly experience
that he'd repeated two more days.

Then, yesterday, he'd borrowed Ryan's car and gone

to pick them up and take them home, prepared to try to discuss the issue calmly and ask Karma to help him search for a solution. But Beachie had told him they'd already been picked up by a friend. In the three days since, he'd called several times and gotten no answer. He'd had to call Jave to reassure himself that Garrett was all right. Then Nancy had told him she'd seen Karma and she appeared to be fine—"physically, at least."

This was a busy time of year for accountants, he knew. And, of course, with a baby, Karma was always busy.

She probably didn't have time to hear him say he was sorry he'd hurt her, but he considered it kinder to admit the truth than to hurt her more deeply later.

But if that was her at the door, he didn't give a damn about later. All he wanted was to see her, to hold her—now!

It was Tom.

"Hi." The bill of his baseball cap faced front and was pulled down low over his eyes. He looked exhausted, but he readjusted his hat to get a better look at Nate's state of undress. "You always answer the door like that?"

Nate sighed. "I thought you were Karma. Come on in." He held the door open, then closed it behind him. He wasn't sure he had the capacity for someone else's suffering at the moment, but he'd give it a shot. It might distract him from his own.

"So…you guys have split up?" Tom asked, pulling out a kitchen chair and sitting down.

Nate, in the act of pouring coffee, turned to frown at him over his shoulder. "How do you know that? I thought you've been out of town."

"Got in this morning," he said. "Had breakfast with Jave."

Nate brought him a steaming cup, then opened the pink bakery box on the table. He'd picked up doughnuts on the way home from the hospital this morning, knowing there'd be no sausages and eggs waiting for him, no fragrant coffee cake hot out of the oven.

"You see the Porters?" He sat opposite Tom with his own cup and reached into the box for an apple fritter.

Tom pulled out a cream-cheese Danish. "I did. We talked for a day and a half. I guess they needed it, too."

"And they don't blame you?"

"No."

"Blockhead. I told you." Nate toasted him with his mug. He thought Tom looked as though he'd been to war and returned alive, but somehow changed. Seeing Davey Porter's parents had apparently helped him square himself with the past to some degree, but he probably felt that nothing would exonerate him completely. Still, it was a step forward. "What happens now?"

Tom chewed a bite of Danish, swallowed, and took a long, slow sip of coffee. "I'm working up my courage to go see Amy," he said reluctantly.

"She's great," Nate said encouragingly. "We all love her."

Tom nodded. "It's just hard to admit you've been a jerk."

Nate angled him a grin. "You should be used to it."

"Hey," Tom said, with a smile that made him look a little more like himself. "I'm feeling a little fragile here. Cut me some slack."

Tom finished his Danish, then carried his cup to the

counter. "What happens now with you and Karma?" he asked.

Nate rubbed a hand over his burning eyes. "Nothing. I think it's over."

Tom came back to the table and frowned down at him judiciously. "I thought you were 'dealing' with your fears."

Nate scraped his chair back and stood. "So did I," he admitted grimly. "Then Garrett was choking, and I was sure the whole time I was going to lose him. I can't deal with the responsibility of having to keep him safe."

"Pardon me," Tom asked, "but did you miss the fact that because of you he's alive today?"

"No. I just know how easily it could have gone the other way."

Tom raised an eyebrow at him, then waved his own words in his face. "So, it's easier to hurt than to get better?"

Nate raised an eyebrow, too. "How the hell would you know?"

But Tom did know. He was better. Nate could see it in his face. But it also looked as though it had cost him something.

"I do," Tom said simply. Then he changed his tone as he took another Danish and started for the door. "You coming to Jo and Ryan's for Christmas Eve? Housewarming and wedding planning, I understand."

"Good for them," Nate said, but he shook his head as he followed him. "I switched with our rent-a-doc. I'm doing his swings for a couple of days. He's got a date with Joanie Christmas Eve."

"You're a chicken," Tom said accusingly.

Nate nodded. "But you're a weirdo."

Chapter Fourteen

The woman was skin and bone, and not as old as Nate had thought her to be when Baldwin and Prentice brought her in. The Dumpster she'd been sleeping in had been hit by a drunk driver, and she'd been bruised, but he could find no broken bones or sign of internal injuries.

He saw her look up at the IV that was dripping normal saline and a piggyback of Ancef into her. Then her eyes went to the red and green paper garlands strung around the room, to the Santas and snowmen on the window that separated the ER from the waiting room.

"Christmas," she said. "My folks is in Tennessee. Won't get to see them, though."

I hear you, Nate thought, moving to inspect the open ulcer above her ankle. My family's right here, but I won't get to see them, either.

"I drink too much," she added, lying quietly as he examined her. "Families and alcohol don't mix."

Nate looked into her eyes and saw the deadness that was the other side of desperation. She was beyond trying. She knew the addiction was stronger than she was.

"There's a good program through the shelter, Patty,"

he said. "You could be better in time to see your family for Easter."

She looked at him as though he were an innocent. "I been in programs."

"Then you'll be good at it."

Joanie joined him, giving him a look that said almost the same thing Patty's had said, just from a different perspective.

Many of the ER staff had long ago given up on the homeless, the druggies, the battered and the broken, some of whom they saw time and time again, mired in their weaknesses and the vagaries of fate.

Patty hadn't been in before, but her odor, and the circumstances in which she'd been found, suggested she'd been living at the bottom for a long time.

But he had a license to heal, and he figured that related to the inside, as well as the outside.

Her bleary brown eyes looked into his, and he felt a frail connection.

"Where is this shelter?" she asked.

"Downtown," he replied, exploring the ulcer. It was silver dollar size and bright right around the edges. There was scarring around it, suggesting a burn that had healed, but this part of the injury had gone much deeper. "It's right behind the park. Want me to call and have somebody from the shelter pick you up?" He turned to Joanie. "Rinse with normal saline. Polysporine ointment, adaptic dressing and fluffs. Wrap in Kerlix."

Patty sighed. "I don't know."

"You think about it," he said, "while Joanie fixes you up. This burn looks pretty old. Haven't you seen someone about this before?"

"Millie put some stuff on it for me."

"Millie?"

"She was with me the night of the fire."

Nate had reached for her chart, then stopped and turned, some sixth sense in him kicking on.

"We didn't even know nothin' was wrong," Patty went on. "We'd gone in to try to keep warm in the basement of the hotel. I woke up 'cause of the smoke and the noise, then the wall fell in and it was like all the fires o' hell was after us. I screamed at Millie, and screamed, and shook her till she was on her feet. That's when I got burned."

Nate listened to the words—then felt the ripple effect of their meaning like the resounding echoes of a gong only inches from his face. The Harmony Hotel fire? In a town the size of Heron Point, there weren't that many fires, and everyone remembered them. "I screamed at Millie," she'd said, "and screamed..."

"The Harmony Hotel fire?" he asked.

"Yeah. That one that was empty. Used to stand over by the bus station." She pointed a grimy finger in the general direction.

He wanted to be absolutely sure. "Tell me again what happened."

She frowned fearfully. "I didn't do it. Me and Millie was just—"

He shook his head quickly. "No, I know you didn't do it. It was a problem with the wiring. But tell me again about you and Millie."

She repeated the story, emphasizing again how she'd had to scream to wake Millie.

Nate stared at her, unable to believe it. Well. Life did have its little trade-offs. He'd had a loss, but he was going to score a win for his buddy.

As he looked up, April walked in with a tray of coffee. "April!" he called. "Is Dr. Nicholas still here?"

She nodded. "I just saw him in the cafeteria."

"Will you tell him I need him to meet me here in ten minutes? Room one." It was the only room with a door.

"Sure."

"Patty," he said to the woman, who still looked worried over his sudden interest in her relationship to the fire. "I want you to tell this story to a friend of mine. We're going to keep you overnight, get you feeling better, then I'll have somebody from the shelter pick you up in the morning. And I promise you a plane ticket to go see your family when you're finished with the program."

Her eyes widened. "Just…to tell the story?"

"Yes."

"But I didn't start it. Me and Millie was—"

"I know. Nobody thinks you did anything wrong. I just want you to tell the story one more time, okay?"

"A plane ticket to Tennessee?"

"I promise."

Her eyes lost their focus for a moment, and he saw her exploring all the possibilities a trip home might entail. She laughed nervously. "Honest?"

"Swear to God."

She smiled. It illuminated her face. "Okay."

Nate called Tom. "I need you to come down to the hospital now," he said.

There was a surprised silence on the other end of the phone. "The hos— Nate, I'm finishing a dollhouse I'm making for Malia. I can't…"

"Finish it for next Christmas. I need you here now."

"Nate—"

"Now! The ER. Ten minutes."

"The ER—?"

Tom arrived looking harried, his baseball cap and his hooded black sweatshirt speckled with sawdust. He looked at Jave, sitting on the edge of a small table, and at Nate, leaning a shoulder against the wall. Then he frowned at the patient on the gurney.

"Look," he said to Nate. "I know you two have come to depend on me for every little thing, but I'm a busy man. I've come running to you this time, but from now on I'm unavailable for medical consultations."

Nate and Jave looked at each other. Jave shook his head. "I'm sorry. When my mother was carrying him, she was frightened by Henny Youngman."

Nate straightened and indicated Patty.

"Tom, this is Patty. Patty, my friend, Tom."

Tom pulled off his hat and offered his hand. "Hi, Patty."

Nate decided that was why he loved him. There wasn't a superior bone in his body.

"Patty has a story we'd like you to hear," Nate said.

Jave reached out to push a chair toward Tom. "Sit down," he said.

Tom frowned in confusion. "She have a wooden leg?" he whispered. "And you need me to—?"

Jave pointed to the chair. "Sit. And shut up."

"Right."

Nate touched Patty's arm encouragingly. "Tell him everything about the night you and Millie slept in the old building."

She looked at Nate, wide-eyed. "And you're gonna give me the plane ticket?"

"I promise."

"Okay. Was a year ago, maybe a little longer...." She joined both hands in her lap, and began to recount the story, telling Tom how she and Millie had been friends for a long time, only she died last year of pneumonia and drink. "We went in the old building to keep warm," she said, "and we was drinkin' wine, 'cause somebody at the church had given Millie five dollars."

Tom glanced in confusion at Nate but nodded politely to Patty.

"We got toasty warm and fell asleep, and we didn't know nothin' was wrong till we heard this rumblin' noise, then sirens. Then the wall fell down and fire came in like somebody was hosin' it at us."

Tom sat absolutely still, his expression frozen.

"What building was it, Patty?" Nate asked.

"The old hotel by the bus station."

A spasm crossed Tom's face.

"What happened after the wall fell?"

"Well, I started screamin' for Millie to get up, to get out, but it took me a while to wake her up."

"How did you do it?"

"I just kept screamin'."

Tom stared at her one more moment, eyes dark in utter disbelief. Then he got slowly to his feet. He was white.

"How," he asked weakly, "did you get out?"

"There was all these police outside. So we went down the basement. They're all connected under the street, you know, from the old days. We came up through the bus station's back room. It's got a broken window. That's how we always got in."

Tom closed his eyes. His mouth contorted, and he put a hand to it. Jave stood and went to put an arm around his shoulders.

"Somebody screamed." Tom choked the words out, leaning against him. "I told you somebody screamed."

"You're the only one who doubted you," Jave said, his voice shaky.

Nate, his throat tight and his eyes burning, smiled at Patty. "Good job," he said. "We'll admit you for tonight, and tomorrow I'll bring your airline tickets to the shelter." Having them in her possession, he hoped, would see her through detox.

Nate stood to go for a wheelchair, but then the back of his lab coat was caught in a fist and he was yanked to a stop. Tom pulled him into his arm, and the three of them stood in the tiny office, arms entangled, laughing, crying.

"How did you find out?" Tom asked, his eyes still glazed with disbelief.

Nate shrugged. He explained what had brought Patty to the ER. "She had a burn scar, I asked about it, she told me, and I knew she was your screamer from that night."

Tom pulled him into his arms, almost paralyzing him. "Thank you."

"Hey. You harass me," Nate said in a strangled voice, "I move sun and moon for you. It's a fifty-fifty friendship."

There was a brisk knock on the door, and then it burst open and Amy Brown stood there, pale and wide-eyed in a pink sweater and pants, her new hairstyle slightly disheveled. "What is it?" she demanded. "I heard that Tom was rushed here...." She looked from one man to the other, then saw Tom, obviously fit, and sagged visibly with relief. "Well, you look all right," she finished accusingly.

"He wasn't *rushed* here," Nate told her, "but hurried here on his own."

"Why?"

He shrugged innocently. "To see you, I imagine." He turned and winked at Tom. "The rest is up to you, buddy. Don't mess up. Come on, Jave. We'll find a room for Patty, then I'll buy you a Coke in the cafeteria."

"A Coke? How come *I* don't get plane tickets?"

KARMA WAS PACING the floor with Garrett for the third night in a row, thinking that she really didn't blame him for raising such a ruckus. She'd give anything for the freedom to scream at the top of her lungs as he'd done incessantly for time beyond measure. But she was the mom. She had to try to keep it together.

Only it had all dissolved on her. There was no laughter in her world, no happiness, no warmth, no comfort. She had Garrett, but he was as miserable as she was, and she couldn't seem to find a way to comfort him.

Christmas surrounded her—mocked her. She had a tree in the living room, gifts under the tree for the Nicholas children, for Chelsea, and a dozen things for Garrett. Carols blared from the radio and the television, and she had several floral arrangements around the room and a fruit basket from clients wishing her Happy Holidays.

The woman who'd once thought the Christmas holidays were a lot of hype punctuated by dollar signs finally believed in love and miracles and hope reborn. And now that Nate wasn't here to share all those qualities, their absence hurt far more than when she hadn't believed in them at all. Even Garrett seemed to want no part of her.

I WANT NATE! Where is he? I thought we were finally all together, and I haven't seen him in days! I want a fa-

ther! I can't face Malia and Chelsea tomorrow night without a father. So, where is he? What have you done with him?

KARMA SAT in the rocker with Garrett, remembering the fun and excitement of the Christmas party. That reminded her of the little girl who'd been thrilled with the rag doll she'd been given by the Santa she didn't believe in.

She'd had such an admirable grasp on life, Karma thought. She'd known what was real and what wasn't, and she'd taken it all in stride. The hospital people, she'd said, were the real Santas.

Karma felt philosophy abandon her as she tried to cope with the probability that Nate was out of her life forever. As a profound sadness overtook her, she remembered that night in his bed, how tender he'd been, how changed she'd felt.

Then came the image of his grandmother's sampler on the wall. All Things Bloom With Love, it had read.

She sat up with a start. Garrett shrieked.

NATE SAT in the empty cafeteria and listened to the sounds of the cooler and the pop machine. His shift was over, Tom had left much earlier with Amy, and Jave had gone home to Nancy.

He was going home to emptiness.

Of course, that was his own fault. He would have been the first to admit it. It was beginning to occur to him that his decision had deprived him of Karma and Garrett anyway, though nothing horrible had happened to them. They were hale and hearty, only a mile away from him—and as beautiful and wonderful as Karma was, and as cute and endearing as Garrett was, some other guy with guts was going to make them a part of *his* life.

He'd been stupid and cowardly, and now it was probably too late.

Then he remembered Patty and the light he'd seen in her eyes when he convinced her she had another chance.

He sat up as it occurred to him that it was possible *he* could have another chance. Maybe he could decide to approach it a day at a time, concentrate on what he had instead of what he could lose, tell Karma he loved her and beg her to forgive him.

It was a lot to ask, but he had nothing to lose. Without them, he felt as if there was nothing left anyway.

He crushed the pop can in his hand, tossed it at the recycling box, and looked at the clock—12:45 a.m. He couldn't wake her at this hour. He'd go home, take a shower, and stare at the ceiling until eight o'clock.

BY THE TIME HE GOT HOME, he'd convinced himself that it was a dumb idea and she'd slam the door in his face. But he decided that he deserved that, and he wouldn't let it stop him.

He heard a baby screaming when he walked up the steps. Memories of Garrett, he thought. Wishful thinking.

It grew louder as he put his key in the door. He looked around. Not a soul in sight. It must be exhaustion.

He pushed the door open and knew instantly that the screams were real. And they were Garrett's. He felt simultaneous bursts of joy and panic. Was Karma here? Was something wrong?

"Karma?" he shouted, flipping on the living room light. She bloomed out of the darkness like somebody's attic angel in ratty sweats, her ponytail dragging, long, straight strands of hair hanging around her eyes and temples.

Her cheeks were pink and puffy, her eyes damp and tired. He felt their sadness like his own pain.

He stopped about a foot from her, both ecstatic and confused by her presence. Was she here for personal or medical reasons? Garrett was screaming, and she looked as though she might collapse at any moment.

"What?" he asked gently.

She swallowed, and it looked as though it hurt. "Garrett's been crying for four days," she said, her voice raspy.

Was that medical or personal? He still wasn't sure. He closed the space between them and took the baby from her. "Here, let me see him."

AAAAGGGHHH! Aaagghh! Aagghh! Oh, hi. Well, it's about time. Where have you been? I've been calling for you for days! Look, are we all together, or what? Because there's a party tomorrow, or today—you've had me so upset I don't know if it's day or night—and if I don't have a father by then, I'm not going. Those girls are going to lord it over me again, and I'm just not up to it. So, what's it going to be?

Or is that the wrong approach? You like it when I smile, don't ya? How's that? And when I grab your finger. Feel that? I've been working out. I've got this new mobile, and I can almost reach it.

So what do you say? I know you're concerned because of that episode the other night, but, hey, I'm over that, and I promise not to do it again. I'm not going to be a reckless kid. I'm her *son. How foolhardy do you think I'll be?*

I can reach my toes now, and pretty soon I'll learn to count. I might go into accounting, too.

NATE LOOKED AT KARMA as Garrett quieted, smiled and grabbed his index finger. "I think," he said, "that he just wanted me."

Karma watched her son at work and couldn't shake the feeling that he'd somehow intended this all along. All right. She was on his side.

She squared her shoulders and tugged on her sweatshirt, trying to lend herself some shred of dignity. When she'd decided to come here, she'd run out of the house without even a glance in the mirror.

"Well, he gets that from me, you know," she said, hope swelling in her because Nate's eyes were burning into her. But she also felt a painful lump in her throat. Could it be that she was simply seeing in Nate what she wanted to see?

Nate couldn't quite believe his ears. He opened his mouth to speak, and couldn't.

Afraid he didn't care, Karma pressed her case. "There's Christmas stuff all over the place, and *you*—" she stabbed a finger at him accusingly "—filled me with the spirit, and now it's worse than if I'd never had it, because you took it away! All the things I used to be able to do alone don't work anymore, because I got used to doing them with *you*. I hate my little house now that I've lived in this one, I can't eat my cooking 'cause you're not there to tell me how good it is, I can't sleep because you're not there to hold me. And because I'm not in that bed with your grandmother's sampler over it. All things bloom with love, remember?"

EASY, Mom. You're going to spook him.

SHE RESISTED the impulse to throw herself into his arms, to burst into tears. Instead, she swallowed and tried to make sense.

"Nate," she said reasonably, though her voice quaked, "we love each other. Don't you think if we try, we could both bloom? You'll grow to learn to cope with having a child, and I'll grow to be more understanding, more flexible, more…"

Nate looked into her anguished eyes and had to stop her with his fingertips to her mouth. "You don't have to be more anything. I'm the one who—"

He stopped abruptly as he realized what she was giving him. Another chance.

"You love me," he asked, "after I left you at your baby's bedside?"

Karma looked into his eyes and did see love burning there, she was sure of it. It was there when he looked at Garrett. And it flamed when he looked at her.

She sniffed and folded her arms. "That *was* pretty crummy." She glanced up at the vaulted ceiling. She felt a tear spill over and swiped it away. "Does this house come with you?"

Nate couldn't believe this, but he wasn't going to question it. He had to clear his throat. "Yes, it comes with me."

"Then, yes," she said. "I want you."

He pulled her to him, and she fell against him, sobbing happily, wrapping her arm around Garrett to enclose him in their circle.

"I'm sorry," Nate said. "I was being irrational, I guess. That scared the hell out of me, and in my business fear often means failure."

She hugged him hard. "We're going to be able to do

this, I'm sure of it. With my organizational skills and your ability to make fun out of nothing, I think we can have a deliriously happy marriage, and raise a healthy, happy child.''

I'M NOT WORRIED.

''Ah, speaking of organizational skills,'' Nate said, kissing the top of her head. ''Have you misplaced your car? I didn't see it when I drove up.''

She grinned sheepishly up at him. ''I left it at the park and walked a block. I was afraid if you didn't want to see me, you'd take off at the sight of my car.''

He rolled his eyes. ''I've thought about nothing but you and Garrett for days. I called, but you weren't home.''

She nodded. ''I turned the ringer off a few times when Garrett fell asleep out of sheer exhaustion. He's been horrid, and I've been like a zombie. Ah...'' She drew out of his arms to go to the sofa, where she'd left Garrett's carrier. She pulled a long, thin box out of it and handed it to him, taking the baby so that Nate could open it. ''Merry Christmas from Garrett and me.''

Nate pulled the paper off and lifted the lid. Inside were a dog collar and a white envelope.

''Ah...what are you suggesting here, my love?'' he asked.

She swatted his shoulder. ''Open the envelope, you nit.''

He did, and found American Kennel Club papers for a four-month-old harlequin Great Dane registered as Skywalker of Stratford.

''You can pick him up at the breeder's on the twenty-sixth,'' Karma said, her heart melting at the deep-down delight in his eyes. "We can give him a less pretentious name."

He wrapped her in his arms. "Thank you. It feels good to have you endorse my dreams." Then he put her away from him and went to the kitchen table, which was covered with gifts. He sorted through them and returned to her with one roughly the same shape her box had been. He took Garrett back.

Karma unwrapped it and found a legal-looking document inside. She read it and screamed.

"A year's rent paid on the office with the skylight in the Chambers Building!"

She hugged Nate fiercely. "Thank you! I've wanted that office for so long. I can't believe you remembered I said that. So...you endorse my dreams, too?"

"Completely. We're going to have a great time."

"I know." She leaned lazily against him, clutching the box. Her eyelids drooped heavily. "I'm so happy."

"You also look exhausted. Maybe we should go to bed," he said. "I had rather a big day myself."

YAWN. Me, too. Crying that much is very tiring. I almost hyperventilated twice.

KARMA leaned lazily against Nate as he walked toward the stairs. "What happened?"

He told her about Patty, and how she had finally resolved Tom's questions about the night of the fire. "So, when we get up," he said, "I have to get her airline tickets to Tennessee."

They reached the top of the stairs, and she turned to kiss him soundly. "So, you're the real Santa?"

He hugged her to him. "Santa isn't real, according to the little girl at the party."

"She said he was a front for 'the hospital people.'" She leaned back to smile at him, thinking that she hadn't known it was possible to be this happy. "That's you. The real Santa. So, am I going to be Mrs. Santa, or Mrs. Foster?"

"Well, how would it sound?" Nate asked, sitting on the edge of the bed with her and Garrett. "Karma Santa."

"I don't think so," she said.

"Right. Karma Foster."

"That's elegant."

DON'T FORGET ME. Garrett Joseph Santa. I don't think that cuts it. I go for Foster.

"GARRETT FOSTER," Nate said. "What do you think of that?"

Garrett waved both arms. They laughed.

Karma looked at Nate, her heart in her eyes. "I love it. And I love you."

YES. It has a ring to it. "Garrett Foster pilots the first spacecraft to Mars." Or "Garrett Foster, Olympic gold medalist in boxing, flyweight division…" Or—this would be cool!—"Garrett Joseph Foster was elected fiftieth president of the United States by a landslide. Insiders attribute his success to the promise to make Christmas a yearlong celebration."

"Yeah. I like it. Merry Christmas, Mommy. Merry Christmas, Daddy."

Coming in December from

◆ HARLEQUIN®

AMERICAN *Romance*®

Triplets, Quads & Quints:
Multiple births lead to
remarkable love stories.

When Maitland Maternity Hospital opens a new
multiple-birth wing donated by the McCallum family,
unforgettable surprises are sure to follow. Don't miss the
fun, the romance, the joy…as the McCallum triplets find
love just outside the delivery-room door.

Watch for:

TRIPLET SECRET BABIES
by Judy Christenberry
December 2001

QUADRUPLETS ON THE DOORSTEP
by Tina Leonard
January 2002

THE McCALLUM QUINTUPLETS
(3 stories in 1 volume)
featuring *New York Times* bestselling author Kasey Michaels,
Mindy Neff and Mary Anne Wilson
February 2002

Available at your favorite retail outlet.

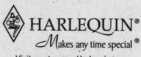

HARLEQUIN®
Makes any time special®

Visit us at www.eHarlequin.com

HARMAIT

*Together for the first time
in one Collector's Edition!*

New York Times bestselling authors

Barbara Delinsky

Catherine Coulter

Linda Howard

Forever Yours

**A special trade-size volume containing three
complete novels that showcase the passion,
imagination and stunning power that these
talented authors are famous for.**

Coming to your favorite retail outlet in December 2001.

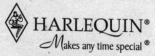

HARLEQUIN®
Makes any time special ®

Visit us at www.eHarlequin.com

PHFY

TRUEBLOOD, TEXAS

Coming in January 2002...

THE BEST MAN IN TEXAS

by

Kelsey Roberts

Lost:

One heiress. Sara Pierce wants to disappear permanently and so assumes another woman's identity. She hadn't counted on losing her memory....

Found:

One knight in shining armor. Dr. Justin Dale finds himself falling in love with his new patient...a woman who knows less about herself than he does.

Can the past be overcome, so that Sara and Justin may have a future together?

Finders Keepers: bringing families together

HARLEQUIN®

Makes any time special ®

Visit us at www.eHarlequin.com

TBTCNM5

Who needs Cupid when you've got kids?

Sealed with a Kiss

A delightful collection
from *New York Times*
Bestselling Author

DEBBIE MACOMBER

JUDITH BOWEN

HELEN BROOKS

Romance and laughter abound as
the matchmaking efforts of some
very persistent children bring
true love to their parents.

HARLEQUIN®
Makes any time special ®

Available in January 2002...just in time for Valentine's Day!

Visit us at www.eHarlequin.com

PHSK

Look to the stars
for love and romance
with bestselling authors

JUDITH ARNOLD
KATE HOFFMANN
and GINA WILKINS

in

WRITTEN
IN THE
STARS

Experience the joy of
three women who dare to
make their wishes for love
and happiness come true in
this *brand-new* collection
from Harlequin!

Available in December 2001
at your favorite retail outlet.

HARLEQUIN®
Makes any time special ®

ADDED BONUS:
As a special gift to our readers, a 30-page 2002
Love Guide will be included in this collection!

Visit us at www.eHarlequin.com

PHWS

If you enjoyed what you just read,
then we've got an offer you can't resist!

Take 2
bestselling novels FREE!
Plus get a FREE surprise gift!

Clip this page and mail it to The Best of the Best™

IN U.S.A.
3010 Walden Ave.
P.O. Box 1867
Buffalo, N.Y. 14240-1867

IN CANADA
P.O. Box 609
Fort Erie, Ontario
L2A 5X3

YES! Please send me 2 free Best of the Best™ novels and my free surprise gift. After receiving them, if I don't wish to receive anymore, I can return the shipping statement marked cancel. If I don't cancel, I will receive 4 brand-new novels every month, before they're available in stores! In the U.S.A., bill me at the bargain price of $4.24 plus 25¢ shipping and handling per book and applicable sales tax, if any*. In Canada, bill me at the bargain price of $4.74 plus 25¢ shipping and handling per book and applicable taxes**. That's the complete price and a savings of over 15% off the cover prices—what a great deal! I understand that accepting the 2 free books and gift places me under no obligation ever to buy any books. I can always return a shipment and cancel at any time. Even if I never buy another book from The Best of the Best™, the 2 free books and gift are mine to keep forever.

185 MEN DFNG
385 MEN DFNH

Name	(PLEASE PRINT)	
Address	Apt.#	
City	State/Prov.	Zip/Postal Code

* Terms and prices subject to change without notice. Sales tax applicable in N.Y.
** Canadian residents will be charged applicable provincial taxes and GST.
All orders subject to approval. Offer limited to one per household and not valid to current Best of the Best™ subscribers.
® are registered trademarks of Harlequin Enterprises Limited.

BOB01   ©1998 Harlequin Enterprises Limited

Coming in January 2002,
from Silhouette Books
and award-winning, bestselling author

ANNETTE
BROADRICK

*Secret
Agent
Grooms*

**Three heartbreaking men who'll risk their lives—
but not their hearts!**

In ADAM'S STORY, a man in search of his enemy
finds love where he least expected it....

In THE GEMINI MAN, an undercover agent assigned
to protect a damsel in distress finds himself bringing
his work home with him!

In ZEKE, a woman who thinks Zeke has been
assigned to protect her learns he's really after
her uncle. But he's not quite through
with her yet, either....

SECRET AGENT GROOMS:
They're always around when you need them!

Available at your favorite retail outlet.

Silhouette®

Where love comes alive™

Visit Silhouette at www.eHarlequin.com

BR3SAG